W9-BMJ-253

THE MAGILL BIBLIOGRAPHIES

The American Presidents, by Norman S. Cohen, 1989
Black American Women Novelists, by Craig Werner, 1989
Classical Greek and Roman Drama, by Robert J. Forman, 1989
Contemporary Latin American Fiction, by Keith H. Brower, 1989
Masters of Mystery and Detective Fiction, by J. Randolph Cox, 1989
Nineteenth Century American Poetry, by Philip K. Jason, 1989
Restoration Drama, by Thomas J. Taylor, 1989
Twentieth Century European Short Story, by Charles E. May, 1989
The Victorian Novel, by Laurence W. Mazzeno, 1989
Women's Issues, by Laura Stempel Mumford, 1989
America in Space, by Russell R. Tobias, 1991
The American Constitution, by Robert J. Janosik, 1991
The Classic Epic, by Thomas J. Sienkewicz, 1991
English Romantic Poetry, by Brian Aubrey, 1991
Ethics, by John K. Roth, 1991
The Immigrant Experience, by Paul D. Mageli, 1991
The Modern American Novel, by Steven G. Kellman, 1991
Native Americans, by Frederick E. Hoxie and Harvey Markowitz, 1991
American Drama: 1918-1960, by R. Baird Shuman, 1992
American Ethnic Literatures, by David R. Peck, 1992
American Theater History, by Thomas J. Taylor, 1992
The Atomic Bomb, by Hans G. Graetzer and Larry M. Browning, 1992
Biography, by Carl Rollyson, 1992
The History of Science, by Gordon L. Miller, 1992
The Origin and Evolution of Life on Earth, by David W. Hollar, Jr., 1992
Pan-Africanism, by Michael W. Williams, 1992
Resources for Writers, by R. Baird Shuman, 1992
Shakespeare, by Joseph Rosenblum, 1992
The Vietnam War in Literature, by Philip K. Jason, 1992
Contemporary Southern Women Fiction Writers, by Rosemary M. Canfield Reisman and Christopher J. Canfield, 1994
Cycles in Humans and Nature, by John T. Burns, 1994
Environmental Studies, by Diane M. Fortner, 1994
Poverty in America, by Steven Pressman, 1994
The Short Story in English: Britain and North America, by Dean Baldwin and Gregory L. Morris, 1994
Victorian Poetry, by Laurence W. Mazzeno, 1995

Human Rights in Theory and Practice, by Gregory J. Walters, 1995

Energy, by Joseph R. Rudolph, Jr., 1995

A Bibliographic History of the Book, by Joseph Rosenblum, 1995

Psychology, by The Editors of Salem Press (Susan E. Beers, Consulting Editor), 1996

The Search for Economics as a Science, by The Editors of Salem Press (Lynn Turgeon, Consulting Editor), 1996

Art, Truth, and High Politics, by John Powell, 1996

Popular Physics and Astronomy, by Roger Smith, 1996

Paradise Lost, by P. J. Klemp, 1996

World Mythology: An Annotated Guide to Collections and Anthologies, by Thomas J. Sienkewicz, 1996

Ref
BL
311
.Z99
.S53

World Mythology

An Annotated Guide to Collections and Anthologies

Thomas J. Sienkewicz

Magill Bibliographies

The Scarecrow Press, Inc.
Lanham, Md., & London
and Salem Press
Pasadena, Calif. / Englewood Cliffs, N.J.
1996

SEP 4 1997

492536

SCARECROW PRESS, INC.

Published in the United States of America
by Scarecrow Press, Inc.
4720 Boston Way
Lanham, Maryland 20706

4 Pleydell Gardens, Folkestone
Kent CT20 2DN, England

Copyright © 1996 by Thomas J. Sienkewicz

All rights reserved. No part of this publication may be reproduced,
stored in a retrieval system, or transmitted in any form or by any
means, electronic, mechanical, photocopying, recording, or otherwise,
without the prior permission of the publisher.

British Cataloguing-in-Publication Information Available

Library of Congress Cataloging-in-Publication Data

Sienkewicz, Thomas J.
World mythology : an annotated guide to collections and anthologies / by
Thomas J. Sienkewicz.
    p.   cm. —(The Magill bibliographies)
Includes bibliographical references and indexes.
1. Mythology—Bibliography. I. Title. II. Series.
Z7836.S54   1996   [.BL311]   016.2911'3—dc20   96-10156   CIP

ISBN 0-8108-3154-6 (cloth : alk. paper)

⊖™ The paper used in this publication meets the minimum requirements of
American National Standard for Information Sciences—Permanence of
Paper for Printed Library Materials, ANSI Z39.48–1984.
Manufactured in the United States of America.

In fond memory of my sister Doris

CONTENTS

INDEXES

ACKNOWLEDGMENTS

This project could not have been completed without the enthusiastic cooperation of the staff of the Hewes Library at Monmouth College. Beth Cox and Eleanor Gustafson, in particular, patiently dealt with my mountains of interlibrary loan requests. Dean Bill Julian, members of the Faculty and Institutional Development Committee, and others at Monmouth College supported this project by granting the sabbatical which guaranteed the bibliography's timely completion. I would also like to thank my wife, Anne, and my children, who bore my efforts with forbearance and understanding. Finally, I would like to thank Jim Betts for sharing his editorial skills with me and for letting me use his cave to hibernate.

INTRODUCTION

Sisyphus, the great sinner of Greek mythology, was doomed to roll a rock up a hill forever in the Underworld. Whenever he was just short of the top, the rock slipped and fell back to the bottom. Telling the story of myth is a task worse than Sisyphean. Not only can it never be completed, but, even worse, myth is a much more slippery and intangible rock than any Sisyphus had to roll. Despite centuries of debate and interpretation, the boundaries of myth remain unfixed and its mass unweighable.

Such uncertainty challenges the general reader, for whom this annotated bibliography is intended. The purpose of this introduction is to provide some context for approaching the mythologies of the world for the first time. Collections and anthologies of mythology form the bulk of the material represented here. While some scholarly works are included, the emphasis is on material which offers significant retellings, translations, and summaries of myths rather than erudite analysis and interpretation. Thus, this bibliography deals with the myths themselves more than with theories of myth. Citations in this book are further restricted to English-language material; many interesting collections are not included because they appear only in the original language. For example, Manuel J. Andrade's *Folk-Lore from the Dominican Republic* (Vol. 23 in *Memoirs of the American Folk-Lore Society*. New York: American Folk-Lore Society, 1930) is an important collection of 304 folktales about Tar Baby, Cinderella, trickery, death, and the Devil. Unfortunately, all are recorded only in Spanish without English translation, and so Andrade's collection does not appear here.

The subject matter of myth is unlimited. Myths include creation stories, aetiological tales explaining the origin of persons, places, or customs, legends about heroes, and folktales about ghosts, witches, and supernatural occurrences. What do all these stories have in common? Some might say that they are all fiction or falsehood, that the basic meaning of "myth" is untruth—hence the use of the word to refer to an untruth, such as white supremacy, or to imaginary people, events, or phenomena, such as the abominable snowman. Such a definition of "myth" is not, however, the one on which this annotated bibliography is based. Books dealing with modern economic or political myths are not included here.

Rather, in this bibliography, myths are understood in the context of the Greek word *mythos*, which means "speech" or "story." In this sense, myths are essentially traditional stories, narratives handed down from generation to generation within a community.

Such narratives are usually divided into three or four categories, according to subject matter. Myths proper deal with gods, creation, and the origin of things. Legends and sagas tell the life stories and great deeds of heroes or extraordinary mortals. Folktales, or *Märchen*, are about ordinary people. Fairy tales, about supernatural creatures such as giants, ogres, and fairies, are sometimes grouped with folktales and other times are classified separately. A great deal of overlap exists among these types. Some myths deal with interaction between heroes and gods, such as the relationship between the Greek goddess Athena and the heroes Odysseus and Heracles. Other myths show ordinary mortals encountering or even becoming deities. According to the Inuit myths of the Arctic, for example, Sedna was a mortal woman who was transformed into a goddess terrifying to humans. Although some would argue that the only real myths are those which deal with the gods and creation, folktales and fairy tales cannot legitimately be excluded from mythological collections. Myths about the gods and folktales have much in common. Both types of traditional narrative share themes and motifs. Offense against a god is the core of the mythic conflict between the Titan Prometheus and the god Zeus. The same theme is central to the fairy tale about Sleeping Beauty, in which one fairy is offended because she was not invited to the christening of the infant princess. As much as Sisyphus really would like to divide his rock into more manageable parts, it really cannot be done. Therefore, this annotated bibliography assumes that myths proper, legends, folktales, and fairy tales share features and themes which warrant common treatment.

These myths spill over into so many different areas that, in some ways, the list of possible candidates for inclusion in a bibliography of world mythology becomes almost endless. For example, books of folklore often contain not only traditional narratives but also less mythological materials: personal recollections, superstitions, customs, omens, cures, proverbs, and riddles. Also complementing these myths are modern fictional tales and reinterpretations of myths, such as the creations of Hans Christian Andersen, the great nineteenth-century Danish storyteller, or John Barth's *Chimera* (New York: Random House, 1972), a literary reworking of myths about the Greek heroes Perseus and Bellerophon. While such materials complement the study of mythology, they are not the focus of this bibliography, which concentrates as much as possible on primary rather than secondary treatments of myths.

Seeking a distinction between myth and history does not really help Sisyphus either. It might seem easy for twentieth-century Americans to distinguish the Revolutionary War from the battle in which the Tuatha Dé Danaan, the divine inhabitants of ancient Ireland, gained control of the island from the Fir Bolg. The first is a historical event carefully supported by a variety of reliable documents. The second looks back to a primeval time for which there are no historical records. The difference appears straightforward, yet the historicity of the Trojan War was the subject of similar skepticism until Heinrich Schliemann astonished the world in 1871 by uncovering the ruins of an ancient city on the site of Homer's Troy.

Nor is the line dividing myth from history so easy to discern in other parts of the world. The traditional story of the founding of Rome by Romulus and Remus, who had been nursed by a she-wolf, is told by the Roman historian Livy, yet it is found in all the collections of Roman mythology. West Africa possesses a biographical tradition which conflates legend and history. Sunjata, the subject of these tales, was the thirteenth-century founder of the ancient kingdom of Mali. While he really lived, many of the details in Sunjata's life are far from historically reliable. In their songs the griots of modern Mali, Guinea, Gambia, and Senegal sometimes portray the hero as the champion of Islam, even the descendant of the Prophet Muhammad; other times his antagonist is endorsed by the power of Allah, while Sunjata is sanctioned by animistic forces. Historians have no proof of the hero's actual religious persuasion, but, from a mythological perspective, this ambiguity is neither unusual nor trouble-some. Myth tends to be self-contradictory rather than consistent; it tends to include rather than exclude different versions of the same tale. So, in a society where both religious traditions have historically been strong, Sunjata is both the defender of Islam and its animistic opponent. In a similar way, the figure of Raven in the Pacific Northwest is both creator and trickster. He can make the world better for humankind by bringing light to the world, but he also teases humankind unmercifully in the process.

Despite the ambiguity of personality which they share, Sunjata remains more historical than the anthropomorphic Raven. His major accomplish-ment, the founding of a great kingdom, is plausible enough. At the same time, details of his life story tip the scales back in favor of myth. In particular, the griots tend to exaggerate Sunjata's conception, gestation, birth, and childhood. Imaginative details are used to enhance Sunjata's life and to make it extraordinary. Even more precocious than the Greek god Hermes, who steals his brother Apollo's cattle on the day he is born, Sunjata's fetus occasionally sneaks out of his mother's womb to play. As a child, Sunjata remains unable to walk for many years, sometimes not until the age of twelve. When he finally does walk, it is under dramatic circumstances. Because of her son's infirmity Sunjata's mother has no one to collect baobab leaves for her kitchen and is mocked by other mothers with healthy sons. Goaded by his mother's shame, Sunjata finally walks, uproots a giant baobab tree, and plants it in his mother's courtyard.

These tales of Sunjata's frolicking fetus and the giant baobab tree have no foundation in truth. Both stories transport the biography of the historical Sunjata into the realm of heroic legend, where heroes are marked as special from the moment of conception. This heroic pattern is most fully developed by Lord Raglan (*The Hero: A Study in Tradition, Myth and Drama.* London: Methuen, 1936. 2d ed. New York: Alfred A. Knopf, 1956), who notes similar events in the lives of heroes all over the world. Perseus is conceived in a shower of gold, Oedipus under the shadow of parricide, and Helen by union of mortal woman and god disguised as a swan. So, too, Jesus is made man via immaculate conception, the Buddha experiences a series of births, the birth of King Arthur takes place in the context of infidelity, if not technical illegitimacy, and the conception of the Aztec plumed serpent god Quetzalcóatl is linked with the mysterious disappearance of a beautiful feather found by his mother the goddess Coatlicue. Such parallels cast further doubt upon the historical accuracy of Sunjata's own conception, pregnancy, and birth, but they celebrate Sunjata's mythic features.

Myth and history also intersect in modern times. In the United States, for example, George Washington was certainly the first president, but he probably did not chop down a cherry tree or throw a silver dollar across the Potomac. Davy Crockett was a congressman and the hero of the Alamo, but his feats of marksmanship, personal prowess, and ability to wrestle wild bears parallel the exaggerated accomplishments of Sunjata.

From one point of view, the story of Sunjata's wandering fetus or the tale of Davy Crockett and the bear are fiction. A rationalist can claim that they never happened, yet in some ways these events are just as real, just as true, as historical events. These tales remain alive in the imaginations of those who tell and those who hear the stories. The ability to exist as a fetus outside his mother's womb makes Sunjata stand apart from everyone else and heralds his special, heroic position in society. Anyone who hears the story knows that this child will be a menacing opponent as an adult. Similarly, Davy Crockett's defeat of the bear celebrates his skill as a frontiersman, as a nineteenth-century embodiment of American superiority over the formidable wilderness. Sisyphus' rock becomes heavier.

The heroic lives of both Sunjata and Davy Crockett have a more universal meaning, too. Both the crippled hero's ability to overcome his physical limitations and help his mother and the American frontiersman's successful encounter with ferocious nature provide assurance to all of us that we can overcome the obstacles of our lives and succeed. We can all become Sunjatas and Davy Crocketts. Carl G. Jung, a student of Sigmund Freud, explains the universality of the hero story in terms of a body of unconscious dreams and aspirations which the human community shares. In *Archetypes and the Collective Unconscious* (New York: Pantheon Books, 1959), Jung argues that the lives of heroes such as Sunjata or Davy Crockett contain recurring themes, or archetypes, which reflect basic human psychological needs. We all yearn for heroes who parallel our own lives. They may be greater than we are, but they experience the same hardships and joys. They must grow up, face challenges, succeed, and even die, just as we all do. Sisyphus himself has undergone similar transformation. In the philosophy of the French existentialist Albert Camus, Sisyphus' hopeless task becomes a symbol of the intrinsic absurdity of life. So myth intersects not only with history but also with human psychology and human aspirations. Sisyphus' rock grows larger.

For all of these reasons, this annotated bibliography includes references to material which can be considered semi-historical and religious rather than purely mythic. For the intersection of myth and history the reader is directed to the Sunjata epic in the Sub-Saharan section of Chapter 2 and to tales about Davy Crockett among the modern American myths in Chapter 3. Other semi-historical tales discussed in the bibliography include legends about the early Inca kings of Peru among the South American myths of Chapter 3, the material about the settlement and early history of the Pacific islands in Chapter 5, legends of King Arthur in the section on Celtic myths in Chapter 6, and Scandinavian sagas among the medieval and modern European myths in the same chapter. Philosophical and religious citations appear throughout the bibliography, since discussions of myth narrative dealing with beliefs in god, human fate, death, and the origin of humankind occur in nearly every mythological context.

Legends about historical figures put into perspective the lives of more imaginary heroes such as the Greek Perseus, who flies on the winged sandals of the god Hermes and uses the severed head of the Gorgon Medusa to petrify his enemies. Or the Babylonian hero Gilgamesh, who slays the evil giant Humbaba with the help of his trusty friend Enkidu. Or the trickster Coyote, who, in an emergence tale of the Navajo of the Southwest U.S., cheats Water monster of his fur coat in a game of chance and steals his children. In retaliation, Water monster sends upon the world a great flood, from which Coyote rescues people and animals by leading them from the Fourth World up into the present Fifth World. Perseus' winged sandals, Gilgamesh's monster, and Coyote's great flood, like Sunjata's baobab tree or Davy Crockett's bear, cannot be judged on the standard basis of fact and fiction and lead us to grapple with the truth of myth. At this point, Sisyphus might despair.

Myth, then, is a lie: It invites us to examine its truth but cloaks that truth in fiction. Perseus' winged sandals make no sense, so we reject them as "just a story." We may be tempted to dismiss myths as products of "primitive," untrained minds lacking in the tools of rational thought. Yet the mythic mind is not as naïve as all that. The Greeks themselves were aware that their tales were lies and told the story of the poet Stesichorus, who once blamed the Trojan War on the wantonness of Helen and was struck blind by Zeus, insulted at this unfair accusation of his daughter. Stesichorus responded by composing the first "palinode," or recantation, in which he took it all back and claimed that Helen did not cause the war—that, indeed, she never went to Troy at all, only her ghost did. Of course, Stesichorus' own story places the poet among those special mythic figures marked in some way by god. The storyteller is transformed from mythmaker to myth. The rock and Sisyphus become one.

The Greeks, then, were not troubled by contradictory versions of the same myth. Nor were they necessarily haunted by Helen and her ghost. Rather, the two Helens can be seen as two sides of the same coin, as an examination of the complex role of women in ancient Greek society, just as Sunjata's wandering fetus is both Islamic and animistic. The West African griots, too, recognize the inconsistencies in their story and singers can tell the story in different ways. There is no fixed way of telling the tale; details change at the whim of the storyteller. Sisyphus' rock can undergo metamorphosis as he rolls it up the hill!

If myths are lies, the storyteller is not the only liar. Mythmakers all over the world remind their audiences that they do not invent their stories, but hear them from others. The West African griot, for example, often celebrates his own genealogy, in which he traces his ancestry through a chain of paternal singers back to the time of Sunjata. From this point of view, myth is not a lie, but an oral tradition, the common heritage of a people, and the storyteller's tales represent the collective memory of generations. If the storyteller lies, the ancestors lie, too.

Some ancient Greek storytellers avoid the fate of Stesichorus not by blaming their ancestors but by implicating the gods. The *Iliad* and the *Odyssey* begin with invocations in which the poet prays to the Muse, the Greek goddess of inspiration, to help him tell the story he will sing. In the first book of the *Odyssey*, Penelope, the wife of the hero Odysseus, is grieved when the court singer performs a tale about the missing hero and she rebukes the singer for his lack of tact. Her son Telemachus interrupts his mother and defends the singer with the argument that blame lies not with the singer but with the god Zeus, who sings through him. Here the singer of the *Odyssey* and the authors of the Bible share a belief in divine inspiration. This claim is particularly strong in the poetry of the ancient Greek Hesiod, the author of a creation story called *Theogony*. At the beginning of this poem, Hesiod says that the Muses themselves taught him fine singing as he kept sheep on Mount Helicon. Such personal encounter with deity is not found only in Greek myth. In the myth of Sedna, the chief deity of the Inuit, the shaman serves as the intermediary between the people and their angry goddess. When Sedna withholds food from the people, the shaman intercedes.

If myths are lies, what about biblical tales such as the story of Noah and the flood? Scholars of the Near, or Middle, East have noted parallels between the flood in Genesis and an older Babylonian flood story, which has its own Noah, called Utnapishtim, and includes an aetiology about the rainbow. Great world cataclysms such as floods and fires are a common theme of mythologies all over the world, including China, Oceania, Africa, and the Americas. Here is another challenge for Sisyphus. Why should one flood story be considered true and another false? If the stories of Utnapishtim and of Coyote are just lies, then, one might argue, so is the story of Noah and the ark. Such tales about great primeval world cataclysms are part of a common core of myths about the gods, creation of the world, and the origin of humankind in the mythologies of people all over the world. Within each cultural group, these tales are legitimate attempts to articulate a world view and to explain religious beliefs. Judged from outside the culture, these tales often appear contradictory and even nonhistorical. Yet myths can provide radically different versions of reality which remain legitimate for the people who tell them.

It is difficult, if not impossible to separate mythology from religious beliefs, and we do so inconsistently. We consider our own myths to be religious beliefs and describe the religious beliefs of other cultures as myths. Explaining similarities in flood stories as Hebrew borrowings of a Sumerian tale about the flooding of the Tigris and Euphrates rivers challenges religious belief in a literal interpretation of the Bible. Yet one cannot really discuss the flood myths of Babylonia and ancient Greece without acknowledging parallels in the story of Noah. Rather, references to the Bible and to texts of other world religions illustrate the role of myth in the realm of religion and faith. At one side of the spectrum, myth is a lie. At the other, it is religious dogma. Myth is like Sunjata's wandering fetus. Sometimes it resides in the womb of truth, and sometimes it strays far afield. That is really the point of myth. Myth is not limited by boundaries. It crosses the barrier between truth and untruth, between history and fiction, between religious inspiration and lies. Myths cross disciplinary boundaries and attract the attention of poets, dramatists, theologians, philosophers, psychologists, historians, and anthropologists.

So the discussion of myth is no frivolous matter. It confronts us not only with history but with deity, forcing us to rethink our views of truth and religion. It poses for us questions which can have no answer. How did we come to exist? Why do we die? What happens after we die? These basic questions and concerns of humankind will never be answered to our satisfaction, any more than we will ever really know whether Washington chopped down the cheery tree or if Sunjata relocated the baobab tree. The task is as futile, and as unending, as that of Sisyphus.

Myth also crosses the boundaries of media. The first myths were probably spoken, not written down. Such orally based myths still exist today. Many of the myths recorded in the Americas, Africa, and Oceania are written down not by the storytellers but by ethnologists. The same is true even for modern urban myths, such as tales about the choking Doberman recorded in American cities by Jan Harold Brunvand. While in Florence a few years ago, I was not surprised to hear an Italian version of Brunvand's urban myth about the Mexican pet which turned out to be a rat. Sisyphus' rock may not reach the top of the hill, but it travels far.

Connected with this oral tradition is myth's long-standing relationship with ritual and ceremony. Indeed, some scholars in the early twentieth century argued that all myths originally were related to rituals which they explained or reenacted. Many Navajo myths, for example, are linked with Chantway ceremonies. The Babylonian creation epic *Enuma Elish* is associated with the festival of the New Year. The Greek mysteries at Eleusis are thought to have described the myth of the goddess Demeter's search for her daughter Persephone. Myth and ritual developed a particularly important bond in ancient Athens, where the Greater Dionysia, an annual festival in honor of the god of wine, became the occasion for dramatic performances of myth. Occasionally Dionysus himself was the subject of these tragedies, as he is in Euripides' *Bacchae*, but, more often, the Athenian playwrights sought their material in legends about the heroes, and, especially, about the Trojan war. Nor did they hesitate to tamper with the traditional story. The self-blinding of the hero Oedipus does not appear to have been part of the hero's myth before the time of Sophocles' great tragedy *Oedipus Rex* (c. 427 B.C.). At least Homer makes no mention of the hero's blindness. Whether Sophocles himself invented this detail or borrowed it from someone else, the fact remains that his tragedy made Oedipus' blindness an essential part of the tale.

As the human race developed culturally, the media used to express myth expanded accordingly to include the visual. Cave paintings of neolithic humans in France, the Sahara, and America depict scenes which may represent myth narratives. Potters in Athens of the sixth and fifth centuries B.C. frequently decorated their work with mythological scenes, some of which have no written corollary. One magnificent pot in the Vatican Museum, for example, depicts the Greek hero Jason half-consumed by the dragon guarding the Golden Fleece. The goddess Athena stands at his side, apparently ready to rescue him, yet how, or whether, Jason actually escapes we do not know, because no one but this artist tells us the story.

With the invention of writing, myths underwent another metamorphosis. Ancient mythological texts are preserved in hieroglyphics on the walls of Egyptian pyramids, in cuneiform on Mesopotamian clay tablets, and in alphabetic writings on papyrus and parchment. Indeed, the tales of many ancient peoples are known today only because they were written down. The myths of the Aztec, Maya, and Inca of Central and South America survive because they were preserved in indigenous documents or recorded by early Spanish missionaries. The Babylonian epic of Gilgamesh was rediscovered in a spectacular archaeological find in the early nineteenth century. Canaanite mythology resurfaced only in the early twentieth century, as a result of archaeological work on the site of the ancient city of Ugarit, near the modern Syrian town of Ras Shamra. Those ancient myths which were never written down were not so fortunate. The weight Sisyphus' rock sheds with these lost texts is no consolation, but any study of world mythology must recognize the contribution of archaeologists and linguists whose work in excavation, decipherment, and translation has ensured that many ancient texts are known in the modern world. Some of this work is included in the bibliography, but only when it is accessible to the general reader. Original texts without English translation, for example, are not included.

While some ancient myths were preserved primarily as visual expressions and others in written form, some myths have enjoyed expression in both media, which have been layered on each other over the ages to extend and enrich the myths they tell. Many citations in this bibliography demonstrate how visual and written versions of myths complement each other. Anthologies and collections of world myths are frequently enhanced by artistic illustrations of mythological iconography. Sometimes illustrations and texts are a coherent artistic whole, as they are on the walls of Egyptian pyramids and tombs. Contemporary Navajo sand paintings retell and reinterpret the traditional Navajo world view and myth of emergence. Artwork can also be inspired by text. *Perseus,* Benvenuto Cellini's seventeenth-century bronze masterpiece in the Piazza della Signoria in Florence, is based ultimately on Ovid's description of the Greek hero in the *Metamorphoses.* Occasionally, written myths are needed to understand mythological artwork. For example, many painted images of the Indian god Krishna are difficult to interpret without consulting textual versions of the god's myths.

Another medium in which myth functions is music. Sometimes the tales are sung rather than spoken. Some musical accompaniments, such as those for the odes in Greek tragedy, are lost, but occasionally musical scores accompany versions of the myths, especially those recorded by modern ethnologists. Myths and legends have also inspired musical compositions such as Nikolay Andreyevich Rimsky-Korsakov's symphonic suite *Scheherazade* or even the score to Walt Disney's *Aladdin*, both based on the *Thousand and One Nights* of ancient Persia and Arabia. This bibliography notes references to musical scores in transcriptions and translations but does not incorporate other musical material, such as recordings available on video- and audiotapes. Sisyphus will have to roll this rock mostly without music.

Today we can use the word "myth" to refer not only to stories told by oral, theatrical, written, musical, and visual means but also to those that appear in the media of our modern age: the comic pages of the daily newspaper, cartoons in *The New Yorker*, even the computer screen. The media of myth are as varied as the shapes the ogre could display to Puss in Boots, as changeable as the Greek sea god Proteus, who could take on any shape he desired. Many of these media are represented in this bibliography.

Myth is not only protean in its media; it is also universal in its geography. Myth-telling is a human phenomenon. The history of mythography in European scholarship illustrates the ever-growing web of myth. Until the early nineteenth century the study of mythology basically meant the study of Greco-Roman myths. Some ancient texts, such as Ovid's *Metamorphoses* and Vergil's *Aeneid*, were well known in the medieval world. The Italian Renaissance, with its rediscovery of things Greek, gave the myths of the ancient Greeks and Romans a new vitality. In the fourteenth century Giovanni Boccaccio wrote a monumental mythological treatise in Latin entitled *Genealogia Deorum Gentilium* (c. 1350-1375; genealogy of the gods of the Gentiles). Early in the fifteenth century, the hero Hercules and other figures from Classical myth appear on the doors of old St. Peter's in Rome and on the Porta della Mandorla on the cathedral in Florence, and, later in the century, Lorenzo de' Medici amused himself by composing a song about the marriage of Bacchus and Ariadne.

This focus on Greco-Roman mythology did not really change until the European Enlightenment in the eighteenth century, when scholars began to examine the world from different perspectives. Two developments in mythology reflect this trend. The first is the publication by Jacob and Wilhelm Grimm's collections of German fairy tales and legends published as *Kinder- und Hausmärchen* (*German Fairy Tales*) in 1812 and *Deutsche Sagen* (*German Legends*) between 1816 and 1818. The work of the Brothers Grimm recognized the value of the oral traditions of the common folk of Europe and stands at the beginning of the modern science of folkloristics. The second is the announcement by Sir William Jones in 1786 that the Sanskrit, Greek, and Latin languages sprang from a common source. Jones's work in what is now called Indo-European Linguistics opened the door not only to the science of historical linguistics but also to studies in comparative mythology. Linguistic links were found to bind the sky gods of many ancient peoples of Europe and Asia. The Sanskrit sky god Dyaus, called *pita*, or "father," was recognized to have names and functions similar to the Greek god Zeus (also known as Dios Pater), to the Latin Jupiter, and even the Germanic Tiw Vater. The names of all these deities share two common Indo-European root words, *deiw**-, which means "to shine," and *pater**- or "father."

From the Indo-European mythologies, comparativists moved further afield later in the nineteenth century. The European exploration and colonization of Africa opened up vast opportunities for collection of mythological material. The oral literature which the German anthropologist Leo Frobenius gathered in the early twentieth century is only partially available to the English reader today. Other early collections of African myths were originally written in English and remain accessible, especially in reprint form. Similar work has been done in the Pacific and among the Native Americans of North America by anthropologists such as Paul Radin, Elsie Clews Parsons, George Bird Grinnell, and William Wyatt Gill. In the twentieth century the modern sciences of anthropology and folkloristics have been refined, and anthropologists and folklorists have become more sensitive to the cultures being recorded. Nineteenth-century views of "primitive" peoples have, for the most part, given way to work which aims at authenticity. Some of these are even bilingual, such as the edition of legends of the Papago and Pima of Arizona by Dean Saxton and Lucille Saxton. The culmination of this trend is reflected in mythological collections made by or in collaboration with members of the culture, such as the Navajo texts produced by Ekkehart Malotki and Michael Lomatuway'ma. Such original-language texts with English translation have been available for ancient Greek and Latin materials since the nineteenth century. Only recently has this phenomenon become more standard, especially for Native American texts. Despite the evolutionary nature of this material, many of the nineteenth- and early twentieth-century ethnographic collections of world mythology have been reprinted. Approached cautiously, the material remains a valuable resource for the general reader at the end of the twentieth century.

Ranging wide in the territory it covers, this bibliography is intentionally inclusive but not exhaustive in its Sisyphean task. Priority has been placed upon listing the widest possible cultural range of anthologies, collections, and translations of myths. In accordance with this worldwide scope, the chapters of this bibliography are organized geographically, except for Chapter 1, which deals with comparative studies and collections of myths from more than one part of the world. The remaining chapters move from east to west around the world, beginning in Chapter 2 with the myths of ancient Egypt and Sub-Saharan Africa. The oral traditions of the Americas in Chapter 3 are followed by Oceanic legends and myths of the Pacific and Australia in Chapter 4. Grouped together in Chapter 5 are the many different mythologies of Asian peoples such as the Babylonians, Hebrews, Indians, Chinese, and Japanese. Special care has been taken to offer a broad survey of these mythological materials from Africa, the Americas, Oceania, and Asia, because they are, in general, somewhat unfamiliar to the average English-reader and have become, for the historical reasons discussed above, the object of special scholarly interest only in recent decades.

The mythologies of Europe present a different kind of challenge. So much published material is available on the myths of the ancient Greeks, Romans, Celts, and Norse, not to mention more modern European traditions, that an exhaustive treatment of this continent would split Sisyphus' rock in two and would require a second bibliographic volume for Europe alone. Just the legends surrounding King Arthur have generated a formidable list of of more than 12,000 titles. For this reason, citations on European myths in this bibliography represent only a sampling of some of the best and most widely accessible work in this area. One criterion for exclusion from the European chapter is the availability of other bibliographic resources. For example, although the Homeric epics and fifth-century Athenian tragedies are considered central mythological texts for ancient Greece, this material is not emphasized here in part because annotated bibliographies on Greek epic and tragedy exist in the Magill Bibliographies series and elsewhere.

In the metamorphosing world of myth, even such a broad geographic organization can present occasional problems. While some of these challenges and difficulties are addressed in more detail in the chapter introductions, three specific cultural examples warrant observation here. The Gypsy peoples of Europe, Asia, and the Americas share a common folk tradition that crosses political borders. Chapter 1 serves as the logical repository for such cross-regional works. A second group which crosses continental boundaries is composed of the indigenous peoples of the Arctic and sub-Arctic, including the Inuit of North America and Greenland, the Eskimo of Siberia, and the Lapps of Finland and Russia. While the literature on their mythology is sometimes comprehensive, more often it focuses on the peoples of northern Canada, Alaska, and Greenland. Consequently, citations dealing with the mythology of the Arctic peoples can be found in several different chapters of this bibliography. Most belong with the North American material in Chapter 3 and a few with the Asian material in Chapter 5. Works dealing with the whole geographic range of Arctic cultures appear in Chapter 1. A third geographically diverse mythological tradition is that of the Jewish people. Rooted in the soil of ancient Israel and Palestine, the Jewish people possess a wealth of tales which they share with Christians and Muslims through the Old Testment. At the same time, the Jewish tradition did not stagnate after the fall of Jerusalem and the destruction of the third temple in A.D. 70. More Jewish legends and myths survive in medieval literature such as the Midrash, and Jews of the diaspora have maintained their own myths and legends wherever they have lived. Since Jewish traditions cross many geographical boundaries, bibliographic references to Jewish myth appear in two separate chapters. Discussions of biblical tales appear with similar Babylonian, Canaanite, and Sumerian stories among the West and Central Asian myths in Chapter 5. The legends and folktales of medieval and modern Jews, however, have equally strong ties with the general folklore tradition of Europe and America—a cross-boundary tradition—and for this reason, several important works on Jewish mythology and folklore appear among the general anthologies, commentaries, and translations in Chapter 1.

Myths can be presented in a variety of ways. Sometimes editors offer transcriptions of oral texts recorded in the field, accompanied by literal translations or plot summaries. The fullest treatment of this sort is done by anthropologists who provide detailed ethnographic information about the people and careful documentation about the storytellers and the circumstances of recording. Other authors offer only paraphrases or free retellings of myths. Occasionally violent or sexual details are censored, especially in versions for children. Sometimes the primary sources for a myth are literary. This is especially true for ancient cultures such as the Egyptians, Greeks, Babylonians, and Maya, for whom the recording of myths in the field is no longer possible. Actually, no single technique of recording is better than the others, and each technique addresses different needs and audiences. This bibliography does not emphasize any particular type of mythological record. Even children's versions of myths can prove valuable to a scholar interested in different transformations of a particular myth. Sisyphus' rock must be variegated in every possible way. For this reason the bibliography includes myths told and illustrated for young children or juvenile readers as well as myths presented in a more scholarly format. Some of this material is readily available in many public and undergraduate college libraries. The rest can be obtained by the general reader via interlibrary loan.

Another problem is one of nomenclature. Ancient Greeks and Romans sometimes used different names for the same mythological figure. The Greek god Zeus, for example, is identified with the Roman deity Jupiter. The Greek hero Heracles is the equivalent of the Roman Hercules. The Greek Odysseus is the Roman Ulysses. For Greek names, one is faced with the further problem of differing orthographic systems. *Herakles* is a more faithful Greek transliteration of the more latinized spelling *Heracles*. *Oedipus* can also appear as *Oidipous*. Nor are spelling problems confined to the Mediterranean. In North America, one is faced with a variety of spellings for Native American nations—*Navajo* or *Navaho*, *Algonquin* or *Algonkin* or *Algonquian*—and for mythological figures such as the trickster *Glooskap/Gluscap/Gluskap*. Occasionally, variation in orthography is part of the process of mythmaking. The African trickster spider is known as *Anansi* or *Ananse* in African contexts but becomes *Nancy* among African Americans in the Caribbean and in the United States. Nomenclature is also connected with the issue of political correctness. Many of the authors cited in the section on North American myths lived before the word "Indian"—an inaccurate label used by Europeans ignorant of their geographical whereabouts when they "discovered" the Americas—came into disfavor. The peoples of eastern Canada and the Arctic prefer the indigenous name *Inuit* to the ubiquitous *Eskimo*, while the name Yup'ik is used by the people of the Bering Strait and Inupiat by inhabitants of the north slope of Alaska. In the face of such problems, consistency of nomenclature is an important goal in this bibliography. While spelling is not changed in titles, citations aim toward standardized spellings. The more familiar latinized forms Greek names are used in Greek contexts, and Latin names are used in Roman contexts. The word "Indian" is replaced within citations by the term "Native American." The word "tribe" is studiously avoided, especially in dealing with American and African peoples.

By this point Sisyphus would no longer recognize his rock, which has undergone repeated metamorphosis and which has taken on unbelievable weight. He has learned, however, that his rock is universal and encompasses all aspects of human life. It is fiction and truth, history and legend, religious belief and fable, art, literature, drama, music, psychology, and a good story well told all rolled up into one. Sisyphus may never succeed in rolling his rock to the top of the hill, but the reward is in the effort.

Monmouth, Illinois
November, 1995

Chapter 1
GENERAL COLLECTIONS AND ANTHOLOGIES

The citations in this chapter cross the geographic boundaries used in the rest of the bibliography. Some deal with mythologies from all around the world. Others focus not on world mythology but on a narrower yet cross-regional, geographic range. For example, Egyptian religion and mythology, usually treated separately, are often discussed in the context of Middle Eastern cultures. Those citations which deal with both Egypt and the Middle East appear here. The mythologies of two peoples, in particular, cut across traditional geographic boundaries. A broad geographic context is necessary for the discussion of many Jewish myths, which may spring from an ancient heritage in the Middle East but which also have strong ties to the European folktale tradition. Some Jewish material with a special Middle Eastern focus is included with the West Asian myths in Chapter 5. Most of the Jewish material, however, is found here in Chapter 1. Although the peoples of the Arctic regions of North America, Europe, and Asia share a common culture, most handbooks focus on the myths of the native peoples of Canada, Alaska, and Greenland and are treated with the North American Myths in Chapter 3. Where authors acknowledge a broader geographic context for the Arctic peoples, the citations are included here. Some of the books cited in this chapter are arranged around particular themes such as creation myths from around the world. Others illustrate different treatments of the same folktale, such as "Cinderella." Also included in this chapter are several general bibliographies and research guides.

Anderson, George K. *The Legend of the Wandering Jew.* Providence, R.I.: Brown University Press, 1965.
A historical analysis of the medieval tale of the wandering Jew and its variations as Ahasuerus stories. Traces the beginning of the legend and its treatment in various European countries and in America and follows its transformations into the nineteenth and twentieth centuries. Appendices include a bibliographic discussion of scholarly studies of the legend, a note on Hungarian treatments of the legend, and notes on stories about the wandering Jewess. Endnotes and index.

Ausubel, Nathan, ed. *A Treasury of Jewish Folklore.* New York: Crown Publishers, 1948.
This rich anthology of the oral tradition of the Jewish people arranged thematically includes not only myths and folktales, but also jokes,

proverbs, riddles, songs, and dances. Among the many mythological categories represented are tales about heroes, sages, saints, *schnorrers* or "beggars," the fools of Chelm, tricksters, and rabbis, as well as folktales, demon tales, animal fables, and legends based upon the Bible, the ten lost tribes of Israel, and the afterlife. General introductory essay on sources and characteristics of Jewish folklore. Some tale types are also preceded by introductions. Glossary and index.

Bailey, John, Kenneth McLeish, and David Spearman. *Gods and Men.* New York: Oxford University Press, 1981.
Thirty traditional short tales from around the world are retold for the general reader. Ten creation myths are followed by eleven tales of good and evil, including stories about the first sin and flood myths from Sumeria, Israel, and China, and nine legends about heroes such as King David of Israel, Beowulf, and St. George, and the prophets Moses and Elijah. No sources for the tales are provided, but each selection is introduced by brief commentary. Illustrated with black-and-white drawings by Derek Collard, Charles Keeping, and Jeroo Roy. Short introduction by Bailey; bibliography.

Ballou, R. O., ed. *The Bible of the World.* New York: Viking Press, 1939.
religious texts from eight major world religions are gathered together in translation in this anthology, which is arranged according to religion. While some of these selections concentrate on moral teachings and religious principles, others contain significant mythological narrative, including creation and flood myths in the Hindu *Satapatha-Brahmana*, the Zoroastrian *Zend-Avesta*, and the Bible. Mythological material also includes the *Gathas*, or hymns of the Persian Zoroaster, and legendary lives of Buddha and Zoroaster. Introductory essay, endnotes, bibliography, glossary, and index.

Brunvand, Jan Harold. *Folklore: A Study and Research Guide.* New York: St. Martin's Press, 1976.
This introduction to folklore and annotated bibliography is intended for the beginner, especially the college undergraduate. In Chapter 1 Brunvand provides a historical perspective for the study of folklore and discusses leading folklore theories. Chapter 2 is a reference guide with bibliographic discussions. Some sections are arranged according to the form of the material (reference, journal, survey, textbook, etc.). Others are arranged thematically and deal with folklore theories, genres, stylistics, and geography. In Chapter 3 Brunvand offers a

detailed guide to writing a research paper on a folklore topic. Includes a sample paper, glossary, and index of authors.

Bulfinch, Thomas. *The Age of Fable*. Boston: S. W. Tilton, 1855.
The first of Bulfinch's highly popular compilations of mythological tales has been reissued numerous times, with and without illustrations. Bulfinch's selections reflect the nineteenth century's emphasis on Greek and Roman myths complemented especially by the legends of other Indo-European peoples, such as the Persians, Hindi, Germans, and Celts. Also deals with some myth theories, tales about imaginary beasts, and medieval legends. In the introductory chapter Bulfinch surveys the Greco-Roman pantheon and in the following thirty-two chapters tells Greco-Roman myths, mostly borrowed from Homer, Ovid, and Vergil. The stories of Prometheus and Pandora are followed by various tales from Ovid's *Metamorphoses* and legends of the heroes, the Trojan war, and Vergil's *Aeneid*. In Chapter 34 Bulfinch deals with Pythagoras, Egyptian deities, and oracles. He considers several theories about the origin of mythology in Chapter 35, several mythological monsters in Chapter 36, Zoroastrian, Hindu, and Buddhist mythologies in Chapter 37, Norse mythology in Chapters 38-40, and druids in Chapter 41. In the preface Bulfinch states that his goal is to illustrate the link between mythology and European literature. For this reason his text is filled with poetic quotations with mythological references from poets such as Edmund Spenser, John Milton, and Henry Wadsworth Longfellow.

_____. *Bulfinch's Mythology*. New York: Thomas P. Crowell, 1913. Reprint. Edited by Richard P. Martin. New York: HarperCollins, 1991.
Brings together into one volume all three of Bulfinch's popular retellings of mythology. In the first thirty-three chapters of *The Age of Fable* (1855) Bulfinch deals with the myths of the ancient Greeks and Romans, and in the remaining eight chapters he also considers myth theory and the myths of the Egyptians, Asians, Scandinavians, and Celts. In *The Age of Chivalry* (1858) Bulfinch retells medieval legends of the British Isles, including the story of King Arthur, the Welsh *Mabinogion*, *Beowulf*, and Robin Hood. In *The Legends of Charlemagne* (1863) Bulfinch deals with tales connected with European romances about Charlemagne, including the adventures of Rinaldo and Orlando, Huon of Bordeaux, and Ogier the Dane. In appendices are a collection of proverbial expressions, a list of illustrative literary passages cited in the text, and a combined mythological dictionary and

index by Edward Everett Hale. Although this volume has been reissued frequently, with and without illustrations, Martin's annotated edition offers some special and valuable features. Martin precedes each chapter of *The Age of Fable* with headnotes placing Bulfinch's work in historical perspective and showing how interpretations of these myths have changed. For *The Age of Chivalry* and *The Legends of Charlemagne* Martin uses introductory chapters instead of headnotes, for the same purpose. In a general introductory essay, Martin reviews Bulfinch's career and discusses the continuing influence of his works. Martin's edition also includes four maps, five genealogical charts, line drawings by Sabra Moore, and a bibliography.

Bynum, David E. *The Daemon in the Wood: A Study of Oral Narrative Patterns.* Cambridge, Mass.: Harvard University Press, 1978.
Woven into this technical study of tree motifs in oral tales are forty-three illustrative tales from all over the world. Offers tales from a wide variety of traditional contexts, including biblical legends, selections from the Babylonian epic *Gilgamesh*, selections from *Beowulf*, honey-trickster tales from the Lamba of Africa, folktales of North Carolina, and Serbo-Croatian tales. A list of these tales can be found at the beginning of the appendix. Sixty-seven figures illustrating traditional scenes and ancient artwork, endnotes, and index.

Cavendish, Richard, ed. *Legends of the World.* New York: Schocken Books, 1982.
Thirty-four British scholars collaborated to create this collection of legendary stories from all over the world, including tales about supernatural battles with monsters, love and loyalty, historical events and battles, saints, magicians, and craftsmen. Contains five geographic sections with chapters on forty-three different cultural groups. Besides more common regions, areas such as Burma, Ethiopia, and the Balkans receive separate treatments. Some emphasis on European legends, with several chapters on Celtic tales and legends dealing with medieval Christian Europe, while the many cultures of Sub-Saharan Africa and of the Americas are treated collectively. Appendix with a comparative thematic survey of world legends. Seven full-page illustrations by Eric Fraser. Endnotes, bibliography, and index.

_____, ed. *Mythology: An Illustrated Encyclopaedia.* New York: Rizzoli International, 1980. Also published as *An Illustrated Encyclopoedia of Mythology.* New York: Crescent Books, 1984.

Essays by twenty-seven scholars prominent in various areas of myth study are arranged in six geographic groupings: Asia, the Middle East (including Egypt), the West, Africa, the Americas, and the Pacific. Each essay offers a broad overview of the mythology of the culture with some summary and analysis of specific myths. Individual essays are often accompanied by a map, chronological charts, genealogies, glossaries, and many illustrations of artwork and sites associated with mythology. Special areas covered in this anthology are the mythologies of Tibet, Islam, the Slavs, the Caucasus region, and Voodoo. The Arctic is the only major geographic region not represented in this collection. General glossary, bibliography, and index.

Cole, Roger W. *Edith Hamilton's Mythology: A Critical Commentary.* New York: American R. D. M. Corp., 1966.

This study guide and companion to Hamilton's *Mythology* begins with an introductory and background chapter on the meaning and interpretation of mythology, the early history of the Greeks, and general features of the Greek gods and religion. In Chapter 2 Cole offers structural analyses and summaries of the myths, followed by some notes and commentary. These analyses and notes follow the order used by Hamilton and concentrate on the mythology of the ancient Greeks plus a short section on Norse mythology. In Chapter 3 Cole discusses some of the aims of Hamilton's book, her approach, and her style. List of suggested study topics and annotated bibliography.

Colum, Padraic. *Orpheus.* New York: Macmillan, 1930. Reprinted as *Myths of the World.* New York: Grosset and Dunlap, 1972.

This collection of myths from all over the world was gathered from unspecified sources. The arrangement is both geographic and loosely chronological. Egyptian, Babylonian, Persian, and Jewish myths are followed by Greek, Roman, and Greco-Roman tales. The rest of Europe is represented by one Finnish and several Icelandic tales. From East Asia are Indian, Chinese, and Japanese myths. Four tales from Polynesia are followed by nine from the Americas. Emphasis is on myths about creation and the gods. Includes the Egyptian story of Osiris and Isis, a selection from the Babylonian *Gilgamesh*, the Greek tale of Cupid and Psyche, Icelandic, Chinese, Japanese, and Polynesian tales about the beginning of things, and a Zuñi tale about the origin of corn. Accompanied by twenty black-and-white engravings by Boris Artzybasheff.

Cox, Marian Roalfe. *Cinderella.* London: The Folk-Lore Society, 1893.

A pioneering collection of 345 variants of the Cinderella story. Part 1 consists of abstracts of the tales with special themes and motifs highlighted. These abstracts are arranged in four groups: Cinderella tales with an ill-treated heroine and recognition by means of a shoe, Catskin tales with an unnatural father and flight of the heroine, Cap o' Rushes tales with a King Lear judgment and an outcast heroine, and indeterminate tales. Part 2 offers more detailed tabulations or summaries of these tales arranged according to sources. Part 3 contains abstracts and tabulations of hero tales with incidents common to Cinderella variants. Introductory essay on the Cinderella folktale tradition by Andrew Lang. Detailed preface by the author on methodology, characteristics of the tale, and its historical tradition, with charts showing geographic distribution and a chronological list of variants. Endnotes.

Creighton, David. *Deeds of Gods and Heroes*. New York: St. Martin's Press, 1969.

This survey of world mythology is designed for schoolchildren. Summaries and retellings of myths are accompanied by study material. A preliminary chapter on the meaning of myth is followed two North American myths, one from ancient Egypt, two from the Middle East, three about the gods of ancient Greece, four about the Greek heroes Theseus, Perseus, Heracles, and Jason, three about the Trojan War heroes Achilles, Odysseus, and Aeneas, and three about Norse gods and heroes. Each geographic section and each chapter is introduced by some background and comparative material. The study material in an appendix includes bibliography, references to artistic and musical adaptations of the myth, and questions for comprehension and comparison. Numerous illustrations of artwork and sites, genealogical tables, charts, and pronouncing index.

de la Mare, Walter. *Animal Stories*. New York: Charles Scribner's Sons, 1939.

A collection of forty-two animal stories interspersed with forty-six traditional poems on the same theme. Includes well-known folktales such as "Puss in Boots" retold by Charles Perrault and "The Traveling Musicians" by the Brothers Grimm; familiar children's tales such as "The Three Little Pigs" and "The Story of the Three Bears"; and stories by more modern authors such as "Running Wolf" by Algernon Blackwood and de la Mare's own "The Hare and the Hedgehog." Also in the collection are Gypsy folktales and stories told in Scottish dialect. In an introductory essay, de la Mare provides some background and sources for these tales, discusses the general characteristics of *Märchen*, myths, sagas, and aetiologies, and considers special features of animal tales.

Doane, Thomas William. *Bible Myths and Their Parallels in Other Religions*. New York: Truth Seeker, 1882. Reprint. New Hyde Park, N.Y.: University Books, 1971.

This book was strongly influenced by Godfrey Higgins' *Anacalypsis* (1833) and is the product of the Freethought movement of the late nineteenth century. Despite its original publication date, Doane's book remains a valuable study of comparative religion and mythology. Doane's goal is to compare legends in both the Old and New Testaments to parallel tales in other world cultures. A significant portion of the book consists of retellings and paraphrases of biblical, Indian, Chinese, Babylonian, Greek, and other tales. Part 1 deals with the Old Testament and contains chapters on the creation and the fall, the flood, the tower of Babel, the sacrifice of Isaac, Jacob's ladder, the exodus, the ten commandments, Samson, Jonah, and circumcision. Most of Part 2 is concerned with events in the life of Jesus, with additional chapters on the Eucharist, baptism, worship of the Virgin, Christian symbols, Christmas, the trinity, pagan elements in Christianity, the success of Christianity, and the antiquity of the pagan religions. Essays in appendices deal with Native American mythologies, myths about heavenly bodies, fairy tales, and early historical references to Jesus and to Christians. Bibliography and combined glossary and index. In a foreword to the reprint, Leslie Shephard provides valuable commentary on the life of Doane and the scope of this book.

Doria, Charles, and Harris Lenowitz, eds. and trans. *Origins: Creation Texts from the Ancient Mediterranean*. Garden City, N.Y.: Anchor Press, 1976.

This collection of more than sixty myths is divided into two groups: myths about creation through speech and myths about creation by elemental forces. Includes selections from Egyptian Pyramid texts and the Book of the Dead, the Hebrew Old Testament, the Babylonian *Enuma Elish*, the Hurrian *Song of Ullikummi*, Greek texts such as Apollonius of Rhodes' *Argonautica* and Aristophanes' *Birds*, and Roman works such as Ovid's *Metamorphoses* and Vergil's *Eclogue* 6. All the translations are printed in verse form. A brief introduction appears at the beginning of each selection. Appendix of numerical creation texts from ancient Greece and Egypt. Introduction by the editors and a preface by Jerome Rothenberg. Bibliography.

Dundes, Alan, ed. *Cinderella: A Folklore Casebook*. New York: Garland
Press, 1982.

In this collection of essays, scholars and folklorists analyze and interpret different versions of the folktale commonly known as "Cinderella." Contains translations of three early versions of the story from
Western Europe: Giambattista Basile's Italian version published between 1634 and 1636, Charles Perrault's French version of 1697, and
the 1812 German version of the brothers Jacob and Wilhelm Grimm.
Also summarizes or retells versions of the tale from China, Japan,
Africa, Java, Iran/Afghanistan, Russia, India, Tuscany, and elsewhere.
Preceding each version Dundes provides useful background information and commentary. Endnotes follow each article. Bibliography.

Eliade, Mircea. *From Primitives to Zen: A Thematic Sourcebook of the
History of Religions*. New York: Harper & Row, 1967.

This anthology of readings about ancient religions by an important
scholar os the psychology of myth contains translations of traditional
and scholarly documents from all over the world. Many are of mythological interest. Contains descriptions of deities and prayers from
Africa, the ancient Middle East, Greece and Rome, North America, the
Pacific, China, and Japan. Judaeo-Christian texts are not included.
Selections from eighteen cosmogonical myths are accompanied by six
describing the creation of humankind, two flood stories, and five
describing the origin of death. Texts include references to ritual sacrifices, oracles, hymns, initiations, shamans, ethical teachings, descriptions of the afterlife, and myths of descent into the underworld,
including several variations on the Greek legend of Orpheus. Each
selection is followed by information about sources and occasional
endnotes. Bibliography and index.

Gaster, Moses, trans. *Ma'aseh Book*. 2 vols. Philadelphia: Jewish Publication Society of America, 1934.

An English translation of 254 medieval Jewish tales and legends
originally written in Judeo-German. The title refers to the Judeo-German word for an old grandmother's tale. Sources for these tales include
the Talmud as well as the oral tradition of individual Jewish commu-
nities, especially in German-speaking Europe. The collection includes
tales about biblical figures and devout rabbis, moral stories, miracles,
religious persecution, and wondrous adventures. In an introductory
essay, Gaster discusses the history of Jewish folklore and provides a
history of the *Ma'aseh Book*. One illustration, endnotes, and index.

Gayley, Charles M. *The Classic Myths in English Literature and in Art*. Rev. ed. New York: John Wiley & Sons, 1939.

Part 1 is a retelling of Greek, Roman, and Norse myths based originally on Bulfinch's *The Age of Fable* with extensive illustrations and quotations from art and literature, particularly from British authors and artists. Begins with Greek creation stories and emphasizes myths about the Greek gods and goddesses. Several chapters devoted to Greek hero legends, the Trojan war, Homer's *Odyssey*, Vergil's *Aeneid*, and Norse mythology. Part 2 is a history of myth, with chapters on the origin and elements of myth, the distribution of myths, and their preservation. An interpretative and illustrative commentary accompanies the text. Fifteen full-page illustrations and 189 black-and-white figures. Pronunciation guide to mythological names, index of modern authors and artists, and index of mythological subjects.

Gilliland, Hap. *The Flood*. Billings: Montana Indiana Publications, 1972.

Seventeen flood myths from around the world are retold for children. Some groups represented are the Apache, Athabasca, Delaware (Lenni Lenape), Squamish, Tlingit, and Yakima of North America, the Yanawamo of South America, the Tamil of Sri Lanka, the Shasta of Africa, Filipinos, Chinese, ancient Babylonians, ancient Hebrews, and ancient Greeks. Two tales are not identified with a specific cultural group. Short introduction.

Goodrich, Norma Lorre. *Ancient Myths*. New York: New American Library, 1960.

Retells legends from the ancient Middle East, Egypt, India, Greece, and Rome. Each of the seven geographically arranged chapters begins with some background and commentary. Included are the stories of the Sumerian hero Gilgamesh in Chapter 1, the Egyptian god Horus in Chapter 2, the Greek heroes Minos and Theseus in Chapter 3, the Trojan princess Cassandra in Chapter 4, the Persian hero Rustan in Chapter 5, the Indian Rama in Chapter 6, and the travels of the Trojan Aeneas and his war in Italy in Chapter 7. Four maps, five line drawings, four charts, and an index.

Grimal, Pierre, ed. *Larousse World Mythology*. Translated by Patricia Beardsworth. New York: G. P. Putnam's Sons, 1963.

More than twenty scholars have contributed essays to this basic reference source edited by a prominent professor at the Sorbonne. Examines myths from every major area of the world. Separate sections on Egypt, the Middle East, the Semites, Greece, Rome, India, China, Japan, Celts,

Germans, Slavs, Balts, Finns, Siberia, and the Arctic. The peoples of
North America, South America, Central America, Oceania, and Africa
are dealt with more generically in the last five sections. Combines basic
description and interpretation with many visual illustrations, paraphrases of mythic narratives, and occasional quotation in translation
from original sources. Six hundred illustratations, including forty-nine
in color. Bibliography and index.

Groome, Francis Hindes. *Gypsy Folk-Tales*. London: Hurst and Blackett,
1899. Reprint. New York: Arno Press, 1977.
A collection of seventy-six Gypsy tales arranged in nine geographic
groupings. Tales of Turkish Gypsies in Chapter 1 are followed by those
of Romanian Gypsies in Chapter 2, Burkowina Gypsies in Chapter 3,
Transylvanian Gypsies in Chapter 4, Slovak, Moravian, and Bohemian
Gypsies in Chapter 5, Polish Gypsies in Chapter 6, English Gypsies in
Chapter 7, Welsh Gypsies in Chapter 8, and Scottish Tinkers in Chapter 9. These tales are often based upon supernatural elements such as
dragons, the devil, magic, wizards, and vampires. In a detailed introductory essay, Groome discusses various Gypsy groups around the
world, their language, and their origin; offers a history of Gypsy
folkloristics; and discusses characteristics of their folktales, with some
comparative comments.

Guirand, Felix, et al., eds. *New Larousse Encyclopedia of Mythology*.
Translated by Richard Aldington and Delano Ames. New York: Hamlyn, 1968.
This monumental reference book on world mythology offers seventeen
essays by a group of mostly French scholars. The emphasis is on the
mythologies of Europe and the ancient Mediterranean, with separate
studies of Egyptian, Assyro-Babylonian, Phoenician, Greek, Roman,
Celtic, Teutonic, Slavonic, and Finno-Ugric myths. The rest of the
world is discussed in less detail, with studies of the myths of ancient
Persia, India, China, Japan, the Americas, Oceania, and Sub-Saharan
Africa. Introductory essay by Robert Graves on some characteristics
and interpretations of myths from around the world. About six hundred
illustrations, including thirty-two color plates, depicting artifacts connected with the myths. Bibliography and index.

Hamilton, Edith. *Mythology*. New York: New American Library, 1942.
A popular handbook of Greco-Roman and Norse mythology. Summaries of the myths of the major gods and heroes are accompanied by
quotations from various ancient sources. Part 1 deals with the various

Greek deities, creation, and early human life. Part 2 is devoted to Greek tales of love and adventure such as the myths of Cupid and Psyche, Orpheus and Eurydice, and Jason and the Argonauts. Four other parts tell the stories of great Greek heroes before or during the Trojan War and tales of the great mythological families of Greece. The last part includes an introduction to Norse mythology, especially the Norse gods, creation stories, wisdom literature, and the stories of Signy and Sigurd. Illustrations, genealogical tables, and index.

Henderson, Joseph L., and Maud Oakes. *The Wisdom of the Serpent: The Myths of Death, Rebirth, and Resurrection*. New York: George Braziller, 1963.
This rich collection of fifty world myths illustrating the themes of death, rebirth, and resurrection contains excerpts from a variety of published translations. Especially prominent are Hindu and Indian myths, but Aztec, Greek, African, Middle Eastern, and Native North American tales are also represented. The myths are arranged into the following thematic groups: death and rebirth as a cosmic pattern; death and rebirth as cycles of nature; initiation as a spiritual education; initiation as a psychic liberation; and myths of resurrection. Each thematic group is preceded by the authors' introduction. Some myths have separate introductions. In an appendix are four illustrations of the theme of death and rebirth in the poetry of Emily Dickinson, Samuel Taylor Coleridge, and Walt Whitman. In an introductory essay, Henderson discusses each of the themes in the context of Carl G. Jung's theory of myth as an expression of the collective unconscious. Eighteen line drawings and thirty-two plates illustrating some of these myths in artistic contexts. Endnotes for the plates, bibliographic endnotes, and index.

Herzberg, Max J. *Classical Myths*. 1935. Rev. ed. *Myths and Their Meaning*. Boston: Allyn and Bacon, 1966.
This traditional survey of the myths of ancient Greece, Rome, the Celts, and Scandinavia has served as an introduction to mythology for several generations of American schoolchildren. Part 1 has seventeen chapters on Greek cosmogony, Greek deities and heroes, the Trojan war, the adventures of Aeneas, Roman divinities, and myths in Latin literature. In Part 2 are three chapters on the gods and heroes of northern Europe and Celtic fairies. Summaries of the myths are followed by sections illustrating their use in Western literature, bibliographies, numerous exercises, word studies, and quizzes. In an introductory section, the author considers the meaning of myth. In a concluding

section, he summarizes some influences of the myths in the modern world. Illustrated with many black-and-white photographs of ancient and modern art. Additional tests, projects, and bibliography in an appendix. Index.

Jewkes, Wilfred Thomas. *Man the Myth-Maker*. New York: Harcourt Brace Jovanovich, 1973.

This school anthology brings together a wide variety of mythological texts, including retellings of original myths by scholars such as W. H. D. Rouse, Paul Radin, and Ella Elizabeth Clark, and literary works by William Wordsworth, William Butler Yeats, and Mark Twain which make significant reference to mythological figures and themes. The selections are arranged in six thematic chapters. In Chapter 1 Greek, Chinese, and Ugandan myths are accompanied by modern poems and essays about god. In Chapter 2 the Greek myth of Prometheus and a Crow myth about Old Man are followed by more modern texts dealing with contributions to human life by a god-teacher. Chapter 3 illustrates the theme of human Paradise lost with the Greek myths of Pandora, Phaëthon, Arachne, and Pegasus, Blackfoot and Hottentot myths about death, and selections from twentieth-century novels. Chapter 4 deals with the theme of the great flood, especially in its Greek and Mesopotamian versions. In Chapter 5 the theme of metamorphosis is illustrated by Greek myths about Daphne, Baucis and Philemon, Midas, Pygmalion, and Narcissus. In Chapter 6 the themes of immortality and the seasons are developed by means of the Greek myths of Persephone and of Adonis, an Aztec lamentation, a Norse myth about the May Queen, and a variety of nineteenth- and twentieth-century pieces. Study questions follow each selection. Illustrated with line drawings by Alan E. Cober and with numerous photographs in color and black-and-white. Short introduction.

Kaster, Joseph. *Putnam's Concise Mythological Dictionary*. New York: G. P. Putnam's Sons, 1964.

This dictionary is a complete revision of *A Dictionary of the Deities of All Lands* (1931), edited by Bessie G. Redfield for the general reader. Names of deities, heroes, and concepts from all over the world are listed alphabetically. Most of the approximately 1,100 entries consist of a short phrase or sentence offering basic descriptions and cultural identifications. The reader is guided to related entries by words printed in small capitals within an entry. Greek, Roman, and Hebrew terms dominate, but words from ancient Egypt, Babylonia, India, and the Americas are also present. Bibliography.

Knappert, Jan. *Islamic Legends: Histories of the Heroes, Saints and Prophets of Islam.* 2 vols. Leiden: E. J. Brill, 1985.

A collection of traditional tales by storytellers all over the Islamic world, including Turkey, South Asia, and Africa, as well as Arabia and other parts of the Middle East. These oral tales, which complement the official Islamic text, the Koran, are legends, not historical records, tracing events from creation to the time of Muhammad. Five groups of tales appear in these volumes: creation and the lives of the early prophets, the prophet Muhammad and his followers, legends of the saints of Islam, tales of heroism and morality, and stories about the afterlife. In an introduction at the beginning of Volume 1, Knappert provides some background to these tales, including a useful list of Islamic prophets and their biblical equivalents. Bibliography.

Kramer, Samuel Noah, ed. *Mythologies of the Ancient World.* Garden City, N.Y.: Doubleday, 1961.

A group of scholars surveys in separate chapters the mythologies of the ancient Egyptians, Sumerians, Hittites, Canaanites, Greeks, Indians, Iranians, Chinese, Japanese, and Mexicans. Individual chapters may include extensive quotations from ancient sources in translation as well as bibliographies, endnotes, chronological charts, and glossaries. General introduction and index.

Lang, Andrew, ed. *The Fairy Books of Many Colours.* 12 vols. London: Longmans, Green, 1889-1910. Reprint. New York: Dover Publications, 1966-1968.

Lang, a major British folklorist of the late nineteenth century, consulted a variety of sources to produce this extremely popular series of fairy-tale collections from all over the world for children. The title of each volume is identified by a different color. Beginning in the earlier volumes with the European material from the works of folklorists such as Charles Perrault, Madame d'Aulnoy, and William Morris, Lang later incorporated primary materials from around the world, including Africa, the Americas, and the Pacific. Lang also did not hesitate to include stories by Hans Christian Andersen and other writers who produced children's stories modeled on the fairy-tale tradition. This collection remains a valuable resource not only for children but also for the general reader. Standard tales such as "Puss in Boots," "Cinderella," and "Snow White and Rose Red" are accompanied by more unfamiliar tales. Often stories from different regions of the world repeat the same plot with different character names. Minimal source information is provided at the end of each tale. Each volume includes additional source material in a preface. Illustrated with black-and-white drawings by H. J. Ford, G. P. Jacomb Hood, and Lancelot Speed.

Lavender, Ralph. *Myths, Legends and Lore*. Oxford: Basil Blackwell, 1975.

This pedagogical overview of world mythology considers why and how myths are taught to children. In Chapter 1 the author discusses some sociological, anthropological, historical, psychological, and aesthetic reasons for studying mythology. In Chapter 2 Lavender suggests techniques teachers can use in the classroom. Chapters 3-6 consist of annotated bibliographies of mythology numbered sequentially and organized according to age group. While material from all over the world is included, a special emphasis on the myths of the British Isles can be noted. In Chapter 7 Lavender reviews some of the audiovisual and reference materials useful in the teaching of mythology. Musical scores are listed in an appendix. Regional, character, and general indexes.

Leach, Marjorie. *Guide to the Gods*, edited by Michael Owen Jones and Frances Cattermole-Tally. Santa Barbara, Calif.: ABC-Clio, 1992.

This monumental dictionary offers comprehensive references to deities from all over the world. The gods are grouped alphabetically in fifty-three categories under the general headings of cosmogonical, celestial, atmospheric, and terrestrial deities, and gods dealing with the cycle of life and death, economic activities, sociocultural concepts, and religious activities. Some gods appear in more than one category. Entries include short descriptions of the gods, their functions and attributes, and their geographic range, followed by bibliographic references for further study. Glossary, bibliography, and index.

Lee, Frank Harold. *Folk Tales of All Nations*. New York: Tudor Publishing, 1930.

A rich and geographically diverse collection of 360 folktales gathered from a variety of literary sources. The arrangement is generally alphabetical by region, but some groups, including African, American, and Celtic tales, are divided into subcategories. For example, the Americas are represented by categories such as "Eskimo," North American Indians, Louisiana (Cajun), Mexico and Peru, Pueblo "Indians," South Carolina, and "Negro." While not every American group is included, the diversity of cultures represented is impressive. Represented in general headings are Basque, Breton, Chinese, Cossack, Gypsy, and Japanese tales. Contains animal fables from southern Nigeria, traditional tales of the Australian Aborigine and the Fiji Islands, ancient tales from Greece, Egypt, and India, and modern tales from Greece, Italy, and Portugal. Each regional section begins with a short introduction to the area and its people. General introduction on the nature of folktales. Occasional explanatory footnotes.

Leeming, David Adams. *Mythology: The Voyage of the Hero.* 2d ed. New York: Harper and Row, 1981.
A collection of readings about heroes from all over the world. Includes stories about Heracles, Oedipus, and Odysseus from ancient Greece; Isis and Horus from Egypt; Moses and Abraham from ancient Israel; and Siegfried and King Arthur from Europe. Also represented are the founders of world religions such as Jesus, Muhammad, and Buddha, as well as Quetzalcóatl of the Aztec, Bear Man of the Cherokee, and the Hittite Telepinu. Arranged according to the stages of the hero's life pattern: miraculous conception, childhood, quest, death, descent to the underworld, rebirth, and apotheosis. Each section contains paraphrases and readings from original sources and from modern handbooks and concludes with a general commentary. Artistic illustrations accompany some themes. Each section is followed by a brief commentary by the author. In appendices are examples of seven different creation myths and two flood myths as well as an introduction to Carl G. Jung's approach to mythology. Footnotes, bibliography, and index.

_____, ed. *The World of Myth.* New York: Oxford University Press, 1990.
This broad-ranging anthology of readings in mythology is intended to be comprehensive but not exhaustive. Includes tales from the Sub-Saharan Africa, Greece, Egypt, Babylon, China, and Polynesia. Readings from ancient and modern literature are placed alongside traditional oral tales, mythological handbooks, and religious and scientific writings, in order to illustrate the universality of mythological thought. Myths about creation, the flood, the afterlife, and apocalypse are contained in Part 1; myths about the gods in Part 2; hero legends in Part 3; and tales about places and objects in Part 4. Integrated into the readings are explanations and commentary by the editor. Each part is followed by a short bibliography. Index.

Long, Charles H. *Alpha: The Myths of Creation.* New York: George Braziller, 1963.
An anthology of forty-five creation myths including selections from the Babylonian *Enuma Elish*, the Orphic creation myth and Hesiod's

Theogony from ancient Greece, Brahman creation from an egg from India, and the Hebrew creation story in the Bible, as well as myths of native North and South Americans, Polynesians, Japanese, Maya, and the Mande of West Africa. Substantial portions of original texts are provided for each myth. Arranged in five major types of creation myth: emergence myths, world-parent myths, stories of creation from chaos and from the cosmic egg, creation from nothing, and earth-diver myths. Each chapter begins with a discussion of the characteristics of each type followed by several representative myths. In appendices two additional types of creation myth are represented: creation through sacrifice and an Australian myth in which ancestors are creators. Introductory essay on the history of religion in the modern world, characteristics of mythical thought, and creation myths. Thirty-two black-and-white plates illustrating creation myths in art. Also five line drawings depicting several cosmic systems and deities. Endnotes, bibliography, and index.

Lum, Peter. *Fabulous Beasts*. New York: Pantheon Books, 1951.
A survey of mythological beasts from all over the world in twenty-one chapters, including an introductory essay on the beast in fable. Studies the unicorn and lizard-like basilisk of medieval Europe, the serpentine Nnagas, the crocodile-like makara and the elephant-headed gansha of India, and the chimera, sphinx, phoenix, and Pegasus from ancient Greece. Also contains chapters on dragons, mermaids, and sea-monsters. Eighty-two illustrations from ancient manuscripts, pottery, and artwork. Bibliography and index.

Luquet, G. H."Prehistoric Mythology." In *New Larousse Encyclopedia of Mythology*, edited by Felix Guirand et al. Translated by Richard Aldington and Delano Ames. New York: Hamlyn, 1968.
Uses early burials, painting, and sculpture from France, Germany, Britain, Egypt, Africa, and South America to illustrate the religion and cult of the dead among prehistoric humans. Evidence of magicians, hunting and fertility magic, and burial customs among these peoples suggests the presence of religious and, perhaps, mythological beliefs among paleolithic peoples. Sixteen black-and-white illustrations are accompanied by one in color.

Maclagan, David. *Creation Myths*. London: Thames and Hudson, 1977.
This meditation on various ways that humankind has explained creation and the world order contains some reference to and quotation from myths in textual form but concentrates on visual examples of these

myths. Includes 149 illustrations, nineteen in color, depicting the creation of the world and the cosmic structure from many different cultural contexts. Manuscript illuminations from India, ancient Egypt, Mesoamerica, and medieval Christian Europe are juxtaposed with Navajo sandpaintings, Dogon and Australian Aboriginal drawings, and modern European artwork. Bibliography.

Marasinghe, M. M. J. "Theravada Buddhism." In *Mythology: An Illustrated Encyclopaedia*, edited by Richard Cavendish. New York: Rizzoli International, 1980. Also published as *An Illustrated Encyclopedia of Mythology*. New York: Crescent Books, 1984.
A short essay on the mythic tradition of Buddhism in Sri Lanka, Burma, and Southeast Asia. Includes sections on the legendary life of Buddha, myths about the defeat of titanic demons called Asuras, descriptions of the realms of god and humans, the relationship between Buddha and his antagonist demon Mara, the realm of purgatory ruled by Yama, and changes in Buddhist beliefs. Map and illustrations of artwork related to the myths.

Marchal, C.-H. "The Mythology of Indo-China and Java." In *Asiatic Mythology*, edited by M. J. Hackin. Translated by F. M. Atkinson. New York: Thomas Y. Crowell, 1963.
Examines the gods, cosmic views, and legends among the Khmer and Cham of Indochina and the Malayo-Polynesian peoples of the island of Java. These mythologies are based on various religious movements, especially Buddhism and Hinduism. Explains Buddhist scenes of hell and Paradise and episodes from the Hindu epics *Mahābhārata* and *Rāmāyana* on the temples of Angkor-Vat. Also contains episodes from the life of Buddha on the temple of Borobodur on Java. Forty-seven black-and-white figures and one color plate.

Meyer, Marvin W., ed. *The Ancient Mysteries: A Sourcebook*. San Francisco: Harper and Row, 1987.
Offers a broad selection of ancient texts describing the mystery religions of the Mediterranean world. Includes chapters on the Eleusinian mysteries of the Greek goddess Demeter, the Andanian mysteries of Messenia, the worship of the god Dionysus, the Anatolian mysteries of the Great Mother and the Syrian Goddess, the Egyptian cults in honor of Isis and Osiris, the Roman worship of Mithra, and elements of mystery religion in Judaism and Christianity. Short introductory essay by the editor, some illustrations of ancient representations of these deities, and glossary.

Murray, Alexander S. *Manual of Mythology*. Rev. ed., by William H.
Klapp. New York: Tudor Publishing, 1935.

This handbook of ancient mythology and religion by a curator at the
British Museum is designed for the general reader. Most of the book
is devoted to ancient Greece and Rome, with sections on their creation
stories, Olympian deities, other deities, and heroes. Shorter treatments
of Norse and Old German mythology, the Vedic and Brahmanic deities
of the Hindi, and ancient Egyptian deities. The appearance and attributes of each god and hero are described and important myths are
summarized. Introductory essay on Greek mythology and on Greek
religion, ceremonies, and rituals. Includes 182 black-and-white illustrations, sixteen of which are full-page photographs of ancient and
modern artwork. Genealogical chart and index.

Nahmad, H. M., ed. *A Portion in Paradise and Other Jewish Folktales*.
New York: Viking Press, 1970.

Forty-one stories collected from biblical sources and from Jewish
traditions in the East and in the West. Grouped according to the
following themes: tales of the prophet Elijah, tales of kings David and
Solomon, wisdom and the folly of women, the righteous and the pious,
tales of wit and wisdom, and the *golem* or "human figure made of clay."
At the beginning of each section, the editor considers the character and
background of the stories. Preface on the nature of Jewish legends and
folktales and their sources.

Norman, Howard A., ed. *Northern Tales: Traditional Stories of Eskimo
and Indian Peoples*. New York: Pantheon Books, 1990.

The Arctic and sub-Arctic peoples represented by these 116 traditional
tales cross continental boundaries and include groups from northern
Canada, Alaska, Greenland, and Siberia. Most of the tales have already
appeared in a variety of printed sources, but some were obtained from
personal archives and correspondence. All are offered here in translation for the general reader. Organized in eight thematic groupings:
stories about village life; tales about creation and the origin of various
aspects of human life and the natural world; tricksters and culture
heroes; animal stories; shaman tales; encounters with dangerous animals, monsters, giants, and ghosts; hunting adventures; and stories
about marriage, especially human unions with animals. Introductory
essay on the northern peoples, their storytelling traditions, and the
history of the study of their folklore. Maps, endnotes on sources, and
bibliography.

Oinas, Felix J., ed. *Heroic Epic and Saga: An Introduction to the World's Great Folk Epics.* Bloomington: Indiana University Press, 1978.
While the focus of this collection of essays is the literary form of oral epics from around the world, many of the epics discussed deal with mythological themes. Of particular note are essays about the Homeric epics of Greece, *Gilgamesh* and other sagas of Mesopotamia, the great Sanskrit epics *Rāmāyaṇa* and *Mahābhārata,* heroic epics from Europe, and the African heroic epic. Essays are contributed by various scholarly experts and are followed by separate endnotes and bibliographies. General introduction on epics by Richard M. Dorson. Index.

Olcott, William Tyler. *Star Lore of All Ages.* New York: G. P. Putnam's Sons, 1911.
Discusses myths and traditions about the stars and constellations of the Northern Hemisphere. Sections are arranged alphabetically according to constellation. Combines scientific information about these constellations with explanations of their astronomical symbols and mythological names. Summarizes star legends of various ancient peoples, including Egyptians, Greeks, Romans, Scandinavians, and North Americans. Accompanied by many drawings of the constellations and by fifty-eight illustrations, especially of Greco-Roman artwork associated with the constellations. Appendix with charts containing scientific information about major stars. Bibliography and index.

_____. *Sun Lore of All Ages.* New York: G. P. Putnam's Sons, 1914.
A collection of myths and folklore about the sun from a variety of cultures and time periods, including the ancient Greeks, Norse, Aztec, and, especially, many Native North American nations. Some of these myths are briefly paraphrased while others are told in fuller narrative. Devotes several chapters to myths about the creation of the sun, ancient ideas about the sun and the moon, sun worship, sun-catching, solar festivals, solar omens, traditions and superstitions, the solar significance of burial customs, and symbolic forms of the sun. In the last chapter scientific information about the sun is provided. Artwork, shrines, and sites associated with the sun from all over the world are depicted in thirty black-and-white illustrations. Bibiliography and index.

Powell, Barry B. *Classical Myth.* Englewood Cliffs, N.J.: Prentice Hall, 1995.

While concentrating especially on the myths of the ancient Greeks, this anthology of readings also contains significant texts from ancient Mesopotamia, including translated excerpts from the Babylonian *Enuma Elish* and the Sumerian *Gilgamesh*. Also includes a collection of texts dealing with Roman myths, especially legends of the Roman monarchy and the early Republic. The last part of the book offers a sweeping historical survey of theories of myth, beginning with ancient Greek theories about allegory and euhemerism and ending with twentieth-century theories based upon anthropology, linguistics, psychology, and structuralism. Maps, genealogical charts, and many illustrations of ancient and modern art. Bibliographies at the end of every chapter. Footnotes and index.

Pritchard, James B., ed. *The Ancient Near East*. Princeton, N.J.: Princeton University Press, 1958.
Texts selected from Pritchard's *Ancient Near Eastern Texts Relating to the Old Testament* are combined with 197 illustrations of Middle Eastern artifacts in order to make these documents more accessible to the general reader. Major Egyptian and Middle Eastern documents are here translated by eleven scholars of the region, including William F. Albright, Samuel Noah Kramer, and John A. Wilson. In addition to legal, historical, and epistolary texts, the collection includes translations of six Egyptian myths, tales, and divine hymns, a Sumerian myth about a great flood, a Hittite myth about Telepinu, Ugaritic myths about the gods Baal and Anath, and an epic about the hero Aqhat. Akkadian myths receive the fullest treatment, with translations of a creation epic, the *Epic of Gilgamesh*, a cosmological incantation, the story of Adapa, the *Descent of Ishtar*, and the legend of Sargon. All translations follow the original documents closely and include careful indications of original text numbers, restorations, and doubtful readings. Some translations are preceded by short introductions. Includes 197 illustrations of Middle Eastern artifacts. Footnotes, map, indexes, and glossary.

_____. *The Ancient Near East in Pictures*. Princeton, N.J.: Princeton University Press, 1954.
This collection of illustrations dealing with various aspects of life in ancient Egypt and the Middle East has several parts on mythological topics. Part 6 deals with the gods of Syria, Mesopotamia, Anatolia, and Egypt and their emblems. Part 7 includes sections on monsters and demons and on myth and legend. Part 8 focuses on Mesopotamian cylinder seals with depictions of deities, their human worshipers, heroes, and monsters. Accompanying the illustrations is a descriptive

catalogue with bibliography. Introductory essay on the selection of photographs and their arrangement. Maps and index.

_____, ed. *Ancient Near Eastern Texts Relating to the Old Testament*. 3d ed. Princeton, N.J.: Princeton University Press, 1969.
Part 1 of this scholarly collection of ancient legal, historical, religious, and didactic texts contains translations of Egyptian and Middle Eastern myths, epics, and legends by John A. Wilson, Samuel Noah Kramer, E. A. Speiser, Albrecht Goetze, H. L. Ginsberg, A. K. Grayson, and others. The material is arranged geographically and includes Egyptian creation stories, heroic tales, and mortuary texts, Sumerian and Akkadian stories of Gilgamesh and the flood, Hittite tales about kingship in heaven, and Ugaritic poems about the god Baal. In Part 4 are Egyptian, Sumerian, and Hittite prayers and incantations of some mythological interest. Each translation is preceded by a brief introduction which includes original sources for the text. All translations follow the original documents closely and include careful indication of original text numbers, restorations, and doubtful readings. Footnotes and indexes.

Quinn, E. C. *The Quest of Seth: For the Oil and Life*. Chicago: University of Chicago Press, 1962.
Traces the origin, motifs, and development of a medieval Latin legend about Set, the son of Adam, and his search for the oil of mercy. The myth is briefly paraphrased in the introduction. Shows how this tale, which is blended with the Holy Cross legend of St. Helena, is represented in medieval literatue and art. Includes references to earlier traditions of the myth in ancient Egypt and Babylonia. Endnotes, bibliography, and index.

Ranelagh, Elaine L. *The Past We Share*. London: Quartet Books, 1979.
In this comparative study, Ranelagh argues that the roots of Western culture include not only Greco-Roman and Judaeo-Christian elements but also Arabian ones. To illustrate this cultural overlap, Ranelagh incorporates into his text translations of biblical, medieval Christian, medieval Jewish, and Islamic stories. The seven main story lines are those of Joseph and Potiphar's wife, Solomon and the Queen of Sheba, Alexander the Great, the legend of the sixth-century 'Antar known through the Arabic *Sirat 'Antar* or "Romance of 'Antar," the Arabic tales of the twelfth-century *Disciplina Clericalis* of Petrus Alfunsus, the stories of the *Thousand and One Nights*, and Washington Irving's "The Arabian Astrologer." Placed on facing pages between chapters

are Eastern and Western versions of folktales such as "The Emperor's New Clothes" and "The Taming of the Shrew." Twenty-five illustrations, especially of woodcuts and manuscript illuminations. Endnotes, tale type and motif index, and general index.

Rappoport, Angelo. *The Folklore of the Jews*. London: Soncino Press, 1937.
An overview of Jewish folklore with special attention to popular beliefs, practices, superstitions, and traditional tales. Two introductory chapters on the nature, sources, and characteristics of Jewish folklore are followed by eight chapters dealing with the themes of nature and creation, flora and fauna, demons, magic and omens, the human body, birth, marriage and death, folk-medicine, and various customs and practices. A chapter on the origin of Jewish folklore precedes representative selections of folktales, legends, and moral tales, as well as variants and parallels in folklore from other cultures. Each story is followed by information about sources. The last two chapters deal with proverbs and maxims and the relationship between Jewish folklore and the Jewish religion. Bibliography and index.

Riches, David, and Piers Vitebsky. "The Arctic Regions." In *World Mythology*, edited by Roy Willis. New York: Henry Holt, 1993.
A short overview of the mythology of the Inuit and other peoples of the far north with separate sections on the religious beliefs of the peoples of Siberia and of Canada and Greenland. Subsidiary sections on a Canadian myth about the origin of the Sea Spirit and a Yakut tale about a contest between a shaman and a Communist Commissar. Seven color illustrations, mostly in color, of Arctic artifacts. Map.

Riordan, James, and Brenda Ralph Lewis. *An Illustrated Treasury of Myths and Legends*. New York: Exeter Books, 1987.
This collection of twenty-five world myths retold for children is accompanied by numerous color drawings by Victor Ambrus. From the ancient world are tales about the Greek heroes Theseus and Perseus, the Egyptian goddess Isis, the Roman twins Romulus and Remus, and the Babylonian hero Gilgamesh. From northern and medieval Europe come legends about Roland, William Tell, El Cid, Siegfried, and the Russian Danko. The British Isles are represented by King Arthur, Robin Hood, Beowulf, the Irish girl Deirdre, and the Welsh lord Pwyll. Also two stories about the Norse gods as well as one each from Finland, Iceland, China, Kenya, Australia, Polynesia, India, and the Chippewas

of North America. Each tale is preceded by a short introduction. In a postscript, the authors comment on the origin and value of myths.

Rosenberg, Donna, ed. *World Mythology.* 2d ed. Lincolnwood, Ill.: NTC Publishing Group, 1994.
A schoolbook collection of fifty-nine myths from all over the world, including ancient Greece, the Middle East, Northern Europe, the Far East, Africa, and the Americas. Each selection, often abridged and sometimes paraphrased, is preceded by a brief introduction and is presented in simple prose translation. Selections include portions of the Homeric epics, the *Enuma Elish, Gilgamesh, Beowulf,* the Arthurian romance, and the *Sunjata.* Endnotes on sources, bibliography, index of characters with pronunciation guide, and study questions.

Schwartz, Howard, ed. *Lilith's Cave: Jewish Tales of the Supernatural.* San Francisco: Harper & Row, 1988.
Fifty tales about demons, wizards, witches, enchantment, magic, and exorcism collected from published sources and retold by the author. Most were originally published in Yiddish or Hebrew and represent Jewish traditions from Eastern Europe, Germany, the Middle East, Egypt, and North Africa. The title is borrowed from one of the tales, a Tunisian story about a haunted house. Detailed commentary about the stories and their sources in an appendix. Introductory essay by the editor on Jewish beliefs and superstitions and their role in folklore. Black-and-white illustrations by Uri Shulevitz. Bibliography, glossary, and index.

_____, ed. *Miriam's Tambourine: Jewish Folktales from Around the World.* New York: Seth Press, 1986.
These fifty tales and legends have been collected from published sources and retold by the author. Most were originally published in Yiddish or Hebrew and represent Jewish traditions from both Eastern and Western Europe, the Middle East (especially Babylon), North Africa, and even India. The title is taken from the first tale, which tells about a rabbi in Babylon who searches with his son for the tambourine of Moses' sister Miriam. Apocryphal legends about biblical personages such as Daniel, David, and Solomon, are accompanied by supernatural tales about demons and *golems* and stories of enchantment and magic. Detailed commentary about the stories and their sources in an appendix. Foreword by Dov Noy discussing what is Jewish about Jewish folklore. Introductory essay by the editor on the Jewish folktale tradi-

tion. Accompanied by illustrations, some in color, by Lloyd Bloom. Glossary.

Schwarzbaum, Haim. *Studies in Jewish and World Folklore*. Berlin: Walter De Gruyter, 1968.
A scholarly analysis and comparative study of Jewish folktales based upon Naftoli Gross's *Ma'aselech un Mesholim*, a collection of 540 tales told in Yiddish and published in 1955. In the core of this book, Schwarzbaum offers plot summaries of these tales, analyzes them in terms of Aarne-Thompson types folktale types, and compares them to folktales from all over the world. These stories deal with themes such as biblical figures, rabbis, Yeshiva students, merchants, craftsmen, misers, soldiers, gentiles, apostates, lunatics, and animal fables. In a detailed introductory essay, the author provides a history of Jewish folkloristics and offers some general comparative comments. Also includes extensive annotated bibliographies on Jewish folk narratives and other genres such as songs, proverbs, and customs. Tables of tale types and narrative motifs and general index.

Seymour, St. John Drelincourt. *Tales of King Solomon*. London: Oxford University Press, 1924.
Traditional legends about King Solomon of Israel are gathered from all over the world for the general reader. Seymour's sources include the Koran, medieval Jewish and European tales, the Arabian *Thousand and One Nights*, and storytellers in Ireland and the Malay Peninsula. Some of this material is translated into English for the first time from French and German sources. The tales are organized chronologically around Solomon's life, with separate chapters on his birth, wisdom, power, and magic carpet, birds and beasts, the finding of Shamir, the construction of the temple, the Queen of Sheba, Pharaoh's daughter, and Solomon's death and exile. In an introductory essay, Seymour discusses his sources and some characteristics of these tales. Five color drawings, chapter endnotes, and index.

Shah, Idries, ed. *World Tales*. New York: Harcourt Brace Jovanovich, 1979.
Retells sixty-five folktales from a variety of literary sources and accompanies them with drawings by a number of modern artists. Also contains some reproductions of ancient art. Each tale is preceded by a short introduction noting treatments of the tale in other cultures. Includes "The Tale of Two Brothers" from an ancient Egyptian papyrus manuscript, several selections from Geoffrey Chaucer's *The Canter-*

bury Tales, Voltaire's version of an Eastern tale called "The Hermit," and ancient stories from China, Serbia, Russia, and other parts of the world.

Sharwood-Smith, John. *The Bride from the Sea*. London: Macmillan, 1973.

The title of this book refers to the Greek myth about the marriage of Peleus and Thetis which serves here as an introduction not only to Greek mythology but to mythology in general. Written especially for schoolchildren, with several maps, genealogies, and an index with pronunciation guide. Examples of legends, folktales, and pure myths include not only major Greek myths such as the stories of Oedipus, Perseus, and the fall of Troy but also Grimm fairy tales, the British legends of Dick Whittington and King Arthur, and semi-historical tales about Charlemagne and Roland. Surveys several modern theories of myth, including the psychological theories of Sigmund Freud and Carl Jung and the anthropological theories of ritual explanation, charter theory, and structuralism. Also a short section on the possible origins of Greek myths and an epilogue on the use of Greek myths in later literature and art. Original drawings by Jonathan Wolstenholme.

Smith, Ron. *Mythologies of the World: A Guide to Sources*. Urbana, Ill.: National Council of Teachers of English, 1981.

A professor of English offers a geographically organized bibliographic survey of world mythology with sections on worldwide, West Asian, South and East Asian, European, American Indian, African, and Oceanic mythologies. Most of these sections contain further geographic subdivisions. For example, West Asia is divided into sections on Mesopotamian, Hittite, Canaanite, Persian, biblical, and Islamic myths. Generally, each subdivision contains background information on the people and their culture, as well as discussions of collections of their myths, translations, and works on religion, on historical and cultural background, and on archaeology, language, and art. Short bibliographic notices and evaluations of individual books are incorporated into these discussions. Introductory essay on the study of mythology and its modern history and on the structure of the book and how to use it. Appendix on contemporary mythology, especially in the United States.

South, Malcom, ed. *Mythical and Fabulous Creatures*. New York: Peter Bedrick Books, 1987.

Part 1 consists of a collection of essays about twenty imaginative beasts from all over the world, arranged taxonomically. Under the category of birds and beasts are the unicorn, dragon, phoenix, roc, griffin, chimera, and basilisk. Composites of humans and animals are the manticora, mermaid, siren, harpie, gorgon, sphinx, Minotaur, satyr, and centaur. Creatures of darkness are the vampire and the werewolf. Giants and fairies are also discussed in separate chapters. In each essay a different scholar traces the history of a particular creature in a comparative context and includes a bibliography and significant quotation in translation from a variety of original sources. General introductory essay with bibliography by the editor. In Part 2 South offers a miscellany and taxonomy in which these twenty creatures are grouped in five categories with other mythological beasts. Glossary of fabulous creatures, illustrations of some creatures, especially from early book plates. General bibliography and index.

Sproul, Barbara C., ed. *Primal Myths: Creation Myths Around the World.* San Francisco: HarperCollins, 1979.
The creation myths from all over the world in this anthology were selected from a variety of published sources. The myths are grouped geographically. Part 1 contains thirteen myths from Sub-Saharan Africa, including Mande, Bushongo, and Bushmen tales of creation and the ordering of the world, and Swahili, Bulu, and Ngombe stories of the first humans. The Middle Eastern myths in Part 2 include tales of ancient Egypt as well as Mesopotamia. Some of these myths are arranged under religious categories such as the Bible, Zoroastrian myths, gnostic myths, and Islam. Among the European myths in Part 3 are selections from the works of the Greek Hesiod and the Roman Ovid as well as short pieces from Celtic, Norse, and Finnish sources. Part 4 contains examples of Hindu, Jain, Buddhist, and tribal myths of India. The creation myths of China and Japan in Part 5 are followed by tales from Siberia and the Arctic peoples in Part 6. Creation and destruction tales of sixteen North American peoples, including the Apache, Hopi, Huron, and Salinan, appear in Part 7. Six examples of creation tales from Central and South American are found in Part 8. The myths of Australia and the Pacific in Part 9 include Maori and Tahitian cosmologies, creation myths from Melanesia, and a cosmic chant from the Tuamotu Islands. Some selections are presented in verse form. Each selection is preceded by an introduction by the editor and is followed by bibliographic source. General introductory essay and index.

Sykes, Egerton. *Who's Who in Non-Classical Mythology*. 2d ed. revised by Alan Kendall. New York: Oxford University Press, 1993.
Alphabetical listing of more than 2,500 entries with information about mythological characters from all over the world. Each entry includes geographical, historical, and cultural information. Entries for deities, heroes, mythological places, and major literary sources are accompanied by thematic entries on topics such as "Egyptian Creation Legends" and "Black Magic." Introduction and bibliography.

Thompson, Stith. *The Folktale*. Berkeley: University of California Press, 1977.
This broad introduction to the nature and function of folktales begins with the terminology of folktales and illustrations of their universality. Part 2 surveys folktales in the Indo-European world from Ireland to India with chapters on complex tales, simple tales, the folktale in ancient literature, and the use of Indo-European folktales on other continents. Part 3 is devoted to folktales of Native North Americans with chapters on creation myths, trickster tales, tests and hero tales, journeys to the otherworld, and stories about animal spouses. Part 4 deals with folktale theory, collection, classification, history, and scholarship. Thompson uses a series of motifs to show how folktales are based on a limited number of narrative themes known as Aarne-Thompson motifs. These motifs are listed in two appendices. Footnotes, bibliography, and general index.

_____, ed. *One Hundred Favorite Folktales*. Bloomington: Indiana University Press, 1968.
This collection of traditional stories is intentionally selective and includes tales which are representative of their folktale type, which come from the part of the world where this type is best known, and which are well-told tales. Except for an Egyptian tale, all stories come from European sources. Includes selections from ancient Egyptian papyri, from the ancient Greek writers Homer and Herodotus, from Basile's seventeenth-century collection of Italian Neapolitan tales, and from the well-known anthologies of Charles Perrault, Hans Christian Andersen, and the Brothers Grimm. The appendix contains a list of sources and notes on the Aarne-Thompson tale types represented by each story.

Trankell, Ing-Britt, and Roy Willis. "Southeast Asia." In *World Mythology*, edited by Roy Willis. New York: Henry Holt, 1993.

This short, thematic survey of Southeast Asian mythology and religious beliefs also includes some material from Indonesia. Sections on creation myths, culture heroes, encounters with magical powers, and myths about rice. Subsidiary sections offer retellings of a Balinese creation myth about the serpent and the turtle, a Laotian myth about the three divine ancestors of humankind, an Indonesian tale about the wild woman Bota Ili, and a Thai tale about Sujata's gift to Buddha. Eight color illustrations of sites and artifacts. Map and time chart.

Van Over, Raymond, ed. *Sun Songs: Creation Myths from around the World*. New York: New American Library, 1980.
A collection of myths about the beginning of the world and about the creation of humankind. Each part begins with a short introduction to the creation stories of a particular geographic region and contains translations of the myths without commentary. Begins with North American myths, especially those of the Zuñi, Crow, Maidu, and Inuit. Part 2 includes Central and South American stories of the Maya, Xingu, Inca, and the Lengua of Paraguay. Part 3 deals with northern Europe and central Asia and offers myths of Romania, Finland, and other areas. In Part 4 contains myths of ancient Babylon, Arabia and Phoenicia. Greek myths, especially cosmogonies from the works of Hesiod, Aeschylus, and Plato, appear in Part 5. Sub-Saharan Africa is poorly represented in Part 6, with only three short creation myths. Part 7 includes Judaeo-Christian creation stories from the biblical books of Genesis, Psalms, the Gospel of John, Revelation, and a few selections from the Jewish Midrash. Egyptian creation myths, especially in the Book of the Dead, receive separate treatment in Part 8, while Persian myths and stories from ancient India such as the Upanishads and the *Mahābhārata* are combined in Part 9 on the Middle East. Japanese, Chinese and Tibetan myths appear in Part 10. Part 11 is devoted to creation myths of Oceania, especially the Maori and Malay. In an introductory essay, the editor discusses the meaning of myth and various myth theories. Footnotes and bibliography.

Vilnay, Zev. *Legends of Galilee, Jordan and Sinai*. Philadelphia: Jewish Publication Society of America, 1978.
This book is the third in a series of volumes based upon a monumental collection of tales of the Holy Land originally published in Hebrew. Here Vilnay offers English translations of 392 tales about three regions in modern Israel, Jordan, and Egypt. These tales reflect the oral heritage of three religious groups, Jewish, Christian, and Islamic, and have been obtained from both the Old and the New Testaments, the Talmud and

other medieval Jewish sources, the writings of the Christian Church fathers, the Koran, and descriptions by Christian pilgrims and Muslim travelers. The tales are arranged geographically around the three regions, with chapters on specific cities and topographical features. Some of these narratives are aetiological. Others associate places with biblical events, supernatural and religious experiences, and historical legends. Sources for the legends are listed in endnotes. Descriptions of these sources appear in an appendix. Sixty-seven illustrations, including photographs, ancient woodcuts and engravings, and artifacts.

_____. *Legends of Jerusalem*. Philadelphia: Jewish Publication Society of America, 1973.

The author began his monumental collection of English translations of tales from the Holy Land with these 319 stories about the holy city of Jerusalem. The tales are arranged in twenty-nine thematic groups dealing with Jerusalem as the center of the world, the Dome of the Rock, the ancient temple and its destruction, Mount Moriah, the Mount of Olives, and features of the medieval and modern city. Sources provided in endnotes. Descriptions of ancient sources are provided in an appendix. Ninety-two illustrations, including photographs, ancient woodcuts and engravings, and artifacts.

_____. *Legends of Judea and Samaria*. Philadephia: Jewish Publication Society of America, 1975.

This second volume in the author's collection of English translations of tales from the Holy Land contains 284 stories about the regions of Judaea and Samaria. The tales are arranged in twenty-eight geographic groups. The tales explain the names and special features of the land and associate the sites with biblical and other events. Sources are provided in endnotes. Descriptions of ancient sources are provided in an appendix. Includes 112 illustrations of photographs, ancient woodcuts and engravings, and artifacts.

Waddell, Helen. *The Princess Splendour and Other Stories*, edited by Eileen Colwell. London: Longmans, 1969.

A collection of nine fairy tales from all over the world retold for children by a prolific Classical scholar and translator of the early twentieth century. These tales of magic, giants, princesses, and supernatural creatures include two from *The Thousand and One Nights* of Arabia, two from Japan, two from Scotland, and two from Ireland. In a preface the editor comments on the sources for these tales and offers a brief biography of Waddell. Illustrated with drawings by Anne Knight.

Watts, Alan W. *The Two Hands of God: The Myths of Polarity.* New York: George Braziller, 1963.

Studies the theme of cosmic polarity, of light versus darkness, of good versus evil, with extensive quotation from a variety of sources ancient and modern. Chapters 1 and 2, "The Primordial Pair" and "The Cosmic Dance," rely heavily on Eastern myths, especially from China and India, which recognize the intrinsic unity of these polar opposites. Chapter 3, "The Two Brothers," uses tales from the Middle East—such as those of the Egyptian brothers Horus and Set, the Hebrew brothers Cain and Abel, and the Zoroastrian Ohrmazd and Ahriman—to illustrate the essential fraternal conflict of good and evil. In Chapter 4, "Ultimate Dualism," passages from a variety of Christian sources, including the Apocalypse of Peter, John Milton's *Paradise Lost*, and Dante Alighieri's *Divine Comedy*, show the Christian polarity between God and the devil, between heaven and hell. In the last chapter, "Dismemberment Remembered," the original unity of these polar opposites is recalled in the myth of the egg in Plato's *Symposium*, the mysteries of Isis in Apuleius' *The Golden Ass*, the apocryphal Acts of Peter, the Gnostic Gospel of Thomas, Islamic tales about the Prophet Muhammad, and meditations about Buddha. Accompanied by twenty-three black-and-white places and six line drawings, mostly illustrating this polarity from artistic sources. Footnotes, bibliography, and index.

Weigle, Marta. *Spiders and Spinsters: Women and Mythology.* Albuquerque: University of New Mexico Press, 1982.

A sourcebook of myths about women from the Americas, the Judaeo-Christian tradition, and ancient Greece and Rome. Translations of original myths, modern poems and novels, scholarly essays, and illustrations of original artwork are integrated into the author's own interpretative essays. Includes chapters on spider and weaving myths, goddesses, female guides and initiators such as Demeter, ritual myths about the moon and menstruation, heroines such as Joan of Arc, and myths of origin and matriarchy such as that of Pandora. Footnotes, bibliography, list of sources, and index.

Wilkins, Cary, ed. *The Andrew Lang Fairy Tale Treasury.* New York: Avenel Books, 1979.

Fifty-two tales, selected from the twelve-volume collection which Andrew Lang published for children as *The Fairy Books of Many*

Colours (1889-1910), are reprinted here with original black-and-white illustrations by H. J. Ford, G. P. Jacomb Hood, and Lancelot Speed. Wilkins has chosen many of the standard European tales such as "Rumpelstiltzkin," "Blue Beard," and "Jack and the Beanstalk" but also includes less familiar tales from India, Russia, Romania, East Africa, and other parts of the world. In an introductory essay, Wilkins offers a biography of Lang and some comments on twentieth-century interpretations of the fairy tale.

Willis, Roy, ed. *World Mythology*. New York: Henry Holt, 1993.
The editor, an anthropologist and an Africanist, introduces this major reference book with an essay on the theories and meaning of myth and with an overview of nine great themes of myth under the headings of creation, cosmic architecture, myths of humanity, supernatural beings, cosmic disaster, heroes and tricksters, animals and plants, body and soul, and marriage and kinship. The rest of the book consists of nineteen essays by various scholars on different mythologies of the world. These essays incorporate summaries of major myths of the region with subsidiary essays on special mythological topics, time charts, maps, genealogical charts, and tables. The text is enhanced by more than 500 color photographs of appropriate cultural artifacts and sites. In a foreword, Robert Walter, the director of the Joseph Campbell Foundation, discusses some of Campbell's views of myth. Bibliography and index.

Wolkstein, Diane. *The First Love Stories*. New York: HarperCollins, 1991.
Seven ancient legends of love, devotion, and metamorphosis are translated from primary sources. The tales are arranged chronologically, beginning with the Egyptian myth Isis and Osiris and ending with the Germanic Tristan and Iseult tale. Also included are the stories of the sacred marriage of the Sumerian Inanna and Dumuzi, the eternal dance of the Hindu Shiva and Sati, the Hebrew song of songs, the marriage of Cupid and Psyche told by the second-century A.D. Roman author Apuleius, and the love of the Arabian Layla and Majnun. Each tale is preceded by a brief introduction. General introductory essay on Wolkstein's tellings of the tales. Glossary and bibliography.

Yolen, Jane, ed. *Favorite Folktales from Around the World*. New York: Pantheon Books, 1986.
More than 150 tales gathered from various literary sources and arranged thematically. Includes telling tales, trickster tales, wonder tales, and stories about fools, heroes, the very young and very old, true and

false love, metamorphosis, the supernatural, ghosts, fooling the devil,
the acquisition of wisdom, death, and the end of the world. Tale sources
are provided in endnotes. In an introductory essay the editor discusses
various aspects of storytelling and types of tales. Several stories are
integrated into this introduction.

Zipes, Jack. *The Trials and Tribulations of Little Red Riding Hood.* South
Hadley, Mass.: Bergin & Garvey Publishers, 1983.
The traditional story known commonly as "Little Red Riding Hood"
is retold here in thirty-one French, British, American, German, Irish,
Italian, French-Canadian, and Chinese versions. Arranged chronologically, beginning with the 1697 French story told by Charles Perrault
and ending with a 1979 Chinese version by Chiang Mi. Translated by
the author. In an introductory essay, Zipes tells the history of the tale
and shows how the story has been transformed according to sociocultural contexts. Attitudes toward sexuality, sex roles, and socialization
modify the tale in significant ways. Accompanied by twenty-eight
black-and-white and nine color illustrations from various editions of
the tale. Notes on the text and on the authors. Selected chronological
bibliography of Little Red Riding Hood tales. Bibliography.

Chapter 2
AFRICA

The continent of Africa is rarely treated as a whole in the study of mythology; a single collection offering material from all over the continent is listed immediately following this introduction. Usually the mythologies and religions of Sub-Saharan Africa and ancient Egypt are treated separately.

Egypt's special position can be explained by its geography. The country's location along a narrow strip of arable land along the Nile River created in antiquity a coherent culture which is the subject of the special field of Egyptology. Cataracts along the river to the south made navigation upriver difficult, while Egypt's position on the delta of the Nile gave it a natural orientation toward the Mediterranean. While ancient Egypt certainly did maintain significant contacts with the rest of the continent, its culture and its mythology can stand alone, as they do here. At the same time, comparison with other Mediterranean peoples can shed additional light on Egyptian topics, and scholars sometimes study the ancient Egyptians along with ancient Middle Eastern peoples such as the Babylonians and Sumerians. In this bibliography, therefore, most of the Egyptian material is found in its own section in this chapter, but for material dealing with both Egypt and the Middle East, the reader should consult the general material in Chapter 1. At the end of the twentieth century, the traditional separation of Egypt from Sub-Saharan Africa raises special concern about Egypt's position in the family of human cultures. The Afro-centrist movement looks to Africa in general, and to Egypt in particular, as the fountainhead of culture both for the ancient Middle East and for the Greeks. Rarely do general works about Egyptian mythology deal with these issues in any detail. For a preliminary discussion of this question, readers should consult the work of Martin Bernal (*Black Athena*, Vol. 1. New Brunswick, N.J.: Rutgers University Press, 1987), which presents some of the linguistic, archaeological, and historical arguments for such a theory.

The geographic category "Sub-Saharan" creates a somewhat artificial barrier across the continent. The myths of Morocco and other Africa countries on the Mediterranean, for example, fit easily in neither category, but are treated here along with the myths of Sub-Saharan Africa proper. The myths of ancient Punic peoples of North Africa such as the Carthaginians are usually treated along with those of other Semitic peoples of the Middle East and, in this bibliography, can be found with the West and Central Asian material in Chapter 5.

General Work

Carpenter, Frances. *African Wonder Tales*. Garden City, N.Y.: Doubleday.
1963.
Retells twenty-four folktales from Africa, including Egypt, for older
children. magic, hunting, mythological beasts, and anthropomorphic
animals are dominant themes in these tales, which are identified by
county or region of origin only. Black-and-white line drawings by
Joseph Escourido. Pronunciation guide.

Egyptian Myths

Allen, Thomas G. *The Egyptian Book of the Dead*. Chicago: University
of Chicago Press, 1974.
This translation of a basic document dealing with Egyptian beliefs
about the afterlife is intended for the general reader and replaces the
early twentieth-century translation by E. A. Wallis Budge with a
version that reflects more recent advances in Egyptology. A short
introductory essay provides some background to the Book of the Dead
and some guide to this translation. The 174 spells in this text are
addressed to the gods and deal with concerns of the deceased. In
Appendix 1, the Book of the Dead is correlated with earlier documents
known as the Coffin and Pyramid texts. Appendix 2 contains a list of
ancient Egyptian documents and their published sources. Footnotes
and index.

Ames, D., trans. *Egyptian Mythology*. New York: Tudor Publishing, 1965.
Originally published in French by Larousse, this general introduction
to Egyptian mythology contains sections on early cults and divinities,
the deities of the "First Time," protective divinities of the pharaohs and
the kingdom, gods of the river and the desert, minor deities of birth and
death, deified humans, sacred animals, and life after death. Numerous
illustrations, twenty-five in color, depicting mythological and religious
scenes from ancient Egyptian art. List of theriomorphic deities. Index.

Anthes, Rudolf. "Mythology in Ancient Egypt." In *Mythologies of the
Ancient World*, edited by Samuel Noah Kramer. Garden City, N.Y.:
Doubleday (Anchor), 1961.
This survey of Egyptian mythology includes sections dealing with the
myth of the heavenly cow (the goddess Hathor), the character of
Egyptian mythology, Egypt's mythological inheritance, the concept of
Horus and his genealogy, the supremacy of the sun god Ra, the

Egyptian concept of the afterlife, the myth of Osiris, Isis, and Horus, and the myth of the eye. Egyptian sources are quoted extensively in translation. Illustration and genealogical chart. Bibliography.

Baines, John, and Geraldine Pinch. "Egypt." In *World Mythology*, edited by Roy Willis. New York: Henry Holt, 1993.
This overview of ancient Egyptian deities and myths includes sections on the first gods, the Ennead or the nine gods of Heliopolis, Osiris, Isis, Horus and Set, solar myths, magic, snakes and scorpions as agents of chaos, goddesses, the pharaoh, priest-magicians, and life after death. Supplementing these discussions are subsidiary sections with paraphrases of myths and short passages translated from ancient sources. Accompanied by thirty color illustrations of ancient Egyptian artifacts. Map, chronology, and genealogical chart.

Barb, A. A. "Mystery, Myth and Magic." In *The Legacy of Egypt*, edited by J. R. Harris. 2d ed. Oxford: The Clarendon Press, 1971.
A historical survey of ancient and modern studies of Egyptian religious beliefs and practices is followed by some discussion of Egyptian beliefs, rituals, and amulets connected with the afterlife, the cults of Osiris and Isis, and various magical beliefs, papyri, and practices. Six figures illustrating magical and religious artifacts from ancient Egypt, footnotes, and bibliography.

Budge, Earnest Alfred Wallis. *The Book of the Dead*. 3 vols. 2d ed. New York: E. P. Dutton, 1928.
The keeper of the Egyptian and Assyrian antiquities at the British Museum translates various hymns and religious texts found in tombs and on sarcophagi, coffins, papyri, and other materials, mostly at Thebes in Egypt. Illustrates ancient Egyptians' attitudes toward their gods and toward death. The book begins with several hymns to the gods Ra and Osiris and includes prayers, petitions, and religious formulae dealing with funerary customs and beliefs. Volume 1 contains an extensive introductory section with a history of the Book of the Dead, an essay on the god Osiris, and a detailed summary of the book, chapter by chapter. The rest of Volume 1 and the two subsequent volumes are devoted to the translation itself. Index at the end of Volume 3. Includes twenty-two color plates and 420 black-and-white illustrations taken mainly from ancient papyri.

—————. *The Gods of Egypt*. London: Methuen, 1904. 2 vols. Reprint. New York: Dover Publications, 1969.

This examination of the gods and myths of the ancient Egyptians has never gone out of date. Volume 1 treats the oldest beliefs and deities of the Egyptians and includes chapters on the conception of god, heaven, the underworld, the myths of Ra, Thoth, and Hathor, and the history of creation and of the destruction of humankind. Volume 2 focuses on the deities of Heliopolis, especially Osiris, Isis, and Amon. Includes several chapters on lesser and foreign gods and numerous hieroglyph texts of myths and legends accompanied by interlinear transliteration and translation. In a preface to Volume 1 Budge provides a short history of the scientific study of Egyptian religion and mythology. The reprint includes the 131 black-and-white text illustrations from the standard edition and an additional 98 color plates from the limited edition. These illustrations are all reproductions from papyri, coffins, and other ancient sources. Index.

_____. *Osiris and the Egyptian Resurrection*. 2 vols. London: P. L. Warner, 1911. Reprint. New York: Dover, 1973.
An attempt to uncover the source of the basic beliefs of the ancient Egyptian religion, and especially of the worship of Osiris. Chapters on the history of Osiris, his name, his myths, his attitude toward practices such as cannibalism, human sacrifice, and dancing. Also chapters on Osiris as ancestral spirit, judge of the dead, moon-god, and bull-god, on his shrines and cultic links with Africa, and on miscellaneous religious practices and beliefs. Extensive quotation of ancient texts, often accompanied by original hieroglyphics in footnotes. The 119 illustrations include seven full-page plates. Translation of three Pyramid texts in an appendix. Footnotes, endnotes, and index.

Cerny, Jaroslav. *Ancient Egyptian Religion*. London: Hutchinson's University Library, 1952.
This short sketch of ancient Egyptian religious practices and beliefs about the gods is intended for the general reader. In an introductory essay Cerny deals with the origin of the Egyptian gods and traces their appearance in textual documents and artistic representations. Chapter 1 considers the nature of the gods, their place in the cosmos, their functions and attributes, and concepts of time and fate. Chapter 2 addresses the relationship between humans and the gods, especially oracles, divine will, and life after death. Chapter 3 describes various forms of cult and divine worship in ancient Egypt. The last chapter considers Egyptian attitudes toward foreign gods, such as the Nubian Dedun and the Semitic Tanat, and the decline of Egyptian religion in the Roman period. Includes some summaries of significant myths and

translated passages from ancient documents. Chronological table, bibliography, and index.

Clark, Robert T. *Myth and Symbol in Ancient Egypt*. New York: Grove Press, 1960.
Uses extensive quotation from ancient texts to explain the mythological system of the Egyptians. An introductory essay deals with features of Egyptian religion and the purposes of their mythology. Includes chapters on the high god in the Old Kingdom and in the period of the Coffin texts, three chapters on Osiris, a chapter on other major deities such as Ra, Set, and Horus, and a chapter on visual symbols, such as the eye, the lotus, and the serpent, and their mythological uses. Argues in a concluding chapter that Egyptian myths are more a religious language than a collection of tales. Chronological tables of Egyptian history and a mythological scheme, charts of Egyptian deities and major religious symbols, list of chief cult centers, and map. Eighteen color plates and forty line drawings of mythological scenes from ancient Egyptian art, especially from late New Kingdom coffins. Introduction, endnotes, and index.

David, Rosalie. "Egypt." In *Mythology: An Illustrated Encyclopaedia*, edited by Richard Cavendish. New York: Rizzoli International, 1980. Also published as *An Illustrated Encyclopedia of Mythology*. New York: Crescent Books, 1984.
This general overview of the mythology of ancient Egypt has sections on myths of creation, the sun-cult of Ra, the religious role of kings and priests, the concept of the temple as an island of creation, festivals, birth, fate, the conquest of death, the judgment of the dead, the afterlife, and the myth of the death and resurrection of Osiris. Illustrations of artwork related to the myths. Map, time chart, genealogy of the gods of Heliopolis, and glossary of major Egyptian deities.

Erman, Adolf. *The Literature of the Ancient Egyptians*. Translated by Aylward M. Blackman. London: Methuen, 1927. Reprint. New York: Arno, 1977.
Originally published in German, this collection of writings from ancient Egypt includes religious and secular poems, narratives, instructional writings, and school exercises. Materials date from the third and second millennia B.C. Of special interest to the study of mythology are a variety of hymns to the gods from various periods and selections from the Old Kingdom Pyramid texts describing beliefs in the blessed dead. Each selection is preceded by a brief editorial note. Chronological chart

of Egyptian history, introductory essay on Egyptian literature, footnotes, and explanatory endnotes.

Faulkner, Raymond O. *The Ancient Egyptian Book of the Dead.* New
York: Limited Editions Club, 1972. Rev. ed. Austin: University of
Texas Press, 1990.
An English translation of the standard collection of funerary texts of
the ancient Egyptians by a prominent British Egyptologist. Accompanied by sixty color and eighty-five black-and-white illustrations from
twenty-four funerary papyri in the British Museum. In an introductory
essay, Carol A. R. Andrews offers some background to the Book of the
Dead. The combination of texts and illustrations creates an overview
of Egyptian deities and attitudes toward death which is perhaps unique
for the English reader. Glossary.

_____. *The Ancient Egyptian Coffin Texts.* 3 vols. Warminster,
England: Aris & Phillips, 1973 (Vol. 1), 1977 (Vol. 2), 1978 (Vol. 3).
This collection of 1,185 spells written on coffins during the Middle
Kingdom is based upon the monumental work of Adriaan de Buck,
who published these texts in their original form between 1935 and
1961. These spells are filled with references to the gods and illustrate
Egyptian beliefs about the afterlife. This translation makes these valuable documents available to the English reader. Each translation is
accompanied by explanatory notes. Index at the end of Volume 3.

_____. *The Ancient Egyptian Pyramid Texts.* Oxford: The
Clarendon Press, 1969.
This English translation of texts carved on the walls of pyramids from
the Fifth and Sixth Dynasties makes use of recent advances in the
knowledge of the language of ancient Egyptian language. These 759
utterances, many consisting of spells and prayers, are accompanied by
editorial notes. In a short preface, Faulkner explains several features
of the translation. List of abbreviations and indexes of divinities,
localities, modern proper names, and selected words.

Fontenrose, Joseph. "God and Dragon in Egypt and India." In *Python: A
Study of Delphic Myth and Its Origins,* by Joseph Fontenrose.
Berkeley: University of California Press, 1959.
In this chapter of a book examining myths of divine or heroic combat
with serpents or dragons in the ancient Mediterranean world, Fontenrose considers examples of dragon combat in Egyptian mythology,
especially in the conflict between the gods Horus and Set. Indicates
folktale themes and motifs from the Aarne-Thompson index which

appear in these Egyptian myths and illustrates in these myths a pattern of conflict between order and disorder, chaos and cosmos, and life and death which is also found in the Greek myth of Apollo and Python and in the Indic struggle between Indra and Vritra. One black-and-white figure.

Frankfort, Henri. *Ancient Egyptian Religion*. New York: Harper & Row, 1961.
An overview of Egyptian religious beliefs, including their concept of god, the role of the state in religious practices and beliefs, ethical teachings, and attitudes toward death. Addresses the relationship between religion and mythology in the last chapter, which deals with change and permanence in ancient Egyptian literature and art. Thirty-two illustrations from ancient monuments, art and papyri, introductory preface, chronological table, and index.

_____. "Kingship and the Divine Powers in Nature." In *Kingship and the Gods*, by Henri Frankfort. Chicago: University of Chicago Press, 1948.
This section of a scholarly comparison of ancient Egyptian and Mesopotamian concepts of kingship concentrates on the divinity of the ancient Egyptian pharaoh. Emphasizes associations between the pharaoh and the Egyptian deities, Ra, Hathor, and Osiris. Through Ra the pharaoh is identified with the sun and the powers of creation. Through Hathor the king is linked with cattle and the forces of procreation. Through Osiris the pharaoh is tied with the cyclic flooding of the Nile, the stages of the moon and constellations, and, ultimately, the process of rejuvenation and resurrection. These associations are demonstrated via references to ancient cults, artistic scenes, and documents. Black-and-white illustrations of some of these scenes are included, as are short passages in translation from ancient texts. Endnotes and index.

Harris, Geraldine. *Gods and Pharaohs from Egyptian Mythology*. New York: Schocken Books, 1982.
This general introduction to Egyptian mythology for juvenile readers includes color illustrations by David O'Connor and line drawings by John Sibbick. Symbols used in the drawings are explained in a brief appendix. Following a short introduction to the land of Egypt are sections on the major Egyptian deities and legends of early Egypt. Later sections deal with folktales and with the reigns of pharaohs such as Akhenaten and Rameses II. The final section describes the history

of Egypt after the pharaohs. Short appendix on writing in ancient Egypt. Map and index.

Hart, George. *Dictionary of Egyptian Gods and Goddesses.* London: Routledge & Kegan Paul, 1986.
This comprehensive dictionary of Egyptian deities, arranged alphabetically, is based upon inscriptional and iconographic evidence from ancient Egypt. Minor gods receive only brief descriptions, but major gods such as Aten and Isis have detailed discussions of iconography, cult, and myth. Frequent reference to ancient documents, especially the Pyramid texts. Many citations are accompanied by drawings based upon tomb paintings, sculpture, and other artifacts from ancient Egypt. Preface, time chart, maps, select bibliography, and list of alternate names for deities.

_____. *Egyptian Myths.* Austin: University of Texas Press, 1990.
This overview of Egyptian mythology, combining summaries of major texts and descriptions of artistic representations of myths, is part of the Legendary Past Series and is intended for the general reader. Offers individual chapters on Egyptian creation legends, the origin of kingship, the myth of cataclysm or the temporary disruption of the relationship between gods and humans, and the journey of the sun god to the underworld. Also contains a discussion of the goddess Isis as a magical healer and stories in which the historical personages Imhotep, Djeheuty, and Rameses II are transformed into figures of legend. Text is accompanied by many illustrations of myths in Egyptian painting and sculpture. Map and short bibliography.

Hollis, Susan Tower. *The Ancient Egyptian "Tale of Two Brothers."* Norman: University of Oklahoma Press, 1990.
A literal translation of a tale about divine brothers, Bata and Anubis, who go through a rite of passage, including attempted seduction, self-mutilation, and deception, before becoming kings. The translation is based upon the papyrus d'Orbiney, discovered in 1852. Uses various signs to indicate inserted words, restorations, and words omitted or capitalized by the Egyptian scribe. Accompanied by seven chapters bringing together a variety of modern disciplines, including folklore studies and anthropology, in order to interpret the narrative and place it in its cultural and historical environment. In these chapters each episode of the tale is analyzed in detail. Passages from the folktale quoted here appear in transliterated Egyptian and in English translation. In a chapter discussing the names and characteristics of the two

brothers hieroglyphics are also used. Selections from a related document, papyrus Jumilhac, in an appendix. Endnotes, bibliography, and index.

Hooke, Samuel Henry. "Egyptian Mythology." In *Middle Eastern Mythology*, by Samuel Henry Hooke. Baltimore: Penguin Books, 1963.
In this chapter of a survey of the mythologies of ancient Middle East, Mesopotamia, Egypt, Ugarit, the Hittite empire, and the Hebrews, a prominent scholar of the early twentieth century recounts some myths of Osiris, Ra, and the Nile River. Explanations of the myths are accompanied by some short examples from ancient texts. Eight pages of black-and-white plates illustrate some of these myths. Endnotes.

Hornung, E. *Conceptions of God in Ancient Egypt: The One and the Many.* Translated by John Baines. London: Routledge & Kegan Paul, 1983.
A major German Egyptologist offers a detailed examination of the gods of ancient Egypt with special attention to their physical descriptions, attributes, powers, and iconographies. A historical introduction is followed by chapters on the Egyptian words for "god," the names of individual gods, their depictions, their characteristics, divine action and human response, and classification of the Egyptian pantheon. Twenty figures and five plates depicting the gods in ancient art. Chronological table, bibliography, glossary of gods, and index.

Ions, Veronica. *Egyptian Mythology.* Rev. ed. New York: Peter Bedrick Books, 1982.
The first part of this general introduction to the myths of ancient Egypt offers a comparison of four different Egyptian cosmogonies, or myths of creation. The central, major portion of this book is devoted to descriptions of individual deities, including their origins, genealogies, concerns, myths, and attributes. The last section describes the spread of the Osiris cult and its links with Egyptian beliefs concerning death and burial. Illustrations on nearly every page, many in color. Chronological chart, short bibliography, and index.

Loew, Cornelius. "Myth in the Egyptian Religious Tradition." In *Myth, Sacred History and Philosophy*, by Cornelius Loew. New York: Harcourt, Brace & World, 1967.
Examines the sacred myths of ancient Egypt and their influence on Christianity's religious heritage. Emphasizes Egyptian conviction in the links between social and cosmic order, the importance of divine kingship, and the growth of concepts of individualism. Particular

reference to sacred Egyptian myths of creation found in Pyramid and Coffin texts. Footnotes and bibliography.

Lurker, Manfred. *Gods and Symbols of Ancient Egypt*. Translated by Barbara Cummings. London: Thames and Hudson, 1980.
This dictionary contains approximately 300 citations on the gods, religious practices, and symbols of the Egyptians. Explanations of the functions of the various deities and how they are depicted visually are preceded by introductory essays on the world of Egyptian symbolism and the cultural and religious history of Egypt. Includes 114 black-and-white illustrations of ancient artifacts and artwork. Map, chronological table, bibliography, and index to the illustrations.

Mackenzie, Donald Alexander. *Egyptian Myth and Legend*. London: Gresham Publishing, 1913.
A historical survey of the myths of ancient Egypt complicated by controversial views about race and theories about racial drift. Begins with the rise of Egyptian civilization and ends with the Greco-Roman period, with individual deities such as Ra, Osiris, and Amon treated during the historical periods when they are most prominent. Myths and legends are paraphrased or cited in English translation in order to illustrate the private lives and religious beliefs of the ancient Egyptians. Frequently cites possible examples of cultural overlap between Egypt and other ancient civilizations, including the Assyrians, Babylonians, Cretans, Hebrews, and Hittites. Seven color and thirty-three black-and-white plates illustrating both ancient art and modern drawings which represent Egyptian deities and myths.

Mercer, Samuel A. B. *The Pyramid Texts in Translation and Commentary*. 4 vols. New York: Longmans, Green, 1952.
Combines English translation and commentary of one of the oldest collections of written material in the world. These texts were inscribed in hieroglyphics on the walls of five pyramids in Sakhara, Egypt, between 2350 and 2175 B.C. They include fragments of myths, legends, astronomical lore, cosmology, and rituals. Volume 1 consists of translations of 714 texts. Commentary is found in Volumes 2 and 3. Volume 4 contains twenty-eight excursive essays on particular topics related to the texts, such as how to get to heaven, magic, and various deities. Several of these are in German or French. Also in Volume 4 are a glossary, a brief chronological table, a list of abbreviations, a map, and four plates.

Morenz, Siegfried. *Egyptian Religion*. Translated by Ann E. Keep. London: Methuen, 1973.
This overview of the religion of the ancient Egyptians includes chapters on their religious development, the gods, the worshipers, divine involvement in human affairs, cults, ethics, theology, cosmogony, death, sacred writings, and contacts with the outside world. In an appendix the characteristics of the most important gods are summarized alphabetically according to the name of the god. Chronological table, bibliography, endnotes, and indexes.

Müller, W. Max. *Egyptian Mythology*. Vol. 12 in *The Mythology of All Races*, edited by Louis Herbert Gray. Boston: Marshall Jones, 1918.
This overview of the myths and religion of the ancient Egyptians begins with a short history of scholarly opinions on this topic. The first chapters describe local deities, sun worship, and gods associated with nature. A chapter on cosmic and cosmogonic myths includes extensive quotation from ancient texts in translation. A chapter on the Osiran circle of deities is followed by another containing ancient texts about these gods. The last part of the book discusses foreign gods, the worship of animals and humans, the afterlife, ethics, magic, and the development of Egyptian religion. Seven plates and 220 figures accompany the text. Endnotes and bibliography. Complete index in Volume 13.

Murray, Margaret A. "Language and Literature." In *The Splendour That Was Egypt*, by Margaret A. Murray. New ed. New York: Hawthorn Books, 1963.
This survey of the language and literature of ancient Egypt discusses various mythological writings such as hymns to the gods and travel tales. Significant portions of some ancient writings are quoted in translation, including the story of the doomed prince and a Ptolemaic tale of a childless couple. Some footnotes.

_____. "Religion." In *The Splendour That Was Egypt*, by Margaret A. Murray. New ed. New York: Hawthorn Books, 1963.
An overview of the ancient Egyptian religion, with sections on local deities, primitive goddesses, the sun god, the relationship between Osiris and the pharaoh, the cult of the pharaoh, ritual, burial customs, temple complexes, ethics, magic, and curses. Seven illustrations and occasional footnotes.

Otto, Eberhard. *Egyptian Art and the Cults of Osiris and Amon*. Translated by Kate Bosse Griffiths. London: Thames and Hudson, 1968.

A study of the cults of the gods Osiris and Amon in the art of ancient Egypt. Part 1 traces the worship of Osiris at Abydos historically from the Early Dynastic Period through the New Kingdom and Late Period. Also contains an account of the myth of Osiris by the Greek historian Plutarch. Part 2 deals with the worship of Amon at Thebes. Chapters include a historical survey, an overview of buildings and cults, and a study of Thebes as a sacred city. Each part includes its own endnotes and notes to plates. Accompanied by fifteen color and fifty-two black-and-white plates. General bibliography. chronological table, glossary of place names, and map.

Piankoff, Alexandre. *The Shrines of Tut-Ankh-Amon*. New York: Pantheon Books, 1955.

Contains translations and reconstructions of the texts written on the shrine found in the tomb of Tut-Ankh-Amon discovered by Howard Carter in 1923. Part 1 consists of a detailed introduction to the worship of the gods Amon-Re and Maat, the theology of Aten, and Egyptian funerary practices. Extensive quotation from ancient texts and myths, including the entire "Book of the Divine Cow," which tells the end of the sun god's earthly reign and the punishment of humankind. Many of the texts of the shrines translated in Part 2 include passages from the Book of the Dead and describe Egyptian beliefs concerning the gods and the afterlife. Sixty-four photographs of the original artifacts are supplemented by fifty drawings depicting details from the shrines. Footnotes, chronological chart, list of plates, and figures.

Posener, Georges. "Literature." In *The Legacy of Egypt*, edited by J. R. Harris. 2d ed. Oxford: The Clarendon Press, 1971.

This survey of ancient Egyptian literature deals with several mythological narratives of the Middle and New Kingdoms. Summarizes the plots of Middle Kingdom tales about the gods, an adventure about a shipwrecked sailor, and New Kingdom stories about Astarte, princes, and heroes, including the "Tale of Two Brothers." Bibliography.

Reymond, Eve A. E. *The Mythical Origin of the Egyptian Temple*. New York: Barnes & Noble, 1969.

Using building texts, especially from the temple of Edfu, Reymond shows how Egyptian temples were constructed in mythological circumstances. The historical building was usually seen as the direct continuation of an edifice built by the gods at the beginning of time. Individual chapters deal with sources, the primeval world of the gods, the second era of the primeval age, the creation of the temple, and the doctrine of the temple's origin. Appendix outlining the history of the

Egyptian temple, eleven illustrations, bibliography, and indexes of names of gods, sacred places, Egyptian words, sacred books of the Edfu temple, and Edfu texts translated.

Rundle, Clark, R. J. *Myth and Symbol in Ancient Egypt*. London: Thames & Hudson, 1959.

This overview of the world of Egyptian mythology studies a select group of myths and their religious symbolism. A short introductory essay on the uses of myths in Egyptian religion is followed by two chapters on the god Ra in the Old Kingdom and in the age of the Coffin texts, three chapters on Osiris and the history of his myth, two chapters dealing with other myths about the great gods and mythological symbols, and a short conclusion. Eighteen plates, forty line drawings, chronological table, mythological scheme, list of chief cult centers, chart of religious symbols, map, endnotes, and index.

Shorter, Alan Wynn. *The Egyptian Gods: A Handbook*. London: Routledge & Kegan Paul, 1937; reprint, 1979.

A general guide to the religion and the gods of ancient Egypt, with extensive quotation in translation from ancient Egyptian religious texts. Creation and the nine great gods are treated in Chapter 1, Egyptian temples in Chapter 2, Osiris and the afterlife in Chapter 3, the Book of the Dead in Chapter 4, and the nature of the gods and the monotheism of King Akhenaten in Chapter 5. Descriptive list of the principal Egyptian gods. Short bibliography, preface, and introductory essay. Four plates.

Simpson, William Kelly, ed. *The Literature of Ancient Egypt*. Translated by Raymond O. Faulkner, E. F. Wente, Jr., and W. K. Simpson. New Haven, Conn.: Yale University Press, 1972.

This selection of readings from ancient Egypt includes translations of several pieces of a mythic or religious nature, including exotic travel tales such as "The Shipwrecked Sailor" and tales about the gods such as "The Tale of the Two Brothers" and "The Contendings of Horus and Seth," as well as ghost stories, tales of magic, and hymns to the gods. Each selection is introduced by some background material about the text and its manuscript source. An introductory essay surveys the different genres of ancient Egyptian literature. Selected bibliography and six illustrations.

Van de Walle, B. "Egypt: Syncretism and State Religion." In *Larousse World Mythology*, edited by Pierre Grimal. Translated by Patricia Beardsworth. New York: G. P. Putnam's Sons, 1963.

60 *World Mythology*

Surveys the religious beliefs of the ancient Egyptians and argues that
the emphasis of Egyptian religion and myth was not dogma, but cult.
Discusses the origin and evolution of religious institutions, with special
attention to the role of the pharaoh and the doctrine of the god Aten
developed by Amenophis IV (Akhenaten) in the Eighteenth Dynasty.
Contains sections on the myths and gods of the different cult centers
at Heliopolis, Hermopolis, Memphis, and Thebes. Paraphrases of
popular myths from the Pyramid texts and the Book of the Dead. These
include the story of Osiris and his relationship with the pharaoh, the
adventures of Horus and Set, the eye of Horus, and the myths of
Apophis and of the cow. Many illustrations of ancient artifacts, some
in color.

Viaud, J. "Egyptian Mythology." In *New Larousse Encyclopedia of Mythology*, edited by Felix Guirand et al. Translated by Richard Aldington
and Delano Ames. New York: Hamlyn, 1968.
Traces the development of Egyptian religious beliefs and concepts of
deity from earliest representations in the middle of the fourth millennium and concentrates in this study on examining deities with genuine
cults and mythologies. Viaud examines the twenty-four gods in the
Ennead or divine company at Heliopolis and in the family of Osiris,
thirteen protective divinities of the pharaohs and of the kingdom, six
river and desert gods, more than fifteen supernatural creatures connected with birth and death, three deified humans, including pharoah,
and seven sacred animals. Each religious figure is treated separately,
with discussions of the god's names, iconography, and major myths.
List of animals associated with Egyptian deities. Fifty-seven black-
and-white and three color illustrations of ancient representations of
these deities.

Wilson, John A. "Egypt." In *The Intellectual Adventure of Ancient Man*,
by Henri Frankfort, H. A. Frankfort, John A. Wilson, and Thorkild
Jacobsen. Chicago: University of Chicago Press, 1946. 2d ed. *Before
Philosophy*. Baltimore: Penguin, 1949.
In this part of a study of myth as a form of concrete speculation about
the universe distinct from the abstract type of thought associated with
philosophy, an Egyptologist at the University of Chicago offers extensive paraphrase and quotation from Egyptian myth sources such as the
Book of the Dead. Illustrates the Egyptian world view of the nature of
the universe, cosmogony, the function of the state and of the pharaoh,
and the purpose and value of human life. Endnotes and bibliography.

_____. "Egyptian Myths and Tales." In *The Ancient Near East*, edited by James B. Pritchard. Princeton, N.J.: Princeton University Press, 1958.

Six major Egyptian texts related to the Old Testament are here translated for the general reader. The mythological material consists of a 700 B.C. document from Memphis describing a theology of creation, a Pyramid text describing the deliverance of humankind from destruction, and a folktale entitled "The Tale of Two Brothers." The other three narratives deal with the voluntary exile of a Middle Kingdom official named Sinuhe, an eleventh-century B.C. journey to Phoenicia, and a description of a great famine in the Third Dynasty (about 2700 B.C.). The translations follow the original documents closely and include careful indication of original text numbers, restorations, and doubtful readings. Each text is preceded by a short introduction. Some of the 197 illustrations of Middle Eastern artifacts in this volume complement these Egyptian texts. Also includes footnotes, map, indexes, and glossary.

_____. "Egyptian Myths, Epics and Mortuary Texts." In *Ancient Near Eastern Texts Relating to the Old Testament*, edited by James B. Pritchard. 3d ed. Princeton, N.J.: Princeton University Press, 1969.

Translations of twenty-four texts from ancient Egypt are here offered in a scholarly format, with careful indication of original text numbers, restorations, and doubtful readings. Arranged thematically are nine narratives about creation and aetiology, the story of the god Ra's deliverance of humankind from destruction, ten tales of heroic deeds by gods and humans, and four mortuary texts describing the afterlife. Each text is preceded by a introductory commentary and bibliography. Footnotes.

Sub-Saharan Myths

Abrahams, Robert D. *African Folktales*. New York: Pantheon, 1983.

The goal of this anthology is to provide a representative sampling of African folktales. Retold especially from previously published material. Thematically arranged in tales of wonder, moral questions, tricksters, great deeds, and outrageous events. Each group includes a short introductory section noting special features and themes. Folktales are identified only by ethnic groups, such as Yoruba, Hausa, and Bantu. Little additional ethnographic information is provided. These aetiologies, animal fables, and hero epics incorporate many songs and proverbs, which are usually marked off in italics. In an introductory essay Abrahams discusses special features of the African folk tradition and the cultural context of the tales. Special emphasis on the context of actual performance and its effect on the narratives. Bibliography and index of tales.

Abrahamsson, Hans. *The Origin of Death*. London: K. Paul Trench, 1952. Reprint. New York: Arno Press, 1977.
This book, originally a doctoral dissertation, is a survey of various Sub-Saharan myths explaining the origin of death. Suggests that in most African myths it is a god who, for one reason or another, allows death into the world. Motivations for the introduction of death vary widely, and these stories are discussed in thematic groups, such as sleep and death, humans desiring or buying death, and death linked with disease or punishment for sins. Geographic distribution of these tales is supported by a series of eighteen maps. Chapter 1 offers a short survey of scholarship dealing with African aetiologies about death. Bibliography and index.

Amadu, Malum. *Amadu's Bundle: Fulani Tales of Love and Djinns*. London: Heinemann, 1972.
These traditional Fulani tales, recorded in Arabic by an Islamic *malum* or "scribe," were collected by Gulla Kell and translated into English by Ronald Moody. Includes animal fables, aetiologies, spells, and stories of marriage, matchmaking, and the supernatural world of *jinns* or "genies."

Arnott, Kathleen. *African Myths and Legends Retold*. New York: Oxford University Press, 1962.
Thirty-four tales about animals, the supernatural, and occult objects from all parts of Sub-Saharan Africa. Many are aetiological in nature. Others deal with rules of human interaction and the place of humankind in the world. Bibliography.

Bali, Esther. *Taroh Folktales*. Ibadan, Nigeria: Spectrum Books Limited, 1990.
A collection of fifteen stories from the Taroh (Yergam) people of Nigeria retold for children by a Nigerian author of children's literature. Mostly animal fables which show the interaction of the natural, human, and supernatural worlds. Short introductory essay on the Taroh and their tales. Glossary of Taroh terms.

Barker, William Henry, and Cecilia Sinclair. *West African Folk-Tales*. London: George G. Harrap, 1917. Reprint. Northbrook, Ill.: Metro Books, 1972.
Thirty-six tales from the Gold Coast of Africa retold for children. Part 1 contains eighteen Anansi or spider tales. Miscellaneous collection of aetiologies and animal tales in Part 2. Introductory essay by Barker with some background about the tales. Twenty-four photographs and drawings by Sinclair.

Bascom, William. "Cinderella in Africa." *Journal of the Folklore Institute* 9 (1972): 54-70. Reprinted in *Cinderella: A Folklore Casebook*, edited by Alan Dundes. New York: Garland Press, 1982.
Offers Neil Skinner's translation of a Nigerian tale originally published in Hausa in 1911 and notes several similarities to the cycle of tales associated with Cinderella. Suggests that this tale was the result of European contact with the Hausa rather than diffusion of the traditional folktale across the Sahara. In a postscript the author summarizes a similar tale from Morocco. Reprint includes useful background information, historical commentary, and bibliography by Dundes. Endnotes.

Bastide, R. "Africa: Magic and Symbolism." In *Larousse World Mythology*, edited by Pierre Grimal. Translated by Patricia Beardsworth. New York: G. P. Putnam's Sons, 1963.
This survey of the mythologies of Sub-Saharan Africa includes sections on the Pygmy, Bushmen, Hottentot, Bantu, Congo, Nilotic, Sudanese, West African seaboard, and Madagascan peoples. The meaning and function of African mythology is discussed in a separate section. Includes descriptions of the Pygmy supreme deity Khonvum, Bushmen animal-spirits, Bantu tales about the origin of humankind, Dogon beliefs, Sudanese ancestor heroes, Ashanti tales about Anansi the spider, legends about Yoruba deities, and Madagascan creation stories. Forty illustrations of African artifacts, two in color.

Beier, Ulli, ed. *The Origin of Life and Death: African Creation Myths*. London: Heinemann, 1966.
A selection of eighteen short creation stories and myths of origin from all over Sub-Saharan Africa. In an introductory essay the editor comments briefly on the general features of African creation myths and their resemblance to biblical mythology. These stories offer African versions of the creation of the world, the relationship between god and humankind, and the origin of death, cripples, fishes, and other aspects

of reality. Tales are identified by ethnic and geographic origin, but no other cultural context is provided.

Berry, Jack. *West African Folktales,* edited by Richard A. Spears. Evanston, Ill.: Northwestern University Press, 1991.
This anthology of 123 tales from English-speaking West Africa, especially Sierra Leone, Ghana, and Nigeria, is the result of the author's own collections in West Africa as well as his selection from printed versions. Includes Anansi or spider tales, tales of the supernatural, morality fables, and aetiologies. Endnotes include short commentary about the tales as well as information on provenance. In a prefatory essay entitled "Spoken Art in West Africa," the author discusses some general characteristics of these tales and provides some background to the study of folklore in West Africa. Introduction by Spears with information about telling a West African tale, the translator, the collection, and the organization of the book. Index and pronunciation guide.

Biebuyck, Daniel. *Hero and Chief: Epic Literature from the Banyanga Zaire Republic.* Berkeley: University of California Press, 1978.
A sequel to *The Mwindo Epic* (listed below), this work includes translated and annotated versions of three songs by Nyanga bards about their hero Mwindo. These texts are accompanied by an extensive introduction to these epics, including linguistic, historical, and social features of the performances, as well as a discussion of the portrayal of the Nyanga hero and characteristics of Nyanga heroic tales. Includes a plot summary of the epic, glossary of personages, bibliography, and index.

Biebuyck, Daniel, and Kahombo C. Mateene. *The Mwindo Epic.* Berkeley: University of California Press, 1969.
The story of Mwindo, the hero of the Bantu-speaking Nyanga people of Zaire, is here translated and annotated. The epic recounts the deeds of a superhuman hero and his travels in search of his father. In an introductory essay the translators include background on Nyanga oral literature, notes on translation, and a summary of the plot. The original Nyanga text follows the English translation. Index.

Bleek, William H. I.. *Reynard the Fox in South Africa.* London: Trübner, 1864.
One of the first English translations of Hottentot legend, this collection contains forty-two tales and fables. Some are translated from the

original Hottentot and others from German manuscripts. Includes stories about the jackal, tortoise, baboon, lion, sun, and moon, as well as folktales about the supernatural and human trickery. In a preface, the author explains how the material for this book was collected and comments briefly on the Hottentots and their myths.

_____. *Zulu Legends*. 1857. Reprint edited by J. A. Engelbrecht. Pretoria: J. L. Van Schaik, 1952.
A limited-edition reprint of twenty-nine Zulu legends collected in Natal in 1855-1856. Legends include creation stories and description of various customs, especially dealing with marriage, birth, and death. Original Zulu texts are accompanied by English translation in parallel columns. Footnotes to the Zulu text and explanatory endnotes. In an introduction to the reprint, the editor provides some background to Bleek's text and its origin and history and analyzes some features of the Zulu used in the original text. He also offers revised versions of the legends in modernized Zulu in an appendix. The reprint includes a portrait of the author, a facsimile of the original title page, an 1856 map of Natal, and Bleek's list of ethnic groups (in German).

Bleek, William H. I., and L. C. Loyd. *Specimens of Bushmen Folklore*. London: George Allen, 1911.
These traditional tales of the Bushmen of South Africa were collected by the authors in the late nineteenth century. Bushmen texts are accompanied on facing pages by English translations. The first half of the book contains myths about the heavenly bodies, animal fables, legends, and poetry. The second half records personal histories of the Bushmen storytellers, adventures about animals and hunting, customs, and superstitions. Fifty illustrations, including portraits of Bushmen and pencil drawings by the storytellers. In an introductory essay, George McCall Theal offers ethnographic and historical information about the Bushmen and information about William Bleek and his recording methods. Footnotes and index.

Brownlee, Frank. *Lion and Jackal, with Other Native Folk Tales of South Africa*. London: George Allen & Unwin, 1938.
These twenty-nine tales include stories about animals, notably the jackal, cannibals, the little hero named Hlakanyana, and fabulous creatures. Explanatory and interpretative notes on the tales appear in Appendix 1. In Appendix 2 the author's essay on the childlike mental horizon of Africans reflects the cultural biases of the European colonists in Africa.

Budge, Earnest A. Wallis. *The Queen of Sheba and Her Only Son Menyelik.* 2d ed. London: Oxford University Press, 1932.

An English translation of the Ethiopian *Kebra Nagast* (the book of the glory of kings), which traces the rulers and people of Abyssinia back to Menyelik, the son of the Queen of Sheba and King Solomon. Woven into this semi-historical document are a variety of legends, folktales, and other traditional writings from Hebrew, Egyptian, Arabic, and Ethiopian sources. Includes stories about biblical figures such as Adam, Noah, and Abraham, tales about Solomon and the Queen of Sheba, and accounts about Jesus. An introductory section on manuscripts of the *Kebra Nagast*, translation of the Arabic version, legends of the Queen of Sheba in the Koran, modern legends about Solomon and the queen, and a summary of the *Kebra Nagast*. Thirty-four plates, mostly details from manuscript illuminations. Index.

Cardinall, A. W. *Tales Told in Togoland.* Oxford: Oxford University Press, 1931.

Retellings of traditional stories told to the author by peasants and hunters in what is now Togo, plus a traditional history of the Dagomba people collected by E. F. Tamakloe. Introductory essay on the ethnography of Togo. Additional chapters are arranged according to the following themes: the origin of things, the sons of God, the Pixie-folk and their ways, hunter lore, cunning versus strength, Anansi the spider, aetiologies, friendship, adversity, the dangers of women, and traditional history. Occasional footnotes and index.

Cendrars, Blaise. *The African Saga.* Translated by Margery Bianco. New York: Payson & Clarke, 1927. Reprint. New York: Negro Universities Press, 1969.

Originally published in 1920 in France as *Anthologie Nègre* (black anthology), this selection of African oral literature was translated freely into French by an important poet and novelist of the period. These 103 pieces are arranged in twenty-one chapters which deal with themes and genres including cosmic legends, fetishism, jinns, charms, totemism, historical legends, the origin of human civilization, aetiologies, wonder tales, anecdotes, moral tales, love stories, humorous tales, fables, proverbs, poems, songs, and modern tales. Each is identified simply by ethnic names such as Hausa, Zulu, and Yoruba. No additional ethnography or information about sources. Short foreword by the author. In an introduction to the English translation, Arthur B. Spingarn comments upon the influence of this anthology in making this literature better known in Western Europe. Bibliography.

Chatelain, Heli. *Folk-Tales of Angola*. Vol. 1 in *Memoirs of the American Folk-Lore Society*. New York: American Folk-Lore Society, 1894. Reprint. New York: Kraus Reprint, 1969.

Fifty tales collected by an American missionary in Angola between 1885 and 1891 are here presented in original Ki-mbundu with a parallel literal English translation. Animal fables, especially tales about an animal hero called Leopard, are accompanied by stories about human hunters, love, metamorphosis, and spirits. Multiple versions of several tales. Some show European influence, such as one modeled on the story of Cinderella. In a preface the author describes how he collected these tales. In an introductory essay he describes the geography of the country, the culture of its people, and the study of Angolan folk-lore, then offers a bibliography of Ki-mbundu literature and a pronunciation guide to the language. Information on informants, dialect, and comparisons with other tales in endnotes. Musical scores in an appendix. Map, bibliography, and index.

Chesaina, C. *Oral Literature of the Kalenjin*. Nairobi, Kenya: Heinemann, 1991.

Includes a variety of traditional oral material collected among the Kalenjin people of western Kenya and the Rift Valley between 1976 and 1984. Part 1 consists of background material on the Kalenjin people, the form, performance, and classification of the oral literature, and a bibliography. In Part 2 the literary materials are arranged according to type: oral narratives, songs, proverbs, and riddles. For the study of myths, the oral narratives are most valuable and include aetiologies, legends, animal fables, trickster tales, and stories of communal life. Each of these narratives is presented both in the Kalenjin language and in English translation. Name and age of narrator and place of origin are provided for each tale. Since this text is intended for use in the schools, each narrative is also followed by several review questions. Map and bibliography.

Courlander, Harold. *The King's Drum and Other African Stories*. New York: Harcourt Brace Jovanovich, 1962.

Twenty-nine tales from a variety of Sub-Saharan peoples and regions, including the Gindo of Mali, the Mende of the Ivory Coast, the Wolof of Senegal, the Hausa of Nigeria, the Ashanti of Ghana, the Bakongo of Zaire, and the Mbaka of Angola. Creation myths were specifically excluded from this collection of folktales, hero legends, and animal fables. Sources and commentary for each of the tales are included in endnotes. Illustrated with drawings by Enrico Arno.

_____. *Tales of Yoruba Gods and Heroes*. New York: Crown, 1973.
Retells thirty-two traditional stories gathered by the author among the Yoruba of Nigeria. Myths about various Yoruba *orishas*, or deities, creation tales, aetiologies, foundation stories, and tales about heroes are preceded by introductory materials on the Yoruba, their gods and heroes, and their calendar week. This collection is followed by various notes and commentary about individual stories. Appendices on Yoruba gods and music in the Americas, especially in Cuba. Map, glossary, pronunciation guide, and selective bibliography.

_____, ed. *A Treasury of African Folklore*. New York: Crown Publishers, 1975.
A sweeping anthology of oral literature from Sub-Saharan Africa gathered from a variety of published sources by a major American folklorist. In a short introductory essay, the editor surveys the features of African literature and describes the scope of this collection, which begins with the Sudanic peoples and moves in turn to the Guinea Coast, Central Africa, East Africa, South West Africa, and then to the East Horn. The tales of each geographic region are introduced by some historical and cultural background. Some of the mythic material includes excerpts from Wolof, Yoruba, Nyanga, and Zulu epics, creation myths from the Ekoi, Shangaan, Venda, Xhosa, and Masai, underworld journeys told by the Bini, Mbundu, Ganda, and Zulu, and trickster tales from the Akan, Bantu, and Hottentot. The collection also includes recollections, wisdom sayings, riddles, and jokes. Bibliography and index.

Courlander, Harold, and Ezekiel Aderogba Eshugbayi. *Olode the Hunter and Other Tales from Nigeria*. New York: Harcourt, Brace & World, 1968.
Gathers and translates eighteen Yoruba and Hausa stories, including morality tales, adventure stories, and animal trickster fables, especially about Ijapa the tortoise. The title story tells of a skilled hunter whose excessive pride proves disastrous. In a series of endnotes, Courlander offers some observations about the tales in general, especially features of the Ijapa stories, as well as interpretative and comparative comments about individual tales.

Courlander, Harold, and George Herzog. *The Cow-Tail Switch and Other West African Stories*. New York: Holt, Rinehart and Winston, 1947.

Seventeen tales collected by the authors in the field or from published sources. A variety of tales, including animal fables and aetiologies, are retold here for children and adults alike. The title story tells of a dead man's miraculous return to life with the aid of his sons and his gift of a beautiful cow's tail to the son who helped him the most. Short introduction by the authors. Sources for the tales are provided in endnotes. Glossary and pronunciation guide. Illustrations by Madye Lee Chastain.

Courlander, Harold, and Wolf Leslau. *The Fire on the Mountain and Other Ethiopian Stories*. New York: Holt, Rinehart and Winston, 1950.
Twenty-four tales told by various peoples of Ethiopia, Somalia, and Eritrea. Many were recorded in the field by the authors and are here translated for the younger reader. Short introduction on the geography and peoples of Ethiopia. Tales come from both Muslim and Christian traditions and tell of heroes, extraordinary deeds, and talking animals. Illustrations by Robert W. Kane. Endnotes offer general commentary, comparison with other folktale traditions, and information on sources. Glossary and pronunciation guide.

Courlander, Harold, and Albert Kofi Prempeh. *The Hat-Shaking Dance and Other Ashanti Tales from Ghana*. New York: Harcourt, Brace & World, 1957.
Twenty-one tales about Anansi, the trickster spider of the Ashanti. Most of these animal tales contain aetiological features and explain the origins of various aspects of the natural and animal worlds. The title story describes a dance performed by Anansi while attempting to hide hot beans under his hat. Includes a brief introduction about the Ashanti and their tales and endnotes with some explanatory and comparative comments about the tales.

Courlander, Harold, and Ousmane Sako. *The Heart of the Ngoni: Heroes of the African Kingdom of Segu*. New York: Crown Publishers, 1982.
A well-known American folklorist collaborates with an African scholar to create this collection of heroic narratives told by the Bambara and Soninke peoples of the Upper Niger River region of Mali between the cities of Bamako and Timbuktu. These tales recall people and events connected with the kingdom of Segu, which flourished from the seventeenth through nineteenth centuries. The legends include the foundation of Segu and the deeds of kings, warriors, singers, and various heroes. Introductory essay on the people and their oral tradition. Selective glossary and bibliography.

Cronise, Florence M., and Henry W. Ward. *Cunnie Rabbit, Mr. Spider and Other Beef.* New York: E. P. Dutton, 1903. Reprint. Chicago: Afro-Am Book, 1969.

These thirty-eight tales collected by missionaries in Sierra Leone and presented in the distinctive English dialect of the region include animal fables about cunning animals such as the spider and the rabbit, aetiologies, moral tales, and ghost stories. In an introductory essay, the authors explain the way these stories were collected and offer some background on West African customs and beliefs, especially storytelling techniques, types, and social purposes. They also compare the Cunnie rabbit tales of West Africa to Brer Rabbit tales of the southern United States and discuss the special dialect used in the tales. In a foreword to the 1969 reprint, Hermese E. Roberts explains the book's continued value despite its colonial view of Africans. Illustrations by Gerald Sichel. Short glossary. Occasional explanatory footnotes.

Dayrell, Elphinstone. *Folk Stories from Southern Nigeria.* New York: Longmans, Green, 1910. Reprint. New York: Negro Universities Press, 1969.

Forty tales from Nigeria are retold with no commentary or information on sources. Most are moralistic or aetiological stories dealing with animals or interaction between humans and animals. In an introduction, Andrew Lang compares each tale to tales in other folktale traditions. One illustration.

Deng, Francis Mading. *Dinka Folktales: African Stories from the Sudan.* New York: Holmes & Meier Publishers, 1974.

A collection of twenty-one stories told by the Dinka, a people who have traditionally herded cattle and farmed in a broad territory along the Nile in Sudan. Recorded in the field and translated by Deng, who is himself a Dinka. These creation myths, animal fables, and stories of the distant and more recent past are preceded by a brief introduction to the Dinka in the author's preface. In a foreword, Michael Reisman illustrates the way certain Dinka folktales teach social values as part of a process of civic acculturation. In an introductory essay, Deng addresses three aspects of Denka tales: their blending of fantasy and reality, the original and present meaning, and the circumstances under which the tales are told. At the end of the collection Deng uses the tales to illustrate Dinka attitudes to courtship, marriage, family, leadership, property rights, and religion. In an appendix Deng lists the names, ages and sexes of the original tellers of these tales, indicates their family relationships, provides some details about their family backgrounds, and comments on the translation. Occasional footnotes.

Doke, Clement M. *Lamba Folk-Lore.* New York: American Folk-Lore Society, 1927.

This collection of folk literature of the Lamba, a Bantu people of Zimbabwe and Zaire, contains aphorisms, songs, and riddles as well as folktales. Original Lamba text and English translation appear on facing pages. The 159 folktales can be divided into animal fables, stories of village life, fairy tales of disappearing princesses and wealth, and tales of supernatural beings such as ogres and gnomes.

Dwyer, Daisy Hilse. *Images and Self-Images: Male and Female in Morocco.* New York: Columbia University Press, 1978.

Thirty-five tales collected by the author in the city of Taroudannt in southern Morocco are told in translation as part of a study of male-female relationships in Arabic-Islamic society. The numbered tales are integrated into five chapters dealing with the image of the female, the transition from girl to woman, the transition from boy to man, the distinction between mother and father, and the custom of female seclusion. The tales tell of biblical personages such as Adam and Eve, Islamic figures such as Fatima daughter of the Prophet Muhammad, widows, saints, and pilgrims. These aetiologies, moral fables, and animal tales are accompanied by two introductory chapters with background on the culture and its folktales. Two concluding chapters summarize the gender roles suggested by these tales. Several tables and figures. Bibliography and index.

Egharevba, Jacob Uwadiae. "Some Ancient Stories of Ancient Benin." In *Some Stories of Ancient Benin*, by Jacob Uwadiae Egharevba. Benin, 1951. Reprint. Nendeln, Liechtenstein: Kraus Reprint, 1971.

A chief of Benin and curator of the museum in Benin City preserves some of the oral traditions of his people by retelling these twenty-eight tales of aetiology, adventure, friendship, morality, and wisdom. Characters include the gods, animals, and humans.

_____. "Some Tribal Gods of Southern Nigeria." In *Some Stories of Ancient Benin*, by Jacob Uwadiae Egharevba. Benin, 1951. Reprint. Nendeln, Liechtenstein: Kraus Reprint, 1971.

A Christian chief of Benin records some of the traditional gods of West Africa, not only from southern Nigeria but also from Benin, Gambia, Sierra Leone, and other areas. Describes various regional deities, their functions, and cults. Also deals with ancestor worship and with the

introduction of Christianity into West Africa. Ends with a chronological table of significant religious events in Benin.

Egudu, Romanus N. *The Calabash of Wisdom and Other Igbo Stories*.
New York: NOK Publishers, 1973.
Twenty-nine stories of the Igbo of Nigeria collected and translated by
the author. Grouped in the following themes: stories of origin, aetiologies, trickster tales, contests, and didactic stories. Accompanied by
drawings by Jennifer Lawson.

Ennis, Merlin. *Umbundu: Folk Tales from Angola*. Boston: Beacon Press,
1962.
Some one hundred tales collected and translated from the Umbundu
language by the author, a Christian missionary in Angola between 1904
and 1944. Grouped according to various themes including family and
kin, property, contests, hunting, famine, death, and animals, especially
the tortoise saga. No specific information about sources and narrators.
In an introductory essay, Albert B. Lord offers an analysis of these tales
and compares them to the folktale traditions and motifs of other
countries. Some Umbundu proverbs are gathered in an appendix.
Glossary.

Evans-Pritchard, Edward Evan. *The Zande Trickster*. Oxford: The Clarendon Press, 1967.
A collection of seventy folktales about a trickster named Ture told by
the Azande people of Central Africa. In many of these tales the clever
hero, whose name means "spider," has encounters with animal characters. This scholarly collection by an anthropologist offers many aids
for the general reader. Occasional footnotes explain unusual words or
phrases. Several tales are offered in multiple versions. Includes a brief
account about Azande society and culture and a full introduction to the
characteristics and origin of these tales. One tale is offered in the
original Zande language with a line-by-line English translation. Indexes and five plates.

Fauconnet, Max. "Mythology of Black Africa." In *New Larousse Encyclopedia of Mythology*, edited by Felix Guirand et al. Translated by
Richard Aldington and Delano Ames. New York: Hamlyn, 1968.
In this limited survey, Fauconnet illustrates some mythological beliefs
in Africa by paraphrasing representative legends from several geographic regions. For the southeast he uses a Malagasy aetiology about
death and rain and a Zambezi story about the creation of humankind.
For the south Fauconnet emphasizes the role of animals in the mythol-

ogy of the Bushmen and of the Hottentots or Khoi-Khoi. In the Congo region he briefly describes various concepts of god and tales of creation. For the Nilotic group he tells several legends about death. His discussion of the Sudan and Volta regions is limited mostly to a belief in fetishes. Finally, in West Africa he describes the gods of the Agni and Gurusi and tells an Ashanti legend about the supreme god Nyamia and a Togo myth about death. Accompanied by eighteen black-and-white and three color illustrations of African artifacts and sites.

Feldman, Susan, ed. *African Myths and Tales.* New York: Dell, 1963.
A collection of 108 sacred and secular stories from all over Sub-Saharan Africa. Sacred tales include myths about primeval times and the origin of death. Among the secular tales are trickster stories, aetiologies, moral fables, and stories of human adventure. In an introductory essay, the editor outlines the distinguishing features of African myths and discusses these tales in a broad comparative context. Bibliography.

Forde, Daryll, ed. *African Worlds.* New York: Oxford University Press, 1954.
A collection of nine essays by an international group of anthropologists and ethnologists. Describes the cosmic view of several African peoples, including the Ashanti of Ghana, the Lεlε of Kasai in Zaire, the Abaluyia of Kenya, the Lovedu of the Transvaal in South Africa, the Dogon of Mali, the Mεnde of Sierra Leone, the Shilluk of the Sudan, the people of Rwanda, and the Fon of Dahomey. Occasionally myths are cited and paraphrased, including Ashanti tales about the Great Spirit, Abaluyia aetiologies about crafts, Dogon myths about social institutions and the world order, and Shilluk tales of origin. In an introductory essay the editor outlines the goals of this volume and considers some of the general features of African world views. Footnotes and index.

Frobenius, Leo. "The Demons of Love." In *The Voice of Africa*, by Leo Frobenius. Vol. 2. New York: Benjamin Blom, 1913; reprint, 1968.
A member of the German Inner African Exploration Expedition of 1910-1912 discusses historical elements in the religious legends of the West African Hausa. Six tales are retold: the legend of Djiberri, the Islamic angel Gabriel, and a war lord of the Hausa; the stories of Alledjenu Sherandeli and Gogobirri Bowa, who are linked with eastern figures such as pharaoh, Noah, and Nimrod; tales of Djengere and

Kundari, supernatural beings who mark humans with signs of their love; and a myth of Serki Rafin, a river god. Illustrations.

_____. "The Fight with the Dragon." In *The Voice of Africa*, by Leo Frobenius. Vol. 2. New York: Benjamin Blom, 1913; reprint, 1968. Compares elements of the Sunjata epic with other West African myths which show a hero's victory over a terrible beast which ravages the countryside. Includes the foundation legend of the Dagomba in Togo, traditional history from Massina in Mali, and a legend of the Hausa. In all these legends the author sees Libyan influence and parallels to European mythology. Some illustrations, especially relating to bronze-working.

_____. "The Giants of the Past." In *The Voice of Africa*, by Leo Frobenius. Vol. 2. New York: Benjamin Blom, 1913; reprint, 1968. Retells three tales of the songai of West Africa: the myth of Owadia, the giant founder of the Soroko of Mali; the story of Nana Miriam, the charmer of the hippopotamus; and the legend of Pa Sini Jobu, a mighty *tungutu*, or female shaman. Three illustrations.

_____. "An Historical Poem." In *The Voice of Africa*, by Leo Frobenius. Vol. 2. New York: Benjamin Blom, 1913; reprint, 1968. A summary of historical records about the thirteenth-century Mande king Sunjata is followed by a paraphrased portion of traditional epic sung about the hero. Includes the story of Sunjata's mother, the hero's birth, circumcision, and flight. Discusses some pre-Islamic features of the legend and its connection with Libya. Includes several illustrations, especially of bronze-work.

_____. "The Idea of the World." In *The Voice of Africa*, by Leo Frobenius. Vol. 2. New York: Benjamin Blom, 1913; reprint, 1968. Describes the world view of the Yoruba of Nigeria. The myths and rituals of the complex trickster deity Edju are discussed in the context of divination via palm nuts associated with Ifa oracles. The spheres of action of Yoruba deities and human beings are arranged according to this oracular system. Includes line drawings illustrating utensils used in Ifa worship.

_____. "The Kingly Thunder-God." In *The Voice of Africa*, by Leo Frobenius. Vol. 2. New York: Benjamin Blom, 1913; reprint. 1968. Deals with the myths and rituals of Shango, the traditional Yoruba god of thunder. The legend of Shango's death and his cult of the ram head are compared to the myths of deities in other regions, such as ram-headed Sudanese gods, the Egyptian ram-god Amon, and even the Germanic thunder-god Thor. Includes photographs of Shango cult sites and line drawings illustrating artifacts of Shango worship.

Frobenius, Leo, and Douglas C. Fox. *African Genesis*. London: Faber and Faber, 1938. Reprint. Berkeley: Turtle Island Foundation, 1983.
Between 1921 and 1924 Frobenius produced in German a multivolume collection of African oral literature called *Atlantis. Volksmärchen und Volksidchtungen Afrikas* (folktales and folk poetry of Africa). Unfortunately, Frobenius' monumental work remains inaccessible to an English-reading public. This book offers a small sampling of what Frobenius had to offer in *Atlantis* and his other books on Africa. Twenty-nine tales, from North Africa, the Sudan, and Zimbabwe, are here translated into English. Part 1 contains five Kabyl creation legends and eight Kabyl animal tales. In Part 2 are four Soninke legends, three from the Nuype, and one each from the Fulbe, Mande, and Hausa. In Part 3 are five Ngona Horn stories and one Wahungwe legend from Zimbabwe. In an introductory essay, Fox offers some ethnographic information and commentary on the folktales. Four maps and fifteen facsimiles of indigenous rock paintings. In a foreword, an anonymous author explains that Frobenius saw in these paintings from both northern and southern Africa evidence for the cultural cohesion of the continent.

Fuja, Abayomi. *Fourteen Hundred Cowries*. London: Lothrop, Lee & Shepard, 1962.
A collection of thirty-one tales of the Yoruba of Nigeria retold by a Nigerian folklorist. These animal fables, aetiologies, and tales of magic and the gods are accompanied by line-drawn illustrations in traditional style by Ademola Olugebefola. Short introductory essay by Anne Pellowski.

Gbadamosi, Bakare, and Ulli Beier. *Not Even God Is Ripe Enough*. London: Heinemann, 1968.
A collection of twenty traditional stories of the Yoruba of Nigeria as told by an ethnographer at the Nigerian Museum in Lagos and a professor of English literature. These folktales and legends are based upon moralistic proverbs and include elements of animal fables, tales of love, and stories of retribution.

Griaule, Marcel. *Conversations with Ogotemmêli*. New York: Oxford University Press, 1965.

These conversations between Griaule, a noted French ethnologist, and Ogotemmêli, a Dogon hunter, took place for thirty-three days in August of 1946. Day by day the world view, cosmology, customs, and religion of the Dogon of Mali are explained. Woven into these conversations are many myths, especially aetiologies. Nine plates and twelve figures, including plans of the Dogon world and social systems and their genealogy. This presentation of the Dogon mythological system has become a standard reference for ethnologists and other scholars. Introductory essay by G. Dieterlen on the work of Griaule and a short preface by Griaule with background about the Dogon and these conversations.

Henries, A. Doris Banks. *Liberian Folklore*. New York: Macmillan, 1966.
These ninety-nine folktales were collected in the field by students at the University of Liberia and are here grouped in the following thematic categories: spider tales, leopard tales, stories about women, aetiologies, and miscellaneous tales. Also contains 199 proverbs grouped according to their ethnic origin. Short introduction by the author. Accompanied by twenty-six line drawings.

Herskovits, Melville J. "Religious Life." In *Dahomey*, by Melville J. Herskovits. Vol. 2. New York: Augustin, 1938. Reprint. Evanston, Ill.: Northwestern University Press, 1967.
This part of an ethnographic study of Dahomey life focuses on the cult and myths of various deities. Individual chapters are devoted to the pantheons of the sky, the earth and thunder, cult organization, fate and divine tricksters, the three souls of humans, the cult of the serpent, magic and charms, and the Dahomean world view. In many of these chapters specific myths are paraphrased and compared. Retellings of the myths appear in bold type. Accompanied by forty-three photographs illustrating Dahomean religious life. Footnotes.

Herskovits, Melville J., and Frances S. Herskovits. *Dahomean Narrative*. Evanston, Ill.: Northwestern University Press, 1958.
A collection of 155 traditional tales recorded in Dahomey, West Africa, in 1931. The narratives are grouped according to the following themes: exploits of the gods, divination, hunger stories, stories of abnormal birth, tales about a glutton named Yo, historical tales, stories about women, aetiological and moral tales, and miscellaneous. Some tales are followed by short endnotes. A major introductory section considers the characteristics of Dahomean narrative, including methodology, problems of classification, form, genre, and value systems. Also has

sections on problems in the study of myth, archetypes, and a general theory of myth.

Heusch, Luc de. *The Drunken King: Or, The Origin of the State*. Translated by Roy Willis. Bloomington: University of Indiana Press, 1982.
Originally published in 1972 in French as *Le Roi ivre: Ou, L'Origine de l'État*. Records and analyzes thirty-three myths told by the Bantu of Central Africa. The myths are integrated into chapters analyzing various myth themes but are easily distinguished by indentation and typescript. In an index Heusch lists the myths recorded and analyzed in this book. Includes aetiological and cosmogonic tales about the origins of the world, divine kingship, fire, salt, and other things, foundation myths about particular kingdoms, social organizations and customs, and tales about rain heroes, parricide, and interaction between the human and the natural world. Many tales are recorded in several versions and are interpreted according to the structural principles of Claude Lévi-Strauss. Introductions by both the author and the translator, occasional footnotes, extensive endnotes, and bibliography.

Hollis, A. C. "Masai Stories" and "Masai Myths and Traditions." In *The Masai, Their Language and Folklore*, by A. C. Hollis. Oxford: The Clarendon Press, 1905. Reprint. Westport, Conn.: Negro Universities Press, 1970.
Two sections of a scholarly study of the language, grammar, and oral tradition of the Masai of East Africa. Twenty animal fables and folktales about hunters, families, and the supernatural in "Masai Stories" and nineteen tales about the origin of the Masai and stories about their gods, creation, and the heavenly bodies in "Masai Myths and Traditions." The original Masai text is accompanied by an interlinear English translation followed by a summary in English. These tales were collected on site by Hollis at the end of the nineteenth century, and his book has become a standard resource for the Masai and their language. The book also includes an introductory essay on the Masai, twenty-seven pages of illustrations, a map, and index.

Horner, George R. "A Bulu Folktale. Content and Analysis." In *The Anthropologist Looks at Myth*, edited by Melville Jacobs and John Greenway. Austin: University of Texas Press, 1966.
Offers a transliteration, literal translation, and free translation of a folktale about a porcupine and her son recorded among the Bulu of Cameroon. The tale tells of the misdeeds of Lindi Ngomo, the porcupine's son, who repudiates his father and steals game from someone

else's traps but who is nevertheless rescued by his father. Supplemented by ethnographic background on the people and their world view and by some notes on literary style and devices in the tale. Endnotes.

Huffman, Ray. "Nuer Folk-Lore." In *Nuer Customs and Folklore*, by Ray Huffman. London: Frank Cass, 1931; 2d ed., 1970.

This chapter in an ethnographic study of the Nuer, a Nilotic people of the Sudan, consists of thirteen tales about the origin and history of the Nuer, animals, birds, and ogres, as well as sixteen riddles.

Idowu, E. Bolaji. *Olodumare: God in Yoruba Belief*. London: Longmans, 1962.

A scholarly examination of the concept of deity among the Yoruba of Nigeria, with special emphasis on Olodumare, their chief deity and creator. An introductory chapter deals, in part, with the role of myths in traditional Yoruba society. Other chapters consider Yoruba creation stories, the name, attributes, and status of Olodumare, the ministers of the deity, his cult, and his role in moral values and human destiny. Traditional literature, including myths, are frequently paraphrased or quoted in translation. Nineteen plates, footnotes, and indexes.

Innes, Gordon. *Sunjata: Three Mandinka Versions*. London: School of Oriental and African Studies, 1974.

Three performances of the West African epic *Sunjata* are transcribed in Mandinka, a language of Gambia, and are translated into English. Each singer recounts legends associated with Sunjata, a thirteenth-century king of Mali. An introduction provides information about the hero, the singers or griots, their audiences, the language of the epic, speech forms, musical accompaniment, and folktale motifs used in the epic. Also summaries and comparisons of the plots of the three performances.

Itayemi, Phebean, and P. Gurrey. *Folk Tales and Fables*. London: Penguin, 1953.

A European scholar collaborates with an African author to retell fifty-two tales from West Africa. More than half are based upon Yoruba stories. The rest come from the Isoko, Sierra Leone, and the Gold Coast (Ghana). Includes tales about brothers, wives, daughters, and wise sons, aetiologies, and animal fables, especially Yoruba tortoise tales and Gold Coast spider (Anansi) stories. Also offers an introductory essay describing various features of these tales, especially their purpose, meaning, and characters.

Jackson, Michael. *Allegories of the Wilderness: Ethics and Ambiguity in Kuranko Narratives.* Bloomington: Indiana University Press, 1982.
A study of 230 traditional narratives recorded among the Kuranko of Sierra Leone. For one tale, the full Kuranko text is provided along with a word-for-word interlinear English translation. An additional thirty-seven tales are published here in English translation only. Stories are grouped according to various themes, such as reciprocity, justice, generational conflicts, friendship, and marriage. Types include animal fables, aetiologies, and morality tales. An introductory chapter describes Kuranko social organization and world view. The narratives are presented in a series of seven chapters, preceded by a short introduction and followed by an analytical commentary. Narratives are interpreted according to the structural approach of Claude Lévi-Strauss. A final chapter summarizes this study and shows how telling these tales helps the Kuranko to resolve some of their social ambiguities and existential dilemmas. Endnotes, glossary of Kuranko words, bibliography, list of narratives, and index.

Johnson, John William. *The Epic of Son-Jara: A West African Tradition.* Bloomington: Indiana University Press, 1986.
An English translation of *Sunjata*, a West African epic about the life of a thirteenth-century king of ancient Mali. Based upon a performance by Fa-Digi Sisòkò, a West African griot. The text is preceded by information concerning the social setting of the epic, the role of the singer in West African cultures, and the characteristics of West African epic. This epic, which has been performed continuously in West African since the thirteenth-century, is an example of history transformed into myth or legend. Annotations, genealogical charts, bibliography, and index.

Johnston, H. A. S. *A Selection of Hausa Stories.* Oxford: The Clarendon Press, 1966.
Eighty-six tales translated by the author from several early twentieth-century collections of Hausa literature. The original Hausa texts for six tales are found in an appendix. Each of these stories—tales of cunning animals (especially the spider or the jackal), fairy tales, and historical legends—is followed by a short note on sources, interpretation, and comparisons with other tales. Introductory essay on the history of the Hausa, their customs, language, and stories.

Kabira, Wanjiku Mukabi, and Kavetsa Adagala. *Kenyan Oral Narratives.* Nairobi, Kenya: Heinemann, 1985.

This collection of thirty-one narratives was made for students at the British secondary level and above. General introduction on the characteristics, types, and methods of collection of these narratives. Most areas of Kenya are represented. Each narrative is introduced by brief information about place of origin, name of narrator, and collector. Includes aetiologies, animal and trickster stories, and moral tales.

Kähler-Meyer, Emmi. "Myth Motifs in Flood Stories from the Grassland of Cameroon." Translated by Uli Linke in *The Flood Myth*, edited by Alan Dundes. Berkeley: University of California Press, 1988.
Discusses several examples of a flood legend in Cameroon. Three versions are provided only in English translation. A fourth is offered both in English and in the original Bali language. The author discusses several themes recurring in these tales, including the motif of the water pot which causes the flood and marriage of the brother and sister who survive the flood. In an introductory note, the editor outlines the scholarly debate concerning the existence of flood myths in Africa. Footnotes and bibliography.

Kesby, John. "East Africa." In *Mythology: An Illustrated Encyclopaedia*, edited by Richard Cavendish. New York: Rizzoli International, 1980. Also published as *An Illustrated Encyclopedia of Mythology*. New York: Crescent Books, 1984.
A general overview of the mythologies of an area reaching from Sudan in the north to Zambia and Mozambique in the south, plus the island of Madagascar. Sections on the patterns of these myths, thematic variations, and the role of myths in the social order are accompanied by summaries of the adventures of two brothers, Mkunare and Kanyanga, with the Little People called Konyingo, the story of Kintu, the first human, and a Bararetta Oromo animal fable about the origin of death. Map and illustrations of artwork and sites related to the myths.

Kipury, Naomi. *Oral Literature of the Maasai*. Nairobi, Kenya: Heinemann Educational Books, 1983.
Includes traditional oral material collected among the Maa-speaking peoples of Kenya. The first two chapters provide ethnographic information about the people, performative context, and style of their oral literature. Four chapters are devoted to the genres of narrative, riddles, proverbs, and songs. The narrative chapter contains the most mythological material with a variety of aetiologies, legends, animal stories, and trickster tales. Each of these chapters begins with an introductory essay by the author. All oral material appears in the original Maa

followed by English translation. Occasional review questions and explanatory notes are also provided for school use. Map and bibliography.

Klipple, May Augusta. *African Folktales with Foreign Analogues*. New York: Garland Press, 1992.
This study was written by a student of Stith Thompson for a doctoral dissertation awarded at Indiana University in 1938. Despite its scholarly context, the general reader will find it both useful and accessible. Offers summaries and comparisons of approximately 300 African tales and their variants, collected from published sources. Deals only with those tales which have parallels in folktale traditions from other parts of the world. For this reason, the tales are arranged according to the numbered tale types and motif types developed by Aarne-Thompson. Within these thematic categories, tales are further arranged in ten geographic groupings. Each tale version is also identified by ethnic group and published source. In an introductory essay, the author offers a brief history of Africa and background on the study of African folktales. In a preface, Alan Dundes places this book in the context of the history of comparative folklore. Lists of ethnic groups and abbreviations. Information about ethnic groups in appendix. Bibliography.

Knappert, Jan, ed. *Bantu Myths and Other Tales*. Leiden: E. J. Brill, 1977.
A scholarly collection of fifty-five representative stories told by the Bantu-speaking peoples of subequatorial Africa, collected and translated by the editor. Arranged in groups representing myths, legends, sagas, fables, proverbs, tales, epic tales, and true stories. The distinguishing characteristics of each group are described in a short introduction at the beginning of each part. A general introduction discusses the Bantu peoples and their religious beliefs. Bibliography, map, and index.

_____. "Central and Southern Africa." In *Mythology: An Illustrated Encyclopaedia*, edited by Richard Cavendish. New York: Rizzoli International, 1980. Also published as *An Illustrated Encyclopedia of Mythology*. New York: Crescent Books, 1984.
This overview of the mythologies of an area reaching from Chad, Sudan, and Cameroon in the north through Zimbabwe and South Africa in the south contains sections on some of the many deities of this region, the role of divine animals in these tales, myths of origin, and beliefs concerning humankind, death, the afterlife, and sorcery. Includes summaries and analyses of the creation myths of the Zulu, the

Bakuba in Zaire, and the Shilluk in Sudan, a Wutu myth about the chameleon and human mortality, and a myth about the Spirit in the tree. Map and illustrations of artwork and sites related to the myths.

_____. *Kings, Gods and Spirits from African Mythology.* New York: Schocken Books, 1986.

This general survey treats the entire continent except Egypt. The organization is thematic rather than geographic. An introductory chapter on the peoples of Africa and their history is followed by chapters on tales about kings, the spirit world, magic animals, monsters, heroes, moral fables, and Islamic saints. Numerous drawings and paintings by Francesca Pellizzoli illustrate many symbols and characters from the myths. Some of these symbols are explained in a short appendix. Map, bibliography, and index.

_____, ed. *Myths and Legends of Botswana, Lesotho and Swaziland.* Leiden: E. J. Brill, 1985.

A selection of seventy-five fables, sagas, and moralistic tales from three kingdoms in southern Africa. These aetiologies, animal fables, and tales about witches, magic, and the supernatural are introduced by short histories of each kingdom, a short section on Swazi religion and myths, and some comments on the functions of these tales in their cultural context. A list of seventy-two Tswana proverbs literally translated, together with their English proverbial equivalents, is provided in an appendix.

_____, ed. *Myths and Legends of the Congo.* London: Heinemann, 1971.

Ninety-one stories representing ten peoples of what is now Zaire, including the Alur, the Bakongo, the Nkundo, and the Ngbandi. Tales are grouped according to the people who tell them, with a short ethnographic introduction to each people and occasional editorial comments at the beginning of individual stories. Many tales of the supernatural about spirits, witches, ghosts, and return from the dead; also, animal and morality tales and aetiological myths about human origin and the origin of individual peoples. Short introductory essay by the editor with comments on the tale selection and storytelling in Zaire. Illustration on the title page by the editor.

_____, ed. *Myths and Legends of the Swahili.* London: Heinemann, 1970.

This sampling of Swahili tales was collected by the editor from Arabic manuscripts, from unpublished material written in Swahili, and from field research. An introductory essay on general features of Swahili tales is followed by eleven chapters of myths grouped according to the following headings: creation, the biblical prophets (especially Abraham, Samson, Moses, and Jesus), the miracles of Muhammad, mysterious destinies, stories of wit and wisdom, the wiles of women, social satire, astute animals, travelers' tall tales, spirits and sorcerers, and just judgments.

_____. *Namibia: Land of Peoples, Myths and Fables.* Leiden: E. J. Brill, 1981.
Retells the myths and songs of the peoples of Namibia, specifically the Bushmen, Dama, Hottentots, Herero, Kwangali, Ambo or Ovambo, and Ndonga or Aandonga of Ondonga. These creation myths, animal fables, and morality tales are introduced by an essay on the geography, population, oral literature, and animal fables of Namibia. Also offers a brief survey of Namibian history to 1980 in Chapter 1. Treats individual peoples and their myths in the next seven chapters. Each of these chapters begins with some ethnographic information about the people and continues with a selection of their myths. A sampling of Namibian proverbs in Chapter 9. Illustrations by Liesje Knappert. Map and index.

_____, ed. *Tales of Mystery and Miracles from Morocco.* Hamilton, New Zealand: Outrigger Publishers, 1976.
Twelve traditional tales collected by the author in the field or from Arabic texts are here translated into English, most for the first time. Tales of love, marriage, and travel in which ordinary people deal with the powerful sultans, the exotic, and the supernatural. In an introductory essay, Knappert provides a brief history of the region and its legends.

Krige, E. Jensen, and J. D. Krige. "Pageants of the Past." In *The Realm of a Rain-Queen*, by E. Jensen Krige and J. D. Krige. New York: Oxford University Press, 1943.
Part of an ethnographic study of the Lovedu, a Bantu people of South Africa. Paraphrases cycles of aetiological and historical legends about Mujaji, a mysterious, semi-mythic queen of the Transvaal. These cycles begin in the seventeenth century and tell the story of origin of the Bantu: their early life and wanderings, their zenith, and their fall in the nineteenth century. The paraphrases are followed by some information on the present status of the Bantu. Footnotes.

Leslau, Charlotte, and Wolf Leslau. *African Folk Tales*. Mt. Vernon, N.Y.: Peter Pauper Press, 1963.

This collection of twenty-five tales includes an Ugandan creation myth, a Zulu animal fable, and tales from various sources about the origins of iron, humankind, mountains, and the Milky Way. Some aetiologies explaining why monkeys live in trees and why nature cannot be changed. Other tales tell of adventure, love, midwives, family relationships, and white men. Few sources beyond geographic location are provided for these stories. Accompanied by drawings by Grisha Dotzenko.

Leslau, Wolf. *Gurage Folklore*. Wiesbaden: Franz Steiner Verlag, 1982.

A collection of thirty-four Gurage folktales from Ethiopia. Texts in three different dialects are accompanied by English translation on facing pages and explanatory footnotes. Tales include animal fables and morality stories. Also contains bilingual collections of folk wisdom, proverbs, riddles, superstitions, and beliefs. A short introduction on the region, its people, and its folk traditions is followed by a list of published sources for these tales. Bibliography and indexes of folktales, riddles, and superstitions.

Lienhardt, G. *Divinity and Experience: The Religion of the Dinka*. Oxford: Oxford University Press, 1961.

This scholarly study of the religious beliefs of the Dinka people of the southern Sudan is divided into two parts. Part 1 deals with the Dinka world view and their gods, with several chapters on the division of the world, the relationship between divinity and human experience, free divinities, and clan divinities. Part 2 is concerned with priests, prayers, sacrifice, and live burial. Throughout the book paraphrases and translations of myths, prayers, and other traditional texts are used to illustrate religious beliefs and the functions and characteristics of various gods. Introductory essay on Dinka life and the importance of cattle in Dinka society. Eight plates and four figures. Index.

Lindblom, Gerhard. *Kamba Tales of Animals*. Cambridge, England: W. Heffer & Sons, 1928.

This collection of thirty animal tales told among the Kamba of Kenya includes the original-language text accompanied by either interlinear translation or translation on facing pages. Linguistic and ethnographic endnotes are followed by notes comparing motifs in these tales to those in other cultural contexts. Most conspicuous in these tales are the cunning hare and the stupid hyena. In an introductory essay, the author describes how these tales were gathered directly from storytellers or were written down by schoolchildren. He groups these Kamba tales into five categories: animal tales, tales about ogres and giants, adventure and hunting tales, myths and legends, and imported tales.

_____. *Kamba Tales of Supernatural Beings and Adventures.* Cambridge, England: W. Heffer & Sons, 1935.
This collection of thirty-two tales told among the Kamba of Kenya includes original-language texts accompanied by English translation on facing pages. Linguistic and ethnographic endnotes are followed by notes comparing motifs in these tales to those in other African and cultural contexts, especially in Africa. In a short introduction, the author explains that this anthology includes not only tales about supernatural beings, especially those known as *eimu,* but also adventure stories, aetiological myths, a cosmology, and a tale borrowed from Arabic sources.

Littlejohn, James. "West Africa." In *Mythology: An Illustrated Encyclopaedia*, edited by Richard Cavendish. New York: Rizzoli International, 1980. Also published as *An Illustrated Encyclopedia of Mythology.* New York: Crescent Books, 1984.
A general overview of the religious and mythological beliefs of the peoples who live along the west coast of Africa from Guinea to Nigeria as well as the inland nations of Mali, Burkina Faso, and Niger. Some analysis accompanies descriptions of Dahomean deities and summaries of a Dahomean tale about a quarrel between the divine brothers Sagbata and Sogbo, an Ashanti story about the first human children, a Dogon creation myth, and a Temne tale about the androgynous demon Anyaroli. Discusses attitudes toward twin and deformed births. Map, genealogical chart of Dahomean deities, and illustrations of artwork related to the myths.

Magel, Emil A. *Folktales from the Gambia.* Washington, D.C.: Three Continents Press, 1984.
Forty-five oral tales collected among the Wolof of Gambia and translated by the author. The Wolof text of one tale, "The Donkeys of Jolof," is included in an appendix. Grouped according to three structural patterns based upon varying sequences of statement, analogy, refutation, and conclusion. Includes animal fables and tales of Islam and the supernatural. Introductory essay on the structure and thematic patterns of the tales and the relationship between the tales and Wolof society. Map and bibliography.

Mbiti, John S. *Akamba Stories*. Oxford: The Clarendon Press, 1966.

These English translations of seventy-eight stories of the Akamba of Kenya were selected from the author's personal collection of 1,500 tales told in the original Kikamba language. Parallel Kikamba and English texts are provided for two of the last tales. The final story is a variant of an earlier tale. The collection contains animal fables, aetiologies, morality stories, and tales of adventure. These stories are preceded by an extensive introductory section containing general ethnographic information about the Akamba, including their social organization, religion, language, and literature. Also contains an interpretative analysis of one tale and a bibliography.

Murgatroyd, Madeline. *Tales from the Kraals*. Cape Town: Howard Timmins, 1968.

Twelve South African tales retold for children with stories explaining how the coral tree got its flowers, how the sugarcane became sweet, how the prickly pear got prickles, and how the water lily came to be. Also contains tales of adventure, war, and magic. Illustrations by Joyce Ordbrown. Short glossary.

Nassau, Robert H. *Where Animals Talk*. London: Duckworth, 1914. Reprint. New York: Negro Universities Press, 1970.

These sixty-one tales of origin, morals, and trickery from equatorial West Africa were translated by the author and are arranged according to three ethnic groups, the Mpongwe, the Benga, and the Fang. Each tale is introduced by a list of dramatis personae and a short explanatory note by the author. These tales take place in a primordial time when animals talked to each other and sometimes interacted with humans. Index of names of animals among five ethnic groups in the region. Pronunciation guide. In a short preface, the author offers some information on these traditional narratives and their narrators.

Niane, Djibril Tamsir. *Sundiata: An Epic of Old Mali*. Translated by G. D. Pickett. London: Longman, 1965.

This literary reworking of the *Sunjata* first brought the West African epic to the attention of the Western reading public, first in France and then, via this translation, in the English speaking world. Niane bases his prose version upon the performances of a griot named Mamadou Kouyaté. This version of the life of a thirteenth-century ruler of ancient Mali includes tales of the hero's mythical conception, childhood, exile, and victory over the sorcerer king Soumaoro Kanté. Map and notes.

Norris, H. T. *Saharan Myth and Saga*. Oxford: The Clarendon Press, 1972.

A scholarly survey of some sagas and tribal chronicles from Saharan Africa. The first half of the book consists of studies of four tale groups: a nautical story about a serpent and a holy man, aetiological tales about the Saharan people of the veil, legendary geographies of the Sahara, and sagas of the Almoravids. Followed by translations of two twentieth-century Arabic manuscripts, "The Ancient History of the Mauritanian Adrar and the sons of Shams al-Din," by Abd al-Wadud, and "A History of the Western Sanhaja," by Shaykh Sidya Baba. Each study and translation is accompanied by footnotes, commentary in endnotes, and original folio page notations. Genealogical and chronological tables in appendices. Six plates, glossary of terms and names, selected bibliography, and index.

Odaga, Asenath Bole. *Thu Tinda! Stories from Kenya*. Nairobi, Kenya: Uzima Press Limited, 1980.
Twenty-six traditional tales told to children among the Luo people of Kenya are translated here. Most are tales about talking animals. Also aetiologies and tales of magic and the supernatural. *Thu Tinda*, the traditional concluding phrase for a Luo tale, means "Let it be, the end."

Ogumefu, M. I. *Yoruba Legends*. London: Sheldon Press, 1929. Reprint. New York: AMS Press, 1984.
A collection of forty Yoruba tales from Nigeria, including legends of Yoruba history, tales of famous rulers, aetiologies, and nine tortoise stories.

Parrinder, Edward Geoffrey. *African Mythology*. Rev. ed. New York: Peter Bedrick Books, 1982.
This overview of African mythological traditions does not treat the continent as a whole but concentrates on the regions south of the Sahara sometimes known as Black Africa. The book is arranged thematically rather than geographically and compares the ways in which such themes as the creator, birth, death, oracles, witches, and animal fables are treated by various black peoples. The use of explanatory myths in the secret societies of Africa and the historical elements of many legends are also considered. Since many myths are preserved in the language of art rather than in written form, the author provides illustrations of artifacts featuring these myths on nearly every page. Map, bibliography, and index.

_____. *West African Religion*. London: The Epworth Press, 1949; 2d ed., 1961.

Four chapters of this study of the religious beliefs and practices of West African peoples such as the Yoruba, the Ewe, and the Akan are devoted to various deities, including the supreme god, gods of the sky and thunder, gods of earth, smallpox, and water, snake gods, and other divinities. Descriptions of the functions, attributes, and names of these deities are frequently accompanied by paraphrases of and references to various myths about these gods. Footnotes, map, bibliography, and index.

p'Bitek, Okot. *Hare and Hornbill.* London: Heinemann, 1978.
These thirty-two traditional stories retold by an important modern African writer and poet include a variety of animal tales, aetiologies, and tales of human life. An introductory essay on the difficulties of accurate retellings of authentic tales.

Posselt, Friedrich W. T. *Fables of the Veld.* Oxford: Oxford University Press, 1929.
These forty-six tales were collected in what is now Zimbabwe and translated by the author. Origin indicated by ethnic group only. Included are aetiologies, morality tales, and animal fables, especially about the cunning hare. Sometimes the animals interact with each other; sometimes they interact with humans. In a short preface, the author discusses some general features of these tales. Occasional explanatory footnotes.

Postma, Minnie. *Tales from the Basotho.* Translated by Susie McDermid. Austin: University of Texas Press, 1974.
This collection of twenty-three traditional tales of the Basotho in Lesotho was originally published in Afrikaans. Some of these tales tell of the origin of humans. Others deal with the problems of childless women. Also present are clever animal stories, tales of a monstrous woman named Moselantja, and love stories, especially about chiefs and their families. A translator's introduction contains information about the Basotho, their stories, the life of Postma, and the origin of the collection. Map, bibliography, and index of folktale types and motifs.

Radin, Paul, ed. *African Folktales.* New York: Schocken Books, 1983.
A collection of eighty-one folktales from Sub-Saharan Africa. Organized into four groups: the universe and its beginnings, animals and their world, the realm of humans, and humans and their fate. In an introductory essay, the editor discusses the history of European attitudes toward African oral literature, the importance of the mythopoeic

imagination in traditional Africa, and the characteristics of native African folk literature. Glossary of African words, bibliography of sources, and index.

Radin, Paul, and James J. Sweeney. *African Folktales and Sculpture*. New York: Pantheon Books, 1952; 2d ed., 1964.
Combines a selection of traditional tales with illustrations of sculpture from Sub-Saharan Africa. The first half of the book contains eighty-one folktales gathered from literary sources by Radin and arranged in the following thematic groups: the universe and its beginnings, the animal and his world, the realm of humans, and human fate. Introductory essay on the nature of native African folktales by Radin. A glossary and bibliography of sources follow the anthology. In the second half, Sweeney has chosen illustrations of 187 representative pieces of traditional African sculpture. None of these illustrations is directly related to the folktale collection in the first half of the book. In the second edition the collection of folktales has not been changed, but additional illustrations have been added. The second edition was revised to reflect political changes in Africa. Map and index.

Rattray, R. Sutherland. *Akan-Ashanti Folk-Tales*. Oxford: The Clarendon Press, 1930.
This scholarly collection of seventy-five tales was gathered in what is now Ghana. Original text and a literal English translation appear on facing pages and are accompanied by illustrations by African artists. Many of the tales are aetiological in theme. Others are Anansi spider tales. In a brief preface, the author considers theories about the origin of Ashanti folktales, the reason for the apparent coarseness in many Akan folktales, and the use of animal names in Ashanti stories.

_____. *Hausa Folklore*. 2 vols. New York: Oxford University Press, 1913.
Traditional tales from the Hausa are presented in three forms on facing pages. The original Hausa script is used on the right, a transliteration into the Roman alphabet on the upper left, and an English translation on the lower left side of the page. Volume 1 contains a short history on the origin of the Hausa and their conversion to Islam plus twenty-one tales about siblings, orphans, fathers and sons, witches, maidens, hunters, and other characters. Many of these explain the origin of animals, human customs, and proverbs. Volume 2 includes nine animal tales with moralistic and aetiological themes, sixteen descriptions of Hausa customs and arts, 133 proverbs, and endnotes for tales in both

volumes. Preface, author's note, chart of the Hausa alphabet, and one illustration in Volume 1. Three illustrations in Volume 2.

Roscoe, John. "Folklore." In *The Baganda*, by John Roscoe. London: Macmillan, 1911. 2d ed. New York: Barnes & Noble, 1966.
This chapter in a monograph dealing with the customs and beliefs of the Baganda of Uganda includes translations of a collection of proverbs and thirteen hunter's legends, animal fables, and aetiologies.

Ross, Mabel H., and Barbara K. Walker. *"On Another Day . . ." : Tales Told Among the Nkundo of Zaire*. Hamden, Conn.: Archon Books, 1979.
These ninety-five traditional tales told by the Nkundo people were collected by Ross with commentary by Walker. Some were told in English while others were told in the Lonkundo language and translated by Ross. Stories are arranged in the following groups: cosmologies and aetiologies, animal tales, stories about human problems and solutions, and dilemma tales. Each tale is preceded by a formal headnote, including name of narrator, location, and date. Walker supplements the tale with general information, observation on the relationship of the tale to others in the volume, identification of the tale type and major motifs, and footnotes. Tale types and motifs are summarized in appendices. General introduction on the Nkundo people, on the scholarship of their oral literature, and on the history and organization of this collection. Also offers a pronunciation guide to Lonkundo and information about the sites and circumstances of narration. In a foreword, Daniel J. Crowley explains why this collection was needed. Map, bibliography, and index.

St. Lys, Odette. *From a Vanished German Colony: A Collection of Folklore, Folk Tales and Proverbs from South-West Africa*. London: Gypsy Press, 1916.
These thirty-one traditional tales from Namibia, formerly the German colony of SouthWest Africa, were collected by the author from materials provided by various European recorders. Animal fables, stories of witchcraft and hunting, and Bushmen tales about the wind and about a quest for god are accompanied by proverbs, riddles, and descriptions of customs and superstitions. Occasional explanatory notes.

Seitel, Peter. *See So That We May See*. Bloomington: Indiana University Press, 1980.

Thirty-four traditional tales told by the Haya people of northwestern Tanzania are translated and analyzed. Together with a colleague, the author collected this material in the field between 1968 and 1970. He shows particular interest in determining the cultural meaning of the tales through analysis of plot development. Two introductory chapters, one on the Haya and their world and another on the storytelling performance, on the translation, and on characteristics of the Haya language. Seven chapters deal with the tales themselves and their interpretation. Plots deal with interpersonal relationships, unusual deeds, supernatural events, and talking animals and their interaction with humans. Arranged according to theme of major dramatic event: parents and children, sisters and brothers, suitors and maidens, new brides, domestic comedy, gluttony and separation, and knowledge and ignorance. Each group of texts is followed by a commentary extracting cultural meaning from the tales. Translations use a system of varied scripts developed by Dennis Tedlock to indicate aspects of performance such as pauses, gestures, and audience participation. Original-language texts of five tales are included in an appendix. Endnotes and index.

Skinner, Neil, trans. and ed. *Hausa Tales and Traditions*. Vol. 1. New York: Africana Publishing Corp., 1969. Vols. 2-3. Madison: University of Wisconsin Press, 1977.
An English translation of *Tatsuniyoyi Na Nausa*, a collection of Hausa tales first published in the original language by Frank Edgar between 1911 and 1913. The collection includes fables, legends, songs, proverbs, riddles, and religious and legal documents. Of most mythological interest are eight animal fables in Volume 1, and *enfant terrible* tales, tall stories, and aetiologies in Volume 3. Each volume includes introductions, glossaries of special terms, and tables cross-referenced to the original edition. Volume 1 contains a foreword by M. G. Smith with a history of Edgar's collection and some background to the Hausa of Nigeria, their tales, and their beliefs. Also in Volume 1, a translator's introduction offers some stylistic comments on the tales.

Smith, Alexander McCall. *Children of Wax: African Folk Tales*. New York: Interlink Books, 1991.
Twenty-seven stories of the Ndebele, relatives of the Zulu who live in Matabeleland in Zimbabwe. Collected by a Zimbabwean of European descent who offers a free translation of his original recordings. Many of the tales describe human dealings with animals. Also contains animal fables. The tale that shares its title with the book tells of children

made of wax whose parents take special care to protect them from the heat of the sun. One boy, however, refuses to stay indoors and is eventually transformed into a bird.

Smith, Edwin W., ed. *African Ideas of God*. London: Edinburgh House Press, 1950.
This collection of twelve scholarly essays deals with various conceptions of deity in Africa. Retells some myths about the gods and their interaction with human beings. Includes several folktales of the Kono in Sierra Leone, Ewe myths about fire, Yoruba explanations of death, and Mɛnde and Ngombe stories about the creation of humans. In an introductory essay, the editor discusses African myths and their views of deity. Map, bibliography, and indexes, including an index of names of deities.

Theal, George McCall. *Kaffir Folk-lore*. London: Sonnenschein, Lew Bas & Lowrey, 1886. Reprint. Westport, Conn.: Negro Universities Press, 1970.
Twenty-one tales of cunning heroes, animal stories, and morality tales by the Kaffir, an indigenous people of the Cape and Natal provinces of South Africa. An introductory chapter on the people, their language, customs, and beliefs. Some proverbs and expressions are collected in the final section. Endnotes.

Todd, Loreto. *Some Day Been Dey: West African Pidgin Folktales*. London: Routledge & Kegan Paul, 1979.
Twenty-four tales told in Pidgin, as spoken on the coast of Cameroon. Pidgin text and English translation on facing pages. Seven tortoise tales are accompanied by a variety of moral tales and stories of cunning. Each tale is followed by explanatory endnotes. An introductory section provides background on the country, the history and characteristics of Pidgin, the collection of the tales, the orthography and type of translation employed, and a bibliography. A formal analysis of the structure of Cameroon Pidgin English follows the tales. Three maps and index.

Troughton, Joanna. *How Stories Came into the World*. New York: Peter Bedrick Books, 1989.
A blending of six West African creation stories retold for children. The framing narrative is a tale of the Ekoi of Nigeria about a mouse, who keeps all the stories of the world's origin to herself until lightning releases them. The five other tales are aetiologies told by the Ekoi, the Efik Ibibio, and the Yoruba. Illustrated by the author.

_____. *Tortoise's Dream*. New York: Peter Bedrick Books, 1986.
A young child's version of a traditional Bantu creation story. This animal fable tells of tortoise's quest for the name of a miraculous tree which is the source of many African fruits and vegetables. Illustrated by the author.

Umeasiegbu, Rems Nna. *The Way We Lived*. London: Heinemann, 1969.
Part 2 of this collection of customs and stories of the Igbo of Nigeria contains fifty-five traditional tales told in English, including aetiologies explaining why women do not grow beards and how humans lost their tails, animal fables, morality tales, stories of the supernatural, and songs. Illustrated.

_____. *Words Are Sweet: Igbo Stories and Storytelling*. Leiden: E. J. Brill, 1982.
These one hundred oral tales were collected by the author among his fellow Igbo of Nigeria. Part 1 consists of detailed background information about the Igbo and their stories with sections on Igbo religion, marriage, traditional economy, and hospitality, on contexts for their storytelling events, on the formal characteristics of their stories, and on gathering these tales in the field. This part is followed by endnotes. In Part 2 the stories are grouped according to the following themes: the tortoise, the church, spouses, people, spinsters, kings, animals, spirit children, and aetiologies. List of sources in an appendix. Bibliography.

Vernon-Jackson, Hugh. *West African Folk Tales*. London: University of London Press, 1958.
Twenty-one tales collected by the author from young men and women in northern Nigeria. The first half deal mostly with animals, while the rest are about people. These stories of humor and adventure, aetiologies, and tales of magic and deceit are accompanied by suggestions for study and discussion to enable African students to practice their English.

Walker, Barbara K., and Warren S. Walker. *Nigerian Folk Tales*. 2d ed. Hamden, Conn.: Archon Books, 1980.
An introduction to traditional Yoruba tales as told to the editors by Olawale Idewu and Omotayo Adu. These thirty-seven tales include aetiologies, moral fables, tales of demon lovers, trickster tales, and stories about fertility. The notes from the first edition discuss the stories in the context of other oral traditions, especially folktale motifs. In the "Supplementary Notes" of the second edition the editors consider other

Yoruba variants of these tales. Illustrated with drawings of Nigerian art objects. Bibliography.

Werner, Alice. *African Mythology.* Vol. 7 in *The Mythology of All Races,* edited by John Arnott MacCulloch. Boston: Marshall Jones, 1925.
This survey of the myths and religious beliefs of Sub-Saharan Africa treats the subject thematically rather than geographically. In each chapter myths from all over the region are cited as illustrations for a variety of thematic topics, including gods, heroes, myths of origin, death, ancestors, nature myths, demons, witchcraft, and imported tales. Special attention is given to animal stories, with separate chapters on hare, tortoise, and spider stories. Includes a short introductory chapter on the general ethnic and linguistic features of Africa and on significant characteristics of African myths. Forty-six plates. Appendix of additional myths from Uganda. Endnotes and bibliography. Complete index in Volume 13.

_____. *Myths and Legends of the Bantu.* London: George G. Harrap, 1933. Reprint. London: Frank Cass, 1968.
Recounts the myths of the Bantu peoples of South Africa, including the Zulu, Xhosa, Basuto, and Bechuana. An introductory chapter on the people, their languages, customs, beliefs, high god, accounts of the origin of humankind, ogres, and animal stories. Nineteen chapters dealing with myths and legends arranged thematically. Each chapter begins with an introductory section followed by the myths, most of which are retold from works by European collectors. Chapters on the legends of the high god, ghosts, heroes, tricksters, monsters, meteorological phenomena, rabbit tales, tortoise tales, and other animal stories are followed by a chapter dealing with stories that appear to be Bantu transformations of tales originally told by other cultures. Thirty-four photographs of the people and their customs. Footnotes, map, bibliography, and index.

Willis, Roy. "Africa." In *World Mythology*, edited by Roy Willis. New York: Henry Holt, 1993.
This overview deals with myths of Sub-Saharan Africa thematically rather than regionally. Includes sections on creation myths, the world of the dead, death, kingship, towers, animal myths, and Eshu the Yoruba trickster. Subsidiary sections treat Gu the divine blacksmith of the Fon, the universe of the Kongo, Kalala Ilunga the rainbow King of the Luba, Chibinda Ilunga king of the Mbangala, the Yoruba deities

Eshu and Ifa, and a San aetiology of fire. Twenty-one illustrations, mostly in color, of African artifacts and sites. Map and time chart.

_____, ed. and trans. *There Was a Certain Man: Spoken Art of the Fipa*. Oxford: The Clarendon Press, 1978.

A scholarly collection and study of oral materials of the Fipa people of Tanzania. Introductory chapter on the people, the types and style of their spoken art, and information on the speakers. Deals with a variety of spoken genres in separate chapters: greetings, stories, proverbs, and authoritative communications. Each chapter begins with a discussion of the genre and its general characteristics, followed by a selection of examples. Many individual texts are preceded by short introductory commentary. For the study of mythology the chapter on narratives is most relevant. Fifty-three stories are recorded and analyzed. All these tales about people, talking animals, and humans interacting with animals are offered in English translation, accompanied by occasional texts in the original Fipa language. All proverbs are presented both in Fipa and in English. The original text of one tale is offered with an interlinear literal English translation in an appendix. Also a note on Fipa grammar and syntax in an appendix. Footnotes and bibliography.

Woodson, Carter Godwin. *African Myths*. Washington, D.C.: Associated Publishing, 1928.

This collection of thirty-nine tales was intended for use by children in the American public schools. It reflects a tendency in the early part of the twentieth century to treat Africa as a single unit and to ignore the great cultural diversity of the continent. Ethnographic contexts are provided for none of the tales, which include a creation myth, aetiologies, and animal fables. Accompanied by two photographs and eighty-six line drawings. Proverbs follow many of the tales.

Zenani, Nongenile Masithathu. *The World and the Word*, edited by Harold Scheub. Madison: University of Wisconsin Press, 1992.

A collection of stories and personal observations by a master Xhosa performer recorded by the editor in the Transkei region of South Africa between 1968 and 1973. The material is arranged according to four themes: birth, puberty, marriage, and maturity. Each section begins with the editor's introductory comments followed by Zenani's own autobiographical and ethnographic material and a series of tales which illustrate her observations. These twenty-four tales deal with the origin of the Xhosa people, interpersonal relationships, interaction between animals and humans, and the supernatural. Twenty-five photographs of Zenani, especially in performance. Map and footnotes.

Chapter 3
THE AMERICAS

The three main mythological traditions represented here are those of Central (or Meso-) Americans, Native South Americans, and Native North Americans. The Central American section deals especially with the myths of the Aztec and Maya, integrated with some material from modern Mexico. Prominent among the South American material are the myths and historical legends of the Inca and anthropological collections of the oral traditions of the peoples of the Amazon basin and the Gran Chaco region of Chile, Argentina, and Paraguay. Represented among the Native North American myths are the traditions of all the major nations of the continent, from the Penobscot in Maine to the Kwakiutl of the North Pacific Coast, from the Navajo and Zuñi of Arizona and New Mexico, to the Inuit of northern Canada and Greenland. As noted in the general introduction, citations combining myths of the Inuit with those of other Arctic peoples can be found in Chapter 1. In addition to these broad geographic groupings, three other categories are used here. The initial, general section contains citations dealing with more than one region of the Americas. The second section considers the oral traditions of peoples of African ancestry from all over the Americas, but especially from the southern portion of the United States and the Caribbean. This section on African American myths precedes the sections on the myths of South, Central, and North America in order to position it closer to the related African material in Chapter 2. The last section in this chapter is an eclectic and selective attempt to recognize the myths and legends of modern America, including frontier stories, ethnic and regional tales, and urban myths.

General Works

Alexander, Hartley Burr. *Latin-American Mythology*. Vol. 11 in *The Mythology of All Races*, edited by Louis Herbert Gray. Boston: Marshall Jones, 1920.
   This overview of the myths of Central and South America is arranged in nine geographical groups: the Antilles, Mexico, the Yucatan, Central America, the northern Andes, the southern Andes, the northern tropical forests, the Amazon, and the far south. Within these groups the author discusses topics such as Taíno myths, the Aztec gods and calendar, regional deities and heroes, El Dorado, and creation myths. In an introductory essay, the author outlines the region's cultural divisions,

describes the general characteristics of the myths, and suggests several reasons that these myths are of particular interest. Forty-two plates and two figures. Endnotes and bibliography. Complete index in Volume 13.

Bancroft, Hubert Howe. *Myths and Languages.* Vol. 3 in *The Native Races*, by Hubert Howe Bancroft. San Francisco: A. L. Bancroft, 1883. Part of an early, comprehensive study of the peoples of the Pacific Coast from Alaska to Mexico and Central America. While the work reflects the cultural prejudices and historical limitations of the nineteenth century and must be consulted critically, Bancroft's mythological survey, often based upon ancient sources in the original languages, offers many valuable summaries and paraphrases of myths and legends. Analyses and interpretations, such as Bancroft's theory on the evolution of human culture in Chapter 1, must be read more cautiously. Chapters are organized thematically rather than geographically. Considers myths about creation, final cataclysms, the physical world, animals, deities, other supernatural beings, and cults, with special attention to the gods of ancient Mexico. Footnotes, many in languages other than English.

Bierhorst, John, ed. *The Red Swan: Myths and Tales of the American Indians.* New York: Farrar, Straus and Giroux, 1976. Reprint. *Myths and Tales of the American Indians.* New York: Indian Head Books, 1992.
Sixty-four myths and tales representing more than forty Native American cultures have been adapted by the editor from a variety of published sources and translators. The tales are organized thematically. Some examples are a Mbayá myth about the creator dream father, Apache and Aztec tales of Mother Earth, a Tenetehara story about the serpent as culture hero, Kwakiutl and Warrau war legends, Arapaho and Menomini hero legends, Crow animal fables, Chippewa and Alabama ghost tales, and Shawnee and Iowa tales of death and renewal. Each tale is introduced briefly by the editor. Endnotes include information on sources. In an introductory essay, the editor suggests four major subject areas for Native American myth, discusses several characteristics of myth in general, and offers an interpretation of myth as passage through death based upon the theories of Claude Lévi-Strauss and Sigmund Freud. Illustrated with early book engravings. Bibliography and glossary.

Brinton, Daniel G. *American Hero-Myths.* Philadelphia: H. C. Watts, 1882. Reprint. New York: Johnson Reprint, 1970.

Combines the tools of comparative religion and comparative mythology in a study of Native American myths about a national hero, sometimes considered the supreme being, who often serves not only as creator but also as the bringer of civilization. Considers in particular the Algonquin myth of the giant rabbit Michabo, the Aztec tale of Quetzalcóatl, the Mayan culture hero legends of Itzamna and Kukulcán, and the story of the Quechua hero-god Viracocha. Paraphrases of the myths are accompanied by analysis and interpretation. Index.

Brunvand, Jan Harold, ed. *Readings in American Folklore.* New York: W. W. Norton, 1979.
This anthology of thirty-six short collections and studies of American folklore, originally published in scholarly journal articles, is intended as an introductory college textbook. A wide variety of traditions are represented, including various states and regions, immigrant groups, and Native Americans. Section 1 contains nine collections of primary oral texts or descriptions of folk traditions. In Section 2 are ten studies of folk traditions in their social and cultural contexts. The eleven selections in Section 3 illustrate a variety of approaches to folklore analysis, including structural, psychological, functional, and comparative methods. In Section 4 six modern American folklorists discuss general folklore theory. Each section and selection is preceded by an introduction by the editor. Footnotes.

Burland, Cottie, Irene Nicholson, and Harold Osborne. *Mythology of the Americas.* New York: Hamlyn Publishing Group, 1970.
Combines three books published separately as *North American Indian Mythology* by Burland, *Mexican and Central American Mythology* by Nicholson, and *South American Mythology* by Osborne. Each is lavishly illustrated in color and black-and-white and offers a broad survey of myths of the ancient peoples of its particular geographic range. Brief introductions to the historical and cultural contexts of the myths are followed by paraphrases of major tales and legends, sometimes with quotation in translation from original ancient sources. Bibliography and comprehensive index.

Fauconnet, Max. "Mythology of the Two Americas." In *New Larousse Encyclopedia of Mythology*, edited by Felix Guirand et al. Translated by Richard Aldington and Delano Ames. New York: Hamlyn, 1968.
This sweeping overview of the mythologies of North, Central, and South America is geographically organized, beginning in the far north and working south. Fauconnet offers significant paraphrases of myths

and legends about the Inuit goddess Sedna, the cosmogony of the Algonquin, and the myth of Morning star of the Great Plains people. Also contains descriptions of the gods and beliefs of ancient Mexico, Central America, the Chibchas of Colombia, the Inca, and the Araucanians of Chile. In a final section, Fauconnet summarizes some myths about Monan and other culture/creator heroes of the Tupi of Brazil. One color and forty-three black-and-white illustrations of Native American artifacts and sites.

Haviland, Virginia, ed. *The Faber Book of North American Legends.* Boston: Faber & Faber, 1979.

An anthology of twenty-nine representative tales from various traditions in North America retold for older children. Among the fourteen Native American stories are a Raven story from the North Pacific Coast, a Coyote tale from the Plains, a Gluskap adventure from the Northeast Woodlands, and the Inuit story of Sedna the Sea Goddess. The five African American contributions consist of a Brer Rabbit tale, three conjurer stories, and a numbskull tale. Also contains five legends told by European immigrants in Appalachia and New England and five tall tales about regional U.S. heroes such as Pecos Bill, Paul Bunyan, and Johnny Appleseed. Some stories are borrowed directly from earlier collections, such as those of George Bird Grinnell. Others have been retold by the editor. Details about sources and editorial comments in endnotes. With illustrations by Ann Strugnell. Bibliography.

Leach, Maria. *The Rainbow Book of American Folk Tales and Legends.* New York: World Publishing, 1958.

A collection of tales and legends from all over the Americas retold for children. The bulk of the material concerns the United States and its westward expansion. Tall tales about legendary figures such as Paul Bunyan, Pecos Bill, Davy Crockett, and Casey Jones are followed by lore about individual states, stories about outlaws like as Billy the Kid and Jesse James, tall tales about floods, mosquitoes and dogs, tales about unusual events, screams and local legends. Also contains eighteen tales of various Native American peoples, including a bear story of the Alaskan Inuit, a Zuñi tale about the center of the world, a story about the Micmac trickster Gluskap, a moral tale of the Miskito of Central America, and an aetiology about fire told by the Toba of the Argentine Chaco. Illustrated with color and black-and-white drawings by Marc Simont. Information about sources in endnotes. Bibliography and index.

Mackenzie, Donald Alexander. *Myths of Pre-Columbian America*. London: Gresham Publishing, 1923. Reprint. Boston: Longwood Press, 1978.

This survey of Central and South American myths before the time of Columbus pursues the controversial possibility of Asian influence on these cultures. Suggests links between the Egyptian and Indian milk goddesses and similar deities in America and between American Tlaloc lore and Chinese and Japanese dragon lore. Other similarities between the cultures and myths of the Old and the New Worlds are also considered. Includes chapters on possible American-Asiatic relations, Pacific sea routes, and migrations. Thirty-four plates, map, and index.

Macmillan, Cyrus. *Canadian Wonder Tales*. London: The Bodley Head, 1918. Reprinted with *Canadian Fairy Tales* as *Canadian Wonder Tales*. London: The Bodley Head, 1974.

Thirty-two tales collected in various parts of Canada and retold for children. Some come from French-Canadian traditions, others from Native American ones. No sources are indicated. Includes tales of magic and the supernatural, aetiologies, and animal fables. Several of the narratives deal with Gluskap, the Algonquin creator deity. Some background to the collection is provided in a short foreword by William Peterson and in a preface by the author. Illustrated in the original edition with drawings by George Sheringham. The reprint is illustrated with black-and-white drawings by Elizabeth Cleaver.

Radin, Paul. *Literary Aspects of North American Mythology*. Museum Bulletin 16 of the Canada Geological Survey. Ottawa: Government Printing Bureau, 1915. Reprint. Norwood, Pa.: Norwood Editions, 1973.

One of the first formal examinations of literary features of the traditional myths of North American peoples. While considering plot, characters, episodes, motifs, and psychological-literary elements, Radin retells and analyzes four trickster myths, an Ojibwa tale about Nenebojo, a deity known elsewhere as Nanabozho or Manabozho, an Omaha story called "The Holy One," a Winnebago tale about a man who visited the thunderbirds, and a Mexican Zapotecan creation myth. Footnotes.

Spence, Lewis. *Myths of Mexico and Peru*. New York: Thomas P. Crowell, 1913.

A survey of the mythologies of the Nahua, Maya, and Inca. Each group of myths is treated separately. Includes creation stories, descriptions of individual deities, historical legends about humankind and its development, migration legends, and tales about great heroes and rulers. Chapters on the civilizations of Mexico and of Peru provide historical and cultural background for the myths. Numerous subtitles within chapters make for easy reference to specific topics, deities, and legends. Generally myths are paraphrased with occasional quotation in translation, sometimes extensive, from ancient sources. Three maps and sixty illustrations, mostly drawings by Gilbert James and William Sewell. Bibliography and a glossary combined with index.

African American and West Indian Myths

Abrahams, Roger D. *Deep Down in the Jungle.* Hatboro, Pa.: Folklore Associates, 1964.

This African American urban folklore was collected in a small Philadelphia neighborhood in the late 1950's. Many of these one hundred tales, toasts, jokes, and verbal contests are based upon traditional stories about trickster animals. Others are based upon personal experience. The author precedes many tales with introductory commentary and analysis according to the Aarne-Thompson index of folktale motifs. Several chapters offer background about the neighborhood, elements of verbal contest, and the heroes of the tales. Glossary of unusual terms, bibliography, index of tale types, and general index.

Beckwith, Martha Warren. *Jamaica Anansi Stories.* Vol. 17 in *Memoirs of the American Folk-Lore Society.* New York: American Folk-Lore Society, 1924. Reprint. Millwood, N.Y.: Kraus Reprint, 1976.

Despite the title, only some of these tales recorded in Jamaica in 1919 and 1921 are about the trickster spider known as Anansi. The 149 tales are arranged in three groups: animal stories, old stories, especially about sorcery, and tales borrowed from the European folk tradition. Some tales are accompanied by musical scores based upon the field recordings of Helen Roberts. Preface on the recording of the tales and the storytelling tradition of Jamaicans. Also included are collections of witticisms and riddles. Explanatory endnotes for tales include some comparative material. Bibliography and indexes to riddles and to informants.

Brewer, John M. *American Negro Folklore.* Chicago: Quadrangle Books, 1968.

Part 1 of this rich collection of African American oral literature contains eighty traditional folktales which combine African elements with the American slave and slavery experience. Contains animal fables, especially about a trickster rabbit, aetiological stories, tall tales about semi-historical figures, ghost stories, other supernatural tales, and anecdotes about real-life situations. Each thematic group is introduced by brief comments by the author. The rest of the collection includes religious tales, songs, personal anecdotes, superstitions, proverbs, riddles, names, children's rhymes, and games. Illustrated by Richard Lowe. Index.

Courlander, Harold. *Terrapin's Pot of Sense*. New York: Holt, Rinehart and Winston, 1957.
These thirty-one tales, collected from African American storytellers in rural Alabama, Michigan, and New Jersey, are retold for children. Several animal fables, especially about Brer Rabbit, are accompanied by tall tales, the story of a talking skull, and tales about Old Master, preachers, and the devil. Endnotes contain explanatory comments and information about sources. Black-and-white illustrations by Elton Fax.

_____. *A Treasury of Afro-American Folklore*. New York: Crown Publishers, 1976.
A rich collection of traditional tales told by people of African ancestry throughout the Western Hemisphere. A short introduction on African influences on these tales is followed by tales from the following geographic regions and cultural groups: Cuba, Haiti, Puerto Rico, Guadeloupe, Carriacou, West African Calypso, Jamaica, Mexico, Surinam, Guyana, Venezuela, Brazil, and the United States. Includes animal fables, slave and slavery tales, songs, cult festivals, spirituals, sermons, and a variety of other forms of folk tradition. Each section is preceded by a brief introduction. Parallel African tales are retold in appendices. Thirty-six photographs illustrating people and places associated with this folklore. Bibliography and index.

Dance, Daryl Cumber. *Shuckin' and Jivin': Folklore from Contemporary Black Americans*. Bloomington: Indiana University Press, 1978.
These 565 tales and songs were collected throughout the United States by the author. Arranged thematically, the tales include aetiologies, ethnic jokes, risqué tales, and stories about heaven and hell, ghosts, conjuring, religion, women, white women and black men, self-degradation, marital infidelity, the cruelty of whites, outsmarting whites, and the "bad nigger." General introductory essay on the character of black

folktales and the origin and purpose of this collection. Additional introductory sections at the beginning of each chapter. All introductions are followed by endnotes. Information about major contributors and the context of recording in appendices. Contains some broad street language. Bibliography.

Dorson, Richard M., ed. *American Negro Folktales.* 2d ed. Greenwich, Conn.: Fawcett, 1967.
Part 1 of this collection of African American tales offers a background essay on the historical and cultural origins of such tales, the storytellers and the geographic regions in which they have been found, and the artistic features of their tales. This part also includes a history of a storyteller named James Douglas Suggs. In Part 2 the tales are grouped in the following categories: animal and bird stories, tales about Old Master and John, lying tales, horror stories, protest tales, and stories about the supernatural, preachers, and the Irish. Bibliography, index of motifs, and index of tale types.

Edwards, Charles Lincoln. *Bahama Songs and Stories.* Vol. 3 in *Memoirs of the American Folk-Lore Society.* Boston: American Folk-Lore Society, 1895. Reprint. Millwood, N.Y.: Kraus Reprint, 1976.
This material was collected among the people of the Bahamas between 1888 and 1893 and is recorded in the local English dialect. In addition to forty songs with lyrics and musical scores in Part 1, the collection contains thirty-eight folktales in Part 2. Many of these tales are about anthropomorphic animals, especially Brer Rabbit. Introductory essay on the islands, the people, and their storytelling traditions. Appendix on African American music. Three photographs. Footnotes.

Faulkner, William J. *The Days When the Animals Talked.* Chicago: Follett Publishing, 1977.
Faulkner retells thirty-three African American tales he heard from Simon Brown and other former slaves. In Part 1 Faulkner offers eleven first-person recollections about Simon and records Simon's tales of slavery, courtship, outwitting the white man, ghosts, witches, and escapes to freedom. Part 2 includes a short introduction followed by twenty-two Brer Rabbit tales told to Faulkner by Brown and other elderly storytellers from South Carolina. In an introductory essay, Faulkner describes his recollections of Brown and the place of storytelling in the experience of African American slaves. In separate forewords, Spencer G. Shaw discusses African American storytellers and their art and Sterling Stuckey comments on Faulkner and his tales.

Afterword on Brown's later years and death. Biography of the author. Illustrated with black-and-white drawings by Troy Howell.

Fauset, Arthur Huff. *Folklore from Nova Scotia*. Vol. 24 in *Memoirs of the American Folk-Lore Society*. New York: American Folk-Lore Society, 1931.
Most of the material in this book was obtained by the author from African Americans in Nova Scotia. The 172 folktales grouped thematically in Part 1 include *Märchen*, animal tales, Pat and Mike tall tales, witch and devil tales, legends about buried treasure, and stories about preachers and neighbors. Themes similar to those found in tales told by African Americans in the American South appear in these tales, but the portrayal of Anansi the spider (here called Nancy) and the story of Tar Baby are so changed that informants could not recognize links with southern variants. The other five parts are devoted to ballads and songs, game songs and counting-out rhymes, nursery rhymes, riddles and riddle tales, and folk notions. Most of the tales are told in English. The few recorded in Gaelic include English translations. Introductory essay on the African American community in eastern Canada and its folk traditions. List of informants.

Harris, Joel Chandler. *Nights with Uncle Remus*. Boston: Houghton Mifflin, 1883. Reprint. Detroit: Singing Tree Press, 1971.
This collection of seventy-one animal tales is based upon the oral traditions of African Americans of the Old American South. Despite a controversial use of stereotypic dialect and Chandler's heavy editorial hand, these versions of the adventures of Brer Rabbit and Brer Fox remain part of the modern American oral inheritance and have been widely retold and re-created in other media. These tales of a trickster rabbit reflect the influence of African animal tales about the crafty tortoise or Anansi the spider upon African American culture. Also evident in these tales are subtle messages about slaves and slavery and the superior intelligence of the black man, who repeatedly manages to trick the unsuspecting white master. Twenty-one illustrations.

Haviland, Virginia, ed. "Black American Tales." In *The Faber Book of North American Legends*, edited by Virginia Haviland. Boston: Faber & Faber, 1979.
Part of an anthology of twenty-nine North American tales told by Native Americans, African Americans, European immigrants, and inhabitants of various regions of the United States. These five traditional African American stories, all originally collected in the late

nineteenth or early twentieth century, are here republished, some slightly edited for older children. A West Virginian version of Brer Rabbit's Tar Baby story is accompanied by three tales about conjurers and a Louisiana numbskull story. Details about sources and editorial comments in endnotes. With illustrations by Ann Strugnell. Bibliography.

Hughes, Langston, and Arna Bontemps, eds. *The Book of Negro Folklore.* New York: Dodd, Mead, 1958.
This collection of the traditional literature of African Americans includes folktales as well as rhymes, sermons, spirituals, songs, poetry, and games. Among the folktales are animal tales such as those of Brer Rabbit and stories about slave and slavery, preachers, God, ghosts, and black magic. In a short introduction, Bontemps discusses the origins and characteristics of African American folklore.

Hurston, Zora Neale. *Mules and Men.* 2d ed. New York: Harper and Row, 1990.
This anthology of the folklore of southern African Americans was gathered, especially in Florida, in the 1930's by a famous storyteller and anthropologist. In Part 1 are seventy traditional folktales, including Slave John stories, aetiologies, and tales about preachers and churches. In Part 2 Hurston describes her encounters with five Hoodoo doctors in Louisiana. This edition contains an introduction by Hurston, a preface by Hurston's mentor Franz Boas, a foreword about Hurston's life and writings by Arnold Rampersad, and an afterword about the importance of Hurston's work by Henry Louis Gates, Jr. Also contains a glossary; appendices of African American songs with music, formulae, and paraphernalia for Hoodoo doctors; a select bibliography of books by and about Hurston; and a chronology of Hurston's life. Illustrated with drawings by Miguel Covarrubias.

Jones, Charles C. *Negro Myths from the Georgia Coast.* Boston: Houghton, Mifflin, 1888. Reprint. Detroit: Singing Tree Press, 1969.
Sixty-one tales collected in the swamp region of coastal Georgia and told in the original vernacular. Most of these are animal tales, especially dealing with Bur Rabbit, the trickster better known as Brer Rabbit. Includes a glossary.

King, Francis. "Voodoo." In *Mythology: An Illustrated Encyclopaedia,* edited by Richard Cavendish. New York: Rizzoli International, 1980. Also published as *An Illustrated Encyclopedia of Mythology.* New York: Crescent Books, 1984.

This brief overview of the Voodoo religion of Haiti and characteristics of its chief deities includes descriptions of Legba, the guardian of the gate between the worlds of humans and spirits; Loco, the god of vegetation; the Guede, the family of dead spirits; Ogu, the divine blacksmith; Zaka, the peasant-god of agriculture; Erzulie, the goddess of love; and her consort Damballah, the hissing serpent. Also contains a section on the role of St. John the Baptist in Voodoo. Emphasizes the African origins of many of these beliefs and the influence of Roman Catholicism. Map and illustrations of artwork and sites related to the myths.

Lester, Julius. *Black Folktales*. New York: Grove Press, 1969.
Twelve traditional tales are retold here by an African American author and folksinger. Stories are arranged in four thematic groups: myths of origin, love, heroes, and people. Includes aetiological stories from Africa, slave and slavery tales from the southern United States, and a semi-historical legend about "Stagolee" sung by urban African Americans. Includes black-and-white drawings by Tom Feelings.

Makhanlall, David. *Brer Anansi and the Boat Race*. New York: Peter Bedrick Books, 1988.
A young children's version of a Caribbean folktale in which Brer Rabbit and Brer Bear challenge the tricky Brer Anansi the spider to a boat race in the middle of a flood. Color illustrations by Amelia Rosato.

Owen, Mary Alicia. *Voodoo Tales*. New York: G. P. Putnam's Sons, 1893. Reprint. Freeport, N.Y.: Books for Libraries Press, 1971.
These twenty-nine tales of sorcery and superstition reflect a unique cultural blending of Native Americans and African Americans in the southwest United States. The author obtained many of these stories from personal experiences and contacts. The tales, recorded in colloquial English with standard English equivalents occasionally indicated in parentheses, center on animal legends, especially those about a red dwarf woodpecker, a fox, a snake, and a rabbit. Fifty-seven line drawings by Juliette A. Owens and Louis Wain. In a short introductory essay, Charles Godfrey discusses Voodooism, some features of these tales, and Owen's connections with them.

Parsons, Elsie Clews. *Folk-Lore from the Cape Verde Islands*. 2 parts. Vol. 15 in *Memoirs of the American Folk-Lore Society*. Cambridge, Mass.: American Folk-Lore Society, 1923.
This material was obtained in 1916-1917 in New England from Portuguese-speaking African American immigrants from the Cape Verde

Islands. Part 1 consists of 133 folktales in English translation. Some are strongly Portuguese or European in theme and content, while others are more African. Prominent are tales about Wolf (Lob') and his nephew. Also contains other animal fables and tales about marriage, magic, tests, and escapes. Part 2 contains the texts of these tales in the original Portuguese dialect, some with musical scores, notes on orthography and phonetics, and collections of riddles, proverbs, and sayings in Portuguese with interlinear English translation. In a preface, Parsons describes how this folklore was collected and provides some background about her informants and their culture. Footnotes, bibliography, and notes on orthography and phonetics.

_____. *Folk-Lore of the Antilles, French and English.* 3 parts. Vol. 26 in *Memoirs of the American Folk-Lore Society.* New York: American Folk-Lore Society. 1933 (Part 1), 1936 (Part 2), 1943 (Part 3).
A monumental collection of folktales gathered in the Caribbean between 1924 and 1927 and arranged geographically beginning with Trinidad in the south and moving north to Haiti. The tales are recorded in the language of the storyteller. Some are in English, but many are in French Creole. Only the first French Creole tale in the collection of each island includes an English translation. Part 1 contains a map, a preface by Parsons describing her experiences in the Caribbean, and the tales of Trinidad, Grenadines, St. Vincent, St. Lucia, Martinique, and Dominica. In Part 2 are the tales of Guadeloupe, Les Saintes, Marie Galante, Montserrat, Antigua, Nevis, St. Kitts, St. Eustatius, Saba, St. Bartholomew, St. Martin, Anguilla, St. Croix, St. Thomas, and Haiti. Each geographic group has a separate list of tales and informants. These tales deal with a variety of themes, including trickster animals, aetiology, contests, boasts, ghosts, witches, and murder. Some have musical scores. In Part 3 are English summaries of all the tales, some with bibliographic references. Also included here are riddles and proverbs arranged by island. Bibliographies and footnotes.

_____. *Folk-Lore of the Sea Islands, South Carolina.* Vol. 16 in *Memoirs of the American Folk-Lore Society.* Cambridge, Mass.: American Folk-Lore Society, 1923.
The 178 folktales recorded here were collected among African American Sea-Islanders in 1919. The tales, preserved in the local dialect, include stories about Brer Rabbit, courting, ghosts, witches, talking animals, buried treasure, murder, and religion. Following the tales are collections or riddles, proverbs, toasts, game songs, and folk customs.

Preface on the Sea-Islanders, their dialect, and this collection of their tales. Footnotes, bibliography, and list of informants.

_____. *Folk-Tales of Andros Island, Bahamas.* Vol. 13 in *Memoirs of the American Folk-Lore Society.* New York: American Folk-Lore Society, 1918.
A collection of 115 tales recorded in the English dialect of the inhabitants of Andros Island. The main characters of these tales can be either animal or human, including Crafty Rabbit, the hero Jack, and the heroine Greenleaf. Common themes are courting, witchcraft, theft, murder, family relationships, and metamorphosis. Introductory essay on the people of Andros Island and their storytelling tradition. Footnotes, list of informants, and bibliography.

Puckett, Newbell Niles. *Folk Beliefs of the Southern Negro.* Chapel Hill: University of North Carolina Press, 1926. Reprint. Montclair, N.J.: Patterson Smith, 1968.
A scholarly study about the folklore and superstitions of southern African Americans. Material was collected in the field by the author and is arranged in the chapters on the following topics: burial customs, ghosts, and witches; Voodooism and conjuration; minor charms and cures; taboos; and prophetic signs or omens. An initial chapter on African survivals in this folklore and a concluding chapter on elements of this folklore in the Christianity of southern blacks. Nine pages of photographs illustrating aspects of this folklore. Footnotes, bibliography, and list of informants.

Sherlock, Philip. *West Indian Folk-Tales.* New York: Henry Z. Walck, 1966.
Retells twenty-one tales of the West Indies, including aetiological stories, several tales of Anansi the spider, and other animal fables. In a short introductory chapter, the author provides a history of the region from the time of the pre-Columbian Arawak to the arrival of African slave with their own oral traditions. With illustrations by Joan Kiddell-Monroe.

Central American Myths

Anaya, Rudolfo A. *Lord of the Dawn: The Legend of Quetzalcóatl.* Albuquerque: University of New Mexico Press, 1987.
A Native American professor of English retells in narrative form the story of Huémac, the last king of the Toltecs, and his antagonistic

relationship with the god Quetzalcóatl. In an introductory essay, David Johnson discusses Quetzalcóatl's origin as a god of creation, his religious cult, and his messianic identity for the Aztec and for the Spanish. Glossary and pronunciation guide.

Bierhorst, John. *The Hungry Woman: Myths and Legends of the Aztecs.* New York: William Morrow, 1984.
Twenty-seven Aztec tales mostly recorded in the sixteenth century. Arranged in five chronological groups: creation myths, tales about the city of Tula and its fall, the story of the founding of Mexico, legends from the days of Montezuma, and tales from the post-Columbian period. Frequently published stories about the flight and return of Quetzalcóatl are accompanied by others about the birth of Huitzilopochtli, the Aztec sun and war god, about the dangerous goddesses Coyolxauqui and Malinalxochitl, and about the cult of the Our Lady of Guadalupe. The title story is about a woman with many mouths who personifies hunger. Illustrated with drawings by sixteenth-century Aztec artists. In an introductory essay, the author discusses the origin of these tales, Aztec cycles of history, features of various deities, and characteristics of Aztec oral literature in general and of Aztec myths in particular. Explanatory endnotes with information about sources, pronunciation guide for Nahuatl, guide to special terms, and bibliography.

_____, ed. *The Monkey's Haircut and Other Stories Told by the Maya.* New York: William Morrow, 1986.
Twenty-two tales of the Maya taken from both ancient and modern sources are retold for juvenile readers. Some originally appeared in the *Popol Vuh* of the ancient Maya. Others show the influence of European and, especially, Christian sources. Contains stories about the gods, the supernatural, metamorphosis, and animal tricksters. In the title story a shave at the barbershop leads to disaster for a talking monkey. In an introductory essay, the editor provides some background about the Maya, their history, culture, and art of storytelling. Also includes an example of personal recollection based upon true events. Illustrated with black-and-white drawings by Robert Andrew Parker. Bibliography and notes on sources and variants.

_____. *The Mythology of Mexico and Central America.* New York: William Morrow, 1990.
An anthology of basic myths of the Aztec and Maya as well as other ancient peoples of Central America. Part 1 offers a historical and cultural introduction to the peoples who have told these myths. In Part

2 myths about the origins of humankind, the flood, the importance of corn and the sun, and journeys to the otherworld are translated from a variety of historical and ethnographic sources. These myths are analyzed and compared in Part 3. Considers Mesoamerican attitudes toward god and the hero and the role of these myths in writing history and in celebrating modern nationalism. The text is accompanied by twenty-five illustrations from ancient manuscripts and drawings, eleven maps, notes on pronunciation and sources, glossary of special terms, references, and index.

_____, trans. "Quetzalcóatl." In *Four Masterworks of American Indian Literature*, edited by John Bierhorst. Tucson: University of Arizona Press, 1984.
The myth of Quetzalcóatl, the plumed serpent Aztec deity, survives in five major fragments which are here translated from the original Nahuatl for the general reader. These narratives include a description of the god's descent into the underworld, the hero's quest for the body of his dead father, the sun, the hero's role as culture hero, the fall of the hero's kingdom of Tula, and a dramatic reenactment of the death of the god and the birth of Cintéotl, the god of corn. Extensive explanatory notes follow the translation. Also contains general comments on the myth and the text in an introductory essay. Part of a volume of translations of four representative pieces of Native American literature. The Aztec myth is accompanied by a Mayan prophecy called *Cuceb* and two ceremonial texts, an Iroquois ritual of condolence and a Navajo night chant. Maps, bibliographies, and general index.

Brotherston, Gordon. "Middle America." In *Mythology: An Illustrated Encyclopaedia*, edited by Richard Cavendish. New York: Rizzoli International, 1980. Also published as *An Illustrated Encyclopedia of Mythology*. New York: Crescent Books, 1984.
Summaries and analyses of several myths of the ancient Maya and Aztec peoples, including the Aztec ages of the world and a great flood, Mayan concepts of world ages, a creation story from the Mayan *Popol Vuh*, a Nahua myth about the creation of humankind from bones, the Toltec tradition about Tlaloc the rainmaker, and the Nahua legend of Quetzalcóatl and his rival Tezcatlipoca. Map, chart of twenty ritual signs, glossary of principal gods, and illustrations of artwork and sites related to the myths.

Brundage, Burr Cartwright. *The Fifth Sun: Aztec Gods, Aztec World*. Austin: University of Texas Press, 1979.

An outline of the Aztec world view with summaries of many myths, especially about gods but also about various aspects of human life, including its origin, war, and death. Chapters deal with Tezcatlipoca, the Aztec god of the night sky, with Quetzalcóatl, the plumed serpent god, with goddesses such as Tonantzin, the mother deity, and with myths about the creation of the universe. Illustrated by Roy E. Anderson with line drawings based upon ancient manuscripts. Endnotes, bibliography, and index.

Burland, Cottie A. *The Aztecs*. London: Orbis Publishing, 1980.

This general introduction to the religious beliefs and myths of the Aztec includes a historical overview of ancient Mexico and a discussion of sources in Chapter 1. Deals in Chapter 2 with the gods of Mexico, their role in the world, Aztec cosmology, and Aztec beliefs about time and the afterlife. The deities Quetzalcóatl and Tezcatlipoca and their powers, cults, and myths are surveyed in individual chapters. Also contains chapters on rituals of daily life, astrology, and the priesthood. A final chapter entitled "The Earthly Confrontation" deals with the Spanish conquest of Montezuma. Illustrated with many color photographs of ancient sites and artifacts. Map, glossary, chronological chart, bibliography, and index.

_____. *The Gods of Mexico*. New York: G. P. Putnam's Sons, 1967.

The first five chapters of this book provide a historical survey of ancient Mexico and trace the development of both the Mayan and the Aztec civilizations and the growth of city-states. In the last eleven chapters Burland describes the gods and religious beliefs which developed in these cultures. Includes chapters on various aspects of the religious calendar, fate, the nature of the gods, Quetzalcóatl, and visionaries. Appendices on early Mexican and Mayan manuscripts and on the ballgame *tlachtli*. Eight pages of photographs and illustrations from manuscripts. Alphabetical list of major deities, pronunciation guide, maps, bibliography, and index.

_____. *Magic Books of Mexico*. Baltimore: Penguin, 1953.

This little book contains sixteen color reproductions of illustrations from Aztec and Spanish documents of the fifteenth and sixteenth centuries. Each illustration is accompanied by a note providing the manuscript source, an explanation of the scene, and, where necessary, a paraphrase of related myths. These scenes depict Aztec deities in ritual and magical contexts. Includes the jeweled turkey of Tezcatlipoca, the birth of the Mixtec people, the corn spirit making offering, and Quetzalcóatl as god of the wind. In an introductory essay, Burland retells the story of the Aztec and the Spanish conquest, briefly describes Aztec cosmogony, and discusses the ancient manuscripts and their history.

Burns, A. *An Epoch of Miracles*. Austin: University of Texas Press, 1983.
An ethnographic examination of the verbal traditions of two Mayan villages in the Yucatan. Most of the book consists of examples of such literature in English translation. Riddles, jokes, lore, and narratives are accompanied by examples of ancient conversations, especially aetiological tales about creation and the discovery of corn. Several of these translations are accompanied by original Mayan texts. In an introductory essay, the author provides background to the people and their oral literature. Bibliography and three photographs.

Carrasco, David. *Quetzalcóatl and the Irony of Empire*. Chicago: University of Chicago Press, 1982.
A professor of religious studies links legends about the Aztec plumed serpent god Quetzalcóatl with a network of urban sites in pre-Hispanic Mexico. Argues that the god played an important symbolic and religious role as the legitimizer of the Aztec urban tradition and as the organizer of the mythic world view of the Aztec. In particular, Quetzalcóatl is associated with the Toltec capital of Tula as both a historical and a mythical site. Sixteen illustrations, mostly photographs of sites and reproductions of manuscript illuminations. Endnotes, map, bibliography, and index.

Caso, A. *The Aztecs: People of the Sun*. Translated by Lowell Dunham. Norman: University of Oklahoma Press, 1958.
A general overview of Aztec religion with short paraphrases and explanations of various myths. Sections on magic, creation of the cosmos and of humankind, the gods, the afterlife, the calendar, and religious organization. Caso pays particular attention to difficulties in interpreting the iconography of Aztec gods. Illustrated with forty-two color drawings by Miguel Covarrubias, mostly based upon depictions of Aztec deities in ancient manuscripts. Sixteen photographs of Aztec artifacts. Some background to Aztec history and to this book in a translator's introduction and in the author's preface. Footnotes and index.

Coe, Michael D. "The Hero Twins: Myth and Image." In *The Maya Vase Book*, edited by Justin Kerr. New York: Kerr Associates, 1989.

Argues that references to the Hero twins Hunahpu and Ixbalanque in the *Popol Vuh* are part of a longer mythic cycle about the brothers and their defeat of the Lords of Xibalba (the underworld). Documents this epic on the pictorial ceramics of the classic Maya. Twenty-nine drawings and photographs of vase paintings and manuscript illuminations.

_____. *Old Gods and Young Heroes*. Jerusalem: The Israel Museum, 1982.
A catalogue of sixty-three artifacts in the Edwin Pearlman Collection of Maya Ceramics in the Israel Museum. Information about provenance, size, date, and previous publication accompany Coe's text. Also contains photographs of each object, some in color, by Justin Kerr. Coe describes each object, explaining the depiction of deities and mythological scenes, particularly in the underworld. In an introductory essay, Coe discusses the iconography of Mayan ceramics. In an appendix, Elizabeth P. Benson and Dan Eban offer an outline of Mayan history and consider several important terms, especially concerning Mayan deities, glyphs, and calendar. Map and bibliography.

Cornyn, John Hubert, trans. *The Song of Quetzalcóatl*. 2d ed. Yellow Springs, Ohio: The Antioch Press, 1931. Reprint. San Antonio: Texas Art Press, 1980.
A verse translation of a pre-conquest Aztec poem about the god Quetzalcóatl by a professor at the National University of Mexico. The song, celebrating the Aztec prophet and god of the wind, is divided into twenty-four sections. Some of these are religious hymns and others are narratives about the god's exile from his home at Tula by the priest enchanter Ttlacáhuan, his wanderings around Mexico, and his return to the Land of the sun in a magic serpent raft. In an introductory essay, Cornyn discusses Aztec literature, its manuscript tradition, aesthetic features of the *Song of Quetzalcóatl*, Aztec history, and sites important to the song. Accompanied by twelve illustrations, including black-and-white drawings based upon the author's photographs of sites and color reproductions of original manuscript illuminations. Explanatory endnotes.

Dorson, Richard M. Foreword to *Folktales of Mexico*, edited by Américo Paredes. Chicago: University of Chicago Press, 1970.
An essay on some important characteristics of Mexican folklore, especially its syncretism of Spanish and Native American elements, elements of revolutionary nationalism, hero cults, and the image of the United States in Mexican folklore. Includes summaries of some myths

such as a Mexican creation myth in which Our Lady of Guadalupe is merged with the Aztec mother goddess Tonantzin. Also contains substantial quotation in translation from original sources such as a ballad about Emiliano Zapata. Footnotes.

Durán, Fray Diego. *Book of the Gods and Rites and The Ancient Calendar*. Translated and edited by Frenando Horcasitas and Doris Heyden. Norman: University of Oklahoma Press, 1971.
English translations of two works by a sixteenth-century Spanish missionary in Mexico. In the twenty-three chapters of the *Book of the Gods and Rites* (c. 1576-1579), Durán presents valuable firsthand information about individual Aztec deities, rites, and ceremonies. Individual chapters are devoted to the gods Huitzilopochtli, Tezcatlipoca, Quetzalcóatl, Tlaloc, Cihuacóatl, Chicomecóatl, Toci, Xochiquetzal, Iztaccihuatl, and Chalchiutlieue, to the feasts of Tezcatlipoca, Tlacaxipehualiztli, Nauholin, Xocotl Huetzi, and the volcano Popocatzin, and to discussions of the high priest Topilzin, human sacrifices, the knights of the sun, the market place, feast day games, and the ballgame. In the *Ancient Calendar* (1579), Durán discusses each of the eighteen months of the Aztec calendar. The original manuscripts of both works included color illuminations. The translations are preceded by a detailed section on the life and works of Durán by the translators. In a bibliographical note, they also offer a history of the Durán manuscripts and earlier printed editions. Foreword on Durán and his work by Miguel León-Portilla. Fifty-five black-and-white reproductions of pages from Durán's manuscripts. Eight of these are also reproduced in color. Pronunciation guide, map, glossary, bibliography, and index.

Gossen, G. *Chamulas in the World of the Sun*. Cambridge, Mass.: Harvard University Press, 1974.
This ethnographic study of the Chamula, a Tzotzil-speaking Mayan people of Chiapas, Mexico, shows that the various genres of their oral tradition must be viewed together in order to articulate a coherent understanding of their world view and social organization. In addition to children's songs, traditional games, prayers, and narratives of recent, historical events, Gossen offers an examination of what the Chamula call "true ancient narrative," stories which recall events about their ancestors in the distant past. Several such texts, describing the creation and destruction of the first people, are quoted in the original Tzotzil with interlinear English translation. An appendix contains short abstracts of 184 other narrative texts, many of them mythic in nature.

Three maps, six figures of charts and schemes, and four drawings by Marian Lopez Calixto. Bibliography, endnotes, and index.

Horcasitas, Fernando. "An Analysis of the Deluge Myth in Meso-america." In *The Flood Myth*, edited by Alan Dundes. Berkeley: University of California Press, 1988.
Surveys sixty-three versions of the flood myth in Central America. These myths are gathered in five ethnographic groups. For each group Horcasitas provides a brief résumé of the plot, résumés of each version in the group, and some comments on problems connected with each group. The American tradition shows little interest in the causes of the flood. Rather, these myths describe the destruction and re-creation of a succession of worlds. Two maps, footnotes, and bibliography.

Laughlin, Robert. *Of Cabbages and Kings*. Washington, D.C.: Smith-sonian Institution Press, 1977.
These 173 myths, legends, and reminiscences were collected between 1960 and 1971 from nine individuals from Zinacantán in Chiapas, Mexico. Biographies of each storyteller accompany each set of tales, which are arranged by storyteller. The original Tzotzil texts usually accompany the English translations. Many stories show a blending of European and indigenous elements. These incredible adventures, animal fables, tales of the supernatural, aetiologies, and flood stories are followed by explanatory endnotes. Appendices include a list of native demons and deities, a geographic gazetteer, a chronology of tale recordings, and a list of tales and tellers. Twelve photographs and figures, eight maps, and bibliography.

_____. *The People of the Bat*, edited by Carol Karasik. Washing-ton, D.C.: Smithsonian Institution Press, 1988.
These dreams and tales were collected in Zinacantán, a Mayan village near Chiapas, Mexico. Part 1 has translations of dreams by nine residents of the village. Biographies of each dreamer precede each collection of dreams. Part 2 contains fifty-one tales collected from these same people and from other sources. Semi-historical legends and conflicts are accompanied by religious tales, journeys to the under-world, animal fables, creation stories, and tales of metamorphosis. Introductory essay on the community, its ethnography, dreams, and tales. Explanatory endnotes, note on pronunciation, and bibliography.

León-Portilla, Miguel. *Aztec Thought and Culture*. Translated by Jack Emory Davis. Norman: University of Oklahoma Press, 1963.

A scholarly examination of the philosophy and culture of the Nahuatl- or Aztec-speaking peoples of Central Mexico before the time of Columbus. Original documents are either summarized or quoted in translation as examples of Aztec metaphysics, theology, and world view. Some of these texts are followed by detailed analysis and commentary. Of particular mythological interest are Aztec accounts about the creation of the universe, the cosmic order, the creation of humankind, and the origins of culture. Appendices on ancient sources and biographies of seventeenth- through twentieth-century investigators of Aztec thought. Footnotes, bibliography, and index.

_____. "Mythology of Ancient Mexico." In *Mythologies of the Ancient World*, edited by Samuel Noah Kramer. Garden City, N.Y.: Doubleday, 1961.
This short introduction to the myths of ancient Mexico begins with historical background and a note on sources. In a section on myths of origin, the author discusses the supreme dual deity (Ometéotl), the cosmic ages, the reestablishment of humans on earth, and the finding of corn. Also contains sections on the Toltec cycle of Quetzalcóatl and Aztec myths and rites. Some early sources are quoted in English translation. Bibliography.

_____. *Pre-Columbian Literatures of Mexico*. Translated by Grace Lobanov and Miguel León-Portilla. Norman: University of Oklahoma Press, 1969.
One chapter in this survey of oral literature of Mexico before A.D. 1500 focuses on myths and legends told in Nahuatl and other native languages and preserved in texts such as the *Popol Vuh*. Combines summaries of these myths and of mytho-religious characters such as Quetzalcóatl with translations of specific texts such as an Aztec tale of cosmic origin, world cycles, and the creation of humans and of the birth of the war god Huitzilopochtli. Other chapters deal with additional oral genres such as sacred hymns, lyrics, religious drama, and historical chronicles. Introductory essay on background and sources for these myths. Also contains nine illustrations from ancient manuscripts, footnotes, bibliography, and index.

Markman, Roberta H., and Peter T. Markman. *The Flayed God*. San Francisco: HarperCollins, 1992.
A collection of sacred texts and images illustrating the mythological world of Central America. Fifty-three photographs of ancient artifacts and drawings and twenty texts translated from ancient sources are

juxtaposed with commentary and explanation of their mythological significance. Includes creation myths of the Maya, Aztec, Mixtec, and Izapan, myths of fertility, and tales of heroic journeys, migrations, and rulers. An introductory essay provides a historical and cultural framework for interpreting the myths. Twenty additional maps and figures, twenty-four color plates of artifacts and illuminations from ancient manuscripts, pronunciation guide, endnotes, bibliography, and index.

Mike, Jan M. *Opossum and the Great Firemaker*. Mahwah, N.J.: Troll Associates, 1993.
An animal fable of the Cora people of the Sierra Madre region of Mexico is retold for young children. Iguana, the great firemaker, deprives humankind of his gift, but the smart Opossum tricks Iguana into bringing fire back to earth. Illustrated by Charles Reasoner.

Miller, Mary, and Karl Taube. *The Gods and Symbols of Ancient Mexico and the Maya*. New York: Thames and Hudson, 1993.
An illustrated dictionary of the gods and religious concepts of Mesoamerica, especially of the ancient Aztec and Maya. The alphabetically arranged entries offer both short identifications and extensive commentary on individual deities, concepts, rituals, and sacred sites. Two introductory essays, a cultural history of the region, and an overview of the Mesoamerican religious world view. Also contains a supplementary bibliographic essay. The 260 illustrations include photographs of sites and artifacts, reproductions of manuscript illuminations, and drawings based on ancient glyphs. Subject index and bibliography.

Morley, S. G. "Religions and Deities." In *The Ancient Maya*, by S. G. Morley. 3d ed., revised by George W. Brainerd. Stanford, Calif.: Stanford University Press, 1956.
This overview of Mayan religion includes brief summaries of Mayan creation myths and cosmologies and descriptions of the major deities. Illustrations of name glyphs for many of these deities.

Nicholson, Irene. *Firefly in the Night*. London: Faber & Faber, 1959.
An examination of the poetry and symbolism of ancient Mexico. Centers on the literature and beliefs of the pre-Aztec Nahuas of Mexico. The title of the book is based upon a translation of the Nahuatl word for their oral literature. Translated texts are incorporated into a discussion of the poetry. Includes descriptions of Nahuan cosmology and tales about their poet-kings and warfare. The major deities and

their myths are presented individually. Thirteen illustrations by Abel Mendoza, based upon ancient artwork. Bibliography and indexes.

_____. *Mexican and Central American Mythology.* 2d ed. New York: Peter Bedrick Books, 1985. Also in *Mythology of the Americas,* by Cottie Burland, Irene Nicholson, and Harold Osborne. London: Hamlyn Publishing Group, 1970.

The mythic world of the ancient Aztec and Maya and other peoples of the region is described for the general reader. A brief introduction to the myths in their cultural and historical context is followed by chapters on time, the calendar, nature, the ballgame, the relationship between humans and beasts, the legend of Quetzalcóatl as great king and lawgiver, and other topics. Paraphrases various myths, such as the tale of the Hero twins in the Mayan *Popol Vuh* and the Aztec legend of the five suns. Some quotation from original sources in translation. Text is illustrated with photographs of ancient sites, sculpture, and drawings. Bibliography and index.

Palacios, Argentina. *The Hummingbird King.* Mahwah, N.J.: Troll Associates, 1993.

A Guatemalan legend about the metamorphosis of a young Mayan chief named Kukul is retold for children. Kukul is killed by his uncle despite the protection of a hummingbird. At his death the youth is transformed into his namesake, the quetzal, the national bird of Guatemala, and a symbol of freedom. With color illustrations by Felipe Davalos.

Paredes, Américo, ed. and trans. *Folktales of Mexico.* Chicago: University of Chicago Press, 1970.

A collection of eighty examples of Mexican oral literature in translation. Of particular interest to the study of mythology are the sections devoted to legendary narratives, animal tales, and ordinary folktales. Also contains jokes, anecdotes, and formula tales. Sources, principal motifs, and general features of the tales are provided in endnotes. In an introductory essay, the editor provides a history of Mexican folkloristics and a general description of the book. Foreword by Richard M. Dorson on characteristics of Mexican folklore. Glossary, bibliography, indexes of motifs and tale types, and general index.

Peterson, Frederick. "Religion." In *Ancient Mexico,* by Frederick Peterson. New York: G. P. Putnam's Sons, 1959.

This chapter in a general introduction to pre-Columbian Mexico includes a genealogy of Aztec gods and descriptions of the major deities. Some are accompanied by drawings based upon ancient codices. Other members of the Aztec pantheon are listed in a table which provides the name of the god and its translation, the god's character, the god's human clients, distinctive attributes, and miscellaneous details. Also contains a shorter section on Mayan deities with a similar table.

Recinos, Adrian, Delia Goetz, and Sylvanus G. Morley, trans. *Popol Vuh*. Norman: University of Oklahoma Press, 1950.
This first English translation of the entire *Popol Vuh*, the sacred book of the ancient Maya, is based upon the Spanish translation of Adrian Recinos. This account of cosmogony and historical legends was first recorded in Mayan in the sixteenth century. The narrative includes the migration of peoples and the deeds of gods and ancient heroes, especially the great Quetzalcóatl. It explains how the kingdom of the Maya grew and flourished and concludes with genealogical lists of Mayan kings and lords. The introduction contains background about the chronicles of the Maya, the manuscript, its author, translations of *Popol Vuh*, and a summary of the text. Map, genealogical chart, and three illustrations from the original manuscript. Footnotes, bibliography, and index.

Sahagún, Fray Bernardino de. *Florentine Codex*. Translated by Arthur J. O. Anderson and Charles E. Dibble. 13 vols. 2d ed. Sante Fe, N.M.: School of American Research and the University of Utah, 1970-1982.
The Florentine Codex is an A.D. 1578-1579 manuscript of Sahagún's *Historia general de las cosas de Nueva España*. The original Nahuatl text of Sahagún with a parallel English translation is here published as *General History of the Things of New Spain*. Sahagún went to Mexico in 1529 as a Spanish missionary. He soon learned the Aztec language. His work is a primary resource for information about Mexico before the Spanish conquest. The *General History* contains volumes on many aspects of Aztec life, including rituals, soothsayers, omens, rhetoric, philosophy, the calendar, rulers, merchants, flora and fauna, and the Cortés conquest. For mythological matters see especially Volume 1, with twenty-two chapters on individual deities, and Volume 3, with myths about the origin of the gods in general and Quetzalcóatl in particular. Each volume contains black-and-white illustrations of the original manuscript drawings. Volume 1 contains a bibliography and Sahagún's original Spanish prologues and interpolations, with parallel

English translation by Dibble. Also contains introductory essays by Anderson and Dibble on Sahagún's career, the *Historia*, and the watermarks of the Florentine Codex. Indexes for all thirteen volumes, arranged by subject matter, places, and persons or deities, appear in Volume 1. Footnotes in all thirteen volumes.

Saunders, Nicholas J. "Mesoamerica." In *World Mythology*, edited by Roy Willis. New York: Henry Holt, 1993.

This overview of Mesoamerican mythologies includes a section on Mayan gods and beliefs and sections on early Aztec deities such as the "Were-jaguar," Aztec myths of creation and cataclysm, the Aztec calendar, and the Aztec gods Tezcatlipoca, Quetzalcóatl, Huitzilopochtli, and Tlaloc. Subsidiary notes on the Aztec fire god Huehuetéotl, the fifth sun of the Aztec present age, the wind god Ehecatl, the founding of Tenochtitlán on the site of modern Mexico City, human sacrifice, the Mayan calendar, and the Mayan myth of the Hero twins. Twenty-five illustrations, mostly in color, of Mesoamerican artifacts and sites. Map, time chart, pronunciation guide, and calendar chart.

Séjourné, Laurette. *Burning Water*. New York: Vanguard Press, 1956.

A study of the religious thought and mythic symbols of ancient Mexico. Part 1 starts with the conquest of Mexico by Hernán Cortés and deals especially with the nature of Aztec society, its development, and its fall. Also discusses human sacrifice, historical sources, the Toltec civilization, and especially Quetzalcóatl. Part 2 deals with magic and the religious meaning of the Quetzalcóatl myth. Part 3 discusses the symbolic meaning of Nahuatl words such as "Tollan" (Tula) and "Teotihuacán," the great mythic metropolis, and of images such as Nahuatl signs for solar heat, fire, and water. Detailed examination of specific deities and their symbols in Part 4. Notes at the end of some chapters. Twenty-two photographs of sites and artifacts. The eighty-two drawings by Abel Mendoza are mostly based upon ancient manuscript illuminations. Index.

Simoni, M. "Central America: Gods of Sacrifice." In *Larousse World Mythology*, edited by Pierre Grimal. Translated by Patricia Beardsworth. New York: G. P. Putnam's Sons, 1963.

A general survey of the two major mythologies of Central America, the Aztec and the Maya. Describes the Aztec creation myths, the divine calendar, and important deities, especially Nanahuatzin and Quetzalcóatl. Also contains a discussion of various Aztec religious concepts, such as nahualism, the magical ability to change into animals. The section on Mayan mythology contains a summary of the *Popol Vuh*, the "Book of Advice," and its serial account of creation, the classification of the world by the gods, the origin of humankind, and the legend of the Hero twins Hunahpu and Ixbalanque. Thirty-nine illustrations of sites and artifacts, three in color.

Skinner, Charles M. *Myths and Legends Beyond Our Borders*. Philadelphia: J. B. Lippincott, 1988.
The second half of this book contains thirty-nine tales from Mexico. Some tell of the arrival of Europeans and others deal with later historical legends. Includes tales representing traditional beliefs of the Aztec and Maya, as well as Christian miracle stories. No sources are provided for the tales. Four illustrations.

Soustelle, Jacques. "The World, Man and Time." In *Daily Life of the Aztecs*, by Jacques Soustelle. Translated by Patick O'Brian. New York: Macmillan, 1968.
This chapter in a general overview of life in sixteenth-century Mexico before the Spanish conquest describes the world view of the Aztec. Summarizes Aztec cosmogony, especially the myth of the four suns. Also considers various Aztec deities and religious beliefs about life, death, and rebirth. Thirty-nine illustrations of Aztec sites and artifacts. Endnotes, three maps, bibliography, and index.

Spence, Lewis. *The Gods of Mexico*. New York: Frederick A. Stokes, 1923.
Despite the title, this book deals primarily with the religion of the ancient Aztec, with only passing references the Maya and Quiché. General characteristics of this religion are described in an introductory chapter, with sections on sources, origins, and cults. Spence provides a detailed discussion of Aztec cosmogony and flood myths in Chapter 2 and ten chapters on various gods, their myths, iconography, and cults. Throughout these chapters significant myths are summarized as well as analyzed. A table for each deity lists basic information such as areas of worship, names, relationships with other deities, calendar places, compass directions, symbols, and festivals. Appendix on the Aztec solar calendar and the *Tonalalmatl*, a book of astrology. Occasional footnotes. Seventy-two illustrations, especially drawings based upon ancient manuscripts. A critical bibliography of Mexican religion, arranged chronologically. Pronunciation guide, glossary, and index.

Taggart, James K. *Nahuat Myth and Social Structure*. Austin: University of Texas Press, 1983.

An ethnographic study of two groups of Aztec-speaking Sierra Nahua in Mexico and a comparison of their myths. Shows how each group adapts its myths to its own social structures. Aetiologies, especially about the origin of corn, and tales of the supernatural appear alongside encounters with the devil, Christian stories, and folktales about lazy husbands and jealousy. Translations of thirty tales are included in the main body of the book. Translations of an additional twenty-eight narratives are provided in an appendix. A second appendix contains biographical profiles of the fifteen Nahua who told the stories. Endnotes and index.

Taube, Karl. *Aztec and Maya Myths.* Austin: University of Texas Press, 1993.

This general survey is part of The Legendary Past Series. Using recently deciphered Mayan glyphs and reinterpreted sixteenth-century colonial manuscripts, Taube retells the major myths of the Aztec and the Maya. The chapter on the Aztec includes an overview of the major deities and sections on creation of the universe, the origins of humans and of corn, and the mythology of the Aztec state. The chapter on the Maya offers a summary of the creation myth known as *Popol Vuh* and an explanation of the place of this myth in classic Mayan religion; it also deals with the mythology of the Maya in Yucatan, especially their creation and flood myths and their calendar. In an introductory chapter, Taube offers some background on Mesoamerican history and religion. Also contains a short chapter on sources and scholarship. Accompanied by many illustrations of Mesoamerican art and drawings from ancient manuscripts. Map, bibliography, and index.

Tedlock, Dennis, trans. *Popol Vuh: The Definitive Edition of the Mayan Book of the Dawn of Life and the Glories of Gods and Kings.* New York: Simon & Schuster, 1985.

This major Mayan epic begins with the creation of the world, tells of the first humans and their dealings with the gods, and ends with the deeds of great Mayan lords in Guatemala. Originally written in Mayan glyphs, the narrative is preserved in a sixteenth-century Quiché adaptation in the Latin alphabet. Tedlock's translation is based upon consultation with modern Quiché priests and is accompanied by photographs of Guatemalan sites and drawings based upon ancient paintings. In an introductory essay, Tedlock provides some background to this text and its translation as well as a detailed summary of the narrative. Pronunciation guide, detailed explanatory endnotes, maps, glossary, and bibliography.

Thompson, John Eric. "Maya Religion." In *The Rise and Fall of Maya Civilization*, by John Eric Thompson. 2d ed. Norman: University of Oklahoma Press, 1966.
In this chapter of a historical study of Mayan society, an archaeologist and scholar offers an overview of various religious beliefs. Contains sections on cosmology, the divine pantheon, corn, creation myths, sacrifices and other religious ceremonies, priesthood, dance, and the individual. Occasional paraphrase of Mayan myths.

Toor, Frances. *A Treasury of Mexican Folkways*. New York: Crown Publishers, 1947.
Part 4 of this comprehensive picture of traditional Mexican life contains more than forty myths and tales, including both Aztec and Mayan creation myths, Tzeltal stories about the underworld, a Huichol deluge legend, Yaqui tales of origin and animal legends, Zoque serpent tales, and legends about Pancho Villa and Tepoztecatl. The rest of the book is devoted to a description of Mexican work and worship, social customs, and songs. One hundred drawings and ten color plates by Carlos Merida plus 170 photographs illustrating various aspects of Mexican life. Endnotes, bibliography, glossary, and index.

Vaillant, George C. "Religion." In *The Aztecs of Mexico*, by George C. Vaillant. New York: Penguin, 1961.
This overview of Aztec religion includes a short survey of the Aztec view of the universe and the role of Aztec gods in nature and in human life. Describes the ages of the world, the geography of the universe, including the underworld, and features of the chief gods and goddesses. Further information about the deities is provided in a detailed table illustrating principal members of the Aztec pantheon, their character and spheres of worship, and their place in the Aztec calendar and day. Endnotes.

South American Myths

Basso, Ellen B. *A Musical View of the Universe: Kalapalo Myth and Ritual Performance*. Philadelphia: University of Pennsylvania Press, 1985.
An ethnographic collection and analysis of myths told by the Kalapalo, a small community of Carib-speaking people in central Brazil. Translated versions of the myths are integrated into an anthropological study of performative contexts, structure, and meanings of these myths. These narratives are about death, relationships with Europeans, de-

monic transformations, and fantasies of erotic aggression. Original
Carib versions, accompanied by English translation, are included in an
appendix. Another appendix deals with the transcription and translation of these songs. Eighteen photographs and nine tables. Endnotes,
bibliography, index of myths, and general index.

Baumann, H. "The Sons of the Sun." In *Gold and Gods of Peru*, by H.
Baumann. Translated by Stella Humphries. New York: Pantheon
Books, 1963.
In this chapter of a study of the ancient civilization of the Inca, the
author uses seventeenth-century sources to retell the foundation legends of the Quechua people, who established the Inca empire. An
account of the lives and conquests of the eleven sons of the sun who
ruled over the Inca between A.D. 1200 and 1500. Several illustrations
from early sources. Originally published in German. Glossary, chronological chart, and map.

Bierhorst, John. *The Mythology of South America*. New York: William
Morrow, 1988.
The myths of native South Americans are divided into seven geographic regions in this general survey. In the introduction the author
discusses the distinguishing features of South American myths and
outlines the history of collections of these myths. Creation, tricksters,
and the battle between the sexes are some of the themes represented in
this collection. In addition to occasional direct quotation from original
sources, the stories are generally paraphrased and analyzed by the
author. Twenty-one illustrations of drawings and artifacts related to the
myths. Eight maps, pronunciation guide, note on sources, and index.

Brett, William Henry. *Legends and Myths of the Aboriginal Indians of
British Guiana*. London: Willaim Wells Gardner, 1880.
A Christian missionary records verse translations of the legends of the
Arawaks, Warrau, Carib, and Acawoios, four peoples of what is now
Guyana. Myths about the gods, the origin of living things, individual
ethnic groups, and Europeans are accompanied by flood tales, stories
about the afterlife, animal fables, sorcerers' legends, and historical and
war tales. Brief ethnographic information on each people. Occasional
explanatory footnotes. Eleven illustrations.

Brundage, Burr Cartwright. *Empire of the Inca*. Norman: University of
Oklahoma Press, 1963.

A historical analysis of the myths and legends of the Inca from their beginnings as simple, nomadic, light-skinned agriculturalists through the glorious days of empire prior to the Spanish arrival. Of particular note is an examination of foundation legends about their capital at Cuzco and various Peruvian creation myths. Five maps, twelve photographs, chronology, genealogical chart, notes on sources, and index.

Cobo, Bernabe. *History of the Inca Empire*, translated and edited by Roland Hamilton. Austin: University of Texas Press, 1991.
A translation of that part of Cobo's seventeeth-century *Historia del nuevo mundo* (history of the new world) which deals with the history and culture of the ancient kingdom of Peru. Cobo's book remains a primary source for information about the pre-Columbian civilizations of the Americas. Combines mythic tales about the origin of the Inca with semi-historical accounts of their rulers. Three maps, endnotes, glossary of Spanish loan words from American languages, bibliography, and index.

De Civrieux, Marc. *Watunna: An Orinoco Creation Cycle*. Edited and translated by David M. Guss. San Francisco: North Point Press, 1980.
This collection of stories about heroic deeds reflects the religious and social beliefs of the Makiritare, who live on the upper Orinoco River in Venezuela. Gathered over a twenty-year period by De Civrieux, the tales were translated and arranged in a coherent form by Guss. In these tales a Stone Age people recollect their oral history. Also includes sacred songs about the Makiritare's tribal law, rituals, and heavenly ancestors. Ethnographic history is provided in an introductory essay. Mythological map of the Makiritare on a flyleaf, eight black-and-white photographs, and glossary.

Flornoy, Bertrand. "The Children of the Sun." In *The World of the Inca*, by Bertrand Flornoy. New York: Doubleday, 1958.
In this chapter in the story of the Inca and their conquest by Spain, Flornoy describes several Inca gods and Inca tales of origin. Kon Tiki is one name for Viracocha, the Peruvian conception of god, whose image is carved on the Gate of the sun at Tiahuanaco. Shows how Viracocha is inseparably connected with legends of the earliest Inca ancestors and their first king, Manco Capac. Includes map, an illustration of Viracocha on the Gate of the sun, and drawings of the earliest Inca by a Peruvian named Huaman Poma.

_____. *Inca Adventure*. Translated by Winifred Bradford. London: George Allen & Unwin, 1956.

Part 1 recounts the expeditions of Francisco Pizarro in Peru and his conquest of the Inca. Part 2 deals with the ancient, mythohistorical past of the Inca as recalled in ancient documents. Retells the Inca story of creation, the history of migrations in Peru, and the founding of the Inca empire. Describes the chief god Viracocha and legends connected with the kings of the Inca. Ten plates with photographs of Inca sites and illustrations of early book engravings. Forty-six figures, including maps and drawings based on early manuscript illuminations. List of Inca kings, chronological chart, bibliography, and index.

Goeje, C. H. de. *Philosophy, Initiation and Myths of the Indians of Guiana and Adjacent Countries.* Vol. 44 in *Internationales Archiv für Ethnographie.* Leiden: E. J. Brill, 1943.
A scholarly examination of the religious beliefs and world view of various peoples of Guyana and the Antilles. Examines philosophy and beliefs in spirits and in the afterlife in Part 1. Specific deities and spirits, including Amana, the Virgin-Mother and creator, Tamusi and Yolokantamulu, her twin sons and husbands, and various water and animal spirits, are considered in Part 2. In Part 3 are descriptions of rituals, initiation rites, and the training of medicine men. Part 4 deals with myths and fairy tales. A short discussion of the general character of these myths is followed by summaries of a wide variety of tales, including marvelous voyages, flood stories, myths about the gods, and aetiologies. Bibliography and index.

Kaplan, Joanna O., and M. R. Kaplan. "Tropical South America." In *Mythology: An Illustrated Encyclopaedia*, edited by Richard Cavendish. New York: Rizzoli International, 1980. Also published as *An Illustrated Encyclopedia of Mythology.* New York: Crescent Books, 1984.
This short overview of the mythologies of the the peoples of Brazil and the north coast of South America includes summaries and analyses of a myth about the founding of agriculture by Paraparawa, the culture hero of the Trio of Surinam and Brazil, an aetiology of fire told by the Kayapo-Gorotire of central Brazil, a jaguar legend of the Mundurucu of northern Brazil, a myth about the origin of menstruation from the Piaroa of Venezuela, a comparison of pre-mythic and post-mythic Piaroa tales about the culture hero Wahari, and a story about the world ruled by women told by the Tupi of Brazil. Particular interest in the portrayal of women, cultivation, and society in these myths. Map and illustrations of artwork related to the myths.

La Barre, Weston. "The Aymara: History and World View." In *The Anthropologist Looks at Myth*, edited by Melville Jacobs and John Greenway. Austin: University of Texas Press, 1966.
A collection of fourteen folktales collected among the Aymara on the shore of Lake Titicaca in Bolivia. These eight animal fables and six folk songs are supplemented by short summaries of four other folktales recorded on the opposite shore of the lake. Includes an ethnographic sketch of the Aymara, an anthropological analysis of the tales, and a historical and geographical explanation for the pessimistic ethos portrayed in the folktales. Endnotes.

Lammel, Annamaria. "Historical Changes as Reflected in South American Indian Myths." *Acta Ethnographica* 30 (1981). Reprinted in *The Flood Myth*, edited by Alan Dundes. Berkeley: University of California Press, 1988.
Contrasts seven traditional South American versions of the flood with one created after the Spanish Conquest in order to show how myths can adapt to historical changes. Each myth is summarized and analyzed. Bibliography.

Leicht, Hermann. "Religion and Myth." In *Pre-Inca Art and Culture*, by Hermann Leicht. Translated by Mervyn Savill. London: Macgibbon & Kee, 1960.
Part of a scholarly study of the culture of the pre-Inca people known as Chimu, who flourished along the Peruvian coast between A.D. 1100 and 1400. This chapter examines the origin of the Chimu religion, its belief in totems, moon worship, and its association with dogs. Summaries of several creation and aetiological myths and descriptions of various deities and religious ceremonies. Thirty-three figures of site plans and drawings in the text and forty-eight plates with photographic illustrations of sites and artifacts. Endnotes and bibliography.

Lévi-Strauss, Claude. *The Raw and the Cooked*. Translated by John Weightman and Doreen Weightman. New York: Harper & Row, 1975.
In this seminal study in the structural approach to mythology by a major French anthropologist, "The Macaws and Their Nest," a myth of the Bororo of central Brazil, is the key to a cultural analysis based upon the author's anthropological fieldwork in South America. Variations of this myth from a wide geographic area are retold and interpreted. Suggests that contradictions among the different versions of this myth are based upon an attempt to resolve social, moral, and cultural conflicts via the structure of mythic language. Four photographs by the

author and eighteen figures, including a map and charts. Illustrated bestiary, table of symbols, bibliography, index of myths, and general index.

Lippert, Margaret H. *The Sea Serpent's Daughter*. Mahwah, N.J.: Troll Associates, 1993.
Retells for young children an aetiological legend from the Brazilian rain forest. In this tale the daughter of the Sea serpent receives the gift of darkness from her father. Following the narrative is some ethnographic information about the people of the Brazilian rain forest. Illustrated with color drawings by Felipe Davalos.

Métraux, Alfred. *Myths of the Toba and Pilagá Indians of the Gran Chaco*. Vol. 40 in *Memoirs of the American Folk-Lore Society*. Philadelphia: American Folk-Lore Society, 1946.
Myths collected by the author among peoples of the Argentine Chaco in 1933 and 1939. Arranged in the following thematic groups: star mythology and cosmogony, cataclysm myths, tales about supernatural beings, culture hero stories, myths of origin, tales about a trickster fox, animal stories, and tales about legendary characters. Many myths are followed by commentary. Some are recorded in several versions. Introductory materials on published sources for Chaco folklore, geographical location of the Toba and the Pilagá, ethnographical background to their folklore and its general characteristics, and a comparison of this folklore with that of neighboring ethnic groups. Bibliography.

_____. "South America: Gods of Sacrifice." In *Larousse World Mythology*, edited by Pierre Grimal. Translated by Patricia Beardsworth. New York: G. P. Putnam's Sons, 1963.
A general overview of the mythologies of the native South American peoples, from Guyana to Tierra del Fuego. Considers characteristics of various nature spirits and deities and several accounts of the creation of the world, creators, and culture heroes. Includes sections on the origins of humankind, cultivated plants, fire and death, astral myths, and accounts of the destruction of the world, especially by fire and flood. Fifteen illustrations of sites and artifacts.

Osborne, Harold. *South American Mythology*. 2d ed. New York: Peter Bedrick Books, 1986. Also in *Mythology of the Americas*, by Cottie Burland, Irene Nicholson and Harold Osborne. London: Hamlyn Publishing Group, 1970.

This general survey of the mythologies of native South Americans is lavishly illustrated with photographs of sites, artifacts, and drawings related to these myths. The introductory chapter offers a cultural and historical overview of the peoples of South America and a guide to the sources and types of their myths. The four central chapters are each devoted to a different group of myths: those of the Inca, the coastal peoples of Peru, the Collao of Bolivia, and the marginal, forest, and southern Andean peoples. In the last chapter the author discusses some riddles of South American myth, including the jaguar cults of Bolivia, the myth of Amazon women, and the story of El Dorado, the city of gold. Bibliography and index.

Palacios, Argentina. *The Llama's Secret*. Mahwah, N.J.: Troll Associates, 1993.
A Peruvian legend about a great flood retold for children. A heroic llama saves humans and animals from the ravages of Mamacocha, the rising sea. With color illustrations by Charles Reasoner.

Roe, Peter G. *The Cosmic Zygote: Cosmology in the Amazon Basin*. New Brunswick, N.J.: Rutgers University Press, 1982.
Sixteen myths recorded among the Shipibo, a Panoan-speaking people of the Amazon basin in Peru, are paraphrased in translation and analyzed in a detailed ethnographic and structuralist context. Mostly tales of metamorphosis and aetiology about humans and a variety of animals such as the jaguar and the anaconda. Argues that the myths of the South American tropical forest build a symbolic cosmology around these animal characters and their interaction with human beings. Includes extensive background about the Shipibo, their environmental setting, and a reconstruction of their world view. Twenty-eight figures, including maps, and schematic charts. Three tables of linguistic and cultural groups. Photograph, endnotes, references, and index.

Sallnow, M. J. "The Incas." *In Mythology: An Illustrated Encyclopaedia*, edited by Richard Cavendish. New York: Rizzoli International, 1980. Also published as *An Illustrated Encyclopedia of Mythology*. New York: Crescent Books, 1984.
This overview of the mythology of the ancient Inca contains summaries and analyses of the Inca creation myth, the journeys of the mysterious white culture hero Viracocha, and the founding of the site of Cuzco. Also contains sections on fifteenth-century revisions to earlier myths and on contemporary Andean mythology. Map, chrono-

logical table, glossary of principal deities, and illustrations of artwork and sites related to the myths.

Saunders, Nicholas J. "South America." In *World Mythology*, edited by Roy Willis. New York: Henry Holt, 1993.

This general survey of the beliefs and myths of South American peoples includes sections on ancient religions, origin myths of the ancient Andean societies, the pantheon of Inca deities, Inca beliefs about the sky, the spirit worlds of the Amazon peoples, and origin myths of the Amazon rain forest people. Supplemented by subsidiary sections on the Inca origin myth, El Dorado, the Inca creator god Viracocha, the mythological sky in modern Peru, shamans, and the origin myth of the Yanomami of Venezuela. Fourteen illustrations of artifacts, sites, and people of the region. Map and time chart.

Troughton, Joanna. *How Night Came*. New York: Peter Bedrick Books, 1986.

Retells for young children a folktale of the Tupi of the Amazon region of Brazil. Explains the origin of night, the cycle of night and day, and creation of the animal world as the result of the illness of the daughter of Great Snake. The girl asks her father to free the night from bondage. During the first unending night animals are born from sticks, leaves, and stones. The girl forms birds of morning and evening in order to establish an alternation between daylight and nighttime. Illustrated by the author.

_____. *How the Birds Changed Their Feathers*. 2d ed. New York: Peter Bedrick Books, 1986.

Retells for children an aetiological myth shared by the Arawak of Guyana and other South American peoples. Set in a primeval period when animals talked and lived together in peace with humans, the myth explains how a young boy's cruelty resulted in the brightly colored feathers of birds and how they came to be hunted by humans. Illustrated by the author.

Urton, Gary. *The History of a Myth*. Austin: University of Texas Press, 1990.

Examines the foundation legend of the Inca, whose ancestors are said to have emerged from a cave at Pacariqtambo, or "Inn of Dawn." From this cave, the ancestors travel north and found Cuzco, the capital city of the Inca. Explains how the myth came to be centered on the site of Pacariqtambo and considers the extent to which a historical and ethnographic study of the region around Pacariqtambo provides further meaning for the myth. Argues that the myth of the ancestors is especially concerned with defining geographic boundaries and the social groups who live within these boundaries. A principal source for this historical legend is the sixteenth-century Callapiña Document, which is transcribed, in Spanish only, in an appendix. Ten photographic plates, five maps, five figures (especially genealogical), and seven analytic tables. Endnotes, bibliography, and index.

Villas Boas, Claudio, and Orlando Villas Boas. *Xingu, the Indians, Their Myths*, edited by Kenneth S. Brecher. Translated by Susana Hertelendy Rudge. New York: Farrar, Straus and Giroux, 1970.
This book is based upon the journals of the brothers Villas Boas, who visited the Xingu of the Amazon basin of Brazil in 1946. Part 1 consists of an ethnographic study of the people, their early history, extinct ethnic groups, archaeological past, and mythical history. In Part 2 are translations of thirty-one Xingu myths, including tales about the first human, stories about the dead and the supernatural, culture myths about fire and the bow, aetiologies, animal tales, and a legend about a cataclysmic flood. Illustrated with drawings by a Xingu named Wacupiá. Two maps and glossary.

Weiss, Gerald. *Campa Cosmology*. New York: American Museum of Natural History, 1975.
An anthropological study of the cosmogony of the Campas of eastern Peru. Includes extensive original-language texts collected in the field between 1961 and 1964 and accompanied by interlinear English translation, some with musical transcription. The narratives describe the organization of the universe; the creation of the earth, the sky, the sun, and the moon; the origin of the Campas and the coming of the Europeans; and the place of humankind in the cosmos. These texts are incorporated into the author's explanation and interpretation of the Campas world view. Includes ethnographic background on the Campas in an introductory chapter. Appendices include tables listing Campas vocabulary dealing with this world view and translated versions of other published accounts of Campas cosmology. Bibliography.

Wilbert, Johannes, ed. *Folk Literature of the Gê Indians*. Vol. 4 in *The Folk Literature of South American Indians*. Los Angeles: University of California Press, 1978.
Brings together in English translation 177 tales of the Gê-speaking Cayapo and Timbira of central Brazil originally published between 1914 and 1968 by eight different anthropologists. Information about

these authors and their narratives appears in a short front note. Longer tales are followed by brief plot summaries. All are followed by information about sources and informants and by a list of folktale motifs. Grouped thematically according to tales of origin, animals, and adventures. In an introductory essay, Wilbert provides a history of Gê folklore studies and describes the Gê art of storytelling and the world view featured in their narratives. In four indexes, folktale motifs are grouped by narrative distribution, topic, alphabetical order, and motif group. Map, glossary, and bibliography.

_____, ed. *Folk Literature of the Selknam Indians: Martin Gusinde's Collection of Selknam Narratives.* Vol. 2 in *The Folk Literature of South American Indians.* Los Angeles: University of California Press, 1975.

Martin Gusinde, a Catholic priest from Germany, conducted several anthropological expeditions among the peoples of Tierra del Fuego at the tip of South America between 1918 and 1924. His collection of traditional tales of the Selknam, Yamana, and Halakwulup were published in German between 1931 and 1974. Here Wilbert offers English translations of fifty-nine Selknam tales from Gusinde's collection. Each tale is followed by a brief plot summary, identification of Gusinde's Selknam informant, and a list of folktale motifs. The first group of tales deals with cosmogony and prominent deities and heroes of the primeval period. The second group includes animal myths, aetiologies of Selknam ceremonies, metamorphosis stories, and legends about a great flood and the Selknam habitat, ancestors, shamans, and spirits. In an introductory essay, Wilbert summarizes the work of Gusinde, describes his informants, and provides background for the narratives, their translation, and folktale motifs. In four indexes, folktale motifs are grouped by narrative distribution, topic, alphabetical order, and motif group. Occasional footnotes, two maps, two plates, glossary, and bibliography.

_____, ed. *Folk Literature of the Warao Indians.* Vol. 1 in *The Folk Literature of South American Indians.* Los Angeles: University of California Press, 1970.

An anthology of 209 traditional myths and legends of the Warao of Venezuela and Guyana. Narratives were selected from ethnographic collections by the author and by three other scholars. Where necessary, these narratives have been translated by Wilbert. Each tale is followed by a short plot summary, indication of source, and a list of folktale motifs. The narratives are arranged according to seven unexplained structural motifs. More useful is a second table of contents grouping the narratives thematically. Includes cosmogonies, aetiologies, animal tales, and stories about the supernatural, magic, social taboos, death, fortune, and fate. In an introductory essay, Wilbert offers a short ethnography of the Warao, provides some background to collections of their oral literature, and discusses some features of folktale motif in the narratives. In two indexes, folktale motifs are grouped by topic and in alphabetical order. Glossary and bibliography.

_____, ed. *Folk Literature of the Yamana Indians: Martin Gusinde's Collection of Selknam Narratives.* Vol. 3 in *The Folk Literature of South American Indians.* Los Angeles: University of California Press, 1977.

These sixty-six myth narratives were recorded by Gusinde among the Yamana of Tierra del Fuego at the southern tip of Chile between 1918 and 1924. Wilbert provides a literal English translation of Gusinde's German text, followed by a short plot summary, information about informants, and a list of folktale motifs. The narratives, arranged thematically, include cosmogonies about heaven and earth; the story of a great flood, tales about culture heroes and the invention of various items such as fire, arrowheads, and hunting; myths explaining the origin of animals and human customs; and tales about supernatural creatures such as ogres, spirits, and shamans. In an introductory essay, the editor describes Gusinde's work, his informants, their social context, field conditions, the style and function of the narratives, and aspects of the translation. In four indexes, folktale motifs are grouped by narrative distribution, topic, alphabetical order, and motif group. Occasional explanatory footnotes, two maps, two photographs, glossary, and bibliography.

_____, ed. *Yupa Folktales.* Los Angeles: University of California Press, 1974.

These translations of fifty-four folktales and fragments are based upon the author's fieldwork among the Yupa of western Venezuela in 1960. Part 1 contains a detailed ethnography of the Yupa, their environment, buildings, occupations, society, and life cycle. The narratives in Part 2 include a myth about the creation of humankind and about night and day; a flood tale; aetiologies of the rainbow, fire, corn, and other natural phenomena; a journey to the Land of the Dead; stories about human metamorphosis into animals; and tales of deception and the supernatural. Each is followed by a short summary and a list of folktale motifs. In the introduction, Wilbert explains the history of this collection. In four indexes, the folktale motifs are listed by motif groups, narrative, topic, and alphebetical order. Nineteen photographs of the Yupa and their world. Glossary and bibliography.

Wilbert, Johannes, and Karin Simoneau, eds. *FolkLiterature of the Bororo Indians*. Vol. 7 in *The Folk Literature of South American Indians*. Los Angeles: University of California Press, 1983.
These 111 traditional narratives of the Bororo of the Mato Grosso of central Brazil were originally published in Portuguese by four Salesian missionaries and appear here in English translation for the first time. Brief biographies and photographs of these authors appear at the beginning of the book. Also contains photographs of two Bororo informants. Seventy-three aetiological or cosmological tales about heavenly bodies, the earth, humankind, and various aspects of human and, especially, Bororo life. Thirty-eight tales about humans trans-formed into animals or about anthropomorphic animals such as Júko the trickster monkey and Agúgo the stupid jaguar. All are followed by information about informants and sources and by a list of folktale motifs. Contains summaries for the longer tales. Introductory essay by Wilbert on folkloristic research among the Bororo and characteristics of their narratives. In four indexes, folktale motifs are grouped by narrative, topic, alphabetical order, and motif group. Map, glossary, and bibliography.

_____, eds. *Folk Literature of the Chamacoco Indians*. Vol. 13 in *The Folk Literature of South American Indians*. Los Angeles: University of California Press, 1987.
Most of these 147 narratives of the Chamococo of the Paraguayan Gran Chaco are English translations of tales originally recorded c. 1970-1980 in Spanish by the Argentine anthropologist Edgardo Jorge Cordeu and published here for the first time. The rest were collected by five European anthropologists, working independently in the first half of the twentieth century. Biographical information about these scholars appears in a front note. The thematically arranged groups include cosmogonies and myths about a great flood, aetiologies, tales about deities called the Axnábsero, animal stories, encounters with monsters and supernatural creatures, and miscellaneous narratives. All are fol-lowed by information about informants and sources and by a list of folktale motifs. Also contains summaries for the longer tales. In an introductory essay on the history of Chamacoco folk literature studies, Wilbert summarizes the work of the contributing anthropologists and discusses some general characteristics of these myths. In four indexes,

folktale motifs are grouped by narrative, topic, alphabetical order, and motif group. Map, glossary, and bibliography.

_____, eds. *Folk Literature of the Chorote Indians.* Vol. 10 in *The Folk Literature of South American Indians.* Los Angeles: University of California Press, 1985.

All of these 150 narratives of the Chorote, a Gran Chaco people who live in Argentina, Paraguay, and Bolivia, are translated, mostly from Spanish, from the collections of one Swedish and four Argentine anthropologists. Biographical information about these scholars appears in a front note. Many of these tales explain natural phenomena, physical features of various animals, and the development of Chorote culture. Various creative acts are performed by the sun, moon, and a goddess of love. Several constellations are metamorphosed human children. Some narratives describe great cataclysms, especially floods. Others focus on talking animals, especially a fox and an armadillo. All are followed by information about informants and sources and by a list of folktale motifs. Also contains summaries for the longer tales. In an introductory essay, Wilbert provides a history of Chorote folklore studies and a description of the narratives. In four indexes, folktale motifs are grouped by narrative, topic, alphabetical order, and motif group. Map, glossary, and bibliography.

_____, eds. *Folk Literature of the Gê Indians.* Vol. 5 in *The Folk Literature of South American Indians.* Los Angeles: University of California Press, 1984.

Supplments Wilbert's earlier collection of oral literature of the Gê-speaking Cayapo and Timbira of central Brazil. Contains 183 narratives collected between 1957 and 1982 by eight different anthropologists. Of these, 124 are made available here in English for the first time. Information about these authors and their narratives appears in a short front note. Longer tales are followed by brief plot summaries. All are followed by information about sources and informants and by a list of folktale motifs. The narratives are grouped thematically, including tales of cosmology and origin, battles, and supernatural creatures such as monsters and ogres. In an introductory essay, Wilbert continues the history of Gê folklore studies which he began in Volume 1 and describes some features of these particular narratives. Editor's note on problems of translation and orthography. In four indexes, folktale motifs are grouped by narrative distribution, topic, alphabetical order, and motif group. Map, footnotes, glossary, and bibliography.

_____, eds. *Folk Literature of the Guajiro Indians*. Vols. 11-12 in *The Folk Literature of South American Indians*. Los Angeles: University of California Press, 1986.

These 233 texts represent all the narrative oral literature which has been collected among the Guajiro on the Guajira peninsula of Venezuela from the late nineteenth century through 1979, arranged in four thematic groups: origins, talking animals, various supernatural creatures, and miscellaneous. The myths of origin include several aetiologies and selections from a great epic about Maleiwa, the Guajiro culture hero, and his battle with jaguar. Information about informants, sources, and folktale motif content follows each tale. The longer narratives are also followed by plot summaries. In an introductory essay, Michel Perrin provides some ethnography of the Guajiro, discusses their storytelling method and some characteristics of the myths and legends, and surveys the history of collecting Guajiro oral literature. Each volume contains four indexes grouping folktale motifs by narrative distribution, topic, alphabetical order, and motif group. A short statistical summary for both sets of indexes is found at the end of Volume 2. Identical glossaries and bibliographies at the end of each volume.

_____, eds. *Folk Literature of the Mataco Indians*. Vol. 5 in *The Folk Literature of South American Indians*. Los Angeles: University of California Press, 1982.

These 207 traditional myths and legends were originally collected among the Mataco of the Gran Chaco region of Argentina and environs by Alfred Métraux and four other European or Argentine anthropologists of the early twentieth century. The editors provide literal English translations of these earlier texts plus short plot summaries, information about sources and informants, and a list of folktale motifs for each tale. The narratives are arranged thematically. Includes cosmogonies, star myths, tales of origin, tricksters, animals, and great cataclysms such as floods and fires. Introductory essay by Niels Fock on the ethnography of the Mataco and some characteristics of their folk literature. Front note on the four contributing authors and their narratives. Editor's note on the translation and organization of the book. In four indexes, folktale motifs are grouped by narrative, topic, alphabetical order, and motif group. Eight photographs, maps, glossary, and bibliography.

_____, eds. *Folk Literature of the Mocoví Indians*. Vol. 15 in *The Folk Literature of South American Indians*. Los Angeles: University of California Press, 1988.

These 222 narratives were collected among the Mocoví of the Gran Chaco region of Argentina by five anthropologists working independently. Information about these authors and their narratives appears in a short front note. Most of the tales were recorded since 1970, but a few date from the late eighteenth and the early twentieth centuries. All were originally written in Spanish and are here translated into English for the first time. The collection is arranged according to the following themes: cosmology, origins, especially about a fox and a jaguar, and extraordinary creatures and events. In four indexes, folktale motifs are grouped by narrative, topic, alphabetical order, and motif group. Map, glossary, and bibliography.

_____, eds. *Folk Literature of the Nivaklé Indians.* Vol. 14 in *The Folk Literature of South American Indians.* Los Angeles: University of California Press, 1987.
This collection of 243 tales told by the Nivaklé of the Gran Chaco of Paraguay is the result of independent fieldwork since 1950 by four Argentine anthropologists and one Paraguayan. Information about these authors and their narratives appears in a short front note. Originally written in Spanish, the tales are here translated into English. The tales are arranged in the following thematic groups: cosmology, cataclysms, aetiologies, extraordinary creatures and events, ogres, animals, and unclassified. All are followed by information about informants and sources and by a list of folktale motifs. Also contains summaries for the longer tales. In an introductory essay on the history of Nivaklé folkloristics, Wilbert surveys anthropological studies of this people and considers special features of these narratives. In four indexes, folktale motifs are grouped by narrative, topic, alphabetical order, and motif group. Map and bibliography.

_____, eds. *Folk Literature of the Nivaklé. Folk Literature of the Nivaklé. Folk Literature of the Tehuelche Indians.* Vol. 9 in *The Folk Literature of South American Indians.* Los Angeles: University of California Press, 1984.
These 110 narratives of the Tehuelche of Patagonia are based upon collections made in the field by ten anthropologists working independently. These texts were originally published in Italian, Spanish, or Gaelic between 1894 and 1977 and are made available here in English translation for the first time. Biographical information about these scholars in a front note. The narratives are arranged thematically: seven cosmological legends; forty-nine tales about the culture hero Elal; eighteen stories about the origin of humankind, the seasons, fire, and

a great flood; twenty-nine tales about plants and animals, especially a talking fox; and five stories about shamans and children-snatching ogres. Tales are followed by information about informants and sources and by a list of folktale motifs. Also contains summaries for longer tales. In the introduction, Wilbert offers a history of Tehuelche folklore study and a description of the narratives. In four indexes, folktale motifs are grouped by narrative, topic, alphabetical order, and motif group. Footnotes, map, glossary, and bibliography.

_____, eds. *Folk Literature of the Toba Indians*. Vol. 6 in *The Folk Literature of South American Indians*. Los Angeles: University of California Press, 1982.
This collection of 199 narratives serves as an introduction to the oral literature of the Toba of the Gran Chaco of lower South America. This material was gathered in the field between 1912 and 1980 by seven scholars working independently. Information about these authors and their narratives appears in a short front note. Some of these narratives are published here for the first time. Approximately half were origi-nally recorded in Spanish and are here translated into English. Preface and editor's note provide information on these sources and the trans-lation. Also contains biographical information about these scholars in a front note. Thematic arrangement of the tales. Thirteen cosmological myths, especially dealing with individual stars and constellations. Thirty tales about cataclysmic fires, floods, and long nights. Fifty aetiologies about the world, humankind, women, fire, various animals, and cultural features such as agriculture, weaving, and pottery. Forty-one tales about a trickster fox. Twenty-four other animal fables. Thirty legends about heroes. Seven stories about extraordinary creatures and places. Tales are followed by information about informants and sources and by a list of folktale motifs. Also contains summaries for longer tales. In the introduction, Wilbert offers a history of Toba folklore study, a description of the narratives, and an analysis of specific myth themes. In four indexes, folktale motifs are grouped by narrative, topic, alphabetical order, and motif group. Footnotes, map, glossary, and bibliography.

_____, eds. *Folk Literature of the Toba Indians*. Vol. 16 in *The Folk Literature of South American Indians*. Los Angeles: University of California Press, 1989.
This sequel to the collection of Toba narratives published in 1982 contains an additional 437 texts recorded in Spanish since 1965 by Argentine anthropologists and translated here into English for the first

time. Biographical information about these scholars in a front note. Preface and editor's note provide information on these sources and the arrangement of this book. Tales are arranged thematically: fifty-three cosmological and star myths; nineteen stories about floods, fires, and great darkness; ninety aetiologies about animals, plants, humankind, and fire plus thirty-three animal tales and 182 stories about a trickster fox; sixty-three legends about heroes, especially Hawk; forty-two stories about extraordinary creatures and events; and thirteen miscellaneous tales. Texts are followed by information about informants and sources and by a list of folktale motifs. In four indexes, folktale motifs are grouped by narrative, topic, alphabetical order, and motif group. Also contains summaries for longer tales. Footnotes, glossary, and bibliography.

North American Myths

Adamson, Thelma, ed. *Folk-Tales of the Coast Salish.* Vol. 27 in *Memoirs of the American Folk-Lore Society.* New York: American Folk-Lore Society, 1934.

The editor collected these 190 tales among the Coast Salish peoples of western Washington in 1926-1927. Told in English and arranged ethnically, these tales of the Upper Chehalis, Cowlitz, Humptulip, Wynoochee, Satsop, and three Puget Sound peoples—the Puyallup, White River, and Skykomish—include flood myths, tales of bungling hosts, epic contests, journeys to the Land of the Dead, aetiologies, and stories about heavenly bodies. Information about these peoples and the informants for the tales is offered in an introduction. Nearly all the tales deal with talking animals who lived in the distant past. In appendices are musical scores of songs and abstracts of the tales arranged thematically. Footnotes, map, and phonetic key.

Alexander, Hartley Burr. *North American Mythology.* Vol. 10 in *The Mythology of All Races*, edited by Louis H. Gray. Boston: Marshall Jones, 1916.

This volume, offering summaries of myths and religious beliefs of peoples from all over the continent from the Rio Grande to the Arctic, is valuable despite its early twentieth-century view of Native American mythology as primitive and unsystematized. In an introductory chapter the author charts the development of these beliefs and compares this development to that in the Old World. The remaining chapters are organized geographically, beginning with the peoples of the Arctic and sub-Arctic; moving to forest peoples, the gulf region, the Great Plains, the Rockies, and the Pueblo; and ending with the Pacific Coast. Particular attention is given to cosmogonies or world views. Thirteen plates, some in color, of masks, pictures, and other artifacts illustrating some of the myths. Notes and bibliography. Complete index in Volume 13.

Angus, Charlotte, et al. *We-gyet Wanders On: Legends of the Northwest.* Seattle: Hancock House, 1977.
These fifteen tales of We-gyet, the trickster figure of the 'KSAN people of British Columbia, were collected in 1971 by members of the community. The myths are told first in English translation and then in the original Gitksan language. A tale about the childhood of We-gyet is followed by a series of his adventures with various animals and with natural phenomena such as wind and fire. Illustrated with color drawings by 'KSAN artists. Short introduction on the character of We-gyet. Endnote on the 'KSAN and the history of this collection.

Ayre, Robert. *Sketco the Raven.* Toronto: Macmillan, 1961.
These fourteen Raven tales of the peoples of the Pacific Northwest are re-created here for young readers. The name "Sketco" is a free transliteration of "Tsesketco," Raven's name in the Tahltan tongue. Raven's ambiguous role as both trickster and culture hero is demonstrated in these tales, in which he steals the stars, the moon, and the sun, and brings fire to earth. Illustrated with black-and-white drawings by Philip Surrey. In a brief author's note, Ayre describes the geographic range of the Raven tales.

Bancroft-Hunt, Norman. "Myth and Cosmology." In *People of the Totem,* by Norman Bancroft-Hunt. New York: G. P. Putnam's Sons, 1979.
This chapter of a book on the native peoples of the Pacific Northwest offers a general overview of their traditional myths and legends. A few short excerpts from myths are provided as several story types are surveyed. Most common are tales explaining the origin of natural phenomena, especially stars; tales of transformation; trickster tales featuring Raven, Bluejay, and Mink; stories about journeys to the Land of the Dead; tales about a great flood; Nootkan Wolf myths; and stories about legendary heroes such as Stone-Ribs and Lazy Boy. Thirteen photographs of sites and artifacts, especially masks, by Werner Forman.

Barbeau, Charles Marius. *Haida Myths.* Ottawa: National Museum of Canada, 1953.

Eleven myth themes of the Haida of the Queen Charlotte Islands of British Columbia are here illustrated in text and in argillite carvings. The myths of Volcano Woman, Bear Mother, Yehl the Raven, Thunderbird, Tlenamaw the dragon, Nanasimgat the Haida Orpheus, Wasco the sea wolf, Kagwaai or Stone-Ribs, Su'san or Strong Man, and people swallowed by fish or carried away by an eagle are followed by a separate section on argillite poles with crests and mythic animals. For each myth theme Barbeau provides a summary and analysis of the myth and illustrations of the carvings. Several myth themes include related narratives in English translation. Some information about informants and location is provided in the text. Accompanied by 328 illustrations of carvings. Bibliography.

_____. *Huron and Wyandot Mythology*. Memoir 8 of the Canada Department of Mines Geological Survey. Ottawa: Government Printing Bureau, 1915.

Originally from Ontario, Canada, the Huron and Wyandot have lived in a variety of locations since the mid-seventeenth century. The core of this book consists of English translations of ninety-eight tales collected by the author among the few surviving Huron and Wyandot in Quebec, Ontario, and Oklahoma in 1911-1912. Myths and folktales are arranged separately according to theme: origin of the world and of natural phenomena, giants and dwarfs, power and social standing, charms derived from monsters, magic and folktales about tricksters and heroes, talking animals, and human adventures. In an appendix are an additional ninety tales gathered from earlier sources, some in French. These are arranged in the following categories: cosmogonic and aetiological myths, origin myths of supernatural power, folktales, and traditions and anecdotes. Abstracts of all these narratives follow the appendix. Preface includes a short history of this people and biographies of informants. Introductory essay on characteristics of these tales, information on their performance, and a summary of the Huron-Wyandot world view. List of phonetic signs, twenty-one photographs of sites and informants, and footnotes.

Barnouw, Victor. *Wisconsin Chippewa Myths and Tales*. Madison: University of Wisconsin Press, 1977.

Sixty tales collected between 1941 and 1944 among the Chippewa of the Great Lakes region are here offered in English translation. Before each tale the collectors, narrator, and interpreter are identified. Some tales are followed by explanatory and comparative comments by Barnouw. Contains several creation myths, tales about two sisters called Matchikwewis and Oshkikwe, stories about a cannibal giant called Windigo, animal tales, stories about spells and magical powers, and narratives considered to be of European or of mixed origin, plus an additional four narratives of personal recollection in a separate chapter. In a final chapter, Barnouw analyzes the myths socially and psychologically. He uses Freudian techniques of personality identification in a discussion of anal themes, courtship, and character ideals in the myths. He also outlines the Chippewa belief system based upon themes of metamorphosis, the reversibility of life and death, and a hierarchy of power. Biographical sketches of five Chippewa informants in an appendix. Also contains a discussion of Chippewa use of hallucinogenic drugs. Introductory essay on the Chippewa and on the methodology used in this book. Three maps, distribution table, bibliography, and index.

Barrett, Samuel Alfred. *Pomo Myths*. Vol. 15 in *Bulletin of the Public Museum of the City of Milwaukee*. Milwaukee: City of Milwaukee, 1933.

These free translations of 108 myths of the Pomo of California are based upon transcriptions made in the original language between 1903 and 1915. Most of these tales center on a complex figure called Coyote who creates the world, various animals, and humankind. Coyote is also the destroyer of the world by fire or flood, a great trickster, and even the thief of the sun. Many of these stories are aetiological in content. They are organized in the following groups: creation and the transformation of human beings, destruction, the sun, supernatural beings, tricksters, magic devices, deer and bear children, and miscellaneous. Preceding the tales is a detailed introduction to the people and their myths. At the end of the book are summaries and explanatory notes for each tale. Also contains notes on the use of numbers in Pomo mythology. Explanatory list of catchwords used in the myths. Essay comparing Pomo mythology to that told by other central Californian groups. Glossary, bibliography, and index.

Beckwith, Martha Warren. *Mandan-Hidatsa Myths and Ceremonies*. Vol. 32 in *Memoirs of the American Folk-Lore Society*. New York: American Folk-Lore Society, 1938. Reprint. New York: Kraus Reprint, 1969.

These forty-eight tales were collected between 1929 and 1932 among two Siouan peoples of the Missouri River region. Myths about the Creator and first human, floods, a sacred arrow, and, especially, the trickster Coyote. Also contains tales about the origins of various ceremonies. Information about sources at the head of every tale.

Introductory essay on the history of the Mandan and Hidatsa Sioux, their culture and storytelling traditions, and the author's recording techniques. More than fifteen line drawings by Bears Arm, one of the informants. Ten photographs of informants and their daily life. Explanatory and comparative footnotes. Bibliography and index.

Bell, Corydon. *John Rattling-Gourd of Big Cove.* New York: Macmillan, 1960.

Re-creates for young readers a storytelling session in which a North Carolina Cherokee named Tsan Gen-se-ti, also known as John Rattling-Gourd, tells twenty-four traditional tales of his people. A cosmogony is followed by aetiologies and tales about animals and the natural world. In a preliminary note, the author comments on Cherokee tales and the sources for this collection. Illustrated with line drawings by the author.

Benedict, Ruth. *Tales of Cochiti Indians.* Bulletin 98 of the Bureau of American Ethnology. Washington, D.C.: U.S. Government Printing Office, 1931. Reprint. Albuquerque: University of New Mexico Press, 1981.

Part 1 consists of about 150 myths and legends of the Cochiti of New Mexico in English translation. Some were collected in the field by the author through interpreters in 1924. Others are based upon original-language texts translated by Franz Boas. Tales are grouped thematically. Many of these aetiologies, stories of creation and the flood, legends about mischievous twins, Corncob Boy, and other heroes, novelistic tales about pueblo life, legends about the trickster Coyote, animal fables, stories based upon European folktales, and true stories are offered in several variants. Part 2 offers abstracts and analyses of these tales. In a short preface the author describes her informants. Four additional myths recorded by Boas appear in an appendix. The reprint contains an introductory essay by Alfonso Ortiz describing the Cochiti and Benedict's work with them. Anonymous informants are identified by number only in footnotes.

_____. *Zuñi Mythology.* 2 vols. New York: Columbia University Press, 1935.

A scholarly collection of the folklore of the Zuñi, the largest pueblo group of the southwestern United States. Tales are arranged according to the following themes: origin, adventure, courtship, deserted children, husbands and wives, witches, war and famine, animal tales, and miscellaneous. Variant versions are included for several tales. In detailed notes at the end of each volume, the author compares published versions and analyzes significant features of each tale. In a long introductory essay, Benedict discusses the relationship between Zuñi culture and the major themes of their folklore, and considers the literary problems of Zuñi narrators. Checklist of previously published Zuñi tales and index of incidents.

Bierhorst, John. *The Mythology of North America*. New York: William Morrow, 1985.
Arranges the myths of native North Americans into eleven regions based upon the distribution of themes and myth types such as creation myths, animal fables, hero tales, and trickster stories. Paraphrases and analyzes myths in their cultural and, especially, comparative contexts. Particular emphasis on variants and the way the myths are told. Twenty-one illustrations of the myths, both traditional and modern. Nine maps, bibliography, note on pronunciation, and index.

_____, ed. *The Naked Bear*. New York: William Morrow, 1987.
Sixteen myths and legends of the Iroquois are retold for older children. Included are supernatural tales about ghosts and living skeletons, talking animals such as turtle, and terrifying monster animals such as Naked Bear. Introductory essay about the Five Nations of Iroquois, their storytelling traditions, characteristics of their tales, and the history of collecting Iroquois stories. Illustrated with black-and-white drawings by Dirk Zimmer. Explanatory endnotes and bibliography.

Bloomfield, Leonard. *Menomini Texts*. Vol. 12 in *Publications of the American Ethnological Society*. New York: American Ethnological Society, 1928. Reprint. New York: AMS Press, 1974.
These 122 texts were collected among the Menomini of Wisconsin in 1920-1921. The first three parts contain a variety of oral materials, including stories about daily life, songs, prayers, and sermons. The materials in the rest of the collection are more mythological in content. Part 4 includes narratives of escape, death, talking animals, and sorcery. In Part 5 are sacred tales about a culture hero called Me'napus and the origin of stars. Other sacred stories are collected in Part 6. Four tales of European origin are told in Part 7. All tales are recorded in the original Menomini with English translation on facing pages. Some of these tales appear in more than one version. Bibliography and comments on the Menomini, their culture, and language in a preface.

Boas, Franz. *Bella Bella Tales*. Vol. 25 in *Memoirs of the American Folk-Lore Society*. New York: American Folk-Lore Society, 1932.

Ninety-nine tales collected by the author among the Bella Bella of the Pacific Northwest and told in English translation, arranged thematically. Includes creation myths, a large number of tales about a trickster and culture hero called Raven, various aetiologies, ancestor tales, stories about deserted children, novelistic tales, and stories about encounters with supernatural beings. Names of informants for each tale are indicated in parentheses. No explanatory notes. Preface on the Bella Bella and their tales, with some comparison to the mythologies of other Pacific Northwest peoples. Index.

_____. *Chinook Texts*. Washington, D.C.: U.S. Government Printing Office, 1894.

These myths and traditions of the Chinook of the Pacific Northwest were told to Boas in 1890-1891 by one of the last surviving Chinook. Original Chinook texts with literal interlinear English translations are followed by more literary English versions. Eighteen myths, especially about Coyote and panther. Also contains accounts of Chinook beliefs, customs, and historical tales. No explanatory notes. Short introductory essay on the Chinook people, on Boas' informant, Charles Cultee, and on the Chinook alphabet. Two portraits of Cultee.

_____, ed. *Folk-Tales of Salishan and Sahaptin Tribes*. Vol. 11 in *Memoirs of the American Folk-Lore Society*. New York: American Folk-Lore Society, 1917.

A collection of tales gathered especially by James A. Teit among various peoples of the Pacific Northwest, including the Thompson, Okanagon, Sanpoil, Pend d'Oreille, Coeur d'Alene, Sahaptin, and Nez Percé. In particular, these myths are about Coyote, a great trickster and culture hero. Sometimes Coyote is an animal and interacts with other creatures in the animal world. Other times he is a great chief. Coyote has the power to metamorphose himself and everything around him. Also contains myths about creation and a flood, other animal fables, aetiologies, migration tales, and adventure stories. Short introduction with bibliography. Footnotes.

_____. *Kathlamet Texts*. Bulletin 26 of the Bureau of American Ethnology. Washington, D.C.: U.S. Government Printing Office, 1901.

Thirty-three myths and tales collected among the Kathlamet people at Bay Center, Washington, in 1890-1891. Original Upper Chinook text with literal interlinear English translation is accompanied by more literary English translation on the same page. Part 1 contains myth narratives which deal mostly with talking animals living in a primeval

time. Plots about floods, famines, the supernatural, and encounters
with heavenly bodies. In Part 2 are tales about human beings and their
adventures and misadventures in love, war, and the supernatural.
Abstracts in an appendix. Two photographs.

_____. *Kutenai Tales*. Bulletin 59 of the Bureau of American
Ethnology. Washington, D.C.: U.S. Government Printing Office, 1918.
This collection contains tales of the Kutenai of the Pacific Northwest
collected independently by Boas and by Alexander F. Chamberlain
between 1891 and 1914. In a short preface, Boas describes the origin
of these texts. Kutenai texts are accompanied by interlinear English
translation and a separate, more literary translation. Arranged according to informant. Especially tales about the trickster Coyote and about
ancient chiefs of the Kutenai. Followed by abstracts and notes for the
tales. Note on Kutenai alphabet and Kutenai-English vocabulary.

_____. *Kwakiutl Culture as Reflected in Mythology*. Vol. 28 in
Memoirs of the American Folk-Lore Society. New York: American
Folk-Lore Society, 1935.
Uses myth texts from a variety of published sources, listed in a preface,
to summarize the culture of the Kwakiutl of the Pacific Northwest.
Sections on general culture dealing with material culture, personal and
family life, social organization, ethics, ceremonies, magic, and numbers are followed by more mythological material about the world,
supernatural beings, animals, and plants. Paraphrases plots and describes general characteristics of these myths. A concluding chapter
compares the mythologies of the Kwakiutl and Tsimshian.

_____. *Kwakiutl Tales*. Vol. 2 in *Columbia University Contribu-
tions to Anthropology*. New York: Columbia University Press, 1910.
Reprint. New York: AMS Press, 1969.
These fifty-two traditional Kwakiutl tales of adventure, the supernatural, and metamorphosis are presented with little editorial support for
the reader. Important characters include tribal ancestors such as Thunderbird, the son of the sun, and a chief called Potlatch-Giver. Several
were collected by the author in British Columbia between 1893 and
1900, some with the assistance of Kwakiutl speaker George Hunt. All
of these texts are presented in the original language with English
translation on a facing page. A few tales at the end of the volume were
not obtained in Kwakiutl and are presented in English only. Information about informants and recorders is provided in parentheses following each title. Some footnotes.

_____. *Kwakiutl Tales*. Vol. 26 in *Columbia University Contributions to Anthropology*. New Series. 2 vols. New York: Columbia University Press, 1935. Reprint. New York: AMS Press, 1969.

These sixty-five tales were collected by the author among the Kwakiutl of the Pacific Northwest in 1930-1931. Volume 1 consists of an English translation of these tales. The original Kwakiutl texts appear in Volume 2. Tales of creation, aetiology, a great flood, adventure, dwarfs, and talking animals. Some footnotes, especially comparing these narratives to other published Kwakiutl stories. Names of informants for each tale are indicated in parentheses. Preface on the Kwakiutl alphabet.

_____. *Tsimshian Texts*. Bulletin 27 of the Bureau of American Ethnology. Washington, D.C.: U.S. Government Printing Office, 1902. Reprint. St. Clair Shores, Mich.: Scholarly Press, 1977.

Eighteen texts, recorded among the Athabasca of British Columbia in 1894, are offered in the orginal Tsimshian with interlinear literal English translation together with a free English translation. The plots deal with the trickster Raven and other anthropomorphic animals and with hunting, witchcraft, and star spirits. In a supplement, an additional five tales are presented in English translation only. Plot abstracts for all the tales appear at the end of the volume. Short introduction on the origin and language of the texts. Pronunciation guide.

Bouteiller, M. "North America: Spirits of Good and Evil." In *Larousse World Mythology*, edited by Pierre Grimal. Translated by Patricia Beardsworth. New York: G. P. Putnam's Sons, 1963.

Deals with general features of the mythologies of native North Americans and suggests that some common denominators are an active body of protective or harmful spirits, a link between various worlds in the cosmos and mediation between life and death. Considers characteristics of aetiologies, flood myths, and various animal and human culture heroes, especially Coyote and Raven. Sixteen illustrations of artifacts, one in color.

Brinton, Daniel G. *The Lenâpé and Their Legends*. Philadelphia: D. G. Brinton, 1884. Reprint. St. Clair Shores, Mich.: Scholarly Press, 1972.

This ethnographic study of the Lenâpé of Delaware, Pennsylvania, and New Jersey includes discussions of their origin, history, language, and literature. The last two chapters are of the most interest to the study of mythology. Chapter 7 is an overview of Lenape myths about creation, culture, and national migrations. Chapter 8 deals with the *Walam Olum*, the text of an oral Lenape narrative recorded in the early nineteenth century by Constantine Samuel Rafinesque-Schmaltz. The *Walam Olum* describes the creation of the universe by the Great Manitou, a great flood caused by the Evil Manitou, a migration of the people, and a list of chiefs. Brinton summarizes the life of Rafinesque-Schmaltz and the authenticity of the text, which he accepts. A description and synopsis of the text are followed by the complete Lenape version accompanied by original pictograms and parallel English translation. Footnotes, endnotes, glossary, and index.

Bunzel, Ruth L. *Zuñi Origin Myths*. Annual Report 47 of the Bureau of American Ethnology. Washington, D.C.: U.S. Government Printing Office, 1929-30; reprint, 1932.
Two myths about the origin and early history of the Zuñi, a pueblo people of the western United States, obtained in the field from an unidentified informant. Both myths are published in Zuñi. The first includes a literal interlinear English translation and is followed by a more polished English version. For the second text, Zuñi and English versions appear on facing pages. Both myths are told in a ritual form usually accompanied by masked dancing in the Kachina cult. Short introductory essays precede each myth.

_____. *Zuñi Texts*. Vol. 15 in *Publications of the American Ethnological Society*. New York: G. E. Stechert, 1933. Reprint. New York: AMS Press, 1974.
Consists of original-language texts collected from eight Zuñi informants in 1926 and accompanied by literal English translation. Two types of texts are included: twenty-five ethnological texts on traditional Zuñi life and fifteen mythological tales about the distant past. Includes multiple versions of several tales. The myths deal especially with two brothers named Ahaiyute, the supernatural, and personified animals. This scholarly collection offers a list of informants and a short foreword on the origin of the texts and features of Zuñi phonology, but no reading aids or explanatory notes.

Burland, Cottie. *North American Indian Mythology*. In *Mythology of the Americas*, by Cottie Burland, Irene Nicholson, and Harold Osborne. London: Hamlyn Publishing Group, 1970. Published separately and revised by Marion Wood. New York: Peter Bedrick Books, 1985.
This introduction to the myths of Native North Americans is arranged geographically. Individual chapters on the Inuit of the Far North, the fishermen of the Pacific Northwest, the hunters of the Canadian North Woods, the farmers of the Great Lakes and Northeast, the buffalo

hunters of the Great Plains, the hunters of the Great Desert, the mesa dwellers of the Southwest U.S., and the farmers of the southeastern woodlands. Each chapter offers a description of the lifestyles of the peoples and summaries of their more important myths about the gods, creation, and tribal history. Nearly every page is accompanied by photographs and drawings illustrating the daily life, art, and myths of these Native Americans. Includes a map, a glossary of the chief gods and spirits of North America, a short bibliography, and an index.

Carpenter, Edmund. *Eskimo Realities*. New York: Holt, Rinehart and Winston, 1973.
While this broad study of Inuit culture in northern Canada focuses on the visual arts, it also contains scattered references to traditional myths and beliefs concerning the natural world and the place of humankind in the universe. Analyzes of the myth of Sedna, the tale of a woman abandoned to save the lives of her family. Sedna becomes mistress of the sea creatures so important to the Inuit. The blind-white snow world of the Inuit is visually reinforced by the use of limited areas of black print on large areas of white background. Map.

Caswell, Helen. *Shadows from the Singing House: Eskimo Folk Tales*. Rutland, Vt.: Charles E. Tuttle, 1973.
Eighteen tales of Alaskan Inupiat are retold for children with illustrations by Robert Mayokok. Includes myths about the deified spirit of the moon and about Sedna the sea goddess. Also contains the story of a great flood and several aetiologies. Preface on the Inupiat view of the year cycle and on Inuit tales.

Clark, Cora, and Texa Bowen Williams. *Pomo Indian Myths*. New York: Vantage Press, 1954.
Forty-three tales of the Pomo of the Pacific Coast of California and Oregon as told to the authors by five informants appear in Part 1. This collection includes narratives about the deeds and adventures of Old Man Coyote, the tricky creator deity of the Pomo, and of their hero, Nukuwee, as well as aetiologies about fire, sickness, geographic features, and the Pomo arrival in California. Introductory essays on Pomo religious beliefs, the nature of myth, bird totems, and the Pomo Coyote deity. Part 2 contains an explanation of the religious symbolism of these tales plus analyses and commentary about each of the tales.

Clark, Ella Elizabeth. *In the Beginning*. Billings: Montana Council for Indian Education, 1977.

Eight creation tales of the Chelan, Cree, Salish, Hopi, Assiniboine, Yakima, and Arapaho are retold for children. Illustrated with line drawings by Pat Robinson. These tales describe not only the creation of the world but also the creation of humankind and of individual races and the settlement of the people in their land. Short introductory comments by Clark precede each tale. Information about informants and published sources follows each tale.

_____. *Indian Legends from the Northern Rockies.* Norman: University of Oklahoma Press, 1966.
A collection of myths, legends, and personal narratives of the Nez Percé, Coeur d'Alene, Kutenai, Shoshoni, Arapaho, Sioux, and other groups from modern Idaho, Montana, and Wyoming. A variety of creation tales, legends about Coyote, and aetiological stories are arranged according to linguistic group. In Chapter 1 Clark offers some background on the traditional life of these peoples. In an introductory essay, the author explains the structure of the book and its sources. Endnotes on sources, pronunciation guide to Native American names, bibliography, and index.

_____. *Indian Legends of Canada.* Toronto: McClelland & Stewart, 1960.
Represented among these myths and legends are thirty-one peoples in nine major language families of Canada and the northern United States: Algonquin, Athabascan, Iroqouian, Kituahan, Salishan, Siouan, Skittagetan, Wakashan, and Inuit. These tales are presented in translation for the general reader and are organized around the following themes: primeval time, culture myths, nature myths and beast fables, aetiologies about landscape features, personal and historical narratives, and miscellaneous stories. Fewer tales about creator/tricksters have been included in favor of less commonly known tales. Some selections are not narrative but explanatory commentary excerpted from various printed sources. Each selection is preceded by a brief introduction. Also contains a general introductory essay on Native American stories and storytelling and on the organization of this collection. List of sources in an appendix. Bibliography.

_____. *Indian Legends of the Pacific Northwest.* Berkeley: University of California Press, 1958.
More than one hundred traditional tales told by Native Americans in Washington and Oregon are collected in this anthology. Many were obtained by personal interviews with the storytellers. Five groups,

organized mostly around natural and geographic phenomena, include mountain myths; tales of rivers, rocks, and waterfalls; myths of creation, the sky, and storms; and miscellaneous myths and legends. Each group of stories is introduced by brief background material on beliefs and customs related to the myths. Maps, source notes, bibliography, and a detailed glossary of place, ethnic, and personal names.

Coffin, Tristram P., ed. *Indian Tales of North America*. Philadelphia: American Folk-Lore Society, 1961.
A collection of forty-five tales from all over North America arranged under three headings: "The Way the World Is," "What Man Must Know and Learn," and "The Excitement of Living." Includes "emergence" tales about the origins of humankind, aetiological and charter myths about the social systems, animal fables, and adventure and trickster tales. The editor offers a general introduction and occasional introductions to individual tales in which the plots and themes are described. An appendix contains a chart with bibliographic, linguistic, and geographic information about the stories. Bibliography and index.

Coolidge, Mary Roberts. "Myths and Folktales." In *The Rain Makers*, by Mary Roberts Coolidge. New York: Houghton Mifflin, 1929. Reprint. New York: AMS Press, 1983.
This chapter in a major ethnographic study of the desert peoples of the Southwest U.S. combines some discussion and analysis with retellings of the Zuñi creation myth about Awonawilona, the supreme life-giver, and several stories in the Navajo creation cycle, including the origin of the Turquoise goddess Estsán-atlehi, the quest of her two sons for their father the sun, and their slaying of a monster. Footnotes.

Cooper, Guy. "North America." In *World Mythology*, edited by Roy Willis. New York: Henry Holt, 1993.
A sweeping overview of the mythology and religious beliefs of the native North American peoples, with sections on creation myths, the origins of humankind, divine and human culture heroes such as Coyote, Raven, and Gluskap, shamans, tricksters, Navajo ceremonial myths, mythology of the Great Plains, and animal myths. Supplemented by notes on the Lakota sun Dance, the Lakota deity known as Wakinyan or Thunderbird, the personal recollection of a Kwakiutl shaman, a Navajo legend about Coyote and a giant, the supreme Lakotan deity called Wakan Tanka or the Great Mystery, a Lakota aetiology about the sacred pipe, and a Navajo aetiology about game

animals. Nineteen illustrations of North American artifacts. Map and time chart.

Courlander, Harold. *The Fourth World of the Hopis*. New York: Crown Publishers, 1971.

A collection of myths, legends, and reminiscences gathered among the Hopi between 1968 and 1970. Begins with a cosmogony in which Tawa, the sun Spirit, creates four worlds, and ends with recollections about the arrival of the Europeans and the breakup of a Hopi village. Tales about Hopi migration, adventure, culture heroes, metamorphosis, and a journey to the underworld are followed by explanatory endnotes on each story. Appendix on narrators and informants. Introductory essay on the Hopi migrations. Decorative drawings by Enrico Arno. Map, glossary, and pronunciation guide.

_____. *People of the Short Blue Corn*. New York: Harcourt Brace Jovanovich, 1970.

Seventeen tales of the Hopi of the Southwest U.S. are retold by Courlander for older children and the general reader. This collection is based upon the author's own fieldwork in 1968-1969. Tales about Coyote and talking animals are accompanied by aetiologies, adventure stories, a journey to the Land of the Dead, jokes, and examples of great foolishness or wisdom. Short introduction about the Hopi and more detailed information about their oral literature and this collection in an endnote. Also contains explanatory endnotes for each tale. Pronunciation guide and glossary.

Curry, Jane Louise. *Down from the Lonely Mountain*. New York: Harcourt, Brace & World, 1965.

Twelve tales of the native peoples of California are retold here for children. No information about the specific sources for these tales is provided. All the stories deal with a primeval world of anthropomorphic animals, especially the trickster Coyote and Wus, a clever fox. Myths about the beginning of the world and of California are accompanied by aetiological tales about the theft of dawn and fire. Illustrated with black-and-white drawings by Enrico Arno.

Curtin, Jeremiah. *Creation Myths of Primitive America*. Boston: Little, Brown, 1898.

A well-known folklorist, agent of the Bureau of Ethnology of the Smithsonian Institution and English translator of Henryk Sienkiewicz's *Quo Vadis*, here retells twenty-two creation stories told by the Wintu and Yana of California. Each tale is preceded by a brief introduction and list of personages. In an introductory essay, Curtin analyzes the creation system developed in these tales and compares it to some European world views. Detailed endnotes and list of Native American place names.

_____. *Myths of the Modocs*. Boston: Little, Brown, 1912. Reprint. New York: Benjamin Blom, 1971.
These fifty-nine tales of the Modoc, a people who lived in the Pacific Northwest, were related to Curtin by a Modoc woman in the late nineteenth century. The collection begins with stories about Kumush, the Modoc creator, and includes adventure stories, aetiologies, and animal fables. In a short introduction, M. A. Curtin relates the sad history of the Modoc people. Endnotes.

_____, ed. *Seneca Indian Myths*. New York: E. P. Dutton, 1922.
Senior members of the Seneca people of northern New York State told these ninety traditional tales to Curtin. Included are adventure stories, tales about the natural and animal worlds, and lessons in human relations. The meanings of Senecan character names are explained at the beginning of each tale. Glossary.

Cushing, Frank Hamilton. *Outlines of Zuñi Creation Myths*. Report 13 of the Bureau of Ethnology. Washington, D.C.: U.S. Government Printing Office, 1891-1892; reprint, 1896. 2d reprint. New York: AMS Press, 1976.
An associate of the American naturalist John Wesley Powell, Cushing lived among the Zuñi between 1879 and 1881 and offers here a preliminary summary of their myths of creation and origin. The tales are arranged chronologically, beginning with the creation of the worlds and of human life and ending with the passing of the corn deity Paíyatuma. Myths about the generations of gods, aetiological tales about various customs, migration legends, and, especially, the story of corn. Detailed introductory essay about early Zuñi traits, their interaction with the Spanish, their pre-Spanish history, and the relationship between their myths and their sociological organization. Index.

_____. *Zuñi Folk Tales*. New York: G. P. Putnam's Sons, 1901. Reprint. New York: Knopf, 1931. 2d reprint. Tucson: University of Arizona Press, 1986.
This collection of thirty-three tales remains a basic resource for the folk literature of the Zuñi, a Pueblo people of western New Mexico. Included are several Coyote tales, aetiologies, and tales about the gods. The story about poor Turkey Girl is sometimes compared to the story

of Cinderella. In an essay introducing the original edition, John Wesley Powell discusses features of Zuñi religion. In the introductory essay for the 1931 reprint, Mary Austin comments upon Cushing's work and its importance.

Deloria, Ella C. *Dakota Texts*. Vol. 14 in *Publications of the American Ethnological Society*. New York: G. E. Stechert, 1932. Reprint. Vermillion: University of South Dakota, 1978.

Sixty-four tales collected among the Dakota are here translated by the author. The first thirty-nine tales deal with incredible events of the remote past. In some of these tales, mythological figures such as the divine Dakota spider trickster Iktoma (known among the Sioux as Iktomi or Unkotomi), the ogre Iya, and a malevolent creature called Double-face interact with humans. Other tales in this group describe incredible events which happen to humans without divine intervention. The remaining twenty-five stories deal with more historical events and legends of various geographic locations. Synopses of all the tales are included. In an introduction, Deloria describes the tales and their sources. In an essay introducing the reprint, Agnes Picotte and Paul N. Pavich offer a biography of Deloria and an evaluation of her work.

Deloria, Vine, Jr. *God Is Red*. New York: Grosset & Dunlap, 1973.

A Native American describes traditional beliefs regarding religion, time, space, creation, history, spatial problems, death, human personality, and the place of individuals in social groups. Scattered throughout the book are brief summaries of Native American myths. In particular, Deloria emphasizes differences between the world views of Christians and traditional Native Americans. Notes, appendices, and index.

Dixon, Roland B. *Maidu Myths*. Vol. 17 in *Bulletin of the American Museum of Natural History*. New York: American Museum of Natural History, 1902.

A short introduction to the Maidu of northeastern California, their social organization, and storytelling traditions is followed by English translations and abstracts of twenty-two myths. The collection begins with a creation myth and a quarrel between Coyote and the Earth-Namer and includes tales about fire, metamorphosed people, animals, and heavenly bodies. Footnotes, most indicating the location where the myth was recorded.

_____. "Some Coyote Stories from the Maidu Indians of California." *Journal of American Folklore* 13 (1900): 267-270. Reprinted in *Readings in American Folklore*, edited by Jan Harold Brunvand. New York: W. W. Norton, 1979.

These four legends about the troublesome trickster Coyote who interferes with acts of the creator deity Kodoyanpe were collected on the 1899 Huntington Expedition among the Maidu of the high Sierra of California. In these tales Coyote marries his own daughter and has encounters with grizzly bears, with fleas, and with a great fox. Footnotes. The reprint includes an introduction by Brunvand.

Dorsey, George A. *The Mythology of the Wichita*. Washington, D.C.: Carnegie Institution of Washington, 1904. Reprint. New York: AMS Press, 1974.

An ethnologist at the Field Museum in Chicago collected these sixty tales among the Wichita in Oklahoma between 1900 and 1903, with the support of the Carnegie Institution. In addition to a creation story and four tales about the present, Dorsey includes fifty-five tales of transformation, especially about the trickster Coyote, heavenly bodies such as the stars, and the animal world. Full translations of the myths are supplemented by abstracts in an appendix. The names of informants are indicated in footnotes. Introductory essay on the everyday life, customs, religious beliefs, and myths of the Wichita.

_____. *The Pawnee: Mythology*. 2 vols. Washington, D.C.: Carnegie Institution of Washington, 1906.

In Volume 1 are 148 eight tales of the Pawnee collected between 1903 and 1905 in Oklahoma and told in English translation. Arranged thematically are myths about heavenly beings, including creation tales and aetiologies, legends about a hero called Ready-to-Give, stories about the origin of medicine ceremonies, and tales of the trickster Coyote. Abstracts of these narratives appear in an appendix. In Volume 2 these Pawnee tales are compared with those of other Caddoan peoples in particular and with North American myth traditions in general. Also in Volume 2 are musical scores and lyrics for songs which appear in the myths. Introductory essay on the Pawnee and their tales in Volume 1.

_____. *Traditions of the Arikara*. Washington, D.C.: Carnegie Institution of Washington, 1904.

Eighty-two tales collected among the Arikara in North Dakota in 1903 are told in English translation with abstracts in an appendix. Two tales in which the earth is created by spiders or by Wolf and Lucky Man are accompanied by several stories about the creation of humankind and the cultivation of corn. Also contains myths about culture heroes such as Star-Boy, Sun-Boy, and Burnt-Hands, who free the world from oppressive monsters. Some tales explain the origin of various rites, while others relate Coyote trickster legends and tales of magic and of war.

_____. *Traditions of the Caddo*. Washington, D.C.: Carnegie Institution of Washington, 1905.
Seventy tales collected among the Caddo of western Oklahoma between 1903 and 1905 and told in English. Many of the tales center on the trickster and creator Coyote, who lived in a primeval time. Myths of creation, early migration, a great flood, encounters with horrible monsters, and cannibals are accompanied by stories about human metamorphosis, especially into heavenly bodies, and aetiological tales about death, medicine men, and various animals. Short introduction on the Caddo and the collection of these tales.

_____. *Traditions of the Skidi Pawnee*. New York: American Folk-Lore Society, 1904. Reprint. New York: Kraus Reprint, 1969.
These ninety tales were collected among the Pawnee of the Great Plains between 1899 and 1902 and are here presented in English translation. Six groups of narratives: cosmogony, boy heroes, medicine, animal tales, Coyote legends, stories about people marrying or becoming animals, and miscellaneous. Ethnographic introductory essay. Twenty-three photographs and drawings of the people and their everyday lives. Endnotes, bibliography, and index.

Dorsey, George A., and Alfred L. Kroeber. *Traditions of the Arapaho*. Publication 81 of the Field Columbian Museum. Chicago: Field Museum, 1903.
These 146 tales of the Arapaho of Oklahoma and Wyoming were collected independently by the authors. Myths about the origin of the people and various ceremonial lodges, legends about a great flood, encounters with animals and monsters, tales of metamorphosis, and stories about the Arapaho trickster and creator called Nih'ā^{n}çā^n or Spider, are recorded here in English translation. Several tales about sex and body functions are told only in Latin. The initial of the recorder follows every tale, but names of informants and comparative information follow the tales only occasionally. A collection of plot abstracts follow the tales. Explanatory footnotes.

Du Bois, Cora, and Dorothy Demetracopoulou. *Wintu Myths*. Vol. 28 in *University of California Publications in American Archaeology and Ethnology*. Berkeley: University of California Press, 1931.

These seventy-five myths were collected among the Wintu of central California in 1929 and are presented here in English translation. The main themes found in these tales are cosmology and cataclysmic disasters, the adventures of the trickster Coyote, death, and a dangerous supernatural female called Kukup'iwit. Names of informants are indicated in footnotes. Endnotes and bibliography.

Dutton, Bertha P. *Sun Father's Way: The Kiva Murals of Kuaua*. Albuquerque: University of New Mexico Press, 1963.

An examination of archaeological excavations at a Zuñi pueblo ruin at Coronado State Monument in New Mexico. Assesses the cultural evidence of these murals, including their mythological and religious symbolism. The mythological figures depicted in the murals include Grey Newekwe, who produces jimson weed to cause dreams, a talking bird called Paiyatuma or Between the Sky, and many other deities. In Part 1 Dutton offers historical background on early Spanish activity in the area, the modern archaeological history, and ethnographic information about the paintings. Part 2 contains a detailed analysis of the paintings. Accompanied by 111 photographs of entire murals or portions of them and photographs of the site and artifacts. Twenty-six drawings of petroglyphs by Agnes C. Sims, who also offers in an appendix an essay on rock carvings as a record of folk history. Bibliography, glossary, and index.

Edmonds, Margot, and Ella Elizabeth Clark. *Voices of the Winds: Native American Legends*. New York: Facts on File, 1989.

An anthology of 132 tales representing more than sixty native North American peoples and selected from a variety of previously published sources, especially scholarly journals. Organized in six geographic groupings beginning in the Pacific Northwest and moving to the Atlantic Coast. Each group includes creation tales, stories about tricksters such as Raven and Coyote, and aetiologies about plants, animals, geographic features, and human customs. Each group and tale is preceded by a brief introduction. Information about sources and occasional explanatory notes follow each tale. Short introductory essay on some characteristics of North American mythology. Illustrated with line drawings by Mollie Braun. Map, glossary, bibliography, and index.

Emerson, Ellen Russell. *Indian Myths or Legends: Traditions and Symbols of the Aborigines of America*. Boston: J. R. Osgood, 1884. Reprint. Minneapolis: Ross & Haines, 1965.

This controversial comparative study of North American legends, religious beliefs, and iconography retells many myths within the body of the text. Unfortunately no sources are indicated, and many tales are identified only as "Indian." Many themes are addressed, including the wind, birds, serpents, star worship, the sun, the origin of humankind, legends of the dead, transmigration or transformation, animals, and the deity Manabozho. Emerson's purpose is to show the intellectual capacity of Native Americans by comparing their beliefs with those of Egyptians, Persians, Assyrians, Chinese, Indians, and other peoples. Parallels among the beliefs of these peoples suggest to Emerson the primeval kinship of the human race. Illustrated throughout with line drawings. Bibliography and index.

Erdoes, Richard, and Alfonso Ortiz, eds. *American Indian Legends*. New York: Pantheon Books, 1984.

More than eighty North American peoples are represented in this sweeping collection of 166 tales gathered in the field or from previously published materials by a storyteller and artist and an anthropologist. Some of the previously published material recorded by nineteenth-century writers has been retold here in a more authentic style. Divided into the following ten thematic parts: human creation; world creation; celestial bodies; monsters; warfare; love; tricksters; animals; ghosts and spirits; and death, cataclysm, and the end of the world. Each tale is preceded by a short introductory overview and is followed by brief information about sources. In an introductory essay, the editors discuss the world vision, history, and oral traditions of the North American peoples and explain how these stories were selected. In an appendix, information about the history, name, and homeland of each people is collected alphabetically by the name of each people. Illustrated with black-and-white drawings by Erdoes. Bibliography and index of tales.

Feldman, Susan, ed. *The Storytelling Stone: Traditional Native American Myths and Tales*. New York: Dell, 1965.

A collection of fifty-two myths arranged in three thematic groups: creation myths, trickster tales, and stories of heroes and supernatural journeys. Selections are borrowed from a variety of anthropological and folklore publications and represent ethnic groups from all over the North American continent. In the introduction, the editor offers some general background to and explanation of these tales and compares some ways that they treat various themes. Bibliography.

Field, Edward. *Eskimo Songs and Stories*. New York: Delacorte Press, 1973.
A collection of poems based upon literal English versions of Inupiat tales collected in the field by Arctic explorer Knud Rasmussen and preserved in the Royal Danish Archives. These thirty-four poems deal with creation, the elements, animals, and human encounters with the physical and spiritual worlds. Accompanied by twenty drawings by the Inuit artists Kiakshuk and Pudlo. Short biographies of the artists in an appendix. Introductory essay on Rasmussen's expeditions. Translator's note and bibliography.

Freuchen, Peter. "The Eskimo Mind." In *Book of the Eskimos*, edited by Dagmar Freuchen. Cleveland, Ohio: World Publishing, 1961.
A chapter in a study of the Inuit written by a twentieth-century Danish explorer and companion of Knud Rasmussen and edited by his wife. Deals with Inuit attitudes toward life and death and their world view, illustrated with retellings of their myths and traditional stories and Freuchen's own personal reminiscences. An account of an imaginary hunter Mala and his wife depicts Inuit intimacy with death. In a section on the Inuit idea of the world, Freuchen paraphrases the Inuit version of creation. He also tells three traditional epic tales of metamorphosis and of human interaction with wild animals. Twenty-one illustrations, mostly photographs of Inuit life.

Gatschet, Albert S., Leo J. Frachtenberg, and Melville Jacobs. *Kalapuya Texts*. Vol. 11 in *University of Washington Publications in Anthropology*. Seattle: University of Washington, 1945.
Part 3 in the first anthropological collection of texts collected among the Kalapuya-speaking peoples of the Willamette Valley in western Oregon. The fifty texts are arranged according to geographic location and theme and are presented in the original dialect with parallel English translation. Besides texts dealing with reminiscences and cultural practices are four tales of European origin about Petit Jean and nineteen myths dealing with the adventures of trickster Coyote, panther, and a number of other animals. Map, pronunciation guide, glossary of Chinook jargon words, abstracts with some comparative commentary, and comprehensive index.

Giddings, Ruth Warner, ed. *Yaqui Myths and Legends*. Tucson: University of Arizona Press, 1959.

These sixty-one tales collected among the Yaqui of Arizona in 1942 include animal fables, metamorphoses, a flood story, historical legends about Yaqui and Spaniards, and supernatural stories about enchanted nature and the devil. Many show the syncretism of Yaqui and Christian ideas. Some tales are followed by explanatory notes by the editor. Introductory essays on the culture of the Yaqui and their storytelling. Biographical information about the four Yaqui narrators is provided at the end of the book. Bibliography.

Gifford, Edward W., and Gwendoline Harris Block. *California Indian Nights Entertainment*. Glendale, Calif.: Arthur H. Clark, 1930. Reprint. New York: AMS Press, 1980.

These eighty-two tales representing the principal Native American groups in California are based on previously published anthropological texts. Arranged in the following thematic groups: the origins of the world and humankind, of death, and of fire; the world fire; the sun and the moon; Coyote; death; monsters; the skyland; stars; thunder; adventure; Yosemite; European motives; and miscellaneous. Original bibliographical sources are not provided. The title of each story is followed by the name and geographic home of the Native American group which tells the tale. Included are myths of the Kato, Maidu, Mono, Shasta, and other peoples. Introductory essay on the Native Americans of California discussed by region, with sections on various thematic tale types. Detailed map indicating the location of Native American groups in California, eleven photographs, and index.

Gillham, Charles Edward. *Beyond the Clapping Mountains*. New York: Macmillan, 1943.

The author heard these thirteen tales of Alaska Inuit through an interpreter and retells them here for children. Most of the stories center on animal characters, including Mr. Crow, foxes, a mouse, and various birds. Several tales explain natural phenomena such as the red fur of the fox and how seagulls learned to fly. Illustrated with black-and-white drawings by Chanimun.

Goddard, Pliny Earle. *Jicarilla Apache Texts*. Vol. 3 in *Anthropological Papers of the American Museum of Natural History*. New York: American Museum of Natural History, 1911.

These eighty-seven narrative and descriptive texts were collected among the Apache of New Mexico in 1909 and are presented in the original Jicarilla language with literal interlinear English translation. Free English translations are provided at the end of the volume. The texts are arranged in four thematic groups. Among the myths are twenty-five stories of emergence, the first war, the killing of monsters, the culture hero Naiyenesgani, Coyote, and aetiology. Among the tales are twenty-eight narratives about the adventures of Coyote and other personified animals. The other two groups consist of more historical texts, personal recollections, and descriptions of ceremonies. Introductory essay on the people and their mythology. Pronunciation key, bibliography, and index.

_____. *Myths and Tales from the White Mountain Apache.* Vol. 24, Parts 2 and 4, in *Anthropological Papers of the American Museum of Natural History.* New York: American Museum of Natural History, 1919.

Most of these thirteen myths were recorded in 1910 in the Southwest U.S. Original Apache texts with word-for-word English translations appear in Part 4. Free English translations are provided in Part 2. Includes a creation myth, the *Naiyenesgani* or "dispersion of the tribes," metamorphosis tales, aetiologies, and tales of the trickster Coyote. Several are ceremonial or religious in performative context. Introduction and bibliography in Part 1.

Goodchild, Peter, ed. *The Raven Tales.* Chicago: Chicago Review Press, 1991.

Examines the many versions of stories about a trickster Raven told among the peoples of the Pacific Northwest of North America. Combines plot summaries of some tales with published translations of other tales. These tales deal with Raven's birth, a great flood, the theft of the sun and of fresh water, aetiologies about the colors of birds, and trickster themes. Devotes Chapter 1 to the tales of the Tlingit of southern Alaska and northern British Columbia. Examines Raven tales from other parts of North America in Chapter 2. Summarizes characteristics of these tales in Chapter 3. Compares North America's Raven to equivalents in the Old World in Chapter 4. Decribes the shamanic role of Raven in Chapter 5. Considers some theoretical interpretations of Raven myths in Chapter 6. In a preface and introduction, Goodchild discusses some general features of these Raven tales. Map, bibliography, and index.

Goodwin, Grenville. *Myths and Tales of the White Mountain Apache.* Vol. 33 in *Memoirs of the American Folk-Lore Society.* New York: American Folk-Lore Society, 1939. Reprint. New York: Kraus Reprint, 1969.

These fifty-seven stories were collected among the easternmost group
of Western Apache between 1931 and 1936 and include esoteric holy
tales about the origin of religious ceremonies and supernatural powers
and more general, entertaining stories about creation, the emergence
of the people, a great flood, monsters, and various customs. The
trickster Coyote appears in many of these tales. Introductory essay on
the people, the art of their storytelling, and characteristics of their tales.
Footnotes include explanatory comments and information about informants.

Grinnell, George Bird. *Blackfoot Lodge Tales: Stories of a Prairie People*.
New York: Scribner, 1892. Reprint. Lincoln: University of Nebraska
Press, 1962.
This work by an important nineteenth-century American conservation-
ist and friend of Theodore Roosevelt, remains an important resource
for traditional tales of the Blackfoot. Includes an introductory essay on
the general character of the Native Americans, their ill treatment by
Europeans, and some features of these tales. The thirty-eight tales,
grouped thematically, include stories of adventure, ancient times, Old
Man, and the Three Tribes, aetiological tales about the medicine and
worm pipes, stories about human encounters with the natural and
animal world, and ghost stories. The last section is a history of the
Blackfoot today. Index and biographical note on the author.

_____. *By Cheyenne Campfires*. 2d ed. New Haven, Conn.: Yale
University Press, 1962. Reprint. Lincoln: University of Nebraska
Press, 1971.
Originally published in 1926, these tales were collected among the
Cheyenne by a prominent American anthropologist who served as
naturalist with the Custer Expedition to the Black Hills in 1874 and
who lived with the Cheyenne every summer for forty years beginning
in 1890. Contains eighteen war stories, eighteen tales of mystery and
the supernatural, nine hero legends, three myths about creation and the
early stages of human life, two culture hero tales, and thirteen tales
about Wihio, a white-skinned trickster. Some of these thematic groups
are preceded by short introductions. Also contains an introductory
essay about the Cheyenne and their stories. The second edition includes
biographical information about Grinnell in a foreword by Omer C.
Stewart. Nine photographs by Elizabeth C. Grinnell.

_____. "The Culture Heroes." In *The Cheyenne Indians, Their
History and Ways of Life*, by George Bird Grinnell. Vol. 2. New Haven,

Conn.: Yale University Press, 1923. Reprint. New York: Cooper Square Publishers, 1962.

Part of a detailed ethnography based upon the author's long contact with the Cheyenne. Here Grinnell summarizes their creation story and myths dealing with the culture heroes, the coming of the buffalo, and the discovery of corn. Retells a full version of the story of Sweet medicine, the most important Cheyenne culture hero, who founded several soldier bands and the Massaum or Crazy Dance and who brought the first medicine arrows. Two photographs of the Massaum ceremony. Footnotes.

_____. *Pawnee, Blackfoot and Cheyenne*. New York: Charles Scribner's Sons, 1900; reprint, 1961.

These selections from Grinnell's writings are arranged by ethnic group. Each section begins with an account of the author's own dealings with each people, followed by information on their history and social organization. Selected folktales are included in each section. The Pawnee stories include a hero legend about a Comanche chief and folktales about children, brides, animals, and aetiologies. The Blackfoot are represented by lodge tales and Old Man stories. The Cheyenne have a creation tale, two stories of mystery, and several tales about Wihio the trickster.

_____. *Pawnee Hero Stories and Folk Tales*. New York: Forest and Stream Publishing, 1889. Reprint. Lincoln: University of Nebraska Press, 1961.

These traditional tales of the Pawnee of the Great Plains were collected by Grinnell in 1872. Grinnell retells eight stories about ancient heroes and great warriors and thirteen tales with supernatural and aetiological elements, followed by Grinnell's extensive notes on the Pawnee, their history, customs, warfare, and religion. Introductory notes by Grinnell on the Pawnee and their history. Reprint includes an introduction by Maurice Frink with information about the Pawnee and the career of Grinnell. Some line drawings of Pawnee people and artifacts. Index.

_____. "Religious Beliefs." In *The Cheyenne Indians, Their History and Ways of Life*, by George Bird Grinnell. Vol. 2. New Haven, Conn.: Yale University Press, 1923. Reprint. New York: Cooper Square Publishers, 1962.

In this chapter of his survey of the Cheyenne people, Grinnell describes their deities, the place of the dead, their concept of soul, and their beliefs regarding compass directions, natural phenomena, water spirits, ghosts, animals, prophets, charms, and taboos. Includes summaries and short retellings of tales illustrating these beliefs. Footnotes.

Haile, Berard. *Love-Magic and Butterfly People*, edited by Karl W. Luckert. Flagstaff: Museum of Northern Arizona Press, 1978.
This version of the *ajiee* (Excessway or Prostitutionway) and Mothway myths told to Fr. Haile by a Navajo named Slim Curly in 1930-1931 was published posthumously. The shamanic hero of *ajiee* is a beggar named Scrap-picker Boy, protected by his father the sun. The narrative describes the hero's initiation, transformation, seduction of Hopi virgins, and hunting of antelope. He also encounters Changing Coyote, journeys to visit his grandmother, has an affair with Three-ear Mush Woman, kills White Butterfly for seducing his wives, and ends his life on earth. This narrative celebrating human sexuality is followed by a short version of the Mothway myth centering on Coyote the trickster hero. Part 1 consists of an English translation. The Navajo text appears in Part 2. In Part 3 are Haile's introductions to the 1941 and 1944 unpublished versions of the text, with discussions of ethnographic features of the text. In an introductory essay, Luckert describes Fr. Haile's work. The editor also offers some introductory commentary at the beginning of each chapter in the narrative. Photograph of Fr. Haile. Footnotes.

_____. *The Upward Moving and Emergence Way*, edited by Karl W. Luckert. Lincoln: University of Nebraska Press, 1981.
This performance of a Navajo emergence myth by informant Gishin Biye, recorded by Fr. Haile in 1908, was first published by Mary C. Wheelwright in 1949 in a less authentic English translation. In an introductory essay, the editor comments on this text and on Haile's career and describes the cosmography of the narrative in text and diagram. In this myth, presented in Part 1, the people move through twelve "speeches," or world levels, in three stages called the Dark World, the Red World, and the Blue World until the First Human finally emerges onto the surface of the earth. On earth the first seeds are planted, several monsters are slain, and a great flood covers the land. In Part 2 the ceremony is performed. Footnotes, charts, and diagrams throughout the text.

_____. *Waterway*. Flagstaff: Museum of Northern Arizona Press, 1979.
This version of a myth in the Chantway series of Navajo ceremonials was recorded in 1929 in Arizona by Haile. An English translation is

followed by the complete Navajo text as sung by Haile's informant, Black Mustache Circle. Describes the origin of the Waterway ceremony, which followed the departure of two old women called Riverward Knoll Woman and Scabby Woman from a place called Riverward Knoll. In this narrative Old Man Water monster sings the ceremony. Woven into the narrative are descriptions of prayer sticks and other parts of the ceremony. Short introductory essay. In an appendix, Karl W. Luckert comments upon Waterway mythology and offers with commentary fourteen black-and-white illustrations of Rain- and Waterway sandpaintings. Bibliography and footnotes.

_____. *Women Versus Men*, edited by Karl W. Luckert. Lincoln: University of Nebraska Press, 1981.
An English translation of part of a Navajo emergence myth dictated to Haile by Curly Tó Aheedlíinii in 1932 is here followed by the original Navajo text. The narrative about a primeval time deals with the First Man and the First Woman, their separation and reunion, a *nádleeh*, or shamanistic male-female entity, Coyote the trickster as helper of the First Man, the creation of the heavenly bodies and months, and the creation of the moccasin game by Coyote. In an introductory essay, Haile discusses some features of this myth. Editor's note and footnotes by both Haile and Luckert.

Hall, Edwin S., Jr. *The Eskimo Storyteller: Folktales from Noatak, Alaska*. Knoxville: University of Tennessee Press, 1975.
These 190 folktales were told to an anthropologist through an interpreter by two Yup'ik informants in 1965. Detailed ethnographic information about the people, their land, and their history in Chapter 1. Background on the Noatak storyteller in Chapter 2. The tales are grouped according to informant in Chapters 3 and 4. Autobiographies of both informants. Each story is followed by a list of folktale motifs used and some comparisons with other Yup'ik tales. Includes stories about ideal personality traits, interpersonal relationships, death, life in isolation, unusual physical features, human marriage to animals, warfare, crime and punishment, human interaction with the natural and supernatural worlds, and shamanism. Analysis of these tales in Chapter 5, with emphasis on context of performance, motifs, literary conventions, and story content. In a preface and an epilogue, the author relates some of his personal experiences with these people. Map, fifteen tables, glossary, bibliography, index of motifs, and general index.

Harrington, John P. *Karuk Indian Myths*. Bulletin 107 of the Smithsonian
   Institution Bureau of American Ethnology. Washington, D. C.: U.S.
   Government Printing Office, 1932.
   Twelve tales collected from a Karuk woman in northwestern California
   are offered in the original-language text followed by English translation. These narratives deal with aetiology, the trickster Coyote, a
   journey to the afterlife, an unethical physician, marriage and courtship,
   and anthropomorphic and supernatural animals. Introductory essay on
   the Karuk, the informant, and some characteristics of her tales. Phonetic key and footnotes.

Harris, Christie. *Once upon a Totem*. New York: Atheneum, 1963.
   Retells for older children five tales about totem poles told by the people
   of the Pacific Northwest. These tales explain family emblems and
   names and tell of supernatural creatures and cannibal giants. In a short
   preface and in introductions to each tale, the author provides some
   general background and commentary. Illustrated with woodcuts by
   John Frazer Mills.

Haviland, Virginia, ed. "Indian and Eskimo Tales." In *The Faber Book of
   North American Legends*, edited by Virginia Haviland. Boston: Faber
   & Faber, 1979.
   Part of an anthology of North American tales which includes not only
   Native American stories but also some from the African American,
   European immigrant and regional U.S. traditions. Here fourteen Native
   American tales from all over the continent are retold for older children.
   Some stories are borrowed directly from earlier collections, such as
   those of George Bird Grinnell. Others have been retold by the editor.
   The tales are representative and include a Raven story from the
   Northwest Pacific Coast, a Coyote tale from the Great Plains, a
   Gluskap adventure from the Northeast Woodlands, and the Inuit story
   of Sedna the Sea Goddess. Details about sources and editorial com-
   ments in endnotes. With illustrations by Ann Strugnell. Bibliography.

Hayes, William D. *Indian Tales of the Desert People*. New York: David
   McKay, 1957.
   Twelve myths and legends of the Pima and Papago of Arizona are
   retold for children. Several tales feature the mysterious figure Ee-ee-
   toy, a great spirit with special magical powers. Includes a tale explaining how the divine Earth magician created the world and two stories
   about the adventures of the trickster Coyote. In a preliminary note, the
   author provides a history of the people and discusses some charac-

teristics of their tales. Illustrated by the author with black-and-white drawings.

Hewitt, John Napoleon Brinton. *Iroquoian Cosmology.* 2 vols. Reports 21 and 43 of the Bureau of American Ethnology. Washington, D. C.: U.S. Government Printing Office. 1903 (Vol. 1), 1928 (Vol. 2). Reprint. New York: AMS Press, 1974.

Records several versions of the creation myths of the Iroquois peoples of upper New York State collected in the field by the author between 1889 and 1900. In Part 1, Onondaga, Seneca, and Mohawk versions of creation are presented in the original languages with literal, interlinear English translation plus a free English translation. In Part 2 an Onondaga myth about the Earth-grasper is presented first in free English translation and then in the original language with interlinear English translation. Part 2 also includes an English translation of the myth of De'hodyä'tkä'ewĕⁿ (He-Whose-Body-Is-Divided-in-Twain) and his expedition to the skyland, an essay on Iroquois myths and their storytelling traditions, and endnotes. Introductory essays at the beginning of each volume contain information about the people, their myths, and the informants. Photographs of six Iroquois informants in Volume 1. Revised edition includes a comprehensive index. Footnotes.

Hill, Kay. *Badger, the Mischief Maker.* New York: Dodd, Mead, 1965.

Fourteen Algonquin tales about a young warrior named Badger are retold for young readers. In his pranks and escapades Badger is often protected by Gluskap, the Algonquin creator and protective deity. Black-and-white illustrations by John Hamberger and glossary.

Hinton, Leanne, and Lucille J. Watahomigie, eds. *Spirit Mountain.* Tucson: University of Arizona Press, 1984.

Two scholars of Hawasupai literature, one of them Hawasupai herself, offer an anthology of oral material of the Yuman peoples of parts of Arizona, California, Mexico, and Nevada. In the preparation of individual sections, Hinton and Watahomigie were aided by additional contributors and editors, including Abraham Halpern, Henry O. Harwell, Margaret Landgon, and Mauricio J. Mixco. The material in this collection was obtained from a number of Yuman storytellers and is divided culturally, with sections on Hualapai, Hawasupai, Yavapai, Paipai, Diegueño, Maricopa, Mojave, and Quechan (Yuma) literatures. Most of the texts are presented in bilingual form, with original and English translation in parallel columns. Paipai texts are presented trilingually, with the addition of Spanish. The mythic narratives deal with cataclysmic floods, emergence of the peoples, Coyote the trickster, and animal legends. Other types of oral literature include songs, childhood reminiscences, and recollections about wars and early contacts with Europeans. Each section contains its own map, information on contributors, alphabet chart, and bibliography. In a general introduction, Hinton and Watahomigie describe the history and way of life of the Yuman peoples, their storytelling tradition, and the transcription and translation of this oral material. Photographs of sites and contributors and line drawings.

Hodges, Margaret. *The Fire Bringer*. Boston: Little, Brown, 1972.
A Paiute legend about how Coyote and a young boy brought fire to humankind is retold for children. Illustrated in color by Peter Parnall.

Hogner, Dorothy Childs. *Navajo Winter Nights*. New York: Thomas Nelson and Sons, 1935.
Forty-four tales of the Navajo of Arizona are retold for children. Arranged in four thematic groups: primeval tales about creation, a great flood, and supernatural creatures; legends about a great warrior called Big Long Man; aetiologies about various animals and their physical features; and stories about the great schemer Coyote. Short preface. Black-and-white drawings by Nils Nogner.

Houston, James. *Tikta' liktak*. New York: Harcourt, Brace & World, 1965.
Retells for children an Inuit legend about a young hunter who is stranded in the Arctic wilderness and survives the elements and encounters with wild animals through his own skill and determination. Illustrated in black-and-white by the author.

Howard, James H. "The North American Indians." In *Mythology: An Illustrated Encyclopaedia*, edited by Richard Cavendish. New York: Rizzoli International, 1980. Also published as *An Illustrated Encyclopedia of Mythology*. New York: Crescent Books, 1984.
A sweeping survey of the mythologies of Native Americans north of the Rio Grande River, excluding Alaska and northern Canada. Sections on the religious and mythological beliefs of the nations of the Northeast Woodlands, the Great Plains, the Southwest U.S., and the Pacific Northwest are accompanied by sections on the Underwater panther, Giant Horned Snake, and other animal demons of the Northeast Woodlands. Also offers summaries and analyses of the Algonquin myth cycle about the trickster hare Gluskap, a Creek tale about Corn Woman, Cheyenne tales about bison and corn, an Arapaho myth about marriage of the sun with a mortal woman, Hopi and Zuñi myths about Corn

Maidens, a Wishram tale about the trickster Coyote, and a Tsimshian story about Raven's theft of daylight. Map and illustrations of artwork related to the myths.

Hultkrantz, Åke. "The Orpheus Motif in North America." In *The North American Indian Orpheus Tradition*, by Åke Hultkrantz. Vol. 2 in Ethnographical Museum of Sweden Monograph Series. Stockholm: Ethnographical Museum of Sweden, 1957.
The introductory chapter of a scholarly comparative study of North American myths about a journey to the underworld in search of a deceased loved one. Retells a Comanche version of this tradition, outlines several defining features of the tale, indicates the geographic distribution of the tale, and analyzes specific variations and regional differences. Footnotes.

Jacobs, Melville. *The Content and Style of an Oral Literature*. Chicago: University of Chicago Press, 1959.
A literary analysis of seven Clackamas Chinook narratives collected by the author in Oregon in 1929-1930. In Part 1 Jacobs offers free English translations of the seven tales followed by detailed analysis and interpretation of each narrative. The first two tales are about the trickster Coyote. The others are about the spirit power Fire, theft of brides by warriors called Grizzly and Black Bear, a cannibal ogre called Grizzly Woman, a murderer named Flint, an awl metamorphosed into a woman, and a big-footed boy whose story Jacobs compares to that of the Greek hero Oedipus. In Part 2 Jacobs analyzes the myths as a whole and considers features of content and of style. In separate chapters, he discusses interpersonal relationships, personalities, humor, the concept of the good, the Clackamas Chinook world view, songs, and stylized devices and motifs. General introductory essay and introduction to Part 2. Endnotes and index.

_____. *Coos Myth Texts. University of Washington Publications in Anthropology* 8, no. 2 (1940): 127-260.
Most of these forty-nine traditional stories of the Coos of western Oregon were dictated in 1933-1934 to the author by Mrs. Annie Miner Peterson, who used either Hanis or the near-extinct Miluk dialect. These original versions are accompanied by English translations. Several other tales appear as they were originally told in English by another informant. Myths are grouped according to the language used. Cosmological tales about a series of Worldmaker-tricksters, including Coyote. Also contains tales about ogres, humans acquiring spirit-

powers or marrying supernatural spouses, sexual taboos, and warfare. In an appendix abstracts of all these tales are grouped thematically with abstracts of other Coos tales. Short introduction on the tales and their informants. Explanatory footnotes and index.

_____. *The People Are Coming Soon*. Seattle: University of Washington Press, 1960.
In 1929-1930 the author collected fifty-six tales from one of the last surviving Clackamas Chinook-speaking people in Oregon. Sociocultural analyses of each of these tales are here accompanied by close English translations. The tales are grouped chronologically. Forty-one myths of the primeval period are followed by eight tales of a transitional period of acculturation, six tales about the period before European settlement, and one modern story. The myths include stories about Coyote and other animals. All the tales contain supernatural elements such as ogresses, metamorphoses, and personified stars. Some graphic reference to human sexual and excretory functions. Endnotes.

_____. "Santiam Kalapuya Myth Texts." In *Kalapuya Texts*. Vol. 11 in *University of Washington Publications in Anthropology*. Seattle: University of Washington Press, 1945.
Part 2 of the first anthropological collection of texts collected among the Kalapuya-speaking peoples of the Willamette Valley in western Oregon. These nineteen mythological narratives were dictated and translated in 1928 by Jacobs' informer, John B. Hudson. Fourteen are presented in the original Santiam Kalapuya dialect with parallel English translation. An additional five tales also have translations into the Tualatin dialect. Most of these narratives describe the adventures of the trickster Coyote and other animals. The plots deal with aetiology, a great flood, combat between animals or superhuman people, and even a contest between the sun and the moon. Several contain graphic references to human sexual and excretory organs. In a short preface, Jacobs provides information about the tales and his informant. Abstracts of these myths together with some comparative commentary appear at the end of Part 3. Comprehensive index.

Jones, Louis Thomas. *So Say the Indians*. San Antonio, Tex.: Naylor, 1970.
This collection of tales and commentary includes legends of Native Americans of the Pacific Northwest, California, Alaska, Canada, the Northeast Woodlands, the Southeast U.S., the Great Plains, and the Southwest U.S. These creation myths, aetiologies, trickster tales, and

animal legends are arranged geographically and are integrated into the author's travelogue, personal experiences, and observations about the peoples he calls "Red Men." Some information about sources in the text, in endnotes, and in the acknowledgments. In an introductory essay, Jones comments on some features of this collection and of the tales themselves. Foreword on Jones's work by Carl Shaefer Dentzel. Index.

Jones, William. *Fox Texts.* Vol. 1 in *Publications of the American Ethnological Society.* Leiden: E. J. Brill, 1907.
These fifty-nine tales, collected among the Fox people of Iowa in 1901-1902, are presented in the original Algonquin with parallel English translation. Among the six thematic groupings, two contain mythological material. The twelve miscellaneous myths and traditions in Part 2 include animal fables, star myths, and tales of the supernatural, monsters, and pygmies. In Part 5 are seventeen stories about a culture hero called Wsa'kä who makes the world safe for humankind. In an introductory essay, Jones offers some background to the people, their tales, and their language. Pronunciation guide. Footnotes, the first of which is a plot summary for each tale.

Judson, Katharine Berry. *Myths and Legends of Alaska.* Chicago: A. C. McClurg, 1911.
These sixty-three short tales from Alaska and the Canadian Northwest are based upon the collections of government ethnologists and are intended for the general reader. Includes aetiologies, nature myths, and animal fables. Special attention is given to the Raven myth, which is especially popular in this area. Illustrations include photographs of the people, their artifacts, and their geographic region.

_____, ed. *Myths and Legends of California and the Old Southwest.* Chicago: A. C. McClurg, 1912.
More than sixty traditional tales of the peoples of California, Arizona, and New Mexico are selected from a variety of published sources and are told in translation. Most frequently represented are the Zuñi, Navajo, and Sia of New Mexico and the Pima of Arizona. These myths about the creation of the world and of humankind, a great flood, the origin of animals and of human customs, and Coyote the trickster are not grouped in any particular order. Sources indicated by ethnic group only. Prefatory essay on some characteristics of these myths. Fifty-one photographs.

_____, ed. *Myths and Legends of the Pacific Northwest.* 3d ed. Chicago: A. C. McClurg, 1916.

A collection of sixty tales of the peoples of the Arctic and the Pacific Northwest, including the Klamath, Nez Percé, Kwakiutl, Modoc, and Inuit. While the author retells tales originally published in ethnographic and scholarly contexts, she offers no bibliographic information about sources, and tales are identified only by ethnic group and geographic area. A prominent figure in these tales is the trickster Coyote. Six tales about the creation of the world are followed by aetiologies, especially of fire, and tales about the origin of humankind, the golden age, animals, and ghosts. Prefatory essay on the people and their tales. Forty-nine photographs of the people, their artifacts, and their land.

_____. *Old Crow Stories.* Boston: Little, Brown, 1917.

Twenty-one animal tales of the Crow of the Great Plains are retold for children. Includes tales about the creation of light and of the sun, stories about cunning Raven, and the deeds of Coyote, the trickster and culture hero, especially his theft of fire for humankind. Six drawings by Charles Livingston Bull.

Kilpatrick, Jack F., and Anna G. Kilpatrick, ed. and trans. *Friends of Thunder: Folktales of the Oklahoma Cherokees.* Dallas, Tex.: Southern Methodist University Press, 1964.

More than seventy tales collected among the Cherokee of Oklahoma are translated here into English. Arranged thematically. Stories about storytellers, birds, animals, the giant reptile Uk'ten', monsters, little people, and the trickster figure Tseg'sgin'. Each section and many individual tales are preceded by short introductions by the editors. Followed by a collection of ethnological data about Cherokee life and six historical sketches. Some are told in narrative form and others in conversation between informant and editors. Bibliography, list of informants, and endnotes.

Klah, Hosteen. *Navajo Creation Myth: The Story of Emergence.* Sante Fe, N.M.: Museum of Navajo Ceremonial Art, 1942. Reprint. New York: AMS Press, 1976.

A Navajo medicine man recorded this myth for Mary C. Wheelwright through an interpreter. Transcripts of several ceremonial songs based on the creation myth as sung by Klah. The myth describes the emergence of life from the Four Worlds, the birth of the twin Gods, their slaying of several monsters, a great flood, the creation of humankind and animals, and the journey of the clans to Navajo country. A collection of seventeen black-and-white reproductions of sandpaintings representing *Hozhonji*, the Blessing Chant of the Navajo creation myth. These reproductions are accompanied by explanatory notes and a general essay. In a preface, Wheelwright provides a history of this work. Also contains an introductory essay on Navajo myths, ceremonies, and sandpaintings. Photograph of Klah, endnotes, and glossary.

Kroeber, Alfred Louis. *Indian Myths of South Central California*. Vol. 4 in *California University Publications in American Archaeology and Ethnology*. Berkeley: University of California Press, 1906-1907. Reprint. New York: Kraus Reprint, 1964.
This scholarly monograph by a major early twentieth-century anthropologist includes a collection of forty-one myths of the Costanoa, Miwok, and Yokut of California. Part 1 is an introduction to the mythologies of the various peoples of north-central and south-central California and a comparison of these mythologies. The tales themselves, collected in the field between 1901 and 1906, are recorded in English translation in Part 2. Grouped according to source, these myths include cosmogonies, stories about Coyote, aetiologies about fire and death, and various animal tales. Abstracts of these tales appear in Part 3.

_____. *Yurok Myths*, edited by Grace Buzaljko. Berkeley: University of California Press, 1976.
This collection of myths of the Yurok of northwestern California was published posthumously. Grouped according to Kroeber's twenty-nine informants, with a final section containing fragments and outlines from various informants. Each group is preceded by information about the informant. Types include marvelous and fantastic tales, aetiologies, institutional myths, and stories about monsters and harmful spirits. Many tales center on the adventures of Wohpekumeu, a culture hero and trickster who steals salmon and acorns for humankind. Other major characters are personifications of the sun, the moon, thunder, earthquake, coyote, and porpoises. Introductory essay on Kroeber's work with the Yurok by Timothy H. H. Thoresen and a foreword on the same topic by Theodora Kroeber. Short essay on the geographical setting of the tales by the author. Folkloristic commentary by Alan Dundes. List of recordings of Yurok myths in an appendix. Seven maps, photographs of Kroeber and three informants, footnotes, bibliography, and index.

Kroeber, Alfred Louis, and Edward Winslow Gifford. *Karok Myths*, edited by Grace Buzaljko. Berkeley: University of California Press, 1980.
These two previously unpublished collections of tales of the Karok of northern California were gathered independently in the first half of the twentieth century by Kroeber and Gifford, who were colleagues at the University of California at Berkeley. Based upon original Karok versions and translated into English with the aid of bilingual assistants. Kroeber's tales are arranged according to informant, while Gifford's are arranged thematically. Aetiologies, tales about immortals and humans, legends about the trickster Coyote, and stories about animals. Also contains some magic formulas. In a foreword, Theodora Kroeber describes the careers of Kroeber and Grifford, the lives of the Karok and Yurok, and characteristics of their myths. Folkloristic commentary by Alan Dundes with comments on some folktale and comparative features of the narratives. In a preface, the editor describes some features of the text and of the tales. Five photographs, map, bibliography, index of parallel plot elements, and Karok linguistic index.

Lankford, George E., ed. *Native American Legends*. Little Rock, Ark.: August House, 1987.
This collection of 131 previously published texts of the Natchez, Caddo, Biloxi, Chicasaw, and other peoples of the Southeast U.S. is intended as a resource for the college classroom and as a reference for ethnographic information about the region. In two preliminary chapters, Lankford provides general background on the peoples and their cultures and on the collection of narratives in the Southeast. The tales are grouped thematically by chapters in two groups. Chapters 3-7 deal with the aboveworld of the gods, the underworld of the dead, the middleworld of the living, the social world, and the plant world. Chapters 8-12 contain adventure tales about the twins, Orphan, the Bead-Spitter, tricksters like Coyote, and journeys to the sky and to the underworld. Texts and explanatory commentary are presented together. In an introductory essay, W. K. McNeil offers a history of North American folkloristics. Map, ten line drawings of artifacts, endnotes, and bibliography.

Leekley, Thomas B. *The World of Manabozho*. New York: Vanguard Press, 1965.
Fourteen tales about the *manitou*, or "wonder worker," of the Chippewa, a Sioux people of the Great Plains. Manabozho, or Great Hare, is both trickster and culture hero. His tales deal with the theft of fire, a great flood, and various encounters with animals. In a short introduc-

tory essay and in endnotes, Leekley comments upon these tales. Illustrated with line drawings by Yeffe Kimball.

Leland, Charles G. *The Algonquin Legends of New England.* Boston: Houghton Mifflin, 1884. Reprint. *Algonquin Legends.* New York: Dover, 1992.

A collection of seventy-three myths told by the Wabanaki or northeastern Algonquin, including the Passamaquoddy and Penobscot of Maine and the Micmac of New Brunswick. Collected by the author from a variety of sources, both written and oral. Includes twenty-seven tales about the divinity Gluskap, eight about a trickster lynx called Lox, seven about Master rabbit, four about Thunder Spirits, five about At-o-sis the serpent, five about Partridge the hero, and nine about magic. In an introductory essay, Leland suggests that thematic similarities among Algonquin, Inuit, and Norse tales is the result of ancient migration. Twelve line drawings. Bibliography.

Lévi-Strauss, Claude. "The Story of Asdiwal." In *The Structural Study of Myth and Totemism*, edited by Edmund Leach. London: Tavistock Publications, 1967.

An English translation of a summary and analysis of a Pacific Northwest myth by a major French structural anthropologist. Part of a collection of seven scholarly essays dealing with the work of Claude Lévi-Strauss and his interpretation of myth as a structure of patterned contradictions. Compares several versions of this myth and the ways in which the myth operates on several levels, including geography, economics, sociology, and cosmology. Known in four versions, this Tsimshian myth deals with the adventures of a young warrior named Asdiwal who eventually is lost in the winter snows and is turned to stone. Map, endnotes, and biliography.

Lopez, Barry Holstun. *Giving Birth to Thunder, Sleeping with His Daughter.* Kansas City: Sheed Andrews and McMeel, 1977.

These sixty-eight myths about Coyote, the trickster, creator, transformer, and Old Man of many North American peoples, have been selected by the author from scholarly journals and various general works on North American mythology. Special effort was made to include stories about sex, cannibalism, and body functions often left out of earlier collections, to tell these tales without the artificial aetiological elements added by some non-native retellers, and to illustrate the dichotomy of Coyote as both trickster and fool. Some features of Coyote and his tales are considered in a foreword by Barre Toelken and in an introductory essay by Lopez. Bibliographic note.

Lot-Falck, E. "Eskimo Lands: Man Against Nature." In *Larousse World Mythology*, edited by Pierre Grimal. Translated by Patricia Beardsworth. New York: G. P. Putnam's Sons, 1963.
This overivew of Inuit mythology includes accounts of creation, Sedna the sea goddess, the moon god, the gods Pinga, Asiaq, and Sila, spirits, and monsters. Accompanied by ten illustrations of Inuit artifacts and drawings.

Loverseed, Amanda. *Tikkatoo's Journey*. New York: Peter Bedrick Books, 1990.
An Inuit folktale about a grandson's journey into the sea and into the sky in order to obtain fire from the sun and thus to save his grandfather's life. Retold and illustrated for children.

Lowie, Robert Harry. *Myths and Traditions of the Crow Indians*. Vol. 25 in *Anthropological Papers of the American Museum of Natural History*. New York: American Museum of Natural History, 1918.
These eighty-one tales and legends were collected in English among the Crow people of the Great Plains in 1907 and are grouped thematically. Tales about a creator and trickster called Old-Man-Coyote are followed by hero legends, stories of supernatural patrons, historical traditions, and miscellaneous tales. Abstracts of six additional tales in an appendix. Introductory essay on some general and comparative features of Crow myths. Footnotes and bibliography.

Lummis, Charles F. *The Man Who Married the Moon*. New York: Century, 1894. Reprint. New York: AMS Press, 1976.
Thirty-three Pueblo or Tée-wahn tales retold for children. Many of the stories concern personified animals, especially the trickster Coyote, and the moon and the winds. Also contains tales of aetiology, the supernatural, and the twin gods, known here as Máw-Sahv and Oó-yah-wee. Introductory essay on the Pueblo and their storytelling traditions. Twenty-three drawings by George Wharton Edwards.

McClintock, Walter. *The Old North Trail*. London: Macmillan, 1910. Reprint. Lincoln: University of Nebraska Press, 1992.
An account of personal experiences and of the culture of the Blackfoot people by a member of a U.S. Forest Service expedition who spent four years, between 1896 and 1900, living among them and became the adopted son of a Blackfoot chief. Incorporated into this narrative are

many traditional Blackfoot tales. In Chapter 6 McClintock tells the aetiology of the Beaver medicine ceremony. Several ghost stories are recounted in Chapter 9. In Chapter 25 are a medicine man's mythical accounts of the culture hero called Old Man. Legends about a supernatural grizzly bear are told in Chapter 36. McClintock tells the legend of a star boy called Poïa in Chapter 38. The reprint includes an introductory essay evaluating McClintock and his work by Sidney J. Larson.

Macfarlan, Allan A., ed. *The Heritage Book of American Indian Legends.* New York: Heritage Press, 1968.

This broad-ranging selection of tales from the works of Henry R. Schoolcraft, George Bird Grinnell, Franz Boas, and other nineteenth- and early twentieth-century North American folklorists was edited for older children but is a valuable resource for the general reader. Arranged thematically with tales about the beginning of the world, heroes and culture heroes, supernatural creatures such as giants and monsters, mystery and magic, adventure and enchantment, spirits, sorcery, tricksters, aetiology, and European fairy-tale themes. The origin of each tale is indicated in the table of contents by national name only. Prominently represented are the Inuit, Tsimshian, Thompson, and Maidu of the Pacific coast, the Pima, Pueblo, and Zuñi of the southwestern United States, the Blackfoot, Cheyenne, Dakota, Pawnee, and Sioux of the Great Plains, the Cherokee, Choctaw, and Shawnee of the southeastern United States, and some peoples of the eastern woodlands, including the Micmac, Iroquois, and Algonquin. In an introductory essay, Macfarlan offers some background on the history of these tales, their motifs, the trickster theme, and legendary figures. Occasional color illustrations by Everett Gee Jackson.

McIlwraith, T. F. *The Bella Coola Indians.* 2 vols. Toronto: University of Toronto Press, 1948.

This ethnographic study of the Bella Coola people of British Columbia is based on the author's fieldwork between 1922 and 1924. Considers many aspects of social life, including geography, religion, social organization, potlatch, birth, death, marriage, the supernatural, ceremonial dances, songs, warfare, games, and physiognomy. Of particular interest to the study of mythology in Volume 1 are a discussion of various Bella Coola deities in a chapter on religion, a variety of aetiological stories about the people and geographic places, and stories about supernatural aid and shamanism. Volume 2 includes a collection of supernatural, catastrophic, and historical tales and legends about the Raven, about other animals, and about a monster named *Snınq* Bella Coola words are often incorporated into the translations of these tales, many of which are accompanied by two or more variants. Also contains occasional footnotes and indication of sources. Forty-six photographs, phonetic key, glossary of flora and fauna, and Bella Coola-English dictionary. Index.

McLaughlin, Marie. *Myths and Legends of the Sioux.* Bismarck, N.D.: Bismarck Tribune, 1916.
McLaughlin, part Sioux, here preserves thirty-eight tales of adventure, war, courtship, and aetiology which she heard from Sioux storytellers throughout her life. Many of these tales center on animal characters, especially rabbit and Unkotomi (spider). In the foreword, the author offers a brief autobiography and some comments on the tales and their origin. Includes original drawings and a photographic portrait of the author.

Macmillan, Cyrus. *Canadian Fairy Tales.* New York: Dodd, Mead, 1922. Reprinted in *Canadian Wonder Tales.* London: The Bodley Head, 1974.
Twenty-six folktales collected among the Native American peoples of Canada are here retold for children. Includes stories about Gluskap, the Algonquin creator deity, various animals, especially the tricksters Raven and rabbit, and encounters with supernatural creatures such as giants. No sources are identified. Some Christian and French influences appear in the tales. Short introduction by John Grier Hibben and preface by the author. The original edition is illustrated with twelve color and fourteen black-and-white drawings by Marcia Lane Foster. The reprint is illustrated with black-and-white drawings by Elizabeth Cleaver.

_____. *Glooskap's Country and Other Indian Tales.* Toronto: Oxford University Press, 1922. Reprint. New York: Oxford University Press, 1956.
These thirty-eight stories told by Native Americans of Eastern Canada were first published in 1918. They center on Gluskap, the chief spirit, creator, and magic master of this region. The collection includes many animal tales, such as aetiologies about the first turtle and the first mosquito or how the rabbit lost his tail, as well as adventure tales about human encounters with the natural and the supernatural worlds.

Malotki, Ekkehart. *Gullible Coyote Una'ihu.* Tucson: University of Arizona Press, 1985.

A linguist presents twelve traditional Hopi tales about the Coyote trickster with both Hopi text and English translation in two columns on the same page. The tales were recorded from Hopi storytellers and translated by Malotki. In these legends Coyote has encounters with Maasaw, the Hopi god of death, with a skeleton, and with a variety of animals, including antelopes, ants, owls, cats, and a little turtle. In a preface written in English only, Malotki explains the purpose of a bilingual format and identifies his Hopi informants. In a bilingual introduction, he describes the character of Coyote in Hopi legends and the role of Coyote in Hopi culture. A bibliography follows the introduction. Two-color illustrations by Anne-Marie Malotki. Appendix on the Hopi alphabet and a bilingual glossary.

_____. *Hopitutuwutsi Hopi Tales*. Tucson: University of Arizona Press, 1983.
Ten traditional Hopi tales are here presented in bilingual form with the original Hopi text and English translation on facing pages. These tales were narrated by Herschel Talashoma to Malotki, who recorded and translated them. They deal with several Hopi deities, including the twin war gods Puukonhoya and Palunhoya and Maasaw, the complex keeper of the underworld. The plots center on encounters with monsters, witches, and demons. In an introductory essay, the author analyzes several Hopi words related to storytelling. Illustrated with forty-two line drawings of Hopi artifacts by Anne-Marie Malotki. Glossary and bibliography.

Malotki, Ekkehart, and Michael Lomatuway'ma. *Hopi Coyote Tales. Istutuwutsi*. Lincoln: University of Nebraska Press, 1984.
A linguist and a native Hopi record twenty-one tales about the trickster Coyote in the original Hopi with English translation on facing pages. Coyote has adventures with various animals, a cowboy, a Navajo, an ogre, and sorcery. In a preface, Karl W. Luckert provides some historical background to the study of Hopi Coyote tales. Illustrated with black-and-white drawings by Anne-Marie Malotki. Bilingual glossary and note on the Hopi alphabet.

_____. *Maasaw: Profile of a Hopi God*. Vol. 11 in *American Tribal religions*. Lincoln: University of Nebraska Press, 1987.
Examines the nature of the central Hopi deity Maasaw by means of an ethnographic commentary on 161 texts collected in the field in 1984-1985. Maasaw is a paradoxical god who controls both death and vegetation and is considered both the champion and the antagonist of

humans. All the texts—presented in bilingual form, with the Hopi text and English translation in parallel columns—are integrated into fourteen chapters dealing with topics such as the realm of death; Maasaw's appearance, emergence, enemies, and connections with the land, fire, light, agriculture, disease, hunting, and health; and his role as clan ancestor, trickster, and patron of sacred societies. Twenty-three figures with photographs of Hopi artifacts. Black-and-white drawings by Petra Roeckerath. Footnotes, bibliography, and appendix on the Hopi alphabet.

_____. *Stories of Maasaw, a Hopi God.* Lincoln: University of Nebraska Press, 1987.
Sixteen Hopi tales collected in the field are here presented in bilingual form, with Hopi original and English translation on facing pages. The tales describe the adventures of Maasaw, the Hopi god of the underworld, who goes courting, marries, meets Coyote, the twin deities known as the Pööqangw Brothers, and various humans, and protects people from enemies. In the preface, Malokti provides some information on Maasaw, on his informants, and on the structure of this book. Illustrated with black-and-white drawings by Petra Roeckerath. Glossary and note on the Hopi alphabet.

Marriott, Alice L. *Winter-Telling Stories.* New York: Thomas Y. Crowell, 1947; reprint, 1969.
Ten tales about Sendeh, the culture hero and trickster of the Kiowa of the Great Plains, retold for children. The first group consists of tales of good deeds in which Sendeh, known here as Saynday, brings the sun and buffalo and almost cuts the ant in two. The second group comprises tales of trouble-making in which he gets caught in a buffalo skull, races with a coyote, gets caught in a tree, gives the bobcat his spots, tries to marry the whirlwind, and tricks his white counterpart. In some of these tales, anthropomorphic animals interact with Saynday. Short introduction and conclusion to the tales by Marriott. Reprint includes drawings by Richard Cuffari.

Marriott, Alice L., and Carol K. Rachlin. *American Indian Mythology.* New York: Thomas Y. Crowell, 1968.
Two anthropologists have compiled a collection of thirty-six myths and legends from more than twenty North American peoples. Some of these include Cheyenne and Modoc creation myths, Tewa and Zuñi aetiological legends, Kiowa and Arapaho historical tales, Sauk myths about the afterlife, Cherokee stories about Grandmother spider, and

Hopi tales about the war twins. Each tale is introduced with ethnographic information about the people and some background about the myth and its distribution. Brief documentation concerning sources follows each tale, many of which were recorded in the field by the authors. In a general introductory essay the authors offer a brief history of native North Americans and outline the effects of the European encounter on their world view and culture. They also summarize the contributions of anthropology and folklore studies to the North American record and discuss some general features of these tales. Twenty-eight photographs of artifacts and ritual scenes. Bibliography.

_____. *Plains Indian Mythology*. New York: Thomas Y. Crowell, 1975.

These thirty-one tales were collected by the authors, especially among the peoples of the southern Great Plains. Represented among the stories are the Apache, Arapaho, Cheyenne, Comanche, Crow, Kiowa, Pawnee, Osage, Shoshoni, and Sioux. Part 1 contains seven myths about the creation of the world and of human beings and about the emergence of the people. Seven aetiologies, especially about physical features of animals, in Part 2. References to horses unite the eleven oral recollections from the period of early encounters with Europeans in Part 3. The six tales in Part 4 deal with the time following the resettlements of the people on reservations. The collection includes personal folklore and narrative songs as well as myths and legends. Each piece is preceded by historical and ethnographic information and is followed by the name and background of the informant. In an introductory essay, the authors summarize the history of the peoples of the Great Plains and discuss some ethnographic features, including the use of dogs and horses and social changes which followed European contacts. Short foreword on the types and collection of North American folklore. Thirty-nine photographs of the people of the Great Plains and their world, mostly by Rachlin. Map of the central United States, reconstructing the original location and movements of peoples based upon mythology and history. Bibliography.

Martin, Fran. *Nine Tales of Coyote*. New York: Harper & Brothers, 1950.
Retells for children nine Nez Percé tales about the changer and trickster Coyote. Describes Coyote's journey to the upper world, his intereaction with early humans, and his encounter with a monster in the Kamiah Valley of the Pacific Northwest. Illustrated with color drawings by Dorothy McEntee.

_____. *Nine Tales of Raven*. 1951. Reprint. *Raven-Who-Sets-Things-Right*. New York: Harper & Row, 1975.

Adapts for children ten tales about the trickster and creator Raven of the native peoples of the Pacific Northwest, including the Tlingit, Haida, Tsimshian, and Kwakiutl. Introductory chapter on the people and their culture. In these tales Raven creates the world, teaches useful skills to humans, and disposes of a variety of monsters. Reprint is illustrated with black-and-white drawings by Dorothy McEntee. Bibliography.

Matthews, Washington. *Navaho Legends*. Vol. 5 in *Memoirs of the American Folk-Lore Society*. Boston: American Folk-Lore Society, 1897. Reprint. New York: Kraus Reprint, 1969.

English translations of three traditional stories of the Navajo of Arizona and New Mexico. The Navajo origin legend recounts the beginning of the world, the emergence of the people from the first four worlds into the present fifth world, early events in this world, a myth of the war gods, and the growth of the Navajo Nation. Also contains two incomplete rite-myths and the stories of Natinesthani and of the Great Shell of Kintyel. Detailed introductory essay on the ethnography of the Navajo, with sections on appearance, language, alphabet, social organization, daily life, arts, and ceremonies. Sections on religion and legends contain useful descriptions of Navajo deities and myths. Explanatory and comparative notes include the Navajo text and interlinear English translation for the first ten paragraphs of the origin legend. Also contains texts and translations of various prayers and songs, some with musical scores. Six full-page plates reprint photographs of Navajo country. Forty-two additional photographs depict the people and their daily life. Map, bibliography, and index.

Mechling, W. H. *Malecite Tales*. Memoir 49 of the Canada Department of Mines Geological Survey. Ottawa: Government Printing Bureau, 1914.

Forty-two myths collected among the Malecites of New Brunswick and Maine between 1910 and 1912 are told in English, arranged thematically. There are seven tales about the divine culture hero Gluskap, six about Poktcinskwes, a troublesome woman with supernatural powers, two about a mythical red-skinned people called Mekweisit, nine about war and adventure, and two about the Micmac people. Also contains a group of sixteen miscellaneous myths, including animal stories, aetiologies, and tales of the spirit world. Short preface on the method of collection and informants. Explanatory footnotes.

Melzack, Ronald. *The Day Tuk Became a Hunter*. New York: Dodd, Mead, 1967.
Ten Inuit tales are retold for children. The title story tells of the adventures of a young boy hunting his first bear. Also included are animal fables, a tale explaining how Raven brought light to the world, the story of the sea goddess Sedna, and tales of the supernatural and human transformation into animals. Short introduction to Inuit tales by the author, who also provides information about his literary sources in his acknowledgments. Illustrated with two-color drawings by Carol Jones.

Mooney, James. *Myths of the Cherokee*. Report 19 of the Bureau of American Ethnology. Washington, D.C.: U.S. Government Printing Office, 1900. Reprinted in *History, Myths, and Sacred Formulas of the Cherokees*. Asheville, N.C.: Historical Images, 1992.
Mooney worked for the Bureau of American Ethnology among the Cherokee of western North Carolina from 1887 to 1890 and produced this significant collection of their folk literature. In his introductory material, Mooney provides an extensive history of the Cherokee, discusses some characteristics of their stories, and identifies his Chero-kee informants. The 126 tales are arranged in seven thematic groups: tales of cosmogony and a flood; myths about quadrupeds; tales about birds; stories about snakes, fish, and insects; wonder stories; historical tales; and miscellaneous myths and legends. Many of these myths are aetiologies of natural objects, animals, customs, and ceremonies. In endnotes, Mooney offers some explanatory commentary and discusses parallel myths from other mythologies of the world. Two maps, eigh-teen photographs, two figures, glossary, and index. The reprint includes Mooney's *The Sacred Formulas of the Cherokees* (1891), a biography of Mooney by George Ellison, as well as endnotes and a photograph of Mooney.

Mullett, George Merrick. *Spider Woman Stories: Legends of the Hopi Indians*. Tucson: University of Arizona Press, 1979.
Eleven traditional stories of the Hopi of northern Arizona are retold in English in a version suitable for older children. Includes a creation tale, a story about the trickster Coyote, the adventures of a hero named Tiyo and his encounters with Spider Woman, and legends about her grand-sons, the twin war gods, Puukonhoya and Palunhoya. In a foreword,

Fred Eggan comments upon the Hopi, Mullett's contacts with them, and some characteristics of these tales. In a preface, Suzanne Mullett Smith provides a history of her mother's stories. Bibliography.

Nequatewa, Edmund. *Truth of a Hopi*, edited by Mary-Russell F. Colton. Bulletin 8 of the Museum of Northern Arizona. Flagstaff: Museum of Northern Arizona, 1936. Reprint. Flagstaff: Northland Press, 1967.
Eight tales blending the history and legends of several Hopi clans of Arizona are told by a member of the Sun Forehead Clan. The title narrative is divided into fourteen chapters and traces the story of several clans from their journey out of the underworld to their settlement in Arizona, the arrival of the Spaniards, their negotiations and troubles with the white man, and their resistance to the white man's ways, such as schooling. The other seven tales are shorter and deal with legends of ancient places, the gods, ladder dances, and an encounter with an anthropologist. Several begin with short comments by the editor. In a foreword, Colton describes the tales and associates them with specific Hopi clans. Explanatory endnotes by Colton. Four photographs and bibliography.

Newcomb, Franc Johnson. *Navaho Folk Tales*. Sante Fe, N.Mex.: Museum of Navaho Ceremonial Art, 1967. Reprint. Albuquerque: University of New Mexico Press, 1990.
From the traditional narratives of the Navajo of Arizona and New Mexico Newcomb creates a coherent cycle of tales about primeval times, as originally told to her own children in a powerful, simple English. Describes how the Navajo people emerged from four earlier worlds into the present, fifth world. The animal culture heroes Snail, Coyote, and Frog contribute the benefits of pure water, fire, and rain. Includes stories about a flood, monsters, the trickster Coyote, a hero called Hunter Boy, and the origin of the *hogan* or Navajo home. Introductory essay on the Navajo, their stories, and this collection. In a foreword to the first edition, Bertha P. Dutton, director of the Museum of Navaho Ceremonial Art, offers some information about Newcomb and the history of her book. In a foreword to the reprint, Paul G. Zolbrod supports the accuracy of Newcomb's versions of the tales. Illustrated with drawings by Alfred Clah.

Nicolar, Joseph. *The Life and Traditions of the Red Man*. Bangor, Maine: C. H. Glass, 1893. Reprint. Fredericton, New Brunswick: Saint Annes Point Press, 1979.

The grandson of a Penobscot chief in Maine retells some of the traditions of his people. Chapters 1-3 center on the adventures of the trickster Gluskap, here called Klose-kur-beh, or the Man from Nothing. In these narratives Klose-kur-beh is created and instructed by the Great Spirit, marries, destroys a great serpent, journeys to the north by sea, hunts a moose, assists in the creation of the first corn and tobacco, and disappears. Chapters 4-6 are based on the oral history of the Penobscot and recollect years of famine, the arrival of the Europeans, and warfare. Some influence from Roman Catholicism is present in these tales. In a concluding chapter, Nicolar discusses the meaning of some Penobscot words. Author's preface. The reprint includes a photograph of Nicolar, a bibliography, and an introductory essay by James D. Wherry with information about Nicolar's life and the importance of his work.

Norman, Howard A. *Where the Chill Came From: Cree Windigo Tales and Journeys*. San Francisco: North Point Press, 1982.
Between 1969 and 1980 Norman gathered and translated these thirty-one tales told by the Swampy Cree people of sub-Arctic Canada about a fearsome spirit-being called Windigo and its encounters with human beings. This creature is sometimes an ice skeleton, sometimes a dangerous wandering giant with a heart of ice, and sometimes a starving human crazed by a malevolent spirit. Endnotes include information about tale informants. In an introductory essay, with separate endnotes, Norman uses conversations with Cree elders to illustrate aspects of Cree culture and storytelling traditions.

_____. *The Wishing Bone Cycle: Narrative Poems from the Swampy Cree Indians*. New York: Stonehill, 1976.
This collection of poetic tales was gathered among the Swampy Cree of northern Manitoba and Ontario and is presented here in English translation. The thirty trickster tales about a wishbone with metamorphic powers are not traditional but are the invention of a Cree named Nibènegenesábe. Also contains songs, lullabies, and poems explaining the origin of personal names. More mythological is a tale about Wichikäpache, the Cree creator and trickster. Introductory commentary for each grouping. In a preface, Jerome Rothenberg discusses poetic features of these narratives. Map and endnotes.

Nungak, Zebedee, and Eugene Arima. *Eskimo Stories—Unikkaatuat*. Ottawa: The Queen's Printer, 1969.
A collection of forty-six "legend carvings" made by Povungnituk Inuit of Hudson Bay in Canada. Each legend includes a photograph of the

carving, a transcription (in the Povungnituk language) of the story the carver told about the carving, and an English translation of the story. The subjects of these stories include myths, legends, historical accounts, and observations about the natural world. In an appendix, the authors review some general features of central Inuit mythology, especially attitudes toward spirits, the human soul, the afterlife, shamans, magic, and the natural world. Also contains photographs of carvers and storytellers.

Nusbaum, Aileen. *Zuñi Indian Tales*. New York: G. P. Putnam's Sons, 1926.
Retells for children sixteen Zuñi tales originally recorded by Frank Hamilton Cushing. Includes a foundation legend about Zuñi cities, animal tales about Gopher and Coyote, hunting stories, a journey to the House of the Sun, and tales of the supernatural. Six black-and-white drawings by Margaret Finnan.

Opler, Morris Edward. *Myths and Tales of the Chiricahua Apache Indians*. Philadelphia: American Folk-Lore Society, 1942.
These 103 myths and variants were collected between 1931 and 1935 among the Chiricahua living in New Mexico. Arranged thematically. Includes myths about a destructive flood, deeds of culture heroes, tales of a giant, a contest for daylight called the Moccasin game, many adventures of the trickster Coyote, and stories about the supernatural and foolish or unfaithful people. Short history of the Chiricahua in the preface. In an appendix, David French offers comparative notes indicating the distribution of Chiricahua stories among the Apache peoples. Footnotes and bibliography.

_____. *Myths and Tales of the Jicarilla Apache Indians*. Vol. 31 in *Memoirs of the American Folk-Lore Society*. New York: American Folk-Lore Society, 1938. Reprint. New York: Kraus Reprint, 1969.
A selection of 139 tales collected among the Jicarilla Apache of the Southwest U.S. in 1934-1935. The first thematic group, dealing with the Jicarilla origin myth, includes twenty-three tales about the creation of the world and heavenly bodies, the emergence of the people, aetiologies of various ceremonies, and a great flood. Followed by several small groupings about the Hactcin ceremony, the origin of games and artifacts, agriculture and rain, hunting rituals, and encounters with supernatural animals. The section on animal stories contains sixty-six tales about the trickster Coyote as well as several tales about Antelope. The other groups represent stories about foolish people,

monstrous enemies, and the winning of wives. Excluded from this collection are several common Jicarilla tale types, including war tales, joking relationships between cousins, visits by the sick and dying to the Land of the Dead, and animal fables such as the adventures of Bluejay. In a prefatory essay, Opler includes some conversations with Jicarilla informants, discusses characteristics of their culture and mythology, and explains the organization of this collection. Index.

_____. *Myths and Legends of the Lipan Apache Indians.* Vol. 36 in *Memoirs of the American Folk-Lore Society.* New York: American Folk-Lore Society, 1940. Reprint. New York: Kraus Reprint, 1969.
These 169 tales of the Lipan Apache of the Southwest U.S. were recorded with the help of an interpreter in 1935. The thematic arrangement of tales parallels that in Opler's collection of Jicarilla Apache tales. Seventy-five of the tales deal with the trickster Coyote. Other narratives are myths of emergence and culture heroes, tales about supernatural beings, human encounters with monsters and animals, myths about agriculture, the origin of games and of death, animal tales, and stories about the foolish Spotted Wood People and about war. Some tales appear in several versions. In a prefatory essay, Opler offers a history of the Lipan Apache, discusses their relationship with the Jicarilla Apache and characterstics of their mythology, and explains how these tales were recorded. Explanatory footnotes, bibliography, and index.

Palmer, William R. *Pahute Indian Legends.* Salt Lake City, Utah: Desert Book, 1946.
Retells twenty-five aetiological tales of the Pahute of Utah. These myths explain natural phenomena such as the rising of the sun, Pahute ceremonies and customs, and physical features of animals. Explanation of Pahute astronomy in Chapter 1. In a preface and introductory essay, Palmer provides background about the Pahute and their culture and some information about his informants. Black-and-white drawings by Eugene Palmer. Glossary of Pahute words.

_____. *Why the North Star Stands Still and Other Indian Legends.* Englewood Cliffs, N.J.: Prentice-Hall, 1957.
This collection of twenty-six traditional legends and stories of the Pahute of Utah are written especially for schoolchildren. These tales, which the author originally heard at Pahute gatherings, are accompanied by illustrations by Ursula Koering. Most of the stories are aetiologies and explain features of the animal, natural, or Pahute worlds,

such as why the coyote looks up when he howls, why rocks cannot travel, and why the Pahutes are nomadic. Appendix on Pahute astronomy and a glossary of Pahute words and names.

Parker, Arthur C. *Seneca Myths and Folk Tales*. Buffalo: Buffalo Historical Society, 1923.

These seventy-two traditional tales of the Seneca of western New York are retold in translation by an archaeologist at the New York State Museum who gathered material from Seneca informants in 1903-1904. The myths are arranged thematically. Eight creation myths and aetiological tales about constellations, twelve tales about boys who overcome magic and the supernatural, nine about love and marriage, nine about cannibals and sorcerers, thirteen about talking animals, and eight about giants, pygmies, and monster bears. Also contains thirteen Seneca traditions, especially about witchcraft. Some are followed by explanatory endnotes. Preceding these tales are three sections of background material, including a summary of Seneca religious beliefs and a catalogue of their deities, nature beings, and magical creatures. Lists of typical themes, incidents, and objects which appear in these myths. Also contains a list of components in Seneca cosmological myth. In the introduction, Parker discusses Seneca storytelling customs and explains different techniques in recording folklore. Seven photographs, eleven drawings by a Seneca chief, and nine figures. Bibliography and index.

Parsons, Elsie Clews. *Kiowa Tales*. Vol. 22 in *Memoirs of the American Folk-Lore Society*. New York. American Folk-Lore Society, 1929.

Ninety-seven myths and tales of personal recollection recorded through an interpreter among the Kiowa of Oklahoma in 1927. The first forty-three tales deal with primeval, mythological subjects such as ritual origins, the end of the world, and especially Sendeh, the first human and Kiowa trickster figure. Although Sendeh has the ability to change into the shape of any animal, he is never identified with the Coyote trickster figure common among many peoples of the western part of the continent. The remaining fifty-four narratives describe intersocial relationships, ceremonies, and personal life. In an introductory essay, Parsons offers comments on her method of recording, on her informants. and on some characteristics of Kiowa culture and tales. Information about society memberships, genealogies of narrators, personal names, and terms for kinship, age, and sex in an appendix. List of informants, genealogical chart, and bibliography.

_____. *Taos Tales*. Vol. 34 in *Memoirs of the American Folk-Lore Society*. Philadelphia: American Folk-Lore Society, 1940. Reprint. New York: Kraus Reprint, 1969.

Ninety-eight legends and variants collected by the author among the Taos, a Pueblo people of the Southwest U.S., are here presented in English translation. Many are about Coyote and various talking animals. Includes tales of trickery, origin, and adventure. In an appendix two tales are recorded in the original language with interlinear English translation followed by a free translation. Short preface on the Taos and their tales. Footnotes and bibliography.

_____. *Tewa Tales*. Vol. 19 in *Memoirs of the American Folk-Lore Society*. New York: American Folk-Lore Society, 1926.

Part 1 of this collection consists of seventy-six myths of emergence and animal tales of the Tewa of New Mexico. In Part 2 are thirty emergence myths and novelistic tales of Tewa, who migrated to First Mesa in Arizona at the beginning of the eighteenth century. Variants are provided for some tales. All are told in English translation. These stories are about traditional figures such as the Corn Maidens, war spirits, and, especially, trickster Coyote, who is here known as Water-drag Man. In an introductory essay, Parsons offers a history of the Tewa, discusses characteristics of Tewa storytelling and compares the New Mexico and Arizona tales. Some information about sources in the explanatory footnotes. Bibliography.

Penney, Grace Jackson. *Tales of the Cheyennes*. Boston: Houghton Mifflin, 1953.

Fourteen tales of the Cheyenne of Oklahoma are retold for children. Includes aetiologies, a story about Coyote, and six tales about Wihio, a dwarf trickster. Introductory essay on Cheyenne storytelling.

Phinney, Archie. *Nez Percé Texts*. Vol. 25 in *Columbia University Contributions to Anthropology*. New York: Columbia University Press, 1934. Reprint. New York: AMS Press, 1969.

These forty-one texts were obtained by a prominent American anthropologist from a Nez Percé woman in Fort Lapwai in 1929-1930. The original Sahaptin texts are accompanied by literal, interlinear English translation followed by a free English translation. Abstracts of the tales appear in an appendix. Most of the narratives are about the trickster Coyote and his adventures with other animals and with humans. In an introductory essay, Phinney describes some characteristics of the tales and their language. Footnotes.

Price, Samuel Goodale. *Black Hills: The Land of Legend*. Los Angeles, Calif.: DeVorss, 1935.

A diverse collection of materials on the Black Hills of South Dakota and Colorado. In Part 1 Price retells fourteen legends explaining various geographic features in the region, especially Devil's Tower and Mount Rushmore. In Part 2 are summaries of seven legendary gold rush tales. Part 3 combines historical data and tourist information about specific sites with some folklore of the hills. Several of the selections are written in verse by Francis Halley Brockett. Some information about sources in the preface. Map and thirty-four photographs and drawings.

Radin, Paul. *Some Myths and Tales of the Ojibwa of Southeastern Ontario*. Memoir 48 of the Canada Department of Mines Geological Survey. Ottawa: Government Printing Bureau, 1914.

Included among these forty-five tales are several adventures of Nenebojo, the Ojibwa changer and trickster. Also contains animal fables, tales of human relationships, encounters with animals and the supernatural, and metamorphosis. Names of informants are provided in the heading of each tale.

_____. *The Trickster: A Study in American Indian Mythology*. New York: Greenwood Press, 1969.

Contains two groups of tales of the Siouan-speaking Winnebago of Wisconsin and Nebraska followed by explanatory endnotes. The forty-nine stories in Part 1 are about Wakdjunkaga, or The Tricky One. Part 2 contains twenty-four myths about a talking trickster hare. Also contains summaries of a Tlingit myth about a trickster raven and fifty-two Assiniboine tales about a human trickster called Sitconski. Part 3 is an analysis of this material with information on Radin's Winnebago informant and text, Winnebago history, culture, mythology, and literary tradition. Also contains an interpretation and literary study of the Winnebago trickster figures with some comparison to other North American tricksters. In Part 4 Karl Kerényi compares the Winnebago trickster to the Greek trickster god Hermes. Part 5 is an essay by Carl G. Jung on the psychology of the trickster figure.

Ramsey, Jarold, ed. *Coyote Was Going There*. Seattle: University of Washington Press, 1977.

This collection of Native American tales from Oregon makes available to the general reader 116 tales originally published by scholars such as Franz Boas and Archie Phinney. Not all of the tales deal with the trickster Coyote. In addition to many cosmogonies and aetiological myths, a few selections deal with semi-historical encounters with the White Man. The myths are arranged in six geographic groups. Prominent are tales of the Nez Percé of Northeastern Oregon, the Wishram and Wasco of the Columbia River area, the Chinook and Kalapuya of the Willamette Valley, the Tillamook, Chinook and Coos of the coastal region, the Modoc and Klamath of southwestern Oregon, and the Northern Paiute of the Great Basin. In an introductory essay the editor discusses some cultural and thematic features of these myths. Explanatory endnotes contain information about sources and informants. Note on the language, many photographs, illustrations, musical scores, mythological map of Oregon, and bibliography.

Rand, Silas T. *Legends of the Micmacs*. New York: Longmans, Green, 1894. Reprint. New York: Johnson Reprint, 1971.
Eighty-seven tales of ancient times, magic, war, and a superhuman being called Gluskap as recorded in English by a nineteenth-century Christian missionary who worked among the the Micmac of Nova Scotia for forty years. In a three-part introduction, Helen L. Webster provides a biography of Rand, a bibliography of his lifeworks, and background on the manners, customs, language, and literature of the Micmac. In a preface, Webster describes Rand's work and the origin of this book.

Rasmussen, Knud. *The Eagle's Gift*. Translated by Isobel Hutchinson. Garden City, N.Y.: Doubleday, Doran, 1932.
These fifty tales were collected between 1921 and 1924 among the Inupait of Alaska by Rasmussen, a well-known Danish explorer, and are retold here for the general reader. Includes creation stories, tales of adventure, and encounters with the spirit world. In the preface, Rasmussen explains the origin of the Danish title for this book, *Fest-tens Ga-ve* (how joy came to man). The English title is based upon the second story in the collection, in which a young hunter named Marten slays an eagle and receives a gift from the bird's mother. Each tale is followed by the name and home of Rasmussen's informant. Illustrated with four color and seventeen black-and-white drawings by Ernst Hansen. Map.

_____. *Eskimo Folk-Tales*, edited and translated by W. W. Worster. London and Copenhagen: Gyldendal, 1921.
This selection of fifty-two tales of Greenland Inuit collected by Rasmussen includes legends of emergence, adventure, ghosts, and the

supernatural, monsters, anthropomorphic animals, and aetiology. In translating these narratives, Worster has not hesitated to simplify and abridge the original for the benefit of the general reader. In an introductory essay, Worster discusses some features of Inuit mythology and religious beliefs. Geographic sources for the tales are listed in an appendix. Twelve line drawings by Inuit artists.

Reichard, Gladys A. *An Analysis of Coeur d'Alene Indian Myths.* Philadelphia: American Folk-Lore Society, 1947.
Forty-eight myths collected in 1927 and 1929 from two storytellers among the Coeur d'Alene people of northern Idaho. Grouped into three categories: Coyote myths, myths not in the Coyote cycle, and tales with historical elements. Three introductory chapters deal with the style of the myths, their cultural reflections, and processes of diffusion and distribution. Retellings of the myths are followed by comparisons to versions of the myths told by other North American peoples. Occasional footnotes and bibliography.

Reid, Dorothy M. *Tales of Nanabozho.* New York: Henry Z. Walck, 1963.
Twenty-one tales about the Sleeping Giant of the Ojibwa retold for juveniles. The giant Nanabozho is associated with a rocky promontory in Canada near Lake Superior. The Ojibwa consider this giant to be creator, trickster, and magician and tell tales about his coming, his inventions, his adventures, and his final sleep. Short preface, pronunciation guide, epilogue about the arrival of Europeans, and bibliography. Illustrations by Donald Grant.

Rink, Henrik. *Tales and Traditions of the Eskimo.* Edinburgh and London: William Blackwood and Sons, 1875. Reprint. Montreal: McGill-Queens University Press, 1974.
Many of these 150 tales of the Greenland and Labrador Inuit are folktale adventures about young children, orphans, husbands, and wives, and widows. magic, the supernatural, giants and journeys, even to the underworld, are important themes. Each of these tales is told in English and is preceded by information about sources. Some appear only in abstract. A detailed introductory section includes information about the Inuit way of life, language, social order, religion, culture, history, and contacts with Europeans. In a short introduction written for the reprint, Helge Larsen offers some perspective on the significance of Rink's work. Numerous line drawings by Inuit artists.

Robe, Stanley L. *Hispanic Folktales from New Mexico*. Berkeley: University of California Press, 1977.

Although U.S. citizens since 1848, the Hispanic peoples of southern New Mexico have retained not only their Spanish language but also many aspects of Mexican culture, including folklore. This collection of 205 tales, translated into English, is grouped in four categories: animal tales, ordinary folktales, jokes and anecdotes, and formula tales. Each tale is followed by information about the informant, date and place of recording, and classification according to Aarne-Thompson folktale types. Introductory essay on the culture and the history of this collection. Registers of tale types and motifs. Bibliography.

Robinson, Gail, and Douglas Hill. *Coyote the Trickster*. New York: Crane Russak, 1976.

Two Canadian poets retell twelve tales about the legendary trickster, changer, and culture hero of many North American peoples. Usually this figure is Coyote, but several stories about the Raven trickster are also included. In these tales the trickster steals a blanket and fire, brings light to the world, encounters giants, and even journeys to the Land of the Dead. The origin of each tale is indicated by ethnic group only. Short introductory essay on the North American trickster figure. Illustrated with black-and-white drawings by Graham McCallum.

Ruoff, A. LaVonne Brown. "Introduction to American Indian Literatures." In *American Indian Literatures*, by A. LaVonne Brown Ruoff. New York: Modern Language Association, 1990.

An essay introducing a bibliographic review and selected bibliography of books, films, and other materials dealing with the broad range of Native American literature, both traditional and contemporary. Ruoff provides historical background and discusses general characteristics of both oral and written literature. Of particular interest to the study of mythology is the section on oral narrative, which deals especially with tales of creation, emergence, and trickster figures. Includes significant quotation of original material in translation.

Russell, Frank. "Linguistics." In *The Pima Indians*, by Frank Russell. Vol. 26 in *Report of the Bureau of American Ethnology*. Washington, D.C.: U.S. Government Printing Office, 1908; reprint, 1975.

This section in a detailed ethnological study of the Pima of Arizona includes transcripts, interlinear English translations, and free English translations of a variety of songs and speeches. Of mythological note are several archaic songs about creation, a cataclysmic flood, the netherworld, and the emergence of the people. Names of informants are included. Footnotes.

_____. "Sophiology." In *The Pima Indians*, by Frank Russell. Vol. 26 *Report of the Bureau of American Ethnology*. Washington, D.C.: U.S. Government Printing Office, 1908.
This section in Russell's ethnology of the Pima of Arizona includes English versions and abstracts of two versions of a creation myth called "Smoke Talk," the story of Coyote the trickster, myths about the children of cloud, a metamorphic skull, and the origin of horses, and ten nursery tales, especially about Coyote. Also contains sections on Pima deities, the soul, holy places, and dreams. Names of informants are included. Footnotes.

Sampson, Martin J., and Rosalie M. Whitney. *Swinomish Totem Pole Tribal Legends*. Bellingham, Wash.: Union Printing, 1938.
A little book containing retellings of tales depicted in carvings on a totem pole at Swinomish Reservation in Washington State. These nine legends, told by Sampson to Whitney, are accompanied by drawings of the carvings. They include origins and explanations of natural phenomena, supernatural occurrences, and cunning animals. Some are followed by explanatory commentary. In an introductory essay, Sampson provides a history of the totem pole and some information on the peoples who live on the Swinomish Reservation. Two photographs.

Sapir, Edward. *Wishram Texts*. Vol. 2 in *Publications of the American Ethnological Society*. Leiden: E. J. Brill, 1909.
Despite the title this collection contains not only thirty-eight texts of the Upper Chinookan Wishram of Washington State but also twenty-five tales and myths of the Wasco of Oregon. The Wishram texts were gathered in the field for Sapir by a native interpreter in 1905 and are published here in the original language with English translation on facing pages. The Wasco tales were recorded in the field by Jeremiah Curtin in 1885 and are published here in English translation. Two additional Upper Chinookan texts collected by Franz Boas are found in an appendix. Eighteen Wishram myths, mostly about Coyote, are accompanied by other texts, including descriptions of customs, letters, and non-mythical narratives, arranged according to type. The Wasco narratives are grouped into tales of human adventure, stories about guardian spirits, Coyote stories, myths about a stupid, child-stealing ogress called At!at!a'ia, and miscellaneous tales about animal heroes

and supernatural adventures. Sapir precedes each collection with an introductory essay on the texts and their history. Footnotes.

_____. *Yana Texts with Yana Myths.* Vol. 9 in *University of California Publications in American Archaeology and Ethnology.* Berkeley: University of California Press, 1910. Reprint. Berkeley: Kraus Reprint, 1964.

This collection of myths recorded by Sapir among the Yana of California in 1907 offers the original transcriptions with literal interlinear English translations followed by free English translations. The tales are arranged according to dialect and to type. In Part 1 are nine tales in the central dialect about Flint Boy, the theft of fire and a cataclysmic burning, an incredible journey to the moon, aetiology, the supernatural, and Coyote. In Part 2 four myths, especially about fire and Coyote, are followed by nine narratives and texts describing Yana customs. Supplemented by fifteen texts collected separately by R. B. Dixon. For only two of these are free English translations accompanied by the original Yana text. Dixon's texts deal with animals, Coyote, metamorphic people, the supernatural, and the creation of humankind. Introductory remarks on the Yana language are followed by a pronunciation guide. Footnotes.

Saxton, Dean, and Lucille Saxton. *O'othham Hoho'ok A'agitha: Legends and Lore of the Papago and Pima Indians.* Tucson: University of Arizona Press, 1973.

Two anthropologists and linguists offer bilingual versions of the oral tradition of the Papago and Pima of Arizona. *O'othham* is the Papago and Pima word for themselves. *Hoho'ok A'Agitha* refers to their stories about creatures of extraordinary powers. The tales are arranged in four thematic groups: aetiologies about the world, stars, corn, and a great flood; animal legends, especially about the trickster Coyote; stories of human emergence from the lower world; and tales of great troubles caused by dangerous beings, drought, taboos, and cruel rulers. The original-language versions and literal English translations appear on the same page. Most of the material used by the Saxtons was originally recorded about 1911 by a native Papago named Juan Dolores. Some additional information about this collection and its origins appears in a foreword, acknowledgments, and introduction. Appendices include a bibliography, notes on the legends, an alphabet, and a Papago/Pima-to-English vocabulary. Some footnotes, black-and-white drawings, and a photograph of Juan Dolores.

Schoolcraft, Henry Rowe. *Algic Researches.* 2 vols. New York: Harper & Brothers, 1839. Reprint. Baltimore: Clearfield, 1992.

Often called the father of American folklore, Schoolcraft here offers versions of forty-six Native American myths and legends which are reasonably accurate and retain value despite the original date of publication. Manabozho, an Algonquin hero in this collection, became the prototpye for Henry Wadsworth Longfellow's romantic poem "Hiawatha." Longfellow, not Schoolcraft, originally conflated the Algonquin figure with the Iroquois hero Hiawatha. Other tales in this collection feature aetiology, magic and the supernatural, animal fables, and extraordinary adventures. The term "Algic," a blend of "Alleghany" and "Atlantic," was coined by Schoolcraft to describe the diverse Native American peoples who lived east of the Mississippi. Schoolcraft provides two introductory essays dealing with these peoples and their tales at the beginning of Volume 1. In an introductory essay written for the reprint, W. K. McNeil comments on Schoolcraft's career and works. Footnotes.

_____. *The Myth of Hiawatha and Other Oral Legends.* Rev. ed. Philadelphia: J. B. Lippincott, 1856. Reprint. New York: Kraus Reprint, 1971.

This collection of forty-two tales of Northeast Woodlands peoples is only loosely based on legends about a sixteenth-century Mohawk chieftain. The revised edition is dedicated to Henry Wadsworth Longfellow. In addition to the legend of Hiawatha are aetiologies, encounters with wild animals, journeys to celestial bodies or deities, and legends about the supernatural and ghosts. Each tale is introduced by analysis and commentary by Schoolcraft. While he labels the tales as either Algonquin, Chippewa, Dakota, Iroquois, Ojibwa, or Ottawa, these divisions are uncertain. Chippewa and Ojibwa, for example, refer today to the same people. Schoolcraft's style includes many nineteenth-century embellishments which are no longer considered authentic. A collection of poems based upon traditional tales appears in an appendix. The introductory essay should be read only as an illustration of stereotypical nineteenth-century attitudes toward the native peoples of North America. Footnotes.

Schultz, James Willard. *Blackfeet Tales of Glacier National Park.* Boston: Houghton Mifflin, 1916. Reprint. New York: Gordon Press, 1977.

Worked into a diary recording a Blackfeet's visit back to his family and friends are fifteen Blackfeet tales connected with various geographic features in what is now Glacier National Park. Many of the tales look back to a primeval time when humans talked with animals and include aetiologies about horses and tobacco, ritual stories, and tales of adventure. The first tale records Blackfeet memories of an early European explorer named Hugh Monroe. Twenty-three photographs.

Sheer, George F., ed. *Cherokee Animal Tales.* New York: Holiday House, 1968.

These thirteen tales about talking and superhuman animals were collected by James Mooney among the Cherokee of North Carolina at the end of the nineteenth century and appeared in *Myths of the Cherokee* (1900). They are here republished for young readers with illustrations by Robert Frankenberg. All of these tales explain some physical characteristic of an animal, such as how the groundhog lost his tail or how the deer got his horns. In an introductory essay, the editor provides a history of the Cherokee and some background to Mooney's collection.

Simmons, Leo W. "Legends and Myths of the Hopi." In *Sun Chief: The Autobiography of a Hopi Indian,* edited by Leo W. Simmons. New Haven, Conn.: Yale University Press, 1942.

In this appendix to the life of Don C. Talayesva of Oraibi, Arizona, the editor retells some examples of the traditional stories which the Sun Chief heard as a Hopi child. Paraphrases of the Hopi creation story and a tale of humankind's escape from the underworld are accompanied by stories about early settlements, metamorphosis, the supernatural, and adventurous journeys, even to the House of the Dead.

Skinner, Charles Montgomery. *Myths and Legends Beyond Our Borders.* Philadelphia: J. B. Lippincott, 1898.

The first half of this book contains sixty-five tales from Canada. Some tell of the arrival of Europeans and others deal with later historical legends. Includes tales representing traditional beliefs of the Native American peoples as well as Christian missionary stories. No sources are provided for the tales. Four illustrations.

Smith, Bertha H. *Yosemite Legends.* San Francisco: Paul Elder, 1904.

Retells six legends of the Yosemite of California, including tales about a grizzly bear known as Yo-sem-i-te, the Spirit of the Evil Wind called Po-ho-no, and white water called Py-we-ack, aetiologies of rocks called Hum-moo or Lost arrow and Kom-po-pai-ses or Leaping Frog Rocks, and an unhappy love story about the gods Tu-tock-ah-nu-lah and Tis-sa-ack. No information is provided on sources for these tales. Illustrated with thirteen drawings by Florence Lundborg.

Spence, Lewis. *The Myths of the North American Indians.* London: George G. Harrap & Company. Reprint. New York: Kraus Reprint, 1972.

This general introduction to the mythologies of North America is a result of a keen interest in comparative mythologies at the beginning of the twentieth century. Chapter 1 offers some ethnographic and historical background, with information on the divisions, customs, and history of these peoples. Their world views and religious beliefs are described in Chapter 2, with special attention to beliefs in totemism, fetishism, deities, creation myths, the natural world, death, burial, and medicine men. Individual chapters offer summaries of the myths and legends of the Algonquin, Iroquois, Sioux, Pawnees, and northern and northwestern peoples. Thirty-five illustrations of the myths, linguistic map, bibliography, glossary, and index.

Spencer, Katherine. *Mythology and Values: An Analysis of Navaho Chantway Myths.* Vol. 48 in *Memoirs of the American Folk-Lore Society.* Philadelphia: American Folk-Lore Society, 1957.

This scholarly study examines the Navajo world view and social values as illustrated by eighteen Chantway myths about heroes, their contacts with supernatural creatures, especially the trickster Coyote, and their acquisition of ceremonial powers. Part 7 contains abstracts of these myths. The rest of the book is an analysis of the myths, with sections on plot construction and value themes, elements of story content such as fertility, ritual observance and property, and sanctions and standards concerning property, sex, marriage, family, and interpersonal relationships. Endnotes and bibliography.

Spott, Robert, and Alfred Louis Kroeber. *Yurok Narratives.* Vol. 35 in *University of California Publications in American Archaeology and Ethnology.* Berkeley: University of California Press, 1942.

These thirty-seven narratives were told by Spott and other Yurok of central Washington, to the ethnologist Kroeber between 1933 and 1940. The tales are presented in three chronological groups, beginning with eighteen recollections of personal histories from the nineteenth century and followed by five legends of an earlier time. Most mythological are the fourteen narratives in Part 3. These tales, dealing with a primeval time when a Woge race created the world, tell of an inland whale, the culture hero Wohpekumeu, the origin of humankind, hunting, marriage, great journeys, and ceremonial dances. Each tale is followed by explanatory commentary by Kroeber. In a prefatory essay Kroeber offers a biography of Spott and discusses some characteristics of these tales. Map, list of informants, chronology of historical events, footnotes, bibliography, and index.

Stirling, Matthew W. *Origin Myth of Acoma and Other Records*. Bulletin 135 of the Smithsonian Institution Bureau of American Ethnology. Washington, D.C.: U.S. Government Printing Office, 1942.

These myths of the Acoma Pueblo were collected in 1928 and are presented here in English. Myths of Acoma origin and migration are accompanied by a narrative about the war twins Masewi and Oyoyewi as well three texts dealing with Acoma customs. Although this material was recorded during a sung performance, no musical score is provided. In a preface, Stirling describes the way this material was collected and published. Eight figures and seventeen plates, one in color, of artifacts and sites. Detailed explanatory endnotes for these plates appear in an appendix. Footnotes and bibliography.

Swanton, John Reed. *Haida Texts and Myths*. Bulletin 29 of the Smithsonian Institution Bureau of American Ethnology. Washington, D.C.: U.S. Government Printing Office, 1905.

These texts were gathered from Haida informants on the Queen Charlotte Islands of British Columbia in 1900-1901. The material is arranged according to format. Two texts in Haida dialects accompanied by interlinear and free English translations are followed by twelve tales told in English and followed by Haida texts. The remaining fifty-eight myths are offered only in English. These myths are about Raven, war, hunting, metamorphic people, supernatural powers, and shamans. Names of informants are indicated in brackets. Introductory comments on the source of the material is followed by a pronunciation guide. Five line drawings illustrating Haida artifacts.

_____. *Myths and Tales of the Southeastern Indians*. Bulletin 88 of the Smithsonian Institution Bureau of American Ethnology. Washington, D.C.: U.S. Government Printing Office, 1929.

The 205 tales in this collection were recorded in the field among the Creek, Alabama, Koasati, Hitchiti, and Natchez in Alabama, Louisiana, Texas, and Oklahoma between 1908 and 1914. Tales are generally organized by ethnic group. Within these groups, myths about natural phenomena, a great flood, and ancient heroes are followed by stories about journeys to the Land of the Dead, encounters with animals and supernatural creatures, and animal legends, especially about the trickster rabbit, popular among the peoples of the Southeast U.S. Short introduction. In an appendix themes in these myths are compared to those of other Native American peoples.

_____. *Tlingit Myths and Texts*. Bulletin 39 of Smithsonian Institution Bureau of American Ethnology. Washington, D.C.: U.S. Government Printing Office, 1909.

These 106 myths of the Tlingit of Alaska were collected by the author in 1904 and tell stories about Raven, aetiologies, human metamorphosis into animals, hunting tales, and animal legends. Most were recorded in English and are arranged according to the two locations where they were told. The last eighteen tales were told in Tlingit and are recorded in their original form with interlinear English translation and a more polished English translation at the top of the page. In addition to these narratives, a speech, song lyrics, and the description of a ceremony are offered in Tlingit with interlinear and polished English translations. Abstracts of all myths appear in an appendix.

Teit, James. *Traditions of the Thompson River Indians of British Columbia*. Vol. 6 in *Memoirs of the American Folk-Lore Society*. New York: American Folk-Lore Society, 1898. Reprint. New York: Kraus Reprint, 1969.

Thirty-eight tales of the Nlak'a'pamux-speaking peoples who live on the Fraser and Thompson rivers in British Columbia are accompanied by two tales of the Lillooet, who live to the north. All these tales are recorded in translation and abstracts are provided in an appendix. The plots of many of these narratives center on transformers or culture heroes such as Coyote and the Old Man. In an introductory essay, Franz Boas provides a sketch of the customs of the Thompson River people and the general characteristics of their tales, with detailed analysis of several tales. Endnotes and index.

Thompson, Stith. "The Folktale in a Primitive Culture: North American Indian." In *The Folktale*, by Stith Thompson. Berkeley: University of California Press, 1977.

This broad survey of the nature and function of folktales in North America begins with background on collection techniques and geographical and cultural divisions of the North American people. Uses a series of motifs to show how these folktales are based on a limited number of narrative themes shared with tales from other cultures. These Aarne-Thompson motifs are collected in two indexes. Includes chapters on creation myths, trickster tales, tests, and hero tales, journeys to the other world, and stories about animal spouses. Footnotes.

_____. *Tales of the North American Indians*. Bloomington: Indiana University Press, 1929.

These ninety-six tales are selected and annotated by a prominent American ethnologist. Grouped thematically, they include myths about creation, mythical incidents about the natural world, trickster tales, especially about Coyote, hero tales, journeys to the other world, animal fables, tales borrowed from Europeans, including Aesop's fables, and several Bible stories. Bibliographic sources are provided for each tale. In an appendix the tales are listed geographically. All regions of North America are represented, including the Arctic, Pacific Northwest, California, Great Plains, Northeast Woodlands, the Southeast, and the Southwest U.S. Detailed endnotes in which motifs are explained and compared to other versions. List of motifs, bibliography, and map.

Trejo, Judy. "Coyote Tales: A Paiute Commentary." *Journal of American Folklore* 87 (1974): 66-71. Reprinted in *Readings in American Folklore*, edited by Jan Harold Brunvand. New York: W. W. Norton, 1979.

A Paiute woman accompanies four Coyote tales recalled from her childhood with interpretative comments valuable because of their perspective from inside the tradition. In these graphic tales, the troublesome Coyote is the cause of tornadoes and cyclones, sexually transmitted disease, the appearance of female genitalia, and the pointed ears of the bobcat. The reprint includes an introduction by Brunvand. Footnotes.

Troughton, Joanna. *How Rabbit Stole the Fire*. 2d ed. New York: Peter Bedrick Books, 1986.

This aetiological tale about a crafty rabbit and wonderworker who steals fire from the Sky People for the benefit of earth creatures is based upon the traditions of the Creek, Hitchiti, and Koasati of the Southeast U.S. Troughton retells and illustrates the tale for children. This rabbit figure is known as Manabozho among many Native American peoples east of the Mississippi.

_____. *Who Will Be the Sun?* New York: Peter Bedrick Books, 1985.

This aetiological tale of the Kutenai of Montana is retold for children with color illustrations by the author. The plot centers on a contest among the animals to determine who should be the sun. In the end Lynx becomes the sun while the hot-headed Coyote remains a trickster.

Tyler, Hamilton A. *Pueblo Animals and Myths*. Norman: University of Oklahoma Press, 1975.

Analyzes the roles of various animals in the religion and myths of the Zuñi and other Pueblo peoples of the Southwest U.S. Separate chapters are devoted to the badger, antelope, deer, bison, elk and sheep, rabbits, coyote, bear, mountain lion, and animal souls and gods. In these chapters, Tyler summarizes myths and ceremonies about these animals and discusses their religious significance and roles. Short preface on Pueblo gods, animals, and world view. Maps, bibliography, endnotes, and index.

_____. *Pueblo Gods and Myths*. Norman: University of Oklahoma Press, 1964.
This overview of the gods and other supernatural creatures of the Pueblo contains significant paraphrasings of myth narratives as well as frequent comparisons to ancient Greek deities. Introductory essay on the Pueblo and their culture. Individual chapters are devoted to the deity Maasaw, or skeleton Man, the dead, deities of creation and tales of creation, flood and migration, the Corn Mother goddess, the Hopi corn germinator Muingwu, Pautiwa the deified sun of the Zuñi, Cipikne the god of the Six Directions and the structure of the universe, deities of place, the Zuñi clown god Koyemshi, the war twins, the horned water serpent, and animism. The discussion of Pueblo beliefs in animism makes significant reference to the work of Sigmund Freud and Martin Buber. Maps, table of town names, footnotes, bibliography, and index.

Underhill, Ruth M. *Red Man's Religion: Beliefs and Practices of the Indians North of Mexico*. Chicago: University of Chicago Press, 1965.
This general introduction to the religious beliefs and cults of Native Americans includes some illustration of the relationship between myth and ritual in these cultures. Contains references to myths from several nations, including the Cherokee, Papago, Apache, and Inuit. Themes include myths of origin and the spirit world. Thirty-four illustrations, four maps, and index.

Velarde, Pablita. *Old Father the Storyteller*. Globe, Ariz.: Dale Stuart King, 1960.
A prominent New Mexican painter of Tewa descent retells six traditional tales she heard as a child. Old Father narrates a myth about the constellation Long Sash (Orion), a Cinderella-type tale about Turkey Girl, the story of a human foundling raised by deer, the adventures of an enchanted hunter, the origin of the Tewa butterfly dance, and the contest between a wizard and humorous twin boys. Supplemented by

Velarde's own color illustrations. Introductory essay on the artist and her tales by D. Hancock. Index.

Voegelin, Charles F. *The Shawnee Female Deity.* Vol. 10 in *Yale University Publications in Anthropology.* New Haven, Conn.: Yale University Press, 1936.
This scholarly examination of tales about kohkomhθena (Our Grandmother), the divine creator and supreme deity of the Shawnee of Oklahoma, is based upon field work conducted in 1933-1934. Following an introductory section, Voegelin discusses the goddess's personality, her acts of creation and revelation, and her place in Shawnee religion. Integrated into the text are paraphrases and translations of tales obtained from Shawnee informants identified only by initials. Footnotes.

Voth, H. R. *The Traditions of the Hopi.* Publication 96 of the Field Columbian Museum. Chicago: Field Columbian Museum, 1905.
These 110 tales were collected among the Hopi of Arizona in 1903-1904 and were translated into these English versions by the author. Abstracts for the tales are provided in an appendix. Begins with tales of origin and emergence and includes stories about monsters, hunting, warfare, contact with Spaniards, and animals, especially the trickster Coyote.

Walker, James R. *Lakota Myth,* edited by Elaine A. Jahner. Lincoln: University of Nebraska Press, 1983.
These fourteen myths were collected among the Oglala Sioux of Nebraska by Walker, who served as a physician at the Pine Ridge Reservation between 1896 and 1914. The preface and introduction include information about Walker and his work among the Lakota, a history of this edition and some sources for comparative analysis of these myths. The tales are grouped according to informants. Editorial comments about these informants and their tales precedes each group. Some of these myths are schematized and retold in a more literary style by Walker himself in the last part of the book. Includes tales about creation, about the Lakota spirits, especially Tate, the wind, his four sons, and a female mediator called Wohpe; about Iktomi, a sly, talking rabbit; and about Pte, the buffalo people. Appendices contain lists of manuscripts about Lakota myth and a phonetic key. Endnotes, bibliography, and index.

Waters, Frank. *Book of the Hopi.* New York: Viking Press, 1963.

Some thirty Hopi elders from Arizona told the myths and legends of their people to the author, who reworked this material and supplemented it with his own research. In Part 1, stories about the creation of the four Hopi worlds are accompanied by the author's commentary on the Hopi symbol of emergence. Part 2 consists of legends about the migrations of the clans accompanied by the author's commentary. Part 3 deals with the nine great religious ceremonies of the Hopi year. In Part 4 the author provides a history of the Hopi people from the period of European contact through 1960 and makes some predictions about the future of the Hopi. Sixty-two black-and-white figures illustrating Hopi art. Thirty-seven photographs of Hopi people and their world. Hopi pronunciation key and glossary of Hopi words. Some explanatory footnotes.

Wheelwright, Mary C. *The Myth and Prayers of the Great Star Chant and the Myth of the Coyote Chant*, edited by David P. McAllester. Tsaile, Ariz.: Navajo Community College Press, 1988.

This collection of Navajo myths and prayers is based upon the collection of Wheelwright, who worked among the Navajo from 1925 until 1958. The Sq'tsoh (Great Star) myth also includes chants about the wind and the evil-chaser and tells of an early time when the son of T'iishtsoh, the Great Snake, lived among the Navajo. His Younger and Older Brother travel and struggle to affirm the power of Sq'tsoh on earth. The second group of myths deal with Ma'ii, the trickster Coyote deity of the Navajo. Both sets of myths are followed by an explanatory commentary by McAllester. Twenty-two color plates based upon original Navajo sandpaintings with descriptive commentary. Illustrated by Jason Chee. Glossary and index.

Wherry, Joseph H. *Indian Masks and Myths of the West*. New York: Funk & Wagnalls, 1969.

Illustrates the meaning and vitality of the myths and legends of Native Americans west of the Rockies by a unique combination of retellings of these tales and numerous photographs of related masks, artifacts, and sites. In Chapter 1 Wherry describes the cultures of these peoples in six geographical groups. In Chapters 2-7 the myths are retold in the following thematic groups: creation and the beginning of light, migration myths, spirits of fire and rain, monsters and giants, death and the mystical way of life, and deities as creators and protectors. Includes the Navajo creation myth, a Tlingit tale about Raven's gift of light, a Shoshonie tale explaining how snake brought them rain, Pacific Northwest stories about cannibal giants called "Sasquatch," a northern

California tale about how the trickster Coyote brought death into the world, and the story of the Inuit sea goddess Sedna. In Chapter 8 Wherry discusses masks and their use in religious ceremonies. Maps, bibliography, index of mythical beings, and general index.

Whitehead, Ruth Holmes. *Stories from the Six Worlds*: *Micmac Legends*. Halifax, Nova Scotia: Nimbus, 1988.
Retells twenty-nine tales of the Micmac of eastern Canada and northern New England. The tales are grouped according to the various worlds in the Micmac cosmology: the worlds beneath the earth and the water, the earth world, the worlds above the earth and above the sky, and the ghost world. Each world is inhabited by its own Shape-Changers, including Ki'kwa'ju, an anthropomorphic wolverine, and Weasel Woman. Also contains prominent in the tales is the deity Kluskap, known elsewhere as Gluskap. Explanatory comments and sources are provided in endnotes. In an introductory essay with separate endnotes, White describes the history of the Micmac and their world view. Appendix on Micmac alphabet and orthography. Bibliography.

Wissler, Clark. *Star Legends Among the American Indians*. New York: American Museum of Natural History, 1936.
This pamphlet is a companion to Charles R. Knight's murals in the Hayden Planetarium in the American Museum of Natural History in New York City. These murals depict a series of star myths told by the Blackfoot of Montana. One of Knight's murals is reproduced in black-and-white in the frontispiece. Descriptions of all the murals are followed by translations of four star myths originally narrated to the author by a Blackfoot in 1903. These myths deal with the North star, Blood-Clot or Smoking-Star (probably the Great Nebula of Orion), Scar-Face or Mistaken Morning star, and Gemini or the twins. Short introduction and foreword on the history of the murals and the myths.

Wissler, Clark, and D. C. Duvall. *Mythology of the Blackfoot Indians*. Vol. 2 in *Anthropological Papers of the American Museum of Natural History*. New York: American Museum of Natural History, 1909. Reprint. New York: AMS Press, 1975.
Ninety-six narratives collected between 1903 and 1907 from twenty-one Blackfoot contributors in Montana and Canada are here translated by Duvall and revised by Wissler. The tales are grouped thematically. Narratives about the creator-trickster known as Old Man are followed by star myths, aetiologies about rituals, aetiologies about other cultural practices, and miscellaneous tales about marriage, ghosts, anthropo-

morphic animals, metamorphosis, and other topics. Some tales are told in more than one version. Introductory essay by Wissler on some characteristics of Blackfoot mythology. Footnotes.

Wood, Erskine Scott. *A Book of Tales*. New York: Vanguard Press, 1929.
A former lieutenant in the U.S. Army retells twenty tales he heard on western campaigns between 1875 and 1878. These stories of the Chippewa, Klamath, Nez Percé, Shoshoni, Tlingit, and other peoples tell of the trickster Coyote and of the origin of animals, people, and the natural world. Each tale begins with a short personal recollection identifying informants and describing the circumstances under which the tale was heard.

Wood, Marion. *Spirits, Heroes and Hunters from North American Indian Mythology*. New York: Schocken Books, 1981.
Twenty-six myths from all over the North American continent are retold in this collection, which is accompanied by illustrations in both color and black-and-white by John Sibbick. Includes tales of the Inuit maiden Sedna, the Micmac deity Gluskap, and the Sioux trickster Iktomi, as well as animal fables, aetiologies, and adventure stories. Each tale includes a brief explanatory introduction. The relationship between the stories and objects illustrated at the beginning of each chapter is explained in an appendix. Index and brief note on the pronunciation of Native American names.

Wright, Harold Bell. *Long Ago Told (HUH-KEW AU-KAH)*. New York: D. Appleton, 1929.
Twenty-three tales of the Papago of Arizona desert are retold for children. The stories tell of the creation of the world, the origin of the Papago, warfare, adventure, and aetiologies for various customs and natural phenomena. A Papago version of each title is provided in parentheses. Each tale is introduced by a short description. In a foreword, the author provides some background to the Papago and their tales and explains his contacts with them. Illustrated with black-and-white drawings by Katherine F. Kitt.

Young, Egerton R. *Algonquin Indian Tales*. New York: Easton & Mains, 1903.
Tales of the Algonquin peoples of the Northeastern Woodlands of the United States are retold for children. Arranged in twenty-five chapters, with topical summaries at the beginning of each chapter. Many of these tales deal with Nanabozho, the legendary son of the West Wind, known here as Nanahboozhoo, this hero is sometimes confused with the

Iroquois Hiawatha. In addition to the life and deeds of this hero, tale types include tales of creation and a great flood, encounters with monsters, and aetiologies about fire, medicine, tobacco, and physical features of animals. Twenty-seven drawings and photographs. Introductory essay and glossary.

Young, Robert W., and William Morgan. *Coyote Tales*. Phoenix, Ariz.: Bureau of Indian Affairs, 1949. Reprint. Santa Fe, N.Mex.: Ancient City Press, 1988.

Six traditional Navajo tales about the trickster Coyote are here retold for schoolchildren in simple Navajo with parallel English translation. Introductory essay by Young on Navajo storytelling. Illustrated with line drawings by Andrew Tsihnahjinnie. Navajo-English vocabulary in an appendix. Reprint includes only the English translations and the introduction by Young.

Zolbrod, Paul G. *Diné bahan' : The Navajo Creation Story*. Albuquerque: University of New Mexico Press, 1984.

This translation of the traditional Navajo narrative poem of creation and emergence is based on careful study of earlier translations, especially Washington Matthews' 1897 version and attempts to capture in English the poetic features of the original. It also restores the explicit sexual references often expurgated in earlier translations. Divided into four parts (the Emergence, the Fifth World, Slaying the monsters, and Gathering of the Clans), the narrative moves from the primeval world, to the appearance of humankind, and, eventually, to the origin of the Navajo people. In a detailed introductory essay, Zolbrod describes the goals of his translation and some features of the narrative. Pronunciaton key, endnotes, and bibliography.

Modern American Myths

Allsopp, Frederick W. *Folklore of Romantic Arkansas*. 2 vols. New York: Grolier Society, 1931.

This collection contains a variety of personal recollections, traditions, and legends from all periods of Arkansas history. Except for an initial chapter on prehistory and archaeology, Volume 1 deals with Native American cosmological legends, aetiologies about streams, place names and geographic features, romantic love legends, tales of hidden mines and lost treasures, and stories about notorious outlaws. Volume 2 contains a collection of oral history and legends about Arkansas in the frontier period and later. Chapters 1-4 and 11 deal with more historical topics such as the adventures of early missionaries, European encounters with Native Americans, the settling of the region, and the lives of distinguished Arkansans. Chapters 5-10 contain more legendary materials, including the folklore of African American slaves, Ku Klux Klan lore, hunting and animal stories, and ghost legends. Prefatory remarks by the author at the beginning of Volume 1. Twenty-eight illustrations in Volume 1 and thirty-two illustrations in Volume 2, including photographs of Arkansas sites and famous personages.

Alvord, Thomas G. *Paul Bunyan and Resinous Rhymes of the North Woods*. New York: Derrydale Press, 1934.
In Part 1 Alvord retells the story of the legendary lumberjack Paul Bunyan in verse, beginning with Paul's "five-stork" birth and describing an additional nineteen incredible adventures and deeds of the hero and his great white ox called Babe. In Part 2 are a collection of miscellaneous verse about the North Woods. Published in a limited edition and illustrated with black-and-white drawings by the author.

Barbeau, Marius, and Michael Hornyansky. *The Golden Phoenix*. New York: Henry Z. Walck, 1958.
Retells eight French-Canadian folktales for older children. Ordinary people such as Petit Jean and Jacques Cornaud the Woodcutter encounter kings, princesses, witches, fairies, and supernatural beasts. In the title story Petit Jean journeys in search of a golden phoenix and a bride. Along the way he meets a talking unicorn, lion, and serpent and deals with a difficult sultan. In a short essay following the tales, Barbeau, an important collector of French-Canadian lore, discusses the background of these tales. Illustrated with two-color drawings by Arthur Price.

Battle, Kemp P., ed. *Great American Folklore*. Garden City, N.Y.: Doubleday, 1986.
A collection of almost 300 legends and folklore connected with general life in the United States. Includes tales about mythical characters such as Paul Bunyan and John Henry and historical personages such as Annie Oakley, Wyatt Earp, and Davy Crockett. Chapters are introduced with illustrations by John M. Battle and are arranged thematically in the following groups: travel, pioneers, fights and duels, hunting and fishing yarns, love and marriage, preachers, witches and the supernatural, animal tales, country life and laughter, the wild west, cowboys, tall tales of lies and boasts, and stories about Paul Bunyan. Includes some ballads and verse. Short introductory essay on the types

and origin of these folktales and on the organization of this book. Bibliography and indexes.

Blair, Walter. *Tall Tale America*. New York: Coward-McCann, 1944.
Retells the lives of several legendary and historical heroes in American history in an informal, humorous style. Historical and tall tales about real people such as Christopher Columbus and Davy Crockett are accompanied by more fictionalized heroes such as Paul Bunyan, Pecos Bill, John Henry, and Joe Magarac, the Pittsburgh Steel Man. Concludes with a twentieth-century legend about a Professor Blur, who gets lost in the Pentagon. Bibliography.

Botkin, Benjamin A. *A Treasury of American Folklore*. New York: Crown Publishers, 1944.
This collection of American tales and folk tradition is arranged thematically. In Part 1 tales of heroes and boasters are grouped in the following categories: backwoods boasters, pseudo-bad men, killers such as Jesse James and Billy the Kid, miracle men such as Paul Bunyan and John Henry, and saints such as Johnny Appleseed. Part 2 is a collection of boasts and put-downs. Part 3 deals with jests, pranks and tricks. Part 4 focuses on liars and their tall tales. Part 5 contains a variety of folktales and legends, including tales about animals, witches, ghosts, and the devil. The last part deals with songs, ballads, and rhymes. Each part has a short introduction by the editor. Also contains a general introduction explaining the purpose of this book. Foreword by Carl Sandburg. Index of authors, titles and first lines of songs; and index of subjects and names.

Bowman, James Cloyd. *Pecos Bill*. Chicago: Albert Whitman, 1972.
These nineteen tales about the legendary cowboy Pecos Bill are retold for children. Arranged chronologically, beginning with the hero's strange childhood among the coyotes, his extraordinary accomplishments as a cowpuncher, his strange adventures with wild animals and monsters, and his mysterious disappearance. Short introductory essay on the history of these tales. Illustrated with drawings by Laura Bannon.

Bradford, Roark. *John Henry*. New York: Harper & Bros., 1931.
Retells the story of the fabulous life of the herculean African American hero of the American South. From his very birth John Henry exhibited superhuman strength and abilities. Even in his death the hero was special. Written in the dialect of Southern African Americans. With woodcuts by J. J. Lankes.

Brunvand, Jan Harold. *The Choking Doberman and Other "New" Urban Legends*. New York: W. W. Norton, 1984.

This sequel to *The Vanishing Hitchhiker* (listed below), a collection of modern American urban legends, includes oral stories about vicious dogs, legends about automobiles and recreational vehicles, horror stories, and sex scandals. Each tale is preceded by a short introduction. An appendix contains a sampling of texts from *The Vanishing Hitchhiker*. Prefatory essay on American urban legends. Bibliography and index.

_____. *The Mexican Pet*. New York: W. W. Norton, 1986.

Third in a series of anthologies of American urban legends and their transformations. This collection includes tales about animals, automobiles, horror, contamination, crime, and sex scandals. Each tale is preceded by some information on background and sources. Introductory essay and index.

_____. *The Study of American Folklore*. 3d ed. New York: W. W. Norton, 1986.

A standard introduction to the folklore of the United States with descriptions of types and methodologies. In the introductory Part 1, Brunvand offers a definition of folklore, describes the collecting, classifying, and analyzing of folklore material, and distinguishes the folklore of different occupational, age, gender, regional, and ethnic groups. Part 2 deals with oral folklore in speech and naming, proverbs, riddles, rhymes, myths and motifs, legends and anecdotes, folktales, folk songs, ballads, and folk music. In Part 3 Brunvand considers customary folklore in superstitions, festivals, dances and dramas, gestures, and games. The material folk traditions described in Part 4 include folklife, architecture, crafts, costumes, and food. Particularly useful for the study of American myths and legends are discussions in Chapters 8-10 of Native American myths, theories and origin of myths, religious, supernatural, urban, and personal legends, and folktale motifs and formulas. Many examples are retold or quoted in the text. Bibliographic notes follow each section. In appendices are essays on research in American folklore, on a modern urban legend, on folklore in academia, on the southern mountain cabin, and on the folk blues. Bibliography, combined glossary and index, and general index.

_____. *The Vanishing Hitchhiker: American Urban Legends and Their Meanings*. New York: W. W. Norton, 1981.

These popular tales and legends collected mostly in Indiana and Utah show how the folklore tradition continues in a modern American urban setting. An introductory chapter on the performance and interpretation of urban legends is followed by chapters on the following kinds of legends: automobile, horror, corpses, nudity and other compromising situations, and business ripoffs. Different versions of the legends are analyzed and compared. The last chapter deals with urban legends in the making. Appendix on methods for the collection and study of urban legends. Glossary and index.

Campbell, Marie. *Tales from the Cloud Walking Country*. Bloomington: Indiana University Press, 1958.
These seventy-eight tales were recorded while the author was a schoolteacher in the mountains of eastern Kentucky between 1926 and 1934. In an introductory essay, Campbell offers some background to these tales. Grouped according to Campbell's six informants. Each section begins with information about the storyteller. Many of these tales are regional variations of European folktales such as "Cinderella," "Snow White," and "The Golden Goose." Black-and-white portraits of each informant by Clare Leighton. Endnotes and bibliography.

Carmer, Carl. *The Hurricane's Children*. New York: Farrar & Rinehart, 1937.
These twenty tales of legendary American heroes were originally told by the author on his popular radio program "Your Neck o' the Woods." Includes stories about Mike Fink, Davy Crockett, Old Stormalong, Ichabod Paddock, Pecos Bill, Johnny Appleseed, and Paul Bunyan. Accompanied by black-and-white illustrations by Elizabeth Black Carmer. Bibliography.

Chase, Richard. *American Folk Tales and Songs*. New York: New American Library, 1971.
A collection of traditional stories and ballads collected in the Appalachian hills of North Carolina, Tennessee, and Kentucky. In Part 1 are twenty-nine tales arranged in five thematic groups: ancient tales, Jack tales, fool Irishman tales, and tall tales. Each tale is preceded by information on sources and parallels in other folktale traditions. Part 2 contains a variety of ballads, songs, hymns, dances, and fiddle tunes, often accompanied by music. Introductory essay on the American folk tradition. Bibliography and endnotes.

_____. *Grandfather Tales*. Boston: Houghton Mifflin, 1948.

Twenty-five American-English folktales originally heard by the author in North Carolina, Virginia, Kentucky, and Maine are retold here for children. These tales include reminiscences, unusual occurrences, tall tales, and encounters with the devil. Sources are provided in an appendix. Short preface explaining the origin of the tales. Illustrated with drawings by Berkeley Williams, Jr.

_____, ed. *The Jack Tales*. Boston: Houghton Mifflin, 1943.
Eighteen tales about a boy named Jack and his two brothers, Will and Tom, as they were told to Chase by inhabitants of the Beech mountain section of North Carolina. Also contains three tales from West Virginia. Besides his well-known adventure on the beanstalk, Jack has a series of encounters with animals, both fictional and real, with robbers, with a four-headed giant, and even with the wind. This collection illustrates how an English folktale tradition is preserved and developed in the United States. Although this collection is written expressly for young readers, information about sources and detailed comparison to other folktales are contained in an appendix. Herbert Halpert offers some comments on the study of English folktales in another appendix. Chase provides some background on the Jack tales tradition in the preface. Illustrated with black-and-white drawings by Berkeley Williams, Jr. Glossary.

Clough, Ben C. *The American Imagination at Work*. New York: Alfred A. Knopf, 1947.
A collection of folk and literary tall tales and yarns from the United States. In Book 1 are tales dealing with historical, semi-historical, and pseudo-historical events. Book 2 contains tales about the weather, animals, and, especially, fish. Book 3 offers a collection of exaggerated adventure stories, sea yarns, and newspaper hoaxes. Ghost stories and other tales of the supernatural are in Book 4, tall tales in Book 5, five explorers' tales in Book 6, and a potpourri of "hardy perennial" hoax stories in Book 7. Bibliographic footnotes assist the reader in distinguishing traditional tales and legends from works of pure fiction or personal experiences by writers such as Bennett Cerf, Carl Sandburg, Stephen Vincent Benét, and John James Audubon. Editorial commentary precedes each book and chapter. General introductory essay on American folklore and its history. Footnotes and bibliography.

Collins, Earl. *Folk Tales of Missouri*. Boston: Christopher Publishing House, 1935.

A collection of tales from the Ozarks of Missouri, including legends about heroes such as Johnny Appleseed, tales explaining the names of places, legendary sayings such as "a Calamity Jane," stories about the mysterious and the supernatural, whopper tales, and a tale about mythical Missourians called Pooseyites. Background to the tales in the author's preface and in a short introductory chapter.

Daugherty, James. *Daniel Boone*. New York: Viking, 1939; 2d ed., 1967.
The legend of the eighteenth-century American frontiersman Daniel Boone is retold for children with original lithographs in color by the author. Boone's legend mixes history and legend and includes tales of adventure, settlement, and violent encounters with Native Americans.

Dorson, Richard Mercer. *American Folklore*. Chicago: University of Chicago Press, 1959.
An examination and historical analysis of traditional American folklore. Chapters on the colonial period, folk humor, regional cultures, immigrant folklore, African Americans, folk heroes, and modern folklore. Direct quotation and comparison of some examples. Distinguishes authentic folklore from "fakelore," which reworks traditional material for commercial profit. List of important dates, bibliographical notes, table of motifs and tale types, and index.

_____. *Buying the Wind*. Chicago: University of Chicago Press, 1964.
This anthology is a companion to *American Folklore*. Included are the sea traditions, legends of the hero Barny Beal, tales of witches, local and amusing anecdotes, and local ballads of Maine Down-Easters. Tales of *brauche* or "wizards" and spells, farm folk beliefs, noodle tales, proverbs, riddles, and songs of the Pennsylvania Dutchmen are accompanied by Jack tales, legends, riddles, ballads, and songs of Southern mountaineers, animal fables, supernatural tales, songs, and folkways of the Louisiana Cajuns, tales of ghosts and witches, folktales, games, and songs of the Egyptians of southern Illinois, tales, legends, humorous stories, proverbs, and ballads of Mexican Americans of the Southwest U.S., and legends of saints, local tales, comic stories, and folksongs of Utah Mormons. Introductory essay for each region and comparative headnotes for each tale. General introductory essay on how to collect oral folklore in the United States. Footnotes and bibliography. Indexes arranged according to subject, tale types, motifs, informants, and collectors.

_____, ed. *Davy Crockett.* New York: Spiral Press, 1939. Reprint. New York: Arno Press, 1977.

This collection of 108 tales and legends about the American frontiersman was compiled from almanacs published between 1835 and 1856. The tales are arranged in ten thematic groups, including legends about Crockett's life, tall tales, relationships with women, his friendship with Congressman Ben Harding, arguments and fights, contests with wild beasts, dealings with peddlers and scoundrels, and comic adventures. These accounts are filled with exaggerated and incredible details about ghosts, cannibals, swallowing thunderbolts, and other superhuman feats. Many of these tales are told in the first person. Some are accompanied by the original black-and-white illustrations. Short editor's note on the origin of these tales. In a foreword, Howard Mumford Jones discusses frontier humor and legend. Bibliographical endnotes.

Felton, Harold W. *Pecos Bill Texas Cowpuncher.* New York: Alfred A. Knopf, 1949.

Claims to be a true account of the biography of Pecos Bill written for young readers. Traces the legendary hero's life from his remarkable birth to his early days living with coyotes and the many tall tales connected with his skills as a lassoer. Illustrated with two-color drawings by Aldren Auld Watson. Bibliography.

Flanagan, John T., and Arthur Palmer Hudson. *The American Folklore Reader.* New York: A. S. Barnes, 1958.

A collection of literary retellings of traditional American tales. Twelve sections arranged according to theme or genre. Some selections are in prose, others in verse. Tales about Native Americans, such as Henry Wadsworth Longfellow's poem "Hiawatha," devil tales such as Washington Irving's "The Devil and Tom Walker," ghost tales such as Robert Frost's poem "The Witch of Coös," tales of witchcraft and superstition such as Nathaniel Hawthorne's "Feathertop," stories about buried treasure such as Edgar Allan Poe's "The Gold Bug," tall tales such as "The Celebrated Jumping Frog of Calaveras County" by Samuel L. Clemens (Mark Twain), literary ballads such as John Greenleaf Whittier's poem "Barbara Frietchie," heroic tales linked with Davy Crockett, Yankee tales such as those of James Russell Lowell, African American tales such as the Brer Rabbit stories of Joel Chandler Harris, as well as folk songs and folk wisdom. Each selection is preceded by a brief introduction by the editors. Biographical notes about the authors, bibliography, and index.

Fortier, Alcée. *Louisiana Folk-Tales.* Vol. 2 in *Memoirs of the American Folk-Lore Society.* New York: American Folk-Lore Society, 1895. Reprint. New York: Kraus Reprint, 1969.

A collection of twenty-seven French Creole tales recorded by a professor of Romance languages at Tulane University and presented in the original Creole dialect and English translation on facing pages. Many of the narratives contain elements borrowed from African and French traditions adapted to the experience of Lousiana Creoles. Part 1 contains fifteen animal tales in which *compair*, the Creole word for French *compère* or "brother," is often used along with *bouki*, an African word for hyena, and the French words for "bull," "rabbit," and "bear" in the tradition of the Brer Rabbit tales of the American South. In Part 2 are twelve tales of love and adventure based especially on the European folktale tradition. In an appendix are English translations of fourteen additional Creole tales published previously by the author. Explanatory endnotes.

Gerster, Patrick, and Nicholas Cords. *Myth in American History.* Encino, Calif.: Benzinger Bruce & Glencoe, 1977.

Deals with historical myths or false beliefs traditionally considered to have been real or actual events. Surveys all periods of American history from the colonial period through Vietnam and Watergate and addresses myths about topics such as colonial development, slavery, the Founding Fathers, the settling of the West and American involvement in World Wars I and II. The text is accompanied by a large number of illustrations. Each chapter includes study questions, endnotes, and bibliography. Index.

Haviland, Virginia, ed. "European Tales Brought by Immigrants" and "Tall Tales." In *The Faber Book of North American Legends,* by Virginia Haviland. Boston: Faber & Faber, 1979.

Part of an anthology of traditional North American tales told by Native Americans, African Americans, European immigrants and inhabitants of various regions of the United States. Here five immigrant tales from Appalachia and New England are accompanied by five tall tales about heroes such as Pecos Bill, Paul Bunyan, and Johnny Appleseed. These representative tales have been selected from early collections and are occasionally edited for the younger reader. Details about sources and editorial comments in endnotes. With illustrations by Ann Strugnell. Bibliography.

Jagendorf, Moritz Adolf. *New England Bean-Pot*. New York: Vanguard Press, 1948.
A collection of legends, tall tales, and adventures from the New England states, arranged by state. In these tales sailors, whalers, loggers, travelers, farmers, and others encounter magic, witches, the devil, storms, Native Americans, and wild animals. Short introduction by the author and a foreword about the author by B. A. Botkin. Illustrated with eleven black-and-white drawings by Donald McKay.

_____. *Sand in the Bag*. New York: Vanguard Press, 1952.
These forty folktales from Ohio, Indiana, and Illinois are retold for children and are arranged by state. Includes tales about ghosts, witches, slavers, and settlement, and legendary figures such as John Brown and Abraham Lincoln. Foreword by William T. Utter. Appendix on sources. Illustrated with black-and-white drawings by John Moment.

_____. *Upstate Downstate*. New York: Vanguard Press, 1949.
A collection of fifty-eight folktales and legends from the Middle Atlantic States and the District of Columbia. The tales are organized by state and include legends about George Washington, the devil, ghosts, superstitions, and unusual occurrences. In a front note, the author identifies his sources and describes how he collected these tales. Foreword by Henry W. Shoemaker. Illustrated with eleven drawings by Howard Simon.

_____ *The Life Treasury of American Folklore*. New York: Time-Life Books, 1961.
Retells more than 100 tales and legends dealing with American history. Begins with the exploration of the Atlantic and moves through the colonial period and the settlement of the West and includes tales about industrialization. Arranged in the following chapters: explorers, "Indians," colonists, backwoodsmen, Yankees, Southerners, Westerners, modern folklore, and miscellaneous tales of wit and wisdom. Includes tales about historical figures such as Daniel Boone, Johnny Appleseed, Jesse James, and Billy the Kid as well as more fictional characters such as Casey Jones and Paul Bunyan. Short introductions for each chapter and for each tale, bibliography, and general glossary of persons, places, and events in American folklore. Illustrated with paintings by James Lewicki.

MacKaye, Percy. *Tall Tales of the Kentucky Mountains*. New York: George H. Doran, 1926.

These twelve tall tales based upon the oral traditions of the Appalachian regions of Kentucky are retold here for children in local dialect and orthography. Told through the voice of Solomon Shell, a well-known nineteenth-century yarn-spinner called Ole Sol. Illustrated with drawings by E. MacKinstry.

Malcolmson, Anne Burnett. *Yankee Doodle's Cousins*. Boston: Houghton Mifflin, 1941.
An anthology of twenty-eight tales about legendary American heroes told for young readers. The stories are presented in four geographic groups. Among these heroes are John Darling of the Erie Canal; Captain Kidd the pirate; Stormalong the sailor from the East Coast; Blackbeard and John Henry from the American South; Johnny Appleseed, Mike Fink, Daniel Boone, and Davy Crockett from the Mississippi Valley; and Pecos Bill and Paul Bunyan from the West. Glossary.

Malcolmson, Anne Burnett, and Dell J. McCormick. *Mister Stormalong*. Boston: Houghton Mifflin, 1952.
Ten Tall Tales about Alfred Bulltop Stormalong, the legendary Yankee sailor, are retold for young readers. Describes how Stormalong became a sailor, his incredible adventures, including a fight with an octopus, his incredible inventions, and his death. The authors' acknowledgments include some background to the tradition. Illustrated with black-and-white drawings by Joshua Tolford.

Masterson, James R. *Tall Tales of Arkansaw*. Boston: Chapman & Grimes, 1943.
A collection of tall tales and humorous stories about Arkansas arranged in twenty-one chapters dealing with topics such as Davy Crockett in Arkansas, the Arkansas traveler, and sporting yarns. Discussion incorporates extensive quotation from original sources. Occasional illustrations, endnotes, bibliography, and index.

Pound, Louise. *Nebraska Folklore*. Lincoln: University of Nebraska Press, 1959.
This collection of scholarly articles about Nebraskan oral tradition includes discussions of lore about caves, snakes, and rain, hoaxes about John G. Mather, and legends about weeping water, lover's leaps, the Lincoln Salt Basin, Nebraskan strong men, and a Swedish pioneer named Olof Bergstrom. Also contains some ballads and folk customs. In appendices are essays on the use of dialect in folklore, the science of folklore, and American folksongs. Footnotes.

Roberts, Leonard W. *Old Greasybeard: Tales from the Cumberland Gap.*
Detroit: Folklore Associates, 1969.
A collection of fifty tales told in the Cumberland Gap region of
Tennessee and Kentucky. Arranged thematically. Ten animal tales,
twenty-seven stories about heroes and giants, and thirteen humorous
and tall tales. Some are retellings of well-known European stories such
as "Jack and the Beanstalk" and others are peculiar to the region. In
endnotes, Roberts classifies each tale according to Aarne-Thompson's
types and provides information about the informant and collector of
the tale. In a detailed introduction, Roberts offers a history of the region
and and discusses some characteristics of its folklore. List of Aarne-
Thompson type numbers and index.

Rounds, Glen. *Ol' Paul.* New York: Holiday House, 1949.
Legends about Paul Bunyan are here retold for children as if the author
were an eye-witness to the events. In an introductory chapter, Rounds
describes Bunyan's early life and logging companions. Ten tall tales
are told, including one about how Paul built the Rocky mountains and
another about a giant bullsnake. Illustrated with line drawings by the
author.

Shapiro, Irwin. *Yankee Thunder.* New York: Julian Messner, 1944.
This life of Davy Crockett intentionally celebrates the American frontiersman as a mythic hero rather than historical politician or defender
of the Alamo. In a prefatory note, Shapiro explains how he has
expanded in this book upon tall and fantastic tales about Crockett found
especially in nineteenth-century pamphlets and almanacs. Crockett's
adventures from birth through his departure for Texas are told in
twenty-five chapters and include tales of Native American fighting,
bear hunting, and sharpshooting. In these tales Crockett encounters
Andrew Jackson, deals with a sinister backwoods peddler called Slick-
erty Sam, and woos his future wife Sally Ann Thunder Ann. Black-
and-white drawings by James Daugherty.

Shephard, Esther. *Paul Bunyan.* New York: Harcourt, Brace, 1952.
Retells for the general reader the adventures of the legendary lumberjack of the Pacific Northwest. The twenty-one tales are arranged
chronologically, beginning with the hero's birth in Maine, describing
many of Paul's incredible deeds, and ending with the death of Paul's
companion, Babe the Blue Ox, and Paul's last job. In an introductory
essay, Shephard summarizes the Paul Bunyan legend and its history.

Accompanied by twenty-four full-page drawings and many smaller ones by Rockwell Kent.

Thompson, Stith. "Folk Tales and Legends." In Vol. 1 in *The Frank C. Brown Collection of North Carolina Folklore*, edited by Newman Ivey White. Durham, N.C.: Duke University Press, 1952.

This section of a monumental collection of folklore collected in North Carolina by a Duke University professor in the first half of the twentieth century offers origin legends, strange tales about animals, stories of magic, witches, ghosts, and other mysteries, tales of buried treasure, numbskulls, fools, and jokers, and animal fables. Some are recorded in dialect. Thompson introduces each tale with information about informants and references to his index of folktale motifs. Bibliography.

Chapter 4
OCEANIA

Books on the mythologies of Oceania deal with a broad geographic range which includes Australia, New Zealand, and Indonesia, as well as the smaller islands of the Pacific. The oral traditions of the peoples of Oceania have been the focus of important ethnographic study since the end of the nineteenth century, and many of the citations in this chapter illustrate the variety of materials available. Some early collections, such as those of William Wyatt Gill and R. H. Codrington, remain important resources and are available in reprints. Other citations deal with more recent anthropological work by scholars such as Catherine H. Berndt and Ronald M. Berndt. Also of interest and value are mythological records by natives of the region, such as those by the last Hawaiian king, David Kalakaua.

Anthologies of world mythology often place the mythologies of Oceania last, following material from Europe, Asia, Africa, and the Americas. In this bibliography Oceania appears between the Americas and Asia, not only because of its geographic position but also because of the cultural ties Oceania certainly shares with Asia, and, if Thor Heyerdahl (*Kon-Tiki*. Chicago: Rand McNally, 1950) and his supporters are correct, may also share with the Americas.

Allen, Louis, A. *Time Before Morning: Art and Myth of the Australian Aborigines*. New York: Thomas Y. Crowell, 1975.
Uses the myths and art of the Australian Aborigines to explain their religious beliefs and way of life. In Part 1 Allen provides background on the Aborigines, their myths, regional characteristics of their art, and artistic techniques. Seven creation myths, including *Djanggawul*, *Wagilag*, and *Laindjung*, are retold in Part 2; five aetiologies about natural forces in Part 3; ten myths about husbands and wives in Part 4; ten stories of everyday life in Part 5; and five funeral myths in Part 5. Each collection of myths is preceded by some introductory commentary by Allen and is accompanied by illustrations of original bark paintings and carved figures in the author's own collection. Map, endnotes on both text and photographs, information on artists, bibliography, and index.

Alpers, Antony. *Maori Myths and Tribal Legends*. Boston: Houghton Mifflin, 1966.

Maori myths retold for adults in modern English translation. The first group consists of myths brought in the distant past by the Maori from "Hawaiki," their ancestral homeland, to Aotearoa (New Zealand). These tell of creation and of the birth and deeds of the mischievous demigod Maui. In the second group is a selection of canoe stories or fantastic tales about the settlement of Aotearoa. Illustrated with drawings by Patrick Hanly. Appendix on sources and background, pronunciation guide, glossary, and index.

Andersen, Johannes C. *Myths and Legends of the Polynesians*. Rutland, Vt.: Charles E. Tuttle, 1969.
An examination of the traditional stories of Polynesia for the general reader. An introductory chapter on the people and their history is followed by twelve thematically arranged chapters in which Andersen retells myths about settlement of the islands, navigation and voyages, Chief Uenuku of the Maori, supernatural creatures such as fairies, elves, and monsters, the myth cycle about the god Tawhaki, legends about the demigod Maui and about his sister Hina, Pele the Hawaiian goddess of volcanoes, spirit worlds and contacts with the dead, the gods Io and Tangaroa and stories of cosmic creation, the gods Tane and Rongo and the creation of humankind, and the Tahitian Areoi Society and the hula dance. In a final chapter Andersen surveys the religious practices of Polynesians. Map, forty-nine photographs of the people and their artifacts, and sixteen color plates by Richard Wallwork. Preface, bibliography, note on proper names, glossary, and index.

Beckwith, Martha. *Hawaiian Mythology*. New Haven, Conn.: Yale University Press, 1940. Reprint. Honolulu: University of Hawaii Press, 1970.
This guide to the mythology of the Hawaiian people is intended for the general reader. Descriptions, analysis, and interpretation of tales about gods and heroes incorporate excerpts and paraphrases from actual narratives. Includes some comparison to myths from other parts of Polynesia. In Part 1 Beckwith deals with the gods and offers individual chapters on the coming of the gods, the deities Ku, Lono, Kane, and Kanaloa, worship of Kane, mythical habitations of the gods, lesser deities, gods of sorcery, guardian deities, and the afterlife. In Part 2 the author considers myths about the goddess Pele and about heroic children of the gods, Kamapua'a, Hina, Maui, Aikanaka, Wahieola, and Haumea. In Part 3 are myths and genealogies of early chiefs and in Part 5 myths about the migrations to Hawaii and chiefs of the islands.

Part 4 deals with more fictional tales called *kupua*, including the "Stretching-Tree Kupua," trickster stories, fantastic voyages, riddle contests, legends about the hero Kana, and stories about a swimmer, the legendary Island of Virgins, matchmaking, dance, and romances. In an introduction to the reprint, Katharine Luomala offers a biography of Beckwith and a scholarly analysis of her work and its importance. Following this introduction are endnotes and a bibliography of Beckwith's work. Bibliography and index.

Berndt, Catherine H. "Australia." In *Mythology: An Illustrated Encyclopaedia*, edited by Richard Cavendish. New York: Rizzoli International, 1980. Also published as *An Illustrated Encyclopedia of Mythology*. New York: Crescent Books, 1984.
A survey of the myths of the Aboriginal people of Australia with sections on major deities and figures and on the relationships between myth and territory, between individuals and groups, between myths and reality, and between males and females. Includes summaries and analyses of a Wonkamal myth about the Wapiya girls, a Wotjbaluk tale about sexual differentiation, and the story of the Wawalag sisters from Arnhem Land. Map and illustrations of artwork and sites related to the myths.

_____. "The Ghost Husband: Society and the Individual in New Guinea Myth." In *The Anthropologist Looks at Myth*, edited by Melville Jacobs and John Greenway. Austin: University of Texas Press, 1966.
A New Guinea myth about a girl accompanying her ghost husband to the land of the dead. Recorded by the author south of Kainantu in the Kamano language. A free English translation of the tale is preceded by information on its local and mythological setting and a note on the translation. Analysis of the tale begins by following a techinique of Franz Boas in listing statements about the people's world view and social relations based upon this tale. Similar tales collected by the author are summarized here and compared with this story. Also provides extensive information about the narrator, including summaries, in chronological order, of similar tales she told the author. Emphasizes the multifaceted nature of this tale, which blends personal and autobiographical details about the narrator with social and cultural aspects of her society. An interlinear transliteration and literal translation are provided at the end of the article. Endnotes.

Berndt, Catherine H., and Ronald M. Berndt. "Art and Aesthetic Expression." In *The World of the First Australians*, by Catherine H. Berndt and Ronald M. Berndt. Chicago: University of Chicago Press, 1965.
These two chapters in a systemic examination of the culture of the Australian Aborigines deal with the oral and visual arts. A significant portion of Chapter 11 consists of a selection of twenty-four animal legends and tales of floods, giants, tricksters, and other mythic themes, told in translation. Chapter 12 deals with paintings and carvings on rocks, bark, wood, the human body, and other media and their mythological content.

_____. "Religious Belief and Practice: Totemism and Mythology." In *The World of the First Australians*, by Catherine H. Berndt and Ronald M. Berndt. Chicago: University of Chicago Press, 1965.
This examination of the religion of the Australian Aborigines begins with the concept of totemism and shows how this belief in a mystical bond between a human individual or group and an object representing a specific phenomenon such as the spirit of an animal pervades the lives of Aborigines. The second half of the essay illustrates the role of mythology in Aboriginal religion and ritual with translations of several myths, including the tale of an ancestral hero called Ngurunderi, aetiologies of ritual, the myth of Njirana ("the man") and Julana ("his penis"), the myth of *ubar*, the wooden gong shaped like the uterus which belongs to Ngaljod, goddess of the rainbow, and incidents in the Djanggawul cycle about the two Wawalag star sisters.

Berndt, Ronald M. "The Wuradilagu Song Cycle of Northeastern Arnhem Land." In *The Anthropologist Looks at Myth*, edited by Melville Jacobs and John Greenway. Austin: University of Texas Press, 1966.
A collection of eighteen Australian Aboriginal songs about the Wuradilagu, a female spirit or spirits, as they wander from Groote Eylandt to Arnhem Bay. Songs are presented in interlinear transcription and literal translation followed by free translation and glossary notes. Extensive ethnographic background, structural analysis, and interpretation also provided. Short comparison of this male version of the myth with one sung by a female. The songs lack plot structure but celebrate the link between human action and natural phenomena such as clouds. Suggests that the peculiar style of these song cycles parallels the wider social structure. Two plates illustrating wooden figures of Wuradilagu. Endnotes.

Clerk, Christian. "Polynesia and Micronesia." In *Mythology: An Illustrated Encyclopaedia*, edited by Richard Cavendish. New York: Rizzoli International, 1980. Also published as *An Illustrated Encyclopedia of Mythology*. New York: Crescent Books, 1984.

This overview of the Micronesian and Polynesian mythologies includes both summaries and analyses of myths such as a Nauruan story of creation of earth and sky, a Maori creation myth, a Maori account of the first woman, an aetiology of fire from Yap in Micronesia, an Hawaian story about the culture hero Maui, and a myth about a conflict between the brothers Tangaroa and Rongo from Mangaia in the Cook Islands. Map, chart of ancestry and settlement, genealogical chart of principal deities, and illustrations of artwork and sites related to the myths.

Codrington, R. H. "Stories." In *The Melanesians*, by R. H. Codrington. Oxford: The Clarendon Press, 1891. Reprint. New Haven, Conn.: HRAF Press, 1957.

A collection of thirty-one tales from various islands of Melanesia in an early but major anthropological study of the region. In a short introductory section, Codrington describes how the tales were collected and translated and comments on the place of these stories in Melanesian culture. The narratives are presented in three thematic groups. The six animal stories in Part 1 focus especially on anthropomorphic birds and fishes. Part 2 contains eight aetiological tales about creator spirits such as Tagaro and the origin of the sea, fish, poisoned arrows, and other things. Seventeen tales of wonder about ghosts, ogres, and human metamorphosis appear in Part 3. Tales are identified only by geographic locations.

Colum, Padraic. *Legends of Hawaii*. New Haven, Conn.: Yale University Press, 1937.

Retells for the general reader nineteen tales of old Hawaii, including stories about Pele the volcano goddess, Maui the pan-Polynesian hero, other heroes such as Rata and Pu-nia, Hi-ku's wonderful arrow named Pua-ne, and the extraordinary brothers Ni-he-u and Kana. In a preface, Colum provides some historical background on Hawaiian folkloristics and on the tales in this collection. Explanatory endnotes and black-and-white drawings by Don Forrer.

Danandjaja, James. "A Javanese Cinderella Tale and Its Pedagogical Value." In *Majalah Ilmu-Ilmu Sastra Indonesia* 6 (1976): 15-29. Reprinted in *Cinderella. A Folklore Casebook*, edited by Alan Dundes. New York: Garland Press, 1982.

Offers an English translation of a Javanese version of the Cinderella folktale collected by the author. The original Javanese version is included as an appendix. Uses Aarne-Thompson folktale motifs to place the tale within the Cinderella cycle. Shows how the tale is especially used among the Javanese as a pedagogical device, as a way of teaching patience, detachment, and inner peace. Reprint contains useful background information and commentary by Dundes but does not include the Javanese text. Endnotes and bibliography.

Dixon, Roland B. *Oceanic Mythology*. Vol. 9 in *The Mythology of All Races*, edited by Louis Herbert Gray. Boston: Marshall Jones, 1916.

This survey is divided according to Oceania's five major geographic/ethnographic groups: Polynesia, Melanesia, Indonesia, Micronesia, and Australia. The author provides a discussion of myths of origin and the flood for each region, a chapter on miscellaneous tales, and special chapters for the Maui cycle of Polynesian myths and for Indonesian trickster tales. Each regional section concludes with a chapter summarizing the primary features of these myths. The author also includes some brief introductory and concluding remarks on the history of the region and the development of its mythology. Twenty-four plates and three figures. Map, endnotes, and bibliography. Full index in Volume 13.

Fischer, John L. "A Ponapean Oedipus Tale." In *The Anthropologist Looks at Myth*, edited by Melville Jacobs and John Greenway. Austin: University of Texas Press, 1966.

A tale recorded on Ponape, a Carolinian Island of Micronesia. In this tale father-and-son antagonism begins when the father tells his wife to kill their son at birth and continues as the adult son insults his father and sleeps with his father's sister. An annotated translation of the text is preceded by ethnographic background and is supplemented by an analysis of four major semantic contexts of the myth (time, space, bipolar organization of characters, and sequences of conflict resolution). Also suggests a sociopsychological significance of the myth based upon Sigmund Freud's Oedipus complex. Tables, charts, and endnotes.

Gill, William Wyatt. *Myths and Songs from the South Pacific*. London: Henry S. King, 1876. Reprint. New York: Arno Press, 1977.

A nineteenth-century Christian missionary in the Hervey Group of South Pacific islands describes the mythological world view of the people and paraphrases some of their myths. Occasionally songs and short texts are quoted in the original language with parallel English translation. The material is arranged thematically with chapters on creation, deified humans, astronomical myths, the exploits of the culture hero Maui, tree myths, the fairy voyage of Ina, the spirit world, the story of Veêtini, the first human to die, human journeys to the spirit world, fairies, death, human sacrifice, and the seasons. In a short introduction, Gill shows some of the prejudices of a nineteenth-century Christian missionary and provides information about his informant and assistant and the dialects of the region. In a prefatory essay, the anthropologist F. Max Müller discusses some characteristics of South Pacific myths. Footnotes, diagrams, and index.

Grey, Sir George. *Polynesian Mythology*, Auckland, New Zealand: H. Brett, 1885. Reprint edited by W. W. Bird. New York: Taplinger Publishing, 1970.
These twenty-five tales were collected among the Maori when Grey was governor of the islands in the early nineteenth century. Grey originally published the tales in Maori in 1854. Some were later published with English translation. This edition contains only English translations, including one tale translated for the first time by Bird. The tales tell of human origins, the demigods Maui and Tawhaki, Rupe's ascent into heaven, Kae's stealing of a whale, the discovery of Aotearoa (New Zealand) by the ancestors of the Maori, chief Manaia, sorcery, magic, fairies, and love. In a preface, Grey explains how he collected the tales. Index. The reprint is illustrated with sixteen black-and-white line drawings by Russell Clark.

Kalakaua, David. *The Legends and Myths of Hawaii*. New York: Charles L. Webster, 1888. Reprint. Rutland, Vt.: Charles E. Tuttle, 1972.
The author of this classic description of the ancient tales and traditions of Hawaii was king of Hawaii until his death in 1890. Two years later his sister Queen Liliuokalani was deposed, and in 1898 the islands were annexed by the United States. Kalakaua was a strong advocate for the preservation of traditional Hawaiian culture, and this book provides a unique perspective on the material. An introductory essay on the geography, history, and culture of the islands is followed by paraphrases and descriptions of myths, legends, and historical narratives. Includes tales about the settling of the islands, early chiefs and their families from the eleventh century through the eighteenth century, the

apotheosis of the volcano goddess Pele, great famines, voyages, and wars, cannibals, legends about geographic features, the arrival of Captain Cook, the suppression of the traditional religion, and supernatural folktales about the fourteenth-century princess Laieikawai and of prince Lohiau, who became the lover of Pele's sister, goddess Hiiaka, and Pele's vengeance on Chief Kahavari. Twenty-seven illustrations, including sites, traditional artifacts, and portraits of Kalakaua and his sister. Glossary. In an introduction to the reprint, Terence Brown provides a biography of Kalakaua and an evaluation of his work.

Kamma, Freerk C. *Religious Texts of the Oral Tradition From Western New-Guinea (Irian Jaya)*. Part A. The Origin and Sources of Life. Leiden: E. J. Brill, 1975.
Twenty-five New Guinean myths about the creation of earth, the sun, the moon, and humans, the discovery of fire, and the relationship between life and death. Collected and translated by a Dutch Christian missionary. In an introductory essay, Kamma discusses a definition of myth and offers some comments on the Papuan world view. Endnotes, bibliography, and glossary of Papuan words.

Kolig, Erich. "Noah's Ark Revisited: On the Myth-Land Connection in Traditional Australian Aboriginal Thought." *Oceania* 51 (1981). Abridged in *The Flood Myth*, edited by Alan Dundes. Berkeley: University of California Press, 1988.
Shows how the Aborigines of Australia have transformed the biblical flood tale into a nativistic and xenophobic tale in which Noah's ark, filled with great wealth and technology, came to rest in Australia. Kolig traces the possible development of this myth and its cultural context. Bibliography.

Landtman, Gunnar. *The Folk-Tales of the Kiwai Papuans*. Vol. 47 in *Acta Societatis Scientarum Fennicae*. Helsinki: Finnish Society of Literature, 1917.
A collection of 498 tales recorded by Landtman in New Guinea between 1910 and 1912. Some of these tales were originally told in pidgin English, others in Kiwai. An introductory essay on Landtman's fieldwork and method of recording is followed by an extensive ethnographic study of the life of Kiwai Papuans with information on habitation, language, dress, houses, social organization, implements, canoes, hunting, fishing, war, ceremonies, burial, song and dance, religion and magic, and the ceremonial *gámoda* plant. The plots of all the tales are summarized in twenty thematic groups. Separate English

translations of the tales follow the same groups. Occasionally variants are summarized following individual translations. Contains aetiological legends about the origin of Kiwai Island and its inhabitants; tales of fabulous humans (especially Sido, the first one to die), encounters with dead spirits (especially in Adiri, the Land of the Dead), mythical beings, courtship and marriage, sexual life, the family, and agriculture; culture myths about fire, the harpoon-head, and the drum; and stories about ceremonies, travel and communication, hunting, war, human deformities, fabulous occupations, dreams, children, animals and plants, heavenly bodies, and miscellaneous topics. Forty-two illustrations, including photographs of the people and their surroundings and drawings made by Landtman's informants. Map, list of geographical names, list of recurring incidents, and subject index.

Layton, Robert. "Australia." In *World Mythology*, edited by Roy Willis. New York: Henry Holt, 1993.
This overview of the mythology and religious beliefs of the Aboriginal peoples of Australia includes sections on the primordial flood, death, aetiologies of marriage, tricksters, and travel legends. Subsidiary sections on a ceremonial reenactment of a myth about the Wawilak or Wawalog Sisters, Tiwi funeral poles, an incest myth about Wodoy and Djunggun, two versions of a myth about ancestral heroes called the Bell Bird Brothers, and the journey of ancestral heroines called the Seven Sisters. Eleven color illustrations of artifacts and sites. Map.

Lessa, William. "Discoverer-of-the-Sun." In *The Anthropologist Looks at Myth*, edited by Melville Jacobs and John Greenway. Austin: University of Texas Press, 1966.
A Micronesian tale about Ilofath or Olifat, the trickster of the Caroline Islands, and his relationship with his adopted son, who, in the tale, receives the name Thilpelap, or Discoverer-of-the-Sun. Ilofath helps his son overcome a variety of obstacles, including death itself, and shows him how to seek vengeance against his enemies. Lessa recorded forty-two tales, including this one, on the Ulithi Atoll in 1960. Includes a translation of the tale followed by an interpretation based upon extensive ethnographic information about Ulithian culture and folklore, specifically a comparison with the other forty-one (unpublished) tales in Lessa's collection and a comparison of stylistic features of this tale with responses to a series of psychological tests given to ninety-nine Ulithians by the author in 1948-1949. Endnotes.

Luquet, G. H. "Oceanic Mythology." In *New Larousse Encyclopedia of Mythology*, edited by Felix Guirand et al. Translated by Richard Aldington and Delano Ames. New York: Hamlyn, 1968.

The topic of Oceanic mythology is here divided into discussions of the pantheon of Oceania and the great myths of the region. Describes the spirits of the dead and the physical appearance, attributes, and origins of Oceanic deities. Summarizes myths about the origin of the universe and of specific heavenly bodies, legends about the origin of the earth, fire, living beings, humankind, and social customs, and beliefs concerning death. Accompanied by thirty-three black-and-white and two color reproductions of the art of Oceania.

McConnel, Ursula. *Myths of the Muηkan*. London: Cambridge University Press, 1957.

Thirty-six tales gathered by McConnel especially from female informants among the Muηkan on the Cape York Peninsula in North Queensland, Australia, between 1927 and 1934, are presented here in free English translation. Some sung material appears in the original language with parallel translation. These aetiological tales deal, in particular, with the establishment of religious cults by Muηkan ancestors. Most of the tales are introduced by explanatory commentary, comments on ritual, and, occasionally, information on informants. In a general introductory essay, McConnel describes the life of the Muηkan. In a preface, she describes her fieldwork and some characteristics of these tales. Short foreword by Sir William Mitchell. Six photographs, twenty-two drawings, and two maps.

Mackenzie, Donald Alexander. *Myths from Melanesia and Indonesia*. London: Gresham Publishing, 1930.

This controversial comparative study traces various myths from this region to prototypes in other parts of the world. Suggests that Melanesian and Indonesian culture was influenced by ancient navigators whose visits are sometimes recalled in these myths. In a special study myths dealing with pigs are linked with tales from the Middle East, Egypt, and India. Also contains myths about betel-nut chewing and kava drinking. Several chapters about stone worship in Melanesia are followed by three chapters dealing with Indonesian myths about birds and serpents, aetiology, and dragon jars. Map and thirty-four plates, mostly photographs depicting various features of life in Melanesia and Indonesia. Index.

Melville, Leinani. *Children of the Rainbow*. Wheaton, Ill.: Theosophical
Publishing House, 1969.
A merchant sailor tells of the religion, gods, and legends of his native
Hawaii before the arrival of Europeans. In an introductory chapter,
Melville suggests several reasons why the religion of the Hawaiians
has not been understood by Europeans, especially missionaries. In the
other eight chapters, Melville blends background information with
retellings of traditional material, such as Hawaiian origin myths and
tales of human origin, the destruction of the legendary island of Ta Rua,
the divine father Tane, the eternal creator Teave, and the royal family
of Teave. Includes a translation of *Tumuripo*, the Hawaiian chant of
creation. Ethnological discussion of the origin of the Polynesians in a
postlude. Also contains illustrations of thirty-four sacred symbols of
the Hawaiians with an explanatory key and an essay on the picture
writing of the *tahunas*, the priests and teachers of the ancient religion.

Panoff, A. M. "Oceania: Society and Tradition." In *Larousse World
Mythology*, edited by Pierre Grimal. Translated by Patricia Beardsworth. New York: G. P. Putnam's Sons, 1963.
This survey of the mythologies of Oceania offers summaries and
comparisons of tales from various islands in four geographic sections:
Polynesia, Melanesia, Micronesia, and Australia. Includes Polynesian
myths about the origin of the world, life, and human culture, especially
legends about the culture hero Maui. Melanesian myths about creation
and the origin of culture center on pairs of spirits such as Qat and
Marawa in the Banks Islands. Several Micronesian myths about the
origin of the world, life, and culture are compared. Distinguishes
Aboriginal Australian myths from other tales in Oceania by their closer
links with ritual and the presence of totemism. Emphasis on Australian
myths about the origins of humans, animals, plants and landscapes,
about the migrations of culture heroes, and the origins of human
techniques, institutions, and ceremonies. Forty illustrations of Oceanic
artifacts and cave paintings, nine in color.

Poignant, Roslyn. *Oceanic Mythology*. London: Paul Hamlyn, 1967.
Each part of this general survey includes background on the world view
and oral tradition of an Oceanic group as well as paraphrases, short
quotations, and analyses of individual myths. Part 1 contains descriptions of various Polynesian deities, aetiologies of humankind and of
foods, the legend of the Hawaiian trickster Maui, and Maori stories
about the noble Tawhaki and his son Rata the Strong. Micronesia is
represented in Part 2 by tales of creation from the Gilbert Islands,

heroic deeds (especially about Olifat or Ilofath, the trickster of the Caroline Islands), and animal and ogre legends. Various Melanesian myths of origin, including Papua New Guinea tales about the descent of humans from a sky world or emergence from the underground, appear in Part 3, together with legends about ogres, hostile brothers, death, and great inventors. The myths of the Aborigines of Australia in Part 4 include tales about sky heroes, the creation of woman by the moon, Kummanggur the rainbow snake, the twin fertility goddesses known as the Djanggawul, their daughters the Wawalag Sisters, and the origin of death. Author's note and introductory essay on the people, their land, their myths, and the coming of the Europeans. Twenty-nine color plates and many black-and-white illustrations of artifacts and sites connected with the myths. Map, bibliograpy, and index.

Smith, William Ramsay. *Myth and Legends of the Australian Aboriginals.* London: George G. Harrap, 1932. Reprint. New York: Johnson Reprint Corporation, 1970.
Despite its nineteenth-century perspective on primitive cultures, Smith's work remains an important resource for the oral traditions of the Australian Aborigines. In Chapter 1 the author describes the customs and traditions of the people, interprets some Aboriginal carvings, and offers versions of the creation myth, including the origin of humankind, butterflies, fire, and the lizard, and primeval tales about the peewee bird, the goanna, and the eagle-hawk's relationship with the crow. Chapter 2 includes a flood myth, an aetiology about the creation of Spencer's Gulf, and a collection of animal myths about a selfish owl, frogs, cats, the porcupine and a mountain devil, tortoises, the mischievous crow, and the terrible lizard-like Whowie. In Chapter 3 Smith describes the religion of the Aborigines, the journey of the dead to the Land of Perfection, communication with the Great Spirit, and witchcraft. Chapter 4 deals with marriage customs, family relationships, hunting, fishing, and sport, and contains no traditional narratives. In Chapter 5 Smith adds retellings of fourteen myths about a hermit named Kirkin, the love of two sisters, the destruction of the Keen Keeng race, the cruelty of Newal, his wife, and their dog, monsters, a giant, an encounter with the Evil One, the brothers Perindi and Harrimiah, the life of the legendary warrior Bulpallungga, the wives of the teacher Nurunderi, human reincarnation, and the origins of the bat and the Pleiades. Photographs, figures, and other illustrations, including sixteen drawings depicting scenes from the myths by Alice Woodward. These drawings are in color in the original edition and in black-and-white in the reprint. Footnotes and index.

Stimson, J. Frank. *Songs and Tales of the Sea Kings*, edited by Donald Stanley Marshall. Salem, Mass.: Peabody Museum of Salem, 1957.

A collection of oral literature from Polynesia by an American who lived in Tahiti in the first half of the twentieth century. Material arranged thematically and mostly in verse form. Includes a psalm of creation, songs about youth, daily tasks, royalty, travel, war, and death. The most mythological sections deal with the gods and various tales and legends, including fifteen about Hiro the trickster. Some songs and tales are preceded by editorial comments. In a preface, the editor offers a history of Polynesia and some comments on characteristics of Polynesian oral literature. In a prologue, Van Wyck Brooks describes Stimson's long association with Polynesia. In an introductory essay, the novelist Susanne McConnaughey provides an overview of Polynesian language and traditional culture.

Strathern, Andrew. "Melanesia." In *Mythology: An Illustrated Encyclopaedia*, edited by Richard Cavendish. New York: Rizzoli International, 1980. Also published as *An Illustrated Encyclopedia of Mythology*. New York: Crescent Books, 1984.

This overview begins with some general characteristics of the myths and their role in Melanesian societies and includes summaries and analyses of the myth of an ogre-killing child of the Orokaiva of Papua New Guinea; tales of sex, fertility, and death centering on a hero known as Sido or Soido; tales of brother-sister incest told by the Huli and by the Trobrianders, both of Papua New Guinea; myths about creator deities of the Imbongu and Tolai of Papua New Guinea; and cargo cult myths of the Biak of Irian Jaya and the Mandang Province of Papua New Guinea. Map and illustrations of artwork related to the myths.

Troughton, Joanna. *Mouse-Deer's Market*. New York: Peter Bedrick Books, 1984.

A folktale from Borneo is retold for young children and illustrated in color by the author. In this tale the small mouse-deer falls into a deep hole and escapes by using her knowledge of psychology to trick larger animals into the hole.

_____. *What Made Tiddalik Laugh*. New York: Peter Bedrick Books, 1977.

Retells an Australian Aborigine folktale for young children. In this aetiological tale about the frog's ability to store water within its body, a giant frog called Tiddalik drinks up all the water in the land and causes a drought until a platypus succeeds in making the frog laugh up all the water he drank. Illustrated with color drawings by the author.

Weiner, James. "Oceania." In *World Mythology*, edited by Roy Willis. New York: Henry Holt, 1993.
This overview deals with the religious and mythological beliefs of the peoples of Oceania. Includes sections on creation myths, sky myths, tales of food and fertility, stories about the trickster Maui, the myths of the Maori, Hawaiian ritual cycles about the gods Ku and Lono, and cargo cult myths and *neineya* (or magic formulae) of the Kalauna of Papua New Guinea. Subsidiary sections examine the use of sound in ritual, aetiologies of yams, the Maori world view in architecture, Lono's link with the death of Captain Cook, and cannibalism. Sixteen color illustrations of Oceanic artifacts. Map, time chart, and genealogy.

Westervelt, William Drake. *Hawaiian Historical Legends*. 3d ed. New York: Fleming H. Revell, 1926.
A major early twentieth-century collector of Hawaiian legends discussions some oral traditions about the settlement and history of the Hawaiian Islands. The material is arranged chronologically in twenty-one chapters, beginning with tales of the legendary ancestor Maui and ending with nineteenth-century accounts of the first books printed in Hawaii, the first constitution, and the Hawaiian flag. Also included are tales of migrations from Polynesia, early rulers of the island, Captain Cook, and historical events. In an introductory essay, Sanford B. Dole, the first U.S. governor of the islands, distinguishes historical legends from myth. Short foreword by Westervelt. Pronunciation guide, eight illustrations, and index.

_____. *Hawaiian Legends of Ghosts and Ghost-Gods*. Boston: George H. Ellis, 1916. Reprint. Rutland, Vt.: Charles E. Tuttle, 1963.
In Part 1 Westervelt retells eighteen tales about Hawaiian ghosts. Some are ghosts of ancestors, some are divine, and some are dragon ghosts. In Part 2 he describes Hawaiian beliefs in some of these spiritual beings. An appendix contains notes about several places in Hawaii and aspects of Hawaiian culture. In an introductory essay, Westervelt discusses some themes found in Hawaiian legends. Foreword on Hawaiian folkloristics by J. W. Gilmore. Eighteen black-and-white photographs, pronunciation guide, note on the Polynesian language, and index.

_____. *Hawaiian Legends of Old Honolulu*. Boston: George H. Ellis, 1915. Reprint. Rutland, Vt.: Charles E. Tuttle, 1963.

These twenty-five tales about ancient Honolulu were gathered by the author from Hawaiian storytellers and from published sources. Includes a migration legend, a myth about the creation of humankind, tales about legendary places in Honolulu, aetiologies, and stories about gods and superhuman mortals and animals. In a short introduction, Westervlet explains how this collection was completed. Foreword on Hawaiian legends by George H. Barton. Twenty-one black-and-white photographs, map, pronunciation guide, appendix on the Polynesian language, and index.

_____. *Legends of Ma-ui: A Demi-god of Polynesia, and His Mother Hina.* Honolulu: Hawaiian Gazette, 1910.
These twenty-five tales about an ancient Polynesian demigod and his divine mother, popular across the Pacific from Hawaii to New Zealand to Tahiti, were originally published as magazine articles. Variants from different parts of the Pacific are compared. Eleven stories tell about Maui's home, his adventures as a fisherman, his discovery of fire, his lifting of the sky, his snaring of the sun, and his quest for immortality. One chapter deals with Maui tales localized on the Hawaiian island of Oahu. Four chapters focus on Maui's mother Hina, her adventures with the Wailuku River, and her daughters. In the preface, the author offers a history of Maui and his tales. Nineteen photographs illustrating scenes and activities mentioned in the stories. Pronunciation guide and index.

_____. *Myths and Legends of Hawaii*, edited by A. Grove Day. Honolulu: Mutual Publishing, 1987.
This selection from Westervelt's monumental four-volume collection of Hawaiian myths and legends includes forty-nine tales arranged thematically. Eight tales about the Polynesian demigod Maui are followed by eleven about the volcano goddess Pele and her family, eleven ghost stories, eighteen about the island of Oahu, and a longer tale about a bride from the Land of the Dead. In a foreword, the editor summarizes some features of Hawaiian religious and mythological beliefs and discusses Westervelt's career and contributions to the study of Polynesian mythology.

Wheeler, Gerald Camden. *Mono-Alu Folklore.* London: George Routledge & Sons, 1926.
An ethnographic collection of seventy-eight tales and eleven songs recorded on the islands of Alu and Mono, Bougainville Strait, of the Western Solomon Islands in 1908-1909. Summaries of the tales and

the songs in Part 1 include comparative notes and commentary. The summaries are organized in the following thematic groups: tales of origin and wandering, the taro plant, non-human women, animals, snakes, sexual activity, cannibalism, encounters with ogres, journeys to another world, ghosts and other supernatual beings, and actual events. The original Mono texts are followed by full English translations and endnotes in Part 2. Eight tales are recorded in English only, and all tales about sexual activity are translated and summarized only in Latin. Mono-English glossary and indexes to motives, flora, fauna, and places in Part 3. In an introductory essay, the author provides some ethnographic background to the people and their tales. Footnotes.

Chapter 5
ASIA

The world's largest continent is particularly difficult to treat coherently from a mythological perspective. Indeed, only two of the citations in the "General Works" section at the beginning of this chapter attempt anything like a sweeping geographic survey of Asian mythologies. Generally, mythographers and scholars tend to look at the myths of Asia's many regional cultures under separate geographic headings like India, China, Japan, and the ancient Middle East and Mesopotamia. These four major areas are accompanied in this chapter by a short additional section on the myths of Southeast Asia, including the Philippines. The "West and Central Asian Myths" section includes not only the traditions of the Babylonians, Canaanites, Hebrews, and other peoples of the ancient Middle East and Mesopotamia but also those of Iranians, Arabs, and other more contemporary peoples of western Asia. The term "Near East," preferred by many scholars of the region, is here replaced by the less Eurocentric "Middle East." The tales of the Old Testament are treated with other Middle Eastern material in this chapter, while the broader geographic traditions of medieval and modern Jews are discussed in Chapter 1, where combined discussions of ancient Middle Eastern and Egyptian mythologies also appear. The section on Indian myths reflects the many religious traditions of the region and includes Vedic, Hindu, Buddhist, Jainist, and tribal myths. The diverse traditions of Buddhism, however, appear in all four geographic sections of this chapter. The myths of China present particular difficulties of definition. Excluded from this study is some material which is often cited in books about Chinese myth but which does not directly deal with traditional tales, such as Lo Kuan-Chung's fourteenth-century novel entitled *Romance of the Three Kingdoms*. Also excluded are more philosophic works such as the Taoist book of Lao-tzu. Despite obvious political implications, the myths of Tibet are discussed in the context of the Chinese mythological tradition with which they share many common themes and historical ties.

General Works

Buck, Pearl S., ed. *Fairy Tales of the Orient*. New York: Simon and Schuster, 1965.
A major American author of popular books for children and for the general public has selected from previously published sources thirty-

six tales of Arabia, China, India, Japan, Persia, Russia, and Turkey. Traditional supernatural themes about witches, dwarfs, and demons are preceded by some summary and commentary by Buck. In a foreword, Buck offers some general description and interpretation of these tales. Illustrated with color drawings by Jeanee Wong.

Hackin, J., ed. *Asiatic Mythology*. Translated by F. M. Atkinson. New York: Thomas Y. Crowell, 1963.
Seven scholars of religion at the Musée Guimet in Paris collaborated in this sweeping survey of the mythologies of Asia. Sections devoted to the mythologies of Persia, the Kafir of Afghanistan, Indian Buddhism, Brahmanism, Lamaism (Tibetan Buddhism), Indo-China, Java, Buddhism in Central Asia, modern China, and Japan. The text is accompanied by fifteen color plates and 354 other illustrations of mythic scenes in the art of these regions. A short introductory essay by Paul-Louis Couchoud describes the scope of the book. Index.

Mackenzie, Donald Alexander. *Myths of China and Japan*. London: Gresham Publishing, 1923. Reprint. London: Studio Editions, 1986.
This survey of Chinese and Japanese myths is based upon a controversial theory of cultural drifting and culture mixing which traces many Chinese beliefs and myths to sources in the West, including medieval Byzantium, ancient Egypt, the ancient Aegean, and even Celtic Scotland. The first four chapters offer evidence for such cultural borrowing in trade and the spread of the Egyptian potter's wheel to China. Later chapters trace the spread of copper to China from the West and discuss culture mixing in Japan. The remaining fifteen chapters examine elements in various Chinese and Japanese myths with similar features in Western myths. Chapters on dragon and other animal lore, creation myths, legendary kings and heroes, the symbolism of jade, Taoism, and other topics. Thirty-four illustrations, some in color, especially from Chinese and Japanese paintings. Footnotes and index.

West and Central Asian Myths

Albright, William Foxwell. "Archaeology and the Religion of the Canaanites." In *Archaeology and the Religion of Israel*, by William Foxwell Albright. 3d ed. Baltimore: The Johns Hopkins University Press, 1953.
Part of a scholarly examination of archaeological sources for information about the religions of ancient Syria and Israel, this chapter deals with the religion and mythology of the Canaanite or Phoenician people.

Of particular mythological interest are a description of the Canaanite pantheon and a summary of the Baal epic of Ugarit. Endnotes.

Al-Saleh-Khairat. *Fabled Cities, Princes and Jinn from Arab Myths and Legends.* New York: Schocken Books, 1985.

The world of Arabian stories is presented to juvenile readers with many illustrations by Rashad N. Salim. Symbols used in the illustrations are explained in a short appendix. A brief introduction to the Arabs and their world is followed by sections on the gods and myths of the ancient Arabs, legends of North and South, tales of priests, soothsayers, and wise men and of generosity, honor, and loyalty. Also contains sections on the heavenly and earthly worlds and on angels and jinn. Shahrazad's story in *The One Thousand and One Nights* is summarized, and two of her tales are told: the story of the city of brass and the story of the Queen of the serpents. Pronunciation guide, map, bibliography, and index.

Ananikian, Mardiros H. *Armenian Mythology.* Vol. 7 in *The Mythology of All Races*, edited by John Arnott MacCulloch. Boston: Marshall Jones, 1925.

This survey of the religion and mythology of the people of Armenia highlights Iranian, Asiatic, and national features. In Chapter 1 the author outlines the political and religious development of the region. Deities of indigenous, Iranian, and Semitic origin are discussed in Chapters 2-4. Vahagn, the national deity, is described in Chapter 5, with a more detailed discussion in an appendix. Chapters 6-9 are devoted to nature worship and myths about celestial bodies, fire, water, and the natural world. Concludes with studies of Armenian heroes, the world of spirits and monsters, and Armenian concepts of cosmogony and death in Chapter 6. Six plates and three figures. Map, appendix, endnotes, and bibliography. Complete index in Volume 13.

Beltz, Walter. *God and the Gods: Myths of the Bible.* New York: Penguin, 1983.

This mythological analysis of the legends of the Bible for the general reader starts from the premise that these stories are more symbolic and legendary than historical. Paraphrases of biblical narrative are followed by commentary on the origin and religious meaning of the tales. In Chapters 1-14 Beltz deals with the themes of creation, god, humans, the people of God, the promised land, the law, great sanctuaries and heroes, miracles, legends about kings, Jerusalem, the adventures of Job, Esther, and Daniel, the devil, the life of Jesus and the story of redemption, and the second coming. In Chapter 15 he surveys the transformations of biblical mythology in the medieval and modern worlds. Introductory essay on the history of the ancient Israel and the Middle East, the sources of the biblical tradition, and some characteristics and purposes of biblical myths. Chronological table, glossary, and indexes.

Budge, Earnest A. Wallis. *The Babylonian Story of the Deluge and the Epic of Gilgamesh*. London: British Museum, 1920.

In this pamphlet the keeper of the Egyptian and Assyrian antiquities at the British Museum describes the museum's excavations at ancient Nineveh in 1852-1853 and translates several documents discovered in the excavations for the general reader. In particular, Budge describes George Smith's discovery of the text of the *Epic of Gilgamesh* among the clay tablets excavated at the site, discusses the Babylonian flood myth, and translates Utnapishtim's account of the flood from the *Epic of Gilgamesh*. Also provides a translation of Berosus' version of the flood. Footnotes, plan, twelve photographs of the clay tablets, one illustration, and three portions of tablet transcriptions.

Caquot, A. "Western Semitic Lands: The Idea of the Supreme God." In *Larousse World Mythology*, edited by Pierre Grimal. Translated by Patricia Beardsworth. New York: G. P. Putnam's Sons, 1963.

Uses poems found at Ras Shamra, the ancient Ugarit, to survey the mythology of the ancient Semites, including the Phoenicians, the Carthaginians, and the Hebrews. In particular, Caquot summarizes myths about the gods El, Baal, Anath, and Mot, as well as a royal legend about King Keret. Also considers references to Semite deities in the Old Testament and in Greco-Roman mythology. Paraphrases of the myths are combined with photographs of artifacts and some quotation in translation from original sources.

Carnoy, Albert J. *Iranian Mythology*. Vol. 6 in *The Mythology of All Races*, edited by Louis Herbert Gray. Boston: Marshall Jones, 1917.

Following a short introduction to the ancient Persian religion with some discussion of sources, the author offers a comprehensive study of Iranian myths, especially those about the wars of the gods, creation, primeval heroes, the Indo-Iranian hero Yima, ancient kings, Zoroaster, and beliefs in the afterlife. Particular emphasis is placed on the Iranian concept of duality and on the evolution of Iranian myths toward historical legend. Fourteen illustrations, transcription and pronunciation guide, endnotes, and bibliography. Complete index in Volume 13.

Cassuto, Umberto, ed. and trans. *The Goddess Anath: Canaanite Epics of the Patriarchal Age*. Translated by Israel Abrahams. Jerusalem: Magnes Press, 1971.

A scholarly edition and translation of the Canaanite epic of Baal by a pioneer in the study of Ugaritic texts. The epic was discovered between 1928 and 1939 on tablets in the ruins of Ugarit, an ancient city located near the modern town of Ras Shamra, Syria. These tables describe a cosmic conflict between life and death, between the gods Baal and Mot. In this struggle Baal is killed, avenged by his warrior sister Anath, and brought back to life. Cassuto's work was originally published in Hebrew in 1951. This English edition includes his Hebrew translation and the transliterated Ugaritic text in parallel columns. Abrahams' English translation appears on facing pages. The scholarly text is accompanied by preliminary notes, descriptions of each tablet, and commentary. In three introductory chapters, Cassuto discusses characteristics of Ugaritic writing, the relationship between biblical and Ugaritic literature, descriptions of the chief Canaanite deities, and a paraphrase of the epic. Extensive use of Hebrew. A translator's foreword and author's preface provide background on the texts and on Cassuto's work. Numerous figures and charts and eight photographic plates of the tablets and of Canaanite artifacts. Footnotes, bibliography, and four indexes.

Childs, Brevard S. *Myth and Reality in the Old Testament*. London: SCM Press, 1960.

A theological scholar shows how myth and the Old Testament have different ways of portraying reality. In Chapter 1, Childs addresses the problem of a definition of myth. In Chapter 2, he illustrates the mythic view of reality in primitive religion and in the myths of the Sumerians, Babylonians, and ancient Egyptians. In Chapter 3, he offers exegeses of seven passages from Genesis, Exodus, and Isaiah in order to show where myth is in conflict with the Old Testament. In Chapter 4, he contrasts the concepts of time and space in myth and in the Old Testament, and in Chapter 5 he addresses some theological problems which follow from these observations. Index.

Colum, Padraic, ed. *The Arabian Nights*. New York: Macmillan, 1923.

The abridged version of *The Thousand and One Nights* as translated by Edward William Lane is here shortened and sanitized for young readers. Many of these tales come originally from the oral storytelling traditions of medieval Persia, India, and Arabia. Ten of the original stories are presented, including the frame tale of Shahrazad and her husband the sultan and narratives about the voyages of Sindibad the sailor, 'Ala-ed-Din (Aladdin) and the lamp, and 'Ali Baba and the forty thieves. Illustrated with three-color drawings by Lynd Ward. In an introductory essay, Colum offers a history of the tales and their English translations.

Curtis, Vesta Sarkhosh. *Persian Myths*. Austin: University of Texas Press, 1993.
This historical survey of the mythologies of Persia for the general reader is part of The Legendary Past Series. Instead of providing a comprehensive overview, Curtis' goal is to illustrate the continuity of Persian mythology from the time of the pre-Zoroastrian deity Ahura Mazda to Islamic transformations of Zoroastrianism in medieval Persia and modern Iran. Following an introductory section on the history of Persia and on sources for knowledge of the country's ancient mythologies, Curtis treats, in separate chapters, the gods of ancient Iran and the creation story of the ancient Iranians, demons, mythical creatures and heroes in the *Avesta*, the legendary rulers in the eleventh-century A.D. *Shah-Nameh* or *Book of Kings* of the poet Firdowsi, *div* or demons and other mythological creatures in the *Shah-Nameh*, legendary biographies of Zoroaster, Cyrus the Great, and Alexander the Great, romantic medieval stories about the lovers Vis and Ramin and Khusrow and Shirin, and Islamic passion plays and the fairy tales in *The Thousand and One Nights*. Concluding section on the continuity of the myths in performances by storytellers and in popular art. Map, bibliography, and index.

Dalley, Stephanie, trans. *Myths from Mesopotamia*. New York: Oxford University Press, 1989.
A Middle Eastern archaeologist and philologist makes use of recent advances in scholarship and lexicography to provide for the general reader accurate and readable translations of ten Akkadian texts. Seven of these, the flood story in *Atrahasis*, the *Epic of Gilgamesh*, the *Descent of Ishtar*, the epics of Adapa and Etana, and the creation story in the *Enuma Elish*, are widely available in English. Less common in English translation are the *Epic of Anzu*, the fragmentary *Theogony of Dunnu*, and *Erra and Ishum*, a conversation in which the gods Erra, Ishum, and Marduk all participate. Translations contain notations indicating restorations, uncertain readings, and gaps in the original texts and are followed by explanatory endnotes. General introduction and individual introductions to each text. Map, chronological chart,

illustrations of the eight mythical monsters mentioned in the translations, glossary, and bibliography.

Delaporte, L. "Phoenician Mythology." In *New Larousse Encyclopedia of Mythology*, edited by Felix Guirand et al. Translated by Richard Aldington and Delano Ames. New York: Hamlyn, 1968.
Following background on the ancient Phoenician site of Gubla, or Byblos in Greek, near modern Beirut, Lebanon, Delaporte offers descriptions of the gods, heroes, and legends mentioned in fourteenth-century B.C. texts of ancient Ugarit (the modern Ras Shamra). In particular, Delaporte considers the annual conflict between the vegetation deities Aleyin and Mot, the deaths of the gods Baal and Aleyin, the description of Baal's temple, the epic of the hero Keret, and a poem about the birth of the gods. From ancient Greek sources, especially Philo of the first century A.D., Delaporte describes the Phoenician cosmogony and the myth and festivals of the vegetation god Adonis. Also contains a short section on the gods of Carthage and of the Hittites. Fourteen black-and-white illustrations of ancient artifacts.

Dresden, M. J. "Mythology of Ancient Iran." In *Mythologies of the Ancient World*, edited by Samuel Noah Kramer. Garden City, N.Y.: Doubleday (Anchor), 1961.
This short overview of Iranian mythology begins with a brief introduction on sources. Compares Zoroastrian and Manichaean views of the world and its origin. Sections on demonology, eschatology, the origin of human beings, and various deities such as Mithra, Haoma, Vayu, and Zurvan. Endnotes and bibliography.

Duchesne-Guillemin, Jacques. *Symbols and Values in Zoroastrianism.* New York: Harper and Row, 1966.
A geographic and historical sketch of Zoroastrianism is followed by a scholarly examination of its religious and iconographic symbols. Chapter 1 deals with the divine entities Mithra and Zurvan. Ritual symbols are discussed in Chapter 2 and religious emblems and insignia of the gods and of humans in Chapter 3. The emphasis is on description and analysis of these religious and mythological symbols rather than on paraphrase and interpretation of mythic narratives. Other chapters consider the place of humankind in the cosmos and Mazdaism in later Sufi literature. Footnotes, five illustrations, and index.

Filby, Fredk. A. *The Flood Reconsidered.* Grand Rapids, Mich.: Zondervan Publishing House, 1970.

A review of various evidence supporting the viewpoint that the flood described in ancient Mesopotamian sources actually took place. The author begins with geological and archaeological materials suggesting the fact of great ancient floods, their causes, and their probable extent. Flood records from many nations, including Mesopotamian and biblical accounts, are examined. Concludes with some theological implications of the flood story. Time charts, footnotes, bibliography, and index.

Follansbee, Eleanor. "The Story of the Flood in the Light of Comparative Semitic Mythology." *Religions* 29 (1939): 11-21. Reprinted in *The Flood Myth*, edited by Alan Dundes. Berkeley: University of California Press, 1988.
Combines a composite version of the Mesopotamian flood myth with an emphasis on the links between myth and ritual and concludes that the myth originally reenacted a fertility ritual. The hero was then a vegetation deity and the ark a religious building constructed as the house of god. Footnotes and bibliography.

Fontenrose, Joseph. "God and Dragon in Mesopotamia." In *Python: A Study of Delphic Myth and Its Origins*, by Joseph Fontenrose. Berkeley: University of California Press, 1959.
In this chapter of a book examining myths of divine or heroic combat with serpents or dragons in the ancient Mediterranean world, Fontenrose considers examples of dragon combat in the mythologies of ancient Sumeria, Assyria, and Babylonia. Uses folktale themes and motifs from the Aarne-Thompson index to compare the contests of the Sumerian hero-god Ninurta and the monster-demon Asag, of the Babylonian Marduk and Tiamat, and of Gilgamesh and the monster Humbaba with the Greek myth about Apollo and Python and other Mediterranean combat myths. Uncovers a common pattern of conflict between order and disorder, chaos and cosmos, and life and death. Four black-and-white figures.

Frankfort, Henri. "Kingship and the Divine Powers in Nature." In *Kingship and the Gods*, by Henri Frankfort. Chicago: University of Chicago Press, 1948.
This section of a scholary comparison of Egyptian and Mesopotamian concepts of kingship shows how Mesopotamian rulers were sometimes associated with deities who die and are resurrected, that is, with suffering gods such as Tammuz, Adonis, and Osiris. While the Mesopotamian ruler was viewed as essentially a mortal burdened with the heavy responsibility of leading humankind in its servitude to the gods,

occasionally these rulers were described as the chosen bridegrooms of a powerful mother goddess such as Ishtar. This theme appears in various ancient cults, artistic scenes, and texts such as *Enuma Elish*, the Babylonian creation myth. Some of this artwork is illustrated in black-and-white figures. Also includes considerable quotation from ancient texts in translation. Endnotes and index.

Frye, Northrop. "Myth II." In *The Great Code*, by Northrop Frye. New York: Harcourt Brace Jovanovich, 1982.
This essay on mythic features of the Bible is part of a study of the Bible as literature by a major literary critic of the twentieth century. Starting from a definition of myth as "sacred narrative," Frye argues that the underlying pattern of the biblical story is a U-shaped progression of fallings-out and restorations between God and humans. In the Old Testament this pattern is reflected in the history of the states of Judah and Israel. In the New Testament this pattern is replaced by a single heroic fall and redemption by Jesus. Frye concludes the essay with an application of this interpretation to the Book of Job.

Frymer-Kensky, Tikva. "The Atrahasis Epic and Its Significance for Our Understanding of Genesis 1-9." *Biblical Archaeology Review* 1978. Reprinted in *The Flood Myth*, edited by Alan Dundes. Berkeley: University of California Press, 1988.
Compares the biblical story of Noah and flood with the eighth-century B.C. Babylonian version known as the Atrahasis epic. The author shows how the composer of Genesis 1-9 has reworked the traditional Mesopotamian myth into a story about pollution. Noah's tale reflects an Israelite emphasis on law and the sanctity of life as fundamental tenets of human existence.

Gaster, Theodor H. *Myth, Legend and Custom in the Old Testament*. New York: Harper and Row, 1969.
A formal examination of 350 sections of the Old Testament containing elements of mythology and comparative folklore. The material is arranged as it appears in the Old Testament, beginning with creation and the story of Adam and Eve and ending with the prophets and the holy writings. Gaster does not retell the myths, but offers a comparative commentary incorporating significant material from Sir James G. Frazer's *Folklore in the Old Testament* (1918). The comparative references come from all over the world, but especially from Egypt and the Middle East. In a preface and introductory essay, Gaster summarizes

some mythological features of the Old Testament and explains the organization of the book. Endnotes and indexes.

_____. *The Oldest Stories in the World.* New York: Viking Press, 1952.
These retellings of thirteen Middle Eastern myths and legends based upon Gaster's own study and translation of the original texts are arranged geographically and are followed by explanatory comments and interpretation for the general reader. The Babylonian tales include the adventures of Gilgamesh, the cosmic war between Apsu and Tiamat, animal lore about the antagonism between the eagle and the serpent, the story of Adapa, and an aetiology of toothache. Among the Hittite tales are the disappearance of Telepinu, the contest between Kumarbi and a stone monster, the capture of a dragon, Kessi the Hunter, and a numbskull bridegroom named Appu. The Canaanite stories tell of a bow-shaped constellation, the forgetful King Keret, and the contest between the gods Baal and Yam. In the preface, Gaster provides some background to the stories, their authorship, form, style, and interpretation. Twelve black-and-white drawings based upon ancient seal engravings and sculpture. Footnotes and index of motifs.

Gibson, J. C. L. *Canaanite Myths and Legends.* Edinburgh: T. and T. Clark, 1978.
A completely revised scholarly version of the mythological material from ancient Ugarit (now Ras Shamra, Syria) originally edited by Godfrey R. Driver in 1956. The core of this book is a series of transliterations of Ugaritic texts with parallel English translation, including the conflict between the gods Baal and Yam, the building of Baal's palace, the conflict between Baal and Mot, the god of death, the legends of King Keret and of Aqhat, son of Dan'el, and poetic hymns to the divine brothers Shachar and Shalim, to the gracious gods, to the goddess Nikkal, and to the daughters of the new moon known as the Kotharat. Several fragmentary texts are added in an appendix in transcription without translation. In an extensive introduction, Gibson offers a description of the discovery of the texts in archaeological excavations between 1929 and 1939 and detailed analysis and interpretation of the texts. Footnotes, concordance of tablets, bibliography, note on Ugaritic phonology, glossary, list of biblical references, and table of Ugaritic signs.

Ginsberg, H. L. "Ugaritic Myths and Epics." In *The Ancient Near East*,
     edited by James B. Pritchard. Princeton, N.J.: Princeton University
     Press, 1958.
     Translations of texts found at Ras Shamra (ancient Ugarit) in Syria
     related to the Old Testament are here presented for the general reader
     with careful indication of original text numbers, restorations, and
     doubtful readings. Poems about the Canaanite fertility god Baal and
     the warrior goddess Anath are followed by the epic tale of Aqhat, the
     son of Dan'el. Each text is preceded by a short introduction. Some of
     the 197 illustrations of Middle Eastern artifacts in this volume com-
     plement this material. Also in the volume are footnotes, map, indexes,
     and glossary.

_____. "Ugaritic Myths, Epics and Legends." In *Ancient Near
     Eastern Texts Relating to the Old Testament*, edited by James B.
     Pritchard. 3d ed. Princeton, N.J.: Princeton University Press, 1969.
     Ras Shamra texts are here translated in a scholarly format, with careful
     indication of original text numbers, restorations, and doubtful readings.
     Poems about the Canaanite fertility god Baal and the warrior goddess
     Anath are followed by the epic tales of King Keret and of Aqhat, the
     son of Dan'el. Each text is preceded by a introductory commentary and
     bibliography. Footnotes.

Ginzberg, Louis. "Jewish Folklore: East and West." In *On Jewish Law
     and Lore*, by Louis Ginzberg. New York: World Publishing, 1962.
     Originally delivered as an address at Harvard University in 1936, this
     essay examines some of the legendary lore found in the Jewish Hag-
     gadah, the traditional, non-legal part of the Talmud. Argues that tales
     about the killing of Cain by Lamech, David's harpstrings, and a
     hermaphroditic Adam are part of an ancient oral tradition filled with
     many foreign influences. Also considers the influence such tales have
     had on the biblical legends in Christianity and Islam. Footnotes.

_____. *The Legends of the Jews*, by Louis Ginzberg. 7 vols. Vols.
     1-2 and Vols. 4-7 translated by Henrietta Szold. Vol. 3 translated by
     Paul Radin. Philadelphia: Jewish Publication Society of America,
     1909-1938.
     A collection of the folklore, fairy tales, and legends from original
     sources in the post-biblical Jewish rabbinic tradition, especially the
     Haggadah. The collection is arranged chronologically and begins in
     Volume 1 with myths about creation, the flood, Abraham, Isaac, and
     Jacob. Volume 2 deals with the stories of Joseph, Moses, and the exodus

from Egypt, and Volume 3 with the wandering in the desert through the death of Moses. In Volume 4 are myths about prophets and kings of Israel, the Babylonian exile and the return from captivity. Endnotes to Volumes 1 and 2 in Volume 5. Endnotes to Volumes 3 and 4 in Volume 6. Comprehensive index in Volume 7.

_____. "Noah and the Flood in Jewish Legend." In *The Legends of the Jews*, by Louis Ginsberg. Vol. 1. Philadelphia: Jewish Publication Society of America, 1909. Reprinted in *The Flood Myth*, edited by Alan Dundes. Berkeley: University of California Press, 1988.
Ginzberg retells Jewish legends related to the flood story in Genesis, including stories about the birth of Noah, the punishment of the fallen angels, the sinful generation which lived before the flood, the holy book of Noah, the passengers on the ark, the flood, Noah's departure from the ark, and his drunkenness.

Goetze, Albrecht. "A Hittite Myth." In *The Ancient Near East*, edited by James B. Pritchard. Princeton, N.J.: Princeton University Press, 1958.
A scholarly translation of a Hittite myth about the god Telepinu, his anger and disappearance, his search party, his ritual, and his homecoming is here accompanied by careful indication of original text numbers, restorations, and doubtful readings. Each text is preceded by a short introduction. Some of the 197 illustrations of Middle Eastern artifacts in this volume complement this material. Also in the volume are footnotes, map, indexes, and glossary.

_____. "Hittite Myths, Epics and Legends." In *Ancient Near Eastern Texts Relating to the Old Testament*, edited by James B. Pritchard. 3d ed. Princeton, N.J.: Princeton University Press, 1969.
Six Hittite myths are here translated in a scholarly format, with careful indication of original text numbers, restorations, and doubtful readings. Included are the story of how the moon fell from heaven, a description of heavenly kingship, the *Song of Ullikummi*, the son of the god Kumarbi and the mother-goddess, the myth of the dragon Illuyankas, the myth of Telepinu, and a tale of El, Shertu, and the storm god. Each text is preceded by bibliographical information. Footnotes.

Goldstein, David. *Jewish Legends*. 2d ed. New York: Peter Bedrick Books, 1987.
This general introduction to Jewish myths and legends from the Bible contains many illustrations, especially from medieval manuscripts. Following a short introduction on the religious and geographic background to these legends, the author traces the Jewish world view from

creation and the flood through tales of the Patriarchs Abraham, Jacob, and Joseph and stories about the leaders Moses, David, and Solomon. Bibliography and index.

Gordon, Cyrus H. "Canaanite Mythology." In *Mythologies of the Ancient World*, edited by Samuel Noah Kramer. Garden City, N.Y.: Doubleday (Anchor), 1961.
A major scholar of Middle Eastern studies uses texts from ancient Ugarit to describe the myths of the Canaanites who lived in ancient Syria and Palestine. Many of these myths center on themes of fertility, both in the natural world and in human society. Also contains myths about kinship among the gods, especially the myths of the god Baal. Special attention to the influence of Canaanite mythology on ancient Israel. Extensive quotation of ancient documents in English translation. Endnotes and bibliography.

_____. *Ugaritic Literature*. Rome: Pontifical Bible Institute, 1949.
This comprehensive and scholarly translation of all the texts found at Ras Shamra, the ancient Ugarit, includes not only mythological texts in Part 1 but also letters, administrative and diplomatic documents, and inventories in Part 2. Five myths are told in these texts: the story of the gods Baal and Anath, the birth of the gods, the marriage of the moon to the Sumerian lunar goddess Nikkal, and the legends of King Keret and of Aqhat, son of Dan'el. Translations are preceded by a plot summary and editorial comments and include indications of interpolations and lacunae. In a foreword and introductory chapter, Gordon provides some background to these texts and compares them to the Bible. Footnotes and indexes.

Graves, Robert, and Raphael Patai. *Hebrew Myths*. Garden City, N.Y.: Doubleday, 1964.
This analysis of myths from the Book of Genesis is meant to be a companion volume to Graves' *Greek Myths* and follows a similar format, with sixty-one chapters arranged chronologically, beginning with creation and ending with the death of Joseph. For each myth the authors provide summaries of several versions (indicated by lowercase letters) and detailed analyses (indicated by numbers). Introductory essay, three maps, index, an annotated list of abbreviations, sources, and bibliography.

Gray, John. *The Canaanites*. New York: Frederick A. Praeger, 1964.

This general overview of the Canaanite or Phoenician people of ancient Syria and Israel by a scholar at the University of Aberdeen contains chapters on habitat and history, daily life, society, religion, literature, and art. Integrated into the texts are significant quotations in translation from various mythological texts, including the Baal myth and the legends of Keret and Aqhat, son of Dan'el. Literary descriptions of Canaanite deities are complemented by illustrations of artisitc images of the god. Bibliography, fifty-seven figures, sixty-one plates with endnotes, and index.

_____. *The Legacy of Canaan.* 2d ed. Leiden: E. J. Brill, 1965.
A scholarly examination, translation, and analysis of cuneiform texts from Ras Shamra (ancient Ugarit) in Syria. In addition to chapters on the history of Ugarit and its records, the social order reflected in the documents, and a literary and linguistic comparison of the documents with the Old Testament, several chapters deal specifically with mythological themes. Chapter 2 considers the myth of Baal and the Canaanite fertility cult. The legends of Keret and Aqhat, son of Dan'el, are examined in Chapter 3. Both of these chapters include extensive quotation from the original documents with parallel English translation. Chapter 4 contains an overview of the Canaanite religion, including descriptions of various deities. Chart of the Ugaritic alphabet with transliteration, footnotes, bilbiography, and indexes.

_____. *Near Eastern Mythology.* 2d ed. New York: Peter Bedrick Books, 1982.
This general introduction to the mythologies of the ancient Middle East is divided into separate geographic parts on Mesopotamia, Canaan, and Israel. Concepts of divinity and kingship and summaries of major myths are covered in each part. In addition, the historical geography of Mesopotamia and Canaan and the relationships between myth and history and myth and poetic imagery in the Old Testament are also discussed. The text is supplemented by illustrations of artifacts representing these myths. Bibliography and index.

Guirand, Felix. "Assyro-Babylonian Mythology." In *New Larousse Encyclopedia of Mythology*, edited by Felix Guirand et al. Translated by Richard Aldington and Delano Ames. New York: Hamlyn, 1968.
Summarizes the Babylonain creation myth, describes the world of the Babylonian gods, and offers separate treatments of the five great gods, four deities of the stars, storm, and winds, and fire, water, and earth. Each religious figure is treated separately, with discussions of the god's

names, iconography, and major myths. Also contains sections on myths about the origin of humankind and the great flood, on the relationship between gods and mortals, on the underworld, on demigods called *utukku*, and on the gods of Elam. Summaries of the myths about the heroes Etana, Adapa, and Gilgamesh. Frequent quotation in translation from original sources. Thirty-five black-and-white and two color illustrations of artifacts illustrating these gods and heroes.

Güterbock, Hans G. "Hittite Mythology." In *Mythologies of the Ancient World*, edited by Samuel Noah Kramer. Garden City, N.Y.: Doubleday (Anchor), 1961.
Adapted from a chapter from *The Art and Literature of the Hittites*, this essay surveys the myths of the peoples of the ancient Hittite empire in Anatolia (western Turkey), Syria, and northern Mesopotamia. An introduction to the various languages of this region is followed by summaries of native tales such as the myth of the vanquished god and the Dragon Fight myth as well as Hittite versions of Hurrian, Canaanite, and Syrian myths such as the Kumarbi epic. Extensive quotation of ancient documents in English translation. Endnotes.

Habel, Norman C. "The Two Flood Stories in Genesis." In *Literary Criticism of the Old Testament*, by Norman C. Habel. Philadelphia: Fortress Press, 1971. Reprinted in *The Flood Myth*, edited by Alan Dundes. Berkeley: University of California Press, 1988.
Analyzes the story of Noah and the flood in Genesis 6-9 in order to show that the biblical tale is a blending of two separate traditions. Habel, a biblical scholar, illustrates that the flood story contains two separate introductory and concluding sections and two narrative versions, one labeled Yahwist and the other priestly.

Hackin, M. J. "Buddhist Mythology in Central Asia." In *Asiatic Mythology*, edited by M. J. Hackin. Translated by F. M. Atkinson. New York: Thomas Y. Crowell, 1963.
Devoted to Buddhist legends and beliefs popular across a wide geographic belt of central Asia, including modern Afghanistan and Chinese Turkestan. Describes representations of the five Dhyani-Buddhas, the Paradise, the life of the Buddha, the miracles of Avalokitesvara, the Lokapala or guardian kings, and the Bodhisattvas Kshitigarbha, Maitreya, and Samantabhadra. Replaced by Islam by the eleventh century A.D., this Buddhist culture survives in fragmentary manuscripts and statuettes and in reliefs on abandoned monasteries. Nine black-and-white figures and one color plate.

_____. "The Mythology of the Kafirs." In *Asiatic Mythology*, edited by M. J. Hackin. Translated by F. M. Atkinson. New York: Thomas Y. Crowell, 1963.

A short discussion of the mythological beliefs of the people of Kafiristan in Afghanistan before their conversion to Islam at the end of the nineteenth century. Based upon European accounts and idols now in the Kabul Museum. Four black-and-white illustrations of these idols and one color plate of a Kafir family.

Hämmerly-Dupuy, Daniel. "Some Observations on the Assyro-Babylonian and Sumerian Flood Stories." *St. Andrews University Seminary Studies* 6 (1968): 1-18. Abridged in *The Flood Myth*, edited by Alan Dundes. Berkeley: University of California Press, 1988.

This survey of the principal Middle Eastern texts about the ancient flood contains brief descriptions of several Assyrian, Babylonian, and Sumerian versions of the myth followed by some general conclusions. All these versions are said to reflect the same tradition about a major cataclysm marking a radical transition from a prediluvian to a postdiluvian world. Footnotes.

Heidel, Alexander. *The Babylonian Genesis*. 2d ed. Chicago: University of Chicago Press, 1951.

A translation of the *Enuma Elish* and Babylonian and Sumerian creation stories, including tales about Marduk's creation of the world, Anu's creation of the heavens, and several myths about the creation of humans. Several related non-creation myths in an appendix: the slaying of the Labbu, the myth of the storm god Zu, and the Adapa legend. Translations are arranged according to original cuneiform tablets and indicate places where material is missing. A backgound essay on *Enuma Elish* contains sections on the discovery and publication of the tablets, a summary of the story, the date, meter, and subject of the epic, and the Babylonian New Year's festival. Also contains an essay on parallels to these texts in the creation stories of the Old Testament. Footnotes, map, and seventeen black-and-white illustrations of Babylonian art, architecture, and inscriptions related to the myths.

_____. *The Gilgamesh Epic and Old Testament Parallels*. Chicago: University of Chicago Press, 1946.

These translations of the *Epic of Gilgamesh*, the Sumerian version of the flood from Nippur, Berossus' account of the flood, *Descent of Ishtar*, the myth of Nergal and Ereshkigal, and Prince Kummaya's vision of the underworld are intended to complement those in *Babylo-*

nian Genesis. Heidel offers not literary translations but ones which follow carefully the format of the original Akkadian cuneiform tables, with notations of tablet and column numbers, restorations, uncertain readings, and missing text. Passages containing sexual references are presented in Latin only. Preceding the *Epic of Gilgamesh* is an introductory essay on the discovery and publication of the tablets and the hero, theme, sources, and date of the epic, together with a plot summary. The introductions to the other texts are briefer. In two chapters following the transations, Heidel compares the themes of the flood and of death and afterlife in these Mesopotamian texts and in the Old Testament. Footnotes.

Hinnells, John R. *Persian Mythology.* 2d ed. New York: Peter Bedrick Books, 1985.
This general introduction to the mythology of ancient Iran begins with an outline of Persian history and a discussion of the sources of the myths and their nature. A chapter on the gods and heroes of ancient Persia is followed by chapters on later mythologies, including those of Zoroastrianism, Zurvanism, and Mithraism. The relationships between Persian myths and prophets, kings, history, ritual, and religious beliefs are also examined. Photographs of archaeological sites, artwork, and manuscripts related to the myths appear on nearly every page. Map, bibliography, and index.

_____. "Zoroastrianism." In *Mythology: An Illustrated Encyclopaedia*, edited by Richard Cavendish. New York: Rizzoli International, 1980. Also published as *An Illustrated Encyclopedia of Mythology.* New York: Crescent Books, 1984.
Describes the mythological beliefs associated with the followers of the Iranian prophet Zoroaster, who lived c. 1500 B.C. Includes sections on the myth of creation, the opposing forces of good and evil, a myth of renovation, the nature of the world, the bridge of judgment which every dead person has to cross, the nature of humans, a variant belief in Zurvan or deified Time, Zoroastrianism in India, the influence of Zoroastrianism in the West, modern interpretations, especially among the Parsi in India, and burial customs. Map, chronological chart, and illustrations of artwork related to the myths.

Holmberg, Uno. *Siberian Mythology.* Vol. 6 in *The Mythology of All Races*, edited by Louis Herbert Gray. Boston: Marshall Jones, 1927.
Examines the world view and religious beliefs of the peoples of Siberia, especially the Turks, Tartars, and Mongolians. In a short

introduction, Holmberg traces the history and religion of these peoples and identifies sources for this information. Some topics covered individually include cosmology, the creation and destruction of the world, the creation and fall of man, various deities, death, shamans, and natural elements such as thunder, fire, and wind. Twenty-nine plates and fourteen figures illustrating artifacts and sites related to these beliefs. Map, endnotes, and bibliography. Complete index in Volume 13.

Hooke, Samuel Henry. "Babylonian and Assyrian Mythology." In *Babylonian and Assyrian Religion*, by Samuel Henry Hooke. New York: Hutchinson's University Library, 1953.
In this chapter of a general study of Mesopotamian religion, a major Middle Eastern scholar of the early twentieth century illustrates how the Babylonian creation myth known as the *Enuma Elish* is not only a myth of origin but also a ritual myth because of its association with the New Year festival. A detailed summary of this myth is followed by briefer discussions of the myths of Adapa, the first human, of Etana, the first king, and of Zu, the bird god. Some quotation in translation from original documents.

_____. *Middle Eastern Mythology*. Baltimore: Penguin Books, 1963.
This examination of the myths of the ancient Sumerians, Babylonians, Egyptians, Ugaritites, Hittites, and Hebrews makes accessible to English readers a large body of cuneiform and Hittite texts deciphered and translated earlier in the century. Explanations of the myths are accompanied by short examples from the ancient texts. Includes a variety of creation and flood myths as well as the myths of deities such as the Babylonian Ishtar, the Egyptian Osiris, and the Ugaritic Baal. Sixteen pages of plates illustrating various mythological scenes in ancient art. In the last three chapters, Hooke considers mythological elements in Jewish apocalyptic literature, especially in the Book of Daniel, mythic features of the birth and resurrection narratives of Jesus Christ in the New Testament, and the relationship between myth and Christian ritual. In an introductory essay, Hooke discusses several types of myth which are important in the Middle East. Chapter endnotes, bibliography, and index.

_____. "The Pantheon." In *Babylonian and Assyrian Religion*, by Samuel Henry Hooke. New York: Hutchinson's University Library, 1953.

Surveys the major deities of Mesopotamia with special emphasis on two triads of Babylonian deities, each associated with a different goddess. The gods Anu, Enlil, and Enki or Ea are linked with Ninmach, the goddess of childbirth, and Sin, Shamash, and Adad are associated with Ishtar. The relationships of these deities with other gods such as Ereshkigal, the lord of the underworld, and Tiamat, the chaos goddess, are also considered. Attached to this essay is a more detailed excursus on the god Tammuz and his mythic and cultic ties with Ishtar.

Huart, Clement. "The Mythology of Persia." In *Asiatic Mythology*, edited by M. J. Hackin. Translated by F. M. Atkinson. New York: Thomas Y. Crowell, 1963.
This chronological survey of the mythologies of Persia begins with the Achaemenid dynasty (546-330 B.C.). Sections on the mythology of Persia during the Arsacid dynasty (250 B.C.-A.D. 224) are followed by treatments of the Manichaeans of the third through seventh centuries and, especially, Shi'ite Muslims of sixteenth-century Persia. Twenty-two black-and-white illustrations and one color plate depicting mythic scenes in the art of the region.

Jackson, A. V. Williams. "The Host of Heaven." In *Zoroastrian Studies*, by A. V. Williams Jackson. New York: Columbia University Press, 1928. Reprint. New York: AMS Press, 1965.
In this chapter of a scholarly study of the Iranian religion founded by Zoroaster, a prominent professor of Indo-Iranian languages at Columbia University discusses the Iranian concept of deity, *Amesha Spentas* or "archangels," *Yazatas* or "angels," and descriptions of Ahura Mazda or Ormazd, the lord god of Iran, of individual angels and archangels, and of various mythological creatures, such as the three-legged monster known as Kahara. Bibliographies.

_____. "The Legions of Hell." In *Zoroastrian Studies*, by A. V. Williams Jackson. New York: Columbia University Press, 1928. Reprint. New York: AMS Press, 1965.
An outline of Zoroastrian beliefs about the devil and other supernatural creatures of the infernal world and descriptions of Anra Mainyu or Ahriman, the devil of ancient Iran, of individual *Daēvas* or "demons" and *Druj* or "fiends," and of various monsters and evil creatures such as the three-headed half-human, half-monster Azhi Dahāka. Bibliographies.

_____. "The Universe of Man." In *Zoroastrian Studies*, by A. V. Williams Jackson. New York: Columbia University Press, 1928. Reprint. New York: AMS Press, 1965.

Describes ancient Iranian beliefs about the creation, order, and history of the universe in general and of the earth and of humankind in particular. Includes sections on Greek references to Persian cosmological concepts and on ancient Iranian ideas about anthropology, human physiology, and psychology. Bibliographies.

_____. "Zoroaster, the Prophet of Ancient Iran." In *Zoroastrian Studies*, by A. V. Williams Jackson. New York: Columbia University Press, 1928. Reprint. New York: AMS Press, 1965.

In this short sketch, Jackson attempts to sort fact from legend in the life of Zoroaster, the Iranian *magus*, or wise man. Includes sections on sources, his name, homeland and date of birth, early life, prophetic relevation, triumphal conversion of king Kavi Vīshtāspa in 618 B.C., other conversions, later religious developments and death, and the subsequent history of the faith. Bibliography.

_____. *Zoroaster, the Prophet of Ancient Iran*. New York: Columbia University Press, 1926. Reprint. New York: AMS Press, 1965.

A detailed examination of the life and legends of the ancient Persian sage Zoroaster, also known as Zarathustra. The introductory chapter discusses sources and Zoroaster as a historical personage and his place among other ancient religious leaders, especially Buddha. Individual chapters deal with Zoroaster's family history, early life, seven visions, conversion of King Kavi Vīshtāspa, other conversions at his court, the spread of the religion, religious developments, holy wars, Zoroaster's death, and subsequent events. In the last chapter, Jackson offers a summary of Zoroaster's life and some general conclusions. In a series of appendices, Jackson collects etymologies of Zoroaster's name, ancient references to his dates and to the geographic location of events in his life, a Zoroastrian chronology, untranslated passages in Greek and Latin texts which mention Zoroaster, descriptions of literary references to Zoroaster in ancient Armenia, China, Syria, Arabia, and Persia, and representations of the sage in ancient sculpture. Footnotes, genealogies, battle charts, bibliography, map, and index.

Jackson, Danny P. *The Epic of Gilgamesh*. Chicago: Bolchazy-Carducci Publishers, 1992.

A verse translation of the ancient Sumerian epic about the travels of the hero Gilgamesh and his tragic friendship with Enkidu. This text is

designed for teaching and includes references to original tablet numbers, column numbers, and line numbers which facilitate cross-reference to other translations. Each tablet is introduced by the translator's
own thematic headings. An introductory essay offers a brief overview,
a plot summary, a pedagogical approach, an interpretation, a note on
translation, and acknowledgments. Supplemented by illustrations of
eighteen ancient Assyrian objects and fifteen original black-and-white
sketches by Thomas Kapheim. Preface, introduction, map, list of main
characters, and glossary.

Jacobsen, Thorkild. "Enuma Elish: The Babylonian Genesis." In *The
Theories of the Universe*, edited by Milton K. Munitz. New York: Free
Press, 1957.
This short excerpt from *The Intellectual Adventure of Ancient Man*
summarizes the Babylonian cosmology told in the Akkadian epic
known as *Enuma Elish*. The primeval water divinities Apsu and Tiamat
create the world and the young god Marduk brings order out of chaos
through his defeat of Tiamat. Divides the myth into two sections: one
on the basic features of the universe and a second on the establishment
of the present world order. Extensive quotations from the epic in
English translation.

_____. "Mesopotamia." In *The Intellectual Adventure of Ancient
Man*, by Henri Frankfort, H. A. Frankfort, John A. Wilson, and
Thorkild Jacobsen. Chicago: University of Chicago Press, 1946. 2d ed.
Before Philosophy. Baltimore: Penguin, 1949.
Part of a study of myth as a form of concrete speculation about the
universe distinct from the abstract thought associated with philosophy.
Offers extensive paraphrase and quotation from Middle Eastern
sources such as the "Myth of the Elevation of Inanna," the "Myth of
Enlil and Ninlil," the *Enuma Elish*, and the *Epic of Gilgamesh* as the
author illustrates the Mesopotamian world view. The following topics
are addressed in separate chapters: cosmogony and the nature of the
universe, the function of the state, and the purpose and value of human
life. Endnotes and bibliography.

Kirk, G. S. "The Nature of Myths in Ancient Mesopotamia." In *Myth. Its
Meaning and Functions in Ancient and Other Cultures*, by G. S. Kirk.
Berkeley: University of California Press, 1970.
Offers an introduction to the literature, culture, and mythology of
ancient Sumeria and Akkadia and to the approaches of two scholars,
Samuel Noah Kramer and Thorkild Jacobsen. While Kramer interprets

Middle Eastern myths as allegories or rational observations about reality, Jacobsen adds a unique emotional level of interpretation to the myths. Cites the Sumerian myth of Ninurta and Asag about irrigation, the myth of Enlil and Ninlil about fertility, and three myths about the underworld, including "Inanna's Descent to the Nether World," known in both Sumerian and Akkadian versions. Concludes with some comments on the nature of Sumerian and Akkadian myths and argues that Sumerian myths tend to be concerned with the natural world, while Akkadian tales focus on the development of cultural institutions.

Kramer, Samuel Noah. "Mythology of Sumer and Akkad." In *Mythologies of the Ancient World*, edited by Samuel Noah Kramer. Garden City, N.Y.: Doubleday (Anchor), 1961.
Surveys the myths of the ancient Sumerians and Akkadians with extensive quotation in translation from ancient texts. The Sumerian section summarizes creation myths dealing with deities such as the air god Enlil, the water god Enki, the goddess Inanna, and her relationship with her husband Dumuzi. The Akkadian section offers a summary of the creation poem known as *Enuma Elish*. Bibliography.

_____. *Sumerian Mythology*. 2d ed. New York: Harper and Brothers, 1961.
Archaeological excavations of Sumerian sites in the Tigris-Euphrates valley in the nineteenth century uncovered thousands of literary tablets dating from c. 2000 B.C. This study by a prominent Sumerian scholar predates the decipherment of significant tablets which have filled out many details of the myths. Plot summaries, substantial quotation from the original sources, and comparison of various versions of the same myth. Deals especially with myths of origin (i.e., the creation and organization of the universe), the destruction of Kur, Inanna's descent into the netherworld, and the Sumerian version of the flood story. Also discusses the discovery of the tablets and their scope and significance. Includes a map, notes, index, illustrations from the tablets, and a chart describing the origin and development of the Sumerian writing system.

_____. "Sumerian Myths and Epic Tales." In *Ancient Near Eastern Texts Relating to the Old Testament*, edited by James B. Pritchard. 3d ed. Princeton, N.J.: Princeton University Press, 1969.
Eight texts from ancient Sumer are here translated in a scholarly format, with careful indication of original text numbers, restorations, and doubtful readings. Included is the Paradise myth of Enki and Ninhursag, the argument between Dumuzi and Enkimdu, the flood,

stories about Gilgamesh and Agga, Gilgamesh's journey to the Land of the Living, and his death, the descent of Inanna into the underworld, and an inscription on a royal statue describing divine duties and powers. Each text is preceded by detailed introductory commentary and bibliography. Footnotes.

Kramer, Samuel Noah, and E. A. Speiser. "Myths and Epics from Mesopotamia." In *The Ancient Near East*, edited by James B. Pritchard. Princeton, N.J.: Princeton University Press, 1958.
Seven major Sumerian and Akkadian myths and epics related to the Old Testament are here translated for the general reader with careful indication of original text numbers, restorations, and doubtful readings. Kramer translates a Sumerian flood myth and Speiser offers English versions of the Babylonian creation epic called *Enuma Elish*, the *Epic of Gilgamesh*, a cosmological incantation about a worm and a toothache, the story of Adapa, the *Descent of Ishtar*, and the legend of King Sargon. Each text is preceded by a short introduction. Some of the 197 illustrations of Middle Eastern artifacts in this volume complement this material. Also in the volume are footnotes, map, indexes, and glossary.

Lane, Edward William, trans. *The Arabian Nights' Entertainments*. London: Charles Knight, 1839. Reprint. New York: Tudor Publishing, 1927.
Lane's translation of *The Thousand and One Nights* remains for the general English reader a standard introduction to this collection of Arabic tales, fables, and historical anecdotes. A Persian version of *The Thousand and One Nights* existed as early as the tenth century A.D., but the present collection of tales, derived especially from Persian, Indian, and Arabian sources, is based upon an Arabic original first translated into French by Antoine Galland in the early eighteenth century. The tales are told each night by Shahrazad to her sultan husband, who usually kills each of his wives after their wedding night but repeatedly spares Shahrazad in order to hear the conclusions to her stories. These tales of love, marriage, genies, and enchantment include stories about merchants, fishermen, beggars, and slaves, animal fables, and the adventures of Sindibad the sailor. Lane's detailed explanatory endnotes with descriptions of Middle Eastern life and thought, often published separately, appear in an appendix to the reprint. Also in the reprint a preface by unnamed editors provides a short history of *The Thousand and One Nights* and its English translations, as well as a pronuciation guide.

_____, ed. and trans. *Stories from "The Thousand and One Nights."* Revised by Stanley Lane-Poole. New York: P. F. Collier & Son, 1937.

This abbreviated edition of Lane's popular translation includes the original introduction plus thirty tales, selected mostly from the first thirty-six nights, and the eight later adventures of Sindibad the sailor. In an appendix are the well-known stories of the magic lamp of 'Ala-ed-Din (Aladdin) and of 'Ali Baba and the forty thieves, which do not appear in most Arabic editions of the anthology. In an introduction, Charles W. Eliot provides a short history of the collection. Explanatory footnotes.

Lang, David M. "Armenia, Georgia and the Caucasus." In *Mythology: An Illustrated Encyclopaedia*, edited by Richard Cavendish. New York: Rizzoli International, 1980. Also published as *An Illustrated Encyclopedia of Mythology*. New York: Crescent Books, 1984.

This overview of the mythologies of the Caucasus region begins with a summary of the biblical story of the great flood and its association with the Caucasian Mount Ararat. Also contains sections on beliefs of the early Armenians, known as Urartians, the early deities of Armenia, the Georgian location of Golden Fleece of the Greek hero Jason, and the Caucasian site of the sufferings of the Greek Titan Prometheus. Map and illustrations of artwork and sites related to the myths.

Langdon, Stephen H. *The Babylonian Epic of Creation*. Oxford: The Clarendon Press, 1923.

This scholarly edition of the *Enuma Elish* offers a transcription and parallel English translation of the Babylonian creation epic and a fragment describing the death and resurrection of Bel-Marduk. This creation epic commemorates the Babylonian New Year's festival and describes not only the engendering of the world and of the gods by the union of the water deities Apsu and Tiamat, but also the violent cosmic succession leading eventually to the reign of the god Marduk. In a detailed introduction, Langon provides background on the discovery of the text, earlier editions, a plot summary, the epic in Babylonian art, characters, the Babylonian New Year's festival, the gods Marduk and Tammuz, the fragment on the death and resurrection of Bel-Marduk, the ritual of Bel-Marduk, and a list of texts. Footnotes, bibliography, and index.

_____. *Semitic Mythology*. Vol. 5 in *The Mythology of All Races*, edited by John A. MacCulloch. Boston: Marshall Jones, 1931.

Considers the mythology of the peoples of ancient Mesopotamia and
the Middle East, including the Sumerians, Babylonians, Assyrians,
Phoenicians, Hebrews, and Arabians. Offers an overview of the geography and languages of the Semitic peoples and chapters on the
pantheon of the Sumerians and Akkadians, the quest of Etana, the story
of Adapa or Adam (the first human), creation, Paradise, the flood, and
the destruction of humans. Compares biblical tales with versions in
other Semitic sources. Also contains overviews of the epic of Gilgamesh and the myth of the goddess Ishtar and her dying consort
Tammuz. One hundred figures and plates, endnotes, bibliography, and
index. Complete index in Volume 13.

Leach, Edmund. "Genesis as Myth." In *Genesis as Myth and Other
Essays*, by Edmund Leach. London: Jonathan Cape, 1969.
A structural examination of the biblical creation story with concentra-
tion on sexual rules and transgressions. Argues that a consistent so-
cioreligious message exists behind the multiple versions of this tale.
One of these messages is the importance of marriage among close kin.
Charts.

_____. "The Legitimacy of Solomon." In *Genesis as Myth and
Other Essays*, by Edmund Leach. London: Jonathan Cape, 1969.
A biblical story of Solomon's succession to the throne of Israel is
interpreted by a British anthropologist as an illustration of myth as a
mediation of contradiction. Despite Jewish intermarriage in the Prom-
ised Land, the tale is seen to be a celebration of Jewish endogamy.
Analyzes parallel themes in the stories of Tamar, Rachab, Ruth, and
Bath-Sheba. Genealogical chart and map.

Loew, Cornelius. "Myth in the Mesopotamian Tradition." In *Myth, Sacred
History and Philosophy*, by Cornelius Loew. New York: Harcourt,
Brace & World, 1967.
Studies the cosmological convictions found in the sacred myths of
ancient Mesopotamia, especially in the *Epic of Gilgamesh*, and their
influence on Christianity's religious heritage. Looks, in particular, at
biological and sociopolitical images of creation and considers Mesopotamian concepts of divine and human rule, cosmic renewal, suffering,
and death as the pre-Christian religious heritage of the Western world.
Footnotes and bibliography.

_____. "Sacred History and the People of Israel." In *Myth,
Sacred History and Philosophy*, by Cornelius Loew. New York: Harcourt, Brace & World, 1967.

Biblical tales about Israel's tribal confederation—especially stories about covenant, divine law, the exodus, and the early kings—reveal Hebrew convictions about cosmology and the relationship between god and his chosen people. Examines attempts by the prophets to reinterpret this sacred history and open it up to new possibilities of salvation for Israel. Footnotes and bibliography.

Lot-Falck, E. "Siberia: The Three Worlds." In *Larousse World Mythology*, edited by Pierre Grimal. Translated by Patricia Beardsworth. New York: G. P. Putnam's Sons, 1963.
A short survey of the mythologies of the peoples of Siberia, including the Finno-Ugrians, the Turko-Mongols, the Tungus, Eskimos, and the Paleo-Siberian Chukchi, Koryak, and Kamchadal. Describes the creation of the universe, sky gods, earth gods, master spirits, and beliefs about water and the underworld. Accompanied by five indigenous drawings illustrating this mythic world view.

McCall, Henrietta. *Mesopotamian Myths*. Austin: University of Texas Press, 1990.
Part of The Legendary Past Series, this book provides a general introduction to and summary of several myths of ancient Assyria and Babylonia. A preliminary chapter on the discovery and decipherment of the texts of these myths by European travelers and scholars is followed by a chapter on the authors of these texts, their audience, and a list of their gods. One chapter is devoted to the flood stories of the *Epic of Gilgamesh* and the myth of Atrahasis. Another summarizes the Mesopotamian *Enuma Elish*. Several shorter myths, including the *Descent of Ishtar, Nergal and Ereshkigal*, and the *Epic of Erra*, are also described. The ancient tablets are quoted extensively in translation. Text is accompanied by photographs of the tablets and illustrations from ancient Mesopotamian art. Includes a map and short bibliography.

Mackenzie, Donald Alexander. *Myths of Babylonia and Assyria*. London: Gresham Publishing, 1939.
Traces the myths and legends of the ancient Middle East beginning with the early Sumerian age and ending with the death of Alexander the Great in 323 B.C. The author's interest in tracing racial origins and his emphasis on cultural borrowing reflect a controversial bias of the early twentieth century. Emphasizes parallels between these myths and those of other cultures, including Europe, Egypt, and India. Chapters are arranged chronologically with specific studies of creation legends,

flood myths, deified heroes such as Etana and Gilgamesh, the myths of Tammuz and Ishtar, and the legend of queen Semiramis. Map, eight color and thirty-two black-and-white plates, especially illustrations of Babylonian art. Index.

Masson-Oursel, P., and Louise Morin. "Mythology of Ancient Persia." In *New Larousse Encyclopedia of Mythology*, edited by Felix Guirand et al. Translated by Richard Aldington and Delano Ames. New York: Hamlyn, 1968.

This survey of Persian mythology is divided into sections on Zoroastrianism and Islam, the two major religions which have, in succession, dominated Persia. The authors depict Zoroastrianism especially through the *Zend-Avesta*, Zoroastrianism's collection of sacred writings. Includes sections on the cult of fire, the rite of *haoma* or the beverage of immortality, archaic gods, the magi, Mazda or the deity of Persian royalty, Mithraism, Manichaeism, and various minor deities. Summarizes Iranian myths about the cosmogonical antagonism between the gods Ohrmazd and Ahriman, Gayomart the first human, Husheng the first king, and the mythical history of early Persia as recounted in the *Shah-Nameh* or Book of the Kings. The shorter section on Islam contains sections on the myths and deities of the pre-Islamic Arabs, Shi'ite Islam, the legend of the twelve *imams* or directors of the Prophet, astrology, spirits, hagiography, and Persian poets. Accompanied by fourteen black-and-white and three color illustrations of Persian art and sites.

Menasce, J. de. "Persia: Cosmic Dualism." In *Larousse World Mythology*, edited by Pierre Grimal. Translated by Patricia Beardsworth. New York: G. P. Putnam's Sons, 1963.

An overview of the religion and mythology of ancient Persia. Considers the concept of cosmic dualism in a variety of texts, especially those associated with the mysterious Zoroaster (Zarathustra) and with the third-century A.D. Mani, the founder of Manichaeism. Describes the supreme god Ahura Mazda and his relationship with other *Amesha Spentas* (powerful immortals), fate, the mythology of fire, and a variety of minor deities. Summarizes and explains the myth of Zurvan and its concept of time as well as the legendary revelations of Zarathustra himself. Also contains Persian eschatology and several myths about humankind: the myth of the first king Yima, of the primal man Gayomart, of the world conqueror Thraetona, and of the world ruler Kay Us. Deals with the cult of the god Mithra and its acceptance throughout the Greco-Roman world. Illustrations of Persian art, some in color.

Meyouhas, Joseph. *Bible Tales in Arab Folklore*. Translated by Victor N. Levi. London: Alfred A. Knopf, 1928.
These forty-seven tales collected by the author among Palestinian Arabs are freely based upon biblical themes. Part 1 deals with events in the Pentateuch, beginning with creation and telling the stories of Adam, Noah, Job, Ibrahim (Abraham), Lot, Isaac and Yakub (Jacob), Yusef (Joseph), and Moussa (Moses). Part 2 contains later biblical tales about Joshua, Samuel Taluth (Saul), Daoud (David), Suleiman (Solomon), Alhadr (Elijah), Isaiah, Uzair (Jeremiah), and Yunes (Jonah). In a short preface, Meyouhas describes some features of Arab storytelling and of the tales.

Mills, Margaret A. "A Cinderella Variant in the Context of a Muslim Women's Ritual." In *Cinderella: A Folklore Casebook*, edited by Alan Dundes. New York: Garland Press, 1982.
This analysis of the relationship between local ritual and a version of the Cinderella folktale includes a translation of a text recorded in Iran in 1978 as well as a description of the ritual which accompanied it. This tale is performed about, by, and for women. Emphasizes transsexual behavior and the relationship between the girl and her stepmothers. Comparison to similar versions of the tale told in Afghanistan. Essay is preceded by useful background information and historical commentary by Dundes. Endnotes.

Montgomery, John Warwick. *The Quest for Noah's Ark*. 2d ed. Minneapolis: Bethany Fellowship, 1974.
An anthology of readings on the search for Noah's ark by theologians, scientists, and ancient writers such as the Babylonian priest Berosus, the Jewish historian Josephus, and the medieval encyclopedist Isidore of Seville. Records of fourteen explorations of Mount Ararat, including the author's 1970 expedition. Also describes satellite testing for the ark on Ararat. Appendices contain Muslim accounts of the ark, a complete list of ascents of Ararat, and a map of the Ararat region. Bibliography and index.

Norris, H. T. "Islam." In *Mythology: An Illustrated Encyclopaedia*, edited by Richard Cavendish. New York: Rizzoli International, 1980. Also published as *An Illustrated Encyclopedia of Mythology*. New York: Crescent Books, 1984.

An overview of Semitic myths and legends which survive in the Koran and in the Islamic tradition. An introductory section on ways to approach Islamic myth is followed by summaries and analyses of the myths of the sage Luqman al-Hakim and his brother Shaddad Ibn Ad, of King Solomon and Bilqis, the Queen of Sheba, of Alexander the Great, known here as Dhul-Qarnayn (the Two-Horned), of al-Khidr's quest for the water of life, of the legendary city of brass, and of the Prophet's son Ali and the Ogre's Head. Map, time chart, and illustrations of artwork related to the myths.

Obermann, Julian. *Ugaritic Mythology*. New Haven, Conn.: Yale University Press, 1948.

A preliminary look at Semite mythology following the discovery of mythological texts at Ras Shamra (ancient Ugarit) between 1928 and 1939. Focuses on the myth about the god Baal's plan to build a temple, his wedding, and his conflicts with Mot and other adversaries. Chapter 1 consists of some introductory considerations and problems in understanding the text. In Chapters 2-3 Obermann analyzes several significant passages, especially a scene between the goddess Anath and Baal's envoy. Some parallels to the biblical Book of Daniel are discussed in Chapter 4. In Chapter 5 Obermann offers a summary of some motifs and characteristics of the myth. Included in the text are transliterated quotations from the original tablets followed by English translations. In Part 6 Oberman provides translations of other passages from the tables treated in the text. In a preface, he discusses the discovery, decipherment, and linguistic features of the Ras Shamra texts. Two plates, including a photograph of a Ras Shamra tablet, and combined glossary and index.

Parrot, André. *The Flood and Noah's Ark*. New York: Philosophical Library, 1955.

The author begins with the premise that Middle Eastern accounts of the flood are based upon a historical disaster in Mesopotamia. Several versions of the flood are analyzed and quoted extensively in English translation, including two biblical versions, the Babylonian *Epic of Gilgamesh*, the Assyrian *Epic of Atrahasis*, the Sumerian version on a tablet from Nippur, and the account of the Babylonian priest Berosus. In addition Parrot summarizes the archaeological evidence for a real flood in the Middle East. Also contains short sections on the actual appearance of the ark and the religious aspect of the flood. Four illustrations and seven figures include one map, several archaeological site plans, and drawings of Mesopotamian sailing vessels. Bibliography and index.

Pavry, Jal Dastur Cursetji. *The Zoroastrian Doctrine of a Future Life.* 2d ed. New York: Columbia University Press, 1929. Reprint. New York: AMS Press, 1965.
This scholarly study of Zoroastrian religious beliefs concerning the afterlife includes descriptions of the last judgment and of various mythological creatures quoted in translation from four types of ancient sources, the *Gathas*, the *Later Avesta*, Pahlavi writings, and Parsi-Persian literature. An overview of these sources is found in the introductory Chapter 1. In Chapters 2 and 3 the experiences of the souls of the righteous and of the wicked immediately after death are described. Chapters 4-6 deal with the manifestation of *Daēnā* or "conscience" to these souls, and Chapters 7-10 offer various versions of individual judgment at the crossing of Chinvat Bridge. Footnotes, bibliography, and indexes.

Porter, J. R. "The Middle East." In World Mythology, edited by Roy Willis. New York: Henry Holt, 1993.
This overview of myths from the ancient Middle East includes sections on myths from Sumer and Babylon, the *Epic of Gilgamesh*, Ishtar's descent into the underworld, Sumerian creation myths, the flood myth, Ugaritic myths about kingship and succession, Hittite myths, and Zoroastrian myths from Persia. Supplementing these discussions are subsidiary sections with paraphrases of myths and short passages translated from ancient sources such as the Gilgamesh epic and the *Enuma Elish*. Accompanied by seventeen illustrations, most in color, of artifacts from the Middle East. Map, chronology, and genealogical chart.

Powell, Barry B. "Mesopotamian Myth." In *Classical Myth*, by Barry B. Powell. Englewood Cliffs, N.J.: Prentice Hall, 1995.
This anthology of Greco-Roman mythology concentrates on important precursors. Historical background about the ancient Sumerians and Semites and a discussion of their gods are accompanied by discussions of the Babylonian *Enuma Elish*, the Sumerian creation of humans from mud and the myth of Inanna and Dumuzi, several universal flood tales, and the story of Gilgamesh. Incorporates significant selections in translation from the original texts. Four illustrations of ancient Mesopotamian art. Footnotes and bibliography.

Pritchard, James B. "Myth, Legend, and Ritual on Cylinder Seals." In *The Ancient Near East in Pictures*, by James B. Pritchard. Princeton, N.J.: Princeton University Press, 1954.

This section of a collection of illustrations dealing with various aspects of life in the ancient Middle East contains photographs of thirty-four Mesopotamian cylinder seals depicting scenes of myth and ritual. The seals are arranged chronologically and include images of deities, their human worshipers, heroes, and mythological creatures. Accompanying the illustrations is a descriptive catalogue with bibliography.

Puhvel, Jaan. "Ancient Iran." In *Comparative Mythology*, by Jaan Puhvel. Baltimore: The Johns Hopkins University Press, 1987.

An introduction to the culture and mythology of ancient Iran, with an emphasis on the *Avesta*, the holy writings of Zoroastrianism. Notes that the Iranian tripartite social division of king, warrior, and worker parallels the social organization of other Indo-European cultures. In particular, compares Iranian religious beliefs and social structure with features of the ancient Vedics of India. Surveys the major Iranian deities, especially Mithra, and links them with Indic counterparts. Three figures illustrating scenes connected with Iranian mythology. Footnotes and bibliography.

_____. "Epic Iran." In *Comparative Mythology*, by Jaan Puhvel. Baltimore: The Johns Hopkins University Press, 1987.

Illustrates the importance of the *Shah-Nama*, the tenth-century A.D. national epic of Iran, as a mythological text and, especially, as a source of information about ancient Indo-European and Indo-Iran society. Summarizes the plot of the *Shah-Nama*, with its interplay of dynastic, historical details with mythic, cosmic elements. Bibliography.

Richardson, M. E. J. "Mesopotamia." In *Mythology: An Illustrated Encyclopaedia*, edited by Richard Cavendish. New York: Rizzoli International, 1980. Also published as *An Illustrated Encyclopedia of Mythology*. New York: Crescent Books, 1984.

A short overview of myths surviving in Sumerian and Akkadian texts with summaries and analyses of the creation and flood myths, the god Marduk's tablets of destinies, the hero Adapa's quest for immortality, the descent of the goddess Ishtar into the underworld, and the *Epic of Gilgamesh*. Map, glossary of principal deities, and illustrations of artwork related to the myths.

_____. "Syria and Palestine." In *Mythology: An Illustrated Encyclopaedia*, edited by Richard Cavendish. New York: Rizzoli International, 1980. Also published as *An Illustrated Encyclopedia of Mythology*. New York: Crescent Books, 1984.

A survey of the myths of the Canaanite people of ancient Syria and Palestine found on inscribed tablets in Ras Shamra (ancient Ugarit) in Syria. Summarizes the conflict between the god Baal and the sea god Yam, the building of Baal's palace, Baal's contest with Mot, the god of death, and the bow of the hero Aqhat, son of Dan'el. Includes significant quotation in translation from the tablets and a comparison of these myths with biblical tales. Map and illustrations of artwork related to the myths.

Sabar, Yona. *The Folk Literature of the Kurdistani Jews: An Anthology.* New Haven: Yale University Press, 1982.

A collection of oral literature recited among the Jews of Kurdistan in western Asia. Arranged by chapter according to various themes and genres including traditional epics based upon biblical tales, historical legends, folktales, anecdotes, women's laments, folk songs, nursery rhymes, and proverbs. Most tales are preceded by synopses, descriptions of their general character, bibliographies, and lists of sources. Literally translated by the author from Hebrew and Neo-Aramaic sources in prose or verse, as appropriate. Introductory essay on the country and its people, the history of the Jews in Kurdistan, their occupations, economic conditions, religious life, relationship with Israel, and literature. Of most interest from a mythological point of view are nine chapters dealing with tales about biblical figures such as Joseph, Moses, and King Solomon, a chapter of legends about famous rabbis, and a chapter containing twenty-five folktales, especially animal fables. Map and eight photographs illustrating the people and their culture. Footnotes, glossary of important Hebrew terms, bibliography, and indexes, including a folktale motif index.

Saggs, H. W. F. "Literature." In *The Greatness That Was Babylon*, by H. W. F. Saggs. New York: Hawthorn Books, 1962.

In this chapter of a detailed examination of the history and culture of ancient Babylonia, a professor of Semitic languages at the University College of South Wales offers overviews and paraphrases of various Babylonian texts. Sumerian and Akkadian proverbs and other wisdom literature accompany more mythological writings, including epics about Gilgamesh, Adapa, and Tukulti-Ninurta and the creation myths *Enuma Elish*, *Nergal and Ereshkigal*, the *Descent of Ishtar*, and the myth of Zu the storm god. Extensive quotation in translation from the original texts.

_____. "Religion." In *The Greatness That Was Babylon*, by H. W. F. Saggs. New York: Hawthorn Books, 1962.
In addition to Babylonian beliefs in demons and magic, types of religious functionaries, shrines, and temples, this overview of Babylonian religion surveys the gods in the Babylonian pantheon, including Anu, Elil, Ea, Sin, Shamash, Ishtar, Adad, Ninurta, Nergal, and Marduk. Some quotation in translation from original texts, especially spells and prayers. Three figures.

Sandars, Nancy K. *The Epic of Gilgamesh*. Rev. ed. Baltimore: Penguin, 1972.
Accounts of the Mesopotamian king Gilgamesh were written down early in the second millennium B.C. The plot of the epic centers on Gilgamesh's futile quest for immortality and his great friendship with Enkidu, whose death results from an offense against the gods. During his travels Gilgamesh is counseled by Utnapishtim, the survivor of a great flood. This English translation of the epic, first discovered on Assyrian cuneiform tablets in Nineveh in the nineteenth century A.D., includes information derived from the decipherment of fresh tablets. In an introduction, the translator includes a history of the epic, historical and literary background, a plot summary, and comments on the hero, the principal gods, and the diction of the epic. Map, a glossary of names, and an appendix of sources.

_____, trans. *Poems of Heaven and Hell from Ancient Mesopotamia*. New York: Viking Penguin, 1971.
These translations of mythological texts of the Middle East are intended for the general reader. The collection includes the Babylonian creation story called *Enuma Elish*, a short, fragmentary poem called *The Sumerian Underworld*, the Sumerian epic known as *Inanna's Journey to Hell*, a fragmentary epic about Adapa the first human, and a prayer to the gods of night. Each piece is preceded by introductory comments by Sandars. For *Enuma Elish* and *Inanna's Journey to Hell*, these introductory sections are extensive, with interpretative discussions, information on the original texts and translations, and bibliography. Map and glossary.

Smith, George. "The Chaldean Account of the Deluge." *Transactions of the Society of Biblical Archaeology* 2 (1873): 213-234. Reprinted in *The Flood Myth*, edited by Alan Dundes. Berkeley: University of California Press, 1988.

Describes the discovery of a cuneiform Assyrian tablet dated c. 1600 B.C. which contains the earliest known Mesopotamian version of the flood myth. Smith offers evidence for dating the tablet, which he translates and compares both to the biblical version and to the account of the Chaldean historian Berosus. Dundes introduces this paper with comments on its historical significance and with anecdotes concerning Smith's life.

Sollberger, Edmond. *The Babylonian Legend of the Flood*. 2d ed. London: British Museum, 1962.
Offers a short account of the flood story told by the ancient peoples of western Asia. Briefly discusses the universal flood theme in world mythologies and the dependence of the biblical flood story upon the earlier tradition of western Asia. Recounts the modern rediscovery of this tradition, especially in the *Epic of Gilgamesh* found by George Smith in 1872 on Assyrian clay tablets. Describes the deities and mortals who participate in various versions of the tale. Detailed analyses with some direct quotation from the original texts of the Sumerian flood tale, the Babylonian *Epic of Atrahasis*, and the Assyrian *Epic of Gilgamesh*. Bibliography and sixteen illustrations.

Speiser, E. A., and A. K. Grayson. "Akkadian Myths and Epics." In *Ancient Near Eastern Texts Relating to the Old Testament*, edited by James B. Pritchard. 3d ed. Princeton, N.J.: Princeton University Press, 1969.
Nineteen ancient Akkadian texts are here translated in a scholarly format, with careful indication of original text numbers, restorations, and doubtful readings. Cosmogonies, including the creation epic, the story of the creation of humankind by the mother goddess, the cosmological incantation about the worm and the toothache, and a Babylonian theogony are accompanied by epics about the heroes Gilgamesh, Adapa, Atrahasis, and Etana, the myth of the gods Nergal and Ereshkigal, the goddess Ishtar's descent into the underworld, and the legend of King Sargon. Each text is preceded by a detailed introductory commentary and bibliography. Speiser's original translations are supplemented by Grayson's notes and additions. Footnotes.

Spence, Lewis. *Myths and Legends of Babylonia and Assyria*. Boston: David D. Nickerson, 1916.
A survey of the mythological and religious beliefs of ancient Babylonia and Assyria for the general reader. Although significant archaeological discoveries and scholarly work have followed the publication of this

book, the broad outlines and plot summaries which Spence offers remain valuable. Individual chapters are devoted to historical and legendary accounts of Babylonia and Assyria, including flood stories and the decipherment of cuneiform writing, Babylonian cosmogony, early religion, the Babylonian pantheon, star worship, and the god Marduk (here called Merodach). Also contains examinations of the *Epic of Gilgamesh*, the Assyrian pantheon, Babylonian and Assyrian temples and cults, magic, monsters, and tales of kings, a comparison of Babylonian and Assyrian beliefs with other ancient religions, modern archaeological excavations in Mesopotamia, and the fall of Babylonian civilization. Forty-one illustrations, some in color, including photographs of sites and ancient artifacts and modern paintings based on the legends. Glossary and index.

Teeple, Howard M. *The Noah's Ark Nonsense*. Evanston, Ill.: religion and Ethics Institute, 1978.
A Christian scholar responds to fundamentalist quests for Noah's ark with a non-literal interpretation of the story of Noah in Genesis. Teeple reviews the history of scholarship and scientific research concerning the flood and the ark and traces the development of the myth in Mesopotamia. In particular, he condemns as fictional televised docudramas such as "In Search of Noah's Ark." Endnotes and bibliography.

Thomas, D. Winton, ed. *Documents from Old Testament Times*. London: Thomas Nelson and Sons, 1958.
Mythological texts from a variety of ancient Middle Eastern sources are here translated and are related to the Old Testament by twenty-one scholars. Arranged according to sources, these cuneiform texts include excerpts from the Babylonian creation epic *Enuma Elish*, the story of the flood from the *Epic of Gilgamesh*, and Ras Shamra texts about Baal myths and legends of King Keret and Aqhat, son of Dan'el. Also containing mythological material are Egyptian hymns and the "Tale of Two Brothers." Each translated text is accompanied by an introduction, explanatory endnotes, and bibliography. Introductory essay on the types of documents. Photographs of original documents in sixteen plates. Chronological table and indexes.

Viéyra, M. "Empires of the Ancient Near East: The Hymns of Creation." In *Larousse World Mythology*, edited by Pierre Grimal. Translated by Patricia Beardsworth. New York: G. P. Putnam's Sons, 1963.

This section of a sweeping survey of world myth considers the cosmogonies of the ancient Sumerians, Babylonians, Hurrites, and Hittites. Combines paraphrase of myths with photographs of ancient artifacts, some in color, as well as often extensive quotation in translation from ancient texts. The Sumerian section deals with the cosmic tree, paradise in the *Myth of Dilmun*, the divine marriage, the flood, and the reason for humankind in the *Myth of Cattle and Grain*. In the Babylonian section, Viéyra summarizes the *Enuma Elish*, the Babylonian creation poem, and explains its role in ritual. In the last section Hurrite/Hittite theogony, especially in the *Song of Ullikummi*, is described.

Woolley, Leonard. "Stories of the Creation and the Flood." *Palestine Exploration Quarterly* 88 (1956): 14-21. Reprinted in *The Flood Myth*, edited by Alan Dundes. Berkeley: University of California Press, 1988.
Compares the version of the flood in Genesis with those on Sumerian cuneiform tablets and concludes that two forms of the Mesopotamian flood myth exist, one mythic and the other historical. Woolley claims to have found archaeological evidence at Ur in modern Iraq in 1928-1929 that an ancient flood actually took place. In the reprint, the editor offers some background concerning Woolley's work and its influence. Footnotes.

Zaehner, R. C. *The Dawn and Twilight of Zoroastrianism*. New York: G. P. Putnam's Sons, 1961.
This scholarly study of the history of the Zoroastrian religion from its founding in the sixth century B.C. by Zoroaster to its revival in the Sassanian empire of Iran in the third century A.D. and to the fall of Zorastrianism to Islam in A.D. 652 incorporates summary and analysis of various Zoroastrian myths and legends. Of special note are legends dealing with the life of Zoroaster in Chapter 1, descriptions of various deities in Chapter 2, worship of the god Mithra in Chapters 4 and 5, the Zurvanite myth in Chapter 9, Zoroastrian cosmogony in Chapter 12, human life in Chapter 13, and the nature of the afterlife in Chapter 15. Forty-five photographs of artwork and sites; endnotes, bibliography, and index.

Indian Myths

Archer, W. B. *The Loves of Krishna*. London: Allen & Unwin, 1957.
This scholarly study presents the story of the god Krishna as a way for westerners to understand some features of Indian painting. In an

introductory chapter, Archer describes some of the problems westerners encounter in understanding this god and his visual representations. In Chapter 2 he describes the portrayal of Krishna the hero in the *Mahābhārata*. In Chapters 3-4 he discusses the more detailed description of Krishna's life in the *Bhagavata Purāna* with special emphasis on his relationship with the cowgirls. Chapter 5 deals with the portrayal of Krishna in the *Gita Govinda*, the *Rasika Priya* of Keshav Das, and other erotic poetry from the twelfth through sixteenth centuries A.D. These portrayals of the god are used in Chapter 6 to interpret serveral kinds of Krishna paintings. Full-page black-and-white reproductions of thirty-nine of these paintings are accompanied by interpretative descriptions. Footnotes, endnotes, bibliography, and index.

Ayyar, Aiylam Subramanier Panchapakesa. *Famous Tales of India*. Madras, India: V. Ramaswamy Sastrulu & Sons, 1954.
English translations of eleven traditional Indian tales, many from ancient sources. Nine originally in Sanskrit and Pakrit and two in Tamil. Includes aetiological stories about how human sacrifice ceased in India and about the first *sati*, or wife who committed suicide at her husband's death. Summaries of two plays by Kalidasa based upon heroic mythology in the *Vedas*. The tale of the great lover Udayana Vatsaraja. The story of Mahāvīra from the *Sutra*. Selections from *Kovalan and Kannaki*, the great epic of the Tamil. The story of Kovalan's daughter, Manimekalai. Also, two powerful love stories from the *Mahābhārata*. Some explanatory footnotes.

Barnett, Lionel D. *Hindu Gods and Heroes*. New York: E. P. Dutton, 1922.
Based upon a series of scholarly lectures at the School of Oriental Studies in London, this book traces the evolution of Indian religious thought and offers a historical survey of Hindu deities, heroes, and religious beliefs. Chapter 1 deals with the age of the *Vedas*, Chapter 2 with the age of the Brahmanas, and Chapter 3 with the great epics the *Mahābhārata* and the *Bhagavad Gītā*, the religions of Vishnu-Krishna and Shiva, and with various later preachers. In a concluding chapter Barnett notes how Indian religion has been changed by individual religious leaders. A basic premise of this book is that the deities of the Aryans of India were essentially spirits rather than personifications of natural forces and that these deities have mostly disappeared in later religious contexts. Footnotes.

Basham, Arthur Llewellyn. "Religion: Cults, Doctrines and Metaphysics." In *The Wonder That Was India*, by Arthur Llewellyn Basham. 2d ed. New York: Hawthorn Books, 1963.

This chapter in a survey of the culture of pre-Muslim India deals primarily with religious concepts and practices of Hinduism, Buddhism, and Jainism. Also contains significant sections on the gods of the *Rig Veda*, on the legendary life of Buddha, and on various Hindu deities, including the mother goddess and Vishnu, his *avatars* or descents, and his relationship with Shiva. Extensive quotation in translation from original sources. Footnotes.

Brockington, John. "India." In *World Mythology*, edited by Roy Willis. New York: Henry Holt, 1993.

This survey of the mythologies of India includes sections on the origin of the world, on the gods Indra, Brahma, Vishnu, Rama, Krishna, Shiva, and Devi, and on the myths of Jainism and Buddhism. Subsidiary sections provide supplementary material such as paraphrases of myths and short passages translated from ancient sources such as the *Mahābhārata*, the *Rig Veda*, and the *Jākatas* or birth stories of Buddha. Accompanied by twenty-six illustrations, most in color, of Indian artifacts. Map, chronology, and genealogical chart.

Brown, W. Norman. "Mythology of India." In *Mythologies of the Ancient World*, edited by Samuel Noah Kramer. Garden City, N.Y.: Doubleday (Anchor), 1961.

A short survey of Indian mythology with sections on the varieties of religious myths in India, the process of creation in the *Rig Veda*, the Hindu culture hero Rama, Krishna as the concept of deified love in epics such as *Mahābhārata* and *Bhagavad Gītā*, the meditative ascetic god Shiva, the great mother Parvati, the human teacher as savior in Buddhism and Jainism, and the uses of mythology in India. Bibliographical notes and guide to pronunciation and transliteration of Sanskrit words.

Buck, William. *Rāmāyana*. Berkeley: University of California Press, 1976.

This prose retelling is intended to make the great Indian epic poem accessible to twentieth-century English readers. To this end Buck has untangled the complicated plot and even inserted episodes not found in the original. The *Rāmāyana* (Rama's way) is attributed to the poet Vālmīki c. 200 B.C.-A.D. 200 and centers on the adventures of prince Rama. Buck divides the seven books of the 25,000-verse epic into three parts. Part 1, named after Rama's home in Ayodhya, follows the hero in Books 1-2 of the epic from his birth through the fourteenth year of his exile. Part 2, from Books 3-6 of the epic, deals with the hero's exile in a forest along with his wife Sita and his brother Lakshamana, the abduction of Sita by the demon Ravana in the forest, and the battle to rescue her. Part 3 describes the funeral of Ravana, the reunion of Rama and Sita, and Rama's coronation from Books 6-7. In an introductory essay, B. A. van Nooten provides some background to the *Rāmāyana*, its author, cultural context, and features of Buck's translation. An anonymous publisher's preface provides information about Buck and his translating methods and goals. Map, list of characters, and twenty-five line drawings by Shirley Triest.

Buitenen, J. A. B. van, ed. and trans. *The Mahābhārata*. Chicago: University of Chicago Press, 1973 (Book 1), 1975 (Books 2-3), 1978 (Books 4-5).
A translation of the monumental epic *Mahābhārata* by a scholar of Sanskrit and Indic studies. The plot of this epic centers on succession to the kindgom of Kuruksetra in northern India and especially on the efforts of five brothers called the Pāndavas to claim their birthright. While the goal of this project is a translation of all eighteen books of the *Mahābhārata*, these 3 volumes include only the first five books. Book 1, called "The Book of the Beginning," is translated in Volume 1. Book 2, "The Book of the Assembly Hall," and Book 3, "The Book of the Forest," are translated in Volume 2. Volume 3 contains Book 4, "The Book of Vira-ta," and Book 5, "The Book of Effort." The English version of each book is accompanied by the translator's introductory comments and summaries for each section. Each volume includes a map and a concordance of this critical edition with the Bombay edition. At the beginning of Volume 1 the translator offers a pronunciation guide and a general introduction to the epic, including summaries of its complex plots and comments on authorship, the text, editions, knowledge of the epic in the West, the translation, and the annotations. Endnotes and index.

Campbell, Joseph. "The Mythologies of India." In *The Masks of God: Oriental Mythology*, by Joseph Campbell. New York: Viking, 1962.
A historical survey of mythology on the Indian subcontinent including the sudden appearance of the Bronze Age Indus civilization c. 2500 B.C., the introduction of Buddhism (c. 563-483 B.C.), the influence of Rome and the West, and the rise of Islam in India (c. A.D. 1000). Concepts such as the immanent transcendent divinity, the ever-return-

ing cycle, reincarnation, the oriental hero, the world savior, and nirvana are illustrated in myths from a variety of Vedic and Buddhic texts, including the Upanishads, the *Mahābhārata*, and legendary biographies of Buddha. Illustrations.

Conze, Edward, trans. "The Legend of the Buddha Shakyamuni." In *Buddhist Scriptures*, by Edward Conze. Harmondsworth: Penguin, 1959.
In this chapter of a collection of texts chosen to illustrate Buddhist beliefs and ways of life, Conze offers in condensed form a translation of the *Buddhacarita*, or "Acts of Buddha." History and legend merge in this tale of the birth, early life, religious conversion, deeds, and death of the Bodhisattva.

Coomaraswamy, Ananda K. *Hinduism and Buddhism*. New York: Wisdom Library, 1943. Reprint. Westport, Conn.: Greenwood Press, 1971.
Instead of a historical analysis of both religions, Coomaraswamy offers a short theological overview. Summaries of the basic religious myth or world view of each religion is accompanied by short descriptions of their doctrines, ethics, and social orders. Endnotes.

_____. "Literature." In *Buddha and the Gospel of Buddhism*, by Ananda K. Coomaraswamy. London: George G. Harrap, 1928. Rev. ed. New York: Harper & Row, 1964.
Some of the Buddhist literature surveyed here is part of the oral literary tradition of ancient India and includes legends and myths. Of particular note are the book of *Jātakas*, a history of the earlier births of Buddha, the *Chaddanta Jātaka*, a tale of an anthropomorphic elephant and previous incarnation which is quoted at length in translation, a summary of the *Vessantara Jātaka* about a generous prince's encounters with Brahmans, and selections from various verse chronicles and poems.

Coomaraswamy, Ananda K., and Sister Nivedita. *Myths of the Hindus and Buddhists*. 1914. Reprint. New York: Dover, 1967.
A selection of myths from classic Hindu and Buddhist sources are here translated for both Indian and Western readers. Individual chapters on the mythology of the Indo-Aryan races, on the epics *Rāmāyana* and *Mahābhārata*, on the gods Krishna, Buddha, and Shiva, and on other stories from the *Purānas*, epics, and *Vedas*. In the concluding chapter, Indian theology is summarized. Thirty-two black-and-white illustrations of watercolor drawings by several Indian artists.

Davids, Thomas William Rhys. *Buddhist Birth Stories.* Vol. 1. London: Trübner, 1880. Reprint. New York: Arno Press, 1977.

A prolific British scholar of Buddhist religion and philosophy translates forty legendary tales and fables from a Sri Lankan version of the *Jātakas*, an ancient collection of 550 birth stories about the Buddha. In many of these tales animal fables are used to illustrate moral messages for the Buddha's listeners. For each of these *Jātaka* Davids includes the original introductions explaining the circumstances under which the Buddha told the stories of his birth. Davids considers these tales to be the oldest extant collection of folklore in the world. Also included is a translation of the original introduction, called the *Nidāna Kathā*, in which the stories of the Bodhisattvas, or earlier incarnations of Buddha, are traced from the first epoch through the final attainment of Buddhahood. In his own introduction, Davids translates six additional *Jātakas* and illustrates the connection of these tales of Buddha's births with the animal fables of the Greek Aesop, the Latin tales of Babrius and Phaedrus, and St. John of Damascus' eighth-century legend of Barlaam and Josaphat. He also provides a history of the birth stories in India, discusses the authorship of the Sri Lankan *Jātaka* and its place in the Buddhist tradition, and analyzes the structure of the book and its religious purpose. In tables supplementing this introduction, Davids offers bibliographies on Buddhist birth stories, Kalilag and Damnag literature, and the story of Barlaam and Josaphat, as well as five tables, including a list of the Bodhisattvas and places where the tales were told. Subsequent volumes containing the introductory tales for the remaining 510 *Jātakas* were never published. Footnotes and index.

Dimmitt, Cornelia, and J. A. B. van Buitenen, eds. and trans. *Classical Hindu Mythology: A Reader in the Sanskrit Purānas.* Philadelphia: temple University Press, 1978.

A selection of translations from the *Purānas* or "Stories of the Old Days." These tales, written originally in Sanskrit between A.D. 300 and 1000, follow the composition of the *Mahābhārata* and are a basic source for Hindu mythology. The readings, organized thematically, deal with the origins of the cosmos, with the gods Vishnu, Krishna, and Shiva, with Shakti the Hindu goddess, and with seers, kings, and supernatural creatures. Introductory essay on the history and form of the *Purānas.* Footnotes, glossary, notes on sources, bibliography, and index.

Dubois, J. A. "Hindu Fables" and "Hindu Tales." In *Hindu Manners, Customs and Ceremonies*, by J. A. Dubois. Translated and edited by Henry K. Beauchamp. 3d ed. Oxford: The Clarendon Press, 1906.
Abbé Dubois, a French missionary in India between 1792 and 1823, produced a sweeping ethnographic study of Hindu culture which has been translated many times into English and which remains a valuable resource. Dubois analyzes, paraphrases, and retells a variety of tales from a Hindu collection of fables known as the *Pancha-tantra* or "Five Tricks." Includes a variety of tales about a Brahman and his encounters with animals, including a crab, an elephant, and a crocodile. In a separate chapter, Dubois also retells three Hindu tales, one about four deaf men, a second about four foolish Brahmans, and a third about Appaji, the prime minister of King Krishna Roya. Footnotes.

_____. "The Principal Gods of the Hindus." In *Hindu Manners, Customs and Ceremonies*, by J. A. Dubois. Translated and edited by Henry K. Beauchamp. 3d ed. Oxford: The Clarendon Press, 1906.
In this chapter of his monumental ethnography, Dubois surveys the attributes, functions, and myths of the major Hindu deities. In addition to sections on the deities Brahma, Vishnu, Rama, Krishna, Shiva, Vigneshwara, and Indra are separate discussions of Shiva's symbol the *lingam* and the four abodes of bliss. Footnotes.

Dutt, Romesh C., ed. and trans. *The Rāmāyana and the Mahābhārata*. New York: J. M. Dent, 1910. Reprint. New York: Dutton, 1972.
This verse translation offers condensed versions of the two major ancient Indian epics. The *Rāmāyana* describes the adventures of the exiled prince Rama, while the *Mahābhārata* deals with a historical war between the Kurus and the Panchalas in northern India. Each book of the epics is preceded by a plot summary and indication of portions of the original deleted in this version. Short essays by Dutt on the epics and their importance follow each translation. The reprint includes a note on the life and work of Dutt.

Edgerton, Franklin, trans. *The Bhagavad Gītā*. Cambridge, Mass.: Harvard University Press, 1944.
A verse translation with explanatory endnotes followed by an interpretation of the poem. In Part 1 of this interpretation are chapters on the origins of Hindu speculation, the Upanishads and the fundamental doctrines of later Hindu thought, and the prehistory of god in the *Bhagavad Gītā*. Part 2 deals with the teachings of the epic, including soul and body, the nature of god, action and rebirth, the way of

knowledge and the disciplined life, the way of devotion to god, attitudes toward Hindu orthodoxy, and practical morality. Part 3 contains a summary and conclusion. Index of words and subjects, and index of passages quoted.

Elmore, W. T. *Dravidian Gods in Modern Hinduism.* 1913. Reprint. New Delhi: Asian Educational Services, 1984.
This formal study of beliefs and rituals of the Dravidian branch of Hinduism includes some mythological material. In Chapters 3-7 Elmore describes the functions and worship of the major deities known as the Seven Sisters, the *Perantalu* or wives whose husbands are still living, the *saktis* or wives of the gods, demons, and the goddesses Kanaka Durbamma and Poshamma. In Chapters 8-9 the author deals with various Dravidian legends, including local aetiologies about the gods, the role of Dravidian gods in Hindu legends, and tales told by the shepherd caste. While some of these tales are paraphrased, Elmore's goal is to use these stories to explain aspects of Dravidian religion and worship. Bibliography and index.

Elwin, Verrier. *The Myths of Middle India.* London: Oxford University Press, 1949. Reprint. Ann Arbor, Mich.: Xerox University Microfilms, 1975.
Gathers together in English translation examples of myths of origin from India. Part 1 deals with creation of the world and of humankind and myths about heavenly bodies, air, water, and fire. In Part 2 myths of the natural world describe metals, minerals, plants, arthropods, reptiles, fish, birds, and mammals. Part 3 focuses on the human body, the invention of tools, food, tobacco, spirits, disease, sex, and death. Part 4 deals with religion, witchcraft and magic, custom and taboo, and festivals, dances, and song. Each chapter begins with an introductory section followed by numbered versions of the myths with ethnic and geographic source references. Introductory essay on these myths and their interpretation. Footnotes, glossary of tribes and castes, general bibliography, index of folktale motifs, and general index.

_____. *The Tribal Myths of Orissa.* London: Oxford University Press, 1954.
A collection of almost one thousand tales collected by the author in the Bhattra, Didayi, Gadaba, Kond, and other Orissa tribes of India between 1941 and 1951. With the assistance of interpreters, Elwin translated the narratives in the field. The tales are grouped thematically. In Part 1 are myths about the creation of the world, the structure of the

cosmos, heavenly bodies, the elements, and earthquakes. In Part 2 myths about the vegetable world are grouped in the categories of plants, food, tobacco, and alcoholic beverages. Myths of the animal world in Part 3 are arranged taxonomically, beginning with earthworms and moving to arthropods, frogs and fishes, reptiles, birds, and mammals. Part 4 deals with mostly physical features of humankind, including creation, the body, reproduction, disease, the soul, and death. Myths about social institutions in Part 5 describe the origin of tribes and castes, marriage, religion, magic and witchcraft, and government. Myths about fire, houses, clothing, agriculture, hunting and fishing, and recreation under domestic life in Part 6. In a preface, Elwin provides information about his informants and his method of translation, and in an introductory essay he discusses the storytelling techniques of the Orissa, the background of individual tribes, and special characteristics of the group's tales. Glossary, word list, bibliography, motif index with explanatory endnotes, and general index.

Fontenrose, Joseph. "God and Dragon in Egypt and India." In *Python: A Study of Delphic Myth and Its Origins*, by Joseph Fontenrose. Berkeley: University of California Press, 1959.
In this chapter of a book examining myths of divine or heroic combat with serpents or dragons in the ancient Mediterranean world, Fontenrose considers examples of dragon combat in Indic mythology, especially in the conflict between the gods Indra and Vritra. Indicates in these Indic myths folktale themes and motifs from the Aarne-Thompson index and shows how these myths share with the Greek conflict between Apollo and Python and the Egyptian struggle between Horus and Set a common pattern of conflict between order and disorder, chaos and cosmos, and life and death.

Ghosh, Oroon K., trans. *The Dance of Shiva and Other Tales from India*. New York: New American Library, 1965.
A broad-ranging survey of the many types of traditional tales of India. Arranged thematically are tales of love and adventure, myths and legends, especially aetiologies and stories about the ancient Vedic deities Brahma, Vishnu, and Shiva, are accompanied by selections from the great epics the *Rāmāyana* and the *Mahābhārata*, some tales from the Upanishads, Buddha stories, animal stories from a variety of sources, and other tales such as those about the Mogul emperor Akbar. Each group is preceded by a brief introduction by the translator. General introduction to Indian myth and religion in a foreword by

Arthur Llewellyn Basham. Illustrated with drawings by Baniprosonno. Pronunciation guide and glossary.

Goldman, Robert P., trans. *Bālakānda*. Vol. 1 in The *Rāmāyana of Vālmīki*. Princeton, N.J.: Princeton University Press, 1984.
A scholarly translation of the first book of the Indian epic *Rāmāyana* traditionally associated with the sage Vālmīki. Tells of the deeds of a king named Dasaratha and his four sons, including his favorite, Rama, and ends with the marriages of the sons. The translation is preceded by a detailed introduction in which Goldman offers summaries of all seven books of the *Rāmāyana*, comments on questions of historicity, and offers some general observations about *Bālakānda* and the translation. Also included in the introduction are essays on the text and critical edition by Sheldon I. Pollock and on translating the R3m3yana by Leonard E. Nathan. Endnotes, glossary, bibliography, and index.

Hart, George L., and Hank Heifetz, trans. and eds *The Forest Book of the Rāmāyana of Kampan*. Berkeley: University of California Press, 1988.
A verse translation of Book 3 of a Tamil version of the *Rāmāyana* by an important twelfth-century A.D. Tamil poet named Kampan. In this central portion of the epic, the hero Rama, his wife Sita, and his brother Lakshamana are living in exile in a forest, where they meet a series of demons. At the end of the book the most powerful of these, Ravana, abducts Sita. In an introductory essay, the translators offer background about Kampan, a summary of the entire epic book by book, comparisons of Kampan's work with Western epics, and discussions of aesthetic and cultural features of his work. The translators use the more familiar Sanskrit equivalents for Tamil names. Endnotes, glossary, bibliography, and guide to the transliteration of Sanskrit and Tamil words.

Herbert, J. "Hindu Mythology." In *Larousse World Mythology*, edited by Pierre Grimal. Translated by Patricia Beardsworth. New York: G. P. Putnam's Sons, 1963.
This long essay in Grimal's comprehensive survey of mythology uses various ancient scriptures, especially the *Rig Veda*, to provide an overview of the Hindu world view and its deities. Includes sections on the creation of the worlds and of Brahma, the ancestral god, on Vishnu the god of multipliticy and his *avatars*, or descents, into the world, on the role of Shiva, god of destruction and renewal, and on the concept of the divine mother *Mahasakti* and the wives of Vishnu and Shiva. Also contains descriptions of and myths about some of the many other

gods in the Hindu pantheon, such as Indra, Panis, and Agni, as well as Hindu demons such as Jalamdhara and Sisupala and sages such as Prajapati and Brihaspati. Concludes with Hindu beliefs about the end of the world and of humans. Illustrated with photographs of Hindu artwork, some in color.

_____. "Mythology of Buddhism." In *Larousse World Mythology*, edited by Pierre Grimal. Translated by Patricia Beardsworth. New York: G. P. Putnam's Sons, 1963.
Retells the legends surrounding the life of Gautama Buddha (c. 563-c. 483 B.C.) and of his previous lives, predecessors, and mythical successors. Also contains a section on Buddhist goddesses. Fourteen illustrations from Buddhist art.

_____. "Mythology of Jainism." In *Larousse World Mythology*, edited by Pierre Grimal. Translated by Patricia Beardsworth. New York: G. P. Putnam's Sons, 1963.
A short description of the complex wheel of time in the Jainist world view. Explains the various temporal divisions, especially the *avasarpini* or cycles of twenty-four conqueroring sages known as *tirthamkaras*. Summarizes the lives of some of these sages, such as Rishabha, Parsva, and *Mahāvīra*. Four illustrations from Indian art.

Ions, Veronica. *Indian Mythology.* 2d ed. New York: Peter Bedrick Books, 1984.
Lavish illustrations from Indian art and manuscripts accompany this general introduction tracing the development of Indian mythology from its Dravidian and Vedic beginnings through the contributions of Hindu, Buddhist, and Jainist thought. Most of the book is devoted to myths about the many Hindu deities, including Brahma and Indra. Also contains summaries of the *Mahābhārata* epic and the life of Buddha. Historical legends, religious teachings, and tales about the gods express Indian wisdom about the world and about human life. Bibliography and index.

Herrenschmidt, O. "Tribal Mythologies of Central India." In *Larousse World Mythology*, edited by Pierre Grimal. Translated by Patricia Beardsworth. New York: G. P. Putnam's Sons, 1963.
A short essay on the mythology of Indians outside the caste system offers summaries of two versions of the creation of the world and of humankind, one told by the Birhors and the other by the Bison-Horn Marias. Also contains the myth of Lingal, the mythical hero of the Gonds. Four illustrations from Indian art.

Keith, A. Berriedale. *Indian Mythology.* Vol. 6 in *The Mythology of All Races*, edited by Louis Herbert Gray. Boston: Marshall Jones, 1917.
This sweeping survey of Indian mythology is arranged chronologically according to the literary sources described in an introductory essay. From the deities and mythology of the *Rig Veda* and the *Brahamanas*, the author moves to the gods of the *Rāmāyana* and *Mahābhārata* epics, to the mythology of the *Purānas* narratives, and finally to the beliefs of Buddhism, Jainism, and modern Hinduism. Thirty-two plates and figures. Transcription and pronunciation guide, endnotes, and bibliography. Complete index in Volume 13.

Knowles, James Hinton. Folk-Tales of Kashmir. 2d ed. London: Paul, Trench, Trübner, 1893. Reprint. New York: Arno Press, 1977.
A missionary offers sixty-four tales told to him by Kashmiri informants. The names of these informants are provided in the first footnote for each tale. Themes appearing in these stories include charms and incantations, anthropomorphic animals, miraculous cures, metamorphosis, unusual births, and ogres. Prefatory essay on the collection of these tales. Footnotes, glossary, and index.

Koppers, Wilhelm. "The Deluge Myth of the Bhils of Central India." An abridgment of "Bhagwan, the Supreme Deity of the Bhils: A Contribution to the History of Indian and Indo-European religions." *Anthropos* 35/36 (1940-41). In *The Flood Myth*, edited by Alan Dundes. Berkeley: University of California Press, 1988.
Beginning with a paraphrase of a Bhil flood myth published in 1938, Koppers describes several other Bhil versions he collected in the field. He then compares the Bhil tradition to the Hindu deluge myth and concludes that the Bhil tradition is influenced in places by the later Hindu tradition, but the Hindu version shows no knowledge of the Bhil myth. In an introductory note, Dundes describes the contributions of Koppers' teacher, Father Wilhelm Schmidt, to the study of mythography. Footnotes.

Linossier, Raymonde. "The Mythology of Buddhism in India." In *Asiatic Mythology*, edited by M. J. Hackin. Translated by F. M. Atkinson. New York: Thomas Y. Crowell, 1963.
A short history of Buddhism in India is followed by a discussion of the mythic life of Buddha Sakyamuni and the symbols used in illustrations of his life. Summaries of various *Jākatas*, or didactic birth narratives, including those dedicated to the deities Shaddanta, Mahakapi, Vessantara, Sibi, Champeyya, the one-horned Rishi, and Syama. Also contains

sections on various other deities, including goddesses, and on the Bodhisattvas, the elect in the Dhyani-Buddhas' Paradise in the Mahayana school of Buddhism. Forty-two black-and-white illustrations and one color plate of the birth of Buddha.

Mackenzie, Donald Alexander. *Indian Myth and Legend*. London: Gresham Publishing, 1913.
Deals with Indian myths and legends from Sanskrit literature and from Brahman, Buddhist, and Jainist sources. Special attention is given to the Aryan controversy and to comparative evidence for cultural ties between Vedic India and Indo-European Europe. Chapters 1-6 deal with the deities and myths of the Vedic period. Chapters 7-8 introduce the newer religions and their deities. Summaries of many myths from the *Mahābhārata* and the *Rāmāyana* in Chapters 9-26, beginning with the prelude to the great Bharata war and ending with the abduction of Sita and the fulfillment of Rama's mission. Forty plates, eight in color, of ancient Indian and modern European art depicting scenes from these legends. Index.

McNair, John F. A., and Thomas Lambert Barlow. *Oral Tradition from the Indus*. Rev. ed. Brighton: R. Gosden, 1908. Reprint. New York: Arno Press, 1977.
Most of these nineteen folktales about gurus, miracles, magic, exorcism, and anthropomorphic animals were collected over a thirty-year period by Barlow at the village of Ghazi on the Indus River. They were translated jointly by McNair and Barlow. In an introductory essay, McNair describes the town of Ghazi and the origin of this collection. Map and fourteen black-and-white drawings by L. Fenn.

MacNicol, Nicol, trans. *Hindu Scriptures*. New York: Dutton, 1963.
A selection of readings in translation from Hindu sacred documents. Thirty hymns from the *Rig Veda*, mostly to deities, five Upanishads, and "The Lord's Song" from the *Bhagavad Gītā*. While the choice of readings was intended to illustrate Hindu religious beliefs, many also offer descriptions of deities and references to myth narratives. Introductory essay, occasional footnotes, and glossary.

Masson-Oursel, P., and Louise Morin. "Indian Mythology." In *New Larousse Encyclopedia of Mythology*, edited by Felix Guirand et al. Translated by Richard Aldington and Delano Ames. New York: Hamlyn, 1968.
This sweeping overview of Indian religion and myths is divided into three parts: the ancient Vedic tradition of the Brahmanic *dharma*, or

cosmic social structure, the so-called heretical *dharmas* of Jainism and Buddhism, and the mythology of Hinduism. In their discussion of Brahmanic beliefs and myths, the authors distinguish the priestly caste's beliefs about the deities Agni and Soma from more popular mythology about *asuras*, or demons and their incarnations, and from more abstract Brahamanic myths about the god Brahma, priests, and mythical heroes. The discussion of heretical *dharmas* centers on the Tirthamkaras, or miraculous saviors of the world, the legendary life of Buddha, and the multiplications of Buddhas. The authors divide their study of the mythology of Hinduism into examinations of the religion of the god Vishnu, especially in his incarnation as Krishna, and the ascetic religion of the god Shiva. Accompanied by sixty-two black-and-white and three color illustrations of Indian art and sites.

Meile, Pierre. "Mythology of the Tamils." In *Larousse World Mythology*, edited by Pierre Grimal. Translated by Patricia Beardsworth. New York: G. P. Putnam's Sons, 1963.
A short essay on the mythological traditions of the Tamil of south India. Describes tales from early Tamil poetry, including the mythic Cankam or literary academies, catastrophic floods, legendary scholars and poets such as Agastya, and favorite gods. Three illustrations from Tamil art.

Narasimhan, C. V., trans. *The Mahābhārata*. New York: Columbia University Press, 1965.
This prose translation of selected portions of the *Mahābhārata*, the longest epic in any language, creates a continuous narrative around the epic's main theme, the heroic rivalry between the five Pāndava and the five Kaurava brothers and the great battle of Kuruksetra. The chapters in the translation are correlated in an index with the original Sanskrit verses. In the introduction, the translator offers a plot summary and an analysis of some of the characters in the epic. Some features of this translation are discussed in the preface. Pronunciation guide, genealogical tables, glossary, and list of alternative names of various characters.

Narayan, R. K., ed. and trans. *The Rāmāyana*. New York: Viking, 1972.
This retelling of portions of the epic in English modern prose by a major Indian novelist is based upon the eleventh-century A.D. Tamil version of Kamban. Begins with Rama's initiation and his marriage to Sita and follows the hero's adventures through his battle with Ravana and his coronation. In an introduction, prologue, and epilogue, the author

provides some background for the full epic. Explanatory list of characters and glossary.

O'Flaherty, Wendy Doniger. *Hindu Myths: A Sourcebook Translated from the Sanskrit.* Baltimore: Penguin, 1975.
Includes translations of selected Hindu texts such as the *Rig Veda*, the *Atharva Veda*, *Mahābhārata*, and *Rāmāyana*, arranged around thematic sections on creation myths, the gods Indra (king of the Indic gods), Agni (god of fire), the assimilated deity Rudra-Siva, the dwarf Vishnu who becomes the supreme god, the goddess Devi, and the battle between the gods and demons. Bibliography, notes, and a glossary and index of names.

_____. "Hinduism." In *Mythology: An Illustrated Encyclopaedia*, edited by Richard Cavendish. New York: Rizzoli International, 1980. Also published as *An Illustrated Encyclopedia of Mythology*. New York: Crescent Books, 1984.
A broad survey of Hindu mythologies, with sections on the Vedic creation myths, myths of battles between gods and demons, stories about gods as human benefactors, myths in the *Mahābhārata*, and *Rāmāyana* epics, especially the lives of Rama and of Krishna, stories about the deities Shiva and the Goddess, and mythology in modern Hinduism. Map, time chart, lists of the *avatars* of Vishnu, glossary of Hindu deities and mythological beings, and illustrations of artwork related to the myths.

_____. *The Rig Veda.* New York: Penguin, 1982.
In this anthology 108 hymns from the *Rig Veda*, an ancient collection of Hindu sacred hymns, are translated into English and accompanied by explanatory notes for the general reader. Many of these hymns make reference to early Hindu myths which no longer survive separately. The hymns are arranged here in the following thematic groups: creation, death, sacrifice, the horse sacrifice, Agni the fire god, Soma the drink of immortals, the life of the god Indra, gods of the storm, solar gods, sky, and earth, Varuna the protector of sacred order, the gods Rudra and Vishnu, worldly life, women, and incantations. Introductory essay on the *Rig Veda* and problems of interpretation. Bibliography and indexes.

Parker, Henry. *Village Folk-Tales of Ceylon.* London: Luzac, 1910 (Vol. 1), 1914 (Vols. 2-3). Reprint. New York: Arno Press, 1977.
These 266 tales from what is now Sri Lanka and India were recorded in the field in Sinhalese and translated literally into English by Parker.

Local royalty, *rākshasas* or "ogres," *yakās* or "demons," and anthropomorphic animals, especially crafty jackal, play prominent roles in
these stories about magic, fools, thieves, disabled people, and sudden
wealth and success. The collection is loosely organized according to
castes and regions. Volume 1 contains thirty-seven stories of the
cultivating caste and Vaeddās in Part 1 and thirty-eight stories of the
lower castes, including the tom-tom beaters, the Durayās, the Rodiyās,
and the Kinnarās, in Part 2. All 102 tales in Volume 2 come from the
cultivating caste. In Volume 3 are ten additional tales of the cultivating
caste, thirty-eight stories of the lower caste potters, washermen, and
tom-tom beaters, and forty-two stories from the western province and
from southern India. Volume 3 also contains transliterated versions of
the Sinhalese texts for six tales and a note on the Sinhalese language.
In an introductory essay in Volume 1, Parker describes everyday life
in traditional Sri Lanka, his method of collecting tales, some characteristics of these tales, and a history of the early kings of Sri Lanka.
Occasional footnotes and comparative endnotes. Each volume has its
own index.

Pollock, Sheldon I., trans. *Aranyakānda*. Vol. 3 in *The Rāmāyana of
   Vālmīki*, edited by Robert P. Goldman. Princeton, N.J.: Princeton
   University Press, 1991.
   The third volume in a scholarly verse translation and commentary for
   the entire *Rāmāyana*, *Aranyakānda* deals with the central portion of
   the plot, namely the wanderings of the exiled Rama, his wife Sita, and
   his brother Lakshamana, and the capture of Sita by the demon Ravana.
   In the introductory Part 1, Pollock discusses the problem of interpreting
   Aranyakānda, summarizes the plot of the book, considers the
   Rāmāyana as myth and romance, and addresses the questions of the
   divine king in *Rāmāyana*, Rama's madness, and the nature of the
   cannibalistic *Rāksasas* in the epic. The translation in Part 2 follows
   carefully the section and line divisions of the original Sanskrit. Part 3
   consists of a detailed critical and interpretive commentary. List of
   abbreviations, guide to Sanskrit pronunciation, glossary, emendations
   of the critical edition, bibliography, and index.

Puhvel, Jaan. "Epic India." In *Comparative Mythology*, by Jaan Puhvel.
   Baltimore: The Johns Hopkins University Press, 1987.
   Considers the cultural and, especially, the mythological contexts of the
   Mahābhārata and the *Rāmāyana*, the great Indian epics of the first
   millennium B.C. Detailed summaries of the plots of both epics. Empha-
   sizes the mythological significance of certain tales in the epics which

retain elements of Indo-European and Indo-Iranian myths. Compares the structure of the *Mahābhārata* to that of epics in the Old Norse tradition. Footnotes and bibliography.

_____. "Vedic India." In *Comparative Mythology*, by Jaan Puhvel. Baltimore: The Johns Hopkins University Press, 1987.
Offers an overview of the culture of ancient India, including social structure, literature, religion, and mythology. Describes the origin and functions of the major deities in the Vedic pantheon. Ancient Vedic society was based on a tripartite organization of kings, warriors, and workers which can be found in later Indo-European societies in western Asia and Europe. Detailed analysis of many Indic words. Some quotation in translation from the ancient Indic hymn called the *Rig Veda*. Figure illustrating the ancient god Vishnu. Footnote and bibliography.

Ram, Govinder. *Rama and Sita*. New York: Peter Bedrick Books, 1988.
Retells an excerpt from the *Rāmāyana* for children. In this tale Prince Rama, his wife Sita, and his brother Lakshamana are banished by his stepmothers to the forest of Dandak. The brothers must use supernatural aids to rescue Sita from the demon king Ravana and to return home. Illustrated in color by the author.

Ramanujan, A. K. "Hanchi: A Kannada Cinderella." In *Cinderella: A Folklore Casebook*, edited by Alan Dundes. New York: Garland Press, 1982.
Translates an Indian versian of Cinderella which the author heard in a North Karnatak village in 1955. A Cinderella-type heroine named Hanchi is disguised by a mask. A rich young man discovers her beauty and marries her but their marriage is temporarily marred by the intrigues of a holy man named Guruswami. The tale is followed by a multifacted interpretation of the folktale in its Indian and broader contexts. Makes use of the Aarne-Thompson technique of comparative analysis via tale types, the structural approaches of Vladimir Propp and Claude Lévi-Strauss, and the psychological theories of Sigmund Freud and Carl Jung. Includes useful background information and bibliography by Dundes. Endnotes and bibliography.

Sahai, Bhagwant. *Iconography of Minor Hindu and Buddhist Dieties*. New Delphi: Abhinav Publications, 1975.
An examination of portraits and depictions of some Hindu and Buddhist gods in the sculpture of northern India. In an introductory essay, the author discusses the scope of his topic and its sources and

offers a historical survey of earlier studies. Part 1 deals with sixteen Hindu deities, including Indra, Agni, Yama, and Revanta. The Buddhist deities Jambhala, Trailokya-vijaya, Aparājitā, Parnaśabarī, Mārīchī, and Hāritī are discussed in Part 2. In each discussion the author makes reference to many sculptural representations of the god. Photographs of forty-five of these, especially from museums in India, accompany the text. Footnotes, transliteration table, bibliography, and index.

Shulman, David. "The Tamil Flood Myths and the Cankam Legend." *Journal of Tamil Studies* 14 (1978). Reprinted in *The Flood Myth*, edited by Alan Dundes. Berkeley: University of California Press, 1988. Examines the Tamil flood tradition, in which a deluge completely destroys the world and the Cankam, i.e., the Tamil literary academies are the only survivals. Several flood myths from the Tamil shrine of Maturai are described in the context of several Tamil myths of creation and of survival. Concludes that the Tamil flood myths are basically celebrations of creation and order rather than of chaos and destruction. Footnotes.

Smith, Vincent A. "Ancient India." In *The Oxford History of India*. 3d ed., edited by Percival Spear. Oxford: The Clarendon Press, 1958. The initial chapter in a history of India first published in 1919. Contains a section in which the literature of the Vedic and Epic periods are suveyed. Also contains useful overviews of the *Rig Veda, Rāmāyana, Mahābhārata,* and other early works with strong mythological content. Short selections in translation. Footnotes and bibliography.

Stevenson, Mrs. Sinclair [Margaret]. "The Life of Mahāvīra." In *The Heart of Jainism*, by Mrs. Sinclair [Margaret] Stevenson. New York: Oxford University Press, 1915. Reprint. Ann Arbor, Mich.: University Microfilms, 1973. This survey of the life of the founder of Jainism is part of a larger study of the religion, its history, and its beliefs. Blended into the historical life of Mahāvīra are an heroic pattern of legendary events such as the dreams of the hero's mother prior to his birth, extraordinary events surrounding the actual birth and his childhood, and stories about his extreme devotion to meditation and asceticism and about his death. Footnotes.

_____. "Jaina Mythology." In *The Heart of Jainism*, by Mrs. Sinclair [Margaret] Stevenson. New York: Oxford University Press, 1915. Reprint. Ann Arbor, Mich.: University Microfilms, 1973.

This chapter in a study of the religion founded in India in the sixth century B.C. by Mahāvīra offers a survey of Jainist deities and their concept of time. The gods are discussed by geographic location in hell, in another hell without human sinners called Pātāla, and in the upper regions, especially the highest one, called Svarga. Stevenson also considers the Jainist view of time as an ever-turning wheel and describes each age in this cycle. Footnotes.

Temple, Richard Carnac. *The Legends of the Panjâb*. 3 vols. London: Trübner, 1884 (Vol. 1), 1885 (Vol. 2), 1900 (Vol. 3). Reprint. New York: Arno Press, 1977.
A collection of fifty-eight traditional tales of the Panjâb are presented in bilingual form. Sometimes the English translation follows the original version, and other times the English appears below the original on the same page. Temple himself recorded most of the tales in the field and translated them. Heroic legends, tribal tales, lives of saints, and ballads are presented in no systematic order. Each tale is preceded by some commentary and information about sources. In prefaces to each volume, Temple provides information on his sources and discusses some characteristics of these tales. Index at the end of Volume 3.

Thomas, F. W. "Language and Early Literature." In *The Legacy of India*, edited by G. T. Garratt. Oxford: The Clarendon Press, 1937.
An overview of the linguistic history of ancient India is followed by a survey of early literature, including the *Rig Veda*, the *Mahābhārata*, and the *Rāmāyana*. Includes some plot summary from these works and occasional quotation in translation.

Thomas, P. Epics, Myths and Legends of India. Singapore: Graham Brash, 1913. Reprint. London: Gresham Publishing, 1989.
A survey of the mythology of Hinduism, Buddhism, and Jainism. Combines analysis of the myths with extensive quotation in translation from ancient Indian texts. Begins in Part 1 with the cosmic and cosmogonic myths of the Hindus and with the Hindu pantheon and chapters on demigods, enemies of the gods, death and soul-wanderings, love and sex, the heavenly bodies, flora and fauna, Hindu holidays, and popular legends. Part 2 contains chapters on the legendary life of Buddha, Jātaka tales about the lives of Bodhisattvas, or Buddhas-elect, and the history of Jainism, its beliefs, deities, and legends about its founder Mahāvīra. Includes a descriptive list of the Thirthankaras, or "Ford Finders," the twenty-four world teachers who became liberated souls after death. Introductory essay on the science

of mythology, Indo-European myths, and special characteristics of Hindu mythology. Accompanied by 268 black-and-white illustrations plus one color plate, including sites, people, and artwork related to the myths. Glossary and index.

Troughton, Joanna. *The Wizard Punchkin*. New York: Peter Bedrick Books, 1988.
In this traditional Indian tale retold for children, Prince Chandra saves his brothers from the evil wizard Punchkin by discovering the secret of the wizard's power in a parrot's egg. Illustrated in color by the author.

Wilman-Grabowska, H. de. "Brahamanic Mythology." In *Asiatic Mythology*, edited by M. J. Hackin. Translated by F. M. Atkinson. New York: Thomas Y. Crowell, 1963.
A general survey of the Hindu religions followed by two major divisions, one on the early Vedic mythology and the second on the mythology of Hinduism. Sections on Vedic sky and sacrificial divinities and various aspects of the Hindu Shiva and Vishnu are accompanied by an extensive summary of the legends with quotations from the *Vedas*. Thirty-six black-and-white illustrations and two color plates.

Wood, Ramsay. *Kalila and Dimna*. New York: Alfred A. Knopf, 1980.
Twenty tales, mostly animal fables, are told by a sage, Dr. Bidpai, to Dabschelim, the young ruler of India. Wood selects these stories from the Buddhist *Tales of Bidpai*, written originally in Sanskrit about A.D. 200. Translated into a variety of Eastern languages, this collection of tales is well known from Ethiopia to China. This edition offers in the margins illustrations by Margaret Kilrenny and appropriate quotations from Western sages such as Cicero, Sigmund Freud, Mark Twain, and John Dryden. In an introductory essay, Doris Lessing discusses the origin of the *Tales of Bidpai*, its influence in the East, and its history in the West.

Zaehner, R. C. *Hinduism*. Oxford: Oxford University Press, 1962.
A professor of Eastern religions at Oxford surveys the religious beliefs of Hinduism. Many myths are retold in chapters dealing with the Vedic texts and with the concepts of *brahma* (sacred action), *moksha* (liberation), god, and *dharma* (duty). Includes descriptions of the cosmos and world view of Hinduism and some quotation from original texts in translation. Also contains chapters on the recent history of Hinduism and on the religious ideas of Mahatma Gandhi. Bibliography and index.

Zimmer, Heinrich. *Myths and Symbols in Indian Art and Civilization*,
    edited by Joseph Campbell. New York: Harper and Row, 1946.
    Narratives of Indian myths are combined with descriptions of mythic
    scenes in Indian art. Accompanied by analysis and interpretation of the
    myths. Includes chapters on eternity and time, the mythology of the
    god Vishnu, the guardians of life, the cosmic delight of Shiva, and the
    origin of Diva, the supreme goddess. Uses psychoanalytic methods to
    show how these myths form a comprehensive and ethical vision of the
    world. Seventeen plates illustrating Indian myths in art, especially
    sculpture. Some footnotes. Index.

Chinese and Tibetan Myths

Allan, Sarah. *The Heir and the Sage: Dynastic Legend in Early China*.
    San Francisco: Chinese Materials Center, 1981.
    Examines five legend sets dealing with transfer of rule in ancient China
    (475-222 B.C.). These include the transition from Yao to Shun and from
    Shun to Yu, the succession of Qi, and the foundations of the Xia, Shang,
    and Zhou dynasties. Each legend set is analyzed in a separate chapter.
    Chinese characters are used throughout, but all are accompanied by
    transliteration, translation, and explanation. Uses structuralist methods
    to show how these legends function as myths and serve to mediate
    social conflicts. Five genealogical charts, bibliography, and index.

Birch, Cyril. *Chinese Myths and Fantasies*. London: Oxford University
    Press, 1962.
    Retells eighteen Chinese myths and legends. The tales are organized
    under the following themes: the conquerors of chaos, stories about
    demons, stories about fairies and ghosts, and the story of Aunt Piety,
    Eggborn, and the revolt of the demons. Accompanied by black-and-
    white illustrations by Joan Kiddell-Monroe.

Birrell, Anne M. *Chinese Mythology*. Baltimore, Md.: The Johns Hopkins
    University Press, 1993.
    A collection of more than 300 myth narratives gathered from more than
    100 ancient Chinese texts by a distinguished scholar of Chinese cul-
    ture. The myths are grouped into the following categories: origins,
    culture bearers, saviors, destroyers, miraculous births, the Yellow
    Emperor, Yi the Archer, Yü the Great, goddesses, immortality, meta-
    morphoses, heroes, flora and fauna, strange lands and peoples, and
    foundation legends. Each narrative is translated from its original source

and accompanied by a commentary which analyzes, explains, and interprets the myth. In an introductory essay, the author discusses definitions of myth, approaches to Chinese myth, the comparative method, the nature of Chinese mythic narratives, modern Chinese and Japanese studies of Chinese myth, and future research. Foreword by Yuan K'o, a Chinese scholar of myth. Chronological table, concordance of English and Chinese book titles, bibliography, index and glossary of Chinese names and terms, and an index of concepts.

Bodde, Derk. "Myths of Ancient China." In *Mythologies of the Ancient World*, edited by Samuel Noah Kramer. New York: Anchor Books, 1961.
This short survey of myths in China begins by noting that the Chinese have individual myths but no systematized mythology. Outlines several problems in the study of these myths, including euhemerization, fragmentation, and chronology. Offers five examples of comogonic Chinese myths: the P'an-ku creation myth, the tale of the fashioning deity Nü-kua, stories about the separation of heaven and earth, sun myths, and flood myths. Selected bibliography.

Boord, Martin. "Tibet and Mongolia." In *World Mythology*, edited by Roy Willis. New York: Henry Holt, 1993.
This general summary of Tibetan and Mongolian myths offers short sections on cosmogony, myths about the ancient kings, the legend of the warrior-king Gesar, the relationship between Buddhism and the ancient gods, and Mongolian shamanism. Subsidiary sections describe the apotheosis of the Indian mystic Padmasambhava and the Mongolian yellow book of divination. Accompanied by eight color illustrations of artifacts from Tibet and Mongolia. Map, time chart, and pronunciation guide.

Campbell, Joseph. "Chinese Mythology." In *The Masks of God: Oriental Mythology*, by Joseph Campbell. New York: Viking, 1962.
The mythological and philosophical thought of China is presented in historical context, beginning with distant prehistory and the Chinese feudal age, moving to the writings of great thinkers such as Confucius (551-487 B.C.) and Mo Tzu (c. 480-400 B.C.), and ending with the age of Buddhist, Taoist, and Confucian religious proliferation (c. A.D. 500-1500). Myths are summarized, often with extensive quotation from major sources. Includes myths about the period of the earliest men, the ten mythical monarchs, the rise and fall of historical dynasties,

and cosmic principles such as *yin*, the female principle, and *yang*, the male principle. Several illustrations.

_____. "The Descent to Heaven: The Tibetan Book of the Dead." In *Transformations of Myth Through Time*, by Joseph Campbell. New York: Harper & Row, 1990.
Campbell offers a tour of the soul by paraphrasing and commenting upon the Tibetan Book of the Dead. Campbell describes the seven worlds of the cakras through which the unprepared soul travels on its forty-nine-day journey from the moment of death to the time of its reincarnation. The soul slips from the opportunity of universal consciousness, to a consciousness of deity, to the radiance of Buddha, to the realm of the Lord Judge of the Dead, down to the worlds of ignorance, lust, and malice, and back into the world of the living. Eight illustrations from Tibetan art and manuscripts.

_____. "Tibet: The Buddha and the New Happiness." In *The Masks of God: Oriental Mythology*, by Joseph Campbell. New York: Viking, 1962.
Contemplates the mythic transformations and conflicts between Buddhism and communism after Tibet was captured by the Chinese in 1955. Combines examples of revised lives of Buddha, attempts to displace the traditional gods with the god of communism, and parallels between the traditional *yin-yang* (female-male) dichotomy and the dialectical materialism of Marxism. Vivid descriptions of tortures and executions in 1955 are interpreted in the context of the Tibetan Book of the Dead where a concept of heaven and hell is believed to be present in each individual consciousness.

Chinner, John. "China." In *World Mythology*, edited by Roy Willis. New York: Henry Holt, 1993.
This overview of myths from ancient China discusses the Chinese account of cosmogony, the role of the deities Nü-kua and Fu Xi in the creation of humankind and in a great flood, myths about the heavenly bodies, Chinese Buddhism, Taoist myths, and myths about the family. Subsidiary sections supplement this material with paraphrases of tales such as Chang E and the Moon or Radish and Lady Leek Stem. Accompanied by seventeen color illustrations of Chinese artifacts. Map, pronunciation table, and table of Chinese dynasties.

Christie, Anthony. "China." In *Mythology: An Illustrated Encyclopaedia*, edited by Richard Cavendish. New York: Rizzoli International, 1980.

Also published as *An Illustrated Encyclopedia of Mythology*. New York: Crescent Books, 1984.

This general overview of Chinese mythology includes some detailed paraphrase and analysis of myths. Contains sections on the creation of order from chaos, mythic descriptions of the physical world, the creation of humankind, control of nature by culture heroes, the story of the smith Kan Chiang and his wife Mo Yeh, a tale of human sacrifice called "The Pumpkin Girl," pantheons of Chinese deities, the Buddhist/Taoist story of Monkey, and the heavenly civil service. Map, time chart, glossaries of mythological inventors and principal mythical figures, and illustrations of artwork related to the myths.

_____. *Chinese Mythology*. 2d ed. New York: Peter Bedrick Books, 1985.

This general introduction to the mythology of China begins with historical and archaeological background about the early cultures of China, including the rise of feudalism, the short unification of China, and the Han consolidation. Following a discussion of the myths and their sources are sections on Chinese myths about the creation of the world and the origin of useful arts, peasant myths, animal fables, and beliefs about the gods, plus a section on the use of myths by the twentieth-century communist government of China. Illustrated on nearly every page with artifacts and manuscripts related to the myths. Map, chronology of mythical and historical dynasties, bibliography, and index.

Eberhard, Wolfram. *Folktales of China*. Chicago: University of Chicago Press, 1965.

Seventy-nine Chinese folktales arranged thematically. Folktales of origin, fortune, love, supernatural marriages, magic, supernatural helpers, cleverness and stupidity, and kindness rewarded and evil punished. A foreword by Charles Dorson describes the links between folklore and the rise of Chinese nationalism, summarizes the history of modern Chinese folklore in the context of the New Culture Movement and the use of folklore by the Chinese Communist Party, and considers Western views of Chinese folklore. In a short introduction, Eberhard surveys collections of Chinese folklore. Index of Aarne-Thompson motifs and types, bibliography, and general index.

_____. *The Local Cultures of South and East China*. Translated by Alide Eberhard. Leiden: E. J. Brill, 1968.

Examines myths and beliefs from a number of early localized cultural groups in China, including the Yao, Thai, Yüeh, Liao, and Tungus. These traditional stories are not retold; rather, their chief elements and major variants are analyzed in a series of cultural chains. Reveals a process of social interaction seen as a significant factor in the development of traditional societies. These goals are explained in an introductory essay. Bibliography and index.

_____. "The Story of Grandaunt Tiger." In *Studies in Taiwanese Folktales*. Taipei: The Orient Cultural Service, 1970. Reprinted in *Little Red Riding Hood. A Casebook*, edited by Alan Dundes. Madison: University of Wisconsin Press, 1989.
A translation of a Taiwanese version of "Little Red Riding Hood," collected in Taipei by the author in 1967-1968, is recorded here and analyzed together with 240 other versions of the tale. In this tale a tiger disguised as an old woman eats a woman but is then tricked and killed by the woman's two daughters. Dundes introduces the reprint with useful background information, commentary and bibliography.

Ferguson, John. C. *Chinese Mythology*. Vol. 8 in *The Mythology of All Races*, edited by John A. MacCulloch. Boston: Marshall Jones, 1928.
An outline of Chinese mythology rather than a comprehensive survey. Major myths are paraphrased and mythic characters described. There are chapters on Taoism, the early, prehistoric emperors, early religious beliefs, cosmogony, domestic religious rites, and national heroes. Also discusses folklore, exemplary tales, tales from drama, and Buddhist myths. A brief summary of Chinese history and culture is offered in an introductory chapter. Six plates, fifty-nine figures, bibliography, and index. Complete index in Volume 13.

Hackin, M. J. "The Mythology of Lamaism." In *Asiatic Mythology*, edited by M. J. Hackin. Translated by F. M. Atkinson. New York: Thomas Y. Crowell, 1963.
Examines the narrative elements in the iconography of Buddhism in Tibet. Special attention to the lives of Buddha Sakyamuni and major Buddhist saints such as Manjusri (the incarnation of wisdom) and Tara (subliminated Compassion). Also contains sections on the terrible divinities (including Lha-mo, Mahakala, and Yama), the tutelary divinities known as Samvara and Hevajara, the Lokapala or guardian kings, Padmasambhava and other great sorcerers, and Gsen-rabs-mi-bo (the great prophet of the Bonpos, a pre-Buddhist religion). Fifty

black-and-white figures and three color plates illustrating manuscript illuminations and artwork in the Musée Guimet in Paris.

Hui-ming, Wang, ed. and trans. *West Lake: Folk Tales*. Beijing: Foreign Languages, 1982.
A collection of fifteen folktales set at the West Lake at Hangzhou, the capital of Zheijiang Province. Many of these are aetiological in nature and explain how the lake was formed, how scissors were invented, and why Hangzhou is famous for its silk, tea, and parasols. Eight tales are accompanied by black-and-white illustrations.

Jameson, R. D. "Cinderella in China." In *Three Lectures on Chinese Folklore*. Beijing: North China Union Language School, 1932. Reprinted in *Cinderella: A Folklore Casebook*, edited by Alan Dundes. New York: Garland Press, 1982.
This paper introduced to the Western world a ninth-century Chinese version of the Cinderella folktale. Retells the story and compares it first to several Chinese versions and then to versions from other parts of the world. Considers questions of distribution and origin as well as the possible meanings of the tale. Reprint includes useful background information, historical commentary, and bibliography by Dundes. Endnotes.

Levy, Howard S. *China's Dirtiest Trickster*. Arlington, Va.: Warm-Soft Press, 1974.
A translation of 114 stories about Hsü Wen-ch'ang (1521-1593), an imperial bureaucrat who spent seven years in prison for killing his wife and around whom developed an elaborate folklore tradition similar to the German Til Eulenspiegel. In these stories Hsü becomes a clever and deceitful peasant who outwits people from all levels of society. The collection is divided into eighty-one tales described as "Clean Fun" and fifty-three as "Dirtied Jokes." Index.

Loewe, Michael. *Chinese Ideas of Life and Death*. London: Allen & Unwin, 1982.
This survey of intellectual and religious beliefs in China during the Han period (202 B.C.-A.D. 220) includes several chapters addressing mythological topics. Of special interest are chapters on the order of nature, the universe and the shape of the heavens, and the earth and its creatures. Other chapters deal with the gods, oracles, shamans, the afterlife, and imperial cults. Includes extensive quotation in translation from ancient Chinese documents. Bibliographic endnotes, glossary, list of emperors of the Han dynasty, and index.

Maspero, Henri. "The Mythology of Modern China." In *Asiatic Mythology*, edited by M. J. Hackin. Translated by F. M. Atkinson. New York: Thomas Y. Crowell, 1963.

This survey begins with the status of religious practices and beliefs in twentieth-century China. Considers the status of Confucian, Buddhist, and Taoist clergy, ritual, and concepts in modern society. Discusses deities according to function. Sections on the supreme gods, including the Jade Emperor, his family, and court, are followed by discussion of nature deities such as the sun and the moon and the great dragon kings; the gods in charge of celestial administrative groups such as T'ai-yo ta-ti (the Great Emperor of the Eastern Peak); gods of administrative districts such as Ch'eng-huang (Gods of Walls and Moats) and T'u-ti (Gods of the Place); gods of the house, the door, the bed, and other areas of the house and of ancestor worship; gods of specific professions and trades such as mandarins, the military, peasants, and sailors; deities in charge of various areas of human life such as happiness, children, and health; and gods of the otherworld. Ninety-one black-and-white figures and two color plates.

O'Connor, W. F., ed. and trans. *Folktales from Tibet*. London: Hurst and Blackett, 1906. Reprint. Kathmandu, Nepal: Ratna Pustak Bhandar, 1977.

Twenty-two folktales gathered by the author during his travels in Tibet. While O'Connor mentions in a short preface that some of these tales are borrowed from India or China and others are indigenous, no indication of such sources is offered tale by tale. Most of these stories are animal fables. Illustrated with thirteen color drawings by an anonymous Tibetan artist. Occasional explanatory footnotes.

Ou-I-Tai. "Chinese Mythology." In *New Larousse Encyclopedia of Mythology*, edited by Felix Guirand et al. Translated by Richard Aldington and Delano Ames. New York: Hamlyn, 1968.

This overview of Chinese mythology concentrates on Taoist divinities and myths, with major sections on heaven and its gods, divinities of the natural world and heavenly bodies, deities who protect humankind, popular gods, deities of various professions, and hell. Accompanied by thirty-two black-and-white and four color reproductions of Chinese art.

Sanders, Tao Tao Liu. *Dragons, Gods and Spirits from Chinese Mythology*. New York: Schocken Books, 1980.

This general introduction to the traditional mythology of China in-cludes lavish illustrations by Johnny Pau. A brief cultural and historical introduction is followed by chapters on early gods and heroes, dragons, Buddhist and Taoist tales, and stories about spirits and demons such as the Monkey Spirit. Symbols and literary characters illustrated in the text are explained in an appendix. Another appendix identifies the ancient sources for these stories. Bibliography and index.

Skorupski, Tadeusz. "Tibet." In *Mythology: An Illustrated Encyclopae-dia*, edited by Richard Cavendish. New York: Rizzoli International, 1980. Also published as *An Illustrated Encyclopedia of Mythology*. New York: Crescent Books, 1984.

Deals not only with the myths associated with the special Buddhism of Tibet but also with the myths of a pre-Buddhist religion called Bon. Includes sections on legends about the founder of Bon, Buddhism in Tibet, Buddhist beliefs about the origins of the world, the myth of the monkey and the ogress, myths about the origin of kingship, various Buddhas and Bodhisattvas, the sixteen Arhats or "Worthy Ones," and the Tibetan epic about the hero Gesar. Map and illustrations of artwork related to the myths.

Soymié, M. "China: The Struggle for Power." In *Larousse World Mythol-ogy*, edited by Pierre Grimal. Translated by Patricia Beardsworth. New York: G. P. Putnam's Sons, 1963.

This overview of Chinese cosmogony and world view begins with a brief description of sources and a caution about the difficulty of summarizing the broad range of mythological materials. Describes several scholarly Chinese theories about creation, myths about the structure of the world, the sun, the moon, and stars, legends about culture heroes and the organization of the world, and tales about the organization of society around sovereigns and rebels. Includes para-phrases of the birth of P'an-ku from a hen's egg, the role of the serpent goddess Nü-kua in the creation of humankind, the story of a cata-strophic flood during the reign of the mythical sovereign Yao, and the legend of the Yellow Emperor Huang-Ti and his fight with the monster Ch'i-You. Accompanied by twenty-eight black-and-white illustrations from Chinese art.

Walls, Jan, and Yvonne Walls, eds. and trans. *Classical Chinese Myths*. Hong Kong: Joint Publishing, 1984.

A collection of forty representative myths from various ancient literary sources, such as *The Classic of Mountains and Seas* (*Shan Hai Jing*, first century B.C.). Each tale is accompanied by a full-page black-and-white illustration by Guo Huai-ren. Aetiological tales about the origin of plant and animal life, Taoist and Buddhist myths, and legends about historical figures are intentionally omitted in favor of a systematic arrangement of myths about creation, nature, gods, heroes, cosmic battles, and a great flood. An introductory essay provides background on sources, distinguishing characteristics of Chinese myths, and the use of these myths in contemporary Chinese culture, especially in art and in theater. Appendices offer an alphabetical list of origin myths and a list of themes used by these myths according to the Aarne-Thompson motif index.

Werner, Edward Theodore Chalmers. *A Dictionary of Chinese Mythology.* Shanghai: Kelly and Walsh, 1932. Reprint. New York: Julian Press, 1961.

A basic reference for Chinese mythology, arranged alphabetically. Entries include descriptions of gods and legendary humans and paraphrases of related myths. Descriptive titles of these myths are cross-listed in an index with entry headings indicating where they are discussed. All Chinese names are given in both Chinese and Roman characters. In his preface to the original edition, Werner addresses some features of Chinese deities and mythology. In an introduction to the reprint, Hyman Kublin describes Werner's contributions to the study of Chinese culture. Pronunciation guide, chronology of Chinese dynasties, and bibliography.

_____ . *Myths and Legends of China.* London: George G. Harrap, 1922. Reprinted as *Ancient Tales and Folklore of China.* London: Bracken, 1986.

This loose paraphrase and translation of Chinese myths from various sources, including *Li tai shen hsien t'ung chien*, begins with a sociological study of Chinese political, religious, and private institutions. Chapter 2 offers a historical overview of Chinese mythology and its sources. The remaining fourteen chapters organize the myths according to themes such as creation myths, the gods, myths about nature, myths about disease and exorcism, and animal legends. Thirty-two color illustrations by Chinese artists. Glossary and index with guide to the pronunciation of Chinese words.

Japanese Myths

Anesaki, Masaharu. *Japanese Mythology*. Vol. 8 in *The Mythology of All Races*, edited by John A. MacCulloch. Boston: Marshall Jones, 1928. A systematic overview of Japanese myths and folktales with concise summaries of the stories and discussion of their cultural and historical contexts. Tales are organized by type: cosmological myths, local legends, fairy tales, stories about demons and ghosts, romantic tales, hero legends, animal fables, stories about plants and flowers, and didactic, humorous, and satirical stories. In an introductory essay, the author explains the relationship between the mythology of the Japanese people and their geography, climate, and culture. Appendix on the use of folklore in folk songs. Thirty-eight plates, map, endnotes, bibliography, and index. Complete index in Volume 13.

Aston, W. G., trans. *Nihongi*. 1896. Reprint. London: Allen and Unwin, 1956. 2d ed. Rutland, Vt.: Charles E. Tuttle, 1972. This classic Japanese text of the eighth century A.D. includes myths about creation and the gods, an account of Jimmu Tenno's legendary conquest of Yamato-dake, also known as Yamato-takeru. Also contains a short history of Japan from earliest times to A.D. 697. This English translation includes extensive footnotes. An introductory essay contains information about the history of writing in Japan and the history of *Nihongi* itself. The first two books are the most mythological, with a tale of creation of the universe, a genealogy of the gods, and tales about divine deeds and travels. Some illustrations of Japanese artifacts and artwork. Index.

Bruhl, Odette. "Japanese Mythology." In *New Larousse Encyclopedia of Mythology*, edited by Felix Guirand et al. Translated by Richard Aldington and Delano Ames. New York: Hamlyn, 1968. This overview of Japanese myths and legends begins with a short survey of oral and written sources followed by sections on the great legends, the traditional deities, and Buddhism in Japan. Includes summaries of the Japanese world view, cosmogony, and myths of the divine spouses Izanagi and Izanami, the sun goddess Amaterasu, and Okuninushi, the god of medicine. Contains descriptions of the major deities as well as various nature deities and gods of human life. In her discussion of Japanese Buddhism, the author limits herself to descriptions of only the most important deities and religious concepts. One color and sixteen black-and-white reproductions of Japanese art.

Campbell, Joseph. "Japanese Mythology." In *The Masks of God: Oriental Mythology*, by Joseph Campbell. New York: Viking, 1962.

Places the mythology of Japan in the context of the island's historical and archaeological record, with special emphasis on the influence of China and on indigenous Japanese ideas. Tells a variety of myths, often with extensive quotation from original sources. Myths include legends about the earliest ages of the world, the emergence of Japan's divine rulers, the advent of Buddhism, the concept of *awaré*, or romantic love, the ritual suicide of heroes, and the Japanese tea ceremony.

Davis, F. Hadland. *Myths and Legends of Japan*. London: George G. Harrap, 1913. Reprint. New York: Dover Publications, 1992.

Retells the traditional tales of Japan in thirty-one chapters, beginning with the period of the gods, heroes, and warriors. Chapters on Buddha legends, legends in Japanese art, animal legends, and bird and insect legends. Other chapters are arranged around themes such as tea, bells, trees, mirrors, festivals, fans, and thunder. Especially useful are a glossary of Japanese deities, a genealogy of the age of the gods, a basic bibliography, an index of poetical quotations, and a combined general glossary and index. In a short introductory essay the author discusses some characteristics of Japanese folklore and indicates some of the original Japanese sources for the tales he uses. Accompanied by thirty-two full-page illustrations by Evelyn Paul.

Dorson, Richard M. *Folk Legends of Japan*. Rutland, Vt.: Charles E. Tuttle, 1962.

This collection of representative Japanese legends was made while Dorson was a Fulbright scholar in Japan in 1956-1957. Uses authentic material gathered by the Japanese Folklore Institute in Seijo-machi and translated by several Japanese scholars. The tales are organized according to following themes: shrines, monsters, spirits, metamorphoses, heroes, *chojas* or rich peasants, knaves, and places. Each tale is preceded by a brief introduction and list of sources. In an introductory essay, Dorson offers some background to legends in general and to the Japanese tradition in particular, briefly discusses the history of Japanese legends and the rise of a science of folklore in Japan in the twentieth century, and emphasizes local features of Japanese legends and their use of folk religion. Illustrations by Yoshie Noguchi. Bibliography and indexes of subjects and places.

_____. "Foreword." In *Folktales of Japan*, edited by Keigo Seki. London: Routledge & Kegan Paul, 1963.

In this short essay, a prominent American folklorist summarizes the history of Japanese folklore studies. Includes descriptions of major literary collections of Japanese tales as well as of twentieth-century efforts to record and classify tales throughout Japan. Particular emphasis on attempts to compare Japanese tales with types from other parts of the world, especially according to the Aarne-Thompson folktale index.

_____, ed. *Studies in Japanese Folklore*. Bloomington: Indiana University Press, 1963.

An American scholar collaborates with seventeen Japanese folklorists to produce a survey of Japanese folklore research. Contains scholarly studies of the traditional beliefs, customs, and stories of Japanese rice farmers, fishermen, ironworkers, worshipers, housewives, and youths. Each paper is followed by endnotes and occasionally by a bibliography. Three illustrations, notes on contributors, glossary of names and terms, and index.

Eliséev, Serge. "The Mythology of Japan." In *Asiatic Mythology*, edited by M. J. Hackin. Translated by F. M. Atkinson. New York: Thomas Y. Crowell, 1963.

Surveys Shinto and Buddhist mythologies in separate parts. A historical overview of Shintoism is followed by a description of major deities and myths, especially the celestial kingdom of Amaterasu, his conquest of earth, and various nature deities. The sections on Buddhism address the influence of this religion in modern Japan and several new sects such as Shingon and the Ryobu-Shinto. The last part is an extensive iconography of Japanese Buddhism offering descriptions of specific deities and concepts arranged alphabetically and often accompanied by illustration. Includes forty black-and-white figures and three color plates.

Harris, Omori. *Japanese Tales of All Ages*. Tokyo: Hokuseido Press, 1937.

This collection of thirty-five traditional tales starts with creation, includes a variety of heroic adventures, animal fables, and supernatural episodes, and ends with accounts about individuals who lived in the late nineteenth century.

Joly, Henri L. *Legend in Japanese Art*. London: The Bodley Head, 1908. Reprint. Rutland, Vt.: Charles E. Tuttle, 1967.

An early twentieth-century collector of Japanese art offers 1,120 descriptions of traditional characters and scenes found on various Japanese art objects, including prints, masks, and sword fittings. Arranged alphabetically. Some are based on myth, legends, and folklore, but others are based on citations for historical episodes and religious symbols. For each entry the anglicized word is followed by the Japanese characters, a brief identification, and, where appropriate, a summary of the story. Approximately 700 illustrations, sixteen in color. Introduction, bibliography, and index in Japanese characters.

Kawai, Hayao. *The Japanese Psyche: Major Motifs in the Fairy Tales of Japan*. Translated by Hayao Kawai and Sachiko Reece. Dallas, Tex.: Spring Publications, 1988.
Originally published in 1982 in Japan as *Mukashibanashi to Nihonjin no Kokoro* (fairy tales and psyche of the Japanese). Analyzes nine different Japanese folktale cycles. Retells a representative tale from each cycle in an appendix. Each of these tales represents a different folktale motif. For example "The Bush Warbler's Home" deals with a motif about a forbidden chamber. Compares different Japanese versions of these tales and shows how the same motif is treated in Western folktale equivalents. Illustrates these comparisons in seven tables. Discusses the cultural and psychological meaning of these tales and suggests that the female figures depicted in these folktales are an ideal representation of the Japanese ego. Eight figures, endnotes, and bibliography.

Kennedy, M. "The Origins of Japanese History." In *A Short History of Japan*, by M. Kennedy. New York: New American Library, 1964.
In this first chapter of a sweeping history of Japan from its origins through American occupation after World War II, Kenney shows how early Japanese history is a blending of historical events, local myths, and foreign legends. Includes a traditional chronology, beginning with the first emperor, Jimmu Tenno, in 660 B.C., and paraphrases of the Japanese story of creation and the story of the mirror. Summarizes the evolution of the Shinto religion and its pantheon. Explains the religious status of the first twelve emperors.

Littleton, C. Scott. "Japan." In *World Mythology*, edited by Roy Willis. New York: Henry Holt, 1993.
Retells the myth of the primal couple Izanagi and Izanami, the contest between the storm god Susano and his sister Amaterasu the sun, the consequences of Amaterasu's withdrawl into the cave, the Izumo cycle about Susano's earthly exile and about Okuninushi and the White Rabbit, and sagas about the legendary heroes Jimmu Tenno and Yamato-takeru in the *Kojiki*. Also contains sections on the gods Inari

and Hachiman and three Buddhist figures of mercy, Amida, Kannon-Bosatsu, and Jizo. Supplemented by a description of demons, of Yomi-tsu-kuni (the Japanese underworld), of the sacred weaving wall of Amaterasu, of Susano's conflict with the food goddess, and of Okuninushi's conflicts with his brothers. Accompanied by ten color illustrations of Japanese artifacts and sites. Map, time chart, and genealogy.

McAlpine, Helen, and William McAlpine. *Japanese Tales and Legends.* New York: Henry Z. Walck, 1959.
This collection of twenty-eight stories begins with myths about the birth of Japan and includes selections from a twelfth-century epic about the *Heike*, or noble warriors of ancient Japan, a variety of folktales, including the story of the Peach Boy, and a series of tales of Princess Kaguya. Illustrations by Joan Kiddell-Monroe, some in color. Glossary.

Mitford, A. B. (Lord Redesdale). *Tales from Old Japan.* London: Macmillan, 1903.
This collection of Japanese stories was first published in 1871 by a British diplomat stationed in Japan. True stories are accompanied by a variety of legends, fairy and animal tales, and stories about superstition, ghosts, and devils. Each story is preceded by an introductory essay. Illustrated by Japanese artists.

Ozaki, Yei Theodora. *The Japanese Fairy Book.* London: Constable, 1903. Reprint. Rutland, Vt.: Charles E. Tuttle, 1970.
In this anthology twenty-two traditional tales are retold for English-speaking children. These stories about anthropomorphic animals, ogres, princes, and other imaginative subjects include the tale of Peach Boy and Urashima Taro, the Fisherboy. With sixty-six illustrations by Kakuzo Fujiyama. Preface.

Piggott, Juliet. *Japanese Mythology.* 2d ed. New York: Peter Bedrick Books, 1983.
This general introduction to the myths of Japan begins with tales of origin concerning the country and the natural world. A historical survey of the island-nation is followed by an explanation of the beliefs and deities of Shintoism and Buddhism. Also contains chapters on myths about supernatural spirits, extraordinary mortals, talking animals, and other topics. Numerous photographs of religious shrines, sculpture, and paintings supplement the text. Bibliography and index.

Saunders, E. Dale. "Japanese Mythology." In *Mythologies of the Ancient World*, edited by Samuel Noah Kramer. Garden City, N.Y.: Doubleday (Anchor), 1961.

A short introduction to Japanese myths with sections on written sources, a summary of the central creation myth, myths about the provinces, and some general conclusions. Endnotes, bibliography, and glossary.

Saunders, E. Dale, and B. Frank. "Japan: Cults and Ceremonies." In *Larousse World Mythology*, edited by Pierre Grimal. Translated by Patricia Beardsworth. New York: G. P. Putnam's Sons, 1963.

This survey of Japanese mythology is divided into sections on Shintoism and Buddhism. Deals with the Shinto attitudes toward fertility, purification, and the role of the gods. Also contains descriptions of two ancient Shinto texts, *Kojiki*, or "Records of Ancient Matters," and *Nihongi*, or "Chronicles of Japan." Summaries of tales such as the creation myth of the gods Izanagi and Izanami, the adventure of Susano and the eight-headed serpent, stories about the god Okuninushi in the Izumo cycle, and legends about the popular hero Yamato-dake. The Buddhist section contains an overview of the Buddhist world view and of the history of Buddhism in Japan and detailed descriptions of the principal deities, including the buddhas Shaka-nyorai and Dainichi-nyorai, Bodhisattvas such as Miroku-bosatsu and Kannon-bosatsu, the *Godaimyoo*, or Five Great Kings of Science in Tantrism, and deities such as Daikoku-ten, the god of happiness. Accompanied by thirty-five illustrations, three in color.

Seki, Keigo, ed. *Folktales of Japan*. Translated by Robert K. Adams. London: Routledge & Kegan Paul, 1963.

A Japanese scholar of folklore selected these tales from a larger collection of Japanese tales not available in English. Includes sixty-three tales arranged in the following categories: animal tales, ogres, supernatural spouses, kindness rewarded and evil punished, good fortune, and cleverness and stupidity. Each tale is introduced with editorial comments, especially offering information on sources and placing the tale in the Aarne-Thompson list of folktale motifs. Glossary, bibliography, index of motifs and tale types, and general index. Foreword on the history of Japanese folklore studies by Richard M. Dorson. Translator's note. Short introduction by the editor on the classification of Japanese folktales.

Smith, Richard Gordon. *Ancient Tales and Folklore of Japan*. London: A. & C. Black, 1908.

These fifty-seven tales gathered mostly from anonymous Japanese peasants and fishermen offer a blend of the ordinary and the extraordinary. Great legendary figures or ordinary humans encounter ghosts, spirits, and miracles. Trees, ponds, mountains, and temples are associated with unusual or memorable occurrences. Some are legends dating back to the early imperial period and others date from the nineteenth century. Accompanied by sixty-two full-page color illustrations by Mo-No-Yuki. Many stories include introductory or concluding commentary by the author. Occasional footnotes.

Takiguchi, Susumu. "Japan." In *Mythology: An Illustrated Encyclopaedia*, edited by Richard Cavendish. New York: Rizzoli International, 1980. Also published as *An Illustrated Encyclopedia of Mythology*. New York: Crescent Books, 1984.

This general overview of Japanese mythology begins with the link between politics and mythology in twentieth-century Japan and a summary of the geographic and literary sources of the myths. Summarizes the myths about the creation of land by the brother-sister deities Izanagi and Izanami, Izanagi's search for his dead wife/sister in the underworld, Susano the storm god's ascend to heaven to visit his sister Amaterasu, the sun goddess, Susano's encounter with the eight-tailed dragon, the adventures of his descendant Okuninushi, and the Tensonkorin or the story of Ninigi, grandson of Amaterasu. Ninigi, the ancestor the Japanese imperial family, becomes ruler of the earth and justifies the authority of the emperor. Map, glossaries of the earliest deities and of Japanese Buddhist deities, family tree of the first emperor, and illustrations of artwork related to the myths.

Taylor, Archer. "The Study of the Cinderella Cycle." In *Cinderella. A Folklore Casebook*, edited by Alan Dundes. New York: Garland Press, 1982.

A prominent American comparative folklorist considers Japanese versions of Cinderella as part of a review of the scholarly history of the Cinderella tale. Retells or summarizes three Japanese versions and makes reference to many others. This paper was first read at a folklore conference in Bucharest in 1969 but never published by the author. Essay is preceded by useful background information and commentary by Dundes. Endnotes.

Wheeler, Post. *The Sacred Scriptures of the Japanese*. New York: Henry Schuman, 1952.

A translation of the basic texts of the sacred Shinto myths, especially the *Kojiki* and the *Nihongi*. Scattered fragments are gathered from various sources to create a continuous narrative alternating in setting from sky to earth to underworld. Begins with the creation of the cosmos followed by tales about the first earthly emperor and other early, legendary rulers of Japan. These myths are the basis of belief in a deified emperor which dominated Japanese political life until the end of World War II. The translation is preceded by an introductory essay containing a detailed discussion of ancient sources and explanations about the text, especially problems about pronunciation, alternate names, and transcriptions of names from Japanese into English characters. Most names are translated so that Izanami becomes She-Who-Invites. Includes a synopsis and outline of the narrative. The translation is followed by an analysis concentrating on myth parallels and possible sources in primeval cults such as those of the sun, the sword, and the phallus. Searches for elements of the narrative which may be western (i.e., Korean, Chinese, and Indian), southern (Polynesian), or local. List of personages and endnotes.

—————. *Tales from the Japanese Storytellers*, edited by Harold G. Henderson. New York: Japan Society, 1964.

These twenty-four tales were selected from Wheeler's ten-volume unpublished compilation and translation of myths and historical legends called the *H-Dan-Z* (treasury of tales). The original Japanese tales were told by *hanashika*, or "public storytellers." While some have literary sources, these animal fables, legends about the sage Oöka (1677-1751), and adventure stories have been in the repertoire of Japanese storytellers for generations. Short introductory essay by the editor. Glossary and note on chronology and page decorations, which are based upon Japanese family crests.

Yanagita, Kunio. *Japanese Folk Tales*. Translated by Fanny Hagin Mayer. Rev. ed. Tokyo: Tokyo News Service, 1966.

The tales in this book come from a collection first published in Japanese in 1930 by the founder of folklore studies in Japan. Yanagita's criteria for selection included geographic diversity and suitability for children. Tales include aetiologies, animal fables, stories about ghosts and other supernatural phenomena, folk wisdom, and trickster tales. Hagin's first English translation included 108 tales from Yanagita's collection. In this edition forty-five tales considered legends or popular fiction were replaced by forty-three stories which seemed to be more genuine folktales. In an introductory essay, the translator offers a survey of the anthologies of Japanese folktales used by Yanagita to create his anthology. Translations of Yanagita's original introduction and a postscript to the Japanese edition appear at the end of the book and offer background about the Japanese folktale tradition and a description of the goals of the original collection. Geographic and published sources are listed at the end of each tale. More detailed bibliographic information appears in a reference index. Illustrations by Kei Wakana. Occasional translator's footnotes, geographic index, and map.

Southeast Asian Myths

Demetrio, Francisco. "The Flood Motif and the Symbolism of Rebirth in Filipino Mythology." An abridgment of "Creation myths Among the Early Filipinos." *Asian Folklore Studies* 27 (1968). In *The Flood Myth*, edited by Alan Dundes. Berkeley: University of California Press, 1988. Synopsizes several versions of a flood myth from Ifugaos and other peoples of the Philippines and suggests that each represents the theme of destruction and rebirth. An earlier race of humans is destroyed and a new race is born from the survivors. Footnotes.

Fansler, Dean S. *Filipino Popular Tales.* Vol. 12 in *Memoirs of the American Folk-Lore Society.* New York: American Folk-Lore Society, 1921. Reprint. Hatboro, Pa.: Folklore Associates, 1965.
These eighty-two stories were recorded by the author in English in the Philippines between 1908 and 1914. Arranged in three thematic groups: hero tales and drolls, fables and animal stories, and aetiologies about animals and the natural world. Each tale is followed by explanatory endnotes with detailed comparative studies. Some tales are recorded in more than one variant. An additional fifty-eight tales are told in shorter forms in the endnotes. Short preface by Fansler on the tales and their folk tradition. The reprint includes a foreword by Fred Eggan with a biography of Fansler and a short essay by Fansler on Philippine folk literature. Bibliography and index.

Hart, Donn V., and Harriett C. Hart. "Maka-andog." In *The Anthropologist Looks at Myth*, edited by Melville Jacobs and John Greenway. Austin: University of Texas Press, 1966.

A synthesis of thirty-one tales recorded among Bisayan Christian Filipinos. These tales, which contain elements of an earlier Samaran tradition, deal with a giant named Maka-andog and his family. A detailed story of the giant's death is quoted in full and the rest are summarized. Tales are organized in thematic groups including the giant's kinship relationships, tremendous strength, special powers, and accomplishments. Includes detailed information on informants, methods of collection, and enthnographic context. Map, genealogical chart, and endnotes.

Lindell, Kristina, Jan-Ojvind Swahn, and Damrong Tayanin. "The Flood: Three Northern Kammu Versions of the Story of Creation." *Acta Orientalia* 37 (1976). Reprinted in *The Flood Myth*, edited by Alan Dundes. Berkeley: University of California Press, 1988.
Includes translations of three oral versions of a flood story from Thailand. In these tales the world is repopulated by a marriage between a brother and sister who are the only survivors. The three versions are briefly compared, especially via a list of folktale motifs used in each version. Footnotes.

Schultz, George F. *Vietnamese Legends*. Rutland, Vt.: Charles E. Tuttle, 1965.
Thirty-two traditional Vietnamese tales translated into English prose. Aetiologies include how the tiger got his stripes and how an unfaithful metamorphosed into the first mosquito. Animal fables, adventure stories, and tales of the supernatural are accompanied by stories of adventure, friendship, and filial devotion. Short introductory essay.

Scott, Sir James George. *Indo-Chinese Mythology*. Vol. 12 in *The Mythology of All Races*, edited by Louis Herbert Gray. Boston: Marshall Jones, 1918.
An examination of the mythologies of Burma, Thailand, Vietnam, and Cambodia. In Chapter 1, Scott offers an introduction to the peoples and religions of the area. In Chapters 2-4, he examines a variety of myths and legends, discusses the major religious festivals of these peoples, and describes thirty-seven Burmese deities known as Nats. Twenty-one plates and twelve figures accompany the text. Short note on the transcription and pronunciation of South Asian words. Endnotes and bibliography. Complete index in Volume 13.

Skeat, Walter William. *Malay Magic*. New York: Macmillan, 1900. Reprint. New York: Barnes & Noble, 1966.

Uses extensive quotations from original Malay sources in translation
to survey the folklore, religious beliefs, and magic of the people of the
Malay peninsula, especially the state of Selangor. Most of the mythical
material appears in chapters on creation and natural phenomena, the
origin of humans and their place in the universe, the supernatural
world, and the Malay pantheon. Other chapters deal with magical rites
to control the four elements and rites about human life. The original
Malay texts are provided in an appendix. Some comments on the
author's goals in a preface by Charles Otto Blagden. Also contains a
note on the word *kramat*, or "sacred." Seven figures and twenty-eight
plates. Bibliography and index.

Spencer, Robert F. "Ethical Expression in a Burmese Jātaka." In *The
Anthropologist Looks at Myth*, edited by Melville Jacobs and John
Greenway. Austin: University of Texas Press, 1966.
An abridged version and an interpretation of "Thuwannashan, the
Suvannasama Jātaka," Burmese Jātaka #543, one of the tales of the
previous lives of Buddha. Also contains quotations from Jātaka #142,
"The jackal." Includes a description of Burmese culture and society,
an analysis of the tale, a study of the structure and style of the Jātaka
and a note on the Jātaka as folk literature. Shows how this tale
celebrating filial piety and the other Jātaka play an important role of
ethical instruction in Burmese society. Endnotes.

Tate, Carole. *The Tale of the Spiteful Spirits*. New York: Peter Bedrick
Books, 1991.
A Kampuchean (Cambodian) folktale about the social obligation of
passing on stories is retold for children. In this tale a young man refuses
to retell stories he has heard and is punished on his wedding day by the
spirits of the stories. Illustrated with color drawings by the author.

Chapter 6
EUROPE

The mythologies and folklore of Europe include not only the traditions of the ancient Greeks, Romans, Celts, and Norse, but also significant medieval and modern material. For the most part, the sections in this chapter are geographic. The section "Celtic Myths" deals especially with the mythologies of the Celts of ancient Britain but also include some reference to continental Celts, especially in France. "Central and Eastern European Myths" focuses, in particular, on the traditions of the Slavic and Finno-Ugric peoples. The section on Greco-Roman mythology contains many more references to Greek mythology than Roman mythology, since most Roman myths are derived from the Greek tradition. The distinctive Roman mythological material describes the special deities and cults of the Roman religion as well as the founding of the city of Rome and the legends surrounding the Roman monarchy. The material for the section on Norse myths is mostly based on the medieval poetic and prose *Eddas*, which retell early Germanic legends about the gods and the beginnings of the world. The Norse section also includes references to the Anglo-Saxon epic *Beowulf*. The last section, on medieval and modern European myths, contains a selective but representative collection of citations on continental medieval myths, Christian legends, Icelandic sagas, and modern European folktales and fairy tales, especially those springing from the traditions of Jacob and Wilhelm Grimm.

Celtic Myths

Barber, Richard. *King Arthur in Legend and History*. Totowa, N.J.: Boydell & Brewer, 1974. Rev. ed. *King Arthur: Hero and Legend*. New York: Dorset Press, 1990.

This introduction to the quest for the historical Arthur and the growth of his legend during the medieval period is written for the general reader. In Chapter 1 Barber presents some of the difficulties involved in separating fictional and historical information about Arthur. In Chapter 2 he deals with the image of Arthur as emperor and epic hero, especially as portrayed by Geoffrey of Monmouth. The evolution of tales about members of Arthur's court, especially in Welsh and French romances, is considered in Chapter 3. Later chapters deal with the legend in Germany, in English poetry of 1250 to 1500, and in Sir Thomas Malory's fifteenth-century *Le Morte d'Arthur*; with popular traditions about Arthur; with the nineteenth-century fascination with Arthur; and with twentieth-century revisions of the tale. Fifty-two black-and-white and twenty-eight color illustrations, including a map, photographs of medieval manuscripts, and medieval and modern artistic representations of Arthurian scenes. Marginal notes and index.

Bulfinch, Thomas. *The Age of Chivalry*. Boston: Lothrop, Lee, and Shephard. 1858. Reprint. New York: New American Library, 1962.
This book has served for more than a century as an introduction to the legends and tales of medieval Britain. The mythical history of England in Part 1 is derived especially from Sir Thomas Malory's *Le Morte d'Arthur*. An introductory chapter on topics such as the training of a knight, tournaments, and literary sources is followed by tales of King Arthur and knights of the round table. Part 2 tells tales of early Wales from the *Mabinogion*. Also includes "Knights of English History," from the 1884 edition of Bulfinch by Edward Everett Hale, with legends of King Richard the Lion-Heart, Robin Hood, Chevy Chase, the Battle of Otterbourne, and Edward the Black Prince. This edition includes a foreword by Palmer Bovie with a biography of Bulfinch and an analysis and appreciation of his work. Index.

Campbell, Joseph. "Where There Was No Path: Arthurian Legends and the Western Way." In *Transformations of Myth Through Time*, by Joseph Campbell. New York: Harper & Row, 1990.
Discusses the intellectual and historical background of the Arthurian romances. The heroic tradition of the Germanic Celts combined with a Christian tradition springing from the Middle East to create the concepts of chivalry and courtly love upon which the romances are based. Campbell describes the world of Celtic Britain, the contributions of the Romans in Britain, and the changes brought by Christianity. Eight illustrations from ancient sites, art, and manuscripts.

Corcoran, John X. W. P. "Celtic Mythology." In *New Larousse Encyclopedia of Mythology*, edited by Felix Guirand et al. Translated by Richard Aldington and Delano Ames. New York: Hamlyn, 1968.
This overview of Celtic mythology offers sections on the mythological cycle in Ireland, the deities of Celtic mythology, the Celtic hero figure, the otherworld, Greco-Roman views of Celtic religion, and archaeological evidence. Includes one color and twenty-nine black-and-white illustrations of ancient representations of Celtic deities.

Cross, Tom Pete, and Clark Harris Slover, eds. *Ancient Irish Tales*. New York: Henry Holt, 1936.

Collects translations of more than forty traditional Irish tales from a variety of books and journals. Includes several tales of the Tuatha Dé Danaan, about the divine settlers of Ireland from northern Europe, heroic sagas about eastern Ulster, tales about Finn and his son Ossian, legends about the traditional kings of Ireland, and the story of the fantastic voyage of Bran, son of Febal. Translations combine prose and verse. Each group of tales is preceded by a brief introduction by the editors. Maps, genealogical table, glossary, and two illustrations.

Crossley-Holland, Kevin, trans. *Beowulf.* New York: Farrar, Straus & Giroux, 1968.
A verse translation of the Old English epic about the Danish hero's adventures with the monster Grendel and with a dragon. In an introductory essay, Bruce Mitchell offers a summary of the poem and discusses the authorship, aims, and meaning of the poem. Map, translator's note, glossary, genealogical tables, metrical analysis, and bibliography.

_____, trans. "Beowulf Fights the Dragon." In *Beowulf.* New York: Farrar, Straus & Giroux, 1968. Reprinted in *The Faber Book of Northern Legends*, edited by Kevin Crossley-Holland. London: Faber and Faber, 1977. Also reprinted in *Northern Lights: Legends, Sagas and Folk-Tales*, edited by Kevin Crossley-Holland. London: Faber and Faber, 1987.
This excerpt from a modern translation of the Old English epic describes the elderly Beowulf's decision to fight a dragon which has been attacking his people. Beowulf kills the dragon but is himself mortally wounded. The passage concludes with the king's funeral.

de Blâacam, Aodh. "Olden Ireland." In *A First Book of Irish Literature*, by Aodh de Blâacam. Dublin: Educational Company of Ireland, 1934. Reprint. Port Washington, N.Y.: Kennikat Press, 1970.
This survey of Irish literature from its beginnings in the days of the Druids to the writers of the Gaelic Renaissance in the early twentieth century includes several chapters dealing with mythological materials. Chapter 3 contains brief descriptions of the *Táin Bó Cuailgne* (the book of the dun cow) and other prose epics about the Ulster heroes in the *Craobh Ruadh* or the Red Branch cycle. In Chapter 4, de Blâacam describes the *Urscéalta*, a collection of historical and mythological tales; these concern such topics as a battle with primeval races in *The Battle of Moytura*, a fantastic voyage to a utopia in *Imramha*, and descriptions of wondrous visions experienced by saints. In Chapter 7,

the author deals with the Fenian cycle of legends about the heroes Finn and the band of warriors known as Fianna. Also contains scattered references to legendary lives of saints, especially St. Patrick.

Dillon, Myles. *Early Irish Literature*. Chicago: University of Chicago Press, 1948.
A survey of the Celtic literature and heroic sagas of early Ireland. A variety of mythological material is covered in separate chapters on the Ulster cycle, the Fenian cycle, the mythological cycle, the historical cycle, the *Echtrae* or tales of adventure in the Promised Land, fantastic voyages, and heavenly visions. In the final chapter, Dillon describes some general features of Irish poetry. Throughout the book works of myth and legend such as the *Táin*, the *Acallam Na Senórech* or "The Colloquy of the Old Men," the *Cath Maige Tured* or *The Battle of Moytura*, the adventure of Conle, and the vision of Adamnán are described and summarized individually. Extensive passages in translation from this material are occasionally supplemented by quotations of the original text with parallel English translation. Footnotes and index of titles.

Elwes, Alfred, trans. "Jaufry the Knight and the Fair Brunissende." In *The Pendragon Chronicles: Heroic Fantasy from the Time of King Arthur*, edited by Mike Ashley. New York: Peter Bedrick Books, 1990.
Elwes' translation of a thirteenth-century tale by an unknown Provençal troubaudour first appeared in 1856. This tale tells the adventures of Jaufry, one of Arthur's earliest knights. Jaufry defeats several formidable opponents, including knights and giants, and wins the hand of Brunissende in marriage.

Evans, Emrys. "The Celts." In *Mythology: An Illustrated Encyclopaedia*, edited by Richard Cavendish. New York: Rizzoli International, 1980. Also published as *An Illustrated Encyclopedia of Mythology*. New York: Crescent Books, 1984.
This overview of the mythology of the Celtic peoples of Western Europe contains sections on Celtic religion and on Irish and Welsh saga. Summaries of tales about the Irish mythical warrior class called Tuatha Dé Danaan, the coming of their champion Lug Samildanach, and the sad tale of the Welsh princess Branwen. Map, glossaries of the gods of Gaul, Ireland, and Wales, and illustrations of artwork related to the myths.

Ford, Patrick K., trans. *The Mabinogi and Other Medieval Welsh Tales*. Berkeley: University of California Press, 1977.

This English prose version of the Welsh national epic is less archaic in style than the 1974 translation by Jones and Jones and includes the first English translation of some medieval tales in one hundred years. In addition to the tales of the four branches of the *Mabinogion* represented by Pwyll, Branwen, Manawydan, and Math, Ford translates the traditional tale of Llud and Llefelys, Culhwch's quest for Olwen, the magical story of Gwion Bach, and the tale of Taliesin. An appendix contains a translation of the *Cad Goddeu*, a poem connected with the tale of Taliesin. Each tale is preceded by introductory remarks by the translator. In a preface and introductory essay, Ford gives detailed background and analysis of these tales. Map, glossary, pronunciation guide, bibliography, and index.

Frankland, Edward. "Medraut and Gwenhwyvar." In *An Arthurian Reader*, edited by John Matthews. Wellingborough: Aquarian Press, 1988.

The second episode in a historical novel tracing the history of England from Roman times to the twentieth century. Deals with Arthur's wife Gwenhwyvar (Guinevere) and his nephew, the prophetic minstrel Medraut. Preceded by a short introduction by the editor.

Gantz, Jeffrey, trans. *Early Irish Myths and Sagas*. New York: Dorset Press, 1981.

Thirteen selections from the traditional myths and legends of ancient Ireland are here translated in prose for the general reader. Gantz has made use of all the major ancient sources in the mythological, the Ulster, the Kings, and the Finn cycles, as he tells events such as Midir's wooing of Étain, incidents in the life of the hero Cú Chulainn, the tale of Macc Da Thó's pig, and the comic feast of the mischievous Bricriu. Each selection is preceded by some background and commentary by the translator. In a general introduction, Gantz discusses the history of the Celts and of the ancient Irish, Irish storytelling, manuscript sources for the tales, some characteristics of Irish mythology, and techniques of translation. Map, bibliography, list of Irish geographical names, pronunciation guide, endnotes, and index.

Goodrich, Norma Lorre. *King Arthur*. New York: Harper & Row, 1986.

Analyzes the literary and archaeological evidence from the medieval period in order to separate the legendary from the historical king of Britain. Three chapters in an introductory section outline the problem, describe the world in which Arthur lived, and discuss the historical evidence. In Part 1 Goodrich considers especially the twelfth-century history of Geoffrey of Monmouth and reviews the life of Arthur through his coronation. In Part 2 she studies the story of Queen Guinevere and Lancelot told in several French medieval romances. Part 3 deals with tales of the Holy Grail and Part 4 with the death of Arthur. Particularly valuable is the material in the appendices: a list of ancient Arthurian sources, a list of major Arthurian texts of the High Middle Ages, a list of similar texts from the Late English Middle Ages, a note on Geoffrey of Monmouth, a list of medieval chronicles and chroniclers, biographies of several antecedents and contemporaries of Arthur, a discussion of the stone building known as Arthur's Oven in Scotland, an excerpt in Latin and English translation from the *Chronicle* of Helinand de Froidmont, a chronological chart, and a genealogy. Eight maps, three figures, bibliography, and index.

Green, Miranda J. *Celtic Myths*. Austin: University of Texas Press, 1993.
This overview of the myths and legends of Ireland and Wales intended for the general reader is part of The Legendary Past Series. Introductory chapter on the literary and archaeological sources for these myths. Chapter 2 offers descriptions of individual deities among the *Tuatha Dé Danaan*, the divine race inhabiting Ireland before the Celts, their battle for the island, the Irish concept of sacred kingship, and the cycle of tales centering around the superhuman hero Finn. In Chapter 3 Green deals with legends in the Ulster cycle, especially from the *Táin*, with the heroes Cú Chulainn, Medb, and Conchobar, and with the battle furies. Chapter 4 contains summaries of the major branches of Welsh myth in the *Mabinogion*, especially with Pwyll's encounter with Arawn, lord of the Welsh otherworld, the tale of Bendigeidfran and his sister Branwen, the enchantment of Dyfed, the story of Math, lord of Gwynedd. Also contains a summary of the *Tale of Culhwch and Olwen*. Chapter 5 considers the theme of love and jealousy in Celtic myth and describes pairs of lovers such as Midir and Étain, Oenghus and Caer, Deirdre and Naoise. Features of Celtic sky and sun myths are surveyed in Chapter 6 and supernatural beings and cults of fertility, land, and water in Chapter 7. The role of animals in Celtic mythology and ritual is discussed in Chapter 8, Druids, sacrifice, and ritual in Chapter 9, and Celtic views about death in Chapter 10. Illustrations of Celtic artifacts appear on almost every page. Map, bibliography and index.

_____. *The Gods of the Celts*. Totowa, N.J.: Barnes and Noble Books, 1986.
While the focus of this introduction to Celtic religion is on cult, ritual, and religious symbolism, mythological topics include descriptions of

the gods, their attributes, and powers. Introductory chapter on Celtic religion, surviving evidence, and general aspects. Individual chapters on cults of sun and sky; mother goddesses; war, death, and the underworld; water gods and healers; and animals and animism. In the prologue the author offers some historical background to the Celts and their civilization. Includes 103 illustrations, mostly of ancient Celtic artifacts. Endnotes, bibliography, and index.

Greene, David H., ed. "Myth, Saga, and Romance." In *An Anthology of Irish Literature*, edited by David H. Greene. New York: Modern Library, 1954.
This chapter in a survey of Irish literature offers twelve translations of medieval Gaelic tales, especially from the Ulster and Fenian cycles. Includes narratives about the dream of Angus Og, a master of love, the adventures of Cú Chulainn and of Finn, and the tragic destruction of Deirdre. Some material is presented in prose and some in verse. Attached are three translated excerpts from the works of the eighteenth-century Gaelic poet Michael Comyn, who obtained the material for his poems from the same medieval sources. Footnotes.

Grohskoph, Bernice. "Sutton Hoo and the Age of Beowulf." In *The Treasure of Sutton Hoo*, by Bernice Grohskoph. New York: Atheneum, 1970.
The rich treasure found in the burial of a seventh-century Anglo-Saxon king is a physical remnant of the heroic, mythological world described in the eighth-century poem *Beowulf*. In this chapter from a general documentary study of the dig, the author discusses the relationship between archaeological find and poem, and shows how this archaeological evidence collaborates the description of such wealth in the poem.

Guest, Lady Charlotte, trans. "The Dream of Rhonabwy." In *An Arthurian Reader*, edited by John Matthews. Wellingborough: Aquarian Press, 1988.
A nineteenth-century English translation of a thirteenth-century Welsh story called *Breuddwyd Rhonabwy*. A medieval Welsh prince named Rhonabwy dreams of King Arthur less as the mythical ruler of Camelot than as an heroic warrior who ruled in Britain after the Romans left. Rhonabwy's dream places Arthur in a transcendental and magical world where Arthur and his men refight the battle of Badon. Preceded by a short introduction by the editor.

Jones, Gwyn. *Welsh Legends and Folk-Tales.* Oxford: Oxford University Press, 1955.
Tales of the Welsh from the *Mabinogion* and from other traditional sources are retold for young readers. In Part 1 are stories about Pwyll and his son Pryderi, Branwen, Manawydan, and Lleu from the four branches of the *Mabinogion.* Part 2 contains Arthurian romances about Culhwch's search for Olwen, Tristan and Iseult, Rhitta the Giant, and Rhonabwy's dream. Part 3 offers a miscellaneous collection of ten tales about heaven, the sea, dreams, fairies, and animals. With illustrations, some in color, by Joan Kiddell-Monroe. Map, genealogical tree, and pronuncation guide.

Jones, Gwyn, and Thomas Jones. "The Lady of the Fountain." In *The Mabinogion.* Translated by Gwyn Jones and Thomas Jones. London: J. M. Dent, 1974. Reprinted in *The Pendragon Chronicles: Heroic Fantasy from the Time of King Arthur,* edited by Mike Ashley. New York: Peter Bedrick Books, 1990.
In this story from a medieval collection of Welsh myths, Sir Owain, a knight of King Arthur, disappears and becomes entangled with Lynette, the Lady of the Fountain, and her mistress, the Countess of the Fountain. Owain guards this fountain against assault and eventually marries the countess.

Jones, Gwyn, and Thomas Jones, trans. *The Mabinogion.* Rev. ed. London: J. M. Dent, 1974.
This translation of the medieval Welsh epic known as *Mabinogion* includes eleven separate tales. The four branches or tales of the Mabinogi proper deal with the legendary figures Pywll of Dyfed, Branwen, the daughter of Llyr, her brother Manawydan, and Math, the son of Mathonwy. These are followed by four independent tales about the dreams of the Roman emperor Macsen Wledig and Rhonabwy, the brothers Llud and Llefelys, and the lovers Culwhch and Olwen, the oldest Arthurian tale in Welsh. At the end of the collection are three Norman-French Arthurian legends about the lady of the fountain, Peredur, and Gereint, son of Erbin. In an essay introducing the first edition, the translators offer detailed background and analysis of the eleven tales. In an introduction to the revised edition, Gwyn Jones describes some important advances in early Welsh studies since the first edition appeared. Bibliography and textual endnotes.

Kinsella, Thomas, trans. *The Tain.* New York: Oxford University Press, 1970.

An English translation of the *Táin Bó Cuailnge*, an eighth-century A.D. prose epic in the Ulster cycle of Irish legend. The plot of this epic is a cattle raid in Ulster by the armies of Ailill and Medb, the king and queen of Connacht. Preceding this tale are translations of eight independent *remscéla*, or "pre-tales," describing events leading up to this raid. In a translator's note and introductory essay, Kinsella provides background to the epic and to this translation. Illustrated with brush drawings by Louis Le Brocquy. Maps, bibliography, pronunciation guide, and explanatory endnotes.

MacCana, Proinsias. *Celtic Mythology*. Rev. ed. New York: Peter Bedrick Books, 1985.
This lavishly illustrated overview of the myths of the ancient Celts is intended for the general reader. In an introductory essay, the author provides a history of the people and discusses sources for their mythology. This introduction is followed by seven thematic chapters in which MacCana compares the gods of the Celtic Gauls of France with their equivalents in Britain, retells and interprets tales of early invasion of Britain, especially the divine race called Tuatha Dé Danaan, surveys the ancient gods and goddesses of Britain, highlights heroic tales from the Ulster and Fenian cycles and the Arthurian legends, and considers the Celtic concepts of sacred kingship and the otherworld. In the last chapter MacCana discusses the transition to Christianity in Britain. Nearly every page includes photographs of Celtic artifacts and sites. Bibliography and index.

MacCulloch, John Arnott. *Celtic Mythology*. Vol. 3 in *The Mythology of All Races*, edited by Louis Herbert Gray. Boston: Marshall Jones, 1918.
A survey of the myths associated especially with the Celtic peoples of the British Isles (the Irish, the Welsh, the Scots, and the ancient Britons). Except for a chapter on the myths of the British Celts, the organization is thematic. Includes chapters on the strife of the gods, the mythic powers, loves and anger of the gods, divine assistance of mortals, myths of origins, mythical animals, and the links between paganism and Christianity. Three Celtic heroes receive special attention: Cú Chulainn and Finn of Ireland and Arthur in Britain. In an introduction, the author outlines references to Celtic myths and culture by Classical authors and describes the major sources for Celtic myths. Twenty-six plates illustrating sites, coins, and other artifacts related to the myths. Endnotes and bibliography. Complete index in Volume 13.

MacInnes, John. "The Celtic World." In *World Mythology*, edited by Roy Willis. New York: Henry Holt, 1993.

This overview of the mythology of the ancient Celts includes sections on the Celtic pantheon, the first and second battles of Magh Tuiredh in the Irish mythological cycle, tales of the Ulster hero Cú Chulainn, the myths of Finn and his son Oisin, goddesses, voyages to the otherworld, the Welsh *Mabinogion*, and legends of King Arthur. Accompanied by subsidiary sections on the antlered god Cernunnos, Daghda's cauldron, the death of Cú Chulainn, Finn's Salmon of Knowledge, links between the goddess Bridhid and the Christian Saint Bride of Kildare, and Merlin the magician. Fourteen color illustrations of Celtic artifacts and sites. Map, time chart, and pronunciation guide.

Matthews, Caitlín, and John Matthews. *Guide to British and Irish Mythology*. Wellingborough: Aquarian Press, 1988.

This alphabetically arranged list of names and peoples in the myths and legends of the ancient Britons is intended for the general reader. Each entry includes a brief description and a code-letter associating the name with one of the following geographic and thematic categories: Arthurian; birds, beasts, and fish; Celtic; Greek; Irish; legendary; Norse; Roman and Romano-British; Scottish; saints; Welsh; and heroic figures of history. An introductory essay on the scope of this book is accompanied by descriptions of these categories and a user's key. Black-and-white illustrations by Chesca Potter. Bibliography.

Matthews, John, ed. *An Arthurian Reader*. Wellingborough: Aquarian Press, 1988.

An anthology of narratives and scholarship dealing with the Arthurian legends. Part 1, entitled "The Matter of Britain," deals with the story of Merlin and the adventures of King Arthur. Readings about the Holy Grail are found in Part 2. In Part 3 are some imaginative reworkings of Arthurian tales. Includes excerpts from medieval texts such as the poem "Sir Gawain and the Green Knight," essays by early twentieth-century authors such as A. E. Waite and Clemence Houseman, pieces on Arthurian geography, links between the Holy Grail and the Greek rites of Adonis, and retellings of stories such as that of Guinevere and Lancelot. Each selection is preceded by a brief introductory note. Endnotes follow each chapter. Bibliography and seventeen illustrations from the original texts.

Morgan, Edwin, trans. *Beowulf*. Berkeley: University of California Press, 1952.

This verse translation strives to re-create the Anglo-Saxon epic in accented but unrhymed modern verse which is free from the archaisms common in earlier translations of the epic. In an introductory essay, the author offers a critical review of fifteen earlier English translations of the epic, outlines his own goals as a translator, and notes some of the artistic features of the epic. Original line references in margins. Glossary of proper names.

Murphy, Gerald. *Sage and Myth in Ancient Ireland.* Dublin: Colm O Lochlainn, 1955.
A short overview of the ancient storytelling traditions of Ireland with sections on the oral art of Gaelic bards, mythological tales about the early gods of Ireland, heroic tales in the Ulster cycle, and tales about early kings such as Mac Con and Cormac. Although he does quote extensively from this mythological material in English translation, Murphy concentrates on discussing characteristics of the myths rather than summarizing them. Bibliography and index.

O'Faolain, Eileen. *Irish Sagas and Folk-Tales.* Oxford: Oxford University Press, 1954.
Some of the traditional tales of Ireland are retold for young readers. In Part 1 are three stories about the primeval period when a divine race called Tuatha Dé Danaan inhabited Ireland. These tales tell of the search for the children of Turenn, the love of Midir and Étain, and the children of Lir. Part 2 deals with tales from the Ulster cycle, especially tales about Cú Chulainn and the cattle raid of Cooley. In Part 3 are six episodes from the mythological cycle about Finn and his son Oisin. Part 4 contains seven traditional folktales about the Black Thief, princesses, giants, and enchantment. With illustrations, some in color, by Joan Kiddell-Monroe. Glossary.

O'Rahilly, Thomas F. *Early Irish History and Mythology.* Dublin: Dublin Institute for Advanced Studies, 1946.
This scholarly reconstruction of the history of pre-Christian Ireland combines examination of Celtic myths about the settlement of the island with linguistic analysis of Celtic words, archaeological evidence, and references to Ireland by Greek and Roman authors. Chapter 1 deals with the account of Ireland in the *Geography* of the second-century A.D. Greek author Ptolemy, Chapter 2 with Fir Bolg, the earliest invaders of Ireland, and Chapter 3 with the Ga Bulga or the "lightning-spear." O'Rahilly moves to the Bolgic invasion of the island in Chapter 4, to the language of the invaders in Chapter 5, and to the Laginian

invasion in Chapter 6. In Chapter 7 he discusses Roman references to a tribe of Quariates which may be associated with the Celts. The conquest of Tuathal is described in Chapter 8, the five provinces of the ancient island in Chapter 9, the invader Mug Nuadat in Chapter 10, the Goidelic invasion in Chapter 11, and King Niall of the Nine Hostages in Chapter 12. In Chapter 13 O'Rahilly discusses some dating questions in early Irish annals, and in Chapter 14 he considers the relationship between history and fable in these accounts of early Irish history. He analyzes linguistic features of several gods and mythological objects in Chapter 15, three Celtic gods of craftsmanship in Chapter 16, and the acquisition of wisdom by the hero Finn in Chapter 17. Ten additional topics are discussed in appendices, including the language of the Picts, the early kings of Connacht, and theories about the Goidelic invasion. Footnotes, endnotes, index of authors, linguistic index, and a general index.

Puhvel, Jaan. "Celtic Myth." In *Comparative Mythology*, by Jaan Puhvel. Baltimore: The Johns Hopkins University Press, 1987.
A survey of Celtic religious beliefs culled from ancient Roman sources and from the Irish and Welsh epic traditions. Special emphasis on the chief Celtic deities, Esus, Tyeutates, and Taranis. Searches for parallels with other Indo-European societies, especially in the context of the tripartite structure of king, warrior, and worker. Four figures illustrating artifacts and scenes connected with Celtic mythology. Footnotes and bibliography.

Rolleston, Thomas William. *Celtic Myths and Legends*. London: George G. Harrap, 1917. Reprint. New York: Avenel Books, 1985.
This general survey of the mythological traditions of the ancient Celts begins with two chapters of background material. Chapter 1 offers a summary of ancient references to the Celts and a historical overview of the Celts in the Roman Empire. Chapter 2 deals with aspects of the religion of the Celts, including magic, megalithic monuments, tombs, symbols, the doctrine of transmigration, human sacrifice, and deities. Several mythological traditions are summarized in the remaining six chapters. The legendary invasions of Ireland, especially by the Tuatha Dé Danaan or People of the God Dana and their conquerors the Milesians, are described in Chapter 3. The reigns of the Milesians, the legendary ancestors of the aristocratic families of modern Ireland, are discussed in Chapter 4. In Chapters 5 and 6 Rolleston tells stories in the Ultonian (Ulster) and Ossianic (Fenian) cycles about the heroes Conor mac Nessa and Finn mac Cumhal. The romantic adventure tales

of ancient Ireland are represented in Chapter 7 by a summary of the voyage of Maeldn to a series of imaginary islands. In Chapter 8 Rolleston describes medieval sources for legends about King Arthur and provides summaries of tales about Pwyll, Branwen, Manawydan, and Math from the four branches of the medieval Welsh epic *Mabinogion*, five Arthurian tales, and a story of the mythical bard Taliesin. Forty-six black-and-white illustrations, including photographs of sites and nineteenth- and early twentieth-century paintings of mythological scenes. Preface, footnotes, genealogical charts, and combined glossary and index.

Ross, Anne. *Druids, Gods and Heroes from Celtic Mythology.* New York: Schocken Books, 1986.
The chief myths and legends of the Celtic peoples who dominated most of Europe in the first millennium B.C. are retold for the general reader and are accompanied by illustrations, many in color, by Roger Garland. Includes an introduction to Celtic history and culture as well as chapters on the legend of King Arthur, tales of Irish heroes such as Cú Chulainn and Finn, and myths about the Celtic gods and magic animals. Symbols and characters are illustrated at the beginning of each chapter and are explained in an appendix. Bibliography, index, and a guide to the pronunciation of names.

Roth, G., and P. M. Duval. "Celtic Lands: Myth in History." In *Larousse World Mythology*, edited by Pierre Grimal. Translated by Patricia Beardsworth. New York: G. P. Putnam's Sons, 1963.
This survey of the mythologies of the Celtic peoples includes separate sections on the Continental Celts, especially in France, and on the Insular Celts of the British Isles. Considers the sanctuaries of the Continental Celts, features of their naturalistic polytheism, and anthropomorphic Gallo-Roman deities such as the Gallic Mercury and Ogmios, the Celtic Heracles. Describes the pantheon of the Insular Celts, mythic elements of the Arthurian legend in Britain, and Irish epics such as the *Leabhar Gabhala* or "Book of Invasions," the Ulster heroic cycle, and the cycle of the Fenians. Twenty-two photographs of Celtic sites and artifacts.

Sjoestedt, Marie-Louise. *Gods and Heroes of the Celts.* Translated by Myles Dillon. Berkeley: Turtle Island Foundation, 1982.
First published in French in 1940, this work of an important French linguist is not a mythological summary but an outline of the major characteristics of Celtic mythology. An introductory essay on the Celts,

their mythology, and ancient sources is followed by seven chapters
dealing with the mythological period, the gods of the continental Celts,
the mother goddesses of Ireland, Irish chieftian-deities, the feast of
November 1, tribal heroes such as Cú Chulainn, and extra-tribal heroes
such as Finn. In the concluding chapter, Sjoestedt summarizes the
mythological world view of the Celts. Prefaces to the American edition
and to the English translation discuss the importance of Sjoestedt's
work. Bibliography and endnotes.

Squire, Charles. *The Mythology of the British Islands*. London: Gresham,
1905. Reprinted as *Celtic Myth and Legend*. Hollywood, Calif.: New-
castle, 1975.
A general introduction to the myths of the ancient Celts and Britons.
The first four chapters discuss the importance of Celtic mythology, its
sources, and the identity and religion of the ancient Britons. Eleven
chapters deal with the Gaelic gods and their stories and nine with the
gods of the Britons and the myths of King Arthur. A final chapter
suggests survivals of Celtic paganism in modern customs, such as the
May Day festival. Four color plates and twenty black-and-white illustrations of scenes from Celtic legend, mostly based on modern drawings. Bibliography and index.

Treharne, R. F. *The Glastonbury Legends*. London: Sphere Books Limited, 1971.
A reexamination of the Glastonbury legends about Joseph of Ari-
mathea's journey to England, the Holy Grail, and King Arthur and his
knights. Uses the tools of modern history and archaeology to show how
these basically unhistorical legends do preserve some record of the
prehistoric period when Christianity first entered the island of Britain.
Argues that missionaries first reached the island not from the east but,
as the legend suggests, from the Bristol Channel in the west. Eighty-
eight photographs and bibliographical notes.

Central and Eastern European Myths

Afanas'ev, Aleksandr Nikolaevich. *Russian Fairy Tales*. Translated by
Norbert Guterman. New York: Pantheon Books, 1945.
This first major English translation of Afanas'ev's monumental nineteenth-century collection of Russian folklore contains 178 animal
fables, tales of the supernatural, witches, magic, and the devil, and
stories about saints, canny peasants, and a legendary Prince Ivan. In an

appendix, the linguist Roman Jakobson provides a history of Russian folkloristics, summarizes Afanas'ev's contributions to the field, and discusses some characteristics of Russian folktales. Black-and-white illustrations by A. Alexeieff. Index.

Alexinsky, G. "Slavonic Mythology." In *New Larousse Encyclopedia of Mythology*, edited by Felix Guirand et al. Translated by Richard Aldington and Delano Ames. New York: Hamlyn, 1968.
Uses modern Slavic folklore to reconstruct and retell some of the ancient myths. Sections on the opposing deities Byelobog and Chernobog, the sky god Svarog, Mati-Syra-Zemly or Moist-Mother-Earth, rustic deities, domestic spirits, spirits of the forest called *leshy*, field spirits called *polevik*, *vodyanoi* or water spirits, *rursalka* or drowned maidens, city and war gods, the gods of joy Yarilo and Kupala, and survivals of early mythology among Christian Slavs. Includes seventeen black-and-white illustrations, mostly modern depictions of traditional myths by I. Bilibin.

Biro, Val. *Hungarian Folk-Tales*. Oxford: Oxford University Press, 1980.
Retellings of twenty-one traditional tales from Hungary for young readers. Tales of goblins, dragons, wicked fairies, the supernatural, and talking animals. Illustrated with line drawings by the author.

Ćurčija-Prodanović, Nada. *Yugoslav Folk-Tales*. New York: Henry Z. Walck, 1957.
Two original-language collections of Serbian folktales are the source for this retelling of thirty-two tales for young readers. Tales of a crafty peasant named Ero, stories about anthropomorphic animals and fruit, and encounters with Turks, the Czar, fairies, the devil, and the supernatural. Illustrated with drawings, some in color, by Joan Kiddell-Monroe.

Downing, Charles. *Russian Tales and Legends*. New York: Henry Z. Walck, 1960.
Retells thirty traditional tales of Russia, the Ukraine, and eastern Siberia for young English readers. Part 1 contains twelve selections from *byliny* or heroic poems, including tales about the deeds of Lord Volga Buslavlevich, Ilya of Murom, Stavr Godinovich, and Vasili Buslayevich. In Part 2 are eighteen *skazkas* or folktales about death, the devil, angels, marriage, soldiers, and the supernatural. Glossary and short bibliography.

Franz, Marie-Louise von. "The Beautiful Wassilissa." In *Problems of the Feminine in Fairytales*, by Marie-Louise von Franz. New York: Spring Publications, 1972. Reprinted in *Cinderella: A Folklore Casebook*, edited by Alan Dundes. New York: Garland Press, 1982.

This Jungian analysis of the Cinderella folktale includes the translated text of a Russian version of the folktale in which Cinderella is called Wassilissa. An encounter with a witch named Baba Yaga enables Wassilissa to overpower her stepmother and win the hand of a king in marriage. Uncovers mythic archetypes which express the feminine unconscious and quest for self. Reprint includes useful background information about Jung and a bibliography by Dundes.

Gieysztor, A. "Baltic Lands: Nature Worship." In *Larousse World Mythology*, edited by Pierre Grimal. Translated by Patricia Beardsworth. New York: G. P. Putnam's Sons, 1963.

A short survey of gods of the ancient Baltic peoples, with a historical overview of their religious beliefs. The gods and cults of the early Prussians, Lithuanians, and Latvians are discussed in separate sections. Two illustrations.

_____. "Slav Countries: Folk-lore of the Forests." In *Larousse World Mythology*, edited by Pierre Grimal. Translated by Patricia Beardsworth. New York: G. P. Putnam's Sons, 1963.

This survey of the religious beliefs of the ancient Slavs begins with a history of the people until their conversion to Christianity in the medieval period. Examines in particular the cults of Svarog the sun god, Perun the god of the thunderbolt, and the "strong lord" Svantevit. Also contains sections on various temples and sacred images, as well as supernatural creatures such as witches, forest spirits, and demons of human fatality and fertility. Accompanied by fifteen black-and-white illustrations of Slavic artifacts.

Guirand, Felix. "Finno-Ugric Mythology." In *New Larousse Encyclopedia of Mythology*, edited by Felix Guirand et al. Translated by Richard Aldington and Delano Ames. New York: Hamlyn, 1968.

This overview of the mythology of Finno-Ugric peoples, who include the Voguls of Siberia, the Hungarians, the Finns, the Estonians, the Livonians, and the Lapps, contains a summary of the *Kalevala*, the national epic of Finland, and discussion of magic and shamanism, magic in the *Kalevala*, the gods of the *Kalevala*, and some characteristics of animism among the Finno-Ugric peoples. Accompanied by ten illustrations, mostly depicting traditional artifacts.

Holmberg, Uno. *Finno-Ugric Mythology*. Vol. 4 in *The Mythology of All Races*, edited by Louis Herbert Gray. Boston: Marshall Jones, 1927.
An overview of the mythological world view and religious beliefs of the Finns, Estonians, Hungarians, Lapps, and other peoples of the Baltic and northeastern Europe. In a short introduction, Holmberg describes the linguistic and cultural ties which unite these peoples; he also outlines their traditional religion and surveys the sources for knowledge of their myths. Individual chapters deal with topics such as souls, death, the afterlife, animal worship, family gods, heroes, nature deities, and shamans. Fifty plates and twelve figures illustrating artifacts and sites related to these beliefs. Map, endnotes, and bibliography. Complete index in Volume 13.

Lang, David M. "The Slavs." In *Mythology: An Illustrated Encyclopaedia*, edited by Richard Cavendish. New York: Rizzoli International, 1980. Also published as *An Illustrated Encyclopedia of Mythology*. New York: Crescent Books, 1984.
This overview of the mythological beliefs of the Slavic peoples of eastern Europe contains sections on Iranian influences on the deities of the Slavs, beliefs in animism and totemism, Prince Vladimir's destruction of the idols in A.D. 989 and their stubborn survivals, heretical religious mythologies such as Bogomilism, the legends of Russian Prince Igor and the Polish hero Krak, the witch Baba Yaga, evil spirits such as Koschchei the Deathless, and various folk heroes. Map and illustrations of artwork related to the myths.

Máchal, Jan. *Slavic Mythology*. Vol. 3 in *The Mythology of All Races*, edited by Louis Herbert Gray. Boston: Marshall Jones, 1918.
This study of the mythology and religious beliefs of the ancient Slavic peoples begins with a brief introduction to the literary sources. Part 1 deals with belief in various genies or supernatural spirits such as ancestors, household gods, fate, and nature spirits. The gods of the Elbe Slavs and the gods of the ancient Russians are described in Parts 2 and 3. Several traditional cults and festivals of the Slavs are explained in light of these myths and beliefs in Part 4. A brief overview of myths of the Slavic peoples of the Baltic, especially the Prussians, the Lithuanians, and the Letts, is offered in Part 5. Thirteen illustrations, pronunciation guide, endnotes, and bibliography. Complete index in Volume 13.

Mijatovies, Csedomille. *Serbian Folk-lore*, edited by W. Denton. 1874. Reprint. New York: Benjamin Blom, 1968.

Twenty-six Serbian legends and folktales translated into English. The tales deal with talking animals, trolls, Satan, dreams, magical places, and the legend of St. George. In an introductory essay, the editor discusses some characteristics of the Serbian folklore tradition.

Puhvel, Jaan. "Baltic and Slavic Myth." In *Comparative Mythology*, by Jaan Puhvel. Baltimore: The Johns Hopkins University Press, 1987.
Culls assorted Russian, Germanic, and Slavic sources for information about the lost mythology of the ancient Baltic peoples. Discusses a trio of Lithuanian deities called Patollo, Perkuno, and Potrimpo, drawing parallels to Germanic, Roman, Indic, and other Indo-European peoples with their emphases on the tripartite social structure of king, warrior, and worker. Matches Slavic vocabulary with comparable words from the Vedic sources of ancient India. Also looks briefly at Slavic sagas and their links with ancient mythology. Footnotes.

Ralston, William Ralston Shedden. *Russian Folktales*. London: Smith, Elder, 1873. Reprint. New York: Arno Press, 1977.
Translations of fifty-one stories gathered from the nineteenth-century Russian folklore collections of A. N. Afanasief, I. A. Khudyakof, E. A. Chudinsky, and A. A. Erlenvein. These tales are incorporated into six thematic chapters. In the introductory Chapter 1, Ralston discusses general features of Russian tales and their links with everyday Russian life. Chapter 2 deals with incarnations of evil such as Baba Yaga and other witches, and Chapter 3 with other forms of personification. Tales of magic and witchcraft are found in Chapter 4, ghost stories in Chapter 5, and legends about saints and demons in Chapter 6. Footnotes and index.

Sauvageot, A. "Finland-Ugria: Magic Animals." In *Larousse World Mythology*, edited by Pierre Grimal. Translated by Patricia Beardsworth. New York: G. P. Putnam's Sons, 1963.
A short overview on the Uralian mythology of the ancient Finns and Hungarians with descriptions of their shamanistic beliefs, gods, creation story, world view, and underground spirits.

Sokolov, Yury M. *Russian Folklore*. Translated by Catherine Ruth Smith. New York: Macmillan, 1950.
A survey of Russian folklore by a Soviet scholar, written as a companion school text for the *Anthology of Russian Folklore* by N. P. Andreyev. Following essays on the nature of folklore and its historiography, the author examines various types of oral tradition before the October Revolution of 1918, including tales, laments, and proverbs.

Includes a review of folklore of the Soviet period, again according to genre. Russian transliteration table, index of collectors, investigators of folklore, and popular creative artists.

Utley, Francis Lee. "The Devil in the Arc (AaTh 825)." In *Internationaler Kongress der Volkserzählungforscher in Kiel und Kopenhagen*, by Francis Lee Utley. Berlin: Walter De Gruyter, 1961. Reprinted in *The Flood Myth*, edited by Alan Dundes. Berkeley: University of California Press, 1988.
Surveys the general traits of about 250 versions of a folktale type told especially in eastern Europe with variants throughout the world. This tale, #825 in the Aarne-Thompson folktale motif index, describes Noah's conflicts with the devil on the ark. Utley lists the twelve major parts of this tale and illustrates the stability of the tale throughout the tradition. Includes a complete list of folktales in which this motif appears. Footnotes.

Warner, Elizabeth. *Heroes, Monsters and Other Worlds from Russian Mythology*. New York: Schocken Books, 1985.
Retells traditional tales from old Russia with illustrations, many in color, by Alexander Koshkin. A short introduction to the history and culture of the people, including the gods they worshiped prior to their conversion to Christianity, is followed by a collection of *bylinas* or stories about legendary heroes, such as Vladimir and Dobrynya; *skazkas*, or folktales of magic and fantasy; and *bylichkas*, or stories about the supernatural and the world of the dead. Symbols and characters illustrated in each chapter are explained in an appendix. Guide to the Russian alphabet, bibliography, and index.

Weinreich, Beatrice Silverman, ed., and Leonard Wolf, trans. *Yiddish Folktales*. New York: Pantheon Books, 1988.
A selection of 178 tales from the Yiddish-speaking Jews of nineteenth- and twentieth-century Eastern Europe. Seven parts are organized in the following thematic groups: allegorical tales, children's tales, wonder tales, pious tales, humorous tales, legends, and supernatural tales. Each part begins with a brief discussion of the characteristics of this type of tale. An introductory essay offers background information on the collection of the tales, their nature, and their storytellers, with six photographs documenting the recorders and their sources. Illustrated with examples of *papirn-shnit*, traditional paper-cuttings popular among nineteenth- and twentieth-century Jews in Poland and Russia.

An appendix lists the archival or published source for each tale. Glossary of important Yiddish terms. Endnotes and bibliography.

Weiss, Pola. *Russian Legends*. Translated by Alice Sachs. New York: Crescent Books, 1980.
Nineteen traditional tales from Russia, including an animal fable, the tale of a miraculous flower, a Ukrainian moral tale, and a story about a plague in Moscow. Three stories are by Leo Tolstoy.

Wigzell, Faith. "Central and Eastern Europe." In *World Mythology*, edited by Roy Willis. New York: Henry Holt, 1993.
A short compilation of some myths of the ancient Slavs, with sections on the otherworld, the witch Baba Yaga, Vlasta and her warlike band of Amazon women, ancestors and spirits of the hearth, souls of the dead, and evil spirits such as werewolves and vampires. Subsidiary sections add information on dragons, the Russian tale of Silver Roan, a spirit of the dead called the *vila*, and vampires. Seven color illustrations of Slavic artifacts. Map, time chart, and lists of Slavic linguistic groups and ancient deities.

Wratislaw, Albert Henry. *Sixty Folk-Tales*. London: Elliot Stock, 1889. Reprint. New York: Arno Press, 1977.
Slavic tales of witchcraft, the devil, miracles, unusual events, and the supernatural are here translated from nineteenth-century original-language sources and are arranged geographically. Bohemian, Moravian, Hungarian-Slovenish, Upper and Lower Lusatian, Kashubian, and Polish stories are represented among the West Slavonian tales. White Russian, Galician, South Russian, and Great Russian stories appear in the Eastern Slavonian section. Bulgarian, Serbian, Bosnian, Carniolan, Croatian, and Illyrian-Slovenish stories are found in the Southern Slavonian section. Wratislaw provides some information about each ethnic group and occasional comparative commentary. Wratislaw includes original-language titles and published sources in the table of contents. Short preface on published sources.

Greek and Roman Myths

Apollodorus. *Gods and Heroes of the Greeks: The Library of Apollodorus*. Translated by Michael Simpson. Amherst: University of Massachusetts Press, 1976.
The *Library* of Apollodorus, an Athenian grammarian who lived sometime after the middle of the first century B.C., is the only surviving

ancient handbook of Greek mythology. This annotated English translation is arranged in thirteen chapters instead of the books and epitomes
used in the Greek original. Original section numbers in the margins.
Begins with the birth of the gods and the story of Prometheus and
moves to the myths of Jason, Perseus, Heracles, Oedipus, Theseus, and
other heroes. The last part of the book deals with the House of Atreus,
the Trojan war, and the homecomings of Agamemnon, Menelaus, and
Odysseus. Translator's notes at the end of each chapter offer background to Apollodorus' myths and references to other ancient versions
of these myths. Several drawings by Leonard Baskin illustrating
mythological characters such as Medusa and Typhon. Includes an
index, select bibliography, and introduction.

_____. *The Library of Greek Mythology.* Translated by Keith
Aldrich. Lawrence, Kans.: Coronado Press, 1975.
This translation faithfully follows the organization of the original
Greek handbook in books and epitomes. Original section numbers
appear in the margins. The books are genealogically arranged. Book 1
deals with the birth of the gods, the flood, and tales about the descendants of Deucalion, including Prometheus, Meleager, Sisyphus, and
Jason. Book 2 tells the myths of nine descendants of Inachus and Belus,
including the Danaids, Bellerophon, Perseus, and Heracles. Book 3 is
about the families of Europa, Pelasgus, Atlas, Asopus, and the kings of
Athens. In the epitome Apollodorus tells myths about the descendants
of Pelops, the Trojan war, and the homecomings of the Greek heroes,
especially Odysseus. Following his translation, Aldrich offers explanatory notes and other ancient treatments of the myths. Index with
glossary and some pronunciation guides, one for names mentioned by
Apollodorus and a supplementary index of 400 mythological names
not mentioned by the author. Several drawings by Voula Tsouvelli are
only loosely connected with the text. Brief introduction, bibliography,
and numeration table illustrating the two systems of numbering Apollodorus' book sections.

Athanassakis, Apostolos N., trans. *The Homeric Hymns.* Baltimore: The
Johns Hopkins University Press, 1976.
These verse translations of the thirty-three surviving Homeric hymns
and fragments use the line references of the original Greek text. Some
of these hymns are only short prayers to the gods, but others include
detailed mythic narratives. The most noteworthy of these myths are
Demeter's search for her lost daughter Persephone in hymn 1, the births
of Apollo in hymn 3 and of Hermes in hymn 4, Aphrodite's seduction

of the Trojan Anchises in hymn 5, and Dionysus' encounter with the sailors in hymn 7. General comments on the hymns and their history in a preface and short introduction. Detailed explanatory endnotes.

Austin, Norman. *Helen of Troy and Her Shameless Phantom.* Ithaca, N.Y.: Cornell University Press, 1994.
Contrasts the traditional depiction of Helen of Troy as the archetype of shameless beauty in the poetry of Homer and of Sappho with later Greek repudiations of this myth and the appearance of Helen's so-called phantom, especially in the *Odyssey*, in the poetry of Stesichorus, in the *Histories* of Herodotus, and in Euripides' *Helen*. Historical overview of Helen's image in an introductory essay. Foreword on the Helen problem by Gregory Nagy. Three illustrations, footnotes, glossary, bibliography, and index.

Beard, Mary. "Rome." In *World Mythology*, edited by Roy Willis. New York: Henry Holt, 1993.
This short overview of Roman mythology includes sections on gods and goddesses, the story of Aeneas, and the founding of Rome and its early history. Supplemented by subsidiary sections on the arrival in Rome of the cult of the Great Mother, the legend of Dido and Aeneas, and the story of Tarpeia. Accompanied by fourteen illustrations, most in color, of Roman artifacts and sites. Map, time chart, list of Greek and Roman mythological parallels, and list of the legendary kings of Rome.

Bell, Robert E. *Dictionary of Classical Mythology.* Santa Barbara, Calif.: ABC-Clio, 1982.
This topical dictionary consists of several useful lists. The most substantial is an alphabetically arranged list of symbols, attributes, and associations followed by mythological figures associated with each term. Also contains an alphabetical list of gods and heroes followed by their surnames, epithets, and patronymics. A third list consists of passengers on the *Argo*, members of the Calydonian Boar Hunt, and members of both Greek and Trojan forces in the Trojan war. Each entry includes a brief description and sometimes ancient source references. The final guide is an alphabetical list of cross-references for major mythological personages mentioned in the dictionary. Illustrated with sixteen line drawings by John Schlesinger. Short introduction and guide to citation abbreviations.

——————. *Women of Classical Mythology.* Santa Barbara, Calif.: ABC-Clio, 1991.

An alphabetically arranged reference for females mentioned in the myths of ancient Greece and Rome with more than 2,600 citations. Each entry includes at least a cross-reference or a brief description, sometimes supplemented by ancient source references. Major female figures receive more detailed descriptions, with discussion of variant sources and representations. In an appendix is an alphabetically arranged list of males, both human and divine, with cross-references to women associated with them.

Birchall, Ann, and P. E. Corbett. *Greek Gods and Heroes*. London: Trustees of the British Museum, 1974.
Classical art, especially Greek painted pottery, from the collection of the British Museum accompanies a short introduction to the major gods and heroes of the Greeks. Individual chapters on the Olympian gods, Dionysus, Heracles, Theseus, and the Trojan war, as well as sections on the Gorgons, the Golden Fleece, and Orpheus. Each illustration includes details of provenance and dating as well as a brief description of the scene. List of illustrations and short bibliography.

Blake Tyrrell, William, and Frieda S. Brown. *Athenian Myths and Institutions. Words in Action*. New York: Oxford University Press, 1991.
A group of Greek myths are studied as examples of Athenian myth-making, as illustrations of the ways in which the Athenians transformed traditional tales to express their own social values and customs. Special attention is devoted to the story of the birth of the cosmos in Hesiod's *Theogony*, to the code of the Greek warrior and sacrifice in Sophocles' *Ajax*, to myths of marriage in the Homeric hymn to Demeter and in such Greek tragedies as Sophocles' *Women of Trachis*, Euripides' *Medea*, and Aeschylus' *Oresteia*, to citizenship in Euripides' *Ion*, and to Athenian patriotism expressed in the myths of the Amazon women, centaurs, and Helen. Bibliography and index.

Bremmer, Jan N., and Nicholas M. Horsfall. *Roman Myth and Mythology*. Bulletin Supplement 52. London: Institute for Classical Studies, 1987.
Two Classical scholars offer eight independent essays on topics related to Roman mythology. Horsfall discusses how the Romans used myth, considers the transformation of Livy's story of M. Manlius and the geese from history to legend, surveys the history of the Aeneas legend from Homer to Vergil, and analyzes the myth of Corythus from Vergil's *Aeneid*. Bremmer offers essays on the founding of Rome by Romulus and Remus, links between myth and ritual in the festival of Nonae Capratinae, and the introduction of the worship of Cybele in Rome.

The authors share an essay on the Caeculus myth in the *Aeneid*. Footnotes, map, bibliography, and index.

Brown, Norman O. *Hermes the Thief*. Madison: University of Wisconsin Press, 1947. 2d ed. New York: Random House, 1969.
A major study of the myth about the theft of his brother Apollo's cattle by the newborn god Hermes, as told in the Homeric hymn to Hermes. In addition to paraphrasing and interpreting the hymn itself, Brown discusses the myth in terms of earlier tribal myths and customs and its evolution from cultural and social aspects of the Greek Bronze and Archaic periods. Also contains a chapter on the possible origin of the hymn in Athens in the late sixth century B.C. Discussion of the Greek text of the hymn and of another version of the myth in appendices. Bibliography and index.

Bulfinch, Thomas. *Myths of Greece and Rome*, edited by Bryan Holme. New York: Penguin, 1979.
This edition of Bulfinch's influential *The Age of Fable*, first published in 1855, includes tales about Greco-Roman deities and heroes which Bulfinch derived mostly from Ovid and Vergil. Chapters on the Greek and Roman gods and goddesses and mythological monsters are followed by discussion of the heroes Hercules, Jason, Theseus, Ulysses (or Odysseus), and Aeneas. Bulfinch accompanied his tales with quotations from poetic texts alluding to these myths. His poetic selection, from the works of poets such as Edmund Spenser, John Milton, and John Keats, represents mid-nineteenth-century American poetic tastes. This edition is enhanced by many illustrations of artistic representations of these myths. Paintings and sculpture from ancient Greece and Rome, the Renaissance, and the modern world are included. Some color illustrations. Contains Bulfinch's original preface as well as an introduction by Joseph Campbell. Genealogical chart and index.

Burn, Lucilla. *Greek Myths*. Austin: University of Texas Press, 1990.
This general survey is part of The Legendary Past Series. A short introductory chapter explains the identity of the major Greek gods. The rest of the book offers chapters on the adventures of Greek heroes, including Heracles, Theseus, Odysseus, Jason, Perseus, and Oedipus, and on the Trojan war. Profusely illustrated with ancient sculpture and painted pottery depicting scenes from these myths. Map and short bibliography.

Buxton, Richard. "Wolves and Werewolves in Greek Thought." In *Interpretations of Greek Mythology*, edited by Jan Bremmer. Totowa, N.J.: Barnes & Noble Books, 1986.
Examines Greek ritual and myth about wolves and human transformation into wolves in the context of Aristotelian zoology and general attitudes toward these animals in ancient Greece. The cult of the Arcadian werewolf probably deals with an initiatory rite of passage, while the related myth of Lycaon warns humans about the consequences of transgression against the divine. Endnotes.

Calame, Claude. "Spartan Genealogies: The Mythological Representation of a Spatial Organisation." In *Interpretations of Greek Mythology*, edited by Jan Bremmer. Totowa, N.J.: Barnes & Noble Books, 1986.
Using especially references in the travel guide of the second-century Greek Pausanias, Calame, an outstanding French structuralist, traces Spartan myths and legends about their kings from their autochthonous origin through the arrival of the Heraclidae, the descendants of Heracles. Includes myths about Helen, her brothers Castor and Pollux, and her daughter Hermione. Suggests that these legends received their particular canonical form as part of a Spartan campaign in the late sixth century B.C. to consolidate its rule over most of the Peloponnese. Use of genealogical narrative creates an appropriate mythic and symbolic structure for this political agenda. Map, genealogical chart, and endnotes.

Calasso, Roberto. *The Marriage of Cadmus and Harmony*. Translated by Tim Parks. New York: Alfred A. Knopf, 1993.
A re-creation and reinterpretation of Greek mythology and the world view which it represents. Begins *in medias res*, with the rape of Europa by Zeus and ends with the marriage of Cadmus and Harmonia. In between Calasso moves back in time to the birth of Zeus and ahead to the fall of Troy and the wanderings of Odysseus. He assimilates material from a variety of ancient sources, especially the Homeric poems, but also Herodotus' *Histories* and the *Dionysiaca* of Nonnus. Includes about fifteen engraved illustrations from mythological handbooks published between 1719 and 1940. Index of sources.

Calder, William M. "New Light on Ovid's Story of Philemon and Baucis." *Discover* 3 a(1922): 207-211. Reprinted in *The Flood Myth*, edited by Alan Dundes. Berkeley: University of California Press, 1988.
A Classical scholar uses literary and historical evidence to argue that the flood myth told by Ovid in *Metamorphoses* I grows not out of the

Mesopotamian tradition but out of an Anatolian version based upon the physical features of Lake Trogitis in Turkey. Map and footnotes.

Caldwell, Richard S., trans. and ed. *Hesiod's Theogony*. Newburyport, Mass.: Focus Information Group, 1987.
This poetic translation of Hesiod's poem about the birth of the universe includes an introduction, a commentary, and an interpretative essay, all directed toward the general reader. The introduction contains extensive genealogical charts and gives a background to the poem, its structure, and its possible sources in Middle Eastern mythology. The translation is accompanied by an explanatory commentary in footnote form. In the interpretative essay the editor analyzes the poem as a succession myth and as a psychological study of the processes of individualization, generational conflict, and sexual desire. Appendices contain translated excerpts from the *Library* of Apollodorus and the first 201 lines of Hesiod's *Works and Days*, which describes the myths of Pandora and of the Ages of Man. Index.

_____. "Texts and Contexts." In *The Origin of the Gods: A Psychoanalytic Study of Greek Theogonic Myth*, by Richard S. Caldwell. New York: Oxford University Press, 1989.
This chapter of an interpretation of Greek creation myth based upon the psychoanalytic theory of Sigmund Freud includes Caldwell's own verse translation of Hesiod's *Theogony* as well as excerpts from the *Library* of Apollodorus. Compares the Greek myth with Middle Eastern creation stories, the Babylonian *Enuma Elish* and the Hurrian-Hittite *Kingship in Heaven* and *Song of Ullikummi*. Endnotes.

Carpenter, Thomas H., and Robert J. Gula *Mythology Greek and Roman*. Wellesley Hills, Mass.: The Independent School Press, 1977.
A general introduction to Greek and Roman mythology. Contains nineteen chapters, beginning with Greek myths of creation and the gods and moving to legends of the heroes. Myths about the Trojan war and about Trojan War heroes such as Achilles and Odysseus are not emphasized. Includes some myth narrative but focuses upon identification and description of major characters. Important names and terms are printed in bold type in the text. Additional information is often provided in smaller print. Some chapters are thematic and deal with topics such as myths of death and destruction, abstract divinities, the transformation myth, and prophets and oracles. Separate chapters on Plato's use of myth and on Roman mythology. Genealogical charts throughout the text and thirty illustrations, mostly scenes from Greek

painted pottery. Appendices include an alphabetical catalogue of mythological monsters, a list of transformations in Ovid's *Metamorphoses* arranged according to appearance, a catalogue of divine love affairs arranged according to deity, and a note on methodology with a list of major Greek and Roman authors, a bibliography, and a time chart. Index of selected ancient sources. Combines general index and glossary. Short introduction.

Coolidge, Olivia E. *Greek Myths*. Boston: Houghton Mifflin, 1949.
Selected myths of the Greeks are retold for older children. The myths are organized thematically. Most of the tales are taken from Ovid's *Metamorphoses* or the Homeric hymns. Myths about Zeus and his loves and about the Trojan War are conspicuously absent from this collection. In Chapter 1 are stories of the gods, including the birth of Hermes, the loves of Apollo, Phaëthon, the contest between Athena and Poseidon for the city of Athens, Arachne, Demeter's search for Persephone, and Dionysus' encounter with the sailors. The loves of the gods in Chapter 2 are those of Cupid and Psyche, Narcissus, Adonis, and Tithonus. Chapter 3 deals with creation, Pandora, and the flood. The human rivalries with the gods in Chapter 4 are those of Niobe, Daedalus, and Midas. The human love stories in Chapter 5 include those of Orpheus, Pygmalion, and Alcestis. In the last two chapters are the heroic adventures of Atalanta, Bellerophon, Perseus, Jason, Theseus, and Heracles. Table of chief gods and list of proper names with pronunciation guide. Illustrated with line drawings by Edouard Sandoz.

Croft, Peter. *All Colour Book of Roman Mythology*. London: Octopus Books, 1974.
Uses a combination of illustration and text to tell the myths of ancient Rome. A collection of 100 color illustrations of the myths in ancient and modern art is accompanied by brief descriptions and summaries of the myths, beginning with Aeneas' journey to Italy and the stories of early Rome, such as the birth of Romulus and Remus and the rape of the Sabine women. Also contains chapters on Roman deities, on deities and myths imported from other cultures, and on the sources for these myths. Introduction by Stewart Perowne.

D'Aulaire, Ingri, and Edgar Parin D'Aulaire. *Book of Greek Myths*. Garden City, N.Y.: Doubleday, 1962.
Retells Greek myths for young children. Tales about Mother Earth and the Titans are followed by descriptions of the twelve Olympian gods. Sections on Prometheus, Pandora, Deucalion, and other myths of

transformation from Ovid's *Metamorphoses* are accompanied by discussion of Asclepius, Orpheus, and the Muses. The last section, entitled "Mortal Descendants of Zeus," tells the stories of Europa, Tantalus, Perseus, Midas, Heracles, Theseus, Oedipus, Jason, and Meleager. Ends with the judgment of Paris and a brief summary of the Trojan War and its aftermath. Mentions the wanderings of Aeneas, but not of Odysseus. Maps and many drawings, some in color. Index.

Ferguson, John. "Mystery Religions." In *Mythology: An Illustrated Encyclopaedia*, edited by Richard Cavendish. New York: Rizzoli International, 1980. Also published as *An Illustrated Encyclopedia of Mythology*. New York: Crescent Books, 1984.
Considers myths associated with the following mystery religions in the ancient Mediterrranean: the Greek cult of Demeter at Eleusis, the worship of Dionysus, including a description of the Villa of the Mysteries at Pompeii, Orphism, the special mysteries on the Greek island of Samothrace, the Phrygian cult of Cybele and Attis, the mystery of the Persian god Mithra, and the worship of the Egyptian gods Isis and Osiris. Map and illustrations of artwork related to the myths.

_____. "Rome." In *Mythology: An Illustrated Encyclopaedia*, edited by Richard Cavendish. New York: Rizzoli International, 1980. Also published as *An Illustrated Encyclopedia of Mythology*. New York: Crescent Books, 1984.
A short examination of native Roman myths and Roman transformation of foreign, especially Greek, tales. Special emphasis on legends preserved in Livy's history of early Rome. Includes sections on Roman gods borrowed from Greece, Roman attitudes toward mythology, historical legends about the founding of Rome, the story of Aeneas, the kings and the founding of the Republic, early stories of heroism, and Roman religious myths. Map, glossary of Roman and Greek deities, and illustrations of artwork related to the myths.

Fontenrose, Joseph. *The Delphic Oracle*. Berkeley: University of California Press, 1978.
A scholarly examination of oracles spoken by Apollo's priestess at Delphi and the way these oracles were given. Discusses characteristics of oracles in history and in folklore, their transmission and attribution, questionable responses, structures of oracular verse, and the procedures followed during an oracular session. Rejects as non-genuine almost all the oracles associated with Delphi between 750 and 450 B.C.

Catalogues known Delphic oracles into four groups: historical, quasi-historical, legendary, and fictional. The best-known oracles of Greek mythology, such as the oracles of Laius and of Oedipus, are found among the legendary oracles. For each oracle the following information is provided: consultant, occasion, question, response, mode (command, prohibition, etc.), topic (religion, politics, private life, etc.), sources, and editorial comments. Not all Greek and Latin quotations are translated. Two illustrations and map. Charts and tables. Concordance of modes and topics. Bibliography and indexes.

_____. *Python: A Study of Delphic Myth and Its Origins.* Berkeley: University of California Press, 1959.
The Greek myth of Apollo's combat with the serpent Python at Delphi is the focus of this examination of myths of divine or heroic combat with serpents or dragons in the ancient Mediterranean world. Examines in Chapters 1-3 several versions of the Python myth and also considers several minor tales of combat in Delphi, including the legends of Tityos, Phlegyas, and Cycnus. Deals in Chapters 4 and 5 with myths about the monster Typhon and its combats with both Zeus and Apollo. Provides a comparative perspective in Chapters 7-10, with examinations of the Egyptian tale of Set, Osiris, and Horos, the Babylonian story of Marduk and Tiamat, and the Indic contest between Indra and Vritra. All these myths reflect a common pattern of conflict between order and disorder, chaos and cosmos, life and death. Examines in Chapters 11 and 12 several encounters with dragons or serpents by heroes such as Perseus, Cadmus, and, especially, Heracles. Earlier forms of the Delphic myth, such as tales of Telphusa, Dionysus, and Heracles and the tripod, are discussed in Chapter 13. In Chapter 14, Fontenrose seeks the precursors of the Delphic Python in myths about the Cilician and Corycian caves. Chapter 15 considers the relationship between these combat myths and rituals such as the Greek Pythian festival and the Babylonian New Year festival. Determines that Greek myths about Apollo and Python or Zeus and Typhon are based upon an earlier family of myths which spread through Europe, Egypt, and Asia. Appendices include discussions of the biblical tale of Judith and Holofernes, the story of St. George and the dragon, and combat myths in Germany, the Orient, and the Americas. Sixty-five black-and white figures and maps. Bibliography. Index of folktale themes and motifs. Index locorum. General index.

Fox, William S. *Greek and Roman Mythology.* Vol. 1 in *The Mythology of All Races*, edited by Louis H. Gray. Boston: Marshall Jones, 1916.

Also published separately as *Greek and Roman Mythology*. Boston: Marshall Jones, 1916, 1928.

Summarizes the most typical myths of the Greeks and Romans and interprets them as expressions of religious thought. Introductory essay on characteristics of Greco-Roman myths and their sources. In Part 1 Fox considers the Greek story of creation and heroes such as Perseus, Oedipus, and Minos, with separate chapters on Heracles, Theseus, the Argonauts, the Trojan war, and the afterlife. Part 2 is devoted to the gods. In Part 3 Fox discusses special features of Roman mythology, especially its Etruscan features, the nature of Italic gods, gods of foreign origin, and stories about the early days of Rome. Sixty-three plates and eleven figures illustrating mythological scenes from ancient art. Appendix on modern Greek survivals of ancient gods and myths. Endnotes and bibliography. Complete index in Volume 13.

Galinsky, G. Karl. *The Herakles Theme: The Adaptations of the Hero in Literature from Homer to the Twentieth Century*. Totowa, N.J.: Rowman and Littlefield, 1972.

Traces the transformations of the Greek hero Heracles from his earliest appearances in Greek literature through modern adaptations of his myths. Chapters 1-8 deal with the hero's appearance in Greek and Roman literature. Descriptions of the hero in the archaic poetry of Homer, Pindar, and Bacchylides, his appearances in the tragedies and comedies of fifth-century Athens, his interpretation by ancient philosophers, and his representation in Roman elegiac and epic poetry and in the tragedies of Seneca illustrate the diverse ways that the Heracles theme was used in antiquity. Chapters 9-12 survey the appearance of the hero in literary contexts from the Renaissance through the twentieth century. Ancient authors are quoted only in English translation. Modern authors are quoted in the original. All foreign-language quotations are translated except French. Endnotes following each chapter. General comments on the Heracles tradition in a foreword and introduction. Short preface by W. B. Stanford. Twenty-three illustrations of the hero in ancient and modern art. Bibliography and index.

Gardner, Jane. *Roman Myths*. Austin: University of Texas Press, 1993.

The myths of ancient Rome center on the founding of the city and its early history, moral tales, and aetiological stories about cults and festivals. In this title in The Legendary Past Series, these myths are retold, analyzed, and interpreted. In an introductory chapter, Gardner discusses her chief ancient sources (Livy, Ovid, Dionysius of Halicarnassus, and Plutarch) and compares Roman and Greek gods. Chapters on the story of Aeneas, the founding of Rome, and legends about early Romans such as Horatius, Mucius Scaevola, and Coriolanus, and their relationship with the state are accompanied by stories about legendary women such as Tarpeia and Lucretia, several indigenous Roman gods and their stories, and Roman cults and festivals. Gardner emphasizes the patriotic and moral nature of many Roman myths. Ancient sources are occasionally quoted in translation. Richly illustrated with ancient and modern artwork related to the myths. Map, bibliography, and index.

Gayley, Charles M. *The Classic Myths in English Literature and in Art.* Rev. ed. New York: John Wiley & Sons, 1939.
Contains twenty-seven chapters retelling Greek and Roman myths with extensive illustration and quotation from art and literature, by British authors and artists in particular. Emphasis on myths about the Greek gods and goddesses. Several chapters about Greek hero legends, the Trojan war, Homer's *Odyssey*, and Vergil's *Aeneid*. Fifteen full-page illustrations and 185 black-and-white figures devoted to Greek and Roman myths. A useful index indicates modern authors, artists, and works cited in the text. Additional lists of modern literary and artistic illustrations of the myths can be found in the commentary, which follows the main body of the text. Also contains an index of mythological subjects.

Gibson, Michael. *Gods, Men and Monsters from the Greek Myths.* New York: Schocken, 1982.
The myths of the Greeks, retold for the general reader, are here accompanied by elaborate drawings, many in color, by Giovanni Caselli. Contains separate sections on each of the major gods and heroes as well as the Trojan war, the wanderings of Odysseus, Orpheus and Eurydice, Cupid and Psyche, and several tales of metamorphosis, including Pygmalion, Echo, Narcissus, and Midas. Symbols and characters illustrated in each chapter are explained in an appendix. Index.

Goldhill, Simon. "Greece." In *World Mythology*, edited by Roy Willis. New York: Henry Holt, 1993.
This overview of Greek mythology offers descriptive sections on the relationship between myth and society, the birth of the gods, the origins of humankind, the consorts of Zeus, the underworld, heroes and monsters, the Argonauts, the Trojan war, the homecomings, great sinners, centaurs, Amazon women, metamorphoses, and each of the Olympian gods and major heroes. Supplemented by subsidiary sec-

tions on the symposium, Delphi, the victims of Artemis, satyrs and maenads, and the labors of Hercules, and paraphrases of the beginning of Hesiod's *Theogony* and the myths of Pandora, Phaedra, Andromeda, Medea, Achilles, Agamemnon, and Oedipus. Accompanied by sixty illustrations, most in color, of Greek artifacts and sites. Two maps, time chart, genealogy, chart of Zeus's consorts and offspring, lists of Greek monsters, Argonauts, and heroes of the Trojan war.

Graf, Fritz. *Greek Mythology: An Introduction*. Translated by Thomas Marier. Baltimore: The Johns Hopkins University Press, 1993.
Originally published in German in 1987, this survey of Greek mythology uses synopses of basic Greek mythological texts to illustrate various ways to interpret these myths in both ancient and modern contexts. Synopses of Hesiod's *Theogony*, the Homeric hymn to Apollo, Aeschylus' *Oresteia*, and Euripides' *Orestes*. Emphasizes the close relationship between Greek myth and Greek poetry, ritual, and drama. Considers Greek constructions of myth as history, especially in the Theseus legend, and philosophic uses of myth by the sophists, Plato, and others. Eleven figures illustrating myth scenes in ancient Greek art, especially painted pottery. Endnotes, bibliography, and index.

_____. "Orpheus: A Poet Among Men." In *Interpretations of Greek Mythology*, edited by Jan Bremmer. Totowa, N.J.: Barnes & Noble Books, 1986.
A historical survey and analysis of the five themes associated with Orpheus in ancient Greek myth: his quest for his dead wife Eurydice, the magical power of his music, his death at the hands of women, the story of his severed head, and his adventures with the Argonauts. Suggests that the myth of Orpheus sprang from secret ritual connected with poetry and music. The singer is Thracian rather than Greek in the myth in order to separate him from the ordinary world and associate him with the inspiration of the Muses. Endnotes.

Grant, Michael. *Myths of the Greeks and Romans*. New York: New American Library, 1962.
Each chapter of this book offers a stimulating combination of summary of a Greco-Roman myth, interpretation, myth theory, and discussion of creative interpretations by modern artists and writers. Special attention is given to several myths, grouped according to ancient sources: the Trojan War and its aftermath, as told in the Homeric epics; the gods Zeus, Apollo, and Demeter, as told in Hesiod's *Theogony* and in the

Homeric hymns; Prometheus and Agamemnon, as told in the dramas of Aeschylus; Oedipus and Antigone, as told in the plays of Sophocles; Heracles and Dionysus, as told in the plays of Euripides; the theme of the heroic quest as developed in Apollonius of Rhodes' epic poem about Jason and the Argonauts, in Vergil's versions of Orpheus and Eurydice and of the travels of Aeneas, and in Livy's history of the early days of Rome; and the themes of love and change of form as developed in Ovid's *Metamorphoses* Illustrations, maps, genealogical charts, bibliographical notes, endnotes, and index.

_____. *Roman Myths*. New York: Dorset Press, 1984.
Traces the development of myths and historical legends in the Roman world, where these stories were popular forms of historical explanation (aetiology), morality, and political propaganda. In separate chapters, Grant provides background on sources of information for these myths, on the character of Roman mythology, and on what is known about Rome from archaeological sources. Individual chapters are devoted to the myths of Aeneas, Romulus, the Roman monarchy, and the early Republic. Includes twenty-eight black-and-white illustrations of these myths on Roman coins and in Roman art. Six maps, bibliography and index.

Graves, Robert. *The Greek Myths*. 2 vols. Rev. ed. Baltimore: Penguin, 1960.
An analysis of the Greek myths based upon the controversial theory of a powerful mother-goddess and a subordinate male vegetation deity. Many of the goddesses and heroines of Greek mythology are seen as transformations of this powerful great goddess while Greek gods and heroes are derived from her inferior consort. Argues that Greek mythology developed from a blending of matriarchal "Pelasgian" beliefs with the more patriarchal culture of Indo-European tribes which entered Greece in the Bronze Age. Contains 171 sections with detailed myth summaries, beginning with creation stories and ending with the sack of Troy and Odysseus' wanderings. Each section is accompanied by notes explaining unusual features, listing ancient literary sources, and paralleling tales in other cultures. Maps, detailed endnotes, and index.

_____. *Greek Myths*. New York: Viking, 1981.
This condensed version of the Penguin edition described above is profusely illustrated in color with mythological scenes from ancient art, especially sculpture and vase paintings. Instead of 171 smaller

sections, seven broad-ranging chapters cover topics such as the beginning of the world, the Olympian deities, various heroes and the myths of Crete, Thebes, and Mycenae. One chapter is devoted entirely to the hero Heracles. Index.

Green, Roger Lancelyn. *Heroes of Greece and Troy.* New York: Henry A. Walck, 1961.

Combines in the form of continuous narrative the major myths and legends of ancient Greece told in *Tales of the Greek Heroes* and *The Tale of Troy.* Begins with descriptions of the gods, the conflicts between Uranus and Cronus and between Cronus and Zeus, the births of Hermes and Apollo, and the stories of Prometheus, the flood, and Dionysus. Moves to the adventures of Perseus, Heracles, Theseus, Jason, and Meleager. Ends with the Trojan war, the returns of Agamemnon, Menelaus, and Odysseus, and the end of the Heroic Age. Not included are the stories of Oedipus and his family and many metamorphosis myths, such as those of Narcissus, Hyacinthus, and Echo. The narrative is freely adapted from a variety of ancient sources, especially Apollodorus, Hesiod, Homer, Apollonius of Rhodes, and Vergil. Illustrated with drawings by Heather Copley and Christopher Chamberlain. Maps, list of the names for Greek and Roman gods, and index.

_____. *The Tale of Troy.* Baltimore: Penguin, 1958.

Retells for young readers the story of the Trojan war, beginning with the marriage of Peleus and Thetis and ending with the return of Odysseus to Ithaca. Includes the myth of the judgment of Paris, the story of Helen in Sparta, and the gathering of the Greek troops at Aulis. The events of the *Iliad* are followed by the stories of Neoptolemus and Philoctetes, the theft of the Palladium, the Trojan horse, the fall of the city, and the returns of Agamemnon and of Menelaus. In the final chapter, Green describes the end of the Heroic Age of the Greeks. Some narratives, such as Euripides' tale of Helen's sojourn in Egypt during the Trojan war, have been modified because the author did not consider the original suitable for children. Each chapter is introduced with a quotation from modern poetry with an appropriate mythological reference. Author's note, map, and list of the names for Greek and Roman deities. Illustrated with line drawings by Betty Middleton-Sandford.

_____. *Tales of the Greek Heroes.* Baltimore: Penguin, 1958.

Despite the title, this book includes not only the myths of Greek heroes but also myths about some of the gods. The myths are told in nineteen chapters of continuous narrative, beginning with the birth of the gods and the myth of succession from Uranus to Cronus to Zeus. Because Green retells the myths for children, some violent details, such as the castration of Uranus, are suppressed. In Chapters 2-6 Green continues the story of the gods with the births of Hermes and Apollo, the stories of the Titan Prometheus, the flood, and Pandora, the tale of Philemon and Baucis, the myths of Typhon, Europa, and Cadmus, and the tales of Actaeon, Midas, and Dionysus. Green tells the stories of the hero Perseus in Chapter 7, of Heracles in Chapters 8-13, of Theseus in Chapter 14, of Jason and the Argonauts in Chapter 15, and of Meleager and Atalanta in Chapter 17. He concludes the narrative in Chapters 18 and 19 with the first fall of Troy and the battle between the gods and the giants. Each chapter is introduced with a quotation from modern poetry with an appropriate mythological reference. Author's note, map, and list of the names for Greek and Roman deities. Illustrated with line drawings by Betty Middleton-Sandford.

Grimal, Pierre. "Greece: Myth and Logic." In *Larousse World Mythology*, edited by Pierre Grimal. Translated by Patricia Beardsworth. New York: G. P. Putnam's Sons, 1963.
In this section of his monumental survey of world mythology, a well-known professor at the Sorbonne considers the development of the Greek body of myths and their role in religious and, especially, literary contexts. Paraphrases and explains Hesiod's *Theogony* as well as Homer's *Iliad* and *Odyssey*. Sections on each of the major gods and the heroes Heracles, Theseus, Jason, Meleager, and Perseus. Also contains the Theban cycle, Orpheus, Daedalus, and Minos, and Cupid and Psyche. Includes many photographs, some in color, of Greek artwork illustrating mythological scenes.

_____. "Rome: Gods by Conquest." In *Larousse World Mythology*, edited by Pierre Grimal. Translated by Patricia Beardsworth. New York: G. P. Putnam's Sons, 1963.
Describes the characteristics and cults of various Roman deities, both major and minor, and surveys historical legends about the founding of Rome and the early years of the city. Discusses parallels between these legends and Roman social life and culture. Also contains an overview of Roman use of foreign legends and beliefs, such as Etruscan practices in divination and the Greek legend of Aeneas. Includes thirteen photographs illustrating Roman artwork.

Guerber, Hélène Adeline. *Myths of Greece and Rome*. New York: American Book, 1893. Rev. ed. New York: House & Maxwell, 1967.

Illustrates the influence of Greco-Roman mythology upon Western culture by integrating artistic and literary interpretations into a narrative account of the myths. The author has deleted from this narrative features considered distasteful to her nineteenth-century readers. Contains black-and-white reproductions of artwork from the ancient and modern worlds. In addition to ancient writers such as Catullus, Euripides, and Homer, the author quotes British authors such as William Shakespeare, John Dryden, and Alfred, Lord Tennyson. Chapters on creation, on each of the major gods, goddesses, and heroes, on the Trojan war, and on the adventures of Odysseus and Aeneas. A concluding chapter offers a philological interpretation of these stories as "nature" myths, that is, as expressions of elemental or physical phenomena. Special features include a map, list of illustrations, genealogical table, index to poetical quotations, glossary, and index.

Guirand, Felix. "Greek Mythology." In *New Larousse Encyclopedia of Mythology*, edited by Felix Guirand et al. Translated by Richard Aldington and Delano Ames. New York: Hamlyn, 1968.
A short overview of the Aegean deities and religion of the Bronze Age is followed by a detailed summary of the mythology of Classical Greece. Retells myths about the creation of the world, the gods, and humankind, the Titan Prometheus, and the great flood from the sixth-century B.C. poems of Hesiod. Each of the Olympian deities receives separate treatment, with sections on the deity's attributes, functions, cults, representations, loves, and major myths and legends. Also contains sections on the lesser deities of Olympus, gods of the heavenly bodies and natural elements, the gods Demeter and Dionysus, the life of humankind, and the underworld. Summarizes the lives of the Greek heroes, Heracles, Theseus, Bellerophon, Perseus, Oedipus, Meleager, Peleus, Jason, Orpheus, and Minos. Little attention is paid to myths and heroes of the Trojan war, especially to the stories of Achilles and Odysseus. Includes 107 black-and-white and six color illustrations of ancient representations of the gods and heroes.

Guirand, Felix, and A.-V. Pierre "Roman Mythology." In *New Larousse Encyclopedia of Mythology*, edited by Felix Guirand et al. Translated by Richard Aldington and Delano Ames. New York: Hamlyn, 1968.
Considers some of the native features of Roman religion and mythology, with individual sections on major deities such as Jupiter and Juno, as well as other gods such as Janus, Faunus, and Vertumnus. Some of the lesser deities are grouped in the categories of agriculture, the underworld, the city, and the family. Also contains sections on deified

heroes, such as Hercules, Romulus, Remus, and Aeneas, and on the contributions of Greece and the Orient to Roman religion. Includes thirty-six black-and-white illustrations of ancient representations of Roman deities and religious scenes.

Halliday, William Reginald. *Greek and Roman Folklore*. New York: Longmans, Green, 1927.
Considers some of the folklore of ancient Greece and Rome and its influence. In an introductory chapter, Halliday offers a history of the tradition from 1000 B.C. through the fall of the Roman Empire. Also discusses some of the sources for this tradition and the question of the continuity of this tradition in modern Greece and Italy. In addition to chapters on superstitious beliefs and practices and the Classical origin of some medieval folklore, a chapter on folktales and fables deals with significant features and the origin of a variety of tales, including Aesop's *Fables*, Apuleius' story of Cupid and Psyche, several tales of Herodotus, and such hero legends as those of Theseus, Jason, Orpheus, and Daedalus. Notes parallels in the German collection of the Grimm brothers. Endnotes and bibliography.

Hamilton, Edith. *Mythology*. New York: New American Library, 1942.
A popular handbook offering a general introduction to the Greek gods and heroes, with summaries of basic myths and quotations from various ancient sources. Part 1 describes the various Greek deities, the Greek story of creation, and tales about Prometheus, Io, Narcissus, and other early mythological figures. Part 2 is devoted to stories of love adventure, such as the stories of Cupid and Psyche, Orpheus and Eurydice, and Jason and the Argonauts. Parts 3-5 tell the stories of great heroes before the Trojan War (Perseus, Theseus, Heracles, Atalanta), Trojan War heroes such as Odysseus and Aeneas, and the great mythological families of Atreus, Thebes, and Athens. Part 6 summarizes less important myths, such as those of Midas, Asclepius, and the Danaids. Part 7 provides a brief overview of Norse mythology. Illustrations, genealogical tables, and index.

Harris, Stephen L., and Gloria Platzner. *Classical Mythology*. Mountain View, Calif.: Mayfield Publishing, 1995.
Designed as an American college student's introduction to the myths of the ancient Greeks and Romans, this textbook includes individual chapters on the nature of myths, myth theory, Hesiod's *Theogony*, the fall of humankind, the Olympian deities, the great goddess, Apollo's oracle at Delphi, the god Dionysus, Hades and the afterlife, the hero,

the Trojan saga, the wanderings of Odysseus, the theater of Dionysus, Aeschylus' use of the Prometheus myth, Aeschylus' *Oresteia*, Sophocles' *Oedipus Rex*, Euripides' *Medea*, Euripides' *Bacchae*, Plato's use of mythology, Roman use of Greek myths, Vergil's *Aeneid*, Ovid's *Metamorphoses*, and transformations of myth in modern art and literature. Each chapter begins with a summary of key themes discussed in the chapter and includes significant translated passages from Hesiod, Homer, the Homeric hymns, Greek tragedy, Vergil, Ovid, and modern authors such as John Milton, Alfred, Lord Tennyson, and Wystan H. Auden, as well as a selected list of works which reinterpret Classical myths. Bibliography and questions for discussion and review appear at the end of each chapter. Profusely illustrated with black-and-white photographs of ancient and modern artistic representations of the ancient myths. Maps, charts, genealogies, glossary, general bibliography, and index.

Harrison, Jane. *Mythology*. New York: Cooper Square Publishers, 1963.
Part of the Our Debt to Greece and Rome series, this volume illustrates intersections between Greek myth and Greek religion. The author was a prominent member of the Cambridge School, which argued in the early twentieth century that myths originated in rituals. A short introductory essay on Greek ritual and religious ideas is followed by individual chapters on the gods Hermes, Poseidon, the Mountain Mother, Demeter/Kore, maiden goddesses (Hera, Athena and Aphrodite), Artemis, Apollo, Dionysus, and Zeus. Discussion of the god's origin, development, and rituals is accompanied by extensive quotation in translation from ancient Greek sources. Endnotes and bibliography.

Hathorn, Richmond Y. *Greek Mythology*. Beirut: American University of Beirut, 1977.
Replaces the traditional, genealogical ordering of Greek mythology in favor of one based on archetypes or patterns. Part 1 deals with two basic patterns of myth: death and rebirth and the sacred marriage. Part 2 considers aspects of god as victim, as prophet, and as trickster, and of the mother goddess as mother, lover, and virgin. In Part 3 Hathorn deals with the major cycles about the heroes Oedipus, Jason, Theseus, and Heracles, and with events surrounding the Trojan War and the homecoming of the Greeks. Each section includes a paraphrase of the myth, analysis, interpretation, and bibliographic references. Index.

Hendricks, Rhoda A., trans. *Classical Gods and Heroes*. New York: William Morrow, 1974.

Uses an anthology of her own translations from Classical authors to retell the myths of the Greeks and Romans. Major sources include the Homeric epics, the poems of Hesiod, and Ovid's *Metamorphoses*. A loose chronological organization beginning with myths of creation, early humankind, and the flood, dealing with major heroes such as Perseus, Heracles, Theseus, and Jason and with myths about the Trojan War and its aftermath, and ending with tales of love about Cupid and Psyche, Pyramus and Thisbe, and Pygmalion. Each reading is preceded by a short introduction. In a general introduction, the translator provides some background to the ancient authors, a short history of Greece, and a historical overview of the study of Greek mythology. Short bibliography and glossary.

Henle, Jane. *Greek Myths: A Vase Painter's Notebook*. Bloomington: Indiana University Press, 1973.
Shows how to recognize and interpret mythological scenes painted on Greek pottery. Emphasizes the historical evolution of these mythological scenes and their iconography between the eighth and fourth centuries B.C. Arrangement is thematic, beginning with Zeus and his loves and ending with the Trojan War and the return of Odysseus. Chapters on the lives of heroes such as Heracles, Perseus, Theseus, and Meleager. Seventy-five black-and-white illustrations from painted pottery. Endnotes and bibliography. Index of types with drawings of standard mythological scenes.

Henrichs, Albert. "Three Approaches to Greek Mythography." In *Interpretations of Greek Mythology*, edited by Jan Bremmer. Totowa, N.J.: Barnes & Noble Books, 1986.
A Classical scholar offers a brief survey of the ancient Greek mythographic tradition organized around three different modern approaches to the subject. The first is an examination of a specific mythography, Conon's *Diegeseis*, a neglected work of the first century A.D. Henrichs offers some background to the book and describes some of its fifty stories, mostly local myths and legends. The second is study of a particular aspect of mythography, the use of mythological catalogues. Henrichs discusses some important ancient lists of names, such as the *Catalogue of Women* by Hesiod and the participants in the funeral games of Pelias, and shows how these names made the transition from poetry to mythology. The third is applied mythography, or a study of all available ancient versions of a myth. Henrichs analyzes six versions of the myth of Callisto (including those of Apollodorus, Pausanias, and Ovid), attempts to reconstruct the original myth by comparing story

patterns, and emphasizes the contribution of Greek art and recent papyrus finds to the modern study of Greek myth. Chart and endnotes.

Hesiod. *Theogony.* Translated by Richard S. Caldwell. Cambridge, Mass.: Focus Classical Library, 1987.
This scholarly English translation of Hesiod's poem about the birth of the Greek gods provides original line references in the margins and detailed explanatory footnotes for the general reader. Uses transliterated spellings of Greek words. The detailed introductory essay includes an analysis of the poem's structure with genealogical figures, a description of Greece before Hesiod, commentary on Hesiod and the theogonic tradition, and some comparison with Middle Eastern cosmogonies. A psychological interpretation of Hesiod's succession myth follows the translation of the *Theogony.* In appendices are translations of lines 1-201 of Hesiod's *Works and Days* and excerpts from Book 1 of Apollodorus' *Library.* Index.

_____. *Theogony and Works and Days.* Translated by M. L. West. Oxford: Oxford University Press, 1988.
This careful prose translation of Hesiod's poems by a major Hesiodic scholar includes original line references at the top of every page and explanatory endnotes. Uses latinized spellings of Greek words. Introductory essay on Hesiod and his poems, note on the text and translation, and bibliography.

_____. *The Works and Days; Theogony; Shield of Heracles.* Translated by Richmond Lattimore. Ann Arbor: University of Michigan Press, 1959.
English verse translations of three mythological poems surviving under the name of Hesiod. *Theogony* describes the creation of the cosmos and of the gods. *Works and Days* includes the Hesiodic version of the and the myths of Pandora and Prometheus. The *Shield of Heracles* survives in the Hesiodic corpus but is probably a later interpolation. This poem describes the conception of Heracles, the hero's great shield, and his encounter with the monster Cycnus, the son of Ares. Introductory essay on Hesiod and his poems. Genealogical tables and glossary.

Hesiod and Homer. *Hesiod, the Homeric Hymns and Homerica*, edited and translated by Hugh G. Evelyn-White. Cambridge, Mass.: Harvard University Press, 1914.
This volume in the Loeb Classical Library makes accessible to English readers not only the widely translated Hesiodic *Theogony* and *Works*

and Days and the Homeric hymns but also includes a number of ancient texts not otherwise readily available in English, such as fragments from Hesiod's *Astronomy*, *Precepts of Chiron*, and *Catalogue of Women*, fragments from various epic poems in the Trojan cycle, and a satirical epic called the *Batrachomyomachia*, or "Battle of the Frogs and Mice." Greek text and English prose translation appear on facing pages. Introductory essay on the poems and their history. Occasional footnotes, bibliography, and index.

Hesiod and Theognis. *Theogony, Works and Days, and Elegies*. Translated by Dorothea Wender. New York: Penguin, 1973.
Only the material dealing with the Hesiodic poems are of mythological note. These verse translations by an American Classical scholar contain original line references at the top of every page and explanatory endnotes. Uses transliterated Greek spellings. In an introductory essay, Wender provides some background to Hesiod and his poems. Bibliography and glossary.

Jameson, Michael H. "Mythology of Ancient Greece." In *Mythologies of the Ancient World*, edited by Samuel Noah Kramer. Garden City, N.Y.: Doubleday (Anchor), 1961.
This short survey of Greek mythology begins with a prologue containing an overview of Greek history. Emphasizes the development of these myths and the interaction between hero legends, folktales, and myths about the gods. Three major sections on heroes, on gods, and on Hesiod's *Theogony* contain frequent references to ancient literary and artistic representations of the myths, with summaries of the major Greek plays and epic poems. Chronological chart, glossary of major Greek gods, and bibliography.

Kane, J. P. "Greece." In *Mythology: An Illustrated Encyclopaedia*, edited by Richard Cavendish. New York: Rizzoli International, 1980. Also published as *An Illustrated Encyclopedia of Mythology*. New York: Crescent Books, 1984.
This overview of Greek mythology includes a summary and analysis of the creation myth in Hesiod's *Theogony*, the five in Hesiod's *Works and Days*, the Homeric depiction of humans and gods, the concepts of prowess and honor, especially in the Homeric hymns, the adventures of the hero Heracles, and the stories of Perseus, Jason, and Theseus. Also contains sections on myths as explanations, on myths in Greek tragedy, and on the Greek philosophical concept of death. Map, genealogies of the gods and several heroes, glossaries of Zeus's children

and of the twelve Olympian gods, a list of early sources, and illustrations of artwork related to the myths.

Kerényi, Karl. *The Gods of the Greeks*. London: Thames and Hudson, 1951.

These retellings of Greek myths about the gods are paraphrases especially from Hesiod, Homer, and the Greek tragedians and are intended specifically for adult readers. Chapters on creation, the Titans, other pre-Olympian deities, Aphrodite, the Great Mother, Zeus, Metis and Athena, Leto and her children, Hera and her children, Maia and Hermes, Poseidon, myths about the sun and the moon, Prometheus and humankind, Hades and Persephone, and Dionysus and his followers. Special attention to the various Greek names of the deities. Twenty-six plates and numerous figures illustrating the gods in Greek art. Ancient sources are provided in endnotes. Introductory essay and index.

Kingsley, Charles. *The Heroes*. London: J. M. Dent & Sons, 1856. Reprint. New York: E. P. Dutton, 1963.

A nineteenth-century British scholar and novelist retells the myths of Perseus, Jason, and Theseus for young readers. The twelve labors of Heracles are also told by Grace Rhys. Introductory essay on the influence of Greece on Western culture. The reprint includes four color plates and line drawings by Joan Kiddell-Monroe.

Kirk, G. S. "The Greek Myths." In *The Nature of Greek Myths*, by G. S. Kirk. Baltimore: Penguin, 1974.

This part of a book which frequently reaches far beyond the boundaries of Greek mythology focuses more specifically on the use of myths in Greek culture. In Chapter 5, Kirk provides a sweeping overview of the use of myths in Greek literature, including the Homeric epics, Greek tragedy, the works of Pindar and other lyric poets, and the writings of Plato. Greek myths are divided into two groups. The first group, consisting of cosmogonical myths, tales describing the development of the Olympian gods, and stories about early humans, is discussed in Chapter 6. In Chapter 7, Kirk looks at three groups of legends. "Older" heroes such as Perseus, Theseus, Cadmus and Jason, whose stories take place in a timeless past, are contrasted with "younger" heroes such as Oedipus, Agamemnon, and Odysseus, whose tales exhibit historicizing elements, and with the life of Croesus, which was transformed into a myth in the historical period. In Chapter 8 Kirk analyzes myths surrounding the hero Heracles, whose ambiguous personality is seen to exhibit a tension between nature and culture. In Chapter 9 he offers some suggestions on the ways that hero-myths develop in human societies.

_____. "The Qualities of Greek Myths." In *Myth: Its Meaning and Functions in Ancient and Other Cultures*, by G. S. Kirk. Berkeley: University of California Press, 1970.
Compares Greek myths about gods and heroes and argues for a basic thematic simplicity of the myths. Lists the commonest themes in Greek myths, including tricks, transformations, accidental killings, and giants, as well as a list of more special or extraordinary themes, such as fire, the Golden age, and returns from the underworld. Contains some comparisons with Norse, Egyptian, and Hindu mythology, and, especially, a comparison of the Hurrian Kumarbi with the Greek Cronus, and concludes that the Greeks shared a common world view with the peoples of ancient Mesopotamia. Also analyzes Hesiod's myth about the and comments upon the relationship between mythic thought and the rise of Greek rational speculation.

Lang, Andrew. *Tales of Troy and Greece*. New York: Longmans, Green, 1907. Reprint. New York: Roy Publishers, 1963.
A prolific nineteenth-century folklorist and translator of the Homeric poems here retells for young readers the stories of the heroes of ancient Greece. In Part 1 Lang centers the story of the Trojan War on the hero Odysseus. He begins with the boyhood of the hero and with the marriage and abduction of Helen, paraphrases the plot of the *Iliad*, and concludes with the fall of Troy. In Part 2 Lang tells of the wanderings of Odysseus and the voyage of Jason and the Argonauts. In Part 3 the myths of the heroes Theseus and Perseus are told. Illustrated with line drawings by Edward Bawden. Map.

Lefkowitz, Mary R. *Women in Greek Myth*. Baltimore: The Johns Hopkins University Press, 1986.
Describes how the ancient Greeks portrayed the female experience in myth and suggests that modern, negative interpretations of Greek myths about women are not entirely accurate. Rather, examination of myths such as those about the Amazon women, Clytemnestra, Antigone, and Alcestis suggests that women in Greek myths are more enlightened then their male counterparts and often feared more for their intelligence than for their sexuality. Also examines misogyny and women in Christian martyrologies. Endnotes, bibliography, and index.

Loew, Cornelius. "Philosophy and Hellenic Culture." In *Myth, Sacred History and Philosophy*, by Cornelius Loew. New York: Harcourt, Brace & World, 1967.

This final chapter of a study of ancient Mesopotamian, Egyptian, Hebrew, and Greek myths as the pre-Christian religious heritage of Western civilization traces the development of a Greek world view from myth to philosophy, from the archaic traditions in the poetry of Homer and Hesiod to the contributions of the pre-Socratic philosophers of Ionia and of Socrates and Plato. The cosmological and social order described in Homer's *Iliad* and *Odyssey* and the cosmogony of Hesiod's *Theogony* and *Works and Days* present mythic concepts of fate, justice, and excellence which are reevaluated by later philosophers. Footnotes and bibliography.

Low, Alice. *The Macmillan Book of Greek Gods and Heroes*. New York: Macmillan, 1985.

Greek myths retold for juvenile readers with many color illustrations by Arvis Stewart. Chapters 1 and 2 deal with Mother Earth and the birth of the gods and descriptions of the major deities in the pantheon. In Chapter 3 are myths about the life of early humankind, especially the myths of Prometheus, Pandora, and the flood. Chapter 4, entitled "Triumphs of the Gods," deals with relationships between gods and mortals in myths such as those of Europa, Arachne, Narcissus, Orpheus, and Oedipus. In Chapter 5 are the stories of five major heroes, Persues, Heracles, Jason, Theseus, and Odysseus. The last chapter is devoted to three myths about constellations, Orion, Cassiopeia, and Castor and Pollux. In a foreword and afterword, Barry Katz briefly describes Greek religious beliefs and explains the relationship between Greek and Roman gods. Index.

Mackenzie, Donald Alexander. *Myths of Crete and Pre-Hellenic Europe*. London: Gresham Publishing, 1917. Reprint. Boston: Milford House, 1973.

Written in the decades following the archaeological discoveries of Heinrich Schliemann in Mycenae and of Sir Arthur Evans at Cnossus in Crete, this book reflects controversial theories of cultural drift, racial migrations, and the development of civilization which were popular in the early twentieth century. Uses a chronological arrangement, beginning with Europe in the Ice Age and Paleolithic period. Chapters on history in myth and legends based on Schliemann's discoveries, on Crete as the lost island of Atlantis, on the palaces of Cnossus and Phaestus, and on various features of Cretan life and culture, especially cave deities. Searches for overlap between the myths and legends of ancient Crete and those suggested in the Paleolithic cave paintings of Spain and France. Map, four color plates, and thirty-two black-and-white illustrations, mostly of objects found in ancient Crete. Index.

McLean, Mollie, and Anne Wiseman. *Adventures of the Greek Heroes.* Boston: Houghton Mifflin, 1961.

Retells the deeds of six Greek heroes for older children. The authors have used versions of the myths from the *Odes* of Pindar rather than the more common Homeric poems and Ovid's *Metamorphoses.* Three chapters on Hercules deal with his rescue of Prometheus, his ten labors, and the story of Admetus and Alcestis. The birth of Perseus and his encounters with Medusa, Atlas, and Andromeda are presented in four chapters. The six chapters on Theseus focus on the hero's early life, especially his adventures on the way to Athens, Medea's attempt to poison him, and the slaying of the Minotaur. The story of Orpheus' journey to the underworld is preceded by a separate description of the Land of the Dead. Meleager's story is presented in two chapters, one on his birth and a second on the Calydonian Boar Hunt. The adventures of Jason and the Argonauts are told in two chapters, one on the journey to Colchis and the second on events in Colchis. Short introductory essay on the connections between these tales and the ancient Greek Olympic games. Illustrated with drawings by Witold T. Mars. Pronouncing index.

Macpherson, Jay. *Four Ages of Man.* New York: St. Martin's Press, 1962.

These retellings of Greek myths are organized chronologically, beginning with creation and stories of the gods and moving to the heroes, the Trojan war, and the conclusion of the Greek heroic Age. The title suggests a parallel between Hesiod's four ages of man and the progress of human life as presented in Greek myths. Chapter 1 deals with creation, the War of succession in heaven, Prometheus, Pandora, the flood, and Phaëthon. In Chapter 2, Macpherson tells the stories of Persephone, Adonis, Hyacinthus, Narcissus, and Orpheus. Chapter 3 is devoted to various loves of the gods and stories of metamorphosis, including Syrinx, Daphne, Arachne, Midas, and Philemon and Baucis. The lives of the heroes Perseus, Heracles, Jason, Bellerophon, and Theseus are presented in Chapter 4. Myths about the city of Thebes are found in Chapter 5. Chapter 6 begins with the judgment of Paris and includes the Trojan War and the returns of the heroes Menelaus, Agamemnon, Aeneas, and Odysseus. The story of Cupid and Psyche is told in Chapter 7. In Chapter 8, Macpherson discusses oracles and the influence of Greco-Roman myths in later European culture. Introductory essay on the meaning and interpretation of myths. Throughout the text are quotations from British poets which contain mythological allusions. Illustrated with black-and-white figures. Genealogical chart, chart coordinating mythological and historical events, endnotes, and combined index and glossary.

Mayerson, Philip. *Classical Mythology in Literature, Art, and Music.* Waltham, Mass.: Xerox College Publishing, 1971.
This survey of Greek and Roman mythology combines explication of the myth with illustration of its use in literature, art, and music. Shows how the myths are treated in different media via extensive quotation of literary adaptations of these myths in the ancient and modern worlds and 110 black-and-white illustrations of artistic treatments of the same myths and references to musical adaptations. Following an introductory chapter with background about ancient mythographers such as Homer, Hesiod, and the Greek tragedians, Mayerson treats the myths chronologically. Begins with creation myths and the rise of Zeus. Separate chapters on the Olympian gods, the gods of the underworld, Dionysus and Orpheus, Greek heroes, the Trojan war, the returns of Agamemnon and Odysseus, and the voyage of Aeneas. Map, bibliography, and index.

Moncrieff, A. R. Hope. *Classic Myth and Legend.* New York: William H. Wise, 1934.
A retelling of the Greek myths for adults. An introductory section deals with the growth of myths, theogony, cosmogony, the Greek pantheon, and demigods. The remaining sections deal with various heroes and mortals, including Phaëthon, Perseus, Arachne, Meleager, Atalanta, Hercules, Jason and the Argonauts, the city of Thebes, the Trojan war, the house of Agamemnon, and the adventures of Odysseus. Also contains the tales of Polycrates and Croesus from Herodotus' *Histories* and the "Dream of Er" from Plato's *Republic.* Includes extensive quotation from ancient Greek authors, especially Homer. The last seven sections offer modern adaptations of ancient myths, including "Tithonus" by Alfred, Lord Tennyson and "Laodamia" by William Wordsworth. Forty-eight plates, including eight in color, of ancient and modern artistic versions of these myths. Index and pronunciation guide.

Morford, Mark P. O., and Robert J. Lenardon. *Classical Mythology.* 5th ed. New York: Longman, 1995.

This standard college textbook summarizes the myths of the Classical gods and heroes. Part 1 deals with creation, the gods, and the afterlife. In Part 2 the heroes of Greece and Troy are grouped according to geographic sagas. In Part 3 a chapter on the nature of Roman mythology is followed by two chapters dealings with the survival of Classical myths, first in modern literature and art and then in music and film. Substantial translation from ancient authors, including all of the Homeric hymns, is integrated into the text. Includes 109 illustrations of Classical and modern artwork with mythological themes, twenty-two in color. Numerous maps and genealogical charts. Several bibliographies, including a discography of musical compositions inspired by mythological themes. Glossary on the Greek spelling of names. Indexes.

Nichols, Marianne. *Man, Myth, and Monument*. New York: William Morrow, 1975.

Considers links between Greek mythology and Greek history, especially by comparing details from the myths with archaeological evidence. For example, the myth of Europa is connected with evidence for migrations on the Greek peninsula, myths about centaurs with the introduction of the horse, the legend of Theseus with archaeological evidence for a Greek presence on Crete, and the story of Jason and the Argonauts with knowledge of trade in the ancient world. Fifty-four illustrations of archaeological sites and ancient artwork depicting mythological scenes. Appendices include a chronological chart and a translation of the Parian chronicle. Bibliography and index.

Nilsson, Martin P. *The Mycenaean Origin of Greek Mythology*. Berkeley: University of California Press, 1932.

Combines written and archaeological evidence in order to answer the question, How old is Greek mythology? Concludes that the myths preserved in the *Iliad* and *Odyssey* of Homer and in other traditional literature contain many elements which can be traced back at least to the Mycenaean period (before 1100 B.C.). In particular, Nilsson looks at Greek myths geographically and associates important Mycenaean political centers with specific myth cycles. In addition to the myths associated with specific sites, such as Perseus with the Argolid, Oedipus with Thebes, and Theseus with Athens, Nilsson also considers more pan-Hellenic myths, such as those of Heracles and of the Greek gods. Footnotes and index.

Otto, Walter Friedrich. *Dionysus: Myth and Cult*. Translated by Robert B.
Palmer. Bloomington: University of Indiana Press, 1965.
Examines the theological significance of the god Dionysus and his cult.
In Part 1, Otto considers the relationship between cult and myth. In
Part 2 descriptions of the god in ancient art and literature and myths
about his birth, epiphanies, marriage to Ariadne, and death are analyzed
in terms of their religious power and meaning. Fifteen plates illustrat-
ing the cult and myths of the god. Introductory essay by the translator.
Endnotes and index.

_____. *The Homeric Gods*. Translated by Moses Hadas. New
York: Pantheon Books, 1954.
A scholarly study of religious aspects of the Greek gods rather than a
handbook of myths. Following a short introduction on general features
of Greek religion, Otto examines in Part 2 the relationship between
myth and religion, especially in the Homeric epics and in Aeschylean
tragedy. In subsequent parts, he considers aspects of worship and belief
associated with each of the major Greek deities, the spiritual nature
and form of the Greek gods, manifestations of the gods to humans, the
relationship between Greek gods and humans, and questions of fate.
References to Greek myths are incorporated into discussions of all of
these topics. Endnotes, seven photographs, and index.

Ovid. *The Metamorphoses*. Translated by Horace Gregory. New York:
Viking Press, 1958.
A major twentieth-century American verse translation of Ovid's first-
century A.D. epic collection of myths of changing form. Original book
numbers appear at the head of every page without original line references. The Roman poet combined Greek and Roman sources to produce a continuous mythic narrative, beginning with the creation of the
world and ending with the apotheosis of Julius Caesar. Ovid's poem
has remained popular in the ancient, medieval, and modern worlds and
has inspired frequent imitation. Some of Ovid's better-known transformations are the stories of Phaëthon, Daphne, Daedalus, and Perseus.
Ovid's poem is also popular for its love tales, such as those of Pyramus
and Thisbe and Philemon and Baucis. Introductory essay on the career
of Ovid. With black-and-white drawings by Zhenya Gray. Combined
glossary and index.

_____. *Metamorphoses*. Translated by Rolfe Humphries. Bloom-
ington: Indiana University Press, 1955. Abridged in *Literature of the*

Western World. Vol. 1 *The Ancient World Through the Renaissance*, edited by Brian Wilkie and James Hurt. New York: Macmillan, 1984. Humphries' verse translation of Ovid's poem rivals Gregory's for accessibility to the general reader. Original book and line references appear at the head of every page. The abridged edition contains portions of Books 1 and 11 and all of Book 10, including the stories of creation, the flood, Orpheus and Eurydice, Pygmalion, Adonis, Atalanta, and Midas. The original edition contains a combined index and glossary and an introductory essay on the life of Ovid and on the art of translating.

_____. *The Metamorphoses.* Translated by Mary M. Innes. Baltimore: Penguin Books, 1955.
In order to make this prose translation of the poem more useful to the general reader, Innes has incorporated into the translation some brief identification of unfamiliar names and has eliminated Ovid's frequent use of direct address. Latin line references and descriptive headings at the top of every page. Includes an introductory essay divided into four parts: a summary of the poet's life and works, literary characteristics of the *Metamorphoses*, the influence of the poem on later literature, and a few comments on the translation. Index.

_____. *Metamorphoses.* Translated by A. D. Melville. Oxford: Oxford University Press, 1986.
A British Classical scholar translates Ovid's first-century A.D. mythological epic into English verse. Original book and line references appear at the top of every page. Explanatory endnotes are provided by E. J. Kenny for the general reader. In an introductory essay, Kenny discusses some literary aspects of the epic. Historical sketch of Ovid, bibliography, and combined glossary and index.

_____. *Metamorphoses.* Translated by Frank Justus Miller. 2 vols. New York: G. P. Putnam's Sons, 1925.
This volume in the Loeb Classical Library offers the original Latin text of Ovid's poem on facing pages with a prose English translation. Miller's formal, literal version is probably less accessible to the general reader than those of Rolfe Humphries and Horace Gregory, but the presence of the actual Latin provides a rare opportunity for the English reader to consult the Latin poem and translation simultaneously. Books 1-8 of *Metamorphoses* appear in Volume 1 and Books 9-15 in Volume 2. Combines glossary and index at the end of Volume 2. Footnotes.

Parker, Robert. "Myths of Early Athens." In *Interpretations of Greek Mythology*, edited by Jan Bremmer. Totowa, N.J.: Barnes & Noble Books, 1986.

Traces Attic myths chronologically from the birth of Athena through the story of Cecrops and his daughters to the life of Erechtheus. Does not deal with the Eleusinian myth of Demeter, the apolitical myth of Cephalus and Procris, or the later tales of Theseus. Uses references to Athenian art and literature to show how the Athenians consciously created a political mythology in the late fifth century B.C. to celebrate the greatness of their city and its institutions. Genealogical chart and endnotes.

Pellizer, Enzio. "Reflections, Echoes and Amorous Reciprocity: On Reading the Narcissus Story." Translated by Diana Crampton. In *Interpretations of Greek Mythology*, edited by Jan Bremmer. Totowa, N.J.: Barnes & Noble Books, 1986.

This philosophical reflection on the myth of Narcissus uses semiotic analysis to interpret the myth as a statement on individual identity, love, and otherness. Presents at the beginning of the article versions of the Narcissus myth by three late sources: Conon (first century A.D.), Plutarch (second century A.D.), and an anonymous medieval mythographer. The structure of these three narratives is compared and associated with Aristophanes' story about the origin of love in Plato's *Symposium*.

Perowne, Stewart. *Roman Mythology*. 2d ed. New York: Peter Bedrick Books, 1984.

While most studies of Greco-Roman mythology tend to emphasize the contributions of the Greeks, Perowne offers a general introduction to the development of Roman mythology, cult, and religious beliefs. Lavishly illustrated with photographs of Roman religious sites, sculpture, and painting. Shows how the Romans began with a small pantheon of deities, including Jupiter, Mars, and Minerva, and several important cults such as Lupercalia and the worship of Vesta and her fire, and gradually accepted beliefs from all over the Roman empire. Worship of Hercules and Apollo came from South Italian Greeks and a belief in augury from the Etruscans. Contributions of Greek philosophy, Egyptian and Syrian religions, Judaism, and Christianity are also considered. The importance of state cults in Rome is reflected in the early link between Roman calendar and Roman cults and myths and in the later development of a cult in honor of the divine emperor. Bibliography and index.

Pinsent, John. *Greek Mythology*. 2d ed. New York: Peter Bedrick Books, 1982.

Part of a series called the Library of the World's Myths and Legends, this general survey of the mythology of the ancient Greeks is profusely illustrated with photographs of archaeological sites, ancient sculpture, and painted pottery related to the myths. The myths themselves are arranged chronologically. Greek tales about creation and the gods are followed by legends about early heroes such as Cadmus, Sisyphus, Perseus, and Jason. Later chapters deal with Thebes, Heracles, Athens, Theseus, the Trojan war, and the returns of heroes such as Agamemnon and Odysseus from Troy. Bibliography and index.

Powell, Barry B. *Classical Myth*. Englewood Cliffs, N.J.: Prentice Hall, 1995.

Written as a textbook for a college survey course on Classical mythology. Analyses of the myths are combined with extensive translation of major sources by Herbert M. Howe. Deals in Part 1 with a definition of myth and with the cultural background of Greek myth, including a survey of Mesopotamian myths and an overview of ancient Greek history and society. Myths about the gods are in Part 2, beginning with cosmogony and the origin of humankind and including chapters on the older and younger Olympians, on the fertility myths of Demeter and of Dionysus, on myths of death and the underworld, and on prophets and prophecy. Myths of all the major heroes appear in Part 3. Also includes a separate chapter on Roman myths and legends. Part 4 contains a historical overview of theories of myth from ancient Greece through the twentieth century. Bibliographies at the end of every chapter. Many illustrations from ancient and modern art. Footnotes, maps, genealogical charts, and index.

Puhvel, Jaan. "Ancient Greece." In *Comparative Mythology*, by Jaan Puhvel. Baltimore: The Johns Hopkins University Press, 1987.

A survey of the major Greek deities and their origins in a broad Indo-European context. Also considers elements of Greek saga which include features of inherited Indo-European structures, such as the Book of the Dead (*Odyssey* 11) and the myth of the Dioscuri. Illustrates the complex nature of Greek myth in a comparative context; that is, these tales contain features which are simultaneously unique to Greece and inherited from the Indo-European tripartite structure of king, warrior, and worker. Bibliography.

_____. "Ancient Rome." In *Comparative Mythology*, by Jaan Puhvel. Baltimore: The Johns Hopkins University Press, 1987.
An introduction to the mythology, deities, rituals, and legendary history of ancient Rome and their links with proto-Indo-European features of society, especially the concept of the king, warrior, and worker. Discusses the origins of Roman mythology and its relationship to Greek and Etruscan sources. Emphasis on religious vocabulary, its meaning, and its Indo-European parallels. Considers major deities such as Mars and Juno, as well as more obscure deities such as Lua Mater, the consort of Saturnus. Compares legends of early Rome, such as the story of Romulus and Remus, with similar features from other Indo-European contexts. Quotations in translation of Roman ritual regulations and parallels from Vedic sources in ancient India. Bibliography.

Rose, H. J. *Gods and Heroes of the Greeks: An Introduction to Greek Mythology*. New York: New American Library, 1958.
In contrast to the author's more scholarly *Handbook of Greek Mythology*, this book serves as a general outline of the more important myths of Greece and Rome. In an introductory chapter, Rose divides these stories into three types: myths proper about the gods, sagas about heroes, and folktales or *Märchen* about ordinary people. Subsequent chapters are then devoted to illustrations of each type. Another chapter illustrates how sagas sometimes center on cycles or particular geographic areas, such as Thebes or Troy. In a final chapter, Rose shows how Hellenistic and Roman authors emphasized the regional features of myth and used them for mere literary adornment. Bibliography and index.

_____. *A Handbook of Greek Mythology*. 6th ed. New York: E. P. Dutton, 1959.
Offers a detailed survey of the basic myths of the ancient Greeks and Romans as told by major authors such as Homer, Hesiod, and the Athenian dramatists. Supplemented, in smaller print, by summaries of more obscure, later, and local tales. Each chapter is followed by endnotes providing ancient and modern sources for further study. An initial chapter lists several theories of myth and offers a brief history of mythology. Early chapters deal with creation, the children of Cronus, the queens of heaven, the younger gods, and lesser and foreign deities. Later chapters summarize the heroic cycles, the story of Troy, the use of folktale themes in Classical mythology, and mythical elements in the early history of Rome. Bibliography and indexes.

Rouse, W. H. D. *Gods, Heroes and Men of Ancient Greece*. New York: New American Library, 1957.

Paraphrases of the Greek myths written in simple English for British schoolchildren. The traditional organization, beginning with creation and ending with the Trojan war, is accompanied by treatments of the story of Cupid and Psyche and the death of Pan. Offers sections on each of the major Greek gods and heroes, but certain myths, such as those of Oedipus and Agamemnon, are avoided, probably because of the themes of incest and parricide which they contain. Some dialogue is invented by the author. Genealogical charts and pronouncing index.

Ruck, Carl A. P., and Danny Staples. *The World of Classical Myths: Gods and Goddesses; Heroines and Heroes*. Durham, N.C.: Carolina Academic Press, 1994.

This handbook is meant to serve as an introduction to Classical mythology either for self-study or as part of a formal college course. The text is filled with pedagogical aids. Major names and terms are printed in boldface. A review of major myths and concepts covered in the chapter and questions for discussion and further study are found at the end of every chapter. The archetypal symbols of Carl Jung form a major organizational principle, with a repertory of paradigms or archetypal patterns discussed throughout the book. Emphasizes the evolutionary nature of the Greek deities and Greek hero as liminal, with feet in two worlds. In Chapter 1 a definition of mythology is sought in the contrast between myth and reality. Five chapters on the gods, especially Athena, Apollo, Artemis, and Dionysus, are followed by four chapters on the liminal heroes Perseus, Heracles, Theseus, Jason, and Oedipus, a chapter on the Trojan war, and a final chapter on Persephone as the liminal heroine. Six maps, nine genealogical charts, ninety-four illustrations (especially from Greek art), a note on geography, a list of ancillary readings, bibliography, and index.

Schwab, Gustav Benjamin. *Gods and Heroes*. Translated by Olga Marx and Ernst Morwitz. New York: Pantheon Books, 1946.

An English translation of *Die Sagen des klassischen Altertums*, a standard German handbook of Greek mythology originally published in 1900. Schwab combines a variety of ancient sources to retell the myths in a continuous narrative without adding personal interpretation. Organized chronologically around the lives of heroes. Begins with the myth of Prometheus and the . Emphasizes in Part 1 the stories of the Argonauts, Heracles and his descendants, Theseus, Oedipus, and the Seven against Thebes. Deals in Part 2 with stories connected with the

Trojan war, the death of Agamemnon, and the return of Odysseus. Text illustrated with numerous black-and-white figures from Greek painted pottery. Introduction by Werner Jaeger. Index.

Seltman, Charles. *The Twelve Olympians*. New York: Thomas Y. Crowell, 1960.
Examines the major features of the twelve major deities of Greek mythology. Each of the divinities, including Dionysus, is given a separate chapter which provides a summary of the god's chief characteristics and concerns as well as a historical sketch of the god's worship. A final chapter considers deified mortals such as Heracles, Alexander the Great, and the Roman emperor Augustus. Extensive quotation in translation from ancient sources. Sixteen illustrations, map, bibliography, and index.

Serraillier, Ian. *The Gorgon's Head*. New York: Henry Z. Walck, 1962.
A retelling of the myth of Perseus for children. The story is told chronologically in seven chapters, beginning with the birth of the hero and ending with his return to Greece and the accidental slaying of his grandfather Acrisius. The central events deal with Perseus' encounter with the Gorgon Medusa and his rescue of the Ethiopian princess Andromeda. Illustrated with line drawings by William Stobbs. Short note on sources and bibliography.

Severin, Tim. *The Jason Voyage: The Quest for the Golden Fleece*. New York: Simon and Schuster, 1985.
Describes a project sponsored by the National Geographic Society in which a replica of a Bronze Age Greek seagoing vessel was built and sailed along the traditional route of Jason and the Argonauts from the Aegean through the Black Sea to Colchis (modern Georgia). This expedition proved that a voyage of this type was possible for an ancient Greek vessel. Includes a retelling of the myth of Jason's voyage, a summary of the text of Apollonius of Rhodes' *Argonautica*, drawings of the general layout and riggings of the *Argo*, maps, and illustrations.

Smith, John. *The Bride from the Sea: An Introduction to the Study of Greek Mythology*. New York: St. Martin's Press, 1973.
The myth of Peleus and Thetis is the point of departure for this basic introduction to Greek myths written for British schoolchildren. Chapters on the relationship between myth and history, on folktales, and on the origins and functions of myths. Greek myths are discussed in the context of European legends and folktales, including the legend of King Arthur and folktales in the collection of the Brothers Grimm.

Short epilogue on the influence of Greek mythology on later European life, literature, and art. Illustrations, genealogical charts, maps, and indexes.

Sourvinou-Inwood, Christiane. "Myth as History: The Previous Owner of the Delphic Oracle." In *Interpretations of Greek Mythology*, edited by Jan Bremmer. Totowa, N.J.: Barnes & Noble Books, 1986.

The second half of this deconstructionist essay analyzes the Greek mythic tradition that an earlier goddess, not Apollo, founded the oracle at Delphi. Examines passages from Aeschylus' *Eumenides*, Euripides' *Iphigenia Among the Taurians*, and the two Homeric hymns to Apollo in order to retell the myth and to show that the myth of a previous owner of the oracle has nothing to do with the history of the cult at Delphi but expresses instead a positive image of Apollo and his oracle by identifying Apollo's acquisition of Delphi with Zeus's succession to power in Hesiod's *Theogony*. Both Apollo and Zeus are gods who have brought order out of disorder. Appendix on the Delphic *omphalos* or navel of the world. Endnotes.

Stapleton, Michael. *The Concise Dictionary of Greek and Roman Mythology*. New York: Peter Bedrick Books, 1986.

The alphabetical references to major personages and places in Classical mythology in this dictionary offer summaries of the myths with little interpretation. Some later adaptations of the myths are mentioned. Includes a short introductory essay on Greek mythology, as well as plot summaries of Homer's *Iliad* and *Odyssey*, Vergil's *Aeneid*, the *Argonautica* of Apollonius of Rhodes, and several Greek plays. A list of minor characters and place names lacking their own citations, index, and bibliography.

_____. *The Illustrated Dictionary of Greek and Roman Mythology*. New York: Peter Bedrick Books, 1986.

Includes all the material found in *The Concise Dictionary of Greek and Roman Mythology* (see above) together with black-and-white illustrations of selected myths in art. Scenes from Greek painted pottery are especially well represented, along with reproductions of Greek and Roman sculpture and Roman wall painting.

Usher, Kerry. *Heroes, Gods and Emperors from Roman Mythology*. New York: Schocken Books, 1983.

An introduction to Roman myths and legends for juvenile readers. Following a short introduction to the Romans and their culture, several sections are devoted to the gods, including gods of the countryside, family, the state, and the underworld. The central part of the book summarizes the travels of Aeneas told in Vergil's *Aeneid*. Legends dealing with the founding and early history of Rome are followed by short sections on metamorphoses and on emperors as heroes. Accompanied by many illustrations by John Sibbick. Symbols used in these illustrations are explained in a short appendix. Map and index.

Versnel, H. S. "Greek Myth and Ritual: The Case of Kronos." In *Interpretations of Greek Mythology*, edited by Jan Bremmer. Totowa, N.J.: Barnes & Noble Books, 1986.
Surveys and analyzes the myth of Cronus as it is told by Hesiod and in other ancient sources. Illustrates how the god and his myth contain strikingly contradictory elements. Cronus is both a wise, great king and the violent castrator of his father or cannibalistic consumer of his children. Notes a similar tension in the Cronia, an ancient ritual of the god celebrated on the island of Rhodes. Like the ambiguous god it honors, this ritual is sometimes described as the bloody sacrifice of children or the bloodless sacrifice of cakes. Endnotes.

Warner, Rex. *Greeks and Trojans*. Lansing: Michigan State College Press, 1953. Reprinted in *The Stories of the Greeks*. New York: Farrar, Straus & Giroux, 1967.
Retells the story of the Trojan war. In Part 1 Warner uses various ancient sources, especially Sophocles' *Philoctetes*, to describe the events leading up to the war, including the judgment of Paris and the story of Helen. Part 2, based on Homer's *Iliad*, begins with the quarrel of Achilles and Agamemnon and ends with the death of Hector and the funeral of Patroclus. In Part 3 Warner uses material from Vergil's *Aeneid* and other sources to tell about the death of Achilles and the fall of Troy. The reprint includes an introductory essay describing the format of the book and sources for the tales.

————————. *Men and Gods*. New York: Farrar, Straus and Young, 1951. Reprinted in *The Stories of the Greeks*. New York: Farrar, Straus & Giroux, 1967.
Most of the thirty-two sections in this book are translations of selected passages from Ovid's *Metamorphoses*. Some translations follow Ovid's text closely, while others leave out obscure references. Warner does not follow Ovid's chronological order. Instead he begins with the myth of Pyramus and Thisbe and moves in sequence from the stories of the Thebans Cadmus, Actaeon, Pentheus, and Ino to the myths of Baucis and Philemon and of Daedalus and Icarus. For the stories of

Perseus, Theseus, Hercules, and other heroes, Warner fills in gaps in Ovid's narrative in his own words to create full biographies. He also retells the myth of Jason and the Argonauts from Apollonius' *Argonautica*, the stories of Oedipus and Antigone from the plays of Sophocles, and the story of Cupid and Psyche from Apuleius' *The Golden Ass*. The reprint includes an introductory essay describing the format of the book and sources for the tales.

_____. *The Vengeance of the Gods*. Lansing: Michigan State College Press, 1955. Reprinted in *The Stories of the Greeks*. New York: Farrar, Straus & Giroux, 1967.
Tells the myths connected with the following Greek tragedies: Aeschylus' *Prometheus Bound* and *Agamemnon* and Euripides' *Ion*, *Alcestis*, *Hippolytus*, *Iphigenia at Aulis*, *Orestes*, *Iphigenia Among the Taurians*, and *Helen*. The reprint includes an introductory essay describing the format of the book and sources for the tales.

Wechsler, Herman J. *Gods and Goddesses in Art and Legend*. New York: Pocket Books, 1950.
The topics covered in the ten chapters of this little handbook of Greco-Roman mythology reflect the author's special interest in accompanying myths with artistic treatments by painters from the first through the nineteenth centuries. Beginning with the Greek creation stories, Wechsler highlights tales of love and adventure, such as the story of Venus and the loves of Zeus, which have traditionally been favored by artists. Individual chapters are devoted to the stories of Jason, Hercules, the Trojan war, and the adventures of Odysseus. Short summaries of the myths are accompanied by commentaries on sixty-four paintings treating these themes. Most of the illustrations are in gravure, but four are in color. Paintings from the Italian Renaissance are particularly well represented. Includes brief biographical information about artists, a list of illustrations, and a select bibliography.

Wills, Gary, ed. *Roman Culture: Weapons and the Man*. New York: George Braziller, 1966.
An anthology of short passages from major Roman authors by a wide variety of translators from the Elizabethan period through the twentieth century. Selections are grouped thematically. Includes the stories of Triton, Narcissus, and the from Ovid's *Metamorphoses*.

Wolverton, Robert E. *An Outline of Classical Mythology*. Totowa, N.J.: Littlefield, Adams, 1966.

Part of the Littlefield College Outline series, this book offers the general reader a basic overview of ancient myths arranged thematically and sequentially rather than in alphabetical order. Short summaries of basic mythological plots and characters are provided in separate chapters. Greek, Sumerian, Babylonian, and Hebrew myths of creation and destruction are surveyed in Chapter 1 and the origins and attributes of the Olympians and other deities in Chapters 2 and 3. The loves, quarrels, and battles of the gods are dealt with in Chapter 4 and human offenses against the gods, dying gods and mystery rites, and various myths of the underworld in Chapter 5. Sea deities and sea heroes such as Odysseus and Jason are treated in Chapter 6, followed by the exploits of other heroes in Chapter 7. Myths of Thebes and Troy are outlined in Chapter 8 and various myths about love in Chapter 9. Unusual and useful features of this book include a brief history of Greek art and its use of mythology, in Chapter 10, and a short survey of mythology in astronomy, literature, and vocabulary in Chapter 11. Also useful is a historical survey of ancient Greek and Latin sources for Classical mythology in the introduction. Numerous lists and genealogical charts, bibliography, and index.

Zimmerman, J. E. *Dictionary of Classical Mythology*. New York: Harper & Row, 1964.
A basic guide for the general reader, this dictionary offers approximately 2,100 entries consisting of important deities, heroes, and place names in Greek and Roman mythology. Each alphabetically arranged entry includes a pronunciation guide, followed by variant names and spellings, where appropriate, and a brief description of the subject. Some reference to variant myths. Longer entries also list appearances of the subject in both ancient and modern literature. Cross-references for further information are indicated within entries by words in small capitals. An introductory essay contains sections on the importance, sources, and recurring themes of mythology, an overview of Greek heroes and of the families of Greek deities, lists of works from the nineteenth and twentieth centuries with mythological themes, and notes on the contributions of mythology to English vocabulary and on useful features of the book. Bibliography.

Norse Myths

Bellows, Henry Adams, trans. *The Poetic Edda*. Princeton, N.J.: Princeton University Press, 1936.

An English verse translation of the medieval lay which tells in thirty-five separate poems some traditional tales of Norse gods and heroes. Most of these poems survive in a single fourteenth-century A.D. manuscript. Fourteen myths about the gods are followed by twenty-one about heroes. Original Germanic poem titles are used with English subtitles. The first lay of the gods, *Voluspo*, is translated as "The Wise Woman's Prophecy." The last song of the heroes, *Hamthesmol*, is translated as "The Ballad of Hamther." Each poem is preceded by some background and commentary by the editor. Introductory essay on the origin, history, and literary features of the *Edda*. Footnotes, pronunciation guide, and index.

Branston, Brian. *Gods and Heroes from Viking Mythology*. New York: Schocken, 1982.

This collection of myths about Odin, Thor, Balder, Gylfi, and other Norse gods and heroes is intended for the juvenile reader. Stories about creation, the first humans, the Golden Age, wars between the gods, the adventures of Thor, and the doom of the gods are told to King Gylfi by three mysterious beings who are Odin in disguise. Also contains the legend of Sigurd and Brynhild. Illustrated by Giovanni Caselli. Symbols and characters used in these illustrations are explained in an appendix. Index with pronunciation guide.

_____. *The Lost Gods of England*. London: Thames and Hudson, 1957. Reprint. New York: Oxford University Press, 1974.

Uses both literary and archaeological evidence to reconstruct the gods and beliefs of the early British peoples. In Chapter 1, Branston focuses on the story of Wayland Smith. In Chapters 2 and 3, he provides a history of the early inhabitants of Britain and examines some features of their religion. Chapter 4 deals with the Old English concept of *Wyrd*, or destiny, Chapter 5 with concepts of deity, and Chapters 6-9 with the gods Woden, Thunor (Thor), Frig, and the divine siblings Frey and Freya. Branston considers Balder as an example of the dying god in Chapter 10, compares Old Norse and Old English myth in Chapter 11, and describes the transition from these earlier beliefs to Christianity in Chapter 12. Incorporated into these discussions are summaries and translations of mythic narratives from medieval sources such as the Germanic *Eddas*. Includes 124 illustrations of drawings and photographs of ancient sites and artifacts from Britain and other parts of Europe. Index.

_____. "Thor Goes Fishing with Hymir." In *The Lost Gods of England*, by Brian Branston. London: Thames and Hudson, 1957. Reprinted in *The Faber Book of Northern Legends*, edited by Kevin Crossley-Holland. London: Faber and Faber, 1977.
On a fishing trip with the giant Hymir, the Norse god Thor catches the World Serpent on his hook. Reprint includes an illustration by Alan Howard.

Bray, Olive, trans. and ed. *The Elder or Poetic Edda*. Part 1, *The Mythological Poems*. London: Viking Club, 1908.
This bilingual edition of Part 1 of the Icelandic poem attributed to twelfth-century scholar Saemund Sigfusson offers the original text and Bray's verse translation on facing pages. These poems include the earliest versions of some of the best-known Norse myths about creation, the hammer of Thor, an old and giant sage called Mighty Weaver, the love quests of Odin, the adventures of the god Thor, the love of the goddess Frey for Gerda (the earth), a contest of words between Thor and Greybeard, the earthly reign of the god Heimdall as King Rig, the dreams of Balder, and the mocking of Loki. A detailed introductory essay includes a summary and analysis of each poem. Illustrated with thirty-three line drawings by W. G. Collingwood. Footnotes, bibliography, and indexes.

Colum, Padraic. "Balder's Doom." In *The Children of Odin*, by Padraic Colum. New York: Macmillan, 1920. Reprinted in *The Faber Book of Northern Legends*, edited by Kevin Crossley-Holland. London: Faber and Faber, 1977.
The tale of the death of Balder, the beloved divine son of the Norse god Odin. Despite the gods' attempt to protect him, Balder is killed at games in his honor by a spring of mistletoe. Balder's brother Hermod attempts in vain to ransom Balder. The tale ends with the funeral of Balder. Reprint includes a short epilogue by the editor and an illustration by Alan Howard.

_____. *The Children of Odin*. New York: Macmillan, 1920.
A popular twentieth-century storyteller provides children with tales of the Norse gods and heroes. The tales are arranged chronologically, beginning with the building of the gods' fortress of Asgard and ending with Ragnarok and the twilight of the gods. Part 1 deals with the dwellers in Asgard and includes the stories of Iduna and her apples, Freya's necklace, and Frey's winning of Gerda. In Part 2 are tales of Odin the wanderer, the adventures of Thor and Loki, Aegir's feast, and

the dwarf's hoard. Part 3 centers on the troubles caused by the witch Gulveig, especially the crimes of Loki and the death of Balder. In Part 4 Colum turns to the heroic *Volsung Saga* and tells the adventures of Sigurd, Sigmund, and Brynhild. Illustrated with black-and-white drawings by Willy Pogany.

Coolidge, Olivia E. *Legends of the North*. Boston: Houghton Mifflin, 1951.
Retellings of Norse myths and legends for juvenile readers. The first section contains a creation story and tales about the northern gods from the medieval poems known as the *Elder* and *Younger Edda*, including tales about Thor's hammer, Hymer's caldron, and the binding of Loki. In the second section are tales from the *Volsung Saga*, such as Andvari's gold, Fafnir's end, and the Valkyrie. The last section includes tales from *Beowulf* and from Saxo's twelfth-century *History of Denmark*. Some comments on sources and later adaptations precede each section. Short introductory essay. Illustrations by Edouard Sandoz. Table of the Norse gods and pronunciation guide for proper names.

Crossley-Holland, Kevin. *Axe-Age, Wolf-Age*. London: André Deutsch, 1985.
A selection of twenty-two myths first published in *The Norse Myths* (see below). In a foreword, the author provides some background to Norse myths and describes his goals in retelling these myths. Tales begin with creation and end with Ragnarok, or the end of the world. With line drawings by Hannah Firmin. Glossary.

_____. *The Norse Myths*. New York: Pantheon Books, 1980.
This handbook of Norse mythology for the general reader begins with an introductory essay providing background on the Norse world, its cosmology and pantheon, the sources for Norse mythology, and the literary structure of the myths. The author retells thirty-two myths in new versions, based on the ancient sources. Begins with creation and the war of the Aesir and Vanir and ends with Ragnarok, the end of the world. Some dialogues and dramatic situations are developed and descriptive passages added by the author. Glossary of principal characters in the myths, bibliography, endnotes, and index.

Davidson, Hilda Roderick Ellis. *Gods and Myths of Northern Europe*. London: Penguin, 1964. Reprinted as *Gods and Myths of the Viking Age*. New York: Bell Publishing, 1981.
A survey of the myths and world view of the ancient Germanic peoples, intended for the general reader. Background on the Vikings, written

sources, and archaeological evidence appears in an introductory essay. In Chapter 1 Davidson describes the *Prose Edda* of Snorri Sturluson and summarizes his tales of the gods and their world. In Chapters 2-7 deities are presented according to function. For example, gods of battle such as Odin, the Valkyries, and the Berserkers are discussed in Chapter 2. Other chapters deal with the gods of thunder, peace and plenty, the sea, the dead, and enigmatic deities such as Heimdall, Loki, and Balder. In Chapter 8 Davidson discusses myths about the world tree, creation, and Ragnarok, or the end of the world. Bibliography, glossary, and index.

_____. "Northern Europe." In *World Mythology*, edited by Roy Willis. New York: Henry Holt, 1993.
This general view of Norse mythology contains sections on early and lost gods, cosmology, the trickster Loki and Ragnarok, Odin, Thor, Frey and the Vanir, female deities and spirits, and the dragon-slayers Beowulf and Sigurd. Supplmented by a description of the fortification of the god's realm of Asgard, the story of Balder, Thor's capture of the World serpent, Frey's marriage to Gerda, land spirits, the theft of the golden apples, and Beowulf and the dragon. Twenty-two color illustrations of Norse artifacts. Map, time chart, and lists of deities.

_____. *Scandinavian Mythology*. 2d ed. New York: Peter Bedrick Books, 1986.
The myths of the Norse gods and heroes are told and analyzed for the general reader. A brief introduction on Norse religion and the literary and archaeological sources for the myths is followed by chapters on the cults of Odin and Thor, on the deities of the earth, the family of the gods, Norse cosmology, and interactions between the Norse myths and Christianity. The text is accompanied by photographs illustrating sites and artifacts related to the myths. Bibliography and index.

Dumézil, Georges. *Gods of the Ancient Northmen*, edited by Einar Haugen. Berkeley: University of California Press, 1973.
A scholarly application of the author's theory of a tripartite social class system in Indo-European societies to the mythology of the Norse pantheon. In Part 1, Dumézil shows how the functions of priest, warrior/king, and herder/cultivator function in the tales about the deities, including the Aesir and Vanir, Odin, Balder, Thor, and Freya. Part 2 deals with minor gods such as Byggvir and Heimdall and compares the Scandinavian bestiary to that in the Indic *Rig Veda*. Many Germanic texts are quoted in the original with parallel English trans-

lation. Occasional untranslated Latin. Includes two introductory essays on Dumézil's Indo-European theory and on Dumézil's contributions to the field of Germanic mythology. Footnotes and index.

Farmer, Penelope. "Wayland Smith." In *The Faber Book of Northern Legends*, edited by Kevin Crossley-Holland. London: Faber and Faber, 1977. Also reprinted in *Northern Lights: Legends, Sagas and Folk-Tales*, edited by Kevin Crossley-Holland. London: Faber and Faber, 1987.
A mighty and fabulous smith is captured and crippled by King Nidud. After many years of imprisonment on an island, the smith kills the king's sons, impregnates his daughter, and escapes on wings he made in his workshop. Includes an illustration by Alan Howard.

Gayley, Charles M. *The Classic Myths in English Literature and in Art.* Rev. ed. New York: John Wiley & Sons, 1939.
Includes three chapters retelling Norse myths with extensive illustration and quotation from art and literature, especially from Matthew Arnold's "Balder Dead" and Richard Wagner's *Ring of the Nibelung*. Four black-and-white figures. An useful index indicates modern authors, artists, and works cited in the text. Additional lists of modern literary and artistic illustrations of the myths can be found in the commentary which follows the main body of the text. Also contains an index of mythological subjects.

Grappin, P. "Germanic Lands: The Mortal Gods." In *Larousse World Mythology*, edited by Pierre Grimal. Translated by Patricia Beardsworth. New York: G. P. Putnam's Sons, 1963.
This survey of the mythology of the ancient Germanic peoples begins with a brief ethnography and history of the people and a description of the *Edda*, the great Norse mythological poems. Detailed paraphrases from the *Edda*, including creation stories for the world, the gods, and humankind, and portraits and myths of individual deities such as Odin, Thor, Tyr, Loki, and Balder. Shorter sections on minor deities and creatures such as the Valkyries, elves, and giants. Concludes with a paraphrase of the story of Ragnarok, the end of the world. Forty-two illustrations, one in color.

Green, Roger Lancelyn. "The Curse of Andvari's Ring." In *Myths of the Norsemen*, by Roger Lancelyn Green. Harmondsworth: Penguin, 1970. Reprinted in *The Faber Book of Northern Legends*, edited by Kevin Crossley-Holland. London: Faber and Faber, 1977. Also reprinted in *Northern Lights: Legends, Sagas and Folk-Tales*, edited by Kevin Crossley-Holland. London: Faber and Faber, 1987.

Odin, Hoenir, and Loki offend Hreidmarr the magician by killing his otter son. Loki captures the dwarf Andvari, who is forced to give a treasure of gold to repay Hoenir for his loss. In this treasure is a cursed ring which causes discord between Hoenir and his sons. Reprints include an illustration by Alan Howard.

_____. "Loki Makes Mischief." In *Myths of the Norsemen*, by Roger Lancelyn Green. Harmondsworth: Penguin, 1970. Reprinted in *The Faber Book of Northern Legends*, edited by Kevin Crossley-Holland. London: Faber and Faber, 1977.

The mischievous god Loki steals the hair of Sif, the wife of Bilskirnir, and is forced by Odin to replace it. Loki persuades the blacksmith dwarf Dvalin to spin gold threads as new hair and wages a bet with the dwarf Brok concerning a contest of skill between Dvalin and Brok's brother Sindri. Loki tries to fix the contest, which he loses anyway. As punishment, Brok laces together Loki's lips. Reprint includes a short introduction by the editor and an illustration by Alan Howard.

_____. "Ragnarok." In *Myths of the Norsemen*, by Roger Lancelyn Green. Harmondsworth: Penguin, 1970. Reprinted in *The Faber Book of Northern Legends*, edited by Kevin Crossley-Holland. London: Faber and Faber, 1977.

Describes the last great battle of the Norse gods at Ragnarok, the day of doom. Haid, the sibyl, predicts these coming events to Odin and Odin has visions of rebirth.

_____. *The Saga of Asgard*. 1960. Reprint. *Myths of the Norsemen*. Harmondsworth: Penguin, 1970.

From traditional materials in the medieval *Eddas* and other sources, Green has created for the general reader a continuous narrative about the Norse gods and their adventures. The fifteen chapters are arranged in traditional order, beginning with Yggdrasil the World Tree and the story of creation and concluding with the passing of the gods in Ragnarok. Includes tales of Loki, Balder, Thor, and Freya. Illustrated with twenty-two black-and-white drawings by Brian Wildsmith. Genealogical chart.

Guerber, Hélène Adeline. *Myths of the Norsemen*. London: George G. Harrap, 1909. Reprint. New York: Dover Publications, 1992.

This general survey of Germanic myths and legends is based directly on the medieval *Eddas* and sagas. Despite its original publication date, the book remains a useful resource. Chapters on the Germanic cosmogony and the end of the world known as Ragnarok frame twenty-six chapters on each of the major gods, supernatural creatures such as the Norns and the Valkyries, and the Sigurd and Frithiof sagas. In a final chapter Guerber offers a short comparison of Greek and Norse mythologies. The original edition is illustrated with sixty-four black-and-white reproductions of paintings by nineteenth-century artists. Two of these are omitted from the reprint. Index to poetical quotations, glossary, and general index.

Hamilton, Edith. "The Mythology of the Norsemen." In *Mythology*, by Edith Hamilton. New York: New American Library, 1942.
This part of a basic handbook on Greek mythology provides a short introduction to Norse mythology with frequent quotation from original sources. The stories of Signy and Sigurd are retold, together with sections on the Norse gods, the Norse creation story, and Norse wisdom. Illustrations and index.

Hatto, Arthur Thomas, trans. *The Nibelungenlied*. New York: Viking Penguin, 1965.
This English translation of a thirteenth-century war epic about Siegfried and Kriemhild is intended for the general reader. While the poem is literary, it has strong roots in the oral sagas of the medieval Germans. In the epic Siegfried wins Brynhild for King Gunther and marries Gunther's sister Kriemhild. When Siegfried is murdered by Hagen, one of Gunter's vassals, Kriemhild successfully seeks vengeance for her husband's death. In the foreword the translator provides a short summary of the plot and a comparison with the *Iliad*. Following the translation, Hatto provides a detailed introduction for a second reading, with sections on the poet and his times, the action of the epic, problems in the plot, characterization, dramatic elements, and meaning. Also contains a note on the translation. Additional essays in appendices on the status of the poet, the manuscript tradition, and the date, genesis, and geography of the poem. Glossary.

Hobhouse, Rosa. *Norse Legends*. New York: E. P. Dutton, 1930.
Retells for the general reader some of the tales about Norse gods and heroes from the *Eddas*. Begins the way Snorri Sturluson does in Part 1 of the *Prose Edda*, with the visit of Odin to King Gylfi of Sweden, and ends with Ragnarok, the end of the gods' world. Included in the fourteen chapters are stories about Yggdrasil's ash, the invasion of Asgard by the giant Hrungnir, Balder's dream, Frey's love for Gerder,

an adventure of Siegfried, and the marriage of Svipdager and Menglod. Each chapter is preceded by a brief plot summary. Introductory essay on the tales and their sources.

Hollander, Lee M. *The Poetic Edda.* 2d ed. Austin: University of Texas Press, 1962.
An English translation in verse form of the poetic sources of much extant Norse mythology. Contains all the mythic, didactic, and heroic lays, including the stories of the gods Loki and Balder and tales of Sigurd and Brynhild. In a general introduction and in introductions to each poem, the translator provides historical background, literary background, and analysis, with discussion of manuscripts, content, composition, and poetic form. Footnotes, guide to pronunciation, glossary, bibliography, list of names, and index.

Hosford, Dorothy. "The Apples of Iduna." In *Thunder of the Gods*, by Dorothy Hosford. New York: Henry Holt, 1952. Reprinted in *The Faber Book of Northern Legends*, edited by Kevin Crossley-Holland. London: Faber and Faber, 1977.
The hunger of Odin and Loki leads to a bargain with the giant Thiazi, disguised as an eagle, who wins Iduna, the wife of the god Bragi, along with her apples of youth. Loki, disguised as a falcon, rescues Iduna, and Thiazi is killed. Reprint includes an illustration by Alan Howard.

Keary, Annie. "How Thor Went to Jotunheim." In *The Heroes of Asgard and the Giants of Jötunheim*, by Annie Keary. London: Macmillan, 1857. Reprinted in *The Faber Book of Northern Legends*, edited by Kevin Crossley-Holland. London: Faber and Faber, 1977.
On their journey to Jotunheim, Thor and Loki feast with a mortal family. The son, Thialfi, fails to follow the gods' dining instructions and, along with his sister Roskra, becomes the gods' servant. All eventually compete in contests of strength with a mountain giant called Utgard-Loki. Reprint includes an illustration by Alan Howard.

Kershaw, N., trans. "Gestumblindi's Riddles." In *Stories and Ballads of the Far Past*, by N. Kershaw. Cambridge, England: Cambridge University Press, 1921. Reprinted in *The Faber Book of Northern Legends*, edited by Kevin Crossley-Holland. London: Faber and Faber, 1977. Also reprinted in *Northern Lights: Legends, Sagas and Folk-Tales*, edited by Kevin Crossley-Holland. London: Faber and Faber, 1987.
In a riddle contest with King Heithrek, Gestumblindi is aided by Odin in disguise.

MacCulloch, John Arnott. *Eddic Mythology.* Vol. 2 in *The Mythology of All Races*, edited by John Arnott MacCulloch. Boston: Marshall Jones, 1930.

Provides an account of the mythology and religion described in the Eddic poems of northern Europe. In a short introduction, the author describes these poems and other mythological sources. Individual chapters on major gods such as Odin, Thor, Balder, and Loki follow a general survey of the Norse gods, their powers, names, and personalities. Other topics include nature, animals, elves, dwarfs, giants, trolls, werewolves, magic, the otherworld, cosmogony, and the twilight of the gods. Forty-seven illustrations, endnotes, and bibliography. Complete index in Volume 13.

Mackenzie, Donald Alexander. *Teutonic Myths and Legends.* London: Gresham Publishing, 1912. Reprint. *German Myths and Legends.* New York: Avenel Books, 1985.

Retells the myths and legends of the German peoples, beginning with the story of creation, the deeds of Odin, the fall of Asgard, and the stories of Loki, Balder, Beowulf, Hamlet, Sigurd, and Siegfried. Ends with the adventures of King Dietrich. Includes many excerpts from British poetry inspired by these legends, such as passages from the plays of William Shakespeare, Edmund Spenser's *The Fairie Queene*, and Henry Wadsworth Longfellow's "The Dwarfs." Illustrated with line drawings by Gustave Doré and other nineteenth-century artists. Index. Reprint includes a new foreword by Donald F. Friedmann.

Magnusson, Eirikr, and William Morris, trans. *The Story of the Volsungs*, edited by H. Halliday Sparling. London: Walter Scott, 1888.

An English translation of a prose version of poems about King Volsung and his descendants, Sigmund and Sigurd, in the *Elder Edda* often attributed to Saemund the Wise (1056-1133). The central plot of the *Volsung Saga* is the doomed love of Sigurd and Brynhild in Chapters 27-30. Surrounding this tale are the deeds of Sigurd's ancestors in Chapters 1-26 and the chaotic events following Sigurd's death in Chapters 31-43. Ten songs from the *Elder Edda* are also translated in verse. In an introductory essay, the editor provides historical background to the tales. Translator's preface, list of characters in the *Volsung Saga*, bibliography, and index.

_____. *The Volsunga Saga.* New York: Norroena Society, 1907.

This edition of an English translation of the *Volsung Saga* includes an examination of the legends of the Wagnerian Ring Cycle by Jessie L.

Weston. Synopses of the plots of the operas are accompanied by interpretative essays and comparisons with ancient legend. Also contains translations of other Old Norse sagas related to the *Volsung Saga*, including the stories of Aslog, Frithiof, Ragnar Lodbrok, King Helge and Rolf Kraki, the battles of Bravalla, and Wayland Smith. In an introductory essay, H. Halliday Sparling offers a history of Iceland and its oral literature. Translators' preface, list of characters in the *Volsung Saga*, and four photogravure illustrations.

Morris, William. "How Sigurd Awoke Brynhild upon Hindfell." In *The Story of Sigurd, the Volsung, and the Fall of the Niblungs*, by William Morris. London: Ellis and White, 1877. Reprinted in *The Faber Book of Northern Legends*, edited by Kevin Crossley-Holland. London: Faber and Faber, 1977. Also reprinted in *Northern Lights: Legends, Sagas and Folk-Tales*, edited by Kevin Crossley-Holland. London: Faber and Faber, 1987.
A selection in verse from a translation of the *Volsung Saga* in which the hero Sigurd climbs Mount Hindfell and awakens the sleeping Brynhild. The two swear eternal love, and Brynhild tells Sigurd her story and shares her wisdom with him. He gives her the cursed ring of Andvari. Reprints include a short introduction by the editor.

_____, *The Story of Sigurd the Volsung*. London: Longmans, Green, 1906.
While the use of archaic language may make this verse translation of the *Volsung Saga* less accessible to today's general reader, Morris' translation captures some of the majesty of the original. Book 1 deals with the story of King Sigmund and his death, Book 2 with the birth of his son Sigurd and Sigurd's fatal relationship with Regin the Master of Masters, Book 3 with the story of Sigurd and Brynhild and their deaths, and Book 4 with the marriage of Atli and Gudrun and the death of Gudrun.

_____, trans. *Volsunga Saga*. New York: Collier Books, 1962.
Morris' English translation of the story of King Volsung and his descendants, Sigmund and Sigurd, was actually the work of both Morris and Eirikr Magnusson and was originally published in 1888. In a scholarly introductory essay, Robert W. Gutman provides a summary of the *Volsung Saga*, discusses its origins, and compares it to the *Nibelungenlied*, to Richard Wagner's *The Nibelung's Ring*, and to other modern literature. The prologue is translated in verse. Ten songs from

the *Elder Edda* are also translated in verse. Three genealogical charts, glossary, and bibliography.

Munch, Peter Andreas. *Norse Mythology*, edited by Magnus Olsen. Translated by Sigurd Bernhard Hustvedt. New York: American-Scandinavian Foundation, 1926. Reprint. Detroit, Mich.: Singing Tree Press, 1968.

This general reference by the father of Norwegian historiography was first published in 1840. The English translation is based upon the third edition (1922), edited by Olsen. In Part 1 Munch describes the creation of the world, the gods, and their adventures. This part ends with Ragnarok, the twilight of the gods, and with a section on mythology in the *Eddas*. Heroic legends, especially from the *Volsung Saga*, are found in Part 2. Munch deals briefly with cults, rituals, and temples of the ancient Germans in Part 3. Introductory essay on the origins and sources of Norse mythology. In the preface, the translator offers some comments on the history and importance of Munch's work. Footnotes, endnotes, bibliography, and index.

Page, R. I. *Norse Myths*. Austin: University of Texas Press, 1990.

This general survey is part of The Legendary Past Series. An introductory chapter providing a brief catalogue and description of the Norse pantheon is followed by an overview of the three major sources for Norse mythology, the *Poetic Edda*, the *Prose Edda*, and Skaldic verse. These three documents are quoted extensively in translation throughout the book, which is devoted, in particular, to stories about the individual gods Odin, Thor, Balder, and Loki and to myths about the creation and end of the world. Also includes chapters describing both the relationship between gods and heroes such as Sigmund and Sigurd and the Norse celebration of gods and kings as givers of riches and fertility to humankind. Map, brief bibliography, and illustrations of artistic and archaeological artifacts from the Norse world.

Picard, Barbara Leonie. *Tales of the Norse Gods and Heroes*. London: Oxford University Press, 1953.

This retelling of the myths and legends of the Scandinavian peoples is intended for the general reader. In Part 1 the myths about the gods from the ancient *Eddas* are arranged in twenty chapters in the standard chronological order. The story of creation and the building of Asgard is followed by tales about Iduna and the golden apples, the theft of Miollnir, Thor's journeys and battles, and Loki's deceits. Part 1 ends with the death of Balder, the exile of Loki, and the end of the world.

In Part 2 Picard presents five heroic tales, including the magic love story of Svipdager and Menglod, the legend of Völund or Wayland Smith, the adventures of Siegfried from the *Volsung Saga*, and semi-historical legends about Ragnar Lodbrok and Nornagest. Illustrated with black-and-white drawings by Joan Kiddell-Monroe. Preface, glossary, and pronunciation guide.

Puhvel, Jaan. "Germanic Myth." In *Comparative Mythology*, by Jaan Puhvel. Baltimore: The Johns Hopkins University Press, 1987.
Surveys the main features of Germanic myths and their parallels with other Indo-European mythologies, especially in ancient India and in Rome. Refers to ancient Roman observations about the Germans and to Germanic texts such as the *Elder Edda*. Considers features of the major Germanic deities and their ties with Indo-European counterparts. Also discusses German cosmogony. Contains six figures illustrating objects connected with Germanic myth and culture. Footnotes and bibliography.

Sellew, Catharine F. *Adventures with the Giants*. Boston: Little, Brown, 1950.
Retells fourteen tales of the Norse gods for children. Between tales about the beginning and the end of the world are stories about the loss of Odin's eye, Friga's necklace, Loki's thefts, Thor's voyage to the Land of the Giants, and the death of Balder. Short introduction on the Norse people and their tales. Two-color illustrations by Steele Savage. Pronunciation guide.

Sharpe, Eric J. "Scandinavia." In *Mythology: An Illustrated Encyclopaedia*, edited by Richard Cavendish. New York: Rizzoli International, 1980. Also published as *An Illustrated Encyclopedia of Mythology*. New York: Crescent Books, 1984.
This overview of Norse mythology contains background on the *Eddas* and summaries of Norse cosmogony and concept of chaos, the gods Thor, Odin, and Frey, the killing of Balder, Loki the trickster, Sigurd and the dragon, and the end of the world. Map, glossary of deities, and illustrations of artwork related to the myths.

Snorri Sturluson. *The Prose Edda*. Translated by Arthur Gilchrist Brodeur. New York: American-Scandinavian Foundation, 1929.
A close scholarly translation of the first two parts of the prose handbook of Norse mythology written by the Icelander Snorri in the thirteenth century A.D. Part 1 of Snorri's *Edda* is called the *Gylfaginning* (the beguiling of Gylfi) and consists of a dialogue between the god Odin

and a legendary king of Sweden called Gylfi. Part 2, the *Skaldskapar-mal* (the poesy of Skalds), is a conversation between the god Bragi and a mortal named Aegir. These dialogues incorporate the mythological and legendary background of Norse saga, including the creation of the world, the gods, and humans, the myths of Thor, Yggdrasil, Balder, and Loki, and the destruction of the world. Part 3 of Snorri's *Edda*, a metrical handbook for bards called the *Hattatal*, is not translated here. Introductory essay on the life of Snorri and a critical history of his work. Footnotes and index.

————————. *The Prose Edda*. Translated by Jean I. Young. Berkeley: University of California Press, 1964.
This abridged translation of Snorri's *Edda* is intended for the general reader. "The Beguiling of Gylfi" in Part 1 is translated in its entirety. The longer mythological and heroic narratives scattered throughout the catalogue of figurative expressions in Part 2 are incorporated here into a continuous narrative. The metrical handbook in Part 3 is omitted. Introductory essay by Sigurdur Nordal on Snorri's works and, especially, his use of mythology. In a foreword, Young provides some background for this translation. Index.

Synge, Ursula. "The Building of the Wall of Asgard." In *The Faber Book of Northern Legends*, edited by Kevin Crossley-Holland. London: Faber and Faber, 1977.
Describes how the Norse gods have a wall built around Asgard in order to keep the giants out. They drive a bargain with a frost giant disguised as a mortal mason to do the job. The wall is built, but the gods use deceit to avoid paying the giant. Illustration by Alan Howard.

Taylor, Paul B., and Wystan H. Auden, trans. *The Elder Edda*. New York: Random House, 1969.
A professor of Middle English and a major twentieth-century British poet combine efforts to produce a verse translation of sixteen poems from the *Elder Edda*. Each of the poems is preceded by background information and plot summary. In an introductory essay the translators provide the general reader with information on the poetic tradition of Old Iceland, kennings, riddles and charms, and the Norse deities and cosmology. Bibliography, endnotes, and glossary.

————————. "The Lay of Thrym." In *The Elder Edda*. Translated by Paul B. Taylor and Wystan H. Auden. New York: Random House, 1969. Reprinted in *The Faber Book of Northern Legends*, edited by Kevin Crossley-Holland. London: Faber and Faber, 1977.

In this selection from a verse translation the Icelandic epic, Thor's sacred hammer is stolen by the giant Thrym, who demands the goddess Freya as his bride in exchange for return of the hammer. Thrym, however, is tricked by the gods to accept the god Thor, disguised as the goddess Freya. Reprint includes an illustration by Alan Howard.

Terry, Patricia, trans. *Poems of the Vikings: The Elder Edda*. Indianapolis: Bobbs-Merrill, 1976.
This verse translation, intended for the general reader, includes the poems of the *Elder Edda* as well as the story of Hervor's quest for her father's sword, Tyrfing, from the *Hervarar Saga*. In a preface, Terry describes the traditional poets who told the *Edda*. In an introductory essay Charles W. Dunn provides some background on the gods, heroes, and style of the poem. Bibliography, footnotes, pronunciation guide, and glossary.

Thomas, Edward. "The Making of the Worlds." In *Norse Tales*, by Edward Thomas. Oxford: The Clarendon Press, 1912. Reprinted in *The Faber Book of Northern Legends*, edited by Kevin Crossley-Holland. London: Faber and Faber, 1977.
In this first chapter of a collection of myths about Norse gods and heroes, Thomas tells of the mysterious journey of an Icelandic king named Gangler, who meets three wise kings and learns about the origin of the world and the role of the gods in nature and in human affairs. In Snorri's original *Prose Edda* Gangler is called Gylfi.

_____. *Norse Tales*. Oxford: The Clarendon Press, 1912.
Retells fourteen Old Norse myths. Part 1 contains tales about creation and the gods. Thomas structures the narrative around a conversation between king Gangler and three wise kings. The tale begins with the creation of the world and of the gods and then describes the god Odin at Valhalla, the story of Balder and Loki, the defeats and victories of Thor, other gods and goddesses, and Ragnarok, the end of the world. In Part 2 the legends of the heroes Sigmund, Helgi, and Sigurd from the *Volsung Saga* are retold. Prefatory essay on the sources for these tales.

Thorpe, Benjamin, and I. A. Blackwell, trans. *The Elder Edda and the Younger Edda*. New York: Norroena Society, 1907.
Literal English translations of two basic sources of Norse saga, the poetic *Elder Edda*, attributed here to Saemund Sigfusson (1056-1133), and the prose *Younger Edda* of Snorri Sturluson (1179-1241). Thorpe's prose translation of the *Elder Edda* follows closely the verse numbers

of the original. Blackwell's contribution is a free translation of part of the *Younger Edda* and uses original chapter numeration. The *Gylfaginning*, or "The Beguiling of Gylfi," a dialogue between the god Odin and a legendary king of Sweden called Gylfi, is here translated, but Parts 2 and 3, the *Skaldskaparmal*, or "The Poesy of Skalds," and the metrical handbook called the *Hattatal*, are not included. *Gylfaginning* begins with creation of the world, the giants, the gods, and humans, narrates the stories of Thor and his hammer, Balder and Njörd, the death of Balder, and the capture of Loki, and ends with the destruction of the world. In a preface, Thorpe offers biographies of both Saemund and Snorri, some comments on the legends, and three genealogical charts. Footnotes, four photogravure illustrations, and glossary.

Tonnelat, E. "Teutonic Mythology." In *New Larousse Encyclopedia of Mythology*, edited by Felix Guirand et al. Translated by Richard Aldington and Delano Ames. New York: Hamlyn, 1968.
Following background on the Teutonic people and their history, Tonnelat offers a summary of their creation myths about the cosmos, the gods, and humans and descriptions of the great Aesir or warrior gods Woden, Donar, Tiw, Loki, Heimdall, and Balder, and of the more pacific Vanir, such as Njörd and Frey. Also contains sections on some secondary gods, on goddesses, on Ragnarok (the twilight of the gods), on spirits, demons, elves, and giants, and on norns or mistresses of fate and the Valkyries or goddesses of destiny. Includes one color and forty-four black-and-white illustrations of Norse artifacts and sites.

Turville-Petre, E. O. G. *Myth and Religion of the North. The Religion of Ancient Scandinavia*. New York: Holt, Rinehart and Winston, 1964.
This survey of Norse mythology is heavily based on ancient sources, including the Old Norse poetry of the *Elder* or *Poetic Edda*, the Icelandic histories and sagas, Snorri Sturluson's *Edder Heimskringla* (a saga about the kings of Norway), and Saxo Grammaticus' *Gesta Danorum* (history of the Danes). All are quoted extensively with many shorter passages in both original and English translation. The author provides an introduction to these sources in Chapter 1. Individual chapters are devoted to Odin, Thor, Balder, Loki, Heimdall, and the Vanir. Later chapters treat less well-known deities, the divine kings, the divine heroes, guardian spirits, temples, sacrifice, death, and cosmogony. Forty-nine black-and-white illustrations of sites and artifacts associated with the ancient Scandinavians. Notes, bibliography, and index.

Medieval and Modern Myths of Western Europe

Baring-Gould, Sabine. *Curious Myths of the Middle Ages.* 2 vols. London: Rivington, 1868.

This collection of twenty-four medieval tales, such as "The Wandering Jew," "William Tell," "St. George," "Antichrist and Pope Joan," and "The Piper of Hameln," proved so popular that it went through a series of reprintings in the nineteenth century. Traces in detail the origin, history, and variants of each legend. Incorporates broad geographic and cultural breadth. Analysis of the legend of St. George includes comparative discussion of the myth of Babylonian god Tammuz and parallels to the Greek myth of Perseus.

—————————. *Curious Myths of the Middle Ages,* edited by Edward Hardy. New York: Oxford University Press, 1978.

This abridged version of a popular nineteenth-century book includes all twenty-four medieval tales in the original but has deleted some of Baring-Gould's more flowery passages in favor of a compact presentation of the tales. Includes a paraphrase of each story, often accompanied by extensive quotation in translation from original sources. Also traces the history of each legend and compares different versions of the tale. Accompanied by a short introductory biography of Baring-Gould. Illustrated with twenty-four woodcuts by Albrecht Dürer.

Boss, Claire, ed. *Scandinavian Folk and Fairy Tales.* New York: Avenel Books, 1984.

This collection of more than 200 tales from Denmark, Finland, Iceland, Norway, and Sweden contains not only traditional material but also stories by Hans Christian Andersen. In creating this anthology, Boss consulted sources from the fifteenth through the twentieth centuries, including major Scandinavian folklorists such as Peter Christen Asbjörnsen of Norway, Baron G. Djurlkou of Sweden, and Jón Árnason of Iceland. The tales are arranged by country, with the Swedish material divided into regional subdivisions. The tales from Iceland are grouped thematically. These tales of magic and the supernatural emphasize the role of the devil, giants, witches, elves, water monsters, trolls, ghosts, and goblins. Illustrated with black-and-white drawings, mostly by nineteenth-century artists. Introductory essay on the history of Scandinavian folklore collections.

Boucher, Alan, trans. *Icelandic Folktales.* Vol. 1, *Ghosts, Witchcraft and the Other World.* Vol. 2, *Elves, Trolls and Elemental Beings.* Vol. 3,

Adventures, Outlaws and Past Events. Reykjavik: Iceland Review
Library, 1977.
A three-volume sampling of traditional folktales from Iceland translated from the nineteenth-century collections of Jón Árnason and
Magnus Grimsson. In a brief foreword to the series (repeated at the
beginning of each volume), the translator offers some background to
Icelandic folktales and the history of their compilation and suggests
some of the advantages these tales offer readers. Each volume has a
separate preface. In the first preface, the translator suggests the role of
magic and witchcraft in traditional Icelandic society. In the second,
Icelandic tales about elves and trolls are related to the harsh geography
and climate of the island. In the third, Boucher discusses characteristics
of Icelandic tales of adventure. Twenty-nine stories about the world of
the supernatural and the unknown in Volume 1, thirty-four tales about
elves and trolls in Volume 2, and fifteen stories about Icelandic outlaws
and folk heroes in Volume 3. Endnotes.

Briggs, Katharine Mary. *A Dictionary of British Folk-Tales in the English
Language.* 4 vols. Bloomington: Indiana University Press, 1971.
A representative collection of tales from medieval, nineteenth-century,
and modern traditions. Volumes 1 and 2 deal with folk narratives,
Volumes 3 and 4 with folk legends. The tales are arranged into
subgroups. The narrative categories are fables, fairy tales, jocular tales,
novellas, and nursery tales. The folk legends are grouped according to
theme: black dogs, bogeys, devils, dragons, fairies, ghosts, giants,
historical traditions, local legends, origin myths, saints, the supernatural, witches, and miscellaneous legends. Some tales are quoted in full,
sometimes in dialect; others are abridged or summarized. Published
sources are cited for each tale, which is also cross-referenced in an
index organized around folktale motifs. Includes a general introduction
to each part as well as individual introductions for each narrative and
legend type. Bibliography and indexes.

Briggs, Katharine Mary, and Ruth L. Tongue, eds. *Folktales of England.*
Chicago: University of Chicago Press, 1965.
A collection of ninety-two English folktales arranged thematically.
Part 1 consists of six tales of wonder. In Part 2 are forty-four legends,
including encounters with supernatural beings, curses and ghosts,
giants, saints, historical and semi-historical tales, and modern legends.
The forty-two jocular tales in Part 3 are about devils and spirits,
preachers and the afterlife, children, spouses, masters and servants,
shaggy dogs, and yarns. Some of these are *rhozzums* or short local tales.

At the beginning of each tale the editors offer information on sources and informants and provide some comparative commentary. In an introductory essay, Briggs discusses sources for and types of English folktales. In a foreword, Richard M. Dorson offers a history of English folkloristics. Glossary, bibliography, index of motifs, index of tale types, and general index.

Bulfinch, Thomas. *The Legends of Charlemagne*. Boston: J. E. Tilton, 1863. Reprint. New York: New American Library, 1962.
This American retelling of the legends and tales of medieval European romance has remained popular for more than a century. A short introductory chapter of historical background leads to tales of King Charlemagne and knights such as Roland and Rinaldo and focuses on the defeat of Charlemagne's army by the Saracens at Roncesvalles in A.D. 778. A foreword by Palmer Bovie in the reprint includes a biography of Bulfinch and an analysis and appreciation of his work. Index.

Campbell, Joseph. "In Search of the Holy Grail: The Parzival Legend." In *Transformations of Myth Through Time*, by Joseph Campbell. New York: Harper & Row, 1990.
A short history of the Parzival myth as it was treated by Chrétien de Troyes and by Wolfram von Eschenbach leads to a retelling of the legend. In particular, Campbell emphasizes the concepts of marriage for love, loyalty in marriage, and government for the people which appear in this tradition. Four illustrations from medieval manuscripts.

_____. "A Noble Heart: The Courtly Love of Tristan and Isolde." In *Transformations of Myth Through Time*, by Joseph Campbell. New York: Harper & Row, 1990.
Following some historical background on the Norman conquest of Britain and the life of Eleanor of Aquitaine, Campbell describes the medieval concept of courtly love, summarizes the life and works of Chrétian de Troyes, and then retells the story of Tristan and Isolde. Three illustrations from medieval manuscripts.

Cavendish, Richard. "Christianity." In *Mythology: An Illustrated Encyclopaedia*, edited by Richard Cavendish. New York: Rizzoli International, 1980. Also published as *An Illustrated Encyclopedia of Mythology*. New York: Crescent Books, 1984.
Surveys the Judeo-Christian tradition about creation of the world and of humankind, afterlife, and the supernatural. Includes summaries of the myths of the creation, Adam and Eve, heaven and hell, and the fall of Lucifer from the biblical books of Genesis and Revelation as well

as the medieval myth of the Holy Grail. Also contains discussions of Christian attitudes toward progress, providence, the noble savage, the classical renaissance, alchemy, the Rosicrucians, and witchcraft. Map, diagram of the seven days of creation, and illustrations of artwork related to the myths.

Craigie, William A., ed. and trans. *Scandinavian Folk-Lore*. London: Alexander Gardner, 1896. Reprint. Detroit: Singing Tree Press, 1970. This collection of Scandinavian folklore represents the oral tradition of the peoples of northern Europe and of Iceland. The tales are arranged in ten thematic groups: the old gods such as Thor and Odin, trolls and giants, Berg-folk and dwarfs, elves and *huldres* or Teutonic sirens, *nisses* or brownies, water beings, monsters, ghosts and wraiths, wizards and witches, and churches, treasures, and plagues. Short preface, pronunciation guide, bibliography, endnotes, and index.

Crossley-Holland, Kevin. *British Folk Tales*. New York: Orchard Books, 1987.
A poet and writer returns to original sources to retell fifty-five folktales from the British Isles. These are fairy tales, hero legends, and stories of enchantment include many traditional favorites such as "Jack and the Beanstalk," "Tom Thumb," and "Dick Whittington." While most are written in prose, several are in verse. Scholarly notes on sources and comments on the tales are found in an appendix. Pronunciation guide.

_____. *The Dead Moon*. London: André Deutsch, 1982.
A retelling of eleven tales of East Anglia and the Fen Country of England, including stories about bizarre deaths, supernatural creatures, and fearless mortals. In an appendix, the author identifies his sources and explains how he has modified the dialect and structure of the original versions. Illustrated with line drawings by Shirley Felts. Glossary.

_____, ed. *The Faber Book of Northern Folk-Tales*. Boston: Faber and Faber, 1980.
An anthology of thirty-five folktales from Scandinavia, Iceland, the British Isles, Germany, and Flanders. Aetiologies and animal tales are accompanied by stories of enchantment, trolls, elves, giants, ghosts and other supernatural creatures. Sources, which include the collections of Andrew Lang and the Brothers Grimm, are identified at the end of each tale. Illustrated with line drawings by Alan Howard. Bibliography.

_____, ed. *The Faber Book of Northern Legends*. London: Faber and Faber, 1977.

A collection of twenty-two stories retold in verse and prose from Norse, Germanic, and Icelandic legends. The first six and last four tales deal with the Norse gods and with the end of the world. Seven pieces from Icelandic saga accompany six legends about Beowulf, Sigurd, and other Germanic heroes. Most of these tales are selections from larger works published in the nineteenth and twentieth centuries by authors such as Sir Walter Scott, W. H. Auden, and Crossley-Holland. Three were written for this anthology. In a foreword, the editor provides some background to the history of the Teutonic peoples, the origin of their legends, and important themes in these stories. Illustrated by Alan Howard. Bibliography and index.

_____, ed. *The Fox and the Cat*. New York: Lothrop, Lee & Shepard, 1985.

A collection of eleven animal tales translated from the *Kinder- und Hausmärchen* (*German Fairy Tales*) of Jacob and Wilhelm Grimm (1812-1815). In these German stories animals, not humans, are the heroes and the villains. Well-known tales such as "The Bremen Town Musicians" as well as lesser-known stories such as "The Hedge-king and the Bear" are retold here for children with color drawings by Susan Varley.

_____, ed. *Northern Lights: Legends, Sagas and Folk-Tales*. London: Faber and Faber, 1987.

Combines thirteen legends and sagas previously collected in the *Faber Books of Northern Legends* with twenty-four folktales from the *Faber Book of Northern Folk-tales*. The result is a unique anthology of traditional stories from all over northwest Europe. Tales about heroes such as Beowulf and Sigurd, semi-historical legends about Viking expeditions and feuds are juxtaposed with folktales about animals and supernatural beasts. Some illustrations by Alan Howard are also reprinted from the Faber books. Foreword by the editor and bibliography.

Dasent, George Webbe. *A Collection of Popular Tales from the Norse and North German*. New York: Norroena Society, 1907.

A collection of forty-one folktales from Scandinavia and northern Germany. Includes a tale explaining why the sea is salty. Also contains the legend of Tannhäuser and stories of magic, werewolves, and mysterious adventures. Introductory essay on Norse myths and religious concepts. Sources for the tales are not indicated. Four illustrations. Occasional explanatory footnotes.

Delarue, Paul, ed. *The Borzoi Book of French Folk Tales*. Translated by Austin E. Fife. New York: Alfred A. Knopf, 1956.
Fifty-four French folktales collected from a variety of published sources are translated into English for the general reader. The anthology is arranged in three thematic groups: tales of the supernatural, animal fables, and humorous tales. Endnotes containing explanatory and comparative commentary and information about sources follow the tales. Introductory essay on the history of modern French folklore studies. Illustrated with line drawings by Warren Chappell. Footnotes.

de Valera, Sinéad. *Irish Fairy Tales*. London: Pan Books, 1973.
These twelve Irish tales about fairies, witches, druids, fantasy, and the supernatural were selected for young readers from several Irish anthologies by de Valera, the wife of the president of the Irish Republic. Included are tales about a captive princess, a stolen crown, a disguised prince, and a mountain wolf. Black-and-white illustrations by Chris Bradbury.

_____. *More Irish Fairy Tales*. London: Pan Books, 1979.
These ten Irish tales about fairies, witches, druids, fantasy, and the supernatural were selected for young readers from several Irish anthologies by de Valera, the wife of the president of the Irish Republic. Included are tales about a magic thorn, a disguised princess, a wishing chair, and a magic emerald ring. Black-and-white illustrations by Julek Heller.

Douglas, George Brisbane. *Scottish Fairy and Folk Tales*. London: Walter Scott Publishing, 1901. Reprint. New York: Arno Press, 1977.
These 105 tales of the Scottish Highlands were selected from a variety of nineteenth-century folklore collections and are arranged in the following ten thematic groups: nursery stories, animal fables, stories about giants and monsters, legends and traditions, fairy tales, stories of brownies, demons, and other supernatural creatures, tales of witchcraft, accounts of ghosts and other apparitions, comic tales, and literary tales. Published sources are identified at the beginnings of the tales. Introductory essay on the history of Scottish folkloristics. Twelve black-and-white illustrations by James Torrance. Footnotes.

Dundes, Alan, ed. *Cinderella. A Folklore Casebook*. New York: Garland Press, 1982.

This collection of essays by scholars and folklorists analyzing and interpreting the folktale commonly known as "Cinderella" includes translations of three important versions of the story from Western Europe: Giambattista Basile's Italian version published betweem 1634 and 1636, Charles Perrault's French version of 1697, and the 1812 German version of the brothers Jacob and Wilhelm Grimm. A Russian version of the tale called "The Beautiful Wassilissa" is retold and analyzed using the psychological archetypes of Carl Jung. Also three Italian versions of the tale recorded in modern Tuscany are translated and compared. Preceding each version Dundes provides useful background information, commentary, and bibliography. Endnotes following each article. General bibliography.

_____, ed. *Little Red Riding Hood. A Casebook.* Madison: University of Wisconsin Press, 1989.
This collection of interpretations of "Little Red Riding Hood" includes the translations of two early printed versions, Charles Perrault's French tale of 1697 and the 1812 German version of the brothers Jacob and Wilhelm Grimm. Also includes the text of an oral French version, recorded in 1885, with reference to thirty-four variants. Preceding each version Dundes provides useful background information, commentary, and bibliography.

Duvoisin, Roger. *The Three Sisters.* New York: Alfred A. Knopf, 1954.
This anthology of thirty-seven traditional Swiss tales is based upon a variety of published sources. The tales, divided about equally between French Swiss and German Swiss sources, deal with fairies, dwarfs, ghosts, and other supernatural creatures, and often explain peculiar geographic features. Also contains several animal fables. The title story is about a simpleton named Jean-Marie who takes too seriously a prediction about his donkey's three sneezes. Short foreword on the folklore of Switzerland. Illustrated by the author.

Every, George. *Christian Legends.* Rev. ed. New York: Peter Bedrick Books, 1987
A general survey of some traditional Christian tales as myth. Following an introductory chapter on the relationships between myth and religion and between Christian scripture and legend, Every considers several thematic groups of Christian myth: creation, the flood, and the fall of humankind, the two cities as a duality of good and evil, sacrifice, descent into hell, the lives of Mary and of the saints, and the afterlife. Also contains chapters on the human need for mythology and on

sources for these myths. Richly illustrated with color and black-and-white photographs of ancient, medieval, and modern representations of these legends. Bibliography and index.

Falassi, Alessandro. "Cinderella in Tuscany." In *Folklore by the Fireside: Text and Context of the Tuscan Veglia*, by Alessandro Falassi. Austin: University of Texas Press, 1980. Reprinted in *Cinderella: A Folklore Casebook*, edited by Alan Dundes. New York: Garland Press, 1982.
Records an actual conversation among three modern Tuscans, each of whom tells a different version of the Cinderella folktale. Falassi occasionally interrupts his English translation of an Italian transcript in order to provide his own observations and commentary about the tale and its ties with Italian society. Reprint includes useful background information and bibliography by Dundes. Endnotes.

_____. *Folklore by the Fireside: Text and Context of the Tuscan Veglia*. Austin: University of Texas Press, 1980.
This ethnographic study of the *veglia*, a folklore tradition of Tuscany in Italy, includes translations of several fairy tales, narratives, and folk songs. The *veglia*, held especially during winter nights, is a gathering of family and friends with a ritualized sequence of fairy tales followed by riddles, lullabies, and prayers until the children go to bed. Then the narratives turn to courtship themes and, eventually, to stories about married couples. In Chapter 1, Falassi examines features of the Tuscan society in which the *veglia* functions. Chapters 2-6 are devoted to the different genres of *veglia*, fairy tales, bedtime rituals, courtship songs, and marriage narratives. In Chapter 6, Falassi describes the dances which conclude the *veglia* season at carnival time, and in Chapter 7 he considers the activities and oral traditions of those who prefer the tavern to the *veglia*. Chapter 8 consists of some concluding remarks about the *veglia* in modern Tuscany. Of particular mythological interest are the translations of several fairy tales in Chapter 2, including "Cinderella," "The Princess and the Frog," and "Donkey Skin." Some Italian texts are provided in an appendix. The text is accompanied by many photographs of traditional Tuscan scenes and some musical scores for songs and dances. Foreword by Roger D. Abrahams, Roger D. Short introductory essay by Falassi. Endnotes, bibliography, and index.

Gathorne-Hardy, G. M., trans. "The Expedition of Thorfin Karlsefni." In *The Norse Discoverers of America: The Wineland Sagas*, by G. M. Gathorne-Hardy. London: Oxford University Press, 1921. Reprinted

in *The Faber Book of Northern Legends*, edited by Kevin Crossley-Holland. London: Faber and Faber, 1977. Also reprinted in *Northern Lights: Legends, Sagas and Folk-Tales*, edited by Kevin Crossley-Holland. London: Faber and Faber, 1987.
The adventures of the Viking Thorfin Karlsefni, brother-in-law of Leif Erikson, and his attempts to colonize Vinland. Includes encounters with inhabitants of the New World. Reprints include a short introduction by the editor and an illustration by Alan Howard.

_____, trans. *The Norse Discoverers of America: The Wineland Sagas*. London: Oxford University Press, 1921.
Part 1 is a compilation of three early sources into a coherent prose narrative dealing with medieval Viking voyages to Greenland and lands west. The *Saga of Erik the Red*, Hauk's Book, and the Flatey Book together provide sometimes contradictory versions of Erik the Red's colonization of Greenland, his son Leif Erikson's voyage of discovery to a land he named Vinland, and later expeditions by Thorvald Karlsefni and Thorfin Karlsefni in the eleventh and twelfth centuries. Part 2 is an analysis of this material, with sections on the nature of the evidence, discrepancies, the stories as history, references to a people called Skraelings, and details and problems concerning the voyages. Gathorne-Hardy emphasizes that the core events in these sagas are based upon historical events, but the student of mythology can recognize many elements in these accounts which parallel other tales of fantastic voyages. Maps, chronological and navigational charts, genealogical table, bibliography, and index.

Gilbert, Henry. *Robin Hood*. Chicago: Saalfield Publishing, 1925.
A retelling of the legendary life of Robin Hood for young readers. Describes in Chapter 1 how Robin became an outlaw, in Chapter 2 how he met Little John, in Chapter 3 how he met Friar Tuck, in Chapter 4 the wedding of Alan-a-Dale, in Chapter 5 how Robin slew the sheriff, in Chapter 6 how he met King Richard the Lion-Hearted, in Chapter 7 the death of Marian, and in Chapter 8 Robin Hood's death. Introductory essay on the legend and times of Robin Hood. Illustrated with black-and-white drawings by Frances Brundage.

Goodrich, Norma Lorre. *Medieval Myths*. New York: Mentor Books, 1961.
Includes prose translations of seven medieval hero legends: the Scandinavian Beowulf, Peredur Son of York from the Welsh *Mabinogion*, the Frankish Roland, the French Berta of Hungary, the Austrian Sifrit

from the *Nibelungenlied*, Prince Igor from the Russian poem *Sbornik*, and the Spanish Cid. A preface contains some information about manuscript sources and English translations. Four pages of illustrations and an index.

Grimm, Jacob. *Teutonic Mythology*. Translated by James Steven Stally-brass. 4 vols. London: George Bell and Sons, 1883 (Vols. 1-3), 1888 (Vol. 4). Reprint. New York: Dover, 1966.
Grimm's monumental study of the mythology and religion of the Teutonic peoples, first published in 1800, went through several German editions before it was translated into English by Stallybrass between 1883 and 1888. Although comparative mythology has advanced considerably in the last century, Grimm's work remains a basic resource. Following an introductory chapter on the Christianization of the Germanic peoples and on their mythology, Grimm offers in Volume 1 individual chapters on the concept of deity, worship, temples, priests, gods, Wotan, Donar, Tiw, Frey, Balder, other gods, other goddesses, the condition of the gods, heroes, and wise-women. In Volume 2 are chapters on wights and elves, giants, creation, the elements, trees and animals, the sky and the stars, day and night, summer and winter, time, souls, death, destiny, and personifications. In Volume 3 are discussions of poetry, ghosts, the supernatural translation of bodies, the devil, magic, superstition, sickness, herbs and stones, and spells and charms. In Volume 4 are Grimm's supplemental notes to the fourth edition and his preface to this volume, plus appendices with Anglo-Saxon genealogies, superstitions, and spells, some of which remain untranslated in the English edition. Grimm's preface to the second German edition of 1844, found at the beginning of Volume 2 in the German and original English editions and at the beginning of Volume 3 in the reprint, offers a résumé of his entire subject. Grimm's discussion of features of Teutonic mythology and folklore illustrates the state of comparative folklore studies in the middle of the nineteenth century. In a translator's preface, Stallybrass considers the importance of Grimm's work and some aspects of this translation. Original-language footnotes. Index to Volumes 1-3 at the end of Volume 3. Volume 4 has a separate index.

Grundtvig, Svendt. *Danish Fairy Tales*. Translated by J. Grant Cramer. Boston: Four Seas, 1919. Reprint. New York: Dover Publications, 1972.
Fourteen tales selected from the author's monumental scholarly collection of traditional Danish stories are here translated into English.

The tales deal with typical folktale themes such as human metamorphosis, wicked stepmotherss, exotic journeys, and impossible tasks. Short preface by the translator about Grundtvig and his stories. Reprint includes black-and-white illustrations by Drew Van Heusen.

Guerber, Hélène Adeline. *Myths and Legends of the Middle Ages*. London: George G. Harrap, 1909.

This handbook for the general reader combines retellings of legends from medieval France, Germany, and Britain with quotations from both medieval sources and modern adaptations of the tales. Individual chapters are devoted to the plots of the Anglo-Saxon poem *Beowulf*, the twelfth- or thirteenth-century German poem "Gudrun" about three generations of the heroic Hegelings, the animal tales in the medieval epic "Reynard the Fox," the German epic *Nibelungenlied*, tales in the Langobardian cycle, especially about Leibgart and Wolfdietrich, legends about the hero Dietrich von Bern, *chansons de geste* about Charlemagne, Roland, Aymon of Dordogne, and Huon of Bordeaux, the quest for the Holy Grail and other Arthurian legends, Tristan and Iseult, the saga of Ragnar Lodbrok, and ballads of the Cid. In the final chapter Guerber offers a survey of medieval romance literature. Sixty-four illustrations, including photographs of sites and black-and-white reproductions of paintings by nineteenth-century artists. Index to poetical quotations and combined glossary and index.

Henderson, William. *Notes on the Folk Lore of the Northern Counties of England and the Borders*. London: Longmans, Green, 1866. Reprint. Totowa, N.J.: Rowman and Littlefield, 1973.

A native of this region of England records and explains some of the local legends about human life and death, the days and the seasons, spells and divinations, portents and auguries, charms and spells, witchcraft, local spirits, dragons, occult powers, haunted spots, and dreams. In an appendix sixteen household tales, or fairy tales, mostly from Devonshire and Yorkshire, are retold and analyzed by S. Baring-Gould.

Jacobs, Joseph. *English Fairy Tales*. 3d ed. New York: G. P. Putnam's Sons, 1898. Reprint. New York: Dover Publications, 1967.

This standard nineteenth-century collection of forty-three English tales includes "Jack and the Beanstalk," "The Three Bears," "Whittington and His Cat," and "Tom Thumb." Nine illustrations by John D. Batten. In a preface, Jacobs discusses the tales and his storytelling technique. In endnotes, Jacobs provides sources, parallels, and remarks.

Jones, Gwyn, trans. "Authun and the Bear." In *Eirik the Red and Other Icelandic Sagas*, translated by Gwyn Jones. London: Oxford University Press, 1961. Reprinted in *The Faber Book of Northern Legends*, edited by Kevin Crossley-Holland. London: Faber and Faber, 1977. Also reprinted in *Northern Lights: Legends, Sagas and Folk-Tales*, edited by Kevin Crossley-Holland. London: Faber and Faber, 1987.
The adventures of the Icelander Authun, who buys a bear and brings it to King Svein of Denmark. Svein's gift of a ring eventually saves Authun's life at the court of King Harold of Norway. Reprints include an illustration by Alan Howard.

Jones, Gwyn, trans. *Eirik the Red and Other Icelandic Sagas*. London: Oxford University Press, 1961.
Nine of the approximately 120 surviving family sagas of medieval Iceland are translated into English for the general reader. Imaginative reworking merges with historical fact in these tales of feuds and adventures. Included are tales about the merchant Hen-Thorir, the men of Vapnfjord, Thorstein Staff-Struck, the priest Hrafnkel, the voyages of Erik the Red, the unfortunate death of the youth Thidrandi, Authun's adventure with the bear, Gunnlaug Wormtongue, and King Hrolf and his warriors. In an introductory essay, Jones provides a history of these sagas and discusses some of their sources and literary characteristics. Map, translator's note, and footnotes.

_____. *Scandinavian Legends and Folk-Tales*. London: Oxford University Press, 1956.
Twenty-four stories from Denmark, Iceland, Norway, and Sweden are retold for children with illustrations by Joan Kiddell-Monroe. The tales are divided into the categories entitled "Princesses and Trolls," "Tales from the Ingle-Nook," "From the Land of Ice and Fire," and "Kings and Heroes."

_____, trans. "Thorstein Staff-Struck." In *Eirik the Red and Other Icelandic Sagas*, by Gwyn Jones. London: Oxford University Press, 1961. Reprinted in *The Faber Book of Northern Legends*, edited by Kevin Crossley-Holland. London: Faber and Faber, 1977. Also reprinted in *Northern Lights: Legends, Sagas and Folk-Tales*, edited by Kevin Crossley-Holland. London: Faber and Faber, 1987.
Describes the deeds of Thorstein, son of Thorarin, and his feud with the household of Bjarni. Reprints include an illustration by Alan Howard.

Laing, Samuel, trans. "The Battle of Stamford Bridge." In *The Heimsk-
ringla, or Chronicle of the Kings of Norway*. Translated by Samuel
Laing. London: Longmans, 1844. Reprinted in *The Faber Book of
Northern Legends*, edited by Kevin Crossley-Holland. London: Faber
and Faber, 1977. Also reprinted in *Northern Lights: Legends, Sagas
and Folk-Tales*, edited by Kevin Crossley-Holland. London: Faber and
Faber, 1987.
A description of the Battle of Stamford Bridge, which took place
nineteen days before the Battle of Hastings in 1066. Harald Sigurdsson
(Hardradi), the Norwegian claimant to the throne of English, is de-
feated by the Anglo-Saxon Harold Godwinson. The story is told from
the Norwegian point of view. Reprints include a short introduction by
the editor.

Lang, Andrew, ed. *Perrault's Popular Tales*. Oxford: The Clarendon
Press, 1888. Reprint. New York: Arno Press, 1977.
A facsimile edition Charles Perrault's *Contes* (popular tales), first
published in Paris in 1697. While Lang's edition presents the eight tales
in the original French, the introductory material is accessible and useful
to the general English reader. In addition to a biography of Perrault,
Lang provides a history and comparative study of each tale and
discusses Perrault's use of fairies and ogres. Included are studies of
"The Three Wishes," "The Sleeping Beauty," "Blue Beard," "Puss in
Boots," "Toads and Diamonds," "Cinderella," "Riquet of the Tuft,"
and "Hop o' my Thumb."

MacDougall, James. *Folk Tales and Fairy Lore*, edited by George Calder.
Edinburgh: J. Grant, 1910. Reprint. New York: Arno Press, 1977.
Fifty-seven traditional Scottish tales are recorded in the original Gaelic
with parallel English translation. These legends of knights, dragons,
superhuman feats, fairies, banshees, witches, and other supernatural
themes are arranged in four thematic groups: folktales, stories about
social fairies, stories about solitary fairies, and legends about water
sprites. In a preface, Calder offers some comments on the spelling of
Gaelic. The preface is followed by a biographical introduction about
MacDougall. Endnotes.

Magnusson, Magnus, and Hermann Pálsson, trans. "The Burning of
Bergthorsknoll." In *Njal's Saga*, by Magnus Magnusson and Mermann
Pálsson. Baltimore: Penguin, 1960. Reprinted in *The Faber Book of
Northern Legends*, edited by Kevin Crossley-Holland. London: Faber
and Faber, 1977. Also reprinted in *Northern Lights: Legends, Sagas*

and Folk-Tales, edited by Kevin Crossley-Holland. London: Faber and Faber, 1987.
Describes the tragic climax to the bloody feud which is the subject of an anonymous Icelandic prose saga written about 1280. Njal and many members of his family burn to death in the destruction of Bergthorsknoll, but his son Kari Solmundarson escapes dramatically. Reprints include a short introduction by the editor and an illustration by Alan Howard.

_____, trans. *Njal's Saga*. Baltimore: Penguin, 1960.
This prose saga about the early settlers of Iceland was written c. 1280 by an anonymous author. The central event in the saga, the burning of Bergthorsknoll, can be collaborated by historical documents, but actual events are embellished by oral tradition and the art of the storyteller. The plot deals with the seer Njal Thorgeirsson and the bitter feud which leads to the immolation of Njal and his family in their fortress of Bergthorsknoll. In an introductory essay, Magnusson provides some background to the tale and discusses some of its general features. Translators' note, genealogical tables, glossary, chronological note, and maps.

Megas, Georgios A., ed. *Folktales of Greece*. Translated by Helen Colaclides. Chicago: University of Chicago Press, 1970.
Seventy-seven modern Greek folktales selected from several sources published in the original language are here made available to the English reader. The tales are arranged in six categories: animal fables; wonder tales; stories of kindness rewarded and evil punished; tales of fate; jokes, anecdotes, and religious tales; and legends. Endnotes provide comparative commentary and information on sources. In an introductory essay, Megas provides a short history of Greek culture and a survey of modern Greek folkloristics, and discusses some characteristics of modern Greek folktales. In a foreword, Richard M. Dorson considers the relationship between ancient Greek mythology and modern Greek folklore. Glossary, bibliography, index of motifs, index of tale types, and general index.

Miller, Hugh. *Scenes and Legends of the North of Scotland*. 2d ed. Edinburgh: W. P. Nimmo, 1869. Reprint. New York: Arno Press, 1977.
Gathers together many of the legends of Scotland as they were told in the old shire of Cromarty. In twenty-two chapters, Miller retells historical and religious legends and tales of ghosts, plague, smugglers,

and curious personalities. Includes personal accounts of the author's research and references to various geographic locations in Cromarty.

Moncrieff, A. R. Hope. *Romance and Legend of Chivalry*. London: Gresham Publishing, 1913. Reprint. New York: Bell Publishing, 1978. Treats the historical legends of the medieval European romance. Part 1 is a history of the romance with chapters on the character of chivalric romance, the growth of romance in both prose and verse forms, and the three traditions of historical romance, King Arthur in Britain, Charlemagne in France, and El Cid in Spain. In Part 2 sixteen typical tales of chivalry from these traditions are retold. Included are the stories of the discovery of Sir Gareth, Sir Gawain and the Green Knight, Roncesvalles, and the rescue of Sir Hugo of Tabarie from Saladin. Eight color plates and twenty-seven black-and-white illustrations, mostly by nineteenth-century artists. Index.

Moore, A. W. *The Folk-Lore of the Isle of Man*. London: D. Nutt, 1891. Reprint. S. R. Publishers, 1971. The first five chapters in this collection of traditional material of the Manx on the Island of Man contains paraphrases, excerpts, and retellings of myths and legendary materials. In Chapter 1 are tales about the legendary history of the island. In Chapter 2 are legends about the conversion of the Manx to Christianity and the lives of several Manx saints and other mytho-historical tales. Stories about fairies and other supernatural spirits appear in Chapter 3 and tales about monsters, giants, mermaids, and ghosts in Chapter 4. Tales about magic and witchcraft are in Chapter 5. The remaining five chapters deal with proverbs and sayings and with customs and superstitions pertaining to the seasons, the natural world, birth and death, and law. Introductory essay on the traditional life of the Manx.

Müller-Guggenbühl, Fritz. *Swiss-Alpine Folk-Tales*. Translated by Katharine Potts. New York: Henry Z. Walck, 1958. Thirty-six traditional German-Swiss tales are retold for young readers. The legend of William Tell is told in Part 1. Nine tales of aetiology and the supernatural from the Swiss Alps appear in Part 2. The folk legends in Part 3 include seven tales about historical figures such as Charles the Bold of Burgundy and Charlemagne. Part 4 offers stories about dwarfs and Part 5 seven fairy tales. In Part 6 are eight religious legends, especially about the conversion of the region to Christianity and about the devil. Illustrated with drawings, some in color, by Joan Kiddell-Monroe.

Olenius, Elsa, ed. *Great Swedish Fairy Tales*. Translated by Holger Lundbergh. New York: Delacorte Press, 1973.

A collection of twenty-one traditional Swedish tales about magic, trolls, talking animals, and queens retold for children by nine Swedish authors. Illustrated with forty-six color drawings by John Bauer (1882-1918). A biography of Bauer appears in the introduction.

Olrik, Axel. *The Heroic Legends of Denmark*. Translated and revised by Lee M. Hollander. New York: American-Scandinavian Foundation, 1919.

Originally published in Danish in 1903, this book is part of a comprehensive study of the heroic poetry of Denmark begun by Svend Grundtvig and continued by his student Olrik. Sources for these legends include Danish, Norwegian, and Icelandic histories of the medieval period. An introductory essay on the history and study of Danish heroic legends is followed by ten chapters dealing with Denmark during the time of the migration of nations, the Biarkamal, legends about Hrolf's warriors, the race of Halfdan, the royal residence at Leire, Hrolf's Berserkers, Scyld, the peace of King Frothi, and the Scyldings. In the final chapter, Olrik draws some conclusions about the development of these legends. Prefatory essay by Hollander on Olrik's life and work. List of Scandinavian sources for the legends, table of references to the original Danish edition, footnotes, and index.

Opie, Iona, and Peter Opie. *The Classic Fairy Tales*. London: Oxford University Press, 1974.

In this collection, a team of major twentieth-century folklorists brings together the first printed English versions of twenty-four well-known tales, including "Tom Thumb," "Sleeping Beauty," and "Cinderella." These texts from the seventeenth through the nineteenth centuries are accompanied by original illustrations and by others which record transformations of the tales over time. Some illustrations in color. Each tale is preceded by a summary of its history and important points of interest. In an introductory essay, the authors discuss features of the tales, especially their printed history. Of particular note is information on the collections of Charles Perrault, Madame d'Aulnoy, Madame de Beaumont, Jacob and Wilhelm Grimm, and Hans Christian Andersen. Short preface on the goals of this collection. Bibliography and index.

Parkinson, Thomas. *Yorkshire Legends and Traditions*. London: Elliot Stock, 1888. Reprint. New York: Arno Press, 1977.

This anthology of Yorkshire tales and narratives combines original material collected from chroniclers, poets, and journalists with the author's commentary and summaries. The legends are arranged in nine thematic chapters dealing with the early history of Yorkshire, abbeys and monastic life, the devil, ghosts, the notorious Mother Shipton and her prophecies, dragons and other monsters, battles and battlefields, wells and lakes, and miscellaneous themes. In an introductory essay, the author discusses some characteristics of tradition and legend, especially in Yorkshire.

Picard, Barbara Leonie. "Dietrich of Bern." In *German Hero-Sagas and Folk-Tales*, by Barbara Leonie Picard. New York: Henry Z. Walck, 1958. Reprinted in *The Faber Book of Northern Legends*, edited by Kevin Crossley-Holland. London: Faber and Faber, 1977. Also reprinted in *Northern Lights: Legends, Sagas and Folk-Tales*, edited by Kevin Crossley-Holland. London: Faber and Faber, 1987.
Tells of the legendary life of Dietrich of Bern, his friendship for the great warrior Hildebrand, their adventures together, and his conflicts with his uncle the emperor Ermenrich. Reprints include an illustration by Alan Howard.

_____. *French Legends, Tales and Fairy Stories*. London: Oxford University Press, 1955.
Twenty-three traditional French tales are retold for young readers. The first four tales, about Roland, William of Orange, Raoul of Cambrai, and the battle of Roncesvalles, are from the medieval romances. Included among six medieval courtly tales are stories about the lovers Aucassin and Nicolette, Amis and Amile, and Huon and Claramunda. Thirteen provincial legends deal with metamorphosis, hobgoblins, ogres, and the supernatural. With illustrations, some in color, by Joan Kiddell-Monroe.

_____. *German Hero-Sagas and Folk-Tales*. New York: Henry Z. Walck, 1958.
In Part 1 tales about the heroes Gudrun, Dietrich von Bern, Walther of Aquitaine, and Siegfried are retold for children. In Part 2 are fourteen folktales, including "Til Eulenspiegel," "The Seven Proud Sisters," and "The Mousetower." Illustrations by Joan Kiddell-Monroe.

Reeves, James. *English Fables and Fairy Stories*. London: Oxford University Press, 1954.
Nineteen traditional English tales are retold for children. Well-known tales such as "Catskin," "Tom Thumb," "Jack and the Beanstalk," and

"Dick Whittington" are included among these stories of foolishness, abandoned children, princesses, and the supernatural. With illustrations, some in color, by Joan Kiddell-Monroe.

Ruland, Wilhelm. *Legends of the Rhine*. Cologne: Hoursch & Bechstedt, 1906.
A collection of more than ninety legends and tales associated with various geographic regions and places along the Rhine River in Germany. These tales are translated into English and grouped geographically. These stories of the Upper Rhine, the Black Forest, Alsace, the adjoining valleys and heights, the Romantic Rhine, and the Lower Rhine include supernatural tales and explanations of natural phenomena. Map, photographs, and illustrations.

Rydberg, Viktor. *Teutonic Mythology*. Translated by Rasmus B. Anderson. 3 vols. New York: Norroena Society, 1907.
An English translation of an important Swedish survey of the deities and myths of the ancient Germanic world. These detailed paraphrases, explanations, and comparisons of versions of ancient myths are based upon the controversial assumptions of a culturally and linguistically unified race of Aryans (Indo-Europeans). The myths are occasionally quoted in the original language, sometimes without translation. Volume 1 has an introductory section on the ancient Aryans, their language family, and hypotheses concerning their origin. Offers a survey of various migration sagas, including those suggesting the Trojan descent of the Norse, as well as sagas of the Saxons, Franks, and Burgundians. Also contains myths concerning the creation and early days of humans, including the myth of a great world war. Discussion of Norse myths about the lower world begins in Volume 1 and continues through Volumes 2 and 3. Included in this last group are the Valkyries, descriptions of the kingdom of death, and myths of the moon god. Volume 3 also contains a dictionary of principal proper names and a comprehensive index. Four engraved illustrations in each volume.

Scott, Walter. "The Hauntings at Frodriver." In *Illustrations of Northern Antiquities*, by Henry Weber, R. Ramieson and Walter Scott. Edinburgh: James Ballantyne, 1814. Reprinted in *The Faber Book of Northern Legends*, edited by Kevin Crossley-Holland. London: Faber and Faber, 1977. Also reprinted in *Northern Lights: Legends, Sagas and Folk-Tales*, edited by Kevin Crossley-Holland. London: Faber and Faber, 1987.

The tale of a Hebridean woman named Thorgunna who dies at Froda in Iceland. Failure to follow her deathbed instructions concerning burial leads to hauntings, disease, and death for inhabitants of Froda. Reprints include an illustration by Alan Howard.

Shub, Elizabeth, trans. *About Wise Men and Simpletons*. New York: Macmillan, 1971.
Seventeen stories from the nineteenth-century folktale collection of Jacob and Wilhelm Grimm are here translated from the original German. The tales are accompanied by etchings by Nonny Hogbrogian. Three about elves and four about simpletons are accompanied by stories about wisdom and trickery such as "Rumplestiltskin," "Hansel and Gretel," and "The Bremen Town Musicians." A short foreword provides background to the Grimm collection and to this edition. Concludes with a brief biography of the brothers Wilhelm and Jacob Grimm.

Simpson, Jacqueline. *European Mythology*. New York: Peter Bedrick Books, 1987.
A general introduction to the folklores of medieval western Europe, including stories about fairies, kings, heroes, saints, seers, magicians, and witches, which are part of the culture of Christian Europe. Considers pre-Christian folk festivals such as midwinter and harvest celebrations, legends about figures such as King Arthur and St. Martin of Tours, as well as Christian beliefs about creation, the cosmos, and the afterlife. Supplemented by photographs of artwork, manuscripts, and monuments associated with these myths. Bibliography and index.

——————. *Icelandic Folktales and Legends*. Berkeley: University of California Press, 1972.
A selection of supernatural tales translated from the nineteenth-century collection of Icelandic folktales of Jón Árnason. Arranged thematically, with sections on elves, trolls, water sprites, ghosts, black magic, buried treasure, and the devil. Each tale is followed by a short note on sources and alternate versions. In an introductory essay, the author provides some background to Icelandic tales in general and to this collection in particular. Bibliography and indexes.

——————. *Legends of Icelandic Magicians*. Cambridge, England: D. S. Brewer, 1975.
A representative sample of seven Icelandic tales about magicians. Several come from a nineteenth-century collection and others from oral tradition in the early twentieth century. In an introductory essay,

B. S. Benedikt offers some historical background for the legendary magicians described in these tales. Endnotes, bibliography, and index of tale types and motifs.

Skeels, Dell R. "Guingamor and Guerrehés: Psychological Symbolism in a Medieval Romance." In *The Anthropologist Looks at Myth*, edited by Melville Jacobs and John Greenway. Austin: University of Texas Press, 1966.
The first English translations of the medieval lay of *Guingamor* and its sequel *Guerrehés*, which appears in the *First Continuation* of Chrétien de Troyes' *Perceval*, written by an unknown author at the end of the twelfth century A.D. Considers Breton singers to be the source for both songs and argues that *Guerrehés* uses symbolic material based upon the phallic level of Freudian development. Endnotes.

Ward, Donald, ed. and trans. *The German Legends of the Brothers Grimm*. 2 vols. Philadelphia: Institute for the Study of Human Issues, 1981.
The first English translation of *Deutsche Sagen*, the collection of German folktales first published by Wilhelm and Jacob Grimm between 1816 and 1818. The 585 tales in this book are an important complement to the Grimm brothers' collection of German fairy tales, which is better known in English. These short tales describe events such as encounters with mythical creatures like gnomes, mermen, and dwarfs, unusual and supernatural occurrences, religious experiences, and legends about historical personages. Each volume includes the Grimm brothers' original forewords, notes on sources, and addenda. Preface to the third edition by Herman Grimm. The English translation includes a foreword on the Brothers Grimm by Dan Ben-Amos and analytic and explanatory commentaries by Ward in each volume. In an epilogue to Volume 2 Ward offers comments on the translating of the legends, biographies of the Brothers Grimm, and their contributions to the study of folklore. Bibliography, index, and table of legends at the end of Volume 2.

Westwood, Jennifer. "Walter and Hildegund." In *The Faber Book of Northern Legends*, edited by Kevin Crossley-Holland. London: Faber and Faber, 1977. Also reprinted in *Northern Lights: Legends, Sagas and Folk-Tales*, edited by Kevin Crossley-Holland. London: Faber and Faber, 1987.
A tale about three child hostages of Attila the Hun: Walter of Aquitaine, his sworn friend Hagen of Burgundy, and his beloved Hildegund. The noble Walter becomes like a son to Attila but escapes with his beloved

Hildegund and Attila's gold. Walter eventually falls into conflict with
the disloyal Hagen and his king, Gunther. After a bitter battle all are
reconciled and Walter and Hildegund are married. Includes an illustration by Alan Howard.

Wilson, Barbara Ker. *Scottish Folk-Tales and Legends.* London: Oxford
University Press, 1954.
Twenty-five traditional tales, especially from the Scottish Highlands,
along with seven tales from the Celtic cycle about a hero known in
Scotland as Finn, are retold for young readers. The folktales include
animal fables and stories about Roman times, fairies, brownies, giants,
and the supernatural. The legends of Finn tell of his band of Fians, his
sword, his monstrous Grey Dog, his love triangle with Diarmid and
Grainne, the death of Conan, the Green Isle, and the legend of his long
sleep in Smith's Rock on the island of Skye. With illustrations, some
in color, by Joan Kiddell-Monroe. Map.

Zipes, Jack, trans. *The Complete Fairy Tales of the Brothers Grimm.* New
York: Bantam Books, 1987.
The collections published by Jacob and Wilhelm Grimm in *Kinder-
und Hausmärchen* (*German Fairy Tales*) in seven editions between
1812 and 1857 have been translated into English many times. Zipes
offers an authentic translation and does not edit the coarser, dialectic
features of the original tales. Zipes includes not only the 210 tales in
the standard 1857 edition but also thirty-two tales from earlier editions.
In addition to well-known tales such as "Rapunzel," "Hansel and
Gretel," and "Snow White," the collection contains animal tales,
stories of the supernatural, and religious tales for children. In an
introductory essay, Zipes describes the career of the Brothers Grimm
and compares versions of several tales from different editions of their
book. The black-and-white illustrations by John B. Gruelle first appeared in a 1914 translation by Margaret Hunt. Translator's note and
original sources in endnotes.

AUTHOR'S NOTE

The following three indexes are designed to serve those who wish to follow the varied trails of Sisyphus' rock. The Author and Editor Index is an index of authors, editors, and translators of the works cited in this bibliography. The authorship of mythology books is as indefinite in boundary as is the subject matter of myth. Some books, such as Edmund Nequatewa's *Truth of a Hopi* (Flagstaff: Museum of Northern Arizona, 1936), are attributed to those who actually told the tale. More frequently, however, the myths are identified with the anthropologists or scholars who recorded the tales and brought them into print. Such is the case with Martha Warren Beckwith's *Jamaica Anansi Stories* (New York: American Folk-Lore Society, 1924), which she collected among Jamaicans in 1919 and 1921. Yet other works, such as Levy Howard's version of the sixteenth-century stories of Hsü Wen-ch'ang, *China's Dirtiest Trickster* (Arlington, Va.: Warm-Soft Press, 1974), are cited under the names of those who have translated the tales into English.

The Illustrator Index brings together the names of the artists and photographers whose work accompanies many of the books in this bibliography. This artwork not only illustrates retellings of myths for young children but also complements more scholarly studies of the myths. These visual images enhance the written myths and can bring additional meanings and interpretations to the myth tradition. This index is inevitably incomplete, since much of the sculpture and artwork illustrated in these books is the creation of many nameless artist of ancient Egypt, Greece, India, and Celtic Europe as well as contemporary traditional cultures, especially in the Americas and Africa. Occasionally, however, the title pages of these books do recognized the work of local artist, such as Kiakshuk and Pudlo, the Inuit artists who illustrated Edward Field's *Eskimo Songs and Stories* (New York: Delacorte Press, 1973). Some authors, such as Richard Erdoes and Joanna Troughton, illustrate their own written works. Other illustrations in these books are the creations of well-known artists, such as Albrecht Dürer of Germany, Gustav Doré of France, and John Bauer of Sweden. This index of artists and photographers invites users of the bibliography to approach the myths from the point of view of the visual image as well as the written word.

The Subject Index is actually a multipurpose concordance. Geographic references and names of various peoples and ethnic groups are included in order to supplement the broader continental and regional categories used in the body of the bibliography. Users who wish to consult books about Apache, Jewish, or Welsh myths, for example, are advised to begin with this index. For similar reasons, this index catalogues the titles of various traditional works of mythology, such as Ovid's *Metamorphoses* and the *Mahabharata*, as well as the names of individual characters, heroes, deities, and mythological concepts. Since some users of this bibliography may wish to study these myths thematically, the index also includes a variety of other categories, such as aetiology, demons, the underworld, and various animals. Finally, the Subject Index includes the names of many of the subsidiary contributors to these books, not only the authors of forewords and introductory essays but also informants and earlier scholars who made possible these mythological collections. The trail of prolific scholars such as folklorists Franz Boas and Alan Dundes is difficult to follow without such an index.

Author and Editor Index

Abrahamsson, Hans 62
Adagala, Kavetsa 79
Al-Saleh-Khairat 238
Alexander, Hartley Burr 139
Alexinsky, G. 325
Allen, Louis, A. 220
Allen, Thomas G. 48
Alpers, Antony 220
Alvord, Thomas G. 208
Amadu, Malum 62
Ames, D. 48
Ananikian, Mardiros H. 238
Andersen, Johannes C. 221
Anderson, George K. 15
Angus, Charlotte 140
Anthes, Rudolf 48
Arima, Eugene 185
Arnott, Kathleen 62
Ashley, Mike 314, 318
Aston, W. G. 300
Athanassakis, Apostolos N. 331
Auden, Wystan H. 381
Austin, Norman 332
Ausubel, Nathan 15
Ayre, Robert 140
Ayyar, Aiylam Subramanier
 Panchapakesa 272

Bailey, John 16
Baines, John 49
Bali, Esther 62
Ballou, R. O. 16
Bancroft, Hubert Howe 97
Bancroft-Hunt, Norman 140
Barb, A. A. 49
Barbeau, Charles Marius 140-141,
 208
Barker, William Henry 63
Barlow, Thomas Lambert 283
Barnett, Lionel D. 272
Barnouw, Victor 141

Barrett, Samuel Alfred 142
Bascom, William 63
Basham, Arthur Llewellyn 273
Bastide, R. 63
Battle, Kemp P. 208
Baumann, H. 124
Beard, Mary 332
Beauchamp, Henry K. 277
Beckwith, Martha Warren 101, 142,
 221
Beier, Ulli 63, 75
Bell, Corydon 143
Bell, Robert E. 332
Beltz, Walter 238
Benedict, Ruth 143
Berndt, Catherine H. 222-223
Berndt, Ronald M. 223
Berry, Jack 64
Biebuyck, Daniel 64
Bierhorst, John 97, 109-110, 124, 144
Birch, Cyril 291
Birchall, Ann 333
Bird, W. W. 226
Biro, Val 325
Birrell, Anne M. 291
Blackwell, I. A. 382
Blair, Walter 209
Blake Tyrrell, William 333
Bleek, William H. I. 64-65
Block, Gwendoline Harris 160
Bloomfield, Leonard 144
Boas, Franz 144-147
Bodde, Derk 292
Bontemps, Arna 105
Boord, Martin 292
Boss, Claire 384
Botkin, Benjamin A. 209
Boucher, Alan 384
Bouteiller, M. 147
Bowman, James Cloyd 209
Bradford, Roark 209

Illustrator Index

Subject Index

Wahungwe 75
Wailuku River 234
Waite, A. E. 320
Wakan Tanka 151
Wakashan 150
Wakdjunkaga 190
Wakinyan 151
Walam Olum 147
Wales 267, 312, 314, 316. *See also* Welsh.
Walter of Aquitaine 403
Walter, Robert 45
Wandering Jew 15, 384
Wapiya 222
War 2-3, 6, 8, 17, 20, 23, 25, 69, 73, 86, 97, 109, 111, 117, 124, 143, 146, 156, 158, 161-163, 165, 167-170, 175, 177-179, 181-183, 185, 187, 189, 191, 199, 202-203, 206, 227-228, 231-232, 240, 245- 246, 266, 277, 283, 287, 292, 301, 303-304, 307, 314, 317, 322, 325, 328, 331-334, 336-338, 340-342, 344, 346-349, 353, 355-356, 361- 364, 366-367, 371-372, 375, 383, 395, 399-401
Warao 132-133
Warrau 97, 124
Wasco 141, 191, 194
Washington State 194
Wassilissa 326, 390
Water 5, 80, 86, 88, 120, 126, 161, 163, 165, 184, 197, 202, 205, 232-233, 238, 249, 256-257, 259, 261, 264, 278, 316-317, 325, 384, 387, 396, 402
Water, weeping 217
Water-drag Man 189
Waterfalls 151
Watergate 215
Waterway 165
Wawalag Sisters 222-223, 228, 231
We-gyet 140

Weasel Woman 205
Weaving 44, 138, 304
Webster, Helen L. 191
Welsh 17, 24, 36, 311, 314-320, 322-323, 392. *See also* Wales.
Werewolves 40, 330, 335, 377, 388
West Africa 30, 63-64, 68, 70-74, 76, 78-79, 85-88, 90, 92-93, 102
West Asia 39
West Indies 108
West Slavonian 330
West Virginia 105, 212
Western Solomon Islands 234
Weston, Jessie L. 378
Whales 198, 216, 226
Wheelwright, Mary C. 172-173, 204
Wherry, James 185
White men 84, 103, 184, 191
White Mountain Apache 161
White River 139
White Russian 330
Whitman, Walt 25
Whittier, John Greenleaf 214
Whittington, Dick 39, 387, 401
Wichikäpache 185
Wichita 155
Widows 71, 192
Wights 393
Wihio 162, 189
Willamette Valley 159, 170, 191
William of Orange 400
Wilson, John A. 34-35, 256
Wind 90, 140, 157-158, 176, 204, 212-213, 249, 253
Wind gods 112-113, 120
Wind spirits 197, 203, 206
Windigo 142, 185
Winnebago 100, 190
Wintu 157
Wisconsin 141, 144, 190
Wisdom 25, 32, 38, 46, 68, 71-72, 83-84, 152, 214, 216, 267, 281, 295, 307, 322, 375, 378, 402

ABOUT THE AUTHOR

Thomas J. Sienkewicz is the Minnie Billings Capron Professor of Classics at Monmouth College in Monmouth, Illinois. He has been teaching general undergraduate courses in Classical mythology for twenty years and has been recognized for his outstanding and innovative teaching by Monmouth College, the American Philological Association, and the Illinois Council for the Teaching of Foreign Languages.

He is the author of numerous books and articles, including *Classical Gods and Heroes in the National Gallery of Art* (Washington, D.C.: University Press of America, 1983). With Viv Edwards he is the author of *Oral Cultures Past and Present* (Oxford: Blackwells, 1991), a cross-cultural study of oral performance in traditional and developed societies all over the world. His *The Classical Epic: An Annotated Bibliography* (Pasadena, Calif.: Salem Press, 1991), dealing with Homer's *Iliad* and *Odyssey* and Vergil's *Aeneid*, is part of the Magill Bibliographies series. In 1992-1993 he was visiting director of the Associated Colleges of the Mid-West (ACM) Programs in Florence, Italy. He is also a regular contributor to *Magill's Literary Annual.*